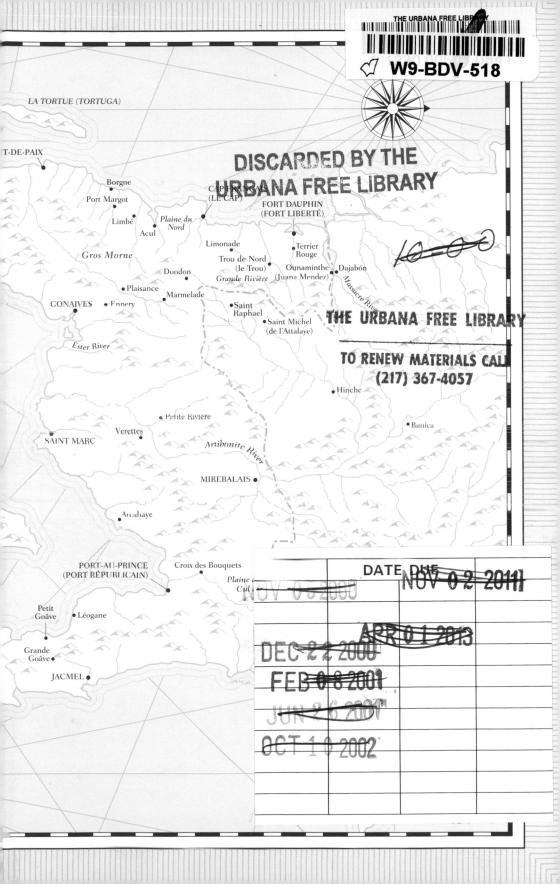

LA TORTUE (TORTUGA)

T-DE-PAIX

Borgne

Port Margot

CAP-FRANÇAIS
(LE CAP)

FORT DAUPHIN
(FORT LIBERTÉ)

Limbé

Plaine du
Nord

Acul

Gros Morne

Limonade

Terrier
Rouge

Trou de Nord
(le Trou)

Dondon

Grande Rivière

Ounaminthe
(Juana Mendez)

Dajabón

Massacre River

Plaisance

Marmelade

GONAIVES   Ennery

Saint
Raphael

Saint Michel
(de l'Attalaye)

Ester River

Hinche

Petite Rivière

Banica

Verettes

SAINT MARC

Artibonite River

MIREBALAIS

Arcahaye

PORT-AU-PRINCE
(PORT RÉPUBLICAIN)

Croix des Bouquets

Plaine
Cul

Petit
Goâve

Léogane

Grande
Goâve

JACMEL

MASTER *of the*
CROSSROADS

MASTER *of the*

CROSSROADS

Madison Smartt Bell

PANTHEON BOOKS   NEW YORK

Pantheon Books and colophon are registered trademarks of Random House, Inc.

Permissions Acknowledgments are on page 735.

Library of Congress Cataloging-in-Publication Data

Bell, Madison Smartt.
    Master of the crossroads / Madison Smartt Bell.
        p.   cm.
    ISBN 0-375-42056-8
    1. Haiti—History—Revolution, 1791–1804—Fiction. 2. Toussaint Louverture,
1743?–1803—Fiction. 3. Slave insurrections—Fiction.
I. Title.

PS3552.E517 M37 2000   813'.54—dc21   00-029835

www.pantheonbooks.com

Book design by Johanna S. Roebas

Printed in the United States of America
First Edition
9 8 7 6 5 4 3 2 1

FOR PÈRE ANTOINE ADRIEN,
WHO HAS OFFERED HIS LIFE TO THIS HISTORY

Michel-Rolph Trouillot, Lóló Beaubrun, Guidel Présumé,
Jean de la Fontaine, Alex Roshuk, Gesner Pierre, Monique
Clesca, Lyonel Trouillot, Sabine Sannon, Rodney Saint-Eloi,
Ephèle Milcé, Carmen, Eddie Lubin, Mimerose Beaubrun,
Russell Banks, Anne-Carinne Trouillot, Edwidge Danticat,
Patrick Delatour, Gabrielle Saint-Eloi, Meg Roggansack,
Richard Morse, Michelle Karshan, Evelyne Trouillot-Ménard,
Georges Castera, Yannick Lahens, Gary Victor, Philippe
Manassé, Claudette Edoissaint, Joel Turenne, Yves Colon,
Anna Wardenberg, Benoit Clément Junior, Bob Shacochis,
Edouard Duval-Carrié, Patrick Vilaire, C. S. Godshalk, Père
Max Dominique, Père William Smarth, Judith Thorne,
Bernard Éthéart, Bryant Freeman, Ken Maki, Didier
Dominique, Rachel Beauvoir, Max Beauvoir, Robert and
Tania Beckham, Dr. Laurent Pierre-Phillipe, Marie Racine,
Stephane D'Amours, Robert Corbett and all citizens of
Corbettland too numerous to mention, Amy Beeder, Hérald
Pérard, Ferry Pierre-Charles, Josette Pérard, Kati
Maternowska, Elizabeth McAlister, Max Blanchet, Kathy
Grey, Faubert Pierre, Marc Christophe, Laetitia Schutt,
Bruce Hoverman, Joel Dreyfuss, Nancy Ménard, Garry
Pierre-Pierre, Paul Ven, Alyx Kellington, Amy Wilentz, Nina
Schnall, Guy Antoine, Daniel Simidor, Beverly Knight
Sullivan, Richard Edson, Uriode Orelien, Baba, RoseMarie
Chierici, Gerard Barthelmy, Fritz Daguillard, Robert Stone,
les jeunes braves du Cap including but not limited to
Martinière, Saint-Jean, Andy, Tidjo, *moun ki mèt nan Morne
Calvaire,* you whose names I have not mentioned, you who
helped me at the crossroads whose names I never knew,

Youn sèl nou pèdi,
Ansanm n'a rive.

10-00 Bt 30.00

Sometimes, if you let a man live,
he is less dangerous
than if you kill him.
If you kill him,
You will never be rid of him.

—Jean-Bertrand Aristide
as quoted by Amy Wilentz
in *The Rainy Season*

CONTENTS

*Most special thanks to Jane Gelfman, Cork Smith,
Dan Frank, Lisa Hamilton, and Altie Karper for arduous,
painstaking work on the manuscript, and to Bill Buford and
Sonny Mehta for taking the chance when the risk was high.*

MASTER *of the* CROSSROADS

Fort de Joux, France

August 1802

Citizen Baille, commandant of the Fort de Joux, crossed the courtyard
of the mountain fortress, climbed a set of twelve steps, and knocked on
the outer door of the guardhouse. When there was no reply, he hitched
up the basket he carried over his left arm and rapped again more smartly
with his right fist. A sentry opened to him, stood aside, and held his
salute. Baille acknowledged him, then turned and locked the door with
his own hand.

"*Les clefs*," said Baille, and the sentry presented him with a large iron
keyring.

"In the future," Baille announced, "I will keep these keys in my own
possession. Whoever has need of them must come to me. But there will
be no need."

Citizen Baille unlocked the inner door and pulled, heaving a part of
his considerable weight against the pull-ring to set the heavy door turning on its hinges. He stooped and picked up a sack of clothing from the
floor, and carrying both sack and basket, passed through the doorway
and turned and locked it behind him.

The vaulted corridor was dimly lit through narrow loopholes that
penetrated the twelve-foot stone walls. Baille walked the length of it,

aware of the echo of his footfalls. At the far end he set down the basket and the sack and unlocked another door, passed through, and relocked it after him.

Two steps down brought him to the floor of the second vaulted corridor, which was six inches deep in the water that came imperceptibly, ceaselessly seeping from the raw face of the wall to the left—the living stone of the mountain. Baille muttered under his breath as he traversed the vault; his trousers were bloused into his boots, which had been freshly waxed but still leaked around the seams of the uppers. Opening the next door was an awkward affair, for Baille must balance the sack and basket as he worked the key; there was no place on the flooded floor to lay them down.

Ordinarily he might have brought a soldier or a junior officer to bear those burdens for him, but the situation was not ordinary, and Baille was afraid—no (he stopped himself), he was not *afraid*, but . . . He could not rid his mind of the two officers of the Vendée who had lately escaped from this place. It was an embarrassment, a scandal, a disgrace, and Baille might well have lost his command, he thought, except that to be relieved of this miserable, frozen, isolated post might almost have been taken as a reward rather than a punishment. He still had little notion how the escape had been possible. There was none among his officers or men whom he distrusted, and yet none could give a satisfactory explanation of what had taken place. The prisoners could not have slipped through the keyholes or melted into the massive stone walls, and the heavy mesh which covered the cell windows (beyond their bars) was not wide enough to pass a grown man's finger.

His current prisoner was vastly more important than those officers could ever dream to be—although he was a Negro, and a slave. From halfway around the world Captain-General Leclerc had written to his brother-in-law, the First Consul, Napoleon Bonaparte himself, that this man had so inflamed the rebel slaves of Saint Domingue that the merest hint of his return there would overthrow all the progress Leclerc and his army had made toward the suppression of the revolt and the restoration of slavery. Perhaps only the whisper of the name of Baille's prisoner on the lips of the blacks of Saint Domingue would be sufficient cause for that Jewel of the Antilles, so recently France's richest possession overseas, to be purged yet another time with fire and blood. So wrote the Captain-General to his brother-in-law, and it seemed that the First Consul himself took the liveliest interest in the situation, reinforcing with his direct order Leclerc's nervous request that the prisoner be kept in the straitest possible security, and as far away as possible from any seaport that might provide a route for his return.

The Fort de Joux, perched high in the Alps near the Swiss border, met this second condition most exactly. One could hardly go farther from the sea while still remaining within French borders. As for security, well, the walls were thick and the doors heavy, the windows almost hermetically sealed. In the case of the recent escape there had most certainly been betrayal. The officers had somehow obtained the files they used to cut their bars, and probably had enjoyed other aid from some unknown person in the fort. For this reason Baille had chosen to wait upon his new prisoner himself and alone, at least for the present, despite the inconvenience it occasioned.

While pursuing this uneasy rumination, he had crossed the third corridor, which was set at a higher level than the one before and therefore was less damp. He opened and relocked the final door and turned to face the openings of two cells. Clearing his throat, he walked to the second door and called out to announce himself. After a moment a voice returned the call, but it was low and indistinct through the iron-bound door.

Baille turned the key in the lock and went in. The cell, vaulted like the passages leading to it, was illuminated only by coals of the small fire. Baille's heart quivered like a jelly, for it seemed there was no one in the room—he saw with his frantically darting eyes the low bed, stool, the table . . . but no human being. He dropped the sack and clapped a hand over his mouth. But now the man was standing before him after all, not five paces distant, as if he had been dropped from the ceiling—or had spun himself down, like a spider on its silk. Indeed the barrel vault over head was filled with dismal shadows, so that Baille could not make out the height of its curve. The vault dwarfed the prisoner, a small Negro unremarkable at first glance, except that he was slightly bandy-legged. Baille swallowed; his tongue was thick.

"Let us light the candle," he said. When there was no response he went to the table and did so himself, then turned to inspect the prisoner in the improved light.

This was Toussaint Louverture, who had thought to make the island colony of Saint Domingue independent of France. He had written and proclaimed a constitution; he had, so rumor ran, written to the First Consul with this arrogant address: "To the first of the whites from the first of the blacks." But now, if this arrogance had not been exactly punished, it had certainly been checked by many rings of stone.

Baille faced his guest with a smile, feeling his lips curve on his face like clay. "I have brought your rations," he said.

Toussaint did not even glance at the basket, which Baille had set down on the table when he struck the light. He looked at the commandant with a cool intensity which Baille found rather unnerving, though he did his best to hold . . . after all, it was not quite a stare. Toussaint's head was disproportionately large for his body, with a long lower jaw and irregular brown teeth. His eyes, however, were clear and intelligent. He wore a madras cloth bound around his head and the uniform of a French general, which was, however, limp and soiled. Apparently he had had no change of his outer garments since he had first been made prisoner and deported from Saint Domingue.

"I have brought you fresh clothing," Baille said, and indicated the sack he had dropped on the floor in his first surprise. Toussaint did not shift his gaze to acknowledge it. Presently Baille picked up the sack himself and stooped to lay out the contents on the low bed.

"This uniform is not correct," Toussaint said.

Baille swallowed. "You must accept it." Somehow he could not manage to phrase the sentence with greater force.

Toussaint looked briefly at the coals in the fire.

"Your uniform is soiled and worn, and too light for the weather," Baille said. "It is already cold here, and soon it will be winter, sir—" This *sir* escaped him involuntarily. He stopped and looked at the woolen clothes he had unfolded on the bed. *"Acceptez-les, je vous en prie."*

Toussaint at last inclined his head. Baille sighed.

"I must also ask that you surrender any money you may have, or any . . ." He let the sentence trail. He waited, but nothing else happened at all.

"Do you understand me?" This time Baille suppressed the *sir*.

"Yes, of course," Toussaint said, and he turned his head and shoulder toward the door. Baille had already begun walking in that direction before he recognized that he had been dismissed, that he should not permit himself to be so dismissed, that it was his clear duty to remain and watch the prisoner disrobe and see with his own eyes that he held nothing back. However, he soon found himself against the outside of the door, unreeling in his mind long strings of curses, although he did not know for certain if it were the prisoner or the assigned procedures he meant to curse.

After a few minutes he called out. The same indistinct mutter returned through the door, and Baille opened it and went back in. Toussaint stood in the fresh clothes that had been given him; his feet, incongruously, were bare. Or rather Baille felt that he himself would have looked absurd and foolish standing barefoot in such a situation, but it detracted in no way from the dignity of the prisoner. Toussaint motioned toward the table with a slight movement of his left hand.

Baille approached. On the table lay some banknotes and coins, a couple of documents of some sort, a watch with a gold chain.

"I will keep my watch," Toussaint said, and already his hand had gathered it up and put it into a pocket, chain and all. There seemed nothing to do but assent; Baille nodded and scooped up the money and papers without looking at them, feeling a stir of shame. Toussaint had stuffed the dirty uniform into the sack in which the other clothes had come. Baille picked up the sack and also collected Toussaint's high-topped military boots—he had furnished a pair of ordinary shoes, but it was not his concern whether the prisoner chose to put them on.

"I have need of pen and ink and paper," Toussaint said. "I must write letters—I must make my report to the First Consul."

"I shall look into the matter," Baille said, and thought of notes somehow forwarded through mesh, through keyholes, folded into minute pellets and passed to confederates outside the prison. No, he would not furnish the writing supplies on his own authority.

"As quickly as possible." A hint of a smile on Toussaint's face, but only a flicker, and his look was stern, commanding. "My duty is urgent."

Baille undertook no direct reply. "Good evening," he said, and swallowed the *sir*, as he made his retreat.

Toussaint stood near the door of the cell, listening to the lock springs snapping, hinges groaning in succession, each sound somewhat fainter than the one before, as Baille receded down the series of passageways. He could hear the commandant's feet splashing in the middle corridor, or thought that he could. Then nothing. He moved from the doorway, his bare feet splaying over the flagstones of the floor. The bell of the castle clock rang with a grating of discontent. Toussaint pulled his watch from the pocket of the coat he had been furnished, and opened the case. It was a quarter past seven. Darkness had come early, or at any rate there was no light at the barred window, but the embrasure had been bricked over two-thirds of the way to the top, and the mesh beyond the bars never strained much daylight through itself, regardless of the hour.

He had learned that now. He replaced the watch and felt the other pockets of the coat from the outside, here and there; he had in fact kept back a few gold coins and a couple of letters from Baille's lackadaisical inspection. The wool coat and trousers fit him loosely, but were warm enough. The uniform of a private soldier, with all insignia cut away. Toussaint coughed thickly and held his hand over the center of his chest, hoping to suppress another spasm. He had caught a heavy cold on his journey from Brest across France to the Fort de Joux, and the cough was lingering. His whole rib cage felt bruised by it. He did not like what Baille had said of the approach of winter . . . which seemed to prove this cell would be no temporary way station. He expected an interview with the First Consul—the opportunity to speak on his own behalf, explain his conduct—he expected, at the least, a trial. It must be a military tribunal before which he would appear in the uniform of his rank in the French army, and therefore he also disliked the clothes he had been given, though they were perfectly serviceable otherwise. Their coarse quality, even their previous use, was no great matter to him; he had known worse.

He walked to the table and turned back the wooden lid of the basket. Salt meat (already cut), a pale, hard, crumbly cheese, a supply of bis-cuit. Ship's rations, more or less. There was a flagon of red wine and what struck him as a meager sack of sugar. Some ground coffee had been included, along with implements for brewing it and some other utensils with which he might warm the food. There were two spoons, but of course no knife. He touched the meat—a corner of it crumbled between his thumb and forefinger. Water had been brought to him sepa-rately beforehand, in a clay pitcher; he might prepare a sort of stew. Toussaint hesitated. In Saint Domingue, he had been careful of poison-ing. Among any company he did not entirely trust (and there was little company he trusted absolutely), he would eat only uncut fruit, a piece of cheese sliced by his own hand from the center of the round, a whole roll or uncut loaf of bread—and drink plain water, never wine.

He raised a scrap of the salt meat and sniffed it, nostrils flaring, then let it fall back into the basket. Turning his head at an angle, he smiled slightly to himself. In this predicament, he would of course be unable to sustain his former precautions. Unless he elected to starve himself, his jailers might poison him whenever they would. Therefore it was useless for him to concern himself about it. He would eat as his appetite com-manded, and without concern. But for the moment he was not hungry.

He took out the wine jug and poured a measure into the cup, then added a small amount of water and drank—red wine, slightly sour. He shook in some sugar from the bag, swirled the cup, and drained the mix-ture. The treacly warmth of the wine seemed to coat his throat against the cough. He closed the lid of the basket and then blew out the candle that Baille had lit when he came in. Firelight spread yellowly, pulsing on the stones of the floor. Toussaint went to the fireplace. The hearth-stone was warm to his bare feet, and thoroughly dry. He stooped and added a single piece of wood to the glow of coals.

More distant from the fireside, the flagstones were clammy, not quite damp. He sat on the edge of the bed and drew on the woollen stockings which had been given him. Cautiously he raised his legs onto the bed and lay back, holding his breath. The roughness thrust up in the back of his throat, but he swallowed it back and managed to exhale without coughing. When he touched the raw stone wall above the bed, his fingers came away moist and slightly chilled. He turned his head away from the wall and looked into the room, lying partly on his side, his legs slightly bent, his palm cupped under the left side of his jaw. An observer might have thought he slept, but he was not sleeping. He watched the fire through slitted eyes and thought of one thing and another: His valet, Mars Plaisir, under lock and key in the neighboring cell; his wife and sons, confined in some other region of France under conditions of which he knew little; the accounting he would make, when pen and paper were brought to him, for the eyes of the First Consul, Napoleon Bonaparte. (And why had Baille been so evasive about this matter? A flicker of worry touched Toussaint, but he let it pass.) The work of writing would require some skill, some artifice. He tried to think how he would begin, but it was difficult without his secretaries, without pen or paper. The words of which his case must be constructed stood apart from him, as if the pen's nib would delve them from the paper; they were not part of his mind.

The castle clock struck another quarter-hour, without Toussaint much remarking it. His concentration was imperfect, and he felt warm and blurry. Perhaps he had a touch of fever, with the cough. The firelight on the hearth narrowed and flattened into a low red horizon . . . sunrise or sunset. From the red-glowing slit expanded a featureless plain, whether of land or water was unclear. A dot interrupted the red horizon; Toussaint blinked his eyes, but the dot persisted. It sprouted spidery limbs, like an insect or stick figure of a man. The form grew larger by imperceptible degrees, as it came over the bare plain and toward him.

Part One

KALFOU DANJERE

1793–1794

Si w konnen ou pa fran Ginen
pa rèt nan kalfou
halfou twa—kalfou danjere
kalfou kat—kalfou règleman
kalfou senk—kalfou pèd pawol
Si w konnen ou pa fran Ginen
pa rèt nan kalfou

    —Boukman Eksperyans,
     "Kalfou Danjere"

If you know you are not an honest believer
don't stop at this crossroad
Third crossroad—dangerous crossroad
Fourth crossroad—crossroad where accounts are settled
Fifth crossroad—crossroad of speechlessness
If you know you are not an honest believer
don't stop at this crossroad

In 1793 the colony of Saint Domingue, once France's most valuable overseas possession, was French in little more than name. Since 1791 a revolt of the colony's African slaves had shredded it from one end to the other. The wars of the Revolutionary French Republic against the royalist nations of Europe were also playing themselves out on the ground of Saint Domingue, and on this battlefield France looked very much like losing.

The French population of Saint Domingue was at war with itself. The large proprietors, slaveowners of royalist predilections, had invited an English protectorate, which would protect their property, including their slaves. The English had invaded from Jamaica, and in an alliance with both the royalist French and a faction of mulattoes who also owned slaves, had taken control of three important ports: Port-au-Prince, Saint Marc, and Môle Saint Nicolas, along with surrounding territory on the coastal plains. The French Republicans defended themselves against the invasion as best they could, with few European troops to support their cause. The mountainous, virtually inaccessible interior of the colony was in a state of anarchy, traveled by bands of armed blacks in revolt against slavery. Some, but not all, of those blacks were nominally in the service of Spain, also at war with the French Republic at this time, and they reported through vari-

ous black leaders to the Spanish military across the border in Spanish Santo Domingo. Other blacks served no one but themselves.

Léger Félicité Sonthonax, the official representative of the French Republic in Saint Domingue, had proclaimed the abolition of slavery, but very few of the blacks in revolt had rallied to that banner. Cap Français, the principal town on the north coast, commonly known as Le Cap, remained technically under French Republican control, but its commanding officer, General Etienne Laveaux, was besieged farther west, at Port-de-Paix, caught between the English on one side and the Spanish on the other. Sonthonax, meanwhile, after losing a battle with the English at Port-au-Prince, had taken the remnants of his force still farther south.

On the same day that Sonthonax proclaimed the abolition of slavery, one of the black leaders in the interior issued his own statement, from a small fort in the mountains called Camp Turel, to the effect that he intended to lead his people to liberty. This leader was nominally in Spanish service, and nominally the subordinate of the black generals Jean-François and Biassou, but in the past couple of years he had been developing a separate reputation as a skilled and dangerous military commander. In the Proclamation of Camp Turel he used, for the first time in any written document, the name of Toussaint Louverture.

I

Midday, and the sun thrummed from the height of its arc, so that the lizard seemed to cast no shadow. Rather the shadow lay directly beneath it, squarely between its four crooked legs. The lizard was a speckled brown across its back, but the new tail it was growing from the stump of the old was darker, steely blue. It moved at a right angle and turned its head to the left and froze, the movement itself as quick and undetectable as a water spider's translation of place. A loose fold of skin at its throat inflated and relaxed. It turned to the left and skittered a few inches forward and came to that same frozen stop. When it turned its head away to the right, the man's left hand shot out like a whiplash and seized the lizard fully around the body. With almost the same movement he was stroking the lizard's underbelly down the length of the long broad-bladed cutlass he held in his other hand.

The knife was eighteen inches long, blue-black, with a flat spoon-shaped turning at the tip; its filed edge was brighter, steely, but stained now with lizard blood. The man hooked out the entrails with his thumb and sucked moisture from the lizard's body cavity. He cracked the ribs apart from the spine to open it further and splayed the lizard on a rock to dry. Then he cautiously licked the edge of his knife and sat back and laid the blade across his folded knees.

At his back was the trunk of a small twisted tree, which bore instead of leaves large club-shaped cactile forms bristling with spines. The man contracted himself within the meager ellipse of shade the tree threw on the dry ground. Sweat ran down his cheeks and pooled in his collarbones and overflowed onto his chest, and his shrunken belly lifted slightly with his breathing and from time to time he blinked an eye, but he was more still than the lizard had been; he had proved that. After a time he looped his left hand around the lizard's dead legs and picked up the knife in his other hand and began to walk again.

The man was barefoot and wore no clothes except for a strip of grubby cloth bound around his loins; he had no hat and carried nothing but the cane knife and the lizard. His hair was close-cut and shaved in diamond patterns with a razor and his skin was a deep sweat-glossy black, except for the scar lines, which were stony pale. There were straight parallel slash marks on his right shoulder and the right side of his neck and his right jawbone and cheek, and the lobe of his right ear had been cut clean away. On his right forearm and the back of his hand was a series of similar parallel scars that would have matched those on his neck and shoulder if, perhaps, he had raised his hand to wipe sweat from his face, but he did not raise his hand. Along his rib cage and penetrating the muscle of his back, the scars were ragged and anarchic. These wounds had healed in grayish lumps of flesh that interrupted the flow of his musculature like snags in the current of a stream.

He was walking north. The knife, swinging lightly with his step, reached a little past the joint of his knee. The country was in low rolling mounds like billows of the sea, dry earth studded with jagged chunks of stone. There were spiny trees like the one where he'd sheltered at midday, but nothing else grew here. He walked along a road of sorts, or track, marked with the ruts of wagon wheels molded in dry mud, sometimes the fossilized prints of mules or oxen. Sometimes the road was scored across by shallow gulleys, from flooding during the time of the rains. West of the road the land became more flat, a long, dry savannah reaching toward a dull haze over the distant sea. In the late afternoon the mountains to the east turned blue with rain, but they were very far away and it would not rain here where the man was walking.

At evening he came to the bank of a small river whose water was brown with mud. He stood and looked at the flow of water, his throat pulsing. After a certain time he crept cautiously down the bank and lowered his lips to the water to drink. At the height of the bank above the river he sat down and began eating the lizard from the inside out, break-

ing the frail bones with his teeth and spitting pieces on the ground. He
gnawed the half-desiccated flesh from the skin, then chewed the skin
itself for its last nutriment. What remained in the end was a compact
masticated pellet no larger than his thumb; he spat this over the bank
into the river.

Dark had come down quickly while he ate. There was no moon but
the sky was clear, stars needle-bright. He scooped out a hollow for his
shoulder with the knife point and then another for his hip and lay down
on his side and quickly slept. In dream, long voracious shadows lunged
and thrust into his side, turning and striking him again. He woke with
his fingers scrabbling frantically in the dirt, but the land was dry and
presently he slept once more. Another time he dreamed that someone
came and was standing over him, some weapon concealed behind his
back. He stirred and his lips sucked in and out, but he could not fully
wake at first; when he did wake he shut his hand around the wooden
handle of the knife and held it close for comfort. There was no one near,
no one at all, but he lay with his eyes open and never knew he'd slept
again until he woke, near dawn.

As daylight gathered he fidgeted along the riverbank, walking a hundred yards east of the road, then west, trying the water with a foot and
then retreating. There was no bridge and he was ignorant of the ford,
but the road began again across the river, beyond the flow of broad
brown water. At last he began his crossing there, holding both arms
high, the knife well clear of the stream, crooked above his head. His
chest tightened as the water rose across his belly; when it reached his
clavicle the current took him off his feet and he floundered, gasping, to
the other bank. He could swim, a little, but it was awkward with the
knife to carry in one hand. When he reached shore he climbed high on
the bank and rested and then went down cautiously to scoop up water
in his hands to drink. Then he continued on the road.

By midday he could see from the road some buildings of the town of
Saint Marc though it was still miles ahead, and he saw ships riding their
moorings in the harbor. He would not come nearer the town because
of the white men there, the English. He left the road and went a long
skirting way into the plain, looping toward the eastward mountains, over
the same low mounds and trees as yesterday. The edge of his knife had
dimmed from its wetting, and he found a lump of smoothish stone and
honed it till it shone again. Far from the road he saw some goats and one
starveling long-horned cow, but he knew it was hopeless to catch them
so he did not try. There was no water in this place.

When he thought he must have passed Saint Marc, he bent his way
toward the coast again. Presently he regained the road by walking along

a mud dike through some rice paddies. People had returned to the old indigo works in this country and were planting rice in small *carrés;* some squares were ripe for harvest and some were green with fresh new shoots and some were being burned for a fresh planting. When he reached the road itself, there were women spreading rice to dry and winnowing it on that hard surface. It was evening now and the women were cooking. One of them brought him water in a gourd and another offered him to eat; he stayed to sup on rice cooked in a stew with small brown peas, with the women and children and the men coming in from the paddies. Some naked children were splashing in a shallow ditch beside the road, and beyond was the rice paddy *bitasyon,** mud-wattled cabins raised an inch or two above the damp on mud foundations.

He might have stayed the night with them, but he disliked those windowless mud houses, whose closeness reminded him of barracoons. Also, white men were not so far away. The French had said that slavery was finished, but the man had come to distrust all sayings of white people. He saw no whites or slavemasters now among these people of the rice paddies, but all the same he thanked them and took leave and went on walking into the twilight.

He was as always alone on the road as it grew dark. The stars appeared again and the road shone whitely before him to help light his way. Soon he came away from the rice country and now on either side of the road the land was hoed into small squares for planting peas, but no one worked those fields at night, and he saw no houses near, nor any man-made light.

In these lowlands the dark did little to abate the heat, and he kept sweating as he walked; the velvet darkness closed around him viscous as seawater, and the stars lowered around his head to glimmer like the phosphorescence he had seen when he was drowning in the sea. He seemed to feel his side was rent by multiple rows of bright white teeth, and he began running down the road, shouting hoarsely and flailing his knife. Also he was afraid of *loup-garous* or *zombis* or other wicked spirits which *bokors* might have loosed into the night.

In the morning he woke by the roadside with no memory of ever having stopped. The sun had beat down on him for half the morning and his tongue was swollen in his head. There was no water. He raised himself and began to walk again.

Now it was bad country either side of him, true desert full of lunatic cacti growing higher than his head. The mountain range away to the east was no nearer than it ever had been. He passed a little donkey

---

*A glossary of Creole and French expressions begins on page 681.

standing by the road, whose hairy head was all a tangle of nopal burrs it must have been trying to eat. He would have helped the donkey if he could, but when he approached, it found the strength to shy away from him, braying sadly as it cantered away from the road. The man walked on. Soon he saw standing water in the flats among the cacti, but when he stooped to taste it, the water was too salty to drink. Presently he began to pass the skulls of cows and other donkeys that had died in this desert place. Somehow he kept on walking. Now there were new mountains ahead of him on the road, but for a long time they seemed to come no nearer.

Toward the end of the afternoon he reached a crossroads and stopped there, not knowing how to turn. One fork of the road seemed to bend toward the coast and the other went ahead into the mountains. *Attibon Legba,* he said in his mind, *vini moin* . . . But for some time the crossroads god did not appear and the man kept standing on the *kalfou,* fearing to sit lest his strength fail him to rise again.

After a time there was dust on the desert trail behind him and then a donkey coming at a trot. When it came near, he saw it bore a woman, old but still slender and lithe. She rode sideways on the wooden saddle, her forward knee hooked around the wooden triangle in front. The burro was so small her other heel almost dragged the ground, as did the long slack straw *macoutes* that were hung to either side of the saddle. She wore a brown calico dress and a hat woven of palm fronds, all brim and no crown, like a huge flat tray reversed over her head.

She stopped her donkey when she reached the *kalfou.* The man asked her a question and she pointed with the foot-long stick she held in her right hand and told him that the left fork of the road led to the town of Gonaives. She aimed the stick along the right-hand fork and said that in the mountains that way there were soldiers—black soldiers, she told him then, without his having asked the question.

She was toothless and her mouth had shrunken over the gums, but still he understood her well enough. Her eyes combed over the scars on his neck and shoulder with a look of comprehension, but at the old wounds on his side her look arrested and she pointed with the stick.

Requin, the man said. Shark.

Requin? the woman repeated, and then she laughed. *B'en ouais, requin* . . . She laughed some more and waved her stick at the dry expanses all around them. The man smiled back at her, saying nothing. She flicked the donkey's withers with her stick and they went trotting on the road to Gonaives.

Too late he thought of asking her for water, but then those straw panniers had looked slack and empty. Still he continued walking with fresh heart. These were dry hills he was now entering, mostly treeless, with shelves of bare rock jutting through the meager earth. The road narrowed, reducing to a trail winding ever higher among the pleats of the dry mountains. At evening clouds converged from two directions and there was a thunderous cloudburst. The man found a place beneath a stone escarpment and filled his mouth and belly with clean run-off from the ledges and let the fresh rainwater wash him down entirely.

The rain continued for less than an hour and when it was finished the man walked on. Above and below the trail the earth on the slopes was torn by the rain as if by claws. By nightfall he had reached the height of the dry mountains and could look across to greener hills in the next range. In the valley between, a river went winding and on its shore was a little village—prosperous, for land was fertile by the riverside. After the darkness was complete he could see fires down by the village and presently he heard drums and voices too, but the trail was too uncertain for him to make his way there in the dark, if he had wished to. It was cool at last, high in those hills, and he had drunk sufficiently. He scooped holes for his hip and shoulder as before and lay above the trail and slept.

Next morning there was cockcrow all up and down the mountains and he got up and walked with his mouth watering. The stream he'd seen the night before proved no worse than waist-deep over the wide gravel shoal where he chose to cross. Upstream some women of the village were washing clothes among the reeds. When he had crossed the stream, he turned back and stooped and drank from it deeply and then began climbing the green hills with the water gurgling in his stomach.

In a little time zigzag plantings of corn appeared in rough-cut terraces rising toward the greener peaks. He broke from the trail and picked two ears of corn and went on his way pulling off the shucks and gnawing the half-ripened kernels, sucking their pale milk. After he had thrown away the cobs his stomach began to cramp. He hunched over slightly and kept on walking, pushing up and through the pain till it had ceased. Now there was real jungle above and below the trail, and plantings of banana trees, and mango trees with fruit not ripe enough to eat.

When he had crossed the backbone of this range, he began to see regular rows of coffee trees, the bean pods reddening for harvest. And not much farther on were many women gathered by the trail's side, with goods arrayed for a sort of market: ripe mangoes and bananas and soursops and green oranges and grapefruit. A woman held a stack of folded flat cassava bread, and another was roasting ears of corn over a small brazier. Also a few men were there, and some in soldiers' uniforms of the Spanish army, though all of them were black.

The man crouched over his heels and waited, the knife on the ground near his right hand. The soldiers made their trades and left—it was only they who seemed to deal in money. Among the others all was barter, but the man had nothing to exchange except his knife and that he would not give up. Still a woman came and gave him a ripe banana whose brown-flecked skin was plump to bursting, and another gave him a cassava bread without asking anything in return. Squatting over his heels, he ate the whole banana and perhaps a quarter of the bread, eating slowly so that his stomach might not cramp. When he had rested he stood up and followed the way the soldiers had taken, carrying his knife in one hand and the remains of the bread in the other.

The opening of the trail the soldiers used was hidden by an overhang of leaves, but past this it widened and showed signs of constant use. The man crossed over a ridge of the mountain and looked down on terraces planted with more coffee trees. In the valley below was a sizable plantation with *carrés* of sugarcane and the *grand'case* standing at the center as it would have done in the days of slavery not long since, but all round the big house and the cane fields was encamped an army of black soldiers.

He was not halfway down the hill before he tumbled over sentries posted there. They trained their guns on him at once and took away his knife and the remainder of his bread. They asked his business but did not give him time to answer. They made him put his hands up on his head and chivied him down the terraces of coffee, prodding him with the points of their bayonets.

In the midst of the encampment some of the black soldiers glanced up to notice his arrival, but most went on about their business as if unaware. The sentries urged him into the yard below the gallery of the *grand'case*. A white man in the uniform of a Spanish officer was passing and the sentries hailed him and saluted. The white man stopped and asked the other why he had come there. Despite the uniform his face was not of the Spanish cast and his accent was that of a Frenchman.

Where is Toussaint? the man said. Toussaint Louverture.

The white officer stared a moment and then turned and sharply saluted a black man, also in Spanish uniform, who was then approaching. The black officer turned and asked the man the same question once more and the man drew himself up and began to recite:

Brothers and friends, I am Toussaint Louverture. My name is perhaps not unknown to you—

The black officer cut him off with a slashing movement of his hand and the man stared back at him, wondering if this could be the person he had sought (as the white officer had seemed to respect him so). But then a silence fell over the camp, like the quiet when birdsong ceases. A large white stallion walked into the yard and a black man in general's uniform pulled the horse up and dismounted. His face was no higher than the horse's shoulder when he stood on the ground, and his uniform was thoroughly coated with dust from wherever he'd been traveling.

The two junior officers saluted again and the black one drew near and spoke softly into the ear of the general. The general nodded and beckoned to the man who had walked into the camp from the mountains, and then the general turned and started toward the *grand'case*. His legs were short and a little bowed, perhaps from constant riding. As he began to mount the *grand'case* steps, he reached across his hip and hitched up the hilt of his long sword so that the scabbard would not knock against the steps as he was climbing. A sentry nudged the man with a bayonet and he moved forward and went after the black general.

On the open gallery the black general took a seat in a fan-backed rattan armchair and motioned the man to a stool nearby. When the man had sat down, the general said for him to say again those words he had begun before. The man swallowed once and began it.

Brothers and friends, I am Toussaint Louverture. My name is perhaps not unknown to you. I have undertaken to avenge you. I want liberty and equality to reign throughout Saint Domingue. I am working toward that end. Come and join me, brothers, and fight by our side for the same cause.

The general took off his high-plumed hat and placed it on the floor. Beneath it he wore a yellow madras cloth over his head, tied in the back above his short gray pigtail. The cloth was a little sweat-stained at his brows. His lower jaw was long and underslung, with crooked teeth, his forehead was high and smooth, and his eyes calm and attentive.

So, he told the man, so you can read.

No, the man replied. It was read to me.

You learned it, then.

Nan kè moin. By heart. He placed his hand above the organ he had named.

Toussaint covered his mouth with his hand, as if he hid a smile, a laugh. After a moment he took the hand away.

It was yourself who made those words, the man said, hint of a question in his voice. Those are the words you made at Camp Turel.

It is so, Toussaint told him, solemnly, with no smile this time, nor any gesture of concealment.

That is good, the man said, lowering his eyes.

Tell me your name, Toussaint said, and your own story.

The white men called me Tarquin, but the slaves called me Guiaou.

Guiaou, then. Why did you come here?

To fight for freedom. With black soldiers. And for vengeance. I came to fight.

You have fought before?

Yes, Guiaou said. In the west. At Croix des Bouquets and in other places.

Tell me, Toussaint said.

Guiaou told that when news came of the slave rising on the northern plain, he had run away from his plantation in the Western Department of the colony and gone looking for a way to join in the fighting. Other slaves were leaving their plantations in that country, but not so many yet at that time. Then *les gens de couleur* were all gathering at Croix des Bouquets to make an army against the white men. And the *grand blancs* came and made a compact with *les gens de couleur* because they were at war with the *petit blancs* at Port au Prince.

Hanus de Jumécourt, Toussaint said.

Yes, said Guiaou. It was that *grand blanc.*

There were three hundred of us then, Guiaou told, three hundred slaves escaped from surrounding plantations that *les gens de couleur* made into a separate division of their army at Croix des Bouquets. They called them the Swiss, Guiaou said.

The Swiss? Toussaint hid his mouth behind his hand.

It was from the King in France, Guiaou said. They told us, that was the name of the King's own guard.

And your leader? Toussaint said.

A mulatto. Antoine Rigaud.

Toussaint called over his shoulder into the house and a short, bald white man with a pointed beard came out, carrying a pen and some paper. The white man sat down in a chair beside them.

Tell me, Toussaint said.

Of Rigaud?

All that you know of him.

A mulatto, Guiaou told, Rigaud was the son of a white planter and a pure black woman of Guinée. He was a handsome man of middle height, and proud with the pride of a white man. He always wore a wig of smooth white man's hair, because his own hair was crinkly, from his mother's blood. It was said that he had been in France, where he had joined the French army; it was said that he had fought in the American Revolutionary War, among the French. Rigaud was fond of pleasure and he had the short and sudden temper of a white man, but he was good at planning fights and often won them.

The balding white man scratched across the paper with his pen, while Toussaint stroked his fingers down the length of his jaw and watched Guiaou.

And the fighting? Toussaint said.

There was one fight, Guiaou told him. The *petit blancs* attacked us at Croix des Bouquets, and fighting with *les gens de couleur* and the *grand blancs,* we whipped them there. After this fight the two kinds of white men made a peace with each other and with *les gens de couleur* and they signed the peace on a paper they wrote. Also there were prayers to white men's gods.

And the black people, Toussaint said. The Swiss?

They would not send the Swiss back to their plantations, Guiaou told. The *grand blancs* and mulattoes feared the Swiss had learned too much of fighting, that they would make a rising among the other slaves. It was told that the Swiss would be taken out of the country and sent to live in Mexico or Honduras or some other place they had never known. After one day's sailing they were put off onto an empty beach, but when men came there they were English white men.

This was Jamaica, where the Swiss were left. The English of Jamaica were unhappy to see them there, so the Swiss were taken to a prison. Then they were loaded onto another ship to be returned to Saint Domingue. On this second ship they were put in chains and closed up in the hold like slaves again. When the ship reached the French harbor they were not taken off.

Guiaou told how his chains were not well set. During the night he worked free of them, tearing his heels and palms, and then lay quietly, letting no one know that he had freed himself. In the night white men came down through the hatches and began killing the chained men in the hold with knives.

Guiaou covered his neck with his right hand to show how the old scars mated there. After several blows, he told, he had twisted the knife from the hand of the white man who was cutting him and stabbed him once in the belly and then he had run for the ladders, feet slipping in blood that covered the floor of the hold like the floor of a slaughterhouse. But when he came on deck the white men began shooting at him so he could only go over the side—

Guiaou stopped speaking. His Adam's apple pumped and he began to sweat.

It's enough, Toussaint said, looking at the tangled scars around Guiaou's rib cage. I understand you.

Guiaou swallowed then, and went on speaking. In the dark water, he said then, the dead or half-dead men were all sinking in their chains, and sharks fed on them while they sank. The sharks attacked Guiaou as well but he still had the cane knife he had snatched, and though badly mauled he fended off the sharks and clambered out of that whirlpool of fins and blood and teeth, onto one of the little boats the killers had used to come to the ship. He cut the mooring and let the boat go drifting, lying on the floor of the boat and feeling his blood run out to mix with the pools of brine in the bilges. When the boat drifted to shore, he climbed into the jungle and hid there until his wounds were healed.

How long since then? Toussaint said.

I didn't count the time, said Guiaou. I was walking all up and down the country until I came to you.

Toussaint looked at the bearded white man, who had some time since stopped writing, and then he called down into the yard. A barefoot black soldier came trotting up the steps onto the gallery.

Take care of him. Toussaint looked at Guiaou.

Coutelas moin, Guiaou said.

And give him back his knife. Toussaint hid his mouth behind his hand.

Guiaou followed the black soldier to a tent on the edge of the cane fields. Here he was given a pair of worn military trousers mended with a waxy thread, and a cartridge box and belt. Another black soldier came and gave him back the cane knife and also returned him his piece of cassava, which had not been touched.

Guiaou put on the trousers and rolled the cuffs above his ankles. He put on the belt and box and thrust the blade of his cane knife through the belt to sling it there. The first black soldier handed him a musket from the tent. The gun was old but had been well cared for. There was no trace of rust on the bayonet or the barrel. Guiaou touched the bayonet's edge and point with his thumb. He raised the musket to his shoulder and looked along the barrel and then lowered it and checked the firing pan. He pulled back the hammer to see the spring was tight and lowered it gently with his thumb so that it made no sound.

The other two black soldiers were almost expressionless, yet they seemed to have relaxed a little, seeing Guiaou so familiar with his weapon. Guiaou lowered the musket butt to the ground and looped his fingers loosely around the barrel. He stood not precisely at attention, but in a state of readiness.

2

The black soldiers were mostly camped in the woods on the rocky slopes above the compound of the *grand'case* and the cane mill, above the flat *carrés* of cane and the ascending terraces of coffee trees. Some of the men were housed in tents but these, someone had told Guiaou, were officers. He was free to make his own *ajoupa,* as the other men had done, and thus he spent part of the afternoon plaiting together long strips of *herbe à panache,* to make a roof he could erect on sticks against a face of rock. All around the place that he had chosen were other such shelters receding in all directions through the trees across and up the mountainside, much farther than he could see. There were more black soldiers here than he could count, many, many hundreds of them.

When he had completed the *ajoupa,* Guiaou sat down in the shade of the plaited roof. He placed his bread and cutlass and the cartridge box on a banana leaf beside him, and held the musket he'd been given across his knees. The air was so very still and hot that even the small movements of weaving his roof had put a gloss of sweat on his bare upper body. He sat motionless, cooling. The view of the fields and the buildings below was clear. After a passage of time Guiaou spoke to his neighbor, one of the soldiers who had outfitted him, whose name was Quamba.

"They are still working the cane in this place," Guiaou said.

"Yes," said the other. "They are working the cane."

"But they are not slaves who work the cane."

"Not slaves," Quamba said. "Soldiers. In return the *habitant* gives land for growing yams and corn. He gives his sheep and goats and pigs."

"It's that," Guiaou said.

"Yes, it's that," Quamba said, who sat beneath a roof improvised in the same manner as Guiaou's and backed into the same shelf of rock. He was looking in the same direction too, down into the compound; neither man had looked directly at the other when they spoke. The general Toussaint Louverture came down from the gallery, hitching up his scabbard to clear the steps and swinging on his plumed hat. He crossed the yard briskly and went into the cane mill.

"*Sé bon blanc, habitant-la,*" Quamba said after a moment. A good white man.

They did not say anything more. The air was growing heavier moment to moment, thick and damp, and everything was darkening, as though the whole of the mountain valley had been plunged underwater. With the subaqueous shading of the light a cold spot appeared in Guiaou's belly and began spreading toward his hands and feet, although his skin was still slick from the heat and his small efforts earlier. His damp palms tightened on the grips of the musket. Below, a white woman with straw-colored hair came hurrying across the compound, leading a little white girl by the hand; with her was a beautiful mulattress who carried a smaller child in her arms. The two women hastened into the *grand'case*, leaving nothing in the yard but a red and gold cock which zizagged aimlessly in different directions, scratching up dust and clucking, then finally darted under the steps to the *grand'case* gallery.

The rain came down all at once as if it had been dumped from a basin on high. No thunder and no turbulence, only a wall of water which closed off Guiaou's view; he could not see the compound of the *grand'case* anymore, nor any of the neighboring *ajoupas*. His own roof held up well enough, with a little water beading around the tight plaits of his weaving. As he'd hoped, the run-off downhill from the rain channeled itself around the rock at his back, so that the area where he was sitting remained quite dry. There was room enough that he might have lain down, even, but he remained sitting with his back against the cool stone. His fingers loosened on the musket, his eyes closed, and he seemed to sleep, although the slightest shift in the pulse of the rain would have been sufficient to arouse him.

*   *   *

Doctor Antoine Hébert lay listening to the rain rush over the roof of the *grand'case.* In the next room, the main public room of the house though it could hardly be called a salon, he could hear the whispering and bustling of the women: his mistress, the *femme de couleur* Nanon, and his sister Elise had just come in with the children. The doctor had been listening for their return for half an hour, and he was relieved that they had beaten the rain to shelter, especially for the sake of the children, for a soaking in this climate might lead to serious illness.

Now he could relax more fully, and he was bonelessly fatigued, for he had been working very hard through the earlier part of the day, further-ing a project he had conceived to divert the course of a mountain spring, both for irrigation and for pleasures he had imagined. He had put his own hands to this work not only for the shortage of *main d'oeuvre* but because it was easier for him so. He had not been in Saint Domingue long enough to accustom himself to slavery (which was now officially at an end in the colony, at least in those areas still controlled by the Republican French) and so he found it simpler to demonstrate his intentions rather than merely ordering that they be accomplished. He had worked most of the day with little respite before the approach of the rain and then had returned to the *grand'case,* where he'd washed himself and undressed to his shirt before stretching out on the bed.

The murmuring of the women faded in the other room and Doctor Hébert lay quietly, listening to the rain. Presently he heard Nanon come in and opened one eye to see her silhouette briefly framed in the door-way to the gallery. The rush of the rain water sounded louder for a moment until she closed the door.

"You're sleeping?" Nanon said in a low voice.

The doctor did not answer her. Because of the rain and the closed jalousies there was not light enough in the room for them to see one another very plainly at all. He closed his eyes as she approached the bed, and soon he felt one of her hands, cool and slim-fingered, smooth-ing over his brow and the sunburned baldness of his head. She paused, then with her other hand turned up his shirt tails and found him there.

"Voilà que ce monsieur reste en réveil, au moins," she said in a sly whis-per. Both her hands withdrew as she straightened from the bed. The doctor could not see her face, only the shadows of her arms unloosing the long scarf that bound her hair. The moist rain-swollen air was cool on the bare exposed fork of him. Her dress dropped in a whispering pool around her feet. When she came to the bed, he raised up onto his elbows and caught the corner of her mouth with a dry kiss.

"And Paul?" he said.

"Zabeth has taken him," Nanon whispered. The warm weight of her breasts pressed into his shirt front, and he dropped backward onto the sheets.

In the small brick-walled office of the cane mill, Toussaint Louverture sat reading drafts of letters by the light of an oil lamp. The rain made a steady roaring sound on the roof, and he had left the outside door open so that he could, at times, glance over and see the rain beyond the sill and eaves, a flowing wall of water. The letters were, in principle, his own, and all addressed to the same person, General Etienne Laveaux, who commanded the Republican French army in the Northern Depart-ment. Indeed there was only one letter, in principle, but Toussaint had not yet selected its final version. He had ordered different drafts from several of his sometime secretaries: Doctor Hébert, a mulatto youth who was called Moustique and who was the son of a renegade French priest, and Captain Maillart, a Frenchman who was now one of Tous-saint's officers but had formerly served under Laveaux and so had the advantage of knowing him personally.

Toussaint arranged and rearranged the three sheets of paper in the soft-edged, yellow circle of lamplight, smoothing them with his large hands. None was yet perfect, no version complete. Another Frenchman had turned up in camp that day, claiming to have recently deserted from Laveaux. Toussaint did not much believe his story, for the Frenchman, who called himself Bruno Pinchon, had more the air of a soldier of for-tune than that of a regular army officer. Nevertheless, he now thought of exploring the newcomer's epistolary style, on the following day, if not later that evening. He had sent Pinchon to dine with the white people who stayed in the *grand'case*.

Now he folded the letters away and turned his chair slightly to face the door and the rain flooding down beyond it. His eyes half-closed, he pictured places and the people in them as if on charts—as he com-missioned letter-writing, so he commissioned the drawing of maps, and one way or another these maps were always drawing themselves before his eyes.

Here was Habitation Thibodet, in the canton of Ennery, and not far from the coast town of Gonaives; here his army was established, the men he had been gathering and training since the first insurrection broke out on the northern plain in 1791. The army of Toussaint Louver-ture was now almost four thousand strong. Gonaives itself was under Toussaint's control, and he maintained a *quartier général* there, with a light garrison, but for the moment he preferred to keep the main body of his force withdrawn at Ennery, under cover of mountains and jungle instead of exposed on the coast. The English occupied Saint Marc, the next important town south on the coastline. The English had invaded from Jamaica and joined forces with the *grand blanc* royalist French and the slave- and property-holding mulattoes—they had restored slavery in whatever territories they could win for the English crown. In the Southern Department the English had made significant gains, Toussaint had heard. In the Western Department, they had most likely taken Port-au-Prince as well as Saint Marc. But news came uncertainly from those areas, which were divided from Toussaint's position by considerable distances ornamented with near-impassable mountains.

To the north lay Cap Français, the Jewel of the Antilles; this port was technically at least under French Republican control, though presently under command of a mulatto officer, Villatte. Toussaint knew that area well, having spent a good period of his life at Habitation Bréda, in the area of Haut du Cap. West of Le Cap, along the northern coast, Laveaux was hemmed in at Port-de-Paix—it was from here that Bruno Pinchon claimed to have defected. At the tip of the northwest peninsula, the English were found again, occupying the naval station of Môle Saint Nicolas.

In between these areas, which Toussaint could flag on his mental maps, all was confusion and uncertainty. He did not know the present position of the French Commissioner Sonthonax, Laveaux's civil superior and the man who had declared the emancipation of all the slaves in the colony. Sonthonax and his co-commissioner Polverel had last been heard of defending Port-au-Prince from the English; rumors of their defeated exodus had begun to reach Toussaint, but he had not yet confirmed them to his own satisfaction.

Eastward in his own rear were mountains and still more mountains, receding to the high range that marked the border with Spanish Santo Domingo, and encamped in these mountains were other black leaders who, like Toussaint himself, were for the moment in the service of royalist Spain and so at war with Republican France. At Marmelade, perhaps, was Biassou, and at Dondon Jean-François. Both were generals of the Spanish army; Toussaint had served beside them both, but now there was discontent between the two. There was discontent between both of them and Toussaint. Biassou and Jean-François commanded more men than he, but less securely; their men were less well trained and perhaps less loyal to their leaders. There was the question of who, ultimately, would be master, if there were to be just one.

Unlike the other black leaders now in the Spanish camp, Toussaint was served by various informants as far away as Europe—a place which he could only construct from their reports, since he had never left the island of his birth. Even as their enemy, he maintained certain contacts among the French Republican whites; it was no accident that his proclamation at Camp Turel had been issued on the same day that Commissioner Sonthonax had announced the abolition of slavery in all Saint Domingue. Yet Sonthonax had made *his* statement from a position of great weakness, as events now seemed to prove.

As for Toussaint himself, his name was not yet known to many—as he had, up to now, preferred. With the proclamation from Camp Turel he had committed himself to step out of the shadows which had hidden and comforted him throughout the first years of the slave rebellion. In which direction ought he to go from here? The English invaders certainly meant to uphold and restore slavery, along with the interests of the white and colored landowners who were their allies in the west. And for all their support of the black rebels, the Spanish also maintained slavery in their own territory, though with considerably less fervor—yet there was no thought of abolition there. The beleaguered French Republicans in the colony were currently declared for general liberty, for the little their actual force was worth, but whether that declaration would be confirmed in Europe was unknown. Toussaint understood the colony to be tossed among the European powers like a precious bauble, a stake or a pawn in their games of war. As yet he did not know enough to reason his way to an outcome. The bits of information he possessed lay quietly in his mind, like seeds.

He narrowed his vision now as he closed his eyes almost completely, his mental map contracting toward its center: his own men camped in concentric rings around the *grand'case* and the cane mill of Habitation Thibodet. Somewhere among them would be the new man who had come today, bearing the useful story about André Rigaud, the mulatto general who was fighting the English in the south. Guiaou. The scars made him memorable, the story more so. He would be resting now, after that long wandering. This thought itself was restful to Toussaint, who spread his hands on his knees and slept, still sitting upright in the chair, until the rain had altogether stopped.

Sometime after full dark the rain broke off with a shock of sudden silence, soon filled with rising voices of insects in the trees. The shift in sound was sufficient to rouse Doctor Hébert from the heavy sleep into which he had fallen. Nanon had gone out, leaving him a lit candle. He washed himself quickly, dressed, and went onto the gallery, where he found his sister Elise and her husband Xavier Tocquet already gathered with the Frenchman who had somewhat mysteriously turned up that morning. Tocquet was drinking a glass of rum and rolling an unlit Spanish cigar in his fingers. He had not troubled to put on shoes, and for that the doctor rather envied him.

"Ah," said Bruno Pinchon, turning to greet the doctor. *"Voilà le propriétaire!"*

"What?" the doctor said, bemused. In point of fact, Habitation Thibodet had passed to Elise on the death of her first husband, and so the plantation now technically belonged to Xavier Tocquet if it could be said to belong to anyone in the current state of affairs. But Pinchon carried on, excitedly, before the doctor could correct him.

"But it's marvelous here!" the guest declared. He was a smallish man, about the doctor's height but thinner, with disheveled wings of black hair and small, dark, moist eyes. He had also been drinking rum, perhaps to excess, the doctor thought.

"The men at work, the fields in good order—practically everything is well in hand," Pinchon enthused. "It's a miracle, you would not believe the disorders I've seen."

"Indeed," said the doctor, who had himself been borne along by several different torrents of fire and blood since the slaves of Saint Domingue had first revolted against their masters almost three years previously. He looked for relief toward the others at the table, but Tocquet had leaned back out of the circle of light, his eyes shadowed in their deep sockets; he nibbled the end of his cigar as if in a trance. As for Elise, she had arranged herself in an almost iconic pose of flirtation, eyes bright and lips just parted, but the doctor knew she might be thinking of almost anything else and that it was unlikely she was listening to anything Pinchon had said.

"Now this little popinjay of a nigger general . . ." Pinchon lowered his voice and become confidential. "That one must be easy enough to lead, no?" He made an obscure movement with his hands, fingers crooked, as if shaping clay. "As he has fallen in with the schemes of the Spanish, he might just as well be directed . . ." Pinchon winked, and waited.

Again the doctor was at a loss for a sensible reply. But at that moment boots came thumping up the steps and captains Maillart and Vaublanc joined the party, moving into the circle of light. Pinchon was distracted by introductions, and immediately following, the black housemaid Zabeth appeared from the kitchen, and with the help of Elise and Nanon began to serve the table.

Dinner was *soupe à giraumon,* followed by barbecued goat with hot peppers, brown peas and rice and chunks of yam. No wine, but a carafe of cool spring water and a bottle of rum stood on the table, along with a pitcher of lemonade. Between serving the courses Elise and Nanon sat and ate with the men; Zabeth had withdrawn to the kitchen. The two children had eaten beforehand and were playing on the gallery. Sophie, nearly four years old, came frequently to pluck at Elise's skirt and prattle. A plate of sliced mangoes was served for dessert and the little girl took bits of it, birdlike, from her mother's fork. Paul, the younger child, had just learned to pull himself to his feet; he crab-walked from one baluster of the gallery rail to the next. Whenever he reached the stairs by this route Nanon must jump up to restrain him from tumbling away into the dark.

Conversation was often thus interrupted, and was desultory in any case. The doctor noticed that Pinchon's garrulity was curbed by his appetite; he ate like one who's been on short rations for some time. When dinner was done, Elise and Nanon went into the house with the children. Zabeth cleared the plates, and when she had finished, Captain Vaublanc produced a greasy pack of cards from his coat pocket.

"Join us," he said to the table at large, as he began to shuffle.

Tocquet twisted his long hair back over his left shoulder, leaning into the candle to light his cigar. "Not at such stakes," he said as he settled back, exhaling.

Vaublanc grunted, unsurprised. His glance passed over the doctor and stopped on Pinchon.

"Eh, I find myself a little out of pocket," Pinchon said. "If the gentlemen would accept my note . . ."

"But of course," said Vaublanc, nodding toward some smudged sheets of accounting which Captain Maillart had just then spread across the table. "Our own notes are . . . most detailed."

Pinchon squinted at the papers, blanched, and retreated. *"Bien, c'est trop cher pour moi,"* he said. Too rich for my blood.

"As you wish," said Maillart with glum resignation. "Though it's tedious with only two."

For a moment it was silent except for the cards snapping on the table. The three nonparticipants watched the play. Tocquet poured himself a half-measure of rum and sipped it slowly while he smoked. Vaublanc and Maillart were gambling for scraps of paper, each inscribed with the name of a slave. The game had been going on in this way for some weeks. Doctor Hébert had no idea how Captain Maillart had first staked himself to it, for he had few assets other than the army commission he had thrown over (as Vaublanc had his own) when news came from France of the King's execution. But Maillart was either the more skillful or more fortunate player, and by this time he had to his credit almost half of the six hundred slaves which Vaublanc, nephew of a wealthy planter of Acul, could claim as his eventual inheritance. Of course the Acul plantation had been burned to the ground in the first insurrection of 1791 (like everything else on the northern plain), its buildings razed, and its slaves scattered who knew where? The officers might as well have been playing for beans or buttons; the doctor thought that Maillart understood this principle well enough, though he could not have said as much for Vaublanc, with whom he was less intimate. It was probable that at least some of the slaves of that Acul plantation were now serving as foot soldiers right here in Toussaint's army.

Tocquet emptied the last swallow from his glass and rose. Without taking leave, he walked barefoot down from the gallery into the yard. Starlight silvered his loose white shirt, and his cigar head glowed and shrank in the darkness.

Pinchon pulled at the doctor's elbow and steered him away from the table. *"Un homme un peu farouche, celui-là,"* he said, looking toward the diminishing glow of Tocquet's cigar. A wild man, that one.

"If he gambles he prefers to choose games he can win," the doctor said.

"I don't mean that," Pinchon said, drawing the doctor along toward the farthest end of the gallery. "All very well to acknowledge one's half-breed bastard—if one must—but to seat one's mulatto whore at table? and with white ladies . . . Well, and the man didn't even have on shoes."

"You're saying that—" the doctor broke off with his mouth still open. He was beginning to grasp the nature of Pinchon's confusions: if the newcomer assumed that he were married to Elise, that would explain he'd been taken for the proprietor of the plantation. A casual observer might well be inclined to pair Nanon with Tocquet, who was certainly the more obviously unconventional of the two white men presently occupying the *grand'case.*

"Nothing serious," Pinchon was going on. He had turned to face the card players again, but spoke to the doctor in a half-whisper, partially shielding his mouth with his hand. "Such conduct might gratify the egalitarianism of our so-called Commissioner Sonthonax, but I tell you that an English protectorate will soon put an end to all such fantasies. I myself, sir, am just come from Saint Marc, with an offer from General Whitelocke for the submission of this rabble here. Of course your Toussaint Whatever-he-calls-himself and the other principal niggers can be paid off . . . but to bring the matter forward I must know who really is in charge of them."

Pinchon closed his mouth and looked at the doctor cannily. The doctor watched the card players, halfway down the gallery, enclosed in a moist nimbus of light. A large green moth swirled toward their candle. Maillart flipped it away with his fingers but it soon returned. Vaublanc cursed the moth and batted it away with his hat.

"Your discretion is admirable," Pinchon said. "Perhaps it's better so. In any case the old buffoon has engaged me to write his letters for him"—he winked—"which should make the affair much easier to conclude."

Still the doctor said nothing. Retracing his way through Pinchon's first remarks, he struck against the phrases *half-breed bastard* and *mulatto whore*. He had been on the verge of explaining to Pinchon the extent of his misapprehensions, but now he decided he had just as well let the man work it out for himself.

At first light Guiaou's eyes opened to greet a small striped lizard poised on the matting of damp leaves just beyond the shelter he had erected. The lizard's tail had been broken off and it was just beginning to sprout a new one from the stump. He made no attempt to catch it; he was not half so hungry as before.

Also he still had his cassava bread, which he took with him when Quamba rose and beckoned him to follow. They followed a well-beaten trail to a clearing where many men were seated in a circle. An old woman was grinding coffee in the hollowed stump of a tree, using a staff as tall as herself for a pestle, and another was roasting corn over a char-coal fire. The men held out gourds or handmade clay vessels or odd-ments of European crockery to receive their coffee ration. Quamba was served by a pretty young woman with glossy black skin, her hair swept up in a red and gold-spangled *mouchwa têt*.

"Merbillay," Quamba said, watching Guiaou's eyes track her as she passed. Quamba shared his cup with Guiaou, who had none of his own, and Guiaou passed him half of the remaining cassava bread. Someone gave each of them a steaming ear of corn.

They assembled for drill behind the cane mill on the flat ground where the *bagasse* was stacked. Guiaou's group was commanded by the same Frenchman in Spanish uniform he'd seen the day before, who was called Captain Maillart. A black officer was with him, the Captain Moyse. Under the orders of these two, the men formed in a square, marched, reversed, shouldered arms, presented them, knelt and aimed but did not fire. The movements were well-schooled, automatic—Guiaou was accustomed to them from his service with the Swiss, though per-haps the drill was a little crisper here. His arms and legs remembered to respond without thinking. No thought was in him, only his limbs answering the voices of the officers and a cool vacant space behind his eyes.

Maillart's voice cracked and the men formed a double column and quick-marched off the improvised drill field. Guiaou's neck and shoulders began to itch. He had been marched in and out of cane fields in columns like this one, encouraged by a whip, and made to sing. He had been marched on and off slave ships with an iron collar riveted around his neck. Now they were marching through the small *carrés* of cane, and other men were working there, but the soldiers did not stop. In silence the double column began to climb the terraces of coffee trees, Captain Moyse at the head and Captain Maillart in the rear. The hillside was steep but Moyse urged them, his voice lower and broader than the white man's, so that they did not slacken speed.

Where the coffee ended a trail began, rising through clumps of bamboo and twisted flamboyants clinging to the cliff side—a red slash in the rocky earth. The men went up in single file, swinging into double time at Maillart's order, stooping low and sometimes scrabbling with the free hand to keep going. When the ground leveled off at the ridge top, Maillart's voice snapped again and the black soldiers dispersed from the trail like a flock of stone-scattered birds, rolling into cover of the brush and taking up firing positions, which they held just long enough for Guiaou to breathe more easily. The air was thick. It was very hot. Below, a long way below, were the buildings and small cane pieces of Habitation Thibodet, tucked into pockets among the sudden hills.

Captain Maillart appeared on the trail, his sword drawn, expression focused—a hundred yards farther, Moyse also showed himself. At the word of Moyse the column re-formed and the men went over the crest of the ridge at a loping dog trot and scrambled down the opposite slope and then climbed the next *morne* at the same fast pace as before. Here there was no trail at all and the ground was wet and slick—a chunk of earth ripped away under Quamba's feet and he began to fall backward, but Guiaou steadied him from behind and urged him on so that they did not lose much speed. At the height of the next hill they scattered from the trail again to find firing positions under cover. Guiaou used the little time to check his cartridges and the mechanism of his musket, and then to breathe. When Captain Maillart showed himself again, he was sweating very much, much more than the black men sweated. Of course he wore a full uniform, and had kept up the pace in the tall, heavy boots he had on his feet, while most of the black soldiers were barefoot and wore little but their trousers and their weapons.

They marched down the hill at an easier pace and traversed the squares of cane at a different angle. By the time they reached the area behind the cane mill, the sun had climbed almost to its height. There they were given a ration of water and then dismissed.

Doctor Hébert was standing knee-deep in water in the swampy area behind and above the *grand'case,* when Captain Maillart, sweat-soaked and breathless, climbed the little colline to find him there. When he saw the captain approaching, the doctor straightened from his work and pulled off the broad-brimmed straw hat he wore to protect his balding head from the sun. He dipped the hat in the water and then replaced it on his head. The hat had been soaked so often it had lost all shape and the brim hung down the back of his neck like a wet rag.

"Je m'excuse," the captain said. He took off his uniform coat and spread it delicately over a thornbush, then removed his shirt and began to wring sweat out of it. The doctor surveyed him with a medical eye. Maillart had lost much weight since his days with the regular French army, so that his ribs showed plainly through the skin and his uniform trousers bagged around his hips, but if he was thin he looked healthy enough.

"News," Captain Maillart said, turning to lay his damp shirt beside the coat. "I am dispatched to General Laveaux— at Le Cap or Port-de Paix or wherever I may find him."

"When?" The doctor stooped to rinse his grimy hands and then climbed out onto the bank, which was now partly reinforced by a dam of mud and stones.

"We leave tomorrow."

"Ah," the doctor said. "But it's dangerous for you—or not?" He knew that Maillart was at least technically a deserter, having decamped from Laveaux's revolutionary command along with a good many other officers of similarly royalist inclinations.

The captain's thin shoulders hitched in the air. "Who harms the messenger who brings good tidings?" He grinned.

"Indeed?" the doctor said, in some surprise.

"Well, we must wait upon events," the captain said. "I am authorized to express . . . receptivity, one might say."

"Ah." The doctor took off his hat and squinted at the sun. He smoothed his damp hands back over his bald spot. "It's an odd moment to choose to join forces with the French," he said. "Their fortunes have hardly been at lower ebb since the first insurrection."

"They?" the captain said. "The French?"

The doctor laughed uneasily. Both he and Maillart were French themselves, but the colony had been fragmented in so many different directions that questions of allegiance had become rather difficult to contemplate.

"That point may press you more closely than it does me."

"True," the captain said, his face briefly clouding.

"This Monsieur Pinchon claims to have an overture from the English at Saint Marc."

"I didn't know," the captain said. He stared down at the pool of water, where three black men were continuing work on the dam. "It's plausible. In general these English prefer to bribe than fight—but they've restored slavery in whatever territory they've taken, so I can't think Toussaint would receive such a proposal. Still . . ."

"Difficult to know his mind, isn't it?"

"Truly," the captain said. "There's his advantage."

The doctor called to Bazau, who led the work gang: "Break off, shall we? Get out of the heat. We will begin again at three." Bazau nodded and all three men came climbing out over the reinforced bank. They smiled at the two white men and started down the hill.

"I meant to ask if you'd go with me," the captain said.

"Tomorrow?" said the doctor. "I don't know. I wouldn't like to leave this work half done."

Both men turned to survey the water project. "A pool just here," the doctor said, "for the children. All this area will be drained." He waved his hand. "We might plant flowers, on the border of the pool." He turned and pointed downhill toward the *grand'case* and the outbuildings. "Then a channel to bring the overflow down past the kitchen . . ."

"Most elegant," the captain said. "Fanciful too, for time of war."

"There's not been much fighting in our area," the doctor said, "as you certainly will have noticed. In any case it's a matter of necessity. All this seepage has already begun to rot out the floors of the *grand'case*."

"But you'll become too bucolic in your habits," the captain said, with a smile that sought to evoke past dissipations—if not debaucheries. "How long has it been since you've seen Le Cap?"

"I believe I've seen it more recently than you," the doctor said, "at which time it was well on its way to burning to the ground. You must ask Xavier—he's more restless than I."

"One might have need of your famous marksmanship along the way," the captain said.

The doctor smiled. "I think you'll find Xavier quite capable," he said, "in case of any such need."

Guiaou and Quamba were working in the stable, brushing mares and geldings and combing out their tails. It was Quamba's regular duty—when a slave, he had been a groom. Guiaou was inexperienced with horses, had never mounted anything larger than a donkey. But with Quamba's directions he began to relax to the work.

In the last stall on the row the big white stallion hung his head over the half-door, whickered and turned restively, and pressed against the door again. Quamba reached up casually and caught hold of his halter.

"The horse of Toussaint," he said in a respectfully low tone. "Bel Argent." He unlatched the door and slipped inside. Guiaou followed, ill at ease. As he entered the stall the stallion jerked his head and danced sideways. Guiaou plastered his back to the wall.

"Be still," Quamba said. It was unclear if he was addressing the horse or Guiaou, who was certainly transfixed to his place and barely breathing. Quamba stroked the stallion's long nose with his free hand, then turned to Guiaou.

"Brush him, as I showed you," he said. "He's wanted soon."

Guiaou did not move from the wall. Quamba sighed. "Hold him, then." And when Guiaou still remained motionless, Quamba took hold of his wrist and brought his hand to the halter. He picked up a brush and began to work down the stallion's right side.

Guiaou looked into the stallion's huge alien face. The stallion's nostrils flared red, his eyes rolled, and he began to rear, lifting Guiaou to his toes.

"Don't look at him like that," Quamba hissed. "You frighten him. Here, don't face him. Turn this way and hold him gently. Be a post."

Now Guiaou and the stallion were shoulder to shoulder, both looking out over the half-door down the hallway of the stable. Guiaou could feel the horse's warm breath flowing over the back of his hand. He took a sidelong glance, then reached and delicately touched the horse above the nostrils. The skin was warm and velvety, astonishingly soft. Both he and the horse now seemed to be growing calmer.

Doctor Hébert walked downhill with the captain and parted from him at the edge of the main compound. Toussaint must be intending to ride out again, he thought, for Quamba and Guiaou had just brought his horse into the yard, saddled and bridled and awaiting its rider. The stallion was stepping high and nervously, hooves slicing in the dust. Muscles twitched under his glossily brushed hide. The doctor turned and slowly began to climb the gallery steps, fatigued and a little giddy from the heat.

"If you please—"

Toussaint's voice. The doctor turned left along the gallery and saw them sitting at the table where they'd dined the night before: Bruno

Pinchon and the colored youth called Moustique. He saw the general's uniform, stiffly formal and correct, the general's hat with its white plumes laid on the table. It was odd, he thought again, how one noticed Toussaint's uniform first—the man inside it reserved into a sort of invisible stillness, until he moved or spoke. Now Toussaint reached across the table to take the sheet of paper Pinchon had been writing on. He sat back, holding the letter close to his face.

The doctor stopped at the table's edge and remained standing. He was a familiar of such scenes. Most likely it was the same letter he had drafted himself the day before. Toussaint liked his various secretaries to compose in ignorance of each other's efforts—he himself would decide upon a final synthesis.

Now Toussaint frowned at the paper. His free hand unconsciously adjusted the knot that secured his yellow headcloth, then dropped below the table, to his waist. Pinchon leaned back, elbow on the gallery rail, a smirk on his face—he seemed to wish to catch the doctor's eye. Toussaint stood up and away from the table with a silent cat-like movement, crumpling the letter with his left hand while with his right he flourished out a flintlock cavalry pistol as long as his own forearm and leveled it at Bruno Pinchon's forehead. He held the pistol rock-steady for just long enough for the Frenchman to register what was happening and then he pulled the trigger.

The firing mechanism snapped. The doctor was acutely aware of a crow calling, then gliding to light on the eave of the cane mill. Pinchon's Adam's apple worked convulsively in an eerie silence. The pistol had not fired. The doctor looked into Toussaint's face, rigid as some inscrutable wood carving. In the yard, Bel Argent kicked and half-reared. Guiaou cried out and broke away while Quamba followed the horse, dragging at the reins.

Toussaint thrust the pistol into its holster, put on his hat and walked quickly down the steps, hitching up the scabbard of his sword. He said something low, indistinguishable, and Bel Argent calmed instantly. Toussaint put the reins over the stallion's head and turned back to the gallery.

"Moustique! Find a donkey."

The boy jumped up and ran for the stables. By the time he returned, astride a small donkey, Toussaint had checked the girth buckles and mounted. He wheeled the stallion and rode out of the yard. Moustique followed on the donkey, at a jouncing trot.

Pinchon had propped his elbows on the table and covered his face with palsied hands. The doctor sat down in the chair Toussaint had occupied. He unfurled the wadded letter, read a line or two and tossed it away with a snort.

"So you didn't write what he dictated."

Pinchon peered at him through the cage of his trembling fingers. "I hardly supposed the man could read."

"Your suppositions are most inexact," the doctor said. "You've insulted his intelligence." He looked down; a large red ant was just surfacing through one of the wider cracks between the boards of the gallery floor. The pistol might have misfired by chance, but the doctor did not much associate that sort of accident with Toussaint Louverture. If he had intentionally spilled the powder from the firing pan before aiming the pistol, he might also have wiped it into a crack with the edge of his boot.

Pinchon took his hands from his face and forced them to steady by bracing them hard against the tabletop. "What must I do?" he said.

"I don't know," the doctor said. "You can't stay here."

3

Moustique's legs were longer than the donkey's; astride, he could hardly keep his bare feet from dragging on the ground. He leaned forward, throwing his own slight weight up the steepening grade, stroking the donkey's mane to encourage it. They were mounting through the coffee trees, Moustique following Toussaint, who rode the white charger. At the edge of the cultivation, high on the hill, Toussaint turned his horse into the forest, onto a still steeper slope. Moustique followed, urging the donkey with a squeeze around his legs, which scissored around the animal's belly so far that his feet could almost touch. Under the trees, a damp, green cool was lingering, welcome now at the day's fullest heat.

Underfoot it was also damp, the earth tearing under the animals' hooves. Moustique watched the white charger, Bel Argent, sleek packets of muscle moving in his hindquarters. Toussaint, with a light pressure of his heels on the horse's flanks and a few clucks of his tongue, negotiated his way around a shelf of raw rock overhung with vines. When he had reached the height of this himself, Moustique looked back once, but there was nothing to see but jungle; Habitation Thibodet had disappeared.

He had never been so high, on this particular mountain. The slope grew still more arduous, so that Moustique believed that Toussaint must surely dismount, but he seemed knitted to the saddle. Bel Argent yawed sideways, scattered wet dirt with his hooves, and finally seemed to scramble up onto some sort of level ground. In a moment Moustique had maneuvered his burro over the same lip; he found that they were standing on a narrow stone road, just wide enough for one mounted man to pass, or possibly two men walking abreast. Toussaint glanced at him dispassionately, wheeled his horse and started westward at a trot. Moustique followed. There was a hoof clack from Toussaint's mount as they went on, as if they were crossing a cobblestone street. Moustique looked down and studied the road's surface; thousands of smallish flints set close against each other and mortared in place by mud. He wondered who possibly could have made it.

"*Les caciques,*" Toussaint said, with a half-turn of his head, as if Moustique had asked the question aloud. The Indians. They were dead now, all of them, their line extinguished. Nearly so. Once, before the insurrection, a band of maroon blacks had passed the little church on the Massacre River, and Moustique's father had pointed out among them a mestizo: the glossy black hair completely straight, the flat, coppery patina of his face. His father had kept a box of small stone objects made by those extinguished Indians, ax heads, laughing and groaning faces, phalluses and animal figures all in a jumble. He was dead now too, Moustique's father.

To the north side of the road, the jungle opened into a sudden, long declivity, which gave view to a fertile valley far below. Beyond were more mountains, chains of them receding from green to distant blue, to the warped misty line of the horizon. Moustique imagined he could see the ocean, or smoke rising faintly over Cap Français, where his father had been executed on the public square, bound and broken on a wheel. The jungle closed over the road again, shut off the view, but Moustique saw in his mind's mirror the executioner's hammer falling to break a shin or elbow, and his father's voice shouting in reply: *Domine, non sum dignus!* He would not weep, and his mother was equally iron-faced, standing beside him in the crowd, only she had bitten through her lips until the blood ran out the corners of her mouth, as if she'd just been killing something with her teeth. Both before and afterward Moustique had been stoned by other boys of his own age and often of his color too; they mocked him for being the son of a priest. That day he felt nothing from the stoning, though afterward he wondered at the wild rainbows of color the bruises raised on his gold skin.

He stopped thinking, let the memory drop. He had learned this, since those terrible days in Le Cap, this emptying, like the passage from dream to sleep, though his eyes were open, all his senses present; he could remark land crabs clinging to the narrow boles of trees, a green parrot gliding silently across the roadcut up ahead, was half aware of the mutual sweat that glued his knees to the donkey's sides, and grateful for the woven straw saddle, round and soft like a coil of bread. A wooden saddle would have broken his hips in the course of the afternoon, he imagined. They rode briskly, with only two brief halts, once to water the animals and drink themselves from a small spring, a second time for Toussaint to dismount and gather herbs.

In the late afternoon, with the air suddenly, ominously cooling, they broke from the road and went down a trail-less jungled slash in the mountainside, so steep that Moustique thought the white horse must surely fall or break a leg, but Bel Argent managed nimbly as a mule, Toussaint remaining mounted all the while. They climbed the other side of the gorge and struck a well-worn trail on the opposite height, a red wound in the dirt deep as the knees of Moustique's donkey. Some passages seemed impossibly steep, but the white war horse went up them like a man mounting stairs. The wind stepped up, sudden and sharp; the trees swayed back away from it, and Toussaint looked over his shoulder to grin briefly at Moustique, the white plumes dancing on his hat, then squeezed and leaned and urged his horse a little faster up the slope.

The wind whistled, carrying a couple of crows over their heads like string-cut kites, and a black pig broke from the undergrowth and stared at them and ran the other way. Not a wild pig, Moustique took note; it was round and complacent, domesticated. A first raindrop came horizontal, like a bullet, and exploded on his cheekbone. Then they had gained a saddle of the ridge and were surrounded by the barking of two tiny savage dogs that snapped from behind a patchy fence of cactus, guarding a small mud-walled *case* planted on a flat area of bare packed earth. Toussaint slipped down from his horse at once. Moustique hesitated—he was afraid of the dogs, but an old woman appeared and cursed the dogs in Creole so that they stopped barking and slunk behind the house.

Toussaint had already stripped saddle and bridle from his horse. He improvised a halter with an end of rope and tied Bel Argent to a sapling's trunk. All around them, the trees were tossing in a whirlpool turbulence; higher on the ridge Moustique saw the crown of a mapou tree thrashing among the others. A younger woman snatched up an iron cauldron from an outside fire and carried it into the shelter of the house. Toussaint grinned and gestured, and Moustique pulled the saddle from his donkey. The bridle was rope, which rain would not harm; he used the reins to fasten the donkey to another tree.

The young woman met them in the doorway, kissing Toussaint at the corner of his mouth for greeting. *"Bon soir,"* she said, and offered Moustique the same formal kiss. The straw saddle kept their bodies separate as lips brushed cheek. She was younger than he'd thought, perhaps even younger than he. Inside the *case* it was quite dark and full of a rich, warm smell from the stewpot. No sooner had they crossed the threshold than the rain dropped down outside like a waterfall.

"N'ap manje," the old woman said out of the darkness. We'll eat.

She passed them halves of hollow gourd and they ate without speaking, sitting crosslegged with the gourds on their knees: a stew of goat meat and brown beans well spiced with small, piquant yellow peppers, and chunks of cassava bread to sop round the edges of the bowl. The girl sat near enough the door that she was covered by the gray rain-streaked daylight, more visible than the others. For every mouthful she swallowed herself she carefully chewed a bite of goat meat and laid it on a piece of bread for the old woman beside her to take in her gums.

When they had finished eating, the old woman stared at the wall of water beyond the doorway for some minutes and then remarked that it was raining. Toussaint agreed that this was true. The old woman waited a few minutes more and then said that they must stay and rest during the rain; Toussaint agreed with this proposal also.

One of the small spotted dogs had crept out of the corner and made itself as agreeable to Moustique as it might, licking the stew scent off his fingers. He lay down on his side, head pillowed on the straw saddle. Through the open door he could see the rain coming down in rivers, and Bel Argent moving a little restively on his tether. The donkey stood still, head lowered mutely under the flow of rain. Its whole near side was covered by an enormous R cut long ago with a hot *coutelas,* the mark of a onetime owner. The little dog curled against Moustique's stomach, and he covered it with his hand, feeling the hot quick pulse of its heart under his fingers, but he was thinking about the girl, watching her breasts rise and recede under the faded blue fabric of her shift as she breathed. The torrent of rain on the thatched roof was no more than a hush.

He did not know that he had slept until Toussaint shook his shoulder to rouse him. The rain had stopped long since and the yard round the *case* was bathed in the light of a moon just short of full. Bel Argent had provided a heap of manure, and Toussaint took a chip of wood and shoveled the droppings into the bush, away from the house.

Moustique saddled the donkey, climbed aboard and followed Toussaint away from the clearing. As they went, he heard from behind him a tap of drums, hollow and uncertain, in the area of the mapou tree. They rode, sometimes startling animals—pigs or goats or perhaps large lizards which made huge noises scattering from their path. So Moustique tried to tell himself, though he was fearful, remembering tales of *loup-garou,* or evil *bokors* who wore the skins of animals to travel in the night. They went on, speechless in the silver night, barred by shadows of the trees. By some trick of acoustics the drumming followed them a long way through the involutions of the mountainside, disappearing and then coming clear again, joined by the sound of singing voices. Moustique wondered if the girl were there among the *hounsis,* if she were dressed in white.

In the moonlight the plumes of Toussaint's hat rode tranquilly as a sail before an easy wind. Even after moonset he kept on at the same urgent pace, through the total darkness. Moustique could see nothing, nothing at all, but his donkey still seemed able to follow. He was numb, sleepy, still a little apprehensive; he wanted to speak but was afraid of being heard. At last a pallor began to dilute the general darkness, and cocks were crowing up and down the mountainside. Then the daylight appeared suddenly from all directions and they were riding into the village of Dondon.

The women of the little town had risen and begun the business of the day, and a few men also went to and fro in the dirt street—all of them black or colored, for the French *colons* had fled the place, those who had not been killed in the insurrection. Some of the men were dressed in oddly assorted rags and tags of European military uniforms. Toussaint halted one of these he seemed to know.

"Koté Jean-François?"

"L'allé . . ." The foot soldier's reply bespoke an eternity of absence, who-knew-where.

Toussaint rode directly to the church, a modest wooden building on a stone foundation. He hitched his horse and entered, sweeping off his hat at the threshold. Moustique tied the burro and followed him, blinking at the change of light. In place of candles they were burning torches of *bois chandel;* the pitchy smoke playing the part of incense. A few black women were scattered on the benches, and a pair of mulattresses dressed in penitential white. Two *blancs* in the uniforms of Spanish officers loitered just inside the door. At the altar stood l'Abbé Delahaye, his arms upraised to consecrate the host.

Toussaint dropped his hat on a backless bench and knelt before the altar, pulling off the yellow *mouchwa têt* he always wore and crumpling it in his left hand. Moustique looked curiously down on his grizzled hair, the bald spot toward the back. Never before had he seen Toussaint bareheaded. Then he remembered to kneel himself, but he still watched Toussaint sidelong, under his lashes, wondering at the docile, lamb-like manner with which he took communion. Next the priest moved toward him with the chalice and the bread, and Moustique closed his eyes completely and received.

After the service, l'Abbé Delahaye entertained his parishioner in the front room of the small house he occupied behind the church. A young black woman came into the room to serve them coffee—she had remained in Delahaye's service of her own volition, though she was no longer a slave. There were no longer any slaves in Saint Domingue. Delahaye smiled privately at the thought, groped in the sack of herbs Toussaint had presented to him, and began to spread the contents on the table: *sonnette, giraumon, tabac à Jacquot,* then something that he didn't recognize. He raised the leaves in his hand and turned to Toussaint.

"*C'est quoi, ça?*"

"*C'est thym à manger.*"

"*Et ça sert à quoi?*"

Toussaint was spooning sugar into his coffee, a great deal of sugar. "It is used," he said, "by women who wish that their children would not be born alive."

Delahaye straightened, stiffened, adjusted his stole.

"*Monpè,*" said Toussaint, "it must be said that oftentimes it is desirable to know of things which one does not intend to use."

Delahaye raised his eyebrows, then nodded, somewhat reluctantly. He opened a notebook, picked up a stick of charcoal, and quickly sketched the herb and its flower on the first blank page. When he had finished, he closed the notebook over the leaves and laid his hand on the cover to flatten it.

"My son," he said to Toussaint, "I see by your uniform that you are still given to the service of kings."

Toussaint didn't answer. His long-jawed black face was almost leadenly impassive. Delahaye had the impression that his sentence had overshot the mark and gone flying out the open door behind his guest, into the yard where the colored youth Toussaint had brought crouched on his heels, chatting idly with the black maidservant. That same mute impassivity was frequent among all those who had been slaves, whether African or Creole, but in this case it could not be assigned to stupidity or incomprehension. In the face of Toussaint's stillness, Delahaye felt utterly at sea. With some difficulty he kept his own silence.

Presently Toussaint loosened a button on his uniform coat and inserted his hand, as if to produce something from an inside pocket. But when he drew forth the hand, it was empty. From outside the door came the faint twittering cry of a swift darting over the *case*.

Delahaye sighed. "I have seen, for example, a letter which you addressed to the republican commander Chanlatte some months ago, wherein you denounce the commissioners, and the republican forces generally, for various cruelties in the field which you allege, but most especially for the cruelty of having executed King Louis XVI in France. In conclusion you say that it is not possible for you and your followers to recognize the commissioners until they have enthroned another king."

"As you know, *monpè*," Toussaint said, "I am merely the junior officer of my generals Biassou and Jean-François—"

"Yes, my son," Delahaye broke in, "I know this even too well, for it was I who spoke to your generals on behalf of the commissioners of the Republic, to which they replied that they had never done anything since the world was made except to carry out the will of kings, and thus they too could not recognize the commissioners until France had enthroned another king."

"It was not I who composed those phrases," Toussaint said.

"Perhaps it was not," said Delahaye. He sighed again and scratched his stiff graying hair, cut carelessly short in the manner of a Roman soldier. "And yet their similarity to those you did compose is remarkable."

"Not so remarkable as the power of your memory, *monpè*."

Delahaye grimaced at the compliment, thin lips tightening against his teeth. "It is true that I study your correspondence with interest whenever it comes my way. In your letter to Chanlatte, for example, you claim that your own party—that is to say, the party of the Spanish and their king—is the only one to truly serve Divine Justice and the rights of man. And yet, if you pride yourself (as your letter also suggests) on the fidelity of your news from Europe, you must also know, or at least suspect, that enthusiasm for the rights of man has overthrown kings, rather than upholding them."

Toussaint had turned his head slightly, so as to look through the open door. Delahaye studied his profile, the durable set of his underslung jaw.

"It is difficult for me to understand you as a warrior for the *ancien régime*," he said. "No doubt you have considered the role played on the coast by the English—good royalists all, and they serve slavery even as they serve their king. As do your Spanish masters, who have not set free *their* slaves."

Toussaint faced him. His hand rose and covered his mouth, as if to block an impulse to reply. Still he did not speak, but Delahaye felt the quickening of his attention.

"Meanwhile," he continued, "the black leaders of the early rebellion have found shelter in the mountains. I think, for example, of Macaya, and of *his* reply to the commissioners. *I am the subject of three kings: the King of the Congo, Lord of all the Blacks; the King of France, who represents his father; the King of Spain, who represents his mother. The three kings are the descendants of those who, led by a star, went to adore the Man-God. Therefore I cannot serve the Republic, as I do not wish to be drawn into conflict with my brothers, who are the subjects of these three kings.*"

"Yes," Toussaint inclined his head. "I have heard that he spoke in that way."

"Indeed," said Delahaye. "I will not call Macaya a savage—I should say, he is a man certainly, yet not a man of your gifts, nor of your attainments. I had thought that you were better instructed than to enter into the simplicity of his thought. Yet you find yourself in agreement with him."

"I have not said that my purpose is the same as his."

"Nor have you said that it is not." Delahaye permitted himself a smile, which Toussaint seemed vaguely to return. "But perhaps your purposes are not the same as those of Biassou and Jean-François either, nor those of the Spanish throne—which, I may observe, is allied with the English against France."

"The Generals Jean-François and Biassou enjoy a higher rank than my own in the army of his Spanish Majesty," Toussaint said, "but I do not answer to their orders. My force is separate from either of theirs."

"That is well," Delahaye said. "You may know—I believe that you must know—that those two generals of yours continue the traffic of slaves. That men and women and children have been taken even on the borders of this town, and brought down to the coast in chains, then loaded like cattle—onto Spanish ships."

"I have heard report of this, but my own eyes have not seen it."

"Yet you support such an abomination?" Delahaye searched the dark face for a sign of reaction.

Toussaint looked at him mutely, waiting. The priest folded his hands and closed his eyes for a moment, breathing slowly.

"My son," he said, "I am convinced that you will find the rights of man of which you have written better served by the French Republic than by any of these nations still ruled by kings. And as you set such store by the quality of your information, I think it would very much interest you to know that the proclamation of Commissioner Sonthonax has been confirmed by the French National Assembly: Slavery has been abolished, once and for all, throughout all our French colonies."

"Is it true?" Toussaint said eventually.

"It's I who tell you."

"*Monpè*, I give you my most perfect confidence."

"Come home to France, my son," breathed Delahaye. "The arms of the Republic are open to receive you."

"*Doucement,*" said Toussaint. "*Doucement allé loin.*"

"*Oui, toujours,*" said Delahaye.

Toussaint set down his coffee cup with a deliberate clatter. "But today I have come on another errand," he said. "The boy—his name is Jean-Raphael, though everyone knows him as Moustique. He is the son of the Père Bonne-chance who was executed at Le Cap for having assisted in the tortures committed by Jeannot against the *blancs* and for having procured white women to be raped by—in any case it must be said that in truth Père Bonne-chance did none of these things, that he was a good and godly man and that his identity was mistaken by the *blancs* who judged him."

"I am familiar with that terrible story," said Delahaye.

"As the boy is the son of a priest, it may be that he is destined for the priesthood," Toussaint said solemnly.

Delahaye turned his face to the wall to hide his smile.

"He is intelligent, and can read and write," Toussaint continued. "I would wish that you take him under your instruction for a time. Perhaps in that way he may find his place in the world at last."

"It is done," said Delahaye.

"I thank you," said Toussaint.

"You'll stay tonight?"

"No." Toussaint shifted in his seat. "I return immediately toward Ennery, today."

"In that case you will have missed Jean-François."

Toussaint displayed his empty palms. "Yes, so it would seem." He leaned forward, reaching for the priest's stole as if he'd touch it, but instead let his hands settle on his knees as he bowed his head, his whole upper body.

"Bless me, *monpè,* for I have sinned; it has been long since my last confession. I have too much mistrusted my fellowmen, I have even shed the blood of my brothers, I have spoken words not entirely true, I have even thought of serving other gods than Holy Jesus . . ."

Delahaye composed himself to listen. He knew from past experience that Toussaint could go on in this vein for a considerable time. And he was amazed, now and for a long time afterward, how the man could use so many words in his confession yet still, in the end, reveal nothing.

4

In a cool, mist-swirling dawn Guiaou woke for no reason that he knew
and saw the fetlocks of the white stallion stepping daintily through the
encampment on the slopes; Bel Argent was moving almost as quietly as
a cat. Toussaint sat the horse as upright and correct as if he were on
parade. He looked neither right nor left, and his face was dark and
unmoving as if it were molded in lava. Guiaou sat up. Quamba was just
then stepping out from the shelter of the next *ajoupa,* and Guiaou rose
also and followed him down toward the stables, in the path of Toussaint. As he passed he saw that others were rousing, tracking the horse
and rider with their eyes. No voice was heard, except for roosters crowing from their perches in the coffee trees all up and down the mountain.
Guiaou knew from the drifting aroma that women had risen and begun
to grind and brew the coffee for the morning.

The mist had already lifted from the flat of the stableyard, and the
light was coming up quick and clear. Toussaint dismounted and passed
the reins to Quamba, while Guiaou stood a few paces back, watching. From this distance he could see that Toussaint's uniform was not
quite so immaculate as it had appeared from farther away: his linen
was grubby at the throat and his breeches were sweat-stained and

shiny from long friction against the saddle. Toussaint nodded briefly at Quamba and looked for a moment at Guiaou out of his yellow-rimmed eyes, as if he were considering something, but he turned away without saying anything and walked toward the *grand'case*, reflexively hitching up his sword hilt as he approached the steps. The beautiful mulattress was drinking coffee on the gallery, and she raised her cup to the black general as he came nearer.

Quamba and Guiaou led Bel Argent to a stall, where they combed and brushed him. Guiaou held his head while Quamba picked out his hooves; he felt calmer with the horse now than he had felt before. Afterward they rubbed his coat all over till it gleamed, then fed him and left him in the stall. By midafternoon Toussaint had ridden out again, with the white doctor and Captain Moyse and twelve other horsemen. One hundred and fifty foot soldiers made up the party, and among them were Quamba and Guiaou.

They went by a different way than the one Guiaou had taken when he'd come to join this army, though roughly in the same direction. On the backbone of the *morne* above Habitation Thibodet they struck a narrow stone road whose like Guiaou had never before seen, and followed it westward through its twists along the ridges, the horsemen riding single file while the foot soldiers marched two by two at a pace just short of a trot. Guiaou went by the side of Quamba, their shoulders sometimes brushing when the jungle edged them closer together. They had marched for perhaps two hours when the rain began, but despite its force they did not stop. At the head of the column, the white plumes of Toussaint's hat drooped and sagged under the rushing weight of water. Guiaou kept pace with the other men, rainwater streaming through his hair and down his bare chest—he sucked in water at the corners of his mouth. At first it was not unpleasant, cooling. He marched, grasping the stones of the road with his toes, covering the lock of his musket with one hand. No one spoke; there was no sound but water pouring over the broad leaves of the jungle trees around the column.

When the rain had stopped, it was fully dark and the men halted for twenty minutes, long enough to dry themselves and eat cold provisions: cassava bread and baked yams that they carried. A rag went round the immediate group of Quamba and Guiaou, and when it came to him, Guiaou used it to dry the mechanism of his musket. His heavy leather cartridge box had been well oiled, and when he looked he found that it had kept his powder dry. While they were eating, there was a little desultory talk.

For some two hours after the meal they continued through the moist night, moonlight silvering the dampness of the leaves around them, until at length they left the road and slip-slid down the slopes of the *morne* to cross a river valley. Here the main body camped for what remained of the night, though Toussaint and six of the mounted men kept going, leaving Moyse in charge of those who stayed.

Next morning they lingered where they had camped for long enough to brew coffee and warm their rations. Toussaint and his party of outriders returned as they were finishing the meal, but they did not dismount even for a moment. Toussaint drank a gulp of coffee in the saddle, and then they all set out once more. All through the morning they threaded their way along the chain of *mornes* that divided the interior from the coastal plain. On the heights, Guiaou now overlooked the cactus desert he had crossed before, in the opposite direction, on his way to reach Toussaint. In the heat of the day they halted for an hour around a small freshwater spring, drinking and dozing a little until the order came to march again. By the hour of the rain, they had come out of the mountains and were marching in low country—they kept going through the rain as before, slowed by the mud that sucked at their legs. When the rain stopped, there were fires ahead on the horizon and they pressed on to reach a rice-growers' village where they were fed and spent the night.

In the morning they went on again through the same terrain. The white masters had fled this territory, and the indigo works were all abandoned or destroyed, unless they had been converted to rice-growing by those of the former slaves who stayed here. All day they marched, skirting the edge of the low marshy plain, never far from the chain of mountains which would shelter any retreat they might suddenly be obliged to make. They saw no trace of any enemy, though now they were coming nearer to the areas thought to be occupied by the English.

In the late afternoon someone at the head of the column called a halt for something he saw in the distance ahead, and when Guiaou shaded his eyes and looked westward, it seemed that he did see a large party of red-coated soldiers advancing across the rice paddies, yet these, when inspected by Toussaint and his officers through a glass, turned out to be nothing but flamingos. Some laughter passed among the horsemen at the recognition of the birds, then the column moved on, quick-marching through another downpour, and that night reached the village of Petite Rivière.

With daylight they entered the town in good order, marching between tile-roofed houses strongly built of stone. Moyse gave permission for the men to take an hour of liberty in the *marché des nègres* behind the church, while the officers attended mass. In the market the people had come from the plantations all around, or from the mountains, and they were selling hats or saddles woven of straw, bags of peas, or sacks of salt collected from the salt pans on the coastal plain. Some had come as far as from Saint Marc with glass beads and iron knives and ax heads, while others offered poultry or meal ground from cassava or simply root provisions with the dirt still clinging to the tubers. A line of small burros stood roped together; one nibbled covertly at a stack of the straw hats. All those vendors there were blacks who had been slaves, except those maroons who had come out of the mountains. The only whites found in Petite Rivière now were a few shabby Spanish soldiers. Guiaou stood for some time admiring and handling long colorful scarves such as a woman might use for a *mouchwa têt*, but he had nothing to barter except his weapons and shot and these he would not trade.

As the bells of the church began to ring, the officers and the white doctor emerged and formed up the line. They marched out of the village, following the Artibonite River valley. Before midday they had changed their direction and crossed a chain of *mornes* into the gorge of the Rivière des Guêpes. From the hilltops they could now see the town of Saint Marc considerably in the distance, with the British flag flying from the ships in the harbor.

A man named Mazarin, walking just ahead of Guiaou, seemed to be distracted by the view and lost his footing on the rocky slope. He fell sideways with his left foot caught in a crevice of the rock, and back down the column they could hear the small bones popping in his ankle like wet sticks crackling in a fire. Mazarin began to cry out but caught himself short by biting his lips. He lay on his back, clutching at the injured leg, while the ripe black gloss of his face faded to a dismal gray.

The column halted and the white doctor dismounted to climb back up to the place where Mazarin lay. Toussaint also came back up the steep defile, but he remained on horseback. Guiaou studied the delicate care with which the big white stallion set his feet. The white doctor stooped over Mazarin and felt around his ankle and questioned him softly. Then the doctor took off his straw hat and turned to smile at Guiaou and Quamba, who were standing nearest to him.

"Hold him, if you please."

Guiaou and Quamba knelt and held Mazarin with his shoulders pressed hard into the turf and shale. The white doctor took hold of his foot and pulled backward as if he meant to detach it from the ankle. Mazarin surged against the hands that held him.

"*Mezi mezami,*" he said instead of screaming. Thank you, friends. The ankle popped again, and Mazarin subsided, releasing his lower lip with blood-stained teeth.

The doctor, who had sent someone else for water, made a poultice of herbs he produced from a bag tucked into his inner coat pocket, and strapped up Mazarin's joint tightly with strips of clean pale cloth. His rust-colored ears waggled unconsciously as he worked; a ring of sweat droplets had started up among the sparse hairs of his balding crown. When he had finished, Mazarin could rise, supported by one other man, and with support could hobble on one leg. With one man helping him, he was dispatched back in the direction of Petite Rivière.

The column resumed its way down the gorge, at a somewhat slower pace than before. In less than an hour they halted on slopes that had recently known cultivation—coffee bushes sprung untended in the jungle, and there were rows of cotton now overtaken by weeds and strangler vine. Moyse circled the group and selected ten men, Quamba and Guiaou among them.

They crept forward, crouching in the overgrown cotton planting, until they reached fresh furrows of the hoe—someone had begun a reclamation of this abandoned place. Across the waves of newly tilled ground they could see the house and mill. In the barnyard were some thirty horses tethered. The black men milling in the compound were armed as soldiers, though some carried hoes too. Also there were some colored men dressed in militia uniforms and white Englishmen wearing the red coats of the British army. Moyse pulled down his lower lip with his forefinger, calculating. Then the whole scouting party returned to the main column.

Toussaint sat his horse, digesting Moyse's report: fifty black soldiers—armed slaves rather, as the English had restored slavery in the area of Saint Marc—with twenty-five or thirty colored militiamen and twenty of the British regular army.

"*Bien,*" said Toussaint, laying his fingertips lightly on Moyse's left epaulette. "You will know how to manage it." His smile had a strange sweetness to it, for what he said. "*Et bon courage.*" He reached into his saddlebag and handed Moyse the brass-bound spyglass they had shared before. Then he touched up his horse and rode away up the river gorge in the direction from which they'd come that morning. Six horsemen, including the white doctor, broke from the line to accompany Toussaint, as if it had all been prearranged.

For most of the next hour, Moyse studied the English through the spyglass, occasionally passing the instrument to a white officer in his company, Captain Vaublanc. They spoke in low tones, discussing the movements of the men in the compound below. At last Moyse chose ten more men to add to the scouting party he had first selected. Vaublanc led the main force farther up the gorge.

Led by Moyse, the smaller group crept down through the cotton planting, crouching for concealment as before, though this effort seemed wasted now, since they were leading two horses whose empty saddles could plainly be seen from the compound. In fact, Guiaou saw the first of the armed slaves take note of the horses; the man straightened from what had been his task, stiffened with attention, then turned to call to one of his fellows. Moyse took a conch shell from his pocket and sounded it; the sound washed over Guiaou in a red wave and he was running across the open ground toward the buildings; all twenty of them were screaming as they charged. Moyse and Quamba vaulted into the saddles and swept ahead of the foot soldiers, Moyse controlling his horse with one hand and still blasting on the *lambi* shell with the other. Quamba was brandishing a burning torch. Guiaou watched him set fire to the barn.

It was all confusion in the compound—the armed slaves milling, crashing into each other, while Quamba and Moyse rode among them, striking in all directions with saber and *coutelas*. The horses tied to the barn rail were bucking and screaming from the smoke. Some of the red-coated English appeared, trying to form a line, a square, but the armed slaves were too frantic to obey them. Guiaou saw two mulatto militiamen dash for the barn; one began cutting the tethers of the horses while the other stove in a wall with an ax to release the animals within. He knelt, as he had been trained to do when he fought with the Swiss, and sighted carefully on one of the red coats before he fired, but the red coat did not fall. He reloaded painstakingly, not too fast, and this time other shots sounded with his own and two of the red coats fell, but from whose shot he didn't know.

Moyse and Quamba were riding back, Moyse shouting for retreat. The horses passed and Guiaou turned and followed them, his musket empty now. As they fled into the cotton planting he tripped and fell headlong, but instead of getting up to run again he turned, knelt, and reloaded. A military drum rattled in the compound. A dozen of the mulatto militiamen and a couple of English officers had managed to mount for pursuit and were coming quickly across the cleared ground while in their rear the other English had formed up the armed slaves in a line now advancing on the double. They were many, and Guiaou choked in the back of his throat, but he swallowed and set his sights on the head mulatto among the horsemen. The man was a honey-colored *sang-mêlé*—the same shade as those men who had betrayed the Swiss and finally sent them to the sharks—and Guiaou waited till the mulatto rider filled his eyes. He wanted to taste the man's death completely, but as he squeezed the trigger someone knocked down the barrel of his gun.

The horse shied and bucked from the shot and the mulatto fell, but rose immediately, cursing but unhurt. Guiaou tore out his *coutelas,* but was undecided whether to attack the enemy before him or the man beside him who'd spoiled his shot and now seemed to be whispering in his ear.

"Leave this one—then we will kill them *all."*

Guiaou was running again, following the other across the cotton—they were the last ones now in the retreat. A pistol ball hummed past him, not too near. Guiaou turned and did a mocking stiff-legged dance, waving his arms and sneering. Another of the mounted mulattoes was coming to ride him down, but at the last possible moment Guiaou broke to the side, slashing his blade at the rider's calf above his boot top. He was running again, stumbling on the stones of the river gorge, with that other man just a pace or two ahead of him, breathless but also seeming to laugh, and he could feel the presence of the other men hidden in ambush all around him, though he could not see them.

He kept scrambling up the gorge, bending forward as the terrain grew steeper. The mulatto militiamen were excellent horsemen (experienced from the *maréchaussée,* no doubt) and managed to remain in the saddle, though their pace was slowed, while the English had all been obliged to dismount and proceed more slowly still. Guiaou dodged behind a boulder at the stream's edge and reloaded his musket, then aimed again and shot the first mulatto out of the saddle. When the man had fallen, Guiaou jumped on top of the boulder, took down his trousers and bent over to waggle his bare buttocks at the enemy. Shots flattened on the rock below his heels and the pursuers howled with outrage. Guiaou did up his trousers and made ready to run again, but when he glanced back he saw that the trap had closed: the larger party under Vaublanc was firing from both rims of the gorge and men were already jumping down to dispatch the fallen with their knives.

Guiaou charged back down the path of his retreat, dragged forward by the rounded point of his *coutelas,* which slipped sweetly between the chest ribs of a colored militiaman, then twisted harshly to shatter the bones. And so with the next, and the next, and the next. At the bottom of the gorge where the ambush had cut off all retreat was an abattoir—the English had mostly already been killed, and the slaves were throwing down their weapons and crying for mercy. Guiaou reached a pair of English soldiers who were fighting back to back, quite skillfully, with their bayonets. His opponent was out of range of the *coutelas* but Guiaou paused a moment to judge the timing of the bayonet thrust, then swept his musket butt in an uppercut that stunned the English-man. He pounced cat-like on the fallen soldier and opened his throat with the *coutelas* as one might let blood from a hog, then immediately turned the corpse face down and tore off the red coat before the blood could spoil it.

He stood up, panting, holding the coat by the shoulders. Everyone near him was dead or surrendered or of his own party. The stranger who had knocked down his gun barrel stood by watching him curiously.

"It looks that you don't like the colored men," he said.

"*Sa*," Guiaou said. "I don't like them." He looked at the other, a small, wiry man with springy clumps of muscle bunched under his velvety skin. "What is your name?"

"I am called Couachy—and you?"

Guiaou folded the coat under one arm and reached out to embrace Couachy—they were each a little sticky from the blood of their enemies, so their skins separated with a slight tacky feel.

"*M rélé Guiaou,*" he said.

Before the end of that day they had reached Petite Rivière again, but they passed on without going into the village, marched an hour after darkness, and camped in the hills. Forty of the slaves who'd been armed by the English marched in the midst of their body, prisoners now. In the night some few of these slipped away and no one interfered with their escape, but on the next morning Moyse spoke to the ones who remained and said that if they would join the army of Toussaint they would be soldiers and free. A man named Jacquot, who seemed to be a leader among them, asked for what white nation or white general they would be fighting for then, and Moyse answered, for none; they would be fighting for their freedom and the freedom of other black people. Jacquot asked if their guns would be given back to them, and Moyse said that they would be given weapons after they had come to the main encampment in the north.

They went on. Guiaou began the day's march wearing the red coat he had taken from the English soldier, but Moyse rode back down the line and ordered all the men wearing such plundered coats to take them off, so they should not be shot from a distance by others who might think that they were English invaders. Guiaou was not discontent—it was hot to wear such a coat and he had more weight to carry than before: the Englishman's boots and his musket and the pistol he had worn in his belt.

All during their return they kept to the *mornes*, avoiding any passage across the open country of the plain. They kept away from any villages or other encampments that they passed, bivouacking in the bush and eating food they carried or could forage. The distance and difficulty of this route added a day's time to their journey, but they went in great good cheer, and during the last afternoon before they came to Ennery, hunters went out and killed wild pigs and goats. That day they reached Habitation Thibodet in time to shelter from the rain beneath their own *ajoupas,* and when the rain had stopped, many fires were built and the air was soon full of the smell of roasting meat.

Moyse and Jean-Jacques Dessalines, who remained in command during the absence of Toussaint, ordered an extra ration of *tafia* for the men who had been in the fighting. Guiaou sat with Quamba and Couachy and the new man, Jacquot, drinking his share of rum and eating goat meat hot from the *boucan.* He wondered where Toussaint had gone, since he had not returned to this encampment, but the thought did not really trouble him and after he had drunk more rum he forgot about it. For the first time he looked into the pockets of the red coat, where he found a thin gold ring which would just fit over the first joint of his smallest finger, and some folded papers with writing on them which he threw onto the *boucan* fire, and a gold case on a chain which looked like a watch but which when he opened it held a picture of a white woman instead. The Englishman's musket seemed better to him than the one he had been given when he joined Toussaint, partly because of the bayonet attached to it, so he gave the other to Jacquot, who had no weapon otherwise.

As they finished eating they began to hear drumming higher up the hill and voices of women singing in the *hûnfor.* The talk among them stopped and for a time they listened, heads lowered and their faces turned away from one another. At last there was a general movement among them, with no word. Guiaou put the chain of the picture case around his neck, and he donned the red coat and walked with the three other men up a twisting path toward the sound of drums and voices. Within the torch-lit clearing the *hûngan* named Joaquim was now calling, *Attibon Legba . . . vini nou . . .* and the *hounsis,* swaying in a line before the drums, sang in response. Attibon Legba, come to us.

The *hûngan* Joaquim stood near a sword driven into the ground, shaking the *asson* to the beat of the deepest drum. With each snap of his wrist the bead chains rattled on the gourd, and Guiaou felt a shadow pass him, swooping, stooping like the small hawks of the mountains. The scream, wild and desperately inhuman, thrilled him with fear and anticipation. A pace away from Guiaou, Couachy had been struck by the god. *Loa* of the crossroads, Legba, had come, to open the way from the world of spirits and dead souls to the world of living people.

Legba kanpe nan baryè, the *hounsis* sang. Legba is standing in the gate . . .

With others, Guiaou moved to support Couachy, who had been staggered by the shock of the descent. His eyes rolled back; when they
reopened, the irises were ringed clear round with white—the fixed and
alien glare of the possessed. He took a limping step toward the rattling *asson,* turning around the vertex of its sound. He limped because
his joints were wracked and twisted; Legba had made of the body of
Couachy the figure of a stooping, grizzled old man, weighed down by a
long straw sack that dragged from his shoulder almost to the ground.
The singing voices surrounded him.

Attibon Legba
Ouvri baryè pou nou
Attibon Legba
Kité nou pasé . . .

Guiaou's hands hummed from his contact with the *loa,* and he felt
that the front parts of his mind were darkening. But it was Jacquot, who
had also moved to support Couachy, who was taken now, he who shuddered and was transformed.

Attibon Legba
Open the gate for us
Attibon Legba
Let us pass through . . .

The gate was open. Maît' Kalfou had risen from beneath the waters to
stand in the body of Jacquot: Master of the Crossroads. Between Legba
and Kalfou the crossroads stood open now, and now Guiaou could feel
that opened pathway rushing up his spine—passage from the Island
Below Sea inhabited by *les Morts et les Mystères.* His hips melted into
the movement of the drums, and the tails of the red coat swirled around
his legs like feathers of a bird. With the other dancers he closed the
small, tight circle around Legba and Kalfou, who faced each other as in
a mirror: the shining surface of the waters, which divides the living from
the dead. Kalfou's bare muscled arms had raised in the form of the
cross, and his head was lowered like a bull's before a charge. He danced
as though he swung suspended from ropes fastened to the dark night
sky. The drums quickened and the *hounsis* sang.

Kalfou sé Kalfou ou yé
Kalfou ouvri rout la
pou moin pasé . . .

Guiaou circulated among the dancers, losing his companions, until he stood before the dancing line of *hounsis,* watching the woman he had watched before, Merbillay, who had served him coffee. He could feel the nearness of his own spirit, the *loa* who was the master of his head. The front of his mind grew more and more dark, and a heavy wing seemed to pass before his eyes with a strong beating movement. With one beat he might find himself looking at some tableau from his past (such as that moment when he stood fixed at the desert crossroads, before he found Toussaint, not knowing which road he must take to pass it), and with the next he would again see what was actually before him.

Kalfou, you are Kalfou indeed
Kalfou, open the road
that I may pass . . .

Behind the *hounsis* were the *petite* and *seconde* Rada drums and between them the big-bellied *maman tambour,* whose player struck it with small mallets, his face fixed and sweat-gleaming. Guiaou saw the flashing of the mallets, a pulse behind his eyes, and the drumming was a pulse in two places where his skull was joined to his neck: Marassa, the divine twins dividing in him, tearing the personal self who was Guiaou from the other that belonged to his *maît'têt,* the *loa* Agwé. The tearing sensation was both painful and pleasant, as a snake might feel ripping out of its skin, but at the same time he wanted to remain in his own senses and to look at Merbillay.

Guiaou was fixed on the crossroads once more, looking down one road and the other, setting his foot forward upon neither. He felt Merbillay's awareness, though she did not look at him. The circle of dancers around Legba and Kalfou blew toward the line of *hounsis* like a hurricane blowing in on a coast. Away from the other women, Merbillay was drawn into its eye, her left arm lifting by the wrist toward Kalfou's outstretched arms. The left hand hung like a chicken claw, slack and will-less, and a flash of alarm passed though Guiaou's whirling head: it was hazardous to give oneself over to Maît' Kalfou, whose intentions were twisted and unknowable. As Kalfou took the proffered wrist, a movement swelled up from the drums through the tightening circle of dancers, through Legba and Kalfou to stop upon Merbillay as if she were the tip of a whip cracking. The whiplash flung her against the ring of dancers; her eyes rolled back suddenly white in her head as she fell backward, legs kicking and arms jerking like the body of a decapitated chicken. The other *hounsis* caught her before she hit the ground, sustained her in a hammock of their arms, and Joaquim came to her and whispered in her ear and rubbed her head with a stiff urgent hand. When she stood again, her eyes were hard and glassy because she had become Ghede.

Ghede stood stiff and erect in the body of Merbillay, upright and rigid as a French *grand blanc*, rigorous even as a corpse (for he was Lord of the Dead, Ghede). Joaquim shook his gourd rattle *asson* behind the ear of Ghede, while one of the *hounsis* tore open a murderously hot pepper and placed a seed from it in the corner of Ghede's eye. Ghede accepted the burn without flinching, without even a blink, though any mortal being would have screamed and collapsed from the pain and fire of it, and so it really was Ghede, Baron Samedi, who called now for his special *clairin,* which was so hotly spiced with pepper too that an ordinary person could not swallow it. But Ghede drank deeply of this rum, then shook off his supporters and looked about himself.

Around the *loa* there was quiet, with here and there an uneasy smile, though farther back the drums were still traveling and the *hounsis* swayed in their line, but in silence. Ghede walked with a high, rubbery goose-stepping gait, looking at one person, then another. His stone-shiny eye was caught by the glitter of the picture case around the neck of Guiaou—he snapped it open and peered at the image of the white woman, then laughed and thrust out his tongue and turned away. Stamping his feet, Ghede turned in a circle, approaching others that hesitated in his area, while Guiaou circulated in an opposite direction, the picture case still dangling open on his bare chest, until Ghede faced him once again. The *loa* reached out to try the fabric of his coat lapel between thumb and forefinger, tugged a little, and fixed Guiaou with his stone eye.

"This *blanc* has gone to be with the dead today," Ghede said. "His coat belongs to me."

The proposition was inarguable—Guiaou surrendered the coat and Ghede slipped into it and puffed up further, springly erect as a man-part aroused, then bowed his legs and began to dance without moving his feet, rolling his hips and grinning ferociously. A three-foot staff appeared between his legs, tipped with a phallus carved in mahogany, whose smooth tip thrust with Ghede's hip roll toward the two oval halves and the hinge of the picture that rested on Guiaou's breastbone. Around them others began to laugh at Ghede's game, and Guiaou felt his own smile spreading over lips still glossy with goat fat, and he answered Ghede's dance with his own crouch and grind, until Ghede lost interest and swung away, the prick-tip of his staff seeking other partners, and then, sated with the sex dance, Ghede fell to eating, sitting splay-legged in a corner of the *hûnfor* with the red coattails fanned out behind him and hurling goat and pork and yams and cassava into the bottomless pit which was the hunger of Ghede.

By that time other *loa* had mounted their servants, Ogûn Badagris and Damballah and Erzulie, and there were more songs and still more potent drumming, until Guiaou was lost to himself and gave up his head to Agwé, so that he knew no more, himself, about anything that happened in the ceremonies. In a later quieter passage of the night he woke in his own *ajoupa* without knowing how he had come there. A dream was moving in him when he opened his eyes, nothing of Agwé but the own dream of Guiaou. All the encampment was quiet but for the sound of people breathing in their sleep.

The dream rose then, and using Guiaou's limbs it stepped outside of the *ajoupa* onto the hillside swimming in moonlight. Then the dream began to walk, carrying Guiaou's body by a way he hadn't known he knew, until it stopped before the shelter where Merbillay slept on her side with her cheek curled in one hand. Behind her a child was sleeping too, wrapped in the red coat which Ghede had claimed.

Guiaou stood still, feet planted on the ground like tree roots, while his body swayed lightly like a tall palm in the breeze and the cool night air prickled on the bare skin of his chest. His dream called in its silent voice to the woman till she woke. She sat up and saw him waiting there; her face was silvered in the moonlight and her eyes were black and swimming. She looked at him for a long time, it seemed, then looked at the child, that he would not wake. As she lay down again, her wrist arched up gracefully and her fingers curved back toward the wrist in a movement that seemed to shape a bridge. Guiaou stooped under the shelter's dry fringe of leaves, lowering his head as he went in to her.

5

A turning of the road from Limbé brought their party between the river of Haut du Cap and the cemetery of La Fossette. Captain Maillart rode beside Xavier Tocquet, flanked by six black soldiers of Toussaint's army who had been sent with them as an escort . . . or guard perhaps, Maillart thought, somewhat uneasily. To his left, Tocquet sat his chocolate gelding, seamlessly joined to the saddle. He had pulled the wide brim of his straw hat down to hide his eyes, and he rocked as easily with the horse's motion as if he were perhaps sleeping, as the blacks sometimes seemed to sleep aboard their burros.

The color was going out of the sky; soon it would be dark. Maillart could see the low roofs of the city of Le Cap, ahead where the river broadened into the bay and anchorage. He was relieved to be reaching the town before nightfall, and yet the passage oppressed him, just in this place. The swampy ground of La Fossette was fetid and unhealthy, putrid with shallowly buried corpses, and the blacks believed it to be frequented by the demons they worshipped—perhaps they were right, the captain thought. He had his own unpleasant associations with the place. He rolled his shoulders and looked toward the river, where a large painted pirogue with a stepped mast and furled sail moved in the brown current toward the town. Two black fishermen in the boat looked at the riders on the road as indifferently as if they were transparent. Ghosts. The fishermen were shirtless, glistening; the one in the stern held a long steering oar motionless in the stream behind him. They would not have looked so, Maillart thought, if they were still in slavery.

The huge sharp rise of Morne du Cap loomed over the road, the town, blocking out a large area of the fading sky. Maillart looked at the faces of the men who rode on either side of him, equally impassive as the fishermen in the boat, and yet he knew them: Ti-jean, Alsé, Pinon-brun. He had himself shared in their training, with a success proven earlier that same day, when brigands had attacked them outside Limbé. Inwardly Maillart smiled at the term—in some quarters they themselves might be called "brigands," by the English for example. The men who had attempted the ambush were perhaps stragglers from the bands of Pierrot or Macaya, who occupied these territories, after a fashion. The area outside Le Cap was contested between the French Republican Army (whatever remained of it) and the black leaders in service of the Spanish, though not too hotly at the moment, it appeared. But the marauders who'd attacked them seemed to be acting on their own agenda. There had been more than twenty of them, though poorly armed and easily dispersed. Maillart felt a warmth of pride in his little squad: they had not wavered. He even felt some small sense of security.

They entered the town by the Rue Espagnole. It was suddenly, deeply dark. Men passed on foot carrying lit torches; some candles were illuminated in the low buildings on either side. Most seemed to have been hastily and partially reconstructed from the fire that had razed the town the year before, when the bands of Pierrot and Macaya had overrun it. In the poor light, Maillart could make out little of the changes. He had not been in the town at the time of the attack, though his friend Antoine Hébert had described it for him in considerable detail.

Tocquet pulled up his horse in front of a hostelry Maillart remembered rather well from his former days in Le Cap, but the captain shook his head at the implied suggestion.

"Let us go directly to the *casernes*," he said, "to find Laveaux."

Tocquet looked at him without comment, then squeezed his horse's flanks and moved on. Maillart rode abreast of him, uneasy. His companion was a strange man, taciturn; they did not know each other well, and Maillart could seldom guess what Tocquet might be thinking. They turned and rode toward the barracks, into the shadow of the mountain at the edge of town. At the torch-lit gate of the *casernes*, Maillart addressed himself to the sentinel, saying that he had come with dispatches for General Laveaux. Without waiting for an answer, he led his little party through the open gate into the yard.

The sentry, a mulatto in French uniform, called to another colored soldier crossing the yard, who responded by bending his way toward the commanding officer's quarters, though without any special haste. Maillart waited, still astride his horse. After a moment he hoisted his canteen and sipped from the last inches of stale water. Now he rather wished that they had stopped at the inn Tocquet had indicated, for a stronger libation if not for a meal. He was saddle-sore, weary, and his heart misgave him rather. He had been billeted in the place for many months, but now he saw no one that he knew.

Presently the black soldiers dismounted one by one; they sat on a curbstone holding their horses loosely by the reins and talking quietly together in Creole. Tocquet got down too, handed over his horse to one of the others, and walked in an aimless circle around the yard, fanning himself with his hat though the air had cooled considerably. A sickle moon hung over Morne du Cap, cradling a star. Maillart kept waiting, to no result. Finally he climbed down from his horse and stalked across to the building where he'd been accustomed to report to his former superiors. When he entered the corridor he could see through the open doorway to his left a mulatto in the uniform of a French colonel, seated at a desk and writing by candlelight. As Maillart crossed the threshold, a black soldier jumped up and barred his passage with a musket held crossways like a stave.

"You must wait!" the soldier said, as he backpedaled Maillart out into the hall. Across the musket stock, Maillart caught the eye of the officer at the desk, who had once styled himself the "Sieur de Maltrot" after the French nobleman who was his father, but was more commonly known as Choufleur.

Then the door closed in his face. Maillart turned and found Tocquet, looking at him coolly, an unlit black cheroot pinched at the corner of his mouth. If not for the other's presence, Maillart might have stamped his feet and shouted; as it was he struggled to contain himself. Tocquet turned away from him without saying anything and went back out into the yard. The man had followed him soundlessly—even wearing riding boots, he walked as quietly as a cat.

Where was Laveaux? Maillart stared at the boards of the door. It occurred to him that he had not seen any white officer or enlisted man since arriving at the *casernes*. Since serving under Toussaint he had grown accustomed to a darker color scheme in the ranks, but here it might well be a trouble sign. After a moment he heard Choufleur's voice in the other room.

"Bring him in."

The door opened. Choufleur did not rise to greet Maillart, or offer him a seat. He continued writing for a moment, the pen's plume wavering between the two candles either side of the paper, before he looked up. His features were African but his eyes were bright green and his skin very pale, except for the spattering of chocolate-brown freckles all over his face—as if the white and Negro blood in him had somehow remained separate in the mix. Maillart had last seen him across the groove of his pistol barrel—had in fact been trying to kill Choufleur, during the mutiny of the mulatto Sixth Regiment.

"I have come with messages for General Laveaux," Maillart said stiffly.

"Yes . . ." Choufleur said, lazily, and as if he were responding to some completely different idea. "Yes, I do remember you—though not your name."

Maillart opened his mouth to supply this information, then stopped himself.

"Of no importance." Choufleur leaned back in his chair and waved his hand airily—a long-fingered, graceful hand, freckled like his face. "You were certainly one of those royalist officers, I recall." He rested his elbows on the desk top and squinted more closely at Maillart, who began to wonder just how well Choufleur might remember their previous encounters.

"I have it now," Choufleur said, snapping his long fingers. "Were you not the friend of that queer little doctor—Hébert? Who had taken up with the *femme de couleur,* Nanon . . . is that alliance still in effect? Where are they now?"

"At Habitation Thibodet, near Ennery." Maillart was surprised into this reponse. He wondered why Choufleur would ask so pointed a question, and on such an irrelevant matter.

"I have come to see General Laveaux," he repeated.

"There was a child, as I recall," Choufleur said musingly. "Of course, one does not know if it were his, in fact—does he acknowledge the child, your friend? Or did it live?"

Maillart felt his neck swelling in the collar of his shirt. "My dispatches are of some urgency," he said.

"As you like," Choufleur said airily, shifting his seat to glance at the dark window. "Laveaux is at Port-de-Paix. In his absence, Villatte commands, but as he is not here at present, you may give your messages to me."

Maillart tightened, aware of a compression of breath and blood in his throat, as though he were being throttled. He drew himself up and touched his waistband. Under the cotton weave of his loose white shirt he could feel the handle of a dirk and the butt of his pistol. He had come on this journey in civilian clothes, dressed in the same fashion as Tocquet, and concealing his weapons as a pirate would. Both a French and a Spanish military uniform were packed in his saddlebags, but it would not have done to come here wearing either.

"J'écoute," Choufleur said.

Maillart willed himself to relax, exhaling consciously, letting his stiff shoulders fall. He thought of Toussaint, not knowing why the image of the black man came to him. Next to the door behind him was a chair and Maillart drew it toward the center of the room, sat down, and crossed his legs.

Choufleur leaned over the desk top toward him. "I remember you, Maillart," he said. "You were one of those who refused to receive me in the Regiment Le Cap—for this." He touched the skin on the back of his left hand, below the braid of his uniform cuff. "But I receive you more generously. I remember too that you are a deserter, Maillart. You might be hanged for a royalist—we conduct such executions here."

Maillart said nothing. The candle flames wavered. Choufleur's shadow distorted itself across the rear corner of the room.

"Your dispatches," Choufleur said.

Maillart kept silence. He felt oddly relaxed now, drained of ill temper, of injured pride. The fatigue of his journey was perhaps responsible. He studied Choufleur in the yellow light: he was rather a handsome man. His close-cut reddish hair showed to advantage the elegant African shape of his head. Maillart's way of observing such details had changed during the time he'd spent in the interior. But the swirl of freckles across Choufleur's face remained constantly perplexing. Maillart said nothing. There was power in silence. If you held your own stillness, your interlocutor might lose his balance, tumble forward into the hollow space you set before him, and fill it with more words. Maillart had sometimes found himself in such a spot with his black general, blurting out sentences he'd never meant to say.

"Je vous attends," Choufleur said, but nothing more. Perhaps he was not to be drawn in such way.

"I mean no offense," Maillart told him. "But my commander's instructions are very explicit. My messages are for the ears of General Laveaux only. I regret to be unable to oblige you."

"Your commander." Choufleur's eyebrows arched. The freckles swam with the movement of his skin.

"I have come directly from Toussaint Louverture."

Choufleur laughed—a startling, silvery sound. The laugh was not bitter or mocking but had a tone of amused astonishment. It struck a note of sincerity for which Maillart was completely unprepared. He was moved to smile himself, but suppressed that response.

"The world is a very strange place," Choufleur said. "Do you not find it so?"

Maillart rose from the chair he'd taken. "Undoubtedly."

"How the world has changed since last we met! That you should serve under an ignorant slave who was, not long ago, the Comte de Noé's barefoot coachman. And who does he serve, your Toussaint 'Louverture'?" Choufleur released the surname with an opprobrious twist. "Who is that old man's master now?"

Maillart remained silent, wondering if Choufleur really believed that Toussaint still had a master. He let himself be the first to break their stare. Choufleur turned to the soldier who'd remained standing at the door throughout their conversation, and barked out orders that he should lead Maillart and his companions to a billet where they could pass the night.

"But we will take lodgings in the town," Maillart protested.

"The gate is closed here for the night." Choufleur's voice was peremptory as before. He was no longer looking at Maillart; he had taken up the plume of his pen. But as Maillart crossed the threshold, Choufleur did look up, as if to halt him with a glance.

"That plantation, what was it called? Near Ennery, you say?"

"What?" Maillart turned in the doorway, mildly confused.

"Hébert, your doctor, and his woman." Choufleur was impatient.

His first flash of anger at this prying felt distant from Maillart, heat lightning on the horizon. He looked at Choufleur for a moment without reply. Then: "The matter seems to interest you."

Choufleur swallowed. "Not particularly."

Maillart went out. The soldier led him and the others to a single room on the opposite side of the barracks. He unlocked a door and gestured at the dim interior, then went away and left them there. Inside were a single low bedframe strung with rope, and hooks for hammocks on the walls, but there were no hammocks or any other bedding.

"We're prisoners, then?" Tocquet's eyes bored into Maillart's face.

"For the night, possibly."

Tocquet struck a light to his cheroot, exhaled; a bloom of smoke spread in the room, before he stepped outside again. Maillart was abashed. His impatience to discover Laveaux—certainly they'd have done better to stop the night at some tavern and present themselves here in the morning instead. He wondered a little about Villatte . . .

another mulatto officer. His stomach whispered discontentedly. There'd been no mention of any kind of rations.

Outside, the new moon hung like a silver knife blade, above the *casernes* courtyard and the black hulk of Morne du Cap. The outline of the mountain was traced by stars appearing in the sky beyond it. Two of their party were just then returning from stabling their horses. Tocquet spoke.

"Gros-jean, Alsé—anou alé, chaché manjé." He made a drinking motion with his hand as well. They departed, Tocquet walking in between the other two. Gros-jean and Bazau had been owned by Tocquet before the insurrections, Maillart knew. Though the two blacks were now enrolled in Toussaint's forces, that had not apparently changed their relation with their former master—which often seemed to be a partnership in mischief. They answered to Toussaint or Tocquet with equal alacrity, and no one had so far found any inconsistency in this arrangment.

Maillart sat down on the single step that raised the door sill from the cobblestones of the barracks yard. A knot of men on the far side of the court seemed to be speaking in ordinary French. Perhaps they were remnants of the republican brigades that had come out with the second commissioners. Maillart did not expect to know them. His own regiment had been deported *en masse* by Sonthonax, sometime after the excecution of the King in France, after his own consequent defection to the Spanish party. The Dillon regiment, where he'd had friends, was transferred to Le Môle on the western peninsula, past Port-de-Paix. He had lost many of his friends before that time, to disease and accident and actions against the Negroes in revolt on the plain outside Le Cap. On the marshy burial ground of La Fossette his regiment had fought an all-out battle with the rebellious mulatto Sixth. Maillart had seen a close friend killed in that engagement, not two paces from where he stood himself. He had fired his pistol at Choufleur but failed to hit him. Now this leader of that mutiny was an officer in apparent good standing with the French military while Maillart himself could not safely choose a uniform to wear. The world had indeed become strange to him.

Tocquet and the others returned across the courtyard, supplied with ship's biscuit and smoke-dried goat meat they had managed to requisition somewhere. There was a gourd of fresh water and, miraculously, another of the new cane rum called *tafia*. Alsé carried a bundle of hammocks under one arm as well. There were no plates or forks or cups. They sat crosslegged in a circle to eat, passing the gourds among them. Maillart was softened by the effects of the rum. He chewed the stone-hard victuals slowly.

When they had eaten, Tocquet produced a pair of dice and they gambled for the sleeping places. Tocquet himself won the second of the four hammocks that had been obtained. Maillart won the rope-strung bed, if that were victory. The last three men stretched out on the bare floor beside him, underneath the heavy sway of the hammocks above. Above and below, their shoulders all touched; the room was close as a ship's cabin.

Ti-jean slapped at a mosquito. "Sweet blood," Tocquet mocked from his hammock. "*Ou gegne sang doux.*" Ti-jean cursed.

Maillart believed he would not sleep at all, then woke near dawn with a rope burn on his cheek. By good daylight they saddled their horses and bluffed their way past the light guard at the gate of the *casernes*. They provisioned themselves at an inn in the town and set out on the road to Port-de-Paix.

Laveaux's force was quartered at the Grand Fort on the Point des Pères—a promontory overlooking Port-de-Paix harbor. In size the structure no longer lived up to its name; it had been sacked and dismantled by enemies and a smaller enclosure erected within the original boundaries. Maillart left Tocquet and the black soldiers to wait for him, sitting on the rubble of the hundred-year-old walls. He climbed to the gate of the newer barrier alone.

In the event he was rather uncomfortable in meeting his former commander. The clothes he wore seemed the badge of his dishonor. He expected Laveaux's glance to rake him collar to cuff, but in fact the general looked him only in the eyes, while taking his hand and greeting him cordially.

Maillart faltered through congratulations on the other's promotion—Laveaux had still been a colonel when last they had met. Laveaux's responding smile was thin, ironical. Deep lines were graven around his mouth and eyes, despite his youth. He had lost flesh from both his face and limbs. He beckoned Maillart into a low stone room of the fort.

"Would that I had wine to offer you," he said. "But we are in a bad case here, officers and men alike. Myself, I take six ounces of bread a day, and drink nothing but water."

"But in Le Cap they seem well enough provisioned," Maillart said. "The . . . colored officers."

"Ah," said Laveaux, with the same thin smile. His chair creaked, or perhaps it was his bones, as he craned his head to look up at the low ceiling beams. "Those gentlemen dispose of private means. Whereas my own have long since been exhausted." He fluttered a stack of correspondence with his left hand. Peering across the table, Maillart recognized, upside down, the florid signature of General Whitelocke, who commanded the English invaders in the Western Department.

"The English offered to repair my fortunes with a bribe of *cinquante mille écus*," Laveaux said. "A modest price for the surrender of my command . . ."

"You're joking." Maillart was genuinely shocked.

"Not at all." Laveaux restacked his papers. "I have the letter somewhere—well, never mind it. The colored commanders have been offered more, I'm told. Rigaud, for instance, in the south. I might perhaps have negotiated a higher price . . ." Laveaux's eyes narrowed and turned inward. "Also they assured me I could keep my property—which is reduced to this." He pinched the threadbare cloth of his coat sleeve. "With my trousers and boots—not that they would bear a very close inspection. And of course my arms." He looked at Maillart. "I must confess I miss tobacco most of all. One does not know what to do with one's hands. It's cheerless to sit here. Let us go out."

Maillart ducked under the low lintel and followed Laveaux into the open air. "But how did you respond to Whitelocke?" he inquired.

"I informed him that, enemy or not, he had no right to offer me such a personal insult," Laveaux said. "I demanded satisfaction—in short, I challenged him to a duel. The choice of weapon to be left to him."

"And then?"

Laveaux laughed, attracting the attention of a soldier who stood watch behind the brick-and-mortar wall. "Why, to be sure a single combat would have been much more to my advantage than his—speaking strictly from the military point of view. Therefore he had small reason to accommodate me. He has shifted his ground, and now sends me appeals to my 'nobility' as he likes to put it, meaning my former title as a count."

Maillart flushed and looked away across the battlements. At the edge of the little town, dark surf strummed on a gravelly beach before a single row of trees. Beyond the breakers, within rowing distance as it looked, the island of Tortuga was gloomy under its cover of jungle.

"It is well for us that the English prefer to purchase their victories," Laveaux said. "Otherwise we might be overwhelmed in half a day here. Look at that one—" He lowered his voice. "Not too directly."

Maillart glanced sidelong at the sentinel, whose tunic and trousers hung in rags. He was barefoot, starveling, a mad glint in his eye.

"He's representative, you see," Laveaux said. "I must send them to post barefoot, like slaves."

"Have you much illness?"

"Fortunately no," Laveaux replied. "The men are well acclimated now—those who survive. The problem is rather starvation. We are dangerously low on both powder and shot. Nothing comes from France, not so much as a word. I write to plead my case, protest my loyalty . . . I would do as well to throw the letters on the fire and hope the smoke might be seen in Paris."

"And the commissioners?" Maillart said. "Sonthonax can procure you no supplies?"

"Both he and Polverel are recalled to France," Laveaux said. "The change in government, you know—they must answer for their excesses." He snorted and spread his arms wide. "I am the highest French authority in all this land!"

The sentinel turned and looked at him strangely, tattered mustachios fluttering in the strong northwest wind from the sea. Laveaux sobered and dropped his arms. He studied a small lizard walking a crevice of mortar in the wall, as if perhaps he'd make a snatch for it.

"Truth," he said. "I will not surrender. I will retreat from hill to hill still fighting. Albeit soon with muskets used as clubs."

"Listen." Maillart's throat worked; he swallowed a portion of his shame. Below the rampart he saw Alsé holding his own horse: French uniform in the left saddlebag, Spanish in the right. Himself in mufti, uncommitted. The horse itself was a stunted specimen, raised on short commons and hard work. Maillart had turned his coat for the death of a king. It seemed foolish now, unconvincing. His connections to the aristocracy of the *ancien régime* were far more tenuous than those of Laveaux, who looked at him now, attentively.

"When I—when I . . . left Le Cap," Maillart swallowed again with some difficulty.

"Yes, man, go on."

"I entered Spanish service." It was said. The words came more readily now. "Since then I have been under orders of one of the black chiefs, he who is known generally as Toussaint Louverture—perhaps you may have heard of him."

Laveaux looked peculiarly interested. "Not only that, but I have tried to send him various messages—through l'Abbé Delahaye. Tell me, do you bring an answer?"

"No—I don't know—not exactly," Maillart stuttered. "I don't know anything about that . . . but it would be like him to open communication on several lines at once. I am to tell you that he would be . . . receptive."

"Receptive." Laveaux's regard was fixed.

"He now commands four thousand troops, or a little more—not the largest force in the interior, yet others might join him were he to change sides. His men are well trained and well disciplined. I myself—"

"Of course, of course," Laveaux said. "What does he ask?"

Maillart looked over the rampart. Tocquet stood smoking, beside the horse, a tendril of smoke curling up from his straw hat. How painful the sight, the odor, must be to Laveaux in his deprivation. Maillart was grateful that he himself had never really taken to the habit.

"I can only convey him your proposals," Maillart said. "But . . ."

"In your opinion?"

"He would wish to retain his rank."

"Which is?"

"In the Spanish service, *maréchal du camp.*"

"But certainly, or no, a promotion even," Laveaux said. "Beyond that? You understand there is no money to be offered . . ."

"I believe that none would be asked. Only liberty—general liberty, for all the former slaves."

"My friend—" Laveaux seized Maillart's hand in both his own. *"C'est assuré."*

Suddenly the two men were hugging and thumping each other on the back. Maillart's throat constricted, his eyes pricked, he felt himself relieved of his guilt, pardoned for the news he'd brought. He had always liked Laveaux, in spite of politics. But for a moment he broke the embrace and leaned over the wall, frightening the lizard, to call down to Tocquet.

"Xavier, come up quickly, and if you please, bring your cigars."

Tocquet and Laveaux struck an amiable acquaintance, which rather surprised Maillart, who had known his traveling companion to be altogether wary of regular army officers. Perhaps it was the cigars, the almost humble gratitude of Laveaux's acceptance, that eased their meeting. But Laveaux was generally without any pretension which might have been associated either with his former title of nobility or his present military rank. A Jacobin? Perhaps at the least he was a truly convinced republican. Maillart mused on the thought, listening to the others talk. Tocquet had become unusually voluble, for him.

"My ancestral home," he announced, gesturing with the tip of his cheroot at Tortuga off beyond the breakers.

"Then you must be a *flibustier,*" Laveaux said.

Tocquet shucked up his shirt sleeve and pumped his arm to raise a vein. "The blood of pirates, Spaniards, Frenchmen, Indians . . ." He traced the blue line on his inner forearm. "Possibly Africans. Certainly whores." He laughed and dropped his arm, looking toward the jungled island. "My grandfathers came out of there, it's true. Buccaneers to the bone, I can testify."

"Then it was they who won this colony for France," Laveaux said with a thoughtful air.

Tocquet's face shadowed. "As you prefer." He tipped ash over the parapet, frowning, reached for a drink that wasn't there. For the moment, no one spoke. A dark cloud hovered over Morne des Pères, behind and above the fort, and in the opposite direction the sea purpled with the approach of night. Someone shouted from below the wall. Tocquet leaned over, called an answer, then turned to Laveaux with his crocodile smile.

"Order them up," he said. "They've been requisitioning."

Presently Bazau and Gros-jean appeared, carrying a stalk of plantains, green-skinned oranges, a rough-surfaced ceramic jug of *tafia,* and two live chickens.

"I'm overwhelmed," Laveaux confessed. He sent one of his barefoot soldiers to find cups.

Tocquet took one of the speckled hens and whipped off its head with a practiced twirl, then handed it to Gros-jean to pluck.

"I'll cook for you," he said. *"Façon boucanière."*

They ate together, the six black soldiers and the three white men, seated on chunks of masonry from the old fallen walls. Tocquet had built his fire in the lee of some few stones still mortared together. He cooked the chickens spitted on a green stick, roasted the plantains in their skins. As they ate, Laveaux quizzed the black soldiers about details of their service with Toussaint. Afterward, they drank rum flavored with chunks of the oranges. The wind had shifted, bringing a swamp smell and clouds of mosquitoes from *l'étang du Coq.* Maillart accepted one of Tocquet's cigars, hoping the smoke would discourage the insects.

Slapping mosquitoes and staring at the fire, they discussed the dispositions of the enemy. The English were well established at Môle Saint Nicolas, though the port was mostly garrisoned by formerly French troops—the Dillon regiment, much distrusted (and justly, it now seemed) by Commissioner Sonthonax. Laveaux had intelligence that Major O'Farrel, Dillon's commander, had turned over the post without a shot.

"I know him," Maillart said.

"Ah," said Laveaux. "A convicted royalist?"

"Merely a bloody Irishman, I should say," Maillart said. "What if I rode that way, tomorrow?"

Laveaux looked at him narrowly across the flames. "What indeed?"

Maillart nodded thoughtfully. Perhaps one success would breed another. If one has turned his coat the first time, why not again? Though this was a thought he kept to himself.

Let Tocquet, then, carry the news to Toussaint at Ennery, Laveaux proposed.

Tocquet looked down into the fire. "Yes," he said, but his pause was noticeable.

"You hesitate," Laveaux observed.

"Hardly." Tocquet roped his long hair between thumb and forefinger and flipped it over his left shoulder. "I had thought to travel east along the coast . . . to Fort Dauphin, perhaps. But your mission is of more importance." He smiled crookedly, tilting his face to the coals. "For the good of France."

"Assuredly," Laveaux said. "You have known Toussaint for a long time."

It was not a question, though Maillart did not understand Laveaux's confidence in presenting it as a fact. Unless perhaps Tocquet's activities as a border smuggler had been reported to the French general. Tocquet looked up, his eyes narrowing as they would do when he had been piqued.

"Horsemen have sought to know him, since his days at Bréda," Tocquet said. "He knows all there is to know of how to school a horse and treat its ailments."

"I see," said Laveaux. "And do you know his mind?"

Tocquet lowered his eyes to the dwindling fire. "No," he said, and then, in a softer murmur, "I don't suppose there's anyone who knows his mind."

The subject fell away in silence. The flames had settled into coals. With his boot toe, Tocquet pushed an ember farther toward the center.

Maillart wondered a little that Laveaux had not pursued his question further. Of course, he was in no position to refuse Toussaint's proffer by reason of mistrust, and perhaps that explanation ought to be sufficient. But he wondered enough to remain wakeful after he and Tocquet had retired to the fort and stretched out on their bedding.

"Why would you go toward Fort Dauphin?" Maillart finally asked the darkness. "You would be at risk from the Spanish along that road."

"I don't expect any difficulty from the Spanish," Tocquet said. "In fact, I meant to cross the border as far as Dajabón, or farther, though I didn't like to tell your general that. You see the shortage of tobacco here—there's money to be made."

Another question balanced on Maillart's tongue, but he did not ask it, for Tocquet had begun to feign a snore.

*   *   *

In the morning they brewed coffee requistioned and ground by Bazau. Maillart's head was heavy from the rum he'd drunk the night before, but as the coffee clarified him, the elation of his success began to return, along with hopes of what he might accomplish when he reached Le Môle.

With Tocquet and four of Toussaint's men he rode to the principal crossroads at the edge of town. There they drew up their horses before parting. Maillart's horse was restive, shying at a red rag bundle tied in a tree near the intersection—the mark of superstition, someone's *ouanga*.

"There's something I wonder," Maillart said.

"Oh?" Tocquet looked down the road he meant to take.

"Why should Toussaint choose *this* moment to join the French Republic? When their forces are at their very weakest. When their chance to win seems nil. And I was struck that Laveaux did not inquire further into the matter."

"Perhaps your general has sense enough not to ask questions without an answer," Tocquet said, and then, quickly, "Sorry! I don't mean to offend."

But Maillart was only struggling with his horse, which had again begun dancing; he sawed on its mouth and turned its head out of view of the red cloth bundle trembling in the tree.

"I'll give you a thought on the subject," Tocquet said. "I don't say it's my own opinion."

Maillart had brought his mount under control. He raised his eyes to meet Tocquet's.

"Suppose that Toussaint has already concluded that he himself is going to win," Tocquet said, with his crocodile smile. "Then he would have only to choose which of the other parties will win with him."

With that, Tocquet tugged down the brim of his hat and quirted his horse down the road toward Ennery, his retainers bringing up his rear. Maillart swung in the opposite direction. For the moment it seemed to him better to ride than think. But he had gone only a few dozen yards when his horse spooked again at another rag in the branches, and turned white-eyed and rearing in a half-circle.

Tocquet had disappeared with no trace of his going. A single tall young woman, balancing a basket of charcoal on her head, traversed the crossroads. She walked slowly, gracefully erect, and sang a song Maillart could not understand. When she had passed, she left the crossroads empty. His horse calm now, Maillart rode for Le Môle.

6

Doctor Hébert woke a little before dawn. He did not know when he had learned this—to assign the moment of his waking before he slept at night—but now the procedure never failed, and he no longer needed anyone to rouse him. Cocks were crowing up and down the mountain gorges surrounding Habitation Thibodet, and he could hear the chink of harness and the snuffling of horses being assembled in the yard outside the *grand'case*.

Nanon slept half turned toward him, her leg hitched up across his hip. The movement of her breath on the bare skin of his shoulder felt very sweet to him. He disengaged carefully, not wanting to wake her. He had laid out what he needed the night before so that now he could find it all by touch and dress quickly and quietly in the dark.

Someone lit a lamp at the table on the gallery beyond their bedroom, and a little light leaked through the slits of the jalousies. The doctor padded across the room and looked at Paul, in the cradle positioned near the window. The little boy slept on his back, lips parted and snoring delicately. He had long black eyelashes, like his mother's. A mosquito whined and lit on the back of the boy's plump hand; Doctor Hébert reached down and extinguished it with a pinch.

Nanon murmured and turned in the bed; her arm flung out heavily across the pillow where the doctor's head had lain. He felt himself quicken and rise, involuntarily. Perhaps she was only feigning sleep, but it was better so; they had no skill for partings. He holstered his two pistols, picked up his rifle and his boots, and went softly out onto the gallery.

The air was cool, misty; there was the green smell of morning and the odor of fresh coffee. Toussaint's hat lay on the table by the lamp and coffee pot; the black general's face was withdrawn in shadow. Hébert's sister, Elise, sat across from him, a shawl wrapped around her shoulder over the cotton shift she wore, both hands curled around the steaming cup she sipped from. The doctor sat down beside her and pulled on his boots. Elise poured him coffee and generously stirred in sugar. Toussaint inclined his head, as if listening, but no one spoke.

The doctor drained the small coffee cup in three rapid gulps. Daylight was beginning to come up now, paling the glow of the lamp. Now they could see each other's faces. Still no one spoke. Elise's face was puffy, comfortable from sleep. The doctor wondered where Tocquet was at this moment, and if she might be thinking the same thing, and where he might be himself in two weeks' time. Toussaint rose, put on his hat. The doctor laid his palm briefly over the warm back of his sister's hand, then followed the black general down the steps. His absence ought to be a brief one, but in fact it was impossible to calculate or predict. He felt a fluttering in his own stomach as he tightened the girth on the brown gelding he would ride. Who knew indeed when he might return, or if . . .

The feeling dissipated once he was mounted and riding with the others up through the coffee plantings toward the backbone of the ridge above. Now and then a thought of Nanon or the child would flick toward him, but he would simply let it pass; such thoughts were painful if allowed to linger. The morning mist was lifting from the trees and the more the light brightened and turned yellow, the louder and more often the little cocks crowed in the jungle on every side. Their party was a strong one: one hundred crack cavalrymen all well-mounted, and the doctor the only *blanc* among them—Toussaint had brought none of his white officers this time. Instead the black officers he most esteemed were present: Moyse, Maurepas, Dessalines. In the middle of the file of riders were several little donkeys loaded with packs and one blue mule whose only burden was an empty saddle.

Coffee and sugar prickled in the doctor's blood, yet at the same time he grew drowsy as the sun grew warmer. The column kept an easy pace, winding over the stone road into the mountains. He scarcely needed to mind his mount; the brown gelding merely followed the horse ahead. The doctor swayed easily in the saddle as if on a wave, the stock of his rifle, sheathed in a woven scabbard, stroking against his knee.

At the height of Morne Pilboreau the doctor twisted in the saddle and looked back in the direction they had come. A twinge touched him as he thought of Nanon and the child. Habitation Thibodet and all the canton of Ennery were hidden by the involutions of the mountains, though beyond the view was clear to the blue haze above the ocean and the coastal town of Gonaives. By now it was very warm and the doctor envied the shirtless soldiers who surrounded him. Immediately ahead of him, riding double behind Quamba, was that new man named Guiaou, his torso bare but for the cross-strap of his cartridge case and the tissue of scars which covered him like a garment. The doctor recalled bits of the man's story, which he had scrawled down at Toussaint's behest, and tried to match them with the scars: there the deep wounds from *coute- las* blows across the forearm, shoulder, and neck, and lower on the rib cage and across the lower spine a crazily mangled area bordered by what suggested the print of a shark's jaw. Still Guiaou carried himself straight and limber, unheedful of the healed tatters of his flesh, as if he were not made of meat at all, but something stronger.

Three men farther up the line, Jean-Jacques Dessalines announced in Creole that it was very hot indeed, then took off his uniform coat and shirt and folded them neatly across his saddle's pommel. The whole of his broad back was a web of cicatrix, thick scars of old whippings criss-crossed, standing raised and pale against the black of his skin, white and wormy as the bellies of fat snakes. The doctor stared with a dull fascina-tion, but when Dessalines sensed his regard and began to turn, he let his gaze go drifting over the jungle. Just at the edge of the narrow path began a long, steep defile which turned stony at the bottom, where a stream belled gently over the rocks. The doctor would have liked to remove his own shirt, but he knew if he did, his weak skin would be broiled raw by the sun.

The trail twisted, corkscrewed upward; on the mountain above them the belly of a blue-white cloud had lowered. Now they were riding up into the sky itself, it seemed; the foliage turned a darker, damper green; a thick, cold fog blanketed the trail. Those who had divested themselves of their coats now put them on again. For periods the fog was so heavy the doctor could see no farther than the tail of Quamba's horse ahead of him. The cries of invisible birds surrounded them, and the purling of streams they could not see. When they stopped to drink and water the horses, the water the doctor scooped into his palms was warmer than he would have expected, and had a slightly sulfurous taste.

They rode on, now down a declining grade, out of the cloud and the rain forest, emerging into the light of the westering sun. Once again it was very hot, so that the doctor felt sweat start immediately, under the layer of cold dampness he'd accrued on the mountain's height. Fleetingly he thought of fever, then abandoned the thought as useless. He checked the priming of his rifle and pistols to be sure that the fog had not dampened the powder. They were riding down the wrinkles of the mountain into a lush green valley below. A cloud detached itself from the mountain behind and darkened and spread over them till all the sky had turned slate gray, but before the evening rain flooded down they had reached the valley floor and taken shelter in the town of Marmelade.

Two thousand of Toussaint's men were quartered here, approximately half his whole command—Marmelade he had also established as a *quartier général*. In the small wooden church, Toussaint took counsel with his officers, while the rainstorm beat the roof above their heads. The doctor sat on a backless pew and noted down their reports on a paper spread across his knee, writing in the smallest characters he could manage, for paper was scarce. When the rain had ended, the men cooked their evening meal out of doors, but after supper Toussaint returned to the church, where he prayed for a long time, kneeling before the altar, and then reconvened his council.

The doctor again served him as secretary, noting what he thought important or whatever Toussaint signaled him to record. He was numb with fatigue, from the long day in the saddle followed by a substantial meal, but Toussaint, who ate little enough at any time, also seemed to need little sleep: three hours possibly, not more than four . . .

They were in the saddle again at dawn, riding down the river valley in a generally southerly direction. As the sun approached its height they began climbing another range of mountains. The doctor, half-drowsing, was startled by the sudden yapping of a gang of snaggle-toothed, vicious-looking little dogs; then around a bend of the trail appeared a little boy two or three years old and stark naked save for a plaited cord around his waist. He stared at them round-eyed, then his teeth flashed and he leapt in the air crying, *"Solda' nèg! Solda' nèg!"* Some other children appeared, running and capering alongside the horses and carrying the same cry forward, "Black soldiers! Black soldiers!" The brown gelding shied at the twirling of a little girl's skirt, and the doctor leaned down to stroke the horse's trembling shoulder. Adult voices called the children harshly away from the trail, and the children disappeared at once, but the barking of the dogs continued, and the doctor was aware of the movement of considerable numbers of people on either side of the trail, though they were obscured by the jungle. There seemed to be a maze of

trails running up the western slope, and through gaps in the undergrowth the doctor caught glimpses of zigzag corn plantings and the roofs
of *ajoupas,* also sections of wooden palisades and even trenches fortified
by angled sharpened stakes.

"Where did these people come from?" he said, not realizing he'd spoken aloud until Guiaou turned back to answer him.

"*Sé marron yo yé.*"

They were maroons then, runaway slaves . . . though the children
were likely born in freedom here. Maybe also some of the adults. The
doctor knew that large bands of maroons had held out in these hills for
several generations. He had himself known such a one, a man named
Riau who could read and write and for a time had served Toussaint both
as scribe and officer, until finally he had deserted or simply disappeared.
He would be with the maroons again now, the doctor thought, if he still
lived. The whooping and barking and sounds of running feet on the hidden trails diminished as they rode on. Then there was silence, followed
by the singing of the birds.

At a broad and shallow spring-fed pool they stopped to drink and
water the animals. Stooping over the ruffled water, the doctor was startled to meet his own visage, blurry and pale among the ripples. His pallor shocked and almost repelled him—he had forgotten that he was
blanc, had come near to forgetting himself entirely. Now he pictured the
little maroon boy they'd surprised on the trail, and felt a twinge of guilt,
for it had been more than twenty hours since he'd remembered Nanon
or the child.

The flash of pain was brief, and left him entirely once they'd all
remounted. As he rode, the doctor quietly took from his pocket a shard
of broken mirror which he always carried. The fragment was trapezoidal
and fit the creases of his palm; it was too small to return him his whole
face, but by turning it this way and that he could glimpse an eye, an ear,
a bit of whiskered lip, like pieces of a puzzle that no longer fit together.
Riau had called the mirror piece his *ouanga,* but if it really were a charm
for magic, the doctor felt that he was ignorant of its use. It was long
since he had seen Riau, who had evaporated from Toussaint's forces
months ago, most likely to return to *marronage;* yet as the mirror shard
returned to him a wheeling vision of the sky, he felt in the same spirit
with him. *In the same spirit* was the phrase that Riau would have used.

He fixed his eyes on the plumes of Toussaint's general's hat, tossing at
the head of the column. So high in the mountains, so deep in the jungle,
direction could no longer be determined, logic failed, it was useless to
think; therefore the doctor's mind became vacant. The white plumes
floating ahead of him were no longer connected to military rank or

political faction or to a man or even to a hat. They were simply there, drifting through the twistings of the trail.

In the afternoon they came out of a cleft of rock onto a wide savannah that stretched almost as far as the eye could see. At the limit of the horizon, the turquoise verdure of the Cibao mountain range was covered by the smoky blue of clouds. The broad plateau rolled gently and smoothly toward the mountains, covered everywhere with tall brindled grasses. Very infrequently there appeared a small contorted tree. Great herds of long-horned cattle roamed the plateau, sometimes tended by one or two herdsmen wearing Spanish flat-brimmed hats, sometimes tended by no one at all.

After an hour or more of riding over the plateau, the doctor's eye was caught by something in the neighborhood of a flamboyant tree, there in the middle distance, near the mouth of a shallow, grassy gulch. But there was nothing, only half a dozen cattle grazing toward the meager shade. Perhaps it was only the tossing of the tree's orange blossoms that had captured his attention, but he kept looking until, when the cattle had drifted nearer, a near-naked black man sprang up from below the tree, made a short determined run and thrust a spear between the ribs of the nearest cow. As the other cows bolted, the one which had been speared let out a moaning bellow and slumped down over its buckling forelegs. Several other men appeared from the tall grass, whirling *coutelas*. One cut the cow's throat immediately while the others whooped and cackled. The sound carried plainly across the quarter-mile distance; a couple of men in Toussaint's column cheered in reply. Guiaou turned toward the doctor again.

"Those are still *maroons*, those people."

The doctor nodded and said nothing. There was no need of a reply. The plain continued; they rode on.

That evening there was no rain, only a rising of the wind with ragged clouds passing swiftly overhead, and then clear sky, with the stars beginning to emerge. Just before darkness had fallen completely, they rode into the town of San Miguel.

Severe Spanish women, sheathed in thick black dresses, regarded them impassively from the doorways as they went by. The town was small and thinly peopled. There were few slaves, few blacks at all in evidence. Some mestizos walked the street, and more of the hard-bitten herdsmen they'd seen on the plateau. The military garrison was light, no more than a handful of Spanish soldiers. Toussaint parlayed with them briefly, then rode to the house where his family was quartered.

By hearsay the doctor knew that Toussaint had a wife and three sons, but he had never met them. Sometime during the first insurrections of

1791, Toussaint had sent them to this place of safety, over the border and across the mountains from the fighting and the burning. The doctor was curious, but could see little through the arched doorway of the house. Toussaint dismounted and went in with Moyse and Dessalines. The doctor heard a child's astonished cry, and thought he also heard the soft tones of a woman's voice. Moyse and Dessalines came out and the door closed behind them. Dessalines detached five men to stand sentry around the house, then led the column to the edge of town.

They bivouacked on the savannah north of San Miguel, just below the crest of a gently rolling rise. The Spanish officer commanding the town issued them two beefs and a barrel of rum, then left them entirely to themselves. The butchers worked efficiently; soon meat was roasting over several fires. Foragers came in with bunches of brightly colored, wrinkly hot peppers and sheafs of lemon-scented leaves. The beef was fat from the rich grazing of the plateau. They'd made their journey so lightly provisioned that they'd eaten very little in two days, and now the doctor feasted with the others, greasing his chops with tallow. Afterward the meat he'd eaten in unaccustomed quantity lay a little heavily on his stomach. He rested on his elbows in the grass, nursing a clay ramekin of rum and listening to the men tell stories around the fire. Now and then one jumped up to illustrate some action of the narrative. Across the fire, Dessalines also watched the storytellers, his smile glossy with grease from the meat. The night was clear and warm enough so they needed no tents or any shelter; they slept in the open on the folded, sweet-smelling grass.

In the morning word came that the Marquis d'Hermonas had arrived with a somewhat larger Spanish force, intending to shower Toussaint with various honors on the part of the Spanish King, whom he now served. But first there must be morning mass. The church of San Miguel was too small to accommodate all the soldiers, but the doctor went in, among the black officers. Toussaint was seated near the altar rail, and beside him his wife, Suzanne, neatly dressed and modestly kerchiefed, her round, brown face respectfully lowered. There too were the sons, Placide, Isaac, and the youngest, Saint-Jean, who looked no more than four or five. Again the doctor felt the mild twinge of absence or regret, and let it pass. Toussaint's sons were well scrubbed and neatly dressed for the church service.

They were singing the Te Deum. Afterward Toussaint confessed, copiously or at least for a long time, then knelt at the altar rail and chanted prayers of penitence in a loud and fervent whisper. The rasp of his devoted voice carried as far as the church door, where the doctor stood near the Marquis d'Hermonas and several of his subalterns. The marquis's eyes were glistening as he regarded Toussaint, and his voice seemed to catch when he spoke: "If God Himself came down to earth, he could inhabit no purer soul than that of Toussaint Louverture."

After communion the mass was completed and all came out blinking into noonday sunlight. Toussaint was presented with an ornamental sword, and informed of an advancement of his rank. He was also given another gift: a small closed carriage in an antique style, crusted with fresh layers of black paint and with Spanish arms in gilt upon the door. The present seemed somewhat impractical—the doctor could not imagine how the coach might be transported over the mountains to the French colony . . . where most roads were impassable for such a vehicle, in any case. But Toussaint beamed with pleasure at the coach. Suzanne got into it, smiling shyly and holding the seat with her hands while all three boys bounced to try the springs.

In the afternoon all the town turned out for a bullfight given in Toussaint's honor. The doctor had heard of such excercises but never seen one himself. He divided his attention between the bullfight itself and the audience that had assembled. The young and unmarried women here made their first appearance—normally they must have remained shut up in their houses (only a few had appeared even at church). Against the yardage of stiff fabrics that encased them, their faces looked small and doll-like, but their little red mouths stretched wide to cry *Olé!* The Spanish men were equally enthusiastic, but most of Toussaint's soldiers seemed bemused or indifferent—surely there were simpler ways to kill a beef.

The bull was one of those longhorns they'd seen on the savannah. Each time the horn points passed the matador, the doctor felt a short, brutal thrill, amplified by the shouts of the Spaniards surrounding him. At the same time he remembered the cow they'd seen speared yesterday by the maroons on the plateau.

Toussaint's elbow brushed his ribs discreetly; the black general spoke from the side of his mouth. *"Votre avis?"*

"A tragedy," the doctor said, his attention on the field. The matador was using a smaller cape now, and had taken out a sword.

"A waste, rather," Toussaint sniffed.

The doctor glanced at his crooked half-smile, then looked back toward the field. The matador leaned in over the bull's horns, probing with his sword, but he missed the mark and was tossed in the air. For a moment he lay breathless on his back in the silty dust, but before the bull could turn and find him with its horns, he was up and scrambling for his hat and sword.

"The man offers himself to death for no purpose." Toussaint spoke behind the hand which covered his smile. On the field, the matador faced the bull again, lowering the furled cape and sighting the sword over the bull's head toward the spot between the humped shoulders.

"And the bull?" the doctor asked.

"The bull does not choose, because he is not free." Toussaint removed his hand from his mouth, which was no longer smiling.

The doctor felt his interest in the spectacle suddenly collapse, though the Spaniards were again shouting all around him. Again he remembered how the maroons had killed their beef on the plateau, and he thought that perhaps their action was not only more useful but even more beautiful than what he was seeing now.

The days that followed began to drag. Toussaint was often in counsel with the Spanish officers, but the doctor was not invited to serve him as amanuensis on these occasions. No reason was given for his exclusion, but he did come to feel he'd been deliberately shut out. Apart from d'Hermonas himself, whose manner was open and frank with everyone, the Spaniards seemed to distrust him a little, perhaps only because he was French.

Most mornings the doctor visited Toussaint's house for coffee, and one evening he was invited there to dine with several Spanish officers and one of Toussaint's black captains, Charles Belair. It struck him again that the Spaniards were uneasy in his presence—possibly it was his imagination but they all seemed to be looking somewhere over his shoulder when they spoke. He fell silent, watching Suzanne, who sat fluidly erect in her place, or sometimes rose and went to supervise the preparation of the next course in the kitchen. She spoke a competent Spanish, the doctor noticed, or anyway it was better than his own. She had the thickness of age, without being heavy; she still seemed light and graceful when she moved. Her kerchief, bound to her brows neat and tightly as a knife's edge, concealed her hair completely, so the doctor could not know if it were gray. Her face was round, pleasant, only a little wrinkled at the corners of the eyes and mouth. She kept her eyes lowered for the most part, and offered little to the conversation of the men.

As the doctor felt alienated from the men's talk himself, he tried Suzanne with various conversational sallies, but her replies gave him little purchase to continue. Finally, at Toussaint's signal, the older boys, Isaac and Placide, came forward to show him samples of their penmanship. The writing was neat, correct, and with a more orthodox spelling than their father commanded. Both boys were well spoken and their French was very proper. The doctor praised them for these qualities and saw their mother smile.

The afternoons were hot and dry and dusty. Sometimes small parties of Toussaint's troop would ride out over the savannah to exercise their horses. It was less dusty there, at least, than in the town. The doctor would have liked to botanize, but as he spoke only a few words of Spanish he could find no one in San Miguel who was knowledgeable about the herbs of the plateau.

Meanwhile, the quality of their rations diminished noticeably, till they were eating nothing but the dried beef which was so plentifully produced here in the Spanish colony—but apparently to the exclusion of almost everything else. There was no corn or rice or beans to be had at all, only a little moldy flour and shriveled dried peas, both imported from Europe at absurdly high prices. Friction developed when it was noticed that d'Hermonas's men, about equal in number to Toussaint's, seemed to have fresh meat to eat. Doctor Hébert discussed the problem with Moyse and Dessalines, and finally agreed to go hunting on the plateau with them and a few others. They rode out several miles from the town to a waterhole where the doctor knocked over a couple of apparently wild cattle with his long rifle.

The others whistled at his markmanship, for the range had been quite considerable. While other men were butchering the meat and loading the pack burros they had brought, the doctor demonstrated the workings of the rifle to Moyse and Dessalines. The gun was something of a rarity here, having been imported from the North American Republic.

That night there was feasting and celebration, but the next day one of those dour and taciturn Spanish herdsmen came forward with a complaint about his lost animals. There ensued a very unpleasant hour during which it appeared that fighting might break out between the Spanish and black soldiers, for the latter were not at all inclined to suffer any punishment or reprimand from whites. In the end the affair was smoothed over for a promise of money, and everyone (the doctor especially) breathed easily again.

Three more days of heat, dust, tedium and dried beef. On the fourth morning, when the doctor visited Toussaint's house for his usual coffee, he found that the former guard had been replaced by a somewhat larger number of Spaniards. No one was allowed to enter; Toussaint was, inexplicably, under house arrest. When the doctor protested and tried to ask an explanation, he was escorted to the end of the block at the point of a bayonet.

He went immediately to d'Hermonas's quarters, where he learned that the marquis had been replaced in his post and indeed had already left the town, by all accounts somewhat unwillingly. In his stead appeared one Don Cabrera, who received Doctor Hébert calmly, no more

than a little coolly. Cabrera could not say why Toussaint had been confined, nor why d'Hermonas had been ordered elsewhere. For such information it would be necessary to apply to Captain-General Don Joaquín
García y Moreno, who had given the orders. The Spanish general's
whereabouts were not precisely known, though most probably he was
now en route to San Miguel from Santo Domingo City.

"Can you doubt Toussaint's fidelity to the Spanish throne and cause?"
The doctor put the question bluntly, though conscious that his phrasing
hardly committed him to a definite belief on that subject.

"Perhaps I have been less impressed with the fervency of his devo-
tions than was the Marquis d'Hermonas," Cabrera said. He smiled
thinly and rearranged some papers on his table. Upside down, at the
foot of a letter, the doctor thought he could make out the name of
Biassou.

"There are some who contend," Cabrera said, "that if Toussaint prays
so long and loud, it is only the better to deceive those who observe him."

The doctor opened his mouth, but nothing emerged. Cabrera looked
at him expectantly.

"I have known this man since the first insurrection in the north of
Saint Domingue," the doctor said carefully. "I would put my life in his
hands with no hesitation. Indeed I can attest that he has already saved it
more than once."

Cabrera nodded, but said nothing. He reached for his pen and
glanced at the door. The interview was at an end.

Doctor Hébert found the junior black officers arguing in their encampment at the edge of town. Dessalines was for sacking San Miguel immediately, or at least for forcing entry to the house so as to liberate
Toussaint and his family from this unjustified detention. Moyse seemed
half persuaded to this course, while Belair and Maurepas were counsel-
ing restraint.

"*Doucement,*" the doctor said. "Let us go softly, gentlemen, and bide
our time a little."

Dessalines looked at him directly, which was rare; the doctor felt the
pressure of his eyes like two palms shoving him smoothly backward. He
forced himself to hold the gaze.

"In such a case, I ask myself," the doctor said, "what would Toussaint
himself do?"

"Nothing," Dessalines said, snorting as he broke the stare. He shifted
his weight and looked down at the blanket where he sat.

"Nothing," the doctor repeated. His eyes ran round the faces of the
others. He was not in the confidence of these men, and he felt an
uncomfortable thrill at the nakedness of the idea between them.

"Watch," Moyse said, "and wait."

Thus it was agreed among the four black officers to await developments, and the arrival of Don García, at least for one more day. The doctor found himself returning toward the town center, in the company of Maurepas—a more comfortable companion, certainly, than Dessalines or even than Moyse. His own question whined in his ears: *What would Toussaint himself do?* What did Toussaint mean to do? It struck him that since they'd left Ennery he had not been much in Toussaint's confidence either.

"No one knows for certain," Maurepas said, quite as if he'd asked out loud, "and so it is with Biassou, and Jean-François as well. They fear Toussaint because he is becoming stronger, and because he has *blanc* officers among us, and other *blancs* like you, and because his understanding with white people was very close before the rising. You have seen men come from Biassou and Jean-François to join with us instead." Maurepas smiled thoughtfully. "Because things are better ordered with Toussaint—one's life may be harder but it is more sure. I think that Biassou has sent a *pwen* upon Don García and Don Cabrera, to poison their minds against Toussaint."

The doctor stopped in his tracks. "I did not know you were enrolled in such superstition," he said.

"It is Biassou who works in that way," Maurepas said, "and my opinion does not matter. Besides, a *pwen* may be sent as a letter or a message, nothing more—and something has worked on the head of Don Cabrera, at least, for this is what we see."

The doctor fell into silence, stroking his short beard to a point as they continued strolling in the general direction of the town's central square. When they turned the next corner, he was fairly astonished to encounter Suzanne, walking toward the market with a basket on her arm and holding the hand of her youngest, Saint-Jean. In his surprise he glanced at Maurepas, but the black officer was no longer there.

Suzanne was flanked by two Spanish soldiers, but they did not prevent the doctor from approaching her, although they did stand near enough to overhear their conversation. On the assumption that they understood both French and Creole, it was out of the question to speak freely. While exchanging banalities with Suzanne, the doctor felt a small hand tugging his trouser leg. He stooped and lifted Saint-Jean into his arms and kissed his cheeks. The boy's fingers brushed his palm, and the doctor closed his hand over a sort of paper bullet, which he put discreetly into his trouser pocket.

As soon as he had turned the next corner, he unballed the paper. Toussaint's crooked writing and phonetic spellings were instantly recognizable—

as was his subtlety of mind. A shadow fell on the paper as he examined it; Maurepas had reappeared, or perhaps simply cast off the cloak of invisibility he had somehow assumed. He and the doctor exchanged a furtive smile and began walking briskly back toward the black encampment.

The letter, addressed to Don García, was part protest, part apology, part self-justification, and part assault on potential enemies. An apparently general thrust went straight to the heart of Biassou, for instance. But all the while Toussaint sustained a tone of humble, bemused, yet honorable simplicity.

At camp, the doctor found his own writing instruments and made a fair copy of the letter, correcting the spelling but leaving the style and argument intact. As a flourish, he managed a passable forgery of Toussaint's signature, complete with the customary three dots closed within the extravagant curlicue of the last letter. He was just wondering where to send the missive when word came that Don García had in fact arrived at San Miguel.

All through the following day, the Spanish general took no apparent action, either on Toussaint's letter or on any other arguments which might have been addressed to him. Toussaint's men fretted, while their leader remained incommunicado, and the tension grew. The next afternoon, Don García rendered himself to the house where Toussaint was detained and stayed there for nearly four hours. That evening the Spanish guard was lifted and Toussaint's officers went in to him, the doctor among them. In a clipped and neutral tone, Toussaint let them know that the following day they would return to the campaign in the French colony, on Don García's order—immediately following morning mass.

Only Maurepas and Charles Belair accompanied Toussaint to services next day. Suzanne and the children were nowhere in sight. When Toussaint uncovered as he entered the church, the doctor was slightly surprised to see that a blood-red *mouchwa têt* replaced the yellow madras headcloth he ordinarily always wore. Toussaint prayed more efficiently than usual, and in a lower, harsher tone, his thumb snapping the beads of his rosary as if he were filing protests before God.

As soon as he had taken communion, he beckoned to the others and stalked out of the church. Dessalines was waiting in the square, at the head of perhaps seventy of the original hundred horsemen. Guiaou tossed the reins of the brown gelding to the doctor, who hurried to mount, seeing that Toussaint was already in the saddle, wheeling his horse. A few Spanish foot soldiers came on the run, calling in unintelligibly accented French. One snatched at the bridle of Dessalines's horse, but Dessalines knocked the arm down with the flat of his sword. Then they were leaving the town at full gallop.

All through the morning they rode hard, as fast as they could go without overheating the horses. There was no pursuit, or reason for any—Toussaint was following Don García's order, however brusque his departure had been. The reason for their haste became more apparent when they overtook the rest of the cavalry at the opening of the first mountain pass on the plateau's edge. Suzanne and the boys were among that group, just climbing out of the Spanish gift carriage.

While the older boys were mounting on burros, several of Toussaint's men quickly unpinned the wheels of the coach and laid them in the closed interior. Suzanne rode the blue mule sidesaddle like a market woman, her forward knee hitched high; she smiled and flicked up the mule on the withers with a foot-long stick she held in her right hand. Saint-Jean rode pillion with Toussaint. Eight of the men dismounted and lifted the carriage by its axles and singletree, and carried it into the mountains at a trot that equaled the pace of the horses.

7

From Port-de-Paix toward the end of the western peninsula, the road wound high on the rim of scrubby hills above the ocean. Dark water foamed and sucked at the rocks below, and there was a steady, salty wind from the north, which had trained all the trees to grow leaning backward, twisting and stooping over the slopes. Still in mufti, Captain Maillart rode westward, leading his small party at a brisk trot. In time his hair grew sticky, clumped by the salt wind. He was second in the short column, following a black soldier named Charlot whom Laveaux had sent out with them as a guide.

The road was a dry, hard surface of bedrock overlain with pale dust and pea gravel. Presently Maillart's horse picked up a stone in his hoof and went slightly lame. The captain dismounted and picked the pebble loose from the tender frog, while one of the black soldiers held the horse and another supported the injured hoof. He walked the animal for twenty minutes, then mounted and rode on as before.

By now the island of Tortuga had dropped out of sight behind the gentle curve of the coast. In the late afternoon a drift of cloud blowing in from the ocean began to grow thicker and darker till it covered the sky, and the seawater itself changed from royal blue to an oily black. The wind twisted and whipped, raising the salt-stiffened locks of the captain's hair and teasing at the mane of his horse. But before the actual downpour began, they had reached the village of Jean Rabel.

The town was tiny, consisting of a mere two streets converging on a square parade ground before a small wooden church. The French tricolor flew from a pole at the center of the square, and as Maillart's party rode in, two black men dressed in tattered French uniform trousers had begun striking the flag against the coming rain. The captain was pleased to see the colors; they were now very near to the English bastion at Môle Saint Nicolas, and he hadn't been completely certain that the sphere of French influence still extended this far. Meanwhile, the wind was lifting coils of dust from the ground and the air grew more heavy and damp at every moment. Charlot parlayed with the two men as they detached the flag from the lanyards and began respectfully folding it. The captain, half stunned from the day's ride, paid small attention to their conversation, though he noticed that Charlot's gestures became broader and more expressive when the rain began in earnest. Maillart was caked with sweat and salt and dust from the road and was almost grateful to be bathed in rain, though he knew a drenching was dangerous, in his state, and could very well lead to fever. But before he was quite soaked to the skin, Charlot concluded an arrangement and one of the flag bearers quickly led them to a warehouse on the edge of town where they might shelter.

The warehouse was a sizable barnlike structure, at the border of the town proper with the land of Habitation Foache. In former times it had been used to store the indigo for which the region of Jean Rabel was noted, but now there was nothing here but a few dozen baskets of coffee beans, still in their red hulls. The men and horses came in together; there was plenty of room for both. Rain swept over the thatched roof with a regular hissing, sizzling sound. In one corner the thatch had rotted through, admitting a silver stream of rainwater and a shaft of rain-streaked daylight. After a moment of hesitation, Maillart stripped off his wet shirt and went over and washed his face and torso under the waterfall, then cupped his hands to take a drink. The black men laughed quietly among themselves, then followed his example.

Maillart tethered his horse to a hook in the wall, unsaddled the animal and dried the leather with a blanket he kept in his saddlebag. He wrapped himself in the blanket and lay down, resting his head on the saddle, half dozing as he listened to the rain and the drone of Creole conversation among the other men. Without knowing it, he must have gone to sleep entirely, for suddenly he woke, shivering a little, aware that the rain had stopped and night had fallen.

The warehouse was empty now except for the horses, but he heard the voices of the men beyond the door, and there was also a cooking smell. Maillart hung up his civilian clothes on the square nails and hooks that studded the walls, to dry as best they might. He put on his French uniform and stepped outside.

His party had grouped around an open fire, covered by an iron stew-pot which an old black woman was stirring with a wooden spoon two feet long. They had been joined by a black man who wore the ragged tunic of a French lieutenant, a bandolier but no trousers—apparently a true *sans-culotte*. At the sight of Maillart, he drew himself up and saluted.

This was the officer who commanded on behalf of the French Republicans in the region of Jean Rabel. In the course of the conversation, Captain Maillart was able to learn that this tattered lieutenant had at his theoretical disposal as many as two hundred men, but that the great majority of these were lately liberated slaves of the region who came and went very much as they pleased, who had no regular military training and whose performance (and attendance) at battles was far from reliable. Meanwhile the English were very well established at Môle Saint Nicolas. The lieutenant had word that they had lately been reinforced from the sea, and that they had mounted an expedition whose result he did not know against Bombarde, another small French post on the south side of the peninsula. Were the English to march on Jean Rabel, the lieutenant could not predict an outcome; he had no more than forty well-trained and reliable men to count on, although, if God so willed, he might compose a force of two hundred fighters of some description.

The captain mused silently on this situation: the French position in the northwest was still more precarious than he'd known for certain . . . and perhaps collapsing, if Bombarde had been lost. The Spanish line came down to the coast at Borgne, which cut off Laveaux, at Port-de-Paix, from the land route east to Le Cap . . . though given what the captain had seen at Le Cap, it seemed unlikely that Laveaux could expect much support from that direction anyway. But the Spanish held Borgne thanks to Toussaint and his men, so if the black general did switch his allegiance, the military map would be quite significantly altered. Maillart carried this thought with him to the woven mat on which he passed that night.

From Jean Rabel they rode along the cliff edge high above the crashing water: the Côte de Fer, where the sea was always high and rough and the rocks lethal to shipping—no vessel could attempt a landing here. But on the shoal of Port d'Écu, a long, sheer drop below, there was a natural salt pan whose crystals shone like diamonds in the rising sun as they passed. Because of the sea wind and the early hour of their leaving, it was cool for the first hours, but by the time they had come down to the Bay Moustique onto the flat, arid plain that ran to the peninsula's furthest tip, the sun was high and scorching and the steady wind off the ocean only seemed to parch them, as it parched the land. All around the country was dry and barren but for desert scrub: prickly pear, raquette trees and nopal cactus.

A mile or two outside the town of Le Môle they fell in with a train of donkeys led by blacks bringing water in from farther up the river. Maillart negotiated a drink for himself and his company, and when they had all quenched their thirst, he dumped the remains of the gourd over his sweat-streaked hair and face, and went on considerably refreshed. In another few minutes they had an overview of the large, deep harbor of Le Môle, where several warships rode at anchor, flying the Union Jack.

They followed the water sellers to the square of the town. The principal street was divided by a small, shallow canal of fresh-looking water running down its middle—indeed each side street was similarly irrigated, so that Maillart wondered at the need for hauling in more water. Perhaps what flowed in those rivulets was not fit to drink, but the sound and sight of the rippling made the town seem cooler and gave the streets a certain charm. There were plenty of people abroad in the streets, blacks and mulattoes and more than a few whites going about their business as usual, and no one seemed especially astonished at the arrival of Maillart and his party.

They rode to the central square, which was bordered on three sides by wild fig trees, in plantings that ran to the steps of the church. Maillart asked a loitering British redcoat where he might find the quarters of the Dillon regiment. The soldier directed him to the barracks at the upper end of the town.

The original French *casernes* were at a slight elevation above the civilian residences. Recently some wooden buildings had been put up, and these now housed recently arrived British troops. When Maillart inquired for the Dillon regiment, he got only a look of bewilderment, but when he asked for Major O'Farrel, someone volunteered to let that officer know that he was wanted.

Maillart waited, alone with his horse in the dense cool shade of another wild fig; he had left his men to scare up lodgings lower in the town. The *casernes* were well situated, he thought—there was a pleasant view and the elevation would be advantageous for the health of the troops billeted here. Presently O'Farrel appeared in the gateway, looking this way and that. Maillart did not instantly recognize him in his British scarlet, for he had known him in French colors, at Le Cap two years before. Moreover, O'Farrel's hairline seemed higher on his head than previously, his sandy mustache rather more speckled with gray. His eyes crossed Maillart with no hint of recognition and went on searching, elsewhere, until Maillart called out his name and stepped toward him, hesitantly holding out his hand.

"I didn't know you," the major said, twisting one end of his mustache, over a smile that might have been a little too ironic for politeness. His cool eye rapidly scanned Maillart's civilian attire.

"Some say it's the uniform makes the man," Maillart replied, and watched to see if O'Farrel would flush in his red coat. But the other returned his gaze, his pale eyes level, and unreadable. At Le Cap they had once come near to quarreling, over a woman, but one or the other or both of them had found enough forbearance that they had not come to blows. The memory of that woman softened Maillart now, and O'Farrel relaxed and smiled and invited him in.

The major's apartment was a good one—in general the officer's quarters at Le Môle were good. However, to Maillart's surprise, it was not O'Farrel who commanded the post.

"But I thought—" the captain said. "I had heard it was you who surrendered Le Môle to the British, at the head of the Dillon regiment."

"As to that you have been misinformed," O'Farrel told him. "The capitulation was arranged by Colonel Deneux, your own superior, might I say?" Again the smile seemed supercilious; Maillart steeled himself not to take offense.

"The ranking British officer here is Major Grant," O'Farrel said. "And for the moment I am serving mostly as his aide-de-camp, for the Dillon regiment is effectively no more."

"Excuse me?"

"Ah." O'Farrel glanced out the window to the yard, where a British sergeant had faced off with a balky mule. "I regret to say that some seventy of my men deserted, once the British flag was raised here. The remnant has just lately been sent down to Saint Marc . . ."

"Deserted—where?"

O'Farrel scratched the back of his head. "Presumably to the Jacobins, you know."

"But I have just come from General Laveaux at Port-de-Paix," the captain said. "There was no one of the Dillon regiment there—not the hair of a single Irishman."

O'Farrel failed to smile at this quip. His eyes narrowed. "From Laveaux, you say?"

"I'll tell the tale, if you've time for it." Maillart composed himself as the major tilted back his chair against the wall. "When news came that the King was guillotined in France, I left Le Cap. To put it plainly, I *deserted*—well, I had been greatly disillusioned—"

O'Farrel nodded. "Of course. Go on."

"I offered my sword to the Spanish crown and was accepted by the Spanish army at Santo Domingo—I am hardly the sole French officer in such a case, you understand. But in this way I came under the command of General Toussaint Louverture."

"I've heard that name, or something like it," O'Farrel said. "Tusan? Wasn't it he who spoiled the capitulation to the British at Gonaives? One of those jumped-up niggers in Spanish uniform . . ."

Maillart looked at the ceiling briefly. "Toussaint commands not only at Gonaives but all the way back along the Cordon de l'Ouest through the mountains as far as the Spanish frontier. Perhaps farther. He has four thousand men at his command and he seems to have the intention of putting them all at the disposal of Governor-General Laveaux."

"You mean . . ."

"I mean to tell you that the wind blows in that quarter now. General Laveaux has accepted my return to the fold. It's not improbable that he might do the same for—"

O'Farrel's front chair legs clacked down on the floor. He stiffened and raised a rigid palm. "Please, no more. There is no question. You understand, even if I wished it—I am not in command here, nor in particularly good odor, regarding the desertion of so many of my troops . . . *wherever* they may have got to. Major Grant would certainly hear nothing of it—I tell you, you only endanger yourself by speaking so. And Colonel Deneux is a royalist, convinced to the core—"

Maillart looked out the window. In the yard, the sergeant was still shouting at the mule, which squatted on its hindquarters. The sergeant began beating it about the muzzle with a short, slim cane of green bamboo.

"No," said O'Farrel, more reflectively, "I'll leave my lot where I've cast it. No nigger general however talented can stand against British troops in the field—or French troops either, I speak without prejudice! But you surprise me, Maillart—by your own account you're a royalist yourself."

"I—well, to begin, I always had a respect for Laveaux, and a liking to boot."

"And I also, to the small extent I knew him."

"And at bottom I suppose I am a Frenchman first, before . . ." Maillart grunted. The picture of himself emerging from the warehouse with a shovel of horse manure entered his mind. "*Au diable.* I don't suppose I know what I am anymore. I find this country damnably confusing."

There was a louder shout from the yard, and a thump of solid impact. Both men stood and moved nearer the window. Outside the sergeant was doubled over with his hands clasping his midsection, while the mule wheeled free, trailing its lead rope, rolling its eyes malevolently.

"After all, you look like you've been through the wars." O'Farrel looked at Maillart with a certain sympathy.

"At least I recognize myself as a soldier still," Maillart said. "I am expected to go through wars."

O'Farrel laughed and clapped him on the back. "But you must come to dinner, at least." He gave the captain the address of a house in the town.

A little after seven in the evening, as the light shaded orange over the sea and the windward passage, Maillart stood with Major O'Farrel in the garden of a small stone house on the Grande Rue. Earlier in the afternoon he had gone to bathe in the river, and afterward changed into his last clean shirt, carefully conserved for such an occasion: a loose blouse of natural-coloured, nubby cotton, the sort of thing worn by planters up the country, or by Xavier Tocquet. Maillart wondered passingly where Tocquet might have got to by this time. When he glanced down at his own sleeve, he realized that he was growing accustomed to seeing himself without the cloth or insignia of anyone else's army. Perhaps in the end he would be content to become the soldier of his own fortune . . .

A black servant appeared, to offer them glasses of rum from a tray, and when they had accepted told them that their host expected to join them shortly. Maillart sipped and turned to admire the garden, lush with hibiscus and bougainvillea and peculiar orchids he had never seen before. Water had been brought into the enclosure from the canal in the street and branched to irrigate all the plantings and to fill both a small pool covered with water lilies and a larger basin with steps leading into it, large enough to fit two men.

"Monsieur Monot is an Acadian, did you know?" O'Farrel asked. "There were a great many who came here thirty years ago, after the English had expelled them from Acadia. But as you see the land is next to worthless here, never mind the merits of the harbor, and the climate did not much agree with them after the cold of North America. Most have gone to Louisiana now, even Monot's own sons, but he has stayed and, as you see, not done so badly for himself. But here he is."

A little man came out of the house, bald, stooped but spry, dressed in an antique manner. He took Maillart's hand and greeted him, smiling.

His eyes were pale blue, under bushy shelf-like eyebrows, with long hairs dangling at the corners like the ends of a mustache. When the servant offered the tray, Monot declined the rum in favor of a glass of grapefruit juice.

Maillart complimented him on the garden and the cunning fashion of its irrigation.

"Yes," said Monot, with enthusiasm. "And you see, the water runs from this basin here"—he indicated the bathing pool—"and out the back, but come and I'll show you."

They followed the rivulet of water through a gate to the kitchen garden at the rear of the house. Here Monot or his minions produced potatoes, peas, herbs, "even *haricots verts,*" as the host declared with some pride.

"*Tout pousse,*" Monot said, a glitter in his eye. "Everything grows, and marvelously, once one brings water to it." The artichokes of the locality, he went on, were perfectly delectable . . .

They returned through the arched gateway to the flower garden. A couple was just coming out of the house: a small dark-haired woman on the arm of a stocky man.

"*Ma belle.*" M. Monot straightened perceptibly and spread his arms wide for an embrace. He moved forward, obscuring Maillart's view, so that he could not see the woman's face until she had accepted Monot's kisses and detached herself. His heart tumbled. She was clothed more modestly than he had known her, in a striped silk dress with a cloud of muslin covering her bosom. Tiny, bright and active as a hummingbird, she was Isabelle Cigny.

The captain bowed, profoundly and extensively, holding his abased posture while the blood rushed to his head. When he straightened, he felt he had at least partially recovered himself.

"*Mais quelle surprise!*" Isabelle said cheerily. She stepped toward him and clasped both his hands. A tension in her elbows discouraged him from coming closer. Maillart remembered the surprising wiriness of her body, which he had in former times traveled inch by inch.

"The surprise is entirely mine," he said, and glanced at O'Farrel, who grinned and quickly turned to look out over the garden wall. It was truly bizarre that he should discover both of them here in this remote corner of the colony after so long, so strange he was moved to wonder if it could be a coincidence. It was Isabelle who had inspired his difference with O'Farrel at Le Cap. Maillart felt a thrust of the old jealousy as he let go of her hands and turned to greet her husband.

"*Monsieur.*"

"*Mon grand plaisir.*" Cigny spoke with no obvious irony in his tone.

His manner of dealing with his wife's suspected lovers had always been opaque. Maillart studied him, sidelong; in former times Cigny had sported a heavy black beard, but now he was clean-shaven, an operation which left his broad face jowly.

"But what happenstance has brought you here?" Maillart said.

"Blown off course," Cigny replied tersely.

Isabelle smiled and dimpled. "We spent a wretched time in the North American Republic, you know, for we had sailed with the fleet of Governor-General Galbaud, when Le Cap was burned and looted by the brigands . . ."

"So I had heard," the captain said.

"We stayed for some little time in Baltimore, then Philadelphia . . ." Isabelle made a pretty flutter of her hands. "But when we got word of *l'appel aux Anglais,* we decided to return here and seek to repair our fortunes—under the standard of our British allies."

"God save the King," Cigny said glumly. "In fact we had meant to land at Saint Marc, but the captain of our ship seems to have exaggerated his abilities."

"Ship, he says!" Isabelle feigned outrage. "It was rather a fisherman's coracle. Fourteen days in an open boat—I expected I should be black as an African by the time we arrived."

Maillart looked at her face more closely. It did seem that a freckle or two had appeared on her nose. He felt a slight pulse of vertigo.

"But by great luck we have fallen among friends." Isabelle took Major O'Farrel's arm, drawing him into the conversation. The major twisted the end of his mustache and smiled in a fashion that slitted his eyes. Maillart's feeling of vertigo worsened.

"And your children?" he forced himself to inquire.

Isabelle's face shadowed momentarily; she let go the major's arm. "I would not bring them into such a situation as we have here now," she said. "They are at school, in Philadelphia."

Monot, meanwhile, had been speaking softly to a servant. *"Messieurs, Madame,"* he announced. "Our table is served."

At dinner they were joined by another young woman, whose name was Agathe, tall and striking, with dark eyes, a slightly aquiline nose, and long, waving black hair parted from the center of her high forehead. An admirable woman. Her lips were very full and red, but she spoke little, except in low tones to Monot himself, at whose right hand she sat, and lowered her head demurely when anyone else addressed her. Sometimes she rose and ambled with a graceful languor to consult with the kitchen between courses, but she had little to contribute to the general conversation.

They began with a plate of artichokes, which quite lived up to Monot's description, and went on to small, deliciously sweet local lobsters. Next came a sort of bourgignon whose delicacy was crushed by the British salt beef that had apparently been used as the primary ingredient. The dish was helped by fresh peas, carrots and onions from the kitchen garden . . . but in any case Maillart had already eaten more than he'd lately been accustomed to. He could not finish all his beef, and only picked at the fruit which followed it.

The food was praised, over Monot's demurrals, and the problems of servants were discussed. Le Môle had never been heavily populated with slaves (for the surrounding land would not support large plantations). A party of some three hundred slaves had been brought in to construct the houses of the whites, and many of these had afterward lived in a river gorge beyond the boundary of the town proper. These persons had been liberated, in principle, by the emancipation proclamation of Commissioner Sonthonax, then subsequently reenslaved, in principle, following the arrival of the British here. The extent to which they were influenced by either principle was not precisely known. Some of them still reported for work, while others had certainly disappeared during all the troubles.

Thus the conversations turned to the troubles themselves, to the military situation and to the hopes and interests of the Cignys in particular. Maillart fell silent, but pricked up his ears. By virtue of his marriage to Isabelle, Cigny had become master of two prosperous sugar plantations, one on the great northern plain east of Le Cap and the other in the region of the Artibonite, farther south. For the nonce, the Plaine du Nord was thought to be completely out of the question—for all the company appeared to believe that that area was firmly under republican control from Jean Rabel east to the Spanish border—and perhaps it would be, Maillart thought privately, if Toussaint did change sides. Present company believed that Laveaux's position at Port-de-Paix was much stronger than was in fact the case. At this juncture, the captain's private knowledge began to make him uneasy, for he saw that O'Farrel was looking at him narrowly from the opposite chair at the table; Maillart shifted position slightly, so that a candlestick blocked the view.

Meanwhile (the discussion proceeded) the British were firmly in position at Saint Marc, and in the southerly direction they were soon expected to take Port-au-Prince if they had not already done so—but north of Saint Marc, where Cigny's Artibonite holdings lay, their advance was impeded by the Spanish at Gonaives—under command of "Tusan," as he was called here. It occurred to Maillart that Cigny, given these accidents of military disposition, might have thrown in with the wrong foreign power so far as his personal ends were concerned, and perhaps Cigny himself was of the same opinion, for he became increasingly plaintive (the more he drank), demanding that O'Farrel explain why more British troops had not been fielded. "Thirty thousand men would wipe this rebellion out in two weeks," he proclaimed.

"Thirty thousand men is far from a trifle," O'Farrel said.

But Isabelle broke off a low-voiced conversation with Agathe, and went to work soothing her husband and smoothing O'Farrel. Cigny, she suggested, had suffered an episode of heat prostration during the day (exacerbated by drinking, the captain thought, if it had existed at all). On this pretext, Isabelle and her husband retired, for they were staying at the Monot house. It was soon determined that Maillart would do the same. His host would by no means permit him to bunk with his Negroes that night, or any other night that he was at Le Môle . . .

As the servants cleared the table, Maillart found himself sharing a final glass of rum with O'Farrel in the garden; Monot had also excused himself, advising his guests to make themselves free. A crescent moon hung over the wall, and the smell of the flowers was sweet.

"And the girl?" Maillart asked, breaking a brief silence. "I couldn't make her out. A daughter? A wife of his old age?"

O'Farrel chuckled in the darkness. The dim moonlight left his face in shadow. "No, she is rather his 'housekeeper'—as they put it here. She manages the servants and the kitchen— I think you'll give her credit for being an excellent cook. In point of view of her bloodlines, she is a *mamélouque*, but no child of Monot, I shouldn't think."

"I had taken her for white," Maillart said.

"For that you might be forgiven. Though if you think more carefully— have you ever seen a white woman move like that?" O'Farrel seemed to sigh in the darkness. "As for her other talents and duties—well, I believe the good Monsieur Monot is incapable, owing to his years."

Maillart could not see the wink, but felt the major must be winking as he went on, "If you have the luck to taste her sweetness, I can only wish you joy."

The captain's room was pleasantly appointed, his bed comfortable enough, the air fresh once he opened the French doors letting on to an iron balcony common to all the bedrooms on the front of the second floor of the house. Along with the cool night air, the braying of the water sellers' donkeys entered the room—it was said the blacks of the town claimed that the donkeys knew the time and reported on the hours.

Maybe it was the intermittent braying that kept the captain awake, or maybe it was the cascade of images of Isabelle, himself with Isabelle: the spiciness of sexual memory stinging like salt on abraded skin. A quick parting of their clothing here and there, flashes of pale thigh or breast, her deeper, rosier openings. He had known her in her own house in Le Cap, where they had carried on in heat and haste, improvising against the chance of discovery by her husband or the servants or even her other swains. He had never seen her wholly naked—no opportunity for such luxury. But though he was astonished by her boldness, they had never been caught outright. It was perhaps her boldness that protected them—she seemed to have no more conscience than a stoat, and could, five minutes following an act of illicit passion, be coolly pouring coffee for her husband in the parlor . . .

He felt certain she must come to him tonight. He tumbled restlessly in the bed; the donkeys brayed and the hours passed, but she did not come. Nor could he sleep. At last he went out on the balcony, his bare toes curling on the cold iron, but all the other French doors were shut and latched and bolted, except the last pair, slightly ajar. When Maillart delicately coaxed the near door open with a finger, it uttered a hideous rusty squeal, and inside Agathe sat bolt upright in bed, sheet clasped to her breast with one hand that rose and fell dramatically. She stared at him, her full lips parted, but made no sound or sign. With that bone trimming of the moon behind him, Maillart knew he was only a shadow to her, she could not see his face. For a long moment he hesitated on the threshold, but at last he returned to his own room, where he slept fitfully, and woke late in the morning with a heavy head.

Maillart took coffee in the garden (alone, for it seemed that Monsieur Monot had gone out on some errand) and ate an omelet slowly, hoping for a glimpse of Isabelle, who did not appear. In spite of the still, arid heat, he called for his horse and rode to the barracks on the hill, thinking to renew his approach to O'Farrel. He had not yet made it clear to the major just what Toussaint's presence on the scene might signify— and had their positions been reversed, Maillart knew that he would have had difficulty grasping this point himself.

He sent in his name at the gate of the casernes, and waited under the same wild fig tree as before. The shade was not adequate now against the noonday heat. Beyond the town and the peninsula's tip, the sea was a flat, turquoise pancake, motionless; there was no wind. After half an hour, when no one had come, Maillart got up and walked in through the gate, fanning himself with his hat. No one challenged him. The British soldiers in the barracks yard seemed disoriented, stunned by the heat. They were not acclimated and many, no doubt, were beginning to fall ill . . . Sweating in their red woollen coats, they stank like wet sheep.

Maillart climbed to O'Farrel's apartment, knocked and waited, but there was no answer. Perhaps the major was at table. Maillart went back down and crossed the yard diagonally toward a building that looked promising, opposite the main gate. A British corporal shouted to him that a horse needed shoeing on the other side of the square. Maillart started, bristled a bit, then went on with an inward smile. Another effect of his civilian garb.

In the stone hallway the heat seemed somewhat less crushing. Maillart put his head in one door and another, looking for an officers' mess. What he found instead was perhaps the commander's council room; at any rate a map of the colony was spread out on a table. Maillart strolled over and glanced down at the map, then leaned closer, bracing his knuckles on the table's edge. The disposition of forces was marked out with colored pins: red for the English, blue for the French, green for the Spanish . . . On the northwestern peninsula, Le Môle was a prick of red in a forest of blue. The British were isolated here, except by sea, commanding nothing but the town and its harbor.

"Your business!"

Maillart shot upright and turned to face a redcoat major in the doorway; balding, mustachioed, and florid either from the heat or irritation.

"Your pardon—I was looking for Major O'Farrel."

"You will not find him here today—he has gone out to Fort Villarie. You are?"

Maillart bowed and stated his name.

"Your business with Major O'Farrel?"

"I—we were acquainted sometime ago. When the major served at Le Cap." Maillart felt his whole face breaking out in pustules of sweat; trickles ran down from his armpits over his ribs.

"Served the Carmagnoles, you mean, your revolutionary rabble?"

"No! Far from it, uh . . ." Maillart closed his fingers loosely against sweaty palms. "No, he took the other part . . ."

The British major stared, then closed his eyes and covered them with his hands for a moment, as if his head pained him terribly. Then he snatched his head upright and shouted, "Winston!"

A sweating guard snapped to attention in the hallway.

"Show this gentleman to the gate."

"Yes, Major Grant!"

The major pointed a forefinger at Maillart. "You, sir, have yourself properly announced if you come here again."

"Of course," Maillart said. "I'll remember that."

"See that you do." Major Grant stamped down the hall.

When he returned to the Monot house, Maillart was sweat-soaked and dizzy from the heat and his own self-disgust. In his bedroom he took off his drenched shirt and sniffed it. True, the sweat of fear had a worse stench than the ordinary. It was the falsity of his position—but this reasoning did little to repair his self-respect.

As best he could determine, the house was still empty except for a couple of servants padding barefoot in the halls. Maillart went down into the garden, hesitated a moment, then shucked off his trousers and lowered himself into the bathing pool. The water was just cooler than tepid and felt very pleasant to his skin. He inhaled and slid completely under, on his back, holding his breath and looking up through the water at the wavery blue of the sky, green smudges of leaves on an orange tree over the pool, fallen leaves and their shadows floating on the surface. His head began to pound, his lungs to burn, and finally he sat up, spouting and shaking his head, then leaned back and rested his elbows on the tiles that flanked the pool. The dizziness passed and he felt much better.

The house door opened just as he had begun to think of calling for a drink but, instead of a servant, Agathe appeared, clothed in a loose white shift belted at the waist, that hung to her bare feet. She looked at him indifferently, as if he were a plant, as she passed toward a table between the lily pool and the garden gate. Maillart noticed that several of her toes were adorned with fine gold rings. O'Farrel had been correct, he thought, as his eyes tracked the flow of her hips underneath the thin cotton. Agathe sat at the table and opened a book and a Chinese fan, spreading her hand over the pages and fanning herself slowly, in profile to him, looking at the flowering vines that hung down over the garden wall. Maillart wondered if she had recognized him after all, last night on the balcony, and what she had thought, and what she might think, tonight, if . . . He felt himself begin to stir, beneath the water.

The house door clacked again, and Maillart lazily turned his head. Isabelle was crossing the garden, more casually dressed than yesterday, in a red-and-blue cotton dress of *faux* peasant fashion, with a straight skirt and tightly laced bodice. She called out something to Agathe, who responded with a smile and a torpid nod, then noticed Maillart with an exaggerated reaction of surprise.

"So . . . you seem to have found your relief from the heat." She kicked off her shoes and settled herself on the tiles by the pool, drawing her bare feet up behind her.

"For a moment, yes," Maillart said. "But at the sight of you I am all at once in a fever again."

Isabelle stretched out opposite him, propping herself on an elbow. "Such gallantry." She inclined her head to look into the water, so shallow, Maillart now realized, that it afforded him little privacy.

"Almost *rampant* gallantry, one might say . . ."

Maillart colored. He would have liked to say something extremely witty, but a swelling in his throat hindered him, and besides no suitable *bon mot* came to his mind. Isabelle lowered her hand into the water, just to her wrist, and made a whirling motion with her fingers—she had not actually touched him, but Maillart felt his natural part swirl into the current she created. He closed his eyes, then opened them as a droplet of water broke on his forehead. Isabelle hovered over him with her wet hand drooping in the gesture of a sorceress.

"I baptise you, in the name of . . . what name shall it be?"

She flicked more water into his face. Maillart shouted, shifted his position and made as if to splash her with his palm. Isabelle scrambled to her feet and took a step backward from the pool.

"I should like to ride out to *le môle*, itself, the breakwater." She pouted. "But I don't like to go alone."

"At your service." Maillart began to stand up from the pool, then caught himself. Coyly, Isabelle turned her back and allowed him to retrieve his trousers.

The wind had come up by the time they left, so that it was considerably cooler. Isabelle rode gracefully, sidesaddle on a small gray mare, her skill somewhat surprising Maillart, who had never been riding with her before. They talked of negligible matters as they crossed the town, sometimes interrupted by pedestrians who greeted Isabelle, but once they rode out onto the peninsula they were alone. *Le môle* itself was a natural breakwater, a narrow spit of stone which sheltered the north side of the bay from the open ocean. Now they rode in silence, except for horseshoes clanging on the stone—the whole surface was black volcanic bedrock, where only a few lichens grew. To their left, the sun lowered on the bay, whose calm surface became a burning plate of gold. On the opposite northern side, tall dark waves rushed against a ten-foot cliff. Out here the wind was stiff indeed, and Maillart pulled his hat low over his eyes so as not to lose it. Isabelle also wore a large floppy-brimmed hat, secured under her chin with a scarf.

At the peninsula's western extremity, Maillart helped Isabelle down from her horse, then slipped the reins under the stirrups. They clambered over the bayside rocks, Maillart lending a hand as necessary, finally swinging her down to the meager beach. Down here, the rocks behind them partially broke the wind. Isabelle let go his hands and took a pace away from him, shading her eyes with hand and hatbrim as she gazed westward into the reddening sunset. Maillart looked in the opposite direction, toward the town, miniaturized by distance and very pretty in the tempered evening light.

Isabelle removed her hat and held it high so that it caught the wind and fluttered, with a whipping sound. She smiled teasingly at Maillart, then let the hat go. He lunged for it hopelessly, and fell to his knees on the sand, as the hat blew out and landed on the bay, floating with the scarf unwinding in the water. He scrambled to his feet, turning to Isabelle, who laughed and threw back her head, her hair blowing loose all around her face. A thin gold chain gleamed on her collarbone. Maillart wrapped his hands around her tiny waist and kissed the white curve of her neck, then her mouth, and felt her quick tongue darting. When his hand rose to her breast she knocked it away.

"No, I don't want it."

Maillart pulled her to him, hand at the small of her back, and thrust once, to make her gasp—the gasp was quite well known to him, encouraging. He kissed her more deeply, inhaling her breath, as his free hand worked loose the bodice laces with a desperate ingenuity. His fingertips brushed something unexpectedly hard and cold, then burrowed toward the more familiar softness. He was trying to pull her down to the sand. Isabelle bit through his lower lip, then, as he recoiled, hit him hard on the cheekbone with her closed hand.

Maillart backed off and spat blood in the sand, touched his finger to his lip, staring at her in astonishment.

"Tu me fais mal." Isabelle tucked her small breast back into her bodice in a businesslike manner, and fastened the laces back up to the neck. "And you've also broken my necklace."

Maillart glanced down at his right hand; the ends of the gold chain unspooled from his fingers. On his palm lay a dark cylindrical object—a carved stone penis, life-sized or near.

"But what *is* that?!"

"Un objèt d'art, évidemment," Isabelle snapped, "A souvenir from the time of the *caciques.*"

Maillart's eyes bulged at the stone phallus. He had seen arrowheads and thunderstones and a few carved fetishes of the long-vanished Arawaks, but nothing remotely resembling this. "They worshipped these?" he asked.

"No more than you worship your own. Bah, you have destroyed the chain."

Maillart's back stiffened. "Allow me to have it repaired for you."

"No, give it to me." Isabelle took the chain, squinted, and closed the broken link with a pinch of her nails. She reached behind her neck to refasten the clasp, then thrust the pendant back into her bosom. Maillart glared as she shook out her hair.

"*Ça va?*" he said with an ironic lift of his eyebrows. He wiped a little blood off his chin.

Isabelle turned toward the west, where the sun was a red disk dissolving in the molten water. "You misunderstand me," she said. "When I come here at this hour, I think of my children."

The captain considered this for a moment. "Accept my apologies," he said.

"But it was I who provoked you," Isabelle said. "After all, you are only a man."

"True," the captain said, with an unaccustomed sense of humility. "I admit that."

His heat had by now completely subsided, and he felt his anger fading too, leaving confusion, then a kind of calm. They stood at arm's length from each other, until the sun had cut entirely through the surface of the water and dropped under like a coin in a slot. Behind was a wake of color streaked across ragged scraps of cloud. Seagulls crossed the red-rippled sky, crying as if the sun was something they had lost.

"We had better go in," the captain said practically. "A horse might break a leg on these rocks in the dark."

Isabelle nodded, speechless. The captain assisted her back to the horses. When she had mounted, she retained his hand a little longer.

"I have still a need for friendship," she said.

"I offer whatever you will accept."

They rode back to the town in the same silence in which they had come. The captain glanced back once to look for Isabelle's hat, but it had either foundered or floated out of sight.

Dinner *chez Monot* was convivial enough—Isabelle seemed rather more animated than usual, and Maillart managed, at last, to rise to the occasion. If Monsieur Cigny suspected anything, he gave no sign of it . . . and after all, this time there was little to suspect. Maillart retired to his room, resolved to stay there, renouncing any adventures on the balcony . . . Beyond the enclosure of the house, the donkeys brayed as usual. He lay down expecting a restless night and was amazed to awaken, what seemed seconds later, to the full light of day.

Major O'Farrel was waiting for him downstairs, fingers drumming on the table. "At last," he said, as Maillart strolled in. "Your horses are fed and watered and saddled and your men are waiting at the gate. As I believe your business here is very much concluded—"

"*Doucement*," Maillart said. "I have not yet breakfasted."

"I would not linger over the meal," O'Farrel said, "unless you want to be hanged for a spy. Major Grant has taken very much against you—he has been making inquiries, since your visit. Were he ever so slightly less muddled, you would have been in the guardhouse since yesterday noon. You understand, I can do nothing—I have already done more than I should."

Maillart sat down and called for coffee. The major jumped up, twitching.

"If you mean to dally after that devil of a woman," he said, "consider if it's worth your life. You waste your time, in any case—she has forsworn her *amours* to devote herself to that swinish husband, for what reason I do not comprehend. Or perhaps she is moved by some other fancy."

Maillart burst out laughing and leaned back in his chair.

"I am delighted to have so amused you," O'Farrel said frostily.

Maillart caught his breath. "I mean no offense," he said. "Indeed I'm grateful for the warning." He touched a cautious finger to the swelling on his cheekbone. "But go—before you're compromised by being seen here. I'll not be ten minutes behind you."

At the edge of town Maillart took counsel with a convoy of water sellers headed for the river, and was directed to a trail barely passable by horsemen, which in theory led directly across the peninsula down to the town of Gonaives. In an hour they had reached the height of the dry mountains. Maillart pulled his horse up sharply and turned back toward Le Môle. He dismounted and, while the black men watched him gravely, took off his civilian shirt, ripped it down the middle and tried to throw it off the cliff. The wind caught the shirt and blew it loosely back so that Maillart's horse shied and bucked. The captain choked up on the reins and calmed his animal, then turned toward the distant sea and began to shout, cursing women and politics equally, mostly in French but with some excursions into English, Spanish and Creole. When he was breathless, the black men laughed and applauded him. Maillart took his French uniform from a saddlebag and put it on, adjusted the epaulettes and pulled the seams straight. Once content with the fit of his coat, he swung back into the saddle and rode on, much relieved.

8

Doctor Hébert had elaborated the water project for Habitation Thibodet many times, both in imagination and in fact, but now it was finally finished in both departments. On the slope above the *grand'case*, a pool had drained the swamp and now fed two channels which divided around the house and then rejoined in a second pool, directly in front of the gallery where the doctor sat now, drinking his morning coffee and nibbling at a sugared piece of flat cassava bread.

The lower pool was edged with stones, laid in a ring without mortar. At its far rim, another channel took the water out, down toward the kitchen garden. The doctor thought the irrigation might reclaim the yard before the house, which had degenerated into a bare expanse of baked clay or mud, depending on the season, trampled by the feet of men and horses. He had already planted a few flowering shrubs around the pool, and four coconut palms which might one day grow tall. He closed his eyes, pictured a fountain, but that was absurd.

"It's lovely . . ." The voice was melodic, soft, but a little teasing too. The doctor opened his eyes to greet his sister, who had just settled into the chair next to his own.

"Lovely . . ." she said again, smiling sleepily at him. "But now how will you fill your days?"

"Haven't I enough to do?" The doctor heard the note of pique in his own voice and realized Elise was right: he would miss his pet project. "There's the coffee and the cane," he said more mildly. "And the infirmary, as always."

"I rather meant some avocation," Elise said, turning languidly to accept a cup of coffee from the maid, Zabeth. "To occupy your imagination. Something apart from ordinary work."

"Yes," the doctor said. "There's a great deal of botanizing I had meant to do. . . ."

His own words echoed back at him from the damp, mist-laden air. It was strange to search for an activity to pass the time, in such a situation, when all of the colony was immersed in war of one kind or another. But ever since Toussaint's party had returned from the Spanish side of the mountains, Habitation Thibodet had been strangely becalmed. Not for the first time, the doctor reflected that this state of affairs was unnatural and perhaps portended ill.

Between Toussaint and Biassou, the situation seemed to be worsening, and the doctor was inclined to suspect the growth of a breach between Toussaint and the Spanish high command. There had been no word from either Maillart or Tocquet on their mission to Laveaux, and though Tocquet's mysterious vanishings were routine, the doctor thought Maillart was overdue.

"Or of course you might devote yourself to further perfection of the arts of love," Elise seemed to be saying.

The doctor renewed his attention to her; she returned his gaze calmly, not to say brazenly, her small rose-petal lips slightly parted, her blue eyes amused. Such a conversation between them would have been unthinkable in France. For that matter, in their father's house Elise would never have thought to appear outside her bed chamber in the extremely diaphanous garment she now wore . . . but in Saint Domingue it was all attributed to the heat. In truth, Elise had thrived here, the doctor had to admit, where many Frenchwomen died or withered or went mad. In most respects, by contrast, his sister seemed to have become a Creole.

He was the first to break their gaze, turning to look back toward the pool. "I should have liked to brick that rim," he said. "But for the moment there's no possibility."

"I think the stones look well enough." Elise's sugar spoon clinked against her coffee cup. She cocked her head toward a child's voice—a peal of laughter, then an indistinguishable word. "Is she—" Elise said. "No, she's going to wake Paul."

"But it does lack something," the doctor said, still staring at the pool.

"A fountain," Elise said, following his glance.

"I thought of that," the doctor said. "But there are no means."

"No." Elise laughed and shook back the blond waves of her hair. "Gold-fish, then."

The doctor snorted. "Why not swans?"

"Or water lilies," Elise said.

"Why yes!" the doctor began, but just then the two children came tumbling out onto the gallery, Paul and Sophie. The little boy toppled over, catching himself on his palms and looking up, puzzled. Sophie, who was not quite two years his senior, stooped soberly to help him up. Zabeth put her head out the doorway, saw that the children were attended to and withdrew. Paul marched over to the doctor, who lifted him to his knee and kissed his solemn, ivory-colored face.

"Bonjour, mon cher."

"Bonjour, Papa."

Paul straddled his father's knee. The doctor jogged him idly, speaking again to his sister.

"Well, there is a place with water lilies . . . of a kind," he said. "A pretty little pond, up in the mountains."

"Is it far?" Elise toyed with her daughter's long black curls, drawing the dark-eyed girl against her hip.

"I'd say an hour's ride," the doctor said. Paul began to twist up in his lap; the doctor tore off a bit of the sugared bread to give him.

Elise became animated. "Oh, do let's go together," she said. "I'm bored with rusticating here—Xavier's been so long away. We might make an outing for the children."

The doctor considered. "Well, if we wait for Nanon to get up . . ."

"But no," Elise said. "She'll sleep till noon—you know her ways. And by then it will be much too hot. No, it's better we should go at once." She stood up and began calling orders to the kitchen.

Within the hour they had left the compound, the doctor carrying Paul before him on the saddle of his horse, and Sophie riding with Zabeth, sidesaddle on a donkey. The children giggled and called to one another, their voices waking voices of the birds. Elise, who had dressed in one of Xavier's piratical blouses and a pair of trousers cut so full that each leg appeared to have a skirt of its own, rode astride a white mule. An unlooked-for talent, the doctor remarked, and certainly an unlooked-for posture. Elise shook her hair back carelessly and let him know that she had ridden mule-back all the way over the mountains from Spanish Santo Domingo, during which journey she had often found herself in postures more unexpected than this one.

The doctor fell silent, listening to the liquid trilling of the birds moving in the trees overhead. They had ridden to the height of the coffee plantation and now were circling the rim above the steep valley of Habitation Thibodet. Through the foliage, they caught glimpses of the buildings below, and the tents and *ajoupas* of Toussaint's military encampment, with smoke beginning to rise from fires where the men were preparing the morning meal. Then they had crossed over the ridge and were descending a snake-like trail that wound the crevices of the far side of the *morne*, twisting through tall, saw-bladed grasses and clumps and clusters of bamboo. The doctor carried a *coutelas* which he used to slash overgrowth from the trail, restraining Paul with his left hand cupped over the child's round, firm belly.

In something over an hour they had arrived at their destination, before it had grown truly hot, though the damp, still air had raised a sweat on them and on their animals. The pool was sheltered on three sides by bearded fig trees and a green calabash, and on the fourth it backed into a face of rock some thirty feet high, overgrown with slender hanging vines that sprouted small, pale flowers. Water seeped from springs in the rock, and the surface of the pool itself was covered with the violet flowers called *bwa dlo*, along with floating, flowering plants that much resembled European water lilies.

Elise dismounted and breathed deeply, hands on her hips as she arched her back to look up at the rock face and the vines. "C'est très joli, ça," she said. "A waterfall of flowers."

She twisted her hair up at the back of her head and, with Zabeth, began spreading a checkered cloth over an area of grass a couple of yards above the edge of the pool. Together the women laid out the food that had been prepared for the excursion: green oranges, small fig bananas, cassava bread, a bit of cold chicken . . . The doctor took a bottle of white wine (Tocquet's extraordinary foraging skills had furnished them a supply) and sank it at the pool's edge where it would cool. He pulled off his boots and stockings, rolled his trousers and waded calf-deep in the water, which was cold enough that he felt the first shock in his teeth. The bottom was covered with fine, shaley gravel. He turned and looked up into the trees surrounding it. Zabeth was staring at the calabash tree and the doctor looked in the same direction; since he'd last come here someone had tied up several of the green gourds to shape them for future use as vessels. Also there were several red rags tied to branches, for no material purpose. The doctor experienced a moment of doubt. The pool was on the trail toward Camp Barade, on the outskirts of Toussaint's direct influence. Stragglers from the camps of Biassou or Jean-François were likely to be much less well disciplined than Toussaint's men . . . still, it was calm here now, and they would not stay too long.

He climbed out of the pool and went to join his sister, who had curled catlike on the cloth, her legs tucked under her, chewing an end of her own hair at the corner of her mouth. The food was still covered with napkins on the plates and woven trays. Paul followed him, suddenly petulant.

"Pa oué Maman?" he complained. "Where's Mama?"

"There now," the doctor said, kissing his forehead absently. "You'll see your mother soon enough. Now go with the Sophie and Zabeth." He turned the boy about and gave a push which sent him trundling back down toward the pool. When he looked up, Elise was frowning.

"You are too indulgent with him," she said.

"One might say the same of you, with Sophie . . ." The doctor's tone was mild enough. It was traditional, after all, for Creole children to be hideously spoiled.

"It is not at all the same."

The doctor looked away. Zabeth had tied up her skirt behind, to wade into the water with the two children. Paul was well distracted now, scooping up flashing bits of mica from the bottom and letting them fall in the sparkling water. It was idyllic here, and yet the doctor sensed a whole hidden agenda in his sister's words. There'd been perhaps a particular reason she'd wished to make this excursion without Nanon.

"You mean the difference of a son from a daughter?" the doctor said, with a certain sense of heaviness. "After all, they are both little children."

"Childhood is sweet," Elise said. "But as adults, those two can never live as cousins. Neither here, nor in France."

The doctor looked at his sister. Her hair was loose around her face, her breasts fell unrestrained against the coarse cloth of her husband's shirt . . . She was wearing trousers, for God's sake; she rode astride a mule. It was very strange to hear her instructing him in the proprieties of this country. Elise was no more *farouche* than many other Creole women, or not much more, and yet whenever he looked at her, he thought of their manner of life in their father's house in France. It now occurred to him, for the first time, that she might be measuring him against a similar standard. His sense of heaviness increased.

"You sound very much like your friend Isabelle Cigny," he said.

"That's reasonable," said Elise. "It was she who first educated me in all the ways of this place."

The doctor looked down at the two children splashing in the pool. Sophie floundered deeper into the water and suddenly sat down, perhaps unintentionally, her skirt spreading on the water around her. She looked distressed at first, but then began laughing. Zabeth laughed with her, a bright smile splitting her dark face, and scooped some water in a mock threat to put it on Sophie's hair. Paul spun aimlessly beside the two of them, his palms stroking the lily pads like fan blades.

"It's well enough for now," Elise said. "But the system here will divide them as they grow. You must see this."

The doctor looked down at the pool again. There was little to choose between the skin tone of the two; Sophie was even slightly the darker, for she had taken her father's coloring—this assuming that her father was in fact Xavier Tocquet, and not Elise's former husband, the late proprietor of Habitation Thibodet.

"What I see is the 'system' here lying in ruins," the doctor said. "With revolution here and in France . . . it is a great uprooting."

Elise sighed. "Some things can never be revolutionized."

The doctor said nothing. Elise sat up straight, crossing her legs like an Indian.

"What of the future?" she said. "There are some who live in such liaisons, and even openly; it is not unheard-of, though—" She looked at him pointedly. "One must never take such a woman to wife. But the children of these unions create difficulties in time."

The doctor felt his first flash of real irritation. "There are irregularities in your own career, *madame ma sœur,* which I have forborne to reproach you with."

Elise failed to blush as expected; she returned his glance calmly, her blue eyes clear.

"To summarize . . ." The doctor tugged at the point of his beard. "I arrive in this country to find you absconded from your husband, absolutely disappeared—yes, I admit he was a brute, but we now speak of law and propriety. You abandon him, you dash off who knows where, to Santo Domingo as I am eventually to learn—I don't know if there were other stops on your itinerary—with a man apparently your lover, this Xavier Tocquet, whose own reputation seems very extraordinary. Let me say that for my part I much prefer your second choice to your first, but still, Madame, your manner of arranging yourself provokes notice, does it not? As for the child of the first marriage, whom you have stolen away in your elopement, I discover—from your bosom friend

Isabelle Cigny, no less—that her legitimacy is somewhat in question. Well, the matter is finally settled decently enough, for across the Spanish border you are married to our Monsieur Tocquet. But I have taken care not to ask the *date* of this marriage, lest it be discovered bigamous, for I do know very well the date of your first husband's demise, since it was I who attended his final illness, during your very conspicuous absence from your place at his side."

Elise, who had caught her lower lip in her top teeth at the mention of the marriage, now released it thoughtfully.

"Are you quite finished?"

"Is it not sufficient?" the doctor said. "I don't mean to quarrel with you, but think of our father's house—our mother, ten years in her grave. Imagine how such an affair would be viewed in Lyons."

"In Lyons, we would make a pretty pair, the two of us." Elise laughed, and after a moment the doctor joined her with a reluctant chuckle.

Sophie came up to the grassy slope, holding out her dripping skirt in a giggling display. Elise made a movement of mock retreat. "Keep your distance, child," she said. "Yes, yes, you *may* take it off."

Sophie undid her skirt and frolicked, naked, back into the pool. The doctor noted that Paul had already disrobed. Zabeth was spreading their wet clothing to dry in the sunshine that poured over the slope.

"The truth of it is," Elise said, "the society here will forgive almost any *faiblesse d'amour,* and much more easily than in Europe—so long as it does not cross the color line. I don't say there's justice in it, but things are as they are. You acknowledge the boy—perhaps it's right that you should. But what of his education? His future, what will it be? And if there should be other children?"

"I have lost the habit of pondering the future here," the doctor said, and realized as he spoke that his words were true. This place seemed to be without a sense of time. There was the moment as you lived it; all others were illusory. Nanon had helped to teach him this, in her somewhat specialized fashion. Then again, there had been many occasions in Saint Domingue when his mere survival to the end of the day, or to the next dawn, had seemed future enough—as much as he could contemplate.

Now Elise had summoned up the future; it appeared before him as a cloudy menace which he had no ability to plan for or control. He stood up, nodding and blinking, and dusted off the back of his trousers.

"Where are you going?" Elise said.

"A little botanizing," the doctor muttered vaguely.

He made a wavering motion with his left hand and turned from her, walking around the borders of the pool and then behind the bearded figs. It was peaceful here, and through the streams of the trees' hanging roots, he caught glimpses of the children, their pale skins flashing in the water, heard them laughing as they splashed each other. But his mind continued to track forward on the path Elise had laid out for it.

What, after all, *would* become of the boy? In the larger scheme of things the doctor knew that his sister was right: such children did bring difficulties, being neither black nor white. In principle they constituted a third race, and their weight in the politics and warfare of this country was considerable. But the doctor had not applied such reasoning to the case of his son Paul, who had, unmistakably, the ears of his own grandfather, who had appeared to him in the guise of a small and amiable human animal. Now the word *son* seemed to thunder in his ears, and also he felt that his conversation with Elise was somehow a betrayal of Nanon (though he himself had said nothing to betray her—had he?). Such thoughts were misery; he must put an end to them somehow.

Meanwhile Toussaint had been some days away from the camp at Ennery, at Marmelade perhaps, or at one of the other strong places that ran from Gonaives back to the Spanish frontier. He explained his comings and goings to no one, arrived and departed with small warning.

At dawn of the day following the family picnic by the lily pond, he appeared on the gallery, and took coffee in silence, failing to rise to any conversational bait that either the doctor or Elise trolled past him. Breakfast done, he retreated to the cane mill.

Doctor Hébert spent the balance of the morning on hospital rounds, changing dressings and attending to some scattered cases of fever or dysentery. There were two infirmaries now: the one he had established for the slaves of Habitation Thibodet, and another in the tented encampment of Toussaint's soldiers. Most of the injuries were accidental at the moment, for there had not been much fighting of late, though some of the black soldiers nursed old wounds, slow to heal. The doctor was attended on his tour by the woman Merbillay, who had a growing skill with herbal brews, and by the newcomer Guiaou, who seemed fascinated with any medical proceeding, his interest perhaps inspired, the doctor thought, by the scars of the terrible wounds from which he had himself recovered.

At the noon hour he lunched with Nanon and Elise on the gallery of the *grand'case*. The meal passed pleasantly enough, but with little conversation. The air was heavy and still and it seemed almost too hot and oppressive to talk at all. The encounter came to a silent conclusion; Tocquet struck fire to his cigar and smoked. The other white people retired for the customary afternoon siesta, retreating from the most intense heat of the afternoon. The doctor lay abed with Nanon, comfortable in her affection, although he was too uneasy in his mind to rise to her caresses. At length he took her hands and folded them together and held them with one of his own; Nanon smiled at him, unoffended, and rolled her back to him. He lay with one hand cupping her belly, breathing the sweet scent of her hair and the nape of her neck and listening to her sleeping respiration, but he himself could not sleep. Or perhaps he dozed, for the light had changed when he finally disengaged himself and rose from the bed. In the crib on the opposite side of the room Paul lay on his back, snoring delicately, his lips slackly apart. The doctor watched him for a moment, then dressed quietly and went out onto the gallery, carrying his boots.

Toussaint sat alone at the round table abstractly looking out over the rail, one hand on the knee of his uniform trousers and the other curled near a tall, clear glass of water. Beads of sweat gathered on his forehead, in the creases below his yellow headcloth. He made no movement to wipe them away, nor did he turn to greet the doctor, who hesitated at the table's edge, but with a motion of his hand invited him to sit. Seated, the doctor looked over the pool he had engineered with a certain satisfaction. There was no sound except for the purling of the water and the cackling of a crow on the eaves of the *grand'case*. Toussaint turned to him with a faint smile and was apparently about to speak, but just then his younger brother Jean-Pierre came dashing up the steps, calling out that Moyse and Charles Belair had been arrested on the order of Jean-François and that they and perhaps some other junior officers were being held under guard at Camp Barade.

Toussaint was on his feet immediately, his fingers brushing his sword hilt and then the grip of his pistol. He called for his coach, which came so quickly that the doctor thought that the horses must already have been harnessed and waiting. Toussaint did not often travel in the coach presented to him by the Spaniards, but on occasions when his progress and arrival required a degree of pomp and circumstance, he did sometimes use it.

Now he beckoned to the doctor to get into the coach with him. There was room enough for four but there were only the two of them, so they sat diagonally opposite each other, their knees knocked together with the jolts of the rough road. Jean-Pierre sat with the driver on the box. Flanked by five outriders, they rolled out from Habitation Thibodet.

Saint Domingue was a wretched country to travel by carriage. Before the insurrection, most colonists unfit for horseback riding had used sedan chairs borne by slaves, rather than risking their bones in wheeled vehicles. The doctor himself much preferred to ride and so, he knew, did Toussaint Louverture. But Toussaint had himself been a coachman, in former times when he was a slave, and so he knew which ways were passable, and how to traverse bad patches of the trails that would have been impassable to others.

The roads were rough and their pace was brisk; the bumps made the structure of the coach creak and groan and sent both passengers flying from their seats. It was almost comical, but the doctor was not moved to laugh, for Toussaint was showing more obvious anger than he had ever known him to do . . . his whole face looked contorted with it. The doctor clung to the edge of the window to hold himself back from lurching into the black general. The coach kept heeling over on one wheel or another, and sometimes it seemed sure to capsize, but in fact they bogged down only once, in the muddy slough of a stream crossing. The outriders dismounted to heave them free, and Toussaint got down to supervise them tersely; in a matter of minutes, the coach was under way again.

Soon after they had climbed back into the coach, the leaves began to rise and lash together in the wind which was bringing the rain in over the mountains. The afternoon was darkening, but there was still sunlight, streaking down through the treetops; a bar of light lay across the lower half of Toussaint's face. The coach yawed and rocked, and Toussaint's expression contorted; he took off his general's bicorne and dug his fingers into his scalp, under the headcloth, molding and massaging as if to assuage some terrible pain, or (the doctor had this peculiar thought) as if to root some alien presence out of his own head. The doctor had never seen him so. Toussaint's eyes squeezed shut from the pressure of whatever he was undergoing. He rocked his head blindly against the sickening lurches of the coach. *"M'pa kab pasé kalfou sa-a,"* he muttered, in a voice much unlike his own. I cannot pass that crossroad . . .

Inexplicably, Toussaint pulled off both his boots. He kicked open the door with his bare heel and was gone. The doctor had barely time to register this departure before the coach heeled over in the other direction and the door slapped shut of its own accord.

Toussaint's plumed hat swayed on a hook above the leather cushion where his head had lately rested. His empty boots bounced against each other on the floor. If not for these traces, the doctor might have doubted he had ever been there. *M'pa kab pasé kalfou sa-a* . . . The doctor closed his eyes and pressed the lids with his fingertips. The thousands of crossroads all over this land seemed to spread against his darkened eyes like glowing nodes of a golden net. At what *kalfou* was he standing now? and at which *kalfou* was Toussaint? and at which stood his friend, Captain

Maillart? or Nanon and Paul, or his sister Elise? or the many men whose wounds and illnesses he had treated without knowing their names, or the other men who had in some fashion become his enemies . . . He knew that the net of *kalfous* connected him somehow to all of these, but he could not read the meaning of the connections. There was a muted thump of thunder, and the doctor opened his eyes and shook his head, dizzily, then peered out the window of the coach. Just here, the trail to Camp Barade crossed a somewhat wider road that ran from Marmelade in the interior down to Gonaives on the coast. The coach passed, one of the outriders clucked to his horse, and again they went under the deep shadows of the trees. The coach went into a tight turn and the doctor felt a cold clutch in his belly. He ran one hand along his belt and realized he was unarmed.

"*Zombi!*" Jean-Pierre's voice, from the box, chilled with fear. The doctor leaned forward, peering out. There was a man on the trail ahead of him, skeletally thin, his breechclout stiff with dirt. He walked in a rigid, unhuman way, arms glued against his ribs, his hips unyielding to his movement. His eyes were ringed clear around with white, and there was something in his face the doctor seemed to recognize. It seemed the horses would strike him down, for he walked toward them as if blind, but at the last possible moment he lurched from the trail and vanished in the brush.

The curve of the road grew tighter still, throwing the doctor up against the door of the coach—he dove out, it seemed to him later, almost before he had heard the first shot, cleared the trail edge and slid down a ravine face down, plowing up grasses and vines and loosening clumps of soft, wet earth. The side of his head butted into a boulder and he caught hold of the edge of it with one hand; the momentum of his fall twisted him onto his back. The spread-eagled form of one of Toussaint's outriders appeared against the sky above him—shot from the saddle. The man landed in a huddle a yard away and the doctor crawled to him, but he was well beyond medical assistance. The doctor appropriated the dead man's musket, which had not been fired, and weaseled his way back to the boulder, which offered cover as well as a prop for the barrel of the gun. Sighting up the ravine, he could see the overturned coach with one wheel still spinning, and some dozen black riders dressed in rags of Spanish uniform, circling, firing pistols into the coach or leaning down from their saddles to slash victims on the ground with their long knives. The doctor closed his left eye and shot one of them in the hollow between his bare shoulder blades—the man stretched out his arms and pitched down from his horse without making a sound, but the next man to him cried out in alarm and stared down the ravine across the mane of his rearing horse.

The doctor hunched further down behind the stone, tasting dirt at the corner of his mouth. Too late he thought of the cartridge box still attached to the dead outrider's belt—he'd have to expose himself to reach it now. But none of the ambushers seemed disposed to return his fire. He heard someone call out an order, and voices shouting in confused reply, then hooves galloping, as it seemed, back down the trail to Camp Barade.

He remained motionless, mashed into the dirt, for a time he could not measure. His ear was swollen where it had struck on the stone, and his head pounded on the same side. Thunder clapped again, but still the rain did not begin. Blood from the body of the man lying near him puddled and trickled across the leaves, and a white butterfly landed there; the doctor was near enough to observe the butterfly's proboscis dip to draw a taste of that thick red nectar. When the birds began to speak again, he raised his head enough to brush the dirt from his cheek. He rubbed grit from his teeth with a finger, spat, then crawled over to retrieve the cartridge box. There was no evidence he had been observed by anyone. He rose to one knee to reload the musket, then stood and scrambled, with the help of his free hand, back up to the trail.

No survivors. Just around the curve from the crossroads the trail had been blocked with heavy tree trunks, but for double assurance the ambushers had shot one of the coach horses in the traces. The other horse was tossing its head and trying to rise from under the splintered singletree. The men were dead. The Spanish coat of arms on the door of the coach was mostly obliterated by a perforation of bullet holes. Across the knees of the dead driver lay the body of Toussaint's brother, Jean-Pierre, riddled with bullet wounds and mutilated by slashes of a *coutelas*. The free coach wheel still ticked on its axle like a cog of a broken watch.

Then the same stiff figure broke from the vines onto the roadway. The doctor covered it quickly with the musket. *Zombi*—a fantasy of the Africans at which he'd scoffed. The doctor had scoffed. The body of a slave laid low by sorcery, then raised from the grave and made to walk, and work, again. Beyond his realm of possibility. The creature advanced toward him blindly, as it had approached the horses. Though fixed in a frozen rictus, the features were those of Chacha Godard, who'd been one of the doctor's captors in the first phase of the insurrection—but Chacha Godard, he *knew*, was dead. That being the case, he wondered if a shot would be effective.

At a yard's distance from his musket barrel, the creature spun away and plunged into the jungle. The doctor pointed the musket in one direction, then another, but it seemed there was now no enemy near. He climbed the barricade of tree trunks, to the height of nearly eight feet. The trail toward Camp Barade was empty. In the other direction, he could see back to the crossroads which Toussaint had not been willing to pass. The light had turned almost completely green, as though filtered through thick green glass, and all the air seemed pregnant with rain which had not yet begun, but a reddish bar of sunlight still lay across the crossroads. Just at that vertex appeared the figure of a stooping, grizzled old man, barefoot and bareheaded, weighed down by a long straw sack that dragged from his shoulder almost to the ground. A singing voice seemed to surround him rather than to come from within him, dark and profound as deep blue water.

Attibon Legba
Ouvri baryè pou nou . . .
Papa Legba
Kité-nou pasé . . .

The doctor covered the old man with the musket for a moment, but the other did not seem to threaten him with any physical harm, indeed he seemed quite unaware of the doctor's presence at the top of the barricade. The doctor lowered the musket. All the same, the hair rose on his arms and the back of his neck, as if he were confronting a ghost or a spirit or someone else's god.

The stooped old man stepped forward from the light of the crossroads into the shadows of the trees and continued to come nearer through the weird green light. He paused to examine the wreckage of the coach, and again to look at the horse struggling under the broken singletree. When he reached the cadaver of Jean-Pierre, he let out a long wolf-like wail and dropped onto his knees; the straw *macoute* went slack on his shoulder. He covered his face with his hands and shuddered. Grief flowed out of him in a black wave which also poured over the doctor, who climbed down from the barricade and left the musket leaning against it. Softly, empty-handed, he approached the old man, who now stopped his wailing and took from the *macoute* a yellow square of cloth and dredged it in the blood that pooled between the knees of Jean-Pierre, then wrung it out and spread it by the corners. From this drenching the cloth had turned a rusty red. The old man bowed and bound the cloth around his head, knotting it firmly at the back. That well-known gesture . . . when the old man raised his head again, he was familiar, but at the same time deeply strange, as he had always been. The doctor went down on one knee himself and stared into the ancient red-rimmed eyes of Toussaint Louverture. A silent flash of lightning lit the space between them starkly white, and then, all at once, the rain came down.

9

Fret not thyself because of evildoers, neither be thou envious against the workers of iniquity.

For they shall soon be cut down like the grass, and perish as the green herb.

Captain Maillart shifted position; his buttocks had already grown numb on the backless bench of the Marmelade church. The mulatto youth at the lectern went on intoning the words of the Thirty-seventh Psalm. His voice was thin, reedy and yet possessed of a peculiar urgency which made it difficult to ignore. Thus Maillart could not doze or drift, as he ordinarily did during his rare appearances in church. Vaublanc, who sat to Maillart's right, seemed more at peace; he breathed with a rasp close to a snore, and his head wobbled on his neck.

Irritably, Maillart studied the colored boy, who was gangly and lean, his acolyte's robe inches too short for him. His kinky hair was close-cropped, his eyes large and almost feminine, floating in the deep hollows of his skull. At last the captain managed to organize his vague sense of familiarity: this was Moustique, who had been a hanger-on at Toussaint's camp at Ennery.

Cease from anger, and forsake wrath: fret not thyself in any wise to do evil.

For evildoers shall be cut off: but those that wait upon the Lord, they shall inherit the earth.

Maillart nudged Doctor Hébert, who sat to the left of him on the pew, and muttered, "That priest's brat from Ennery, is it not?"

The doctor nodded slightly, without turning his head. He sat erect, almost prim, his hands folded on his lap, with the air at least of rapt attention. Maillart moaned inwardly. He looked at the lectern itself; the most elaborate furnishing in all the church. Spread wings of an eagle, carved in mahogany, supported the Holy Writ, but where the eagle's head should have been was some monstrous chimera from an African woodworker's nightmare. A fat globule of sweat purled from Maillart's temple. In a torture of boredom, he let his eyes go unfocused. The voice of the acolyte whined on.

The wicked have drawn out the sword, and have bent their bow, to cast down the poor and needy, and to slay such as be of upright conversation.

Their sword shall enter into their own heart, and their bows shall be broken.

Maillart lowered his moist forehead into his hands, then raised it, looking about himself. The little church was filled past its capacity, with many of Toussaint's junior officers lining the walls, their black faces sweat-shiny and impassive. There was a general stench of too many men perspiring in their woollen uniforms. A hard-shelled flying beetle buzzed over the heads of the congregation and tumbled down the back of Maillart's coat collar. He grunted and clawed at his neck. Toussaint glanced back from between two Spanish officers on the bench ahead. Maillart felt himself flushing. His hand seemed full of splintered beetle legs and wings. Beside him, Doctor Hébert suppressed a laugh.

Toussaint sat uncovered in a posture of devotion, his bicorne hat balanced on his knees. Maillart stared at the glossy black bald spot in the center of his commander's head. He had no clue to Toussaint's thinking. He had delivered Laveaux's invitation—after Tocquet had done the same, after the delegation Laveaux had sent directly from Port-de-Paix had also presented itself at Ennery. And following Maillart's return from Môle Saint Nicolas, Toussaint had held numerous late-night councils with Moyse and Dessalines, Clervaux and Charles Belair. He had sent couriers to all his outposts from Dondon to Gonaives. In the wake of this activity, l'Abbé Delahaye had removed himself and his acolyte from Dondon to the more secure location of Marmelade.

But in the end, if such was the end, Toussaint had done no more than to renew his oath of fealty to the Spanish crown, as represented by the person of the Marquis d'Hermonas. This renewal of vows had taken place yesterday, here at Marmelade, after which Hermonas had ridden back to Saint Raphael, leaving the town with a light Spanish garrison under the command of a Major Verano, who now sat next to Toussaint on the bench. Verano was slight, with a yellowish cast to his skin; he stooped and there was something supercilious in his manner. A straggly beard hung from his chin, and as he listened to the service, or pretended to listen, he would alternately chew on the end of it or roll the dampened hairs between his fingers.

As for Toussaint's intention in all this affair, there was no fathoming it. Maillart dropped bits of crushed beetle on the floor, then scratched again underneath his collar, where he still seemed to feel the scrabble of insect legs—if it were not the Spanish cloth that chafed him.

. . . and as they went on their way, they came unto a certain water, and the eunuch said, See, here is water; what doth hinder me to be baptized?

And Philip said, If thou believest with all thine heart, thou mayest. And he answered and said, I believe that Jesus Christ is the Son of God.

And he commanded the chariot to stand still: and they went both into the water, both Philip and the eunuch; and he baptized him.

And when they were come up out of the water, the Spirit of the Lord caught away Philip, that the eunuch saw him no more: and he went on his way rejoicing.

Moustique had progressed, finally, to the New Testament reading . . . would this service never, ever be concluded? As Maillart released that irritable thought, Moustique closed the heavy book and carried it to the altar. L'Abbé Delahaye, who had been kneeling with his back to the people, rose and turned with a light alacrity, approached the lectern and began to preach.

The white priest's voice was deeper, more sonorous, than the voice of his colored acolyte. Maillart felt himself drifting almost comfortably, back toward his dream of the night before, which he had until this moment forgotten. In dream he had been swimming by moonlight, or rather diving, down through current after current of dark water with ripples lightly silvered by the moon. He was diving in pursuit of something that had slipped from his hand as he swam. He struck the silty bottom with a light rebound and groped in the swirl and murk until his fingers curled through the hilt of a silver sword. Above him, he saw leaves and lily pads and flower petals floating on the moonlit surface of the water. There was a beauty that snatched at his breath, and somewhere behind it the thought of Isabelle Cigny . . . He rose, carrying the heavy sword, and broke a surface of leaves and lilies, but there was no air; he was still covered by the water, and above him plane after plane of petal-sprinkled surfaces; each time he broke through he was somehow still submerged, and at last his limbs went slack and loose, and he was towed back to the bottom by the weight of the silver sword. When he struck against the bottom again, he understood that he should have let the sword go long ago, and now he let it fold into the layers of silt, and rose again more buoyantly, through many planes of leaf and moonlight, but it was too late; his lungs had opened, and he was already breathing in the silver water . . .

The captain popped awake with a jolt. He had slumped over onto Doctor Hébert's shoulder; the doctor shrugged him off with a sardonic smile. But finally the sermon was at an end, and the captain rose and joined the line of people shuffling toward the altar rail. He knelt, and accepted a morsel of bread from the hand of Delahaye. Then Moustique was coming with the wine, murmuring, *the blood of Jesus Christ, the cup of your salvation . . .*

Maillart swallowed, returned to his seat. Dream-fog still covered him, like a spiderweb. He covered the worst of his yawn with his hand. The occupants of the front pews began to file out of the church, following the cross. Maillart rose and marched in line behind Toussaint and the Spanish officers with Doctor Hébert walking immediately behind.

Outside the little building was a flurry of activity. The black captains, Dessalines and Clervaux and Belair, had all hurried to mount their horses, while the priest Delahaye, together with his acolyte and cross-bearer, had vanished as if the earth had swallowed them. A ripple of restlessness ran through the black troops surrounding the church; Toussaint had come to Marmelade in unusual force this time, bringing nearly three thousand of his men. But the black commander himself seemed calm and unhurried. He handed Maillart his bicorne hat to hold, and withdrew from his breast pocket a kerchief unevenly stained a brownish red.

Major Verano watched Toussaint with his slightly slanted, olive-colored eyes, as the black commander pinched the kerchief at diagonal corners, pulling its square into a triangle. Verano put the end of his beard in the corner of his mouth and drew on it as if it were a fine cigar. Maillart, who found this habit revolting, looked away, drumming his fingers absently on the brim of Toussaint's hat. Guiaou and Quamba were leading over Toussaint's horse, the sleek white charger Bel Argent.

"Such a fine devotion," Verano said, pulling his beard out from his lips and molding the damp tip with his dirt-creased fingers. His speech had the Castilian lisp. Maillart was unsure whether his tone of light sarcasm was addressed to himself and the doctor, who stood at his right shoulder, or directly to Toussaint. Verano tasted his beard tip once more, and then withdrew it and squinted at the end. "He fights with the lion's ferocity," he said half mockingly, "but communes with the meekness of the lamb."

Toussaint, flipping the tails of the red kerchief over his head, seemed oblivious to the remark at first. His eyes went white for an instant, as if they were looking through the back of his skull at his fingers tying the cloth. When the knot was accomplished, his eyes came clear; he took his hat back from Maillart and settled it carefully over the red headcloth.

"Blessed are the meek," Toussaint pronounced, "for they shall inherit the earth."

As he spoke, he drew his huge cavalry pistol and shot Major Verano through the center of his chest. At the explosion, Bel Argent jerked his head back against the reins; Quamba and Guiaou restrained him. Verano had snapped over backward like a broken cornstalk; his body sagged into the arms of one of his Spanish subordinates.

"*Vive la France!*" Toussaint cried out, glancing at Maillart as he swung into the saddle, his long, bright sword whirling high around his head. All over the town square the black cavalrymen were riding down the scattering Spanish troops. One of Verano's fellows rounded on Maillart with a shriek of outrage and astonishment. Maillart stood too near to bring a weapon effectively into play. He struck the Spaniard with his fist, then stepped back, hand on his pistol grip, but Guiaou had already skewered the man from behind; the spoon-shaped blade of Guiaou's *coutelas* thrust out for a moment from between the Spaniard's coat buttons, then retracted as the dying man fell.

"*Vive la France!*" Maillart shouted; his voice came back to him with a small, tinny sound, as if someone else had shouted the phrase from a far distance.

He looked for Antoine Hébert, but the doctor had already run to his own mount and was unshipping his long rifle from the scabbard lashed to the saddle. Vaublanc had made it into the saddle and was riding down a side street, his face blank with confusion and his saber pointing at the sky. Maillart scrambled onto his own horse. The snout of his drawn pistol quested this way and that.

"What did you know of this?" he called to the doctor. Hébert, who had remained afoot, bracing his rifle barrel across the saddle of his horse, shook his head. Toussaint had not taken the *blancs* into his confidence . . . Both men held their fire now; there was no target. The black cavalry had swept the Spaniards from the square and were picking off the stragglers in the side streets. A pair of men had already struck the Spanish colors, and begun to run the French tricolor up the flagpole.

"Vive la France," Maillart said again, wonderingly, looking again at the doctor. L'Abbé Delahaye appeared for a moment in the door of the small house behind the church. He made the sign of the cross and then withdrew, pulling Moustique after him as he shut the door. The doctor pulled his rifle down, put it back in the scabbard. Ten minutes and it was already over, the last man of the Spanish garrison wiped out; the French were, in theory at least, masters of Marmelade. Someone tied the Spanish flag to the tail of a donkey and drove the braying animal through the dusty streets, to much laughter and flinging of stones. But fifteen minutes later Toussaint had organized his force and was riding from the town at the head of his cavalry, leading two thousand-odd men on foot at a fast pace toward the north. Maillart rode in the vanguard, following the doctor; they still exchanged bewildered glances, but the euphoria of victory washing over all of Toussaint's troops had caught them up as well.

Biassou, installed at Habitation La Rivière, had not attended church that day. Toussaint's advance guard reached the outskirts of his camp before noon. Biassou had no real pickets posted; Toussaint's men overran a few wanderers gathering wood or wild mushrooms, and silenced them by slitting their throats. The surprise was perfect, for Biassou's camp was still asleep. Only a few breakfast fires had been lit, and most of the men still snored in their shelters. The trampled ground before Biassou's tent, surrounding a pole striped with the serpentine images of Damballah and Ayida Wedo, suggested that the ceremony had gone late the night before. Nearby, a lone old woman pounded coffee in a hollowed stump, her withered breasts flapping as she worked the long stave she used as a pestle. Her mouth popped open when she saw the riders, but no sound came out; she dropped the stave and ran in silence toward the ragged edge of the trees.

Biassou's tent was festooned with snake bones, cat skulls and other *ouangas* strung to the exterior ropes and corners of the canvas. The flaps were down and the tent was quiet, except for a series of little brass bells which gave a ghostly ringing in the breeze. Toussaint pressed Bel Argent into a canter. Not for the first time, Maillart took note of what a superb horseman he was, as he drew his sword and rode down on the tent, handling the weapon with a remarkable dexterity, considering it was more than half the length of his own entire person. Circling on the horse, Toussaint cut all the support ropes, then leaned low from the saddle to strike down the center pole with the flat side of the blade. The tent collapsed on itself like a net drawn tight.

Toussaint's infantry had swept into the camp by this time, moving at a trot with bayonets at the ready. Biassou's men scattered in all directions, still groggy from sleep and perhaps believing themselves caught in some communal nightmare. A couple of Toussaint's men fired into the fallen tent where it flopped with its catch, but Toussaint held up a hand to stop them. He pulled up his horse and waited, straight in the saddle, his sword erect. A neat slit appeared in the canvas and Biassou popped out, holding a short knife in his right hand. He wore his dress uniform coat, bedizened with Spanish ribbons and medals, over his burly torso, but his short legs and his feet were bare. With a glance he assessed his situation and bolted for the trees.

Toussaint rode after him, alone. Biassou's pink heels kicked up under the long tails of his coat. Toussaint's teeth flashed white in his head: *Ou pa blié Jean-Pierre.* His voice was not really a shout, but a speaking tone which carried. You will not forget my brother.

As Biassou reached the edge of the clearing, Toussaint stretched toward him, one hand holding the reins and the horse's mane together while the other struck out with the sword, cleaving Biassou's coat from collar to tail, and opening a red line on his back, such as might have been made by a whip lash. Biassou tumbled over the edge of a shallow ravine and struggled out of sight in the bush. Toussaint reined up and let him go.

A handsome colored woman erupted from the slit Biassou had cut in the tent. Shrieking prettily, she dashed in the same direction as her ravisher, running awkwardly with one hand covering her pudenda. The soldiers began to laugh and applaud, and several of them set off in pursuit of this delicate prize, but Charles Belair called them to halt, and they obeyed him. A commotion had begun at the western fringe of the clearing, and five or six Spaniards in civilian clothes came stumbling toward the center, chivied by black soldiers who pricked them with bayonets. One wore a turban, Arab fashion, the others broad straw hats which now hung down their backs by strings.

"*Yo vann moun,*" said Jean-Jacques Dessalines. They're selling people.

He looked at Toussaint and gestured toward the fringe of woods, where more soldiers were bringing a group of some thirty men and women bound together in a coffle either by iron chains or by split poles carried on their shoulders and lashed with twine to form collars round their necks. Slave traders, Maillart recognized; so the rumors had been true. The turban-wearing Spaniard opened his mouth to speak, but before he could draw breath, Dessalines cracked him across the mouth with the flat of his musket stock, splintering his front teeth and knocking him backward to the ground. At some stage of the attack on Biassou's camp, Dessalines had removed his shirt, as he was wont to do before a fight, and now when he moved with his quick muscular grace the white ropy whip scars on his back crawled as if with a life of their own. He glanced across at Toussaint, who nodded.

"Ou mèt touyé yo," Toussaint said. You may kill them.

Dessalines simply set his boot across the throat of the turbaned man who lay on the ground, rolled his weight forward and held it there until the Spaniard had stopped kicking. Bayonets slammed into the bellies of the others. Maillart tightened the muscle across his own cut, and felt the skin shrinking on his face. An odd moment of indiscipline for Toussaint's command, he thought as he looked quickly away. Other black soldiers were breaking rivets on the chains of the people in the slave coffle, and cutting the lashing on the wooden poles that connected them together in their files. The freed men rubbed their necks and wrists absently; some of the women had begun to cry, and others knelt before Dessalines or the horse of Toussaint Louverture.

By this time, considerable numbers of Biassou's fighting men had regrouped and were filing back down into the clearing, holding their empty hands high to show they were unarmed and submissive. *Papa Toussaint!* many of them were crying, and one who seemed to be their leader went skidding to his knees beside the charger. *Papa Toussaint, nou rinmin ou,* he moaned, and wrapped his hands over the booted foot in the stirrup Papa Toussaint, we love you. Toussaint smiled and placed a palm upon his forehead.

One of the slave traders' severed heads had been hoisted on a pike, and someone had unrolled the turban and ran in circles through the clearing with the purple cloth flagging behind him like a kite tail. Quamba and Guiaou and some other foot soldiers had torn open Biassou's tent and were rooting through the contents, kicking over human skulls and glass bottles and clay *govi*, tumbling the ceremonial drums. Quamba straightened, calling for Toussaint's attention, with a gold watch and chain swinging from one hand and a heavily jeweled snuffbox in the other.

Toussaint drew up to his most rigid martial posture, the saddle creaking as he shifted his weight. "Return those articles to their owner," he declared. "Undoubtedly he will not stop running till he has reached Saint Raphael—return them to him, with my compliments. We are not thieves or pirates—we are soldiers of the Republic of France."

Captain Maillart looked at the doctor and found his own astonishment reflected on the other's face. *"Vive la France!"* the captain shouted. After all, what did he care for slave traders? The words seemed a better fit in his mouth than they had done before.

By nightfall they had swept all the way to Dondon, in the mountain pass above Le Cap and the northern plain. Toussaint raised French colors at every camp along the way; it was the work of moments to eliminate the scatterings of actual Spanish soldiers who opposed them. At every camp from Petite Rivière to Dondon, Toussaint's lieutenants had been prepared in advance for the coup, so that sometimes the Spanish had already been gutted or strung up to the trees by the time Toussaint's own party rode in.

That night in Dondon was a subdued celebration, with a double issue of *clairin*, but no more. Between bites of roast chicken folded in cassava bread, Toussaint instructed Moyse, who commanded at Dondon, to do everything necessary to hold back Jean-François, should the latter attack from his camp, now thought to be at Grande Rivière. If any Spanish had survived the day of massacre, they would probably have fled to join him.

After the meal some of the black infantrymen began drumming around the central campfire, and there was song, a long sonorous chanting in Creole, but the doctor and Maillart and Vaublanc retreated to their bedrolls, where they shared out the second ration of rum, passing a single cup among them in the dark.

"It was neatly done," the doctor said, glancing up at the stars above the treetops and the mountains.

"True enough," Captain Maillart said, twitching a little as he swallowed his share of the raw *clairin*. "We might ourselves be done in as neatly."

"What an extremely unpleasant thought," the doctor said, and lowered his voice to a whisper. "Surely you don't mean to suggest that we should mistrust our commander."

Maillart looked at him narrowly in the starlight, to see to what extent he was joking. "One might say that we ourselves have been mistrusted," he said, "unless you were given more prior notice of this turnabout than I."

"Not in the least," the doctor said, "but one may also argue that the efficacy of a surprise attack depends on secrecy."

Vaublanc drummed his fingers on an unraveling patch of his blanket. "Secrecy is something he has certainly achieved," he said. "I'd give a good deal to know his aims more plainly."

"The French Republic has declared for the general abolition of slavery." The doctor tilted his cup to examine the finger's worth of *clairin* he had conserved there. "Perhaps that is explanation enough."

"And perhaps it isn't," Vaublanc said. "Sonthonax announced abolition nine months ago, and Toussaint did no more than to stake his own competing claim to the fight for general liberty."

The doctor shrugged and sniffed his rum. "Maybe it has taken him until now to remark the inconsistency of his proclamation at Camp Turel with the actual situation . . . with Biassou and perhaps Jean-François still collaborating with the Spanish in the slave trade, as we saw today."

"Do you really think he could have failed to notice that?" Vaublanc retorted.

"Well." The doctor wet his tongue in his ration of rum. "You know I was with him when his coach was ambushed on the road to Camp Barade. Biassou was at the bottom of that attempt, I am certain. And behind his detention at Saint Raphael before that."

"He jumped from the coach before the ambuscade and left you to take the fire meant for him," Vaublanc said, "if I remember your reports of that episode correctly."

"But there was no warning," the doctor said. "I don't think he meant to do what he did then, not in the ordinary sense of intention. It— " He broke off, lost in the strangeness of that hour on the road. "It was as if something had come over him, had taken him over, I mean," he mumbled, shaking his head. Whatever he meant, he could not phrase.

"I see," said Vaublanc. "Then perhaps he neglected to advise anyone of his plan for today because he had not himself formulated it—he was seized with the sudden inspiration as he walked out the door of the church."

"Come," said Maillart. "Are his reasons really so inscrutable? The matter of emancipation must have some weight, and from what Antoine has told us, Biassou and Jean-François have been a long time intriguing against him with the Spanish high command."

"Not to mention trying to murder him," Vaublanc said. "Still and all, it seems a strange moment to join forces with the Jacobins, when they scarcely have a foothold left anywhere on this miserable island."

"May I point out that we are Jacobins ourselves, at least since we left church this morning?" Maillart paused. "You know, Tocquet told me something to that effect before we parted at Port-de-Paix."

"Oh?" said the doctor. With a feeling of resignation he swallowed the remains of his rum and laid his cup aside as the last threads of warmth spread through him.

"He put it that Toussaint didn't need to choose the winning side. That he'd already determined that *he* would win, regardless, so his only chore was to pick his partners in the victory."

Vaublanc laughed softly. "If that's the case," he said, "then we are fortunate indeed that he has chosen us, my friends." He stretched out on his back and pillowed his head on his crossed palms, then added with a tinge of irony, *"Vive la France."*

It seemed they had slept for only a matter of minutes when Clervaux woke them with a shake on the shoulder, although the stars proved to have shifted in the sky. The drums were silent now, and the fires had all been smothered with dirt, but all down the line came the jingle of rings on bits and the squeak of leather as horsemen tightened their girths.

Covering a yawn with his hand, the doctor shrugged at Vaublanc and Maillart, rolled and shouldered his blanket and carried it down the hill to where the horses were tethered at the tree line. His horse turned and whickered at him gently. The doctor fed it a bit of sugar loaf between its lips. It was chilly, and rather damp, so that he shivered and hunched his shoulders up. He changed the priming of his rifle and both pistols before mounting. Maillart and Vaublanc, grumbling under their breath, fell into line behind him.

Two hundred and fifty horses rode westward from Dondon at a quick trot that soon broke into a canter. Doctor Hébert had come to believe that both Toussaint and his white charger must have the night vision of a pair of bats. At times the trails wound clear of cover and their way was lit by wheeling constellations, Bear and Eagle, the Northern Cross, but mostly their way lay under the tight-knit ceiling of tree branches and was dark and tortured and treacherous as the slick bloody twistings of a dragon's entrails. For all that, Toussaint never set a pace slower than a brisk trot, and often enough they seemed to be riding a full gallop through the pitch black of the night.

Twenty minutes were sufficient to secure Gros Morne for the French Republic. It was still full night even when they reached Limbé, did away with a couple of Spaniards hustled from their cots to meet their fate, and informed the black garrison that they had just become French. Toussaint sent a detachment of twenty-five riders to carry the news up the mountain to Port Margot, then on to Borgne, on the north coast, while his main force rode south again, climbing the mountains on trails so steep the doctor had to lie full length across his horse's back to help the balance. At Plaisance, Toussaint left Paparel in charge of the newly republican post, and they rode on with hardly a pause. The stars were just fading when they had reached the height of Morne Pilboreau.

Toussaint called a halt, mysteriously, for there was no settlement, only a goat path running down the precipice, then forking toward Marmelade in one direction and Ennery in the other. Perhaps the *kalfou* had some meaning for him here. At any rate Toussaint got down from Bel Argent and walked backward down the line, murmuring a word or two to different riders, laying a hand of the flank of a horse to be sure it had not overheated. The scabbard of his sword snicked over stones in the path as he walked

Several of the men had begun taking out bread and cold meat from their saddlebags. The doctor saw he would have time to dismount. His legs were rubbery after such a long time in the saddle, and the inseams of his trousers chafed him painfully as he walked. He stood at the trail-head and looked down the dark gulf. It seemed impossible that they should have come so far—full circle or nearly—in the space of a single night. No one could succeed in such a ride; surely he must be dreaming it all. Indeed he did feel half asleep. But somewhere down there in the darkness were Nanon and Paul and Elise and Sophie, as safe as they could be in such a country, he supposed, now that Toussaint had redrawn the lines to surround them. The peaks of the eastern mountains were just discernible against the sky as it gradually lightened into a blue—this was the Cordon de l'Ouest, French now, suddenly, all the way back to the Spanish frontier. All the passways and crossroads along the distance they had come were now charged with the power of Toussaint Louverture.

The doctor walked on his unsteady legs toward the head of the column. After his long riding, the ground seemed to rock up at him in waves. The dragging edge of his boot knocked a stone over the rim and it fell down the dark gorge with no sound of a landing. The doctor came to a halt beside Bel Argent and cocked his head in the starlight. Toussaint stood on the lee side of his horse's shoulder; he was so short that only the white feathers of his hat showed over Bel Argent's mane, but the doctor could hear him muttering, and he heard the click of beads. After a puzzled moment he realized that Toussaint was saying the rosary, murmuring scraps of Latin in a throttled whisper: *Pater Noster, Ave Maria.* A repetition as each wooden bead clicked down the string. The doctor withdrew and walked back to his own horse. Maillart, who had already mounted, looked at him curiously, but the doctor only shook his head and stood staring out over the well of darkness that was the gorge.

Let God save all whom I love from harm, he thought. It was the only prayer he could bring to his mind, and it did not seem to have much authority.

They rode down from Morne Pilboreau through the switchbacks of the dry scrub-covered mountains, silent but for the slap of stirrup leathers and the occasional farting of a horse. The coastal plain was a white-dust-covered desert dotted with small shaley white collines, and at the height of one of these had been raised three spindly wooden crosses outside a rectangular frame of poles, whether for a church or *hûnfor* was uncertain. A woman in a white dress stood at the crest of the hill, looking no bigger than a toothpick doll; she turned her black face to track their descent, her white skirt whipping in the steady wind that came from the sea.

The morning mist had just fully lifted when they rode into Gonaives. A plume of white dust lay over half a mile's worth of their back trail, and a trio of buzzards hung above the column as well, but the Spanish of the garrison were sluggish and off their guard, and in any case knew of nothing to fear from Toussaint Louverture, who found them entertaining a handful of French *émigrés* over a late breakfast of jerked beef and coffee. He and a number of his officers strode into the mess hall, their spurs jingling. the doctor and Maillart bringing up the rear.

There were six or seven of the French, costumed much in the manner of fugitive-slave hunters from the old *maréchaussée*, except for one who wore a black clerk's coat and appeared vaguely familiar to the doctor. The recognition was mutual, for the man winked at him; when his eyes shifted uneasily to Toussaint, the doctor recognized Bruno Pinchon.

Peremptorily for him, Toussaint instructed Belair and Clervaux to escort the French *émigrés* from the room. Six of them rose with studiedly empty expressions; only Pinchon's face betrayed obvious fear. He caught the doctor's sleeve as he passed and drew him out of the room with the group.

In the sunlight outside the barracks, a squad of black soldiers fell in beside the French; the latter had not been disarmed, and now walked with their hands cocked over their pistol grips, except for Pinchon, who appeared to be unarmed, and who whispered urgently in the doctor's ear.

"The pistol will be charged this time—will it not? But I know it."

"What are you talking about?" the doctor said, distracted. The salt smell became stronger as they walked down toward the port, and the light was so bright and hot that he was forced to squint.

"It will be murder, man . . ." Pinchon clawed at the doctor's forearm with both hands. "Help me, do something, can't you? I haven't even a pen knife."

They had just come against the breakwater. There were no real ships at the moorings, only a few small coastal sloops. Charles Belair turned, cleared his throat, and addressed the doctor politely.

"It would be best for you to return to the *casernes*."

At that, Pinchon ducked behind the doctor, seized his collar and with surprising strength began to drag him backward. *"Au secours!"* he kept screaming. *"Sauvez-moi!"*

The doctor was too startled to resist; the other Frenchmen had already fallen—not one had had time to get off a shot or even draw his weapon. He let himself be dragged along the harbor front, his muscles slack, stumbling in his backward steps. Several firearms were aimed their way, but Pinchon had shielded himself too well behind the doctor's body. Belair clucked his tongue regretfully, and tapped his finger on his sword hilt. A couple of the black soldiers took his meaning, drew their knives and began to advance.

Pinchon suddenly released the doctor, pushing him sharply forward. With a frog-like leap, Pinchon cleared the breakwater; a crackle of gunfire from the sloops came almost simultaneously with the splash. The doctor fell on his hands and knees, skinning the butts of his palms as he pitched down. The others of Belair's squad had also taken cover behind the knee-high wall. The doctor peeped over and saw two sloops putting out on the still water, manned by more Frenchmen, some of whom were firing muskets at the shore, while others reached out to haul the water-logged Pinchon aboard their vessels. There were a few moments of cursing and wild rounds whining, but soon enough the little sailboats were out of range and the shooting stopped.

Somewhat belatedly, the doctor followed Belair's advice and walked back up to the *casernes*. Maillart was sitting alone in the mess hall, sipping the dregs of a cup of coffee with a sour expression on his face.

"What's become of the Spaniards?" the doctor inquired.

"It appears that Toussaint has ordered them shot," Maillart said.

The doctor sat down heavily and began rubbing his scalp, where a sunburn was peeling.

"It appears that our compatriots had come up from Saint Marc as emissaries of the English," Maillart said, "who are expected in force here sometime before noon. The English mean to take over Gonaives in order to control the Upper Artibonite valley more effectively—this with the consent of the Spanish, I might add. There was some compact concluded at Santo Domingo City. Toussaint finds himself in a very bad humor about all these developments—his Spanish commanders, if you can imagine it, did not take him into their complete confidence."

"Ah," the doctor said glumly.

"This coffee is cold—ill brewed as well." Maillart drew back the cup as if he meant to dash it against the wall, then changed his mind and set it on the table. He stood up. "No use to brood," he said. "We are good republicans now, after all." He dropped his hand on the doctor's shoulder as he moved toward the door. *"Bon courage—aux armes—vive la France."*

Outside, men were clearing away the bodies of the Spaniards, who had been shot against the side wall of the *casernes*. Toussaint had ordered the cannon of the fort dragged out and brought to bear on the road from the south.

The English arrived in the forenoon, also followed by a flight of vultures. *"Trahison,"* Toussaint hissed between his teeth, when he saw the redcoats coming into focus through the dust, apparently still resentful that his Spanish superiors had not let him into their new compact with the English. All in all, there had been betrayal enough to go round everywhere, the doctor thought, but was prudent enough to keep this notion to himself. Besides, his own glands were humming, and he doubted he could speak without a tremble in his voice.

He sat his horse between Maillart and Vaublanc, who both held their hands grimly on their saber hilts. The smell of horse sweat was sharp and acrid, and the light and the color seemed brighter than was usual. The English kept coming, so near the doctor could see their faces. He had no plan. When he looked over his shoulder he saw the Spanish colors still flying over Toussaint's line. At that moment Toussaint dropped his arm and a volley of grapeshot raked the front line of the English.

"Vive la France!" Many voices took up the cry when Toussaint uttered it, as the cavalry charge swept out from behind the cannon. The doctor's horse moved out with the others, which he had somehow not foreseen. He had no saber, though his pistols were primed—but he did not mean to harm anyone, unless he came under direct attack. Both his hands were knotted in his horse's mane. He watched Maillart, a half-length ahead, chop down a British grenadier who'd raised a bayonet to him. The British were in great disarray, but they were also very numerous.

Toussaint called a retreat, and again the doctor's horse followed the general movement with small direction from the rider. As the cavalry swept back behind the cannon, another round of grapeshot lashed the British line. The redcoats scrambled back out of range, then slowly began to regroup.

The doctor hitched his horse to a gun carriage and began to attend to such of the wounded who were unable to keep their feet. Toussaint was pacing and grinding his jaws, in a very high state of excitement; the doctor had never seen him so agitated. A runner came out from the town and whispered something in his ear. Toussaint grinned as he took off his hat and adjusted the knot of his scarlet headcloth. "Thanks be to God," he said. "They have sent no warships."

But Gonaives had been lightly garrisoned—Toussaint had found few men there to add to his two hundred-odd riders, so the British had them seriously outnumbered. Now they remounted a couple of longer cannons they had been towing backslung behind mules. Presently shells began to fall on Toussaint's force, and the vultures who had settled on the dead between the lines rose and flapped away, troubled by the racket. Meanwhile, the British began a flanking maneuver across the flat open country on the coastal side.

Throughout the next disagreeable hour, the doctor crawled on hands and knees behind the gun carriages, his face pouring sweat, stanching wounds as best he could or sawing off limbs too mangled to be saved. Guiaou helped drag the injured to him, and afterward hauled them farther to the rear. Everything stank of blood and gun powder, and quite often a British cannonball sailed over their heads and plopped down on the dry cracked earth behind them. At one point Maillart came to borrow the doctor's horse, crying that his own had been shot out from under him; the doctor didn't know what became of him after that. Toussaint kept leading sorties to break up the British infantry squares moving in on his right, but the main British line could not be broken.

The cannon balls mostly missed the mark, but the shells exploded after they had fallen and did considerable damage. Wounded men began to drop faster than Guiaou could ferry them. The doctor was half deafened from the explosions, but he did hear a great general shout when it came, and then, farther off, the skirling of conchs and the eerie drone of an African war cry springing at once from a great many throats. He stood up recklessly and shaded his eyes. Two thousand men were coming down from the dry northern hills at a dog trot, led by Jean-Jacques Dessalines. They must have held the same gait for half the night, coming the straightest possible way from Dondon to Gonaives.

The British were even more dismayed than Toussaint's men were heartened. They broke ranks and bolted down the road toward Saint Marc. Dessalines swept over their line, capturing both their cannon. All at once the British were in full flight, tumbling pell-mell across the salt flats and through the cactus of the Savane Désolée, harried by Toussaint's cavalry and pursued at a greater distance by the infantry Dessalines had brought, the horde of men loping along like a pack of dark wolves after the redcoats.

Doctor Hébert tied off a final bandage on the stump of a severed leg; the patient whimpered a little, his eyes glazed with shock, as Guiaou and another man gathered him up and carried him to the rear. The doctor stood up and shaded his eyes to watch the dust of the receding battle. Now the vultures felt enough at ease to settle again on the nearby corpses. Guiaou came up again, leading a big speckled gray pony by a rope bridle.

Guiaou pointed at the dust cloud. No saddle on the pony, the doctor noted. He checked his pistols and looked for his rifle, then remembered that it had gone with Maillart and his own horse. Winding his fingers in the pony's mane, he swung himself astride. Guiaou, with considerably less confidence, scrambled up behind him. The pony tried a buck but the weight was too great, so that he only skittered sideways, cramping his haunches. Guaiou caught the doctor around the waist with one arm and the throat with the other, threatening to strangle him. The doctor broke the choke hold and rejoined Guiaou's hand to the other at his waist. It had been fifteen years since he had ridden bareback, but he gripped with his knees as best he could, and they set off southward at an queasy jog trot.

Even doubled on such a mount, they had soon outdistanced the black foot soldiers. As for the British, their heels had been very much lightened by fear, but after the first couple of miles many began to drop in the white alkaline dust, prostrate from heat and dehydration. Vultures hunched on the ground nearby, waiting for the black infantry to come up and dispatch these victims with thrusts of bayonet or *coutelas*—they were not worth a cartridge. The rout was perfect all the way to Pont d'Ester, but there the British had left a reserve force, which was able to draw up cannon on the south side of the river to cover the crossing of the fleeing redcoats.

Toussaint rode up and down the river bank, in as near to a rage as the doctor had ever seen him. From across the river, the British began firing grape. The doctor was glad enough to slip down from the pony; he covered himself behind the shoulder of his overtaxed mount. Bel Argent reared, and a moment later the doctor saw that Toussaint had been hit, though he himself seemed unaware of it; he gave part of his attention to controlling his horse and the rest to the unfolding of the battle. But red gashes ran backward across his hip as if he'd been raked by the claws of a beast. The doctor ducked under the pony's neck and ran to grab at Toussaint's boot heel.

"Sir! you are wounded!"

Toussaint looked at him without recognition and kicked himself free. Bel Argent wheeled, and the doctor got a mouthful of horse tail for his pains. His palm had come away blood-slick from the boot leather. For a moment he tried to imagine the situation without Toussaint Louverture in command of it. A sour bubble burst in the back of his mouth and spread an evil taste across his tongue.

Maillart and Clervaux came riding up on the other side of Bel Argent. "For the love of—" Maillart began, while Clervaux talked through him, "*Attention, parrain, au blessé . . .*" From a further distance, the mulatto officer called Blanc Cassenave watched with a hooded expression. Another volley of grapeshot flared out, and all the horses laid back their ears and scrambled. The doctor fell in the white alkali dust, finding himself eye to eye with Guiaou for an instant, then rolled to avoid lashing hooves and came up onto his feet. Maillart had drawn his rifle from the scabbard and was thrusting it toward him, at the same time jerking his jaw across the river. The doctor took the weapon and while Guiaou calmed his horse he steadied the octagon barrel across the animal's back and drew his aim on one of the British cannoniers. Blowback from the priming pan stung his cheek when he squeezed the trigger, and kept him from seeing if he had hit his mark, but the British cannon did go silent for a moment, and in the window of quiet the doctor called out to Toussaint.

"You *must* allow me to treat your wound."

Toussaint shook his head, showing the tips of his teeth. If he felt any pain, he did not show it. The doctor wondered about his loss of blood. Maillart shouted, half in anger, "Do you think you can win the whole war in one day?"

"*Mais oui, mon cher—si Dyé vlé, n'ap fé sa.*" Toussaint smiled as easily as if he were sitting on the gallery of the house at Habitation Thibodet. We may do that, if God so wills.

He reached down to stroke the quivering neck of his horse, then rode down the line to attend to the deployment of the captured cannon which had just been dragged across the desert from the north.

For two hours more, and well past sunset, Toussaint kept in the saddle at the head of his men. He was only persuaded to attend to his wound when darkness had completely stopped the fighting. Even then it took the doctor much persuasion to get Toussaint to return to

Gonaives, where he had left his herbs and poultices, and where there would perhaps be a proper bed.

Leaving Blanc Cassenave in command at Pont d'Ester, they rode back in the darkness, a small party, across the Savane Désolée. The sky above them was perfectly clear and in the starlight the cacti cast shadows across the weird white glow of the salt flats. Packs of wild dogs had come out of the desert to growl and quarrel over the carcasses of the slain Britishers, their backs humped up and their jaws thrusting. Whenever the breeze from the west died down, the blood smell was heavy and rank all around them. Toussaint, who had brushed away every offer of assistance, rode fluidly upright in the saddle. Doctor Hébert had noticed some time earlier that his bleeding had stopped or slowed to an imperceptible rate. Perhaps the man had authority to command his own circulation.

Dismounting in the courtyard of the Gonaives *casernes,* Toussaint showed his first sign of weakness; the injured leg would not take his weight. He buckled sideways and was caught by Quamba, who had come up to hold the horse. The doctor took him under the other arm and they made their way across a doorsill to a cot. When Toussaint was once seated, the doctor tried to swing his feet up to the horizontal, but Toussaint brushed his hands away and demanded that his portable writing desk be fetched instead.

"My report," he said. "You will write for me."

"Are you mad?" the doctor asked him.

"Not in the least," Toussaint snapped. "The report must come first, and after . . . as you wish." He stroked a fingertip across the shredded fabric partly covering his wound.

The doctor dragged the fingers of both hands backward over his head, raking up the ring of hair surrounding his bald dome. He went to the door and called for Maillart, who wrote a reasonably legible hand.

"Dictate to him," he said to Toussaint, "but let me examine you at least—I will copy the letter over, afterward, if need be."

Someone brought wine but Toussaint refused it—rare commodity that it was—and took only a few sips of water. After drinking he let himself be eased back on a horsehair cushion. Guiaou was lighting several small string-wicked lamps made from lard congealed in clay jars.

"Write what I say," Toussaint said. *"Toussaint Louverture, général de l'armée de l'Ouest, à Etienne Laveaux, général par interim . . ."*

Maillart's pen began to scratch. The woman Merbillay came into the room carrying a pot of boiled water and some strips of clean rag. Guiaou pulled off Toussaint's boot and went to the door to empty the blood onto the ground outside. The doctor took up a short knife and slit Toussaint's trouser leg to the knee. He cleaned the knife with the hot water, then began using the point to pick shreds of cloth from the edges of the wound. Toussaint's left hand clenched on the canvas of the cot, but his voice went on without faltering.

"It is true, general, that I have been led into error by the enemies of the Republic, but what man can boast to have avoided every trap set by the wicked? In truth, I did fall into their webs, but not for absolutely no reason. You should very well remember that, before the disasters at Le Cap, and by the steps I had taken in your direction, my only goal was to unite our forces to combat the enemies of France."

The steady rhythm of the voice inspired the doctor with a feeling of great calm, so accustomed was he to taking Toussaint's dictation himself. Maillart's pen scraped against the paper, hesitated, scraped again. The whole room seemed mesmerically peaceful. The doctor took a wet cloth from Merbillay and pressed it to the wound to dissolve the crust of dried blood. Toussaint's breath whistled, but he did not flinch. He went on speaking without a break—it was a royal revision of history he had begun, the doctor thought, or perhaps his intentions had always been as he now described them, for no one in his camp had ever plumbed the full depth of his thinking.

"Unfortunately for all concerned, the paths toward reconciliation which I proposed—the recognition of the liberty of the blacks and a general amnesty—were rejected. My heart bled, and I poured out tears for the unhappy fate of my country, foreseeing the misfortunes which would follow. I was not deceived in that regard: fateful experience has proved the reality of my predictions. Meanwhile, the Spaniards offered me their protection, and to support all those who would fight for the cause of kings, and, having always fought for that liberty, I clung to their offers, seeing myself abandoned by the French, my brothers."

The doctor clicked his tongue, withdrawing the rag from the wound. The smoothness of this discourse was truly astonishing. He touched with a fingernail a bit of shrapnel embedded in the wound. Toussaint seemed to raise his voice slightly.

"But a somewhat belated experience opened my eyes to these perfidious protectors and, having taken note of their scoundrel's deceitfulness, I clearly perceived that their intention was to make us slit each other's throats so that our numbers would be reduced, and to load our remnant with chains and tumble us back into our former slavery. No, they will never arrive at their infamous goal, and we will in our turn avenge ourselves on these beings, who are contemptible in every respect. Let us unite forever, and, forgetting the past, concern ourselves only, from now on, with avenging ourselves in detail upon our perfidious neighbors."

Well, this passage was plausible enough, despite the inflated language; it was certainly true that the Spanish commitment to liberating the slaves of Saint Domingue was insincere, and (even without the discoveries at Biassou's camp) no one could have failed to notice that the Spanish part of the island had remained a slave state . . . The doctor flexed his left thumb and forefinger like a set of pincers. At his nod, Guiaou shifted two of the lamps a little nearer. Having lost his forceps in some accident of war, the doctor had grown out and filed the nails of those two digits to replace them. With this homemade instrument and the knife blade he began to dig out bits of the scrap metal from the British grape.

"It is absolutely certain that the national flag flies at Gonaives as well as all the surrounding area, and that I have chased the Spanish and the émigrés from the area of Gonaives, but my heart is shipwrecked by the event which overtook some unfortunate whites who were victims in that affair. I am not like so many others who can watch scenes of horror in cold blood; I have always had humanity to share, and I groan whenever I cannot prevent evil."

Again the statement was more accurate in principle than in precise point of fact, the doctor reflected as he probed the wound—to be sure, Toussaint had himself ordered the execution of at least some of those "unfortunate whites" who had perished during the taking of Gonaives . . . but it was equally true that he disliked useless bloodshed and would not brook cruelty for its own sake from anyone in his command . . . otherwise the doctor himself might have been dead long ago.

Merbillay held up a battered tin pan. The doctor dislodged, slowly, a bullet fragment, what seemed to be a lady's hairpin, the tongue of an iron belt buckle, and finally, with greater difficulty and greater care, a twisted, square cut iron nail. Guiaou's concerned face leaned near Merbillay's in the lard-colored lamplight. The metal shards dropped from the doctor's fingernails and rang on the pan's tin bottom. Toussaint interrupted himself.

"Kite'm oué sa," he said. Let me see.

Merbillay raised the pan under his chin. Toussaint hitched himself up with a grunt. He stirred the bits of metal with a blunt fingertip. Shaking his head, he picked up the hairpin, chuckled at it softly, then let it fall back into the pan and went on with his dictation.

At last the wound was clean. The doctor held a fresh rag over it to stanch the renewed bleeding, while Merbillay soaked herbs in hot water, then composed a compress. The doctor took the damp packet from her hands and bound it loosely to the wound with strips of cloth.

"Salut en patrie," Toussaint concluded. "I will sign it later."

He turned partly on his side, facing toward the stone wall, and fell silent. Though he lay quite still and his breathing suggested sleep, his eyes were open, glittering darkly in the lamplight. Often enough the doctor had seen him rest in this reptilian fashion. Toussaint seemed to need no more than two or three hours of actual sleep each night, and the doctor knew that the letter would be recopied and perhaps redrafted before dawn.

At his rough-carpentered table in the fort at Port-de-Paix, Governor-General Laveaux pulled the edges of the paper tight, and bent his head close to the carefully inked lettering. From time to time he turned the paper over as if to reassure himself that it was a real dimensional object whose meaning was what it seemed to be.

> Gonaives, Gros Morne, the cantons of Ennery, Plaisance, Marmelade, Dondon, Acul and all the surrounding area, including Limbé, are under my orders, and I have four thousand armed men disposed over all these places, not counting the citizens of Gros Morne, who number six hundred.

A miracle. Such a reversal of fortune could only be that. For the first time in many months, Laveaux had the power to march out of Port-de-Paix where he had been cornered for so long, the Spanish and English closing in on him like paired loops of a garrote—could ride freely across the quarter of Borgne, until lately under Spanish control, to rejoin Villatte at Le Cap. Toussaint, meanwhile, had made another lightning strike across the mountains of the Cordon de l'Ouest to scatter the forces of Jean-François (who had temporarily pushed Moyse back from Dondon) and driven them back across the Spanish frontier.

Laveaux rode across the northern plain, catching no glimpse of the maroons or bands of brigands who had so lately been burning and marauding all over that whole area. No one ventured to attack his short column and there was no sign of any disorder; on the contrary the women were working peaceably in their gardens, and on some of the sequestered plantations work gangs were beginning to set out new cane. Laveaux rode into Dondon to see the miracle worker, for the first time, with his own eyes.

Toussaint Louverture was waiting for him in the public square before the church. On horseback he made an imposing figure, but when he dismounted to approach Laveaux on foot, he seemed considerably diminished. His legs were a little bowed from riding and so short that the scabbard of his immense sword cut a furrow in the dirt behind him as he walked. A small, knotty man, with the build of a jockey, a long underslung jaw, and strange deep eyes under the yellow headcloth revealed when he swept off his hat. Laveaux swung down from his own horse to meet him.

"My general," Toussaint said in a clear voice, not particularly loud. "I place the Army of the West under your orders." He made a half-turn and gestured with his hat in a semicircle behind him. The troops were drawn up for review, mounted officers waiting before them, and the foot soldiers ranked in row upon neat row, then in orderly columns running back along the side streets, then in wider ranks again on the slope above the town, black men mostly barefoot and bare-chested, relaxed and holding their arms at the ready.

Laveaux felt the short hairs prickling at the back of his neck and on his forearms under the sleeves of his uniform coat. He returned Toussaint's salute, and stood facing the black officer, a full head shorter than himself, eyes shining up from under the yellow headscarf. Laveaux felt an urge to embrace him, but held himself back. He shook Toussaint's hand. Something more was called for. He took the tallest red plume from his own hat and set it in the center of the white feathers which ornamented Toussaint's bicorne. Toussaint smiled, nodded, adjusted the bicorne carefully on his head. He turned to face his troops, drawing himself up. The red feather bobbed high above the white ones in his hat. There was the silence before thunder, and then four thousand men began to cheer.

Fort de Joux, France

August 1802

Daylight in the vaulted cell always seemed the light of dawn: gray, misty, cold and damp. Toussaint had been accustomed to get up before first light, to be well about his business before the sun had fully risen. He needed little sleep; two or three hours sufficed him ordinarily, so that he could spend half the night composing letters by lamplight, or ride cross-country by the light of the moon. Here in the Fort de Joux, the light of day did not progress; it gathered neither warmth nor energy, and Toussaint was tempted, because of the cold, to remain longer abed, his knees drawn up slightly under the brown woollen blanket, but when his watch advised him that, somewhere outside the thick stone walls that blocked his vision, the sun must have crested the cold mountain peaks, he rose and dressed himself rapidly, holding back a shiver from the chill, then went across the room to tend the fire.

Grâce à Dieu, a few coals had held beneath the gray-black layers of ash. Toussaint knelt carefully, propped himself on his knuckles, and lowered his head to blow the coals to life. When the small flame rose, he sat back on his heels and fed it little splinters of wood, then a couple of larger chunks. A small billow of warmth and orange light swelled out a little way from the hearth—it would not carry across the cell, and was never sufficient to surround him altogether. His supply of wood was insufficient . . . Toussaint warmed his palms against the small balloon of heat for a moment more, before he stood.

The worst of rising was that his cough began, a tickle at the back of his throat that grew to an itch he could not suppress, though he swallowed and swallowed to keep it down, walking barefoot across the cold flagstones of the floor. Ten paces from the grated window opening to the iron-bound door. Five paces from the fireplace to the opposite wall—a raw slab of stone from the mountain's heart—the fire could not throw its heat far enough to absorb the moisture that collected there. The cold shot spearlike up his legs and spine to his back teeth, waking him more effectively than coffee. When the cough began, it echoed from the walls, and Toussaint pressed his forearm across his aching ribs, gathering in the pain of it. In the clammy cold his knees and shoulders pained him in a way he'd never known, and his old wounds reawakened, especially the hip with its bullet wound and the hand that had once been crushed by a cannon.

He spat the proceeds of his cough into his night jar, then quickly recovered the vessel. At the fireside he prepared coffee and, while it brewed, he held his yellow madras headcloth loose before the fire till it heated through, and then retied it over his head—the warm band at his temples seemed to soothe the headache that had lately begun to plague him. As he drank the coffee, thickened with sugar, his cough subsided and became controllable. Yet his ration of sugar was insufficient . . . He softened a piece of hardtack in warm sweetened water and ate it slowly with the coffee; he was not hungry but it was necessary to eat, not only to sustain his strength but to measure regular intervals of the day, though in these confines he was so inactive that he never had real appetite.

The fort's bell gonged eight times slowly as he drained off the syrupy dregs from his coffee cup. He drew on his stockings, then his boots, and walked to the door, then to the window grating with its small, gritty diamonds of pale light. The door, the window . . . This meager exercise was also necessary. It scarcely warmed him, but as he walked his mind loosened and began to work more easily. He had, after all, his report to compose—there was his trial to prepare for, when the tribunal would judge between him and Napoleon's brother-in-law, Captain-General Leclerc. The report must contain just enough truth to be credited and yet reveal nothing that might jeopardize his cause. *Grâce à Dieu,* Toussaint thought, refining phrases as he paced and turned, the truth itself was malleable, ready to change both form and substance as you molded it with your mind and tongue and pen.

Whatever he finally dictated he would himself believe.

The trial . . . Toussaint paused before the window grating, head angled up toward the gritty, colorless light. He turned and paced again toward the door, the diamond shadows of the grate checking his back. The rowels of his spurs rattled with his steps. Baille had not so far sought to confiscate the spurs. By and large this jailer seemed of a decent heart; he had accorded Toussaint the respect due a fellow-soldier, perhaps even a *concitoyen*. His hesitation in providing writing materials was worrisome, however, and in truth Toussaint had even greater need of a secretary, or more than one. In Saint Domingue, through the watches of his nights, he had ridden one scribe after another to exhaustion, then compared the different versions they produced, selecting the most advantageous phrasing from each. Now it mattered more than ever, what the words he chose would make him out to be.

Somehow the admirable opposite of his adversary, Captain-General Leclerc, who was . . . who was what? Impetuous, yes, there was a word. Blame Leclerc with the weakness of an unskilled rider, incapable of controlling the spirited mount he had been given. The forces under his command had escaped his capacity to direct them, he had thoughtlessly let those forces run recklessly abroad. Then too, Leclerc was famously a cuckold, his wife Pauline constantly and ostentatiously unfaithful. Such a man could not but see betrayal in every shadow. It was the disorder of his own mind that had made Leclerc suspect Toussaint of treason.

But he must not blame Leclerc directly—let all that emerge as an effect of contrast. For his own part, against this hotheaded, ill-disciplined, mentally unbalanced commander, Toussaint Louverture, general in chief of the French army of Saint Domingue, opposed his qualities of fidelity and watchfulness. The fierce dog at the gate of France's most prized overseas possession. Endowed with the blind devotion to duty of (why not?) a former slave. When once he had recognized his sacred obligation, he clung to it with the tenacity of an English bulldog. Was that a fault? Perhaps, under certain circumstances, one *might* find blamable a simple old soldier's blind attachment to what he sincerely believed to be the interest of his nation, France . . .

There. Toussaint stopped by the door, half smiling, his head cocked toward the keyhole, for the sentry on the other side had sneezed or shifted his feet. He listened, but there was no further sound. The adjoining cell was empty now, since his personal servant, Mars Plaisir, had been shipped out to some other, unknown destination. Before the valet's departure, they had been in one another's company for a little more than an hour each day. Mars Plaisir had seen to Toussaint's needs and comfort as best he might under such conditions. He had brewed the coffee, sugared the wine, warmed the food—small ceremonies which Toussaint would not now permit himself to regret. Also the companionship. Even when they were apart, each could listen for and sometimes hear the movements of the other in the neighboring cell, though of course they were forbidden to call out.

Toussaint stood listening, but there was nothing more to hear, except the echo of the distant drip and splash in the third corridor, whose floor was always inches deep in water . . . His mental exertion had made him forget the chill, which now cut through to him again. He paced toward the window. Now that the image was complete in his mind, he must search the words to bring that image into being . . .

It is necessary that I account for . . . he began, but no. The phrasing implied too much in the way of external constraint. The impulse to tell the perfect truth must rather come from within the character he was creating. Unconscious of his action, Toussaint sat down in the chair by the fire. He gripped the wooden arms with both hands and focused his concentration.

It is my duty to render an exact account of my conduct to the French government. Yes. *I will report the facts with all the frankness and naïveté of an old soldier.* Yes, that was the tone, the attitude. The flow of his own words began to warm him. He sat with his eyes half-closed, his lips sometimes moving slightly, as he chose the words, reviewed and refined them, and set them down firmly in his memory.

Shortly after the fort's bell had rung twelve times, he heard boots splashing in the third corridor, the sentry's challenge, and then Baille's reply. The huge iron key cried in the lock, but when the door opened it did so almost silently, floating into shadows by the wall. Baille came in with another, smaller Frenchman. The door shut behind them; the key screeched again and the lock snapped shut.

Toussaint did not rise from his chair, but lifted his head ever so slightly to acknowledge the visitors.

"You are well, I trust?" Baille's smile was ever uneasy; his gray hands worked over each other. In one hand he held a white cloth bag.

"I am well enough." Toussaint sniffed, then throttled the cough that tried to rise from the back of his throat. "Apart from the cold."

"You understand, the requisition . . . be it for firewood or . . ." Baille's weak smile guttered as he trailed off, then slowly regained its pale strength. "In the meantime, I have brought you sugar from my own personal supply."

"You do me honor." Toussaint glanced at the small square table.

As if released, Baille walked across and placed the supplementary sugar among the other provisions there. From the corner of his eye, Toussaint measured the package—perhaps two cupfuls.

"As for your other request," Baille nodded to his companion. "I present my personal secretary, Monsieur Jeannin."

Toussaint looked into the fire. The movement concealed his face from the others and so concealed his feeling—a quick rush of relief he much preferred not to reveal. He would certainly have been capable of phrasing the necessary document without the services of a secretary, but he knew that both his spelling and his penmanship were poor.

"*C'est bien,*" he said finally, raising his head.

Baille looked into the corners of the room, then clucked his tongue and rubbed his hands together. "No chair for Monsieur Jeannin to sit," he said. "I will order one to be brought."

Toussaint rose from his own seat, abruptly, as if to dismiss the commandant. "No matter," he said. "Let the chair be brought tomorrow. Today I will dictate standing."

"I will be outside the door," Baille said, taking a step backward. "In case of need." He looked pointedly at Jeannin. His nod to Toussaint was just short of a bow.

The key whined in the lock once more, and the silent shadow of the door floated across the room. Toussaint looked at Jeannin more closely. The secretary wore civilian clothes, a dark blue suit freely sprinkled with lint. He was small and slight, with a ring of stiff, dark curly hair surrounding a scaly bald spot, like a tonsure. His head thrust high from his grubby collar. Under his left arm he carried a wooden lap desk.

"To begin." Toussaint indicated the chair he'd vacated with an unfolding of his right hand. Jeannin hitched the chair to the table, sat down and opened the lap desk. He took out a pen, an inkwell, and several sheets of paper, then looked up and cleared his throat.

"You are ready? Good," Toussaint said. "Write what I say: *It is my duty to render an exact account of my conduct to the French government; I will report the facts with all the frankness and naïveté of an old soldier, adding such reflections as may naturally present themselves . . .*

Jeannin's mouth opened. He dampened the pen point against his tongue, then dipped it in the ink well and began to write.

"You have it? Good." The spiral of Toussaint's steady pacing brought him near enough behind the table and chair that he could see the secretary's hand was fair, and his transcription faithful. He nodded, pursing his lips as he moved toward the window.

"*In the end, I will tell the truth,*" he continued, "*even if it be against myself.*" He waited, listening to the scratching of the pen. A chunk of wood collapsed in the fireplace, scattering coals on the hearthstone.

"A new paragraph," Toussaint said, when Jeannin's pen had stopped. "But first, if you please, attend to the fire."

Jeannin scratched around the edges of his tonsure and looked at him, eyes startled and glittering like a bird's. After a moment, he shrugged, dropped the pen in the inkwell and did as he was bidden, adding a couple of sticks to the fire and, for the want of a proper tool, scraping the coals together with the side of his shoe. Toussaint waited for him to regain his seat.

"To the next paragraph. *The colony of Saint Domingue, which I commanded, enjoyed the greatest tranquillity; both agriculture and commerce were flourishing there. . . .*" Toussaint paused, listening to the pen. Jeannin slumped gradually forward across the table as he wrote, supporting himself on his left elbow, his head turned to one side. When he had finished he pushed himself upright.

"You have all that? Excellent," Toussaint said. *"All that, I am bold to say was my own work."*

In a matter of two weeks the memoir was drafted, recopied and ready for its reader. Toussaint might have finished it in half the time, but he had the services of only a single secretary and that for no more than a couple of hours each day. Yet his consciousness of time fell from him, and when Jeannin was absent he composed and memorized constantly, except for the moments when he ate and the hours when he slept. In a state somewhere between waking and dream (he had taken a slight fever) his mind's eye filled with images of Saint Domingue, where Captain-General Leclerc now found himself more and more severely pressed on every side, as his European soldiers, already decimated by the battles of the spring, died out from yellow fever at a terrifying rate, while his black generals observed the weakening of his situation with what seemed an increasingly ill-concealed satisfaction, for the sly and diabolical policy of Toussaint continued to exercise itself through his former subalterns even in his absence, so that it was worth almost nothing to be rid of him. Everywhere there were risings in the hills, which the black generals never managed, and perhaps never really tried, to suppress completely. Leclerc's program to disarm the population was revealed a wretched failure, and in fact he had no idea how many guns Toussaint might have poured into the countryside, though there seemed to be an inexhaustible supply, as if the weapons grew, like soursops and mangoes and bananas, on the jungle trees. The black generals could neither be trusted nor arrested (for only they controlled the black troops nominally under French command), and more and more it seemed

impossible that the captain-general could ever satisfy Napoleon's imperious demand—"Rid us of these gilded Africans, and we shall have
nothing left to wish for . . ." Sonthonax had been right, Moyse had been
right, Toussaint himself would be right in the end. Dismisally, Leclerc
wrote home to France, "It's not everything to have removed Toussaint,
there are still two thousand chiefs here to be removed."

As Toussaint emerged from the composition of his memoir, time began
to weigh on him more heavily once more; the first day that Jeannin
did not return passed very slowly. Not that the secretary had furnished
conversation—indeed he had never spoken at all, except when, infrequently, he echoed one of Toussaint's own phrases by way of confirmation. After the first hour Toussaint had understood that Jeannin's silence
must have been ordered by Baille or else by someone who stood above
the commandant. This hardly mattered. But Toussaint had been warmed
and distracted by the act of composition and by the sight of the stack of
papers steadily growing under Jeannin's trained hand.

Too little space was here, and too much time. In Saint Domingue, in
(why not admit it, to himself?) his own kingdom, he would have been at
some active work—campaigns or battles or oversight of cultivations—
whenever he finished his *travail du cabinet*. But here he was caged in his
own thoughts. As one chess player imagines the mind of another oppos-
ing him, he pictured Napoleon Bonaparte: a man of slight stature (like
himself), a fine horseman and cavalry commander (like himself) who
had come to political power not only through his military prowess but
through a native political sagacity.

How would he, himself, respond, supposing their situation to be
reversed? In Saint Domingue, certain men had died, ignored, in prison,
such as Blanc Cassenave and Dieudonné—but he, Toussaint, had not
killed these men! Such reproaches were inaccurate, and injust. Dieudonné, for example, had died as the captive of General Rigaud, at Les
Cayes, while Toussaint was at the opposite end of the country, in the
Department of the North. It was said that Dieudonné had been loaded
with so many chains that at last he suffocated under their weight . . .

Now in his cell at the Fort de Joux, Toussaint felt the cold cut
through to him again, and he was sweating, but his sweat was cold, and
there seemed insufficient air in the cell for him to breathe. When Baille
presented himself with the day's rations, Toussaint declared that after
all there was something more. Something different. After all, he would
not send the document he had composed, or would not send it now. In
its place, he would send a letter to Napoleon, no more than a line or

two—five minutes of Monsieur Jeannin's time. Toward nightfall, as the diamonds of weak daylight died on the cell floor, he dictated to the secretary the briefest of notes, which merely said that after all certain matters had been too delicate for commitment to a written memoir—matters it would be best to communicate in person.

When Jeannin had left with this last letter, Toussaint's agitation drained from him. He sat for a while longer in the waning light of the fire, suffused with a sense of renewed calm, a patience too deep even to be aware of itself. The gongs of the fort's bell no longer impressed him. He lay down on his cot and slept, free of dreams.

Part Two

BLACK SPARTACUS

1794–1796

Let righteousness
cover the earth
like the water
cover the sea . . .

—Bob Marley,
"Revolution"

In the spring of 1794, the military map of Saint Domingue was significantly redrawn by Toussaint Louverture's abrupt shift of allegiance from the Spanish monarchy to the French Republic. While in Spanish service, Toussaint had taken pains to reinforce the line of military posts known as the Cordon de l'Ouest, which ran from the seaport of Gonaives through the mountains to the border of Spanish Saint Domingue in the interior. The Cordon de l'Ouest effectively cut off the Northern Department of Saint Domingue, with its important town of Cap Français, from the rest of the colony, whose coast from Saint Marc (the port immediately south of Gonaives) to Port-au-Prince was now occupied by the English invaders or their allies. To control this line improved the French Republican position immeasurably.

Governor-General Etienne Laveaux had technically become the highest French authority in Saint Domingue upon the departure of Sonthonax. The scope of his authority was greatly enlarged by Toussaint's volte-face, which made it possible for Laveaux to return from his hemmed-in position at Port-de-Paix to the seat of government at Cap Français, the northern capital. During Laveaux's protracted absence, Le Cap had become a mulatto stronghold, under the command of the colored officer Villatte, and *members of the colored land- and slave-owning class had substantially rebuilt the town, from which most whites had fled when it was sacked and burned in June of 1793.*

The arrival of Toussaint Louverture in their camp was not necessarily welcomed by this mulatto class. Toussaint did have colored officers in his own force, and he cooperated with Villatte and other colored officers of the Le Cap region, under the command of Laveaux. Nevertheless, the mulatto faction of the north regarded Toussaint's sudden ascendancy, and Laveaux's rapidly increasing dependence on him and his men, with suspicion and even a degree of alarm. This anxiety was shared with the Republican colored party in the south, led by André Rigaud, a general of considerable ability who was fighting the English invaders with some success on the southern peninsula, also known as the Grande Anse. Pinchinat, an elderly colored gentleman respected as a rhetorician and feared as a propagandist, carried messages back and forth between Rigaud in the south and Villatte's party in the northern region.

Toussaint, meanwhile, was busy fighting a war on two fronts. Along the interior border, significant Spanish forces (mostly composed of black auxiliaries) remained to be dealt with. These troops, under the command of Toussaint's erstwhile superiors Jean-François and Biassou, were less well organized and well trained than Toussaint's own men, who were usually successful against them. At the same time, Toussaint's army made repeated but unsuccessful attempts to dislodge the British from Saint Marc and fought numerous engagements in the region of the Artibonite River, the next significant natural boundary south of the mountains of the Cordon de l'Ouest. These areas remained in dispute, but from Dondon in the interior across the mountains to Gonaives, Toussaint—and thus the French Republic—was impregnable.

IO

Papa Legba, we were singing, *Attibon Legba, ouvri baryè pou nou* . . . We sang, and Bouquart, the big Congo maroon with the cross-shaped marks of his people in Guinée paired on his stomach, struck the Asoto *tambou,* there at the center of the *batterie* of three drums. He touched the Asoto drum with his left hand and a small stick crooked like a hammer in his right. Papa Legba, open the gate for us . . . It was Bahoruco Mountain where we danced, on a height above the mouth of one of the great caves, and when the drums played, the cave spoke too in a drum's voice. The drums called Legba to open the crossroads, let the *loa* come up from the Island Below Sea into our heads, and I, Riau, was singing too for Legba, not hearing my own voice any more than I felt the salt water gathering on my face. We call for blessed Legba to come, but sometimes it is Maît' Kalfou who brings himself to the crossroads, the trickster, betrayer sometimes, *magouyé.*

Singing still, I watched Bouquart, his face sweat-shining, with a motionless grin gleaming as he drummed. The fleur-de-lys was branded on his left cheek, to punish him for running away, and for another such punishment his right ear had been lopped off, and for the same reason he wore on each leg a *nabot* the size and weight of a cannonball, welded around his ankles, and yet he had still run as far and fast as Bahoruco. If there had been a forge, I, Riau, might have struck the *nabots* off his feet, using the powers of fire and iron (for that Riau who was a slave had learned blacksmithing from Toussaint), and equally the power of my *maît' têt,* Ogûn-Feraille, but there was no forge at Bahoruco, only the voices, the drums, the low droning out of the caves, then silence with hands fluttering on the drum skins light and soundless as the wings of birds, their gray and white feathers shivering, and the scream that came from Riau's body, stripped the body from the mind, as the god came up from beneath the waters, through heels and spine to flower in his head.

It was not Ogûn who came, they told me after, not the proper master of my head, but Maît' Kalfou who took my body for his horse, though never before had that one mounted Riau. Jean-Pic told me it was so, when Riau came to himself again at dawn, the cool mist rising round him at the edge of the sacred pool. It was quiet then, the birds speaking softly, hidden in the leaves, and only a drum's echo beating slowly somewhere behind my head. Maît' Kalfou, Jean-Pic told me, had walked among the dancers, his arms raised in the shape of the cross and his muscles trembling from their own strength, and had spoken in his wet, croaking voice, but Kalfou's words belonged to the proclamation of Toussaint from Camp Turel.

My name is perhaps not unknown to you. But Maît' Kalfou must have already been recognized by the *serviteurs* there . . . *I have undertaken to avenge you. I want liberty and equality to reign throughout Saint Domingue. I am working toward that end.* How such words must have sounded in the harsh, damp mouth of Kalfou . . . on the morning after my throat ached from his shouting them. *Come and join me, brothers, and fight by our side for the same cause . . .*

Those words were heard before in Bahoruco. Maît' Kalfou had not been the first to bring them here. The words of Toussaint's letter had come from both sides of the border, from the whitemen of France and the whitemen of Spain, and on the same day that the French Commissioner Sonthonax declared that all the slaves were free. Toussaint had signed his letter *Toussaint Louverture,* a name that he had never used before that time, when everyone had called him Toussaint Bréda, from the name of the *habitation* where he had been a slave.

I had not thought much of Toussaint's words when they first came to us, though I saw that he was trying still to use words to sway men at long distances (as Riau had helped him to do, before Bahoruco), sending the words that walked on paper as his messengers, teaching them to speak with the voices of others. But the name . . . he had invented it, so much was sure, unless it was given to him by his *mystère,* but Toussaint always claimed that he served only Jesus, not the *loa,* and no one had ever seen a spirit mount his head. After Kalfou had let Riau's flesh drop in the wind-fallen leaves beside the sacred pool, the understanding came to me, that in calling himself *Toussaint of the Opening* he meant to say it was Legba working through his hands.

But sometimes it is Maît' Kalfou who comes . . .

"Go to the *cacique,*" Jean-Pic said, when I had spoken part of the thought to him. And I got up from the leaves and drank water from a spring nearby, and touched cold water to my face and the back of my head. Jean-Pic and I shared a mango he had picked. We went down toward the cave mouth where the *cacique* was, but the way there was not straight. Below where we walked the *bitasyon* spread among the folds of mountain in and out of sight, the square *cays* built of mud and stick and sometimes fenced with cactus thorn, the corn plantings twisting to follow veins of good earth among rock ledges on the slopes. The path twisted the same way between the corn and the yards of the mud-walled houses. All down the mountain the cocks were crowing and people waking to the day, stepping out upon their packed-earth yards. Farther down the gorges were the palisades of sharpened poles and the mantraps dug and hidden for attackers to fall into, or for anyone. Riau, I myself, might have been so taken, only that I came here with Jean-Pic who knew where the mantraps were dug. Under Santiago the maroons of Bahoruco had promised with the French whitemen to return escaping slaves for a reward of gold, but now Santiago was dead and by the words of Sonthonax there were no more slaves in the land, but still the maroons of Bahoruco mistrusted the coming of any stranger from outside.

The little crook-jawed pin-tooth dogs scampered and turned behind their cactus fences as we passed, but they did not bark or growl because they knew our smell. It was those dogs that gave the warning when the whitemen came, or anyone outside the *bitasyon.* Outside one *cay* a young woman looked up from where she was pounding dried corn into meal to smile at us both as we went by, but there were few women here, and the men were not so many as the whitemen believed they were. They told, when Santiago went to make the peace paper with the French whitemen, he brought one hundred thirty-seven grains of corn to show the number of the people, but that was trickery, there were more. Though not the thousands the whitemen believed, there were some hundreds there.

We walked the twistings of the path, worn deep in rocky earth by people walking, with a stream twisting beside it, lower down, until we turned the point of the ledge and came to the cave opening where the *cacique* was. Bahoruco was a cave of many mouths, and when too many of the whitemen soldiers come, our people knew to run into one mouth and come out at another, far away. The caves were full of the Indian mysteries carved in stone, so that the whitemen did not like to go in, or maybe they were only afraid of the darkness. In times before, enough *blanc* soldiers came to drive our people from Bahoruco back to Nisao, and they burned the corn and wrecked the houses, but afterward the people returned here, and the *bitasyon* had all been rebuilt and had been standing for some years.

The *cacique* had already come out to sit on the ledge before his cave mouth. He was old, with white hair hanging in flat strings, and the gold-colored skin of his face bunched in fine wrinkles. His belly skin was slack and loose and because of an illness he had to carry his balls in a basket when he walked. Now he sat, the basket folded in between his legs, and took the sun on his high cheekbones and his closed eyelids. They called him *cacique* not because he was truly a chief among the Indians but because he was the last Indian in that place. There was still blood mixture to be seen in the maroons of Bahoruco, in the angle of cheekbone, smoothness of the hair or slant of the eye, but it was sinking to the invisible, washed away in the blood of Guinée. Only the *cacique* remained with his Indian blood pure.

We had still the Indian-woven fish traps, the bows with their arrows almost as long as a man was tall, and some said even the gourd and bead *asson* which our *hûngan* shook in time with the drums as the spirits came down, that the *asson* had first been given by an Indian *mystère*. They said the *cacique* knew those mysteries, who had made him wise. Sometimes he could speak in Creole, but today he spoke only his own language, high and quavering as it floated out from his mouth over the green gorges, and the sound of it gave me sadness for my language of Guinée, my mother tongue, which Riau had forgotten.

A basket of *loa* stones, *pierres tonnerres,* lay by the *cacique*'s knee, and I sat down and lifted one, holding it in both my hands. It was black, cone-shaped, and heavier than any ordinary stone, from the weight of the *loa* who stayed inside. I did not know the language the *cacique* was singing over the hills, but understanding came to me. It seemed to come through the palms of my hands, which were both curved to the shape of the *pierre tonnerre*. I saw that Toussaint, when he chose his name at Camp Turel, would have known already what Sonthonax meant to say. He knew many whitemen and was known by them, so that he would have had this knowledge from their councils, before Sonthonax had spoken. He made his message then, choosing the same day, to show it was Toussaint, not Sonthonax, who would open the barrier to freedom.

I went away from the *cacique*'s ledge then, to the *cay* I shared with Jean-Pic and Bouquart and one other. There was no woman in the house, not one among the four of us. Jean-Pic had gone up into the corn plantings, and the others were gone too, so the house was empty. I took from a hole in the clay wall my two pistols and the watch plundered from the body of a whiteman officer long ago, also a box of writing paper and two packets of letters, one tied up with string and the other with blue ribbon—these last things Riau had taken when Halaou ran over a *habitation* in Cul de Sac, and also two long candles of white wax.

I lit one candle and wound the watch, then opened its face so I could see the thin black fingers counting away the bits of time like crumbs falling from a round cassava bread. With all these objects placed before me, alone in a house, I became perfectly like a whiteman, except there was no chair and everything lay on the floor.

Sometimes I would use pieces of sharpened charcoal to copy words and sentences from the letters, so that my skill in writing, which Toussaint had first taught me, would grow larger. By this copying I learned to compose each word with letters that properly belonged to it. Bouquart had interested himself in this art, and sometimes I would try to teach him, but he learned little. I was not such a teacher as my *parrain* Toussaint, who could train a horse and could train a man to train that same horse in place of himself, and who had given me an itch for words on paper which would not leave me, not when Riau first ran from Bréda to join the maroons of the north, not when he ran from Toussaint's army to come to Bahoruco. When I copied the letters to the paper, I was altogether *I*—myself here, the words and paper there, and the whiteman language filled up all the space inside my head, but I knew it was an act of power. When I practiced this writing, I gained more power than my *parrain,* for Toussaint himself did not know how to put the same letters into his words each time he wrote them.

Both packages of letters had been sent to the *gérant*, a whiteman sent out of France to manage the plantation. Those tied with string were from the owners of that *habitation,* who lived in France but wrote mostly complaining to their *gérant,* that too much of money was spent, too small of harvests returned, that the slaves cost too much in money and would not work long or hard enough, that they cost too much in food, and too many ran away to the mountains. The last of those letters, written after the slaves had risen in the north, complained more bitterly of the disasters. But the letters tied with ribbon were sweeter to the taste of eye and mind—they came from two whitewomen of France, the *gérant's* mother and another who sent words of love to him although she did not have his child. BonDyé had not joined these two together before Jesus, but it seemed they wished it, though now the ocean was between them. Those letters spoke words of love to the *gérant*, and went on whispering his name whenever I opened them, though the *gérant* had been dead since that night we had all come to that Cul de Sac plantation with Halaou, and when I copied the words they spoke again. Sometimes I thought of writing such a letter of Merbillay, who had my child—make the love words speak to her from paper. I could write *my son* to Caco, how the letters of the *gérant's* mother always began—*my dear son*. But I did not know if Merbillay was still with Toussaint's camp wherever it had moved to, or if she had gone somewhere else, but wherever she was, she could not read and had never thought of learning.

This day I wrote nothing, copied no word, but sat with my arms wrapped around my knees, looking across the candle flame at the glitter of the watch and the metal pieces on the pistols. In learning to use such tools as these, Riau might enter the mind of a whiteman. Of Toussaint and Sonthonax, which was the greater *magouyé*?

With Toussaint's army Riau was an officer of the rank of *captain*, wearing boots and a sash and cartridge box, with power to order lesser soldiers how to fight, but when he felt too much like a horse in harness, he stripped off those officer clothes and ran with Jean-Pic to Bahoruco. There we heard that Halaou, who was both warrior and *hûngan*, as Boukman had been in the first rising in the north, was killing whitemen on the plain of Cul de Sac. Then I, Riau, I went to see this Halaou with my own eyes—ten thousands of men followed him then, all slaves risen from the *habitations*, so one more was not noticed. Halaou kept his camps across the Spanish border, some way north of Bahoruco, but would come out from his camps to kill whitemen on the plain, or fight against the *grand blanc* Frenchmen who had joined the English of Jamaica to make us slaves again. Halaou was a big man, and he went to the fighting like a *possédé*, and at the ceremonies strong spirits stormed around his head, but at other times he went quietly, so that he was not much noticed, and he always carried in his arms a white cock, tenderly as one carries a baby. In the cluckings of the white cock he heard the voices of his spirits.

Halaou ran to every fight shouting out that the cannon was bamboo, the gunpowder no more than dust. I, Riau, had heard such words before, from the mouth of Boukman (which was lipless now, for Boukman's head was rotting on a stake on the dirt walls outside of Le Cap) and had seen men die because of them. This was not Toussaint's way of fighting. Toussaint was stingy with the lives of his men as a whiteman with his coins. But when Riau followed Halaou to the fighting, there was Ogûn in his head, and the joy of war and battle belonged to Ogûn, and no harm came to the flesh of Riau, though others died and went beneath the waters.

Then Sonthonax came south to Port-au-Prince with his party of the French who were called Republicans, who stood against the *grand blanc* French, the old slave masters, who were with the English at Saint Marc. The *grand blancs* and the English wanted to take Port-au-Prince, where the Republican army was mostly colored men, and no one was certain how those colored men would fight, because many of them, too, owned land and slaves before the risings. Sonthonax did not have many white-man soldiers fighting for his cause. But Halaou had heard that the slaves who were made free now called Sonthonax BonDyé, a god for their freedom, and the white cock clucked that Halaou must go to see this Sonthonax inside of his own eyes.

With ten thousands of his men Halaou went to Port-au-Prince, men beating drums and blowing conch shells and cow horns and trumpets made of metal, swirling bulls' tails around their heads and shouting the name of Halaou. Many were mounted by the *loa* on that journey, but I, Riau, walked with myself alone and saw. The Commissioner Sonthonax came out to the ditches around Port-au-Prince, wrapped in the colored ribbons of France, and kissed Halaou on both his cheeks. He brought Halaou for feasting in the Palais National, and Halaou sat at the table among whitemen and colored officers in their uniforms, himself bare-chested but for the *ouangas* that hung from his neck, and holding the white cock always on his left knee or in the crook of his left arm. Halaou's people had filled up the town, enchanted and shouting to see Halaou feeding the white cock from the commissioner's table, but I, Riau, was silent in myself—I saw how we were many, but that the col-ored soldiers were better organized and armed in their small number. I understood such things from serving with Toussaint, and I saw how the colored soldiers looked at Halaou's men, fingering the locks of their muskets.

After the feasting was done, Sonthonax sent Halaou to make agree-ment with the colored General Beauvais, who commended the Légion de l'Ouest at Croix des Bouquets. Riau went there also, to Croix des Bouquets, and stood with Dieudonné in the council room. Dieudonné had grown strong with Halaou, and the white cock trusted him, so that Halaou liked to keep Dieudonné at his back. As for Dieudonné, he had come to trust Riau. We stood with our backs to the wall, on either side of the window, while Halaou sat at the table with Beauvais and two of his officers. Halaou held the white cock on the table, stroking its feath-ers with his left hand and preening under its neck with his right finger. He and Bauvais were speaking in voices too low for us to understand their words. Afterward some people claimed that secretly Sonthonax had told Halaou to surprise Beauvais and kill him, and others said that the colored men had all along intended to murder Halaou. I did not know anything about it, though I felt that something bad would come from our going to that place. Why did the white cock not warn Halaou away? Two sergeants of the Légion de l'Ouest broke in through Beauvais's office door already shooting, and they shot Halaou many times before he could rise out of his chair, but the white cock crowed and flew between us, out the window. Dieudonné and I turned over the table and went out the window, after the cock.

Then the colored soldiers began to kill the men of Halaou. We were many and they were few, but they had the better guns, and discipline, and Halaou's men were in terror because Halaou was killed and they had seen the white cock fly away, deserting them. They dropped their bulls' tails, which would no longer fan away the bullets, and threw down their *lambi* shells and ran—many were killed there and thrown in the ditches of Croix des Bouquets, and the rest scattered.

After this had happened, Hyacinthe came out of prison, released by Sonthonax. Like Halaou, he was both warrior and *hûngan,* and many of Halaou's men had been with Hyacinthe before, and went back to him now he had returned, but the colored men teased Hyacinthe to a meeting and killed him, as Halaou was killed. Bébé Coustard attacked Croix des Bouquets with men that had been with Hyacinthe and Halaou, and all the colored men were trapped in the church, but one of them came out alone to parlay and killed Bébé Coustard with his musket, and seeing him dead the men were afraid and threw down their weapons and scattered.

I, Riau, went with Dieudonné, who gathered some of those men who had run together again at Habitation Nerrettes. Then the English and the *grand blanc* French came both in ships and overland to attack Port-au-Prince, and Sonthonax had no soldiers left to fight for him except colored soldiers who wanted to go over to the English anyway, so Sonthonax ran away to the colored General Rigaud in the south. When he stopped at Nerrettes plantation, Sonthonax gave his ribbons and the big commissioner's coin to Dieudonné, and said with this gift went all his powers that he had brought out of France, and he warned Dieudonné against the colored men, saying, *Do not forget, so long as you see colored men among your own, you will not be free.* But later on we learned that when Sonthonax came to Rigaud, he gave Rigaud the command of the colony as he had given it to Dieudonné (though only Dieudonné had the medal and the ribbons).

A boat had come from France, bringing a paper of French government that said the slaves of Saint Domingue were free, but Sonthonax climbed into the boat and sailed away. If he was the BonDyé for our freedom, he was gone now, like Halaou's white cock.

Fok nou oué nan jé nou—we must see with our own eyes. Yet I thought it had cost Halaou very much to look at the face of Sonthonax, so I left Dieudonné then and went back to Bahoruco, where I sat inside the clay walls of the *cay* which shut out the sunlight, and looked at the whiteman things by the candle flame. Sonthonax had gone away. In the west wherever the English came they brought back the *grand blanc* French who had been slave masters, and whatever the paper said, there would be slavery under them. Rigaud might say he fought for the Republican French who wrote the freedom paper, yet he and the colored men with him had all been slave masters before the risings. Whatever black leader put his head above the rest was cut down and killed like Halaou. Perhaps after all there was only Toussaint.

The whiteman must know a reason for each thing which he does, but with the people of Guinée, it is not so. I had a spirit walking with me, whether Kalfou or Ogûn-Feraille, and had only to go where the spirit would lead me, as Halaou followed the white cock. I stopped the candle and put the whiteman things back into the hole in the wall and covered them, and then went out of the *cay*. The sunlight was a shock to my eyes, so that I stood blinking. I had not eaten since I woke, but I was not yet hungry. I went up into the provision ground behind the *cay*. Butterflies floated over the flowers on the plants of *pwa rouj*. The beans were not yet ready to pick, but the corn tassels were turning brown. I picked some ears and piled them, and then dug yams with a pointed stick hardened in the fire, until I met Jean-Pic coming the other way along the planting. He looked at all the *vivres* I had gathered and then into my face.

"I am going north," I said. "Will you come?"

Jean-Pic looked all around, at the green trees hanging to the sides of the mountain, the red-earth cliff across the gorge, with terraces to hold up *cays*. He scratched the back of his head, and said, "Was it the *cacique* who told you to do that?"

I lifted my shoulders and let them fall. The *cacique* had not spoken any language that we understood, which Jean-Pic knew as well as Riau, but maybe it was after all because of the *cacique*, or because of Maît' Kalfou.

"*Men* . . ." Jean-Pic scratched his head again, looking all around the *bitasyon*. It was still early-morning light, with the mist still lifting off the slopes around us. "*Sé bon isit-mêm,*" he said. It's good right here.

"*Sé vré,*" I answered, and it was true, and yet I would go anyway. I lifted the *vivres* I had gathered and began walking down toward the *cay*. I had known Jean-Pic for a long time, since we were with Achille's band in the north, but Achille was killed in the first risings, and since then Jean-Pic and I traveled sometimes together, sometimes apart.

Bouquart came after me, out of the corn. He moved in a fast, rolling lope in spite of the two *nabots* fixed to his feet, and caught me with no great trouble.

"You are going," he said. "Why do you go?"

I lifted my shoulders. A whiteman might have answered it was because I hoped to find Merbillay and Caco again, or because of the thoughts in my head about Toussaint, or only because there were few women at Bahoruco. But Riau had no such thought. At other times I had left Dieudonné, and I had left Toussaint's army. I had left Habitation Bréda when I ran away to the maroons and before that I left Guinée to be a slave in Saint Domingue. Now I was leaving Bahoruco. Bouquart stood with a cane knife hanging from his hand, the flat of the blade against his knee, sweat shining over his scarred chest where his breath moved, and his smile uncertain.

"I will go too," he said, and lost the smile when he closed his mouth, watching Riau.

I looked at the two *nabots* on his feet, and at the muscles that swelled up from his ankles to his hips. Bouquart had told the story, how he had limped through his days in the cane field, after the whitemen gave him his *nabots,* but by night he had practiced walking, then running, in the secret dark by the river. Now he could run as fast with his weighted legs as any other man without. If ever the *nabots* were removed from his legs, Bouquart would run faster than a horse.

"*Dako,*" I said, agreed, and Bouquart smiled more fully.

Together we made ready to leave, putting the corn and the yams in a straw sack. I carried the watch and pistols and the candle ends in a smaller straw *macoute* with a strap for my shoulder, and I put the empty writing papers in there too, but the bundles of letters I left in the wall, in case the whiteman words should twist in my sack to betray me.

We left Bahoruco before midday and traveled until dark came, then walked through the next day also, but after that we slept through the days, hiding in the bush, and walked by night, because we did not want to meet any whiteman soldiers. Because the English were at Port-au-Prince we passed on the other side of the salt lake at the end of the Cul de Sac plain, over the Spanish border, and then climbed into the mountains toward Mirebalais. Neither Bouquart nor Riau knew who was holding the town that time, so we went around it on the heights until we came to the south shore of the Artibonite. The river was too deep for Bouquart—his *nabots* would have drowned him, and also there were caymans in the water, or might have been. We passed one day in cutting wood to build a raft, and when we put it in the water we learned that neither Riau nor Bouquart had good skill to guide it, so we drifted a long way downriver before we could reach the other side, almost as far as Petite Rivière. On the north shore people told us that the English had come out from Saint Marc to build a fort at La Crête à Pierrot, above the town, so we went around Petite Rivière to the west, leaving the river, and kept following the mountains north toward Gonaives.

The Savane Désolée was there when we came out of the mountains, all cactus, dust and salt pans, with water too salt to drink. The road was flat and open but Riau was uneasy walking it—we could be seen from a long distance in that open country. While we were walking, a dust cloud rose ahead, toward Gonaives, so we left the road and hid among the cactus and *raquette* trees. The army was a long time passing, with many horsemen, and even more foot soldiers, and mules dragging cannons behind. When it had gone by, and the dust settled, we went back to the road. Some camp followers were still coming along in the rear, women or old men leading donkeys packed with provisions. I called to a woman in a spotted *mouchwa têt* riding sidewise on a little *bourik* with a wood saddle.

"*Ki moun ki pasé la?*" I said. Who are the people passing there?

"*Sé l'armée Toussaint Louvti yo yé.*" She threw her head back, grinning, and whipped the air with the little stick she used to drive her donkey. "*Yo pralé batt l'anglais!*" She rode on.

The army of Toussaint Louverture, going to beat the English. Bouquart wanted to follow them, but Riau wanted to go north, out of the desert to the green of the mountains. We rested through the high heat of the day in the thin, dry shade of the *raquettes,* and I gathered salt from the flats and put it in a cloth bag I carried in my small *macoute.* When the sun turned red and began to fall, we walked on along the road, and in the darkness we turned from Gonaives on the trail toward Ennery. We rested and traveled through that night and at dawn had come to the coffee trees on the heights of Habitation Thibodet.

Most of Toussaint's army had left that place, it was plain, gone to the fighting at Saint Marc. There were some few black soldiers left to guard the *habitation* and the camp, and sick or wounded men in the hospital, where Riau had helped the whiteman doctor Hébert before I ran from Toussaint's army. Many of the women had stayed behind the army, with their children, and now they were coming out of their *ajoupas*, lighting cook fires and beginning to grind meal.

I left Bouquart to rest in hiding in the bush beyond the coffee trees, and I went down softly through the *ajoupas*. That *ajoupa* I had raised was still standing where it had been, but the roof was larger now and someone had woven *palmiste* panels to make walls. The *banza* I had made for playing soft music hung still from the ridgepole where it had hung, and Caco, my son Pierre Toussaint, lay sleeping on a straw mat, curled like a kitten. Merbillay was standing just outside, working a long pestle up and down in a stump mortar. Her arms were smooth and strong and she wore a blue dress and a red headcloth with gold threads on the edges. I plucked a note on the *banza* and she turned and peered into the shadows of the *ajoupa*, first looking to see that Caco slept safely, then finding Riau's face.

"*M'ap tounen, oui,*" I said, no louder than a whisper. Yes, I have come back. Her face went blank as the surface of the sacred pool at Baho-ruco. A moment passed, and then she smiled and came underneath the roof with me.

Riau slept afterward for a time, tired from the long night of traveling. I thought Bouquart must be sleeping too where he was hidden above the coffee trees. When I woke, Merbillay was still by me, lying on her back with her eyes open to the cracks of light in the woven walls. I spread my hand across her belly and felt the hard curled shape of a new child.

Merbillay sat up sharply then, and so did I, turning my shoulder from her. Caco had waked and looked at Riau with his bright, curious eyes.

"*Vini moin,*" I said. "*Sé papa-ou m'yé.*" Caco hesitated, till Merbillay clicked her tongue, and then he came to me quickly. He had grown very much—his legs hung below my waist when I lifted him to my chest. I carried him outside the *ajoupa*, kissing the short hair on top of his head. When he began to squirm, I let him down and he ran away toward the voices of other children.

Merbillay came out from the *ajoupa*, with all her clothes adjusted. Our eyes looked every way but at each other. At last I kissed my fingers to her and began climbing the hill to look for Bouquart. Anger was rising up my throat, but if my thought went outside of Riau, it said that Riau had left with no word or warning and had been gone more than one year. Why would Merbillay not take another man? But the anger with its bit-ter taste was hard to swallow back.

Doctor Hébert had gone to the fighting at Saint Marc, I learned, and in the *grand'case* was his colored woman Nanon with her son and also the doctor's sister with her man, the gunrunner Tocquet, and the child who they had made together. When I studied the *grand'case* from the hill, I saw that the rotten places had all been repaired and much work done to channel the water to a pool in front. Grass began to grow there now, and flowers, where packed earth had been before. But I stayed away from the yard below the gallery of the house, for Tocquet was a man to know one *nèg* from another.

At night I came to Merbillay, bringing Bouquart with me under cover of the dark. She cooked for both of us, and we ate without much talk. That night I lay again beside her, awake for a long time listening to her breath in sleep, until the moon was high, and I went out, down behind the stables, where the forge was dark and untended. A brown horse hung his head over a stall door and whickered to me, and I saw it was Ti Bonhomme. This horse had belonged to Bréda before, and Riau had ridden him with Toussaint's army too. I went to him and gave him salt from the bag I had gathered in the desert, and felt his soft nose breathing on my palm.

During the next day, I carved a wheel for Caco and pinned it to a long stick for him to push and play with. In the night I lay again with Merbillay, but at moonrise I went out quietly and found Bouquart and led him down behind the stables. We fired the forge, Bouquart helping with the bellows, as I showed him. When the forge grew bright, some few people came from the *ajoupas* on the hill and watched from the shadows outside the firelight, but no one challenged Riau, I don't know why. When the forge was well heated I made the tools ready and cut the *nabots* from Bouquart's feet, first the right and then the left. They fell in their hinged halves, like heavy melons, and when each one opened there was a sigh, from the people watching out of the darkness, like a breath of wind.

Bouquart looked up at me, his eyes shining in the firelight. He wet a finger in his mouth and touched it to a spot where the hot metal had blistered his skin. Above his ankles where the *nabots* had been, his leg hair was all rubbed away and the skin was polished and shiny, with black marks on the tendon from chafe wounds that had healed. Bouquart stood up. When he took his first step, his knee shot up so high it nearly hit him in the face. He walked farther, then ran and leapt, so high he touched the barn roof with the flat of his open hand. Ti Bonhomme the horse whinnied from surprise and pulled his head back from the stall door. Bouquart landed in a squat, then stood up, smiling from one ear to the other. In the shadows the people laughed and clapped, and some began to come forward toward the light, the women's hips moving as though they would dance.

*   *   *

We stayed for many days at Habitation Thibodet, I did not count how many. It was calm there all the time. In the daytime the women worked in the coffee or in the provision ground, while the few men who remained did soldier tasks and cared for the horses. All day I kept inside the *ajoupa,* sometimes playing the *banza* softly, with the heel of my palm damping the skin head so that the sound would not carry. Or I would go into the jungle with Caco. I had seen no man there I knew by name (except the *blancs* in the *grand'case*). Those Riau had known in Toussaint's army had all gone to the fighting at Saint Marc, and the whiteman doctor went there also, Merbillay had told me, or perhaps some had been killed, or run away as Riau had done before. But still there might be some man in the camp who would know Riau by sight.

I spent my days in the *ajoupa* or in the trees with Caco far from the camp, and by night I lay with Merbillay. We had not spoken of the new child coming, yet it lay between us whenever our bellies came together.

The news came that Toussaint's army was returning. The English were not chasing them, but still they had come back to Gonaives. It was told that Toussaint had come into the town one time, but the English had sent ships with cannons so that he and his men were driven out again. It was told that a cannonball struck Toussaint in the face, but his *ouanga* was so strong the cannonball did not kill him, though it knocked out one of his front teeth. Toussaint, it was told, had captured Fort Belair and begun to put cannons on Morne Diamant to fire into Saint Marc from above, but during the work a cannon fell on his hand and crushed it, and for this he had come back to Gonaives to wait for healing.

By afternoon more soldiers had come into the camp at Habitation Thibodet, though not Toussaint himself, and not all of his army. From the *ajoupa* I heard the voice of the whiteman Captain Maillart and the voice of Moyse calling out orders, they who had been brother captains with Riau before. All day I stayed in the *ajoupa,* silent, though Caco called me from outside, and I was glad of the woven walls which hid me.

After darkness came and the camp was quiet, I lay beside Merbillay again, but this night we did not touch. It seemed a long time before she slept. Then I got up quietly and took the small *macoute,* which I had made ready before. The moon had not yet risen so it was very dark, but before I had gone many steps from the *ajoupa,* Bouquart rose out of his sleeping place, whispering.

"You are going."

"Yes," I said, "but you can stay." I told him he had only to go to Moyse or the *blanc* Maillart to be made one of Toussaint's soldiers. I had seen his eyes admiring the soldiers in the camp.

"But you." Even in the dark I saw Bouquart's eyes turn to the *ajoupa.*

"*Gegne problèm,*" I said. There was a problem, more than one. Merbillay's new man would be coming back, if he was not killed in the fighting. Riau knew this, though she had not said it. Perhaps I would not have left only for that, but there was another thing I knew. Toussaint would kill a man for running from his army, *desertion* as it was called by whitemen and Toussaint. Riau had felt his pistol barrel against my head one time before, and that was only *petit marronage,* two or three days of hunting in the hills. A year in Bahoruco was *grand marronage.*

I followed Bouquart's eyes toward the *ajoupa.* "Say I will come back," I told him.

Bouquart's head moved toward me through the darkness. "When?"

"*M'ap tounen pi ta,*" I said. I will come back later.

The brown horse Ti Bonhomme had been turned out into a paddock. He came to the fence when I clicked my tongue, and I gave him salt from the bag I had gathered, and made a bridle of a long piece of rope. Holding his mane with my left hand, I swung up onto his bare back. I did not steal a saddle or a leather bridle, though I knew where they were kept, and I would not have taken the horse either except that I needed him to carry me quickly far away.

When the moon did rise, it filled the forest with the light of bones. By moonlight it was easy to ride faster. My spirit led me to a tree where hung the skull and bones of a long-horned goat and the cross of Baron Samedi. Here I reined up my horse, and looked at the ground, the fallen leaves piled under moonlight. The grave had long ago filled in or washed away, but still I felt a hollow. In this place Riau had helped Biassou to take the flesh of Chacha Godard from the ground and make it breathe and walk again, a *zombi.*

I felt fear in my horse's heart, between my knees. I let the reins out and rode quickly on. The night was warm, but a cold straight line was down my back, like death. I took a lump of the desert salt from the sack and held it on my tongue, my jaws shut tight.

II

Cool, and the calm was ruffled only by the wind, shivering the heavy blades of the tall old palms. Above the bunches of their tops, the stars of morning faded, as the cocks took up their cry. A last mosquito, his namesake, whined round his ear, then stung. Moustique, whose hands were both engaged in balancing the priest's slop jar, could not slap it. He let it feed, then fly, and felt his way forward through the warm wet darkness, his ivory toes splaying in the dirt.

L'Abbé Delahaye had assigned him the slop jar to teach him humility, he said. Moustique was meant to share the vessel, during the night, and likewise to share the priest's bedchamber, but he preferred to sleep in the outer room, on a pallet, under the shadows of the chalice and censer on the table, the iron crucifix nailed to the wall—he went outside to relieve his flesh, if he must. The priest snored ferociously, and the bedroom, windowless, was too close and too completely dark.

Delahaye himself had done such tasks, which some might think degrading, during his novitiate in France. He mocked Moustique for rising before first light in hope of hiding his progress with the ordures. One who has attained humility, the priest was wont to say, cannot be humiliated. Furthermore, the boy should count himself lucky that the weather was always dulcet here. As a novice, Delahaye had performed his morning *devoir* walking barefoot across freezing flagstones of his monastery, while outside the roofs and the ground would be covered with snow, that frozen rain that fell lightly as feathers . . . like cotton, the priest explained, but Moustique had not seen cotton either, though once it had been grown in Saint Domingue.

Moustique listened, often without comprehension, and woke each morning well before dawn, to lie listening to the wind bowing the tall palms, the clatter of leaves distant beyond the roar of the priest's snoring through the thin partition. Then he pushed himself up and collected the slop jar and went out into the dark.

It had rained in the night, and the earth beyond the borders of the village was damp beneath his feet. He moved to the edge of the path to avoid a party of charcoal burners he could hear coming down from the mountain with their loaded *bouriks*. They passed him, clucking softly to their animals, the little donkeys snorting at his scent. To his left he could hear the river running over the rocks, and he cut a new path through the reeds and emptied the jar among them, then went on in a long curve to strike the river bank at a lower point. The stars were gone, and daylight was coming up quickly now, framing the mountains and the treetops against a purple sky, new light creating the world all at once out of darkness, as Moustique came out of the reeds onto a gravel shoal.

He stepped shin-deep into the water and crouched down to wash the jar. The morning mist was lifting from the river, and he saw a party of girls upstream, kneeling to dip water for their houses, Marie-Noelle among them. Their laughter belled out when they saw him, ringing with innocent delight that a creature so absurd as himself should have appeared for their amusement. Ducking his head above the cold stream, he felt his face break out with inflamed patches that ran down his throat past the loose collar of his shirt and spread across his collarbone. Delahaye addressed him always as Jean-Raphael, but in a reckless moment he had disclosed his nickname to Marie-Noelle, and this information had become the centerpiece for many pleasantries.

"Ti-moun prêt, sé moustik li yé!" they called after him, and tightened their lips to make the insect whine. The baby priest is a mosquito . . . His gangly limbs were like the legs of a mosquito, his long nose of a *blanc* might give a mosquito's sting. Moustique refused to look back at them, but even if he could not hear their jokes and laughter, he would have been as acutely aware of them, sauntering a few yards behind him, hands and hips lazily swinging, the water jars effortlessly balanced on their heads. He understood that Marie-Noelle tormented him partly from annoyance that he had deprived her of much of her work for

the priest—Delahaye had reassigned the most menial tasks to him, although the girl still came to his house to cook, for the priest would not tolerate Moustique's cooking. There was a limit, he declared, to the mortification of the flesh.

He set the washed jar down on the priest's doorsill, then untied the priest's two donkeys, the jack and the sweet jenny each marked with a crude cross on the flank, and led them out to forage. When he returned, the priest was at matins. Not many of the faithful had assembled, it being a weekday (and in any case all the white planters had been killed or driven into refuge on the coast). Some few black men and women had come down from the hills, hoping for a Jesus *ouanga,* a taste of power from the mighty god of *blancs.* Moustique's own father had been free enough in dispensing such charms, but Delahaye was stricter—he would not baptise anyone more than once, provided that he recognized the convert on a later application. Part of Moustique's duty, indeed, was to identify new Christians who came again to repeat the treatment.

He served at the altar as he had been taught. After the service, Delahaye heard his recitation. Moustique spoke with some difficulty, his mouth full of saliva; he could smell the maize cakes Marie-Noelle was frying over the cook fire behind the house.

" 'For if the first fruit be holy," Moustique carefully pronounced, " 'the lump is also holy, and if the root be holy, so are the branches.

" 'And if some of the branches be broken off, and thou, being a wild olive branch, wert grafted in among them, and with them partakest of the root at fatness of the olive tree;

" 'Boast not against the branches. But if thou boast, thou bearest not the root, but the root thee.' "

Delahaye nodded pensively, signaling with his forefinger for Moustique to continue. The priest assigned him a chapter to memorize each day, first in Latin, which was mere noise to the boy, then in a French version—good French, for if Moustique should lapse into Creole, Delahaye would rap him across the knuckles with the back of a wooden spoon. And yet at other times the priest would drift, captured more by the sense of the passage than the phrasing.

" 'Thou wilt say then, The branches were broken off, that I might be grafted in.

" 'Well, because of unbelief they were broken off, and thou standest by faith, be not high-minded, but fear:

" 'For if God spared not the natural branches, take heed lest he also spare not thee.' "

"Yes . . ." Delahaye said, presenting the flat of his palm to stop the recital. "Yes, that will do." His eyes cleared and focused on Moustique.

"Let us break our fast then," he said, and touched the boy's hand in a kindly manner, as he sometimes would. "My wild olive branch."

Moustique followed him, his puzzlement mute, from the church to the house. As soon as they were seated, Marie-Noelle served them quickly and then withdrew. They ate the maize cakes flavored with dark cane syrup, washed down by cold water from the river. Delahaye discoursed on Latin grammar, comparing certain passages of the morning's text to the French translation. Moustique nodded, miming comprehension, whereas in truth the only thing that he had grasped was that while French was for white men, and Creole for black, Latin was the language spoken by God.

"You may go to the washing," Delahaye told him as they picked at the last crumbs, "after the dishes, of course."

Moustique's heart lowered. Wash day was in some ways his worst experience of an ordinary week. He looked out the open door in the direction Marie-Noelle had gone. A wisp of smoke from the dying cook fire drifted across the open front of the *ajoupa* where the girl had slept, before his own arrival. The little lean-to stood empty now, though Moustique would have gladly slept there himself, farther from the snoring, if Delahaye had allowed it.

"Above all you must beware of concupiscence," Delahaye suddenly announced, drawing the boy's attention back from the world beyond the door. "Lasciviousness, lust of the flesh. Through this sin was your father lost to God."

Moustique flinched, swallowed, and got up to clear the table.

The young girls washed downriver from the older women, and Moustique washed downriver from the girls. On other occasions he had gone upstream from all of them, half-hiding himself in a patch of reeds, but the women frowned and the girls complained loudly that they caught his dirt drifting down the currents. Today he crossed the gravel shoal in full view of their party, swinging his bundle of cloth down on the sand at the water's edge. The sun was hot across his back, but the water was so cold that when he first put a foot in, it shocked him clear to his back teeth. He sighed, unfolded a cassock on the surface of the water, then plunged it under and began to scrub it with a long bar of handmade soap.

This was, absolutely, women's work: another station on his pathway to humility. His father, the French Jesuit Père Bonne-chance, had been a humble man; Moustique had felt this for himself, before his father's execution, and his feeling was confirmed by Delahaye, who had known him reasonably well. *There was much virtue in your father,* Delahaye would lecture him, *even a vocation for martyrdom, as was proved, and yet he shut himself out of the community of saints, because* . . . Because, Moustique reminded himself wearily, he had fallen into the snare of love for women, notably Moustique's mother Fontelle, and had used his male member to plant the seed of children in her belly, the germ of Moustique and his sisters.

He spread a sheet across a boulder and began to scour it with a rounded stone. His palms were wrinkling now from soaking in the water. For some time the girls had been chaffing him in their loud, laughing voices, but Moustique, wrapped up in other thoughts, had scarcely been aware of them. Was this the beginning of humility? The divorce of his mind from his surroundings was certainly something new. And the girls, seeing he did not react to their teasing, had lost interest and begun to splash each other. Moustique understood the source of their resentment—he did not belong here at this hour of the day, no more than any man, and if not for his presence the girls would have been free to strip off the dresses they were wearing and scrub them clean and then swim naked while their clothes dried on the rocks. As it was, the splashing game had soaked the whole pack of them to their necks, so that the wet fabric clung transparently to the rich chocolate flesh, breast and buttocks and belly and the shadowy cleft between the thighs . . . Moustique's mind skittered sideways, crossing over fragmentary passages half-remembered from a very curious French novel his father had kept hidden (so he thought) and which Moustique and his sisters had partially puzzled out in secret sessions, blushing and giggling in embarrassed titillation.

Now his skin was all afire again, and his wicked thoughts were concentrating in the arrow shaft of sin, which sprung forward and strained against the cotton of his breeches. Moustique sank down to his knees, waist-deep in the water, but it was useless now. The girls had begun to grin and gesture—they knew they had him back on the skewer—and the water was not cold enough to quench his heat. But his mind slipped free of his body again, as it had done a few minutes before, and though he felt the physical symptoms of his shame, the blush and bulge, these no longer mattered to him. Was this humility? He stood up out of the water, his empty hands loose at his sides, and looked at the girls frankly, making no effort to conceal himself. The fattest and most impudent of the group cocked her forefinger at his crotch.

"Moustik sa-a, li kab piqué dè fois!" And she erupted into a laugh so powerful she fell over backward into the shallows with a tremendous

splash. It was a fine witticism and the others quickly took it up, shrieking and pointing as they cried, "This mosquito can sting two times!"
Moustique stood still, almost relaxed, and gazed at them with something like indifference. Marie-Noelle, he noticed in a distant way, had
not joined in the laughter of the others.

On Saturday a party of mulattoes came, coffee planters from the hills
roundabout, to dine with the priest before mass on Sunday morning.
Moustique had encountered most of them a time or two before, but had
not learned their names, no more than they had inquired after his . . .
although he saw that he was noticed by appraising, not entirely friendly
eyes. If Delahaye had explained his presence to the guests, he'd done so
out of Moustique's earshot. They were *griffes* or *marabou* mostly, from
the point of view of color, so Moustique was lighter-skinned himself
than any of them.

Marie-Noelle had prepared *griot* of pork with rice and beans and a
few stewed greens, but she remained outdoors beside her fire, while
Moustique served the table. He was not invited to sit down, but caught
snatches of the conversation as he passed the plates and refreshed the
rum and water the company drank in place of wine. Most of the talk
concerned the war. Toussaint had been battering Saint Marc since mid-
summer, and without success, but he had defeated the English almost
everywhere else he had met them, at Marchand and Pont l'Ester and
Verrettes. From this last position he had quickly turned to drive the
Spanish from Petite Rivière. The sheer speed of his maneuvering was
remarkable, all agreed.

Toussaint was certainly a man of cunning, said the oldest man at the
table, fondling his peppery beard as he spoke. Perhaps even a man of
genuine talent—but no one could prevail indefinitely against European
soldiers. A *marabou* youth across the table hotly rejoined that no campaign of the British General Brisbane had managed to dislodge Toussaint from the Cordon de l'Ouest.

"So for the moment he remains our master," said the bearded man,
"for better or for worse," and someone noted that every plantation and
settlement in the mountains was much calmer since Toussaint had
established his chain of posts from Gonaives to the heights above Mirebalais, and someone else complained that his cultivators (he just
stopped short of saying *slaves*) grew restless in the proximity of so many
black soldiers, and many ran away to join Toussaint's army . . .

At the head of the table, Delahaye listened, silently attentive, his fingertips unconsciously worrying a whorl in his close-cropped gray hair, until he noticed Moustique lingering, and gestured at the empty pork platter.

Moustique went outside to the fire. The sky was darkening, slate-blue, the wind shivered the high palms, and crows flew crying among them. In the nearest *bitasyon* above the town, there was a quick, sharp rattle of drums, trailing off, then beginning again. Marie-Noelle refilled the pork platter from the iron kettle, her eyes lowered, almost demure. She was usually quiet, Moustique remembered, when apart from the pack of other girls; still something in her manner seemed to have changed.

When he went back with the dish of pork, the young *marabou* was loudly declaring that Toussaint had a better hope than anyone of driving all the white people from the island once for all. One of the older men pointed out that such a result would hardly be in their own interests— practically all of them had relatives who were collaborating with the British at Port-au-Prince and points farther south.

"Yes," the bearded man agreed, "and equally you must not forget that Toussaint has sold himself to the French, to Laveaux—"

"Laveaux is a good man," Delahaye put in.

"Laveaux is the tool of Sonthonax," the bearded man said, "who would set the most ignorant, savage Africans above us—"

"Sonthonax has left the country," the young *marabou* snapped.

"So he has," the bearded man said, leaning forward as he lowered his voice, "and on the eve of his departure he gave his commissioner's medallion, along with its powers and prerogatives as I have heard, to Dieudonné, who is no more and no less than a wild maroon from the mountains. And he told him—as you may not know—Sonthonax told Dieudonné, *So long as you see mulattoes in your ranks you will never be free.*

A considerable silence followed, during which Delahaye noticed Moustique again and sent him out for more rum and a plate of cut fruit. When he returned, the young *marabou* was in the midst of a hot reply to some resumed thread of the conversation: "—and what of Rigaud, who is of our race, and of the French Republican party? What of Beauvais, who is one of us too, and undoubtedly a man of honor?"

"I do not see that either of those men has thrown in his lot with Toussaint." The bearded *griffe* leaned forward, raising his voice slightly as he balanced his weight toward the younger man. "And perhaps they err in casting their lot with the French Republic. If we gain by being made equal with the *blancs,* we lose as much by having those hordes of wild Africans set equal to us."

"But—" the young *marabou* began.

"I salute your youth—" the bearded man quelled him with an uplifted palm. "But it is no time to be hot-headed, not even for young men. Admire Toussaint if you will—he is admirable both in his courage and his cunning. But he has placed himself at the head of the new-freed slaves, and if he seems to carry them wherever he will, it may just as well be that it is they who are driving him from pillar to post. His shift of allegiance to Laveaux was very sudden, was it not—and are you so completely confident that he will not turn again to some other party, or that he serves any ends but his own? You may very well admire his gifts and his accomplishments, but both before and after, you should fear him."

An assenting murmur ran round the table, as the bearded man braced his palms against the table and sat back. Moustique searched Delahaye's face for a reaction, but the priest remained as inexpressive as Toussaint himself would have in such a case. Since the execution of his father, Moustique had grown to depend upon Toussaint's protection, and so this discussion confused him as much as it evidently had the young *marabou*—so much so that his head began to ache. He left the room without waiting for Delahaye to dismiss him.

It was darker now, the stars appearing, and for the moment the drums had stopped. Marie-Noelle was walking in a spiral pattern between the fire and the trunks of the tall palms, seeming to take pleasure in the light grace of her steps. She was dressed in white, as if for church, and her skirt belled out around her slim legs as she turned. Moustique felt a heart-stirring as he watched her, and wondered if she meant for him to feel it, but her eyes were downcast always, as if unaware of him. She turned and stepped and turned again, the white skirt catching starlight, firelight, starlight.

He lay sleepless in the priest's front room, the sound of Delahaye's snore throbbing at him through the wall, textured by the more distant drumming which the snoring only partly masked. Sleep was like a surface of salt water, so buoyant that it would not let him sink. His mind scuttled spider-like across it, shrinking from the most dreadful images in its store. The scene of his father's execution sometimes still appeared to him in dreams or waking nightmares such as this. They chained his father to a wheel and broke his bones with hammers till he perished. At first, he blessed his executioners but soon enough his prayers turned into screams. And all this was for nothing, for no cause: Père Bonnechance had merely been confused with some other renegade priest who had assisted in tortures and the rape of white women during the first insurrection of '91. Even Delahaye admitted that in this case his father was purely without blame. *Then God has no justice,* Moustique had said. Delahaye smashed his knuckles with the spoon and set him to memorizing long extracts from the book of Job.

Moustique got up cautiously from his pallet, light-headed, at the edge of nausea. He padded barefoot over the floor, lifted the latch and went outside. Just beyond the threshold he paused, listening: the racket of the priest's snoring still shook the walls of the house, uninterrupted. Silvery light spilled over his cheek and his arm. The moon was a crescent, sheltering three stars. When he stepped away from the wall of the house, the jenny raised her head in the corral and came to the palings, whickering softly. Moustique stroked her nose and let her warm breath play over his fingers. In the invisible cleft of the dark hill above, the drumming became more insistent.

He walked through pools of moonlight from the church and square to the edge of the town, and with scarcely a beat of hesitation began climbing the corkscrew path that curved over an extended claw of the mountain's foot. Darkness enveloped him, the moon cut off by the trees. His mind worked, but with no influence over his legs. Delahaye would be furious, if he should find out. Moustique's own father would have disapproved, perhaps more mildly. Moustique did not know one drum from another, so he did not know if he was bound for a secular celebration—*bamboche* or *calenda*—or a service for the pagan gods of Africa. In Jeannot's camp, where Père Bonne-chance had carried his mission in the first months of the rebellion, drums and ceremonies had been a prelude to the slow, elaborate, fatal torture of *blanc* captives. But all this information and the business of thinking about it became more and more distant, miniaturized, the higher Moustique climbed on the trail, while much more fully present were the drums and his own response: his limbs coming into tune with his heartbeat and the strengthening pulse at the base of his skull. From the darkness above, an unearthly cry broke out, an otherworldly entity that voiced itself on a human tongue. Moustique's arms flowered into gooseflesh, but he could not make out if the sensation was pleasure or fear.

He kept following the twistings of the path, scarcely aware of the embedded stones that gouged into the arches of his bare feet. Someone, maybe more than one, was coming down from the *hûnfor,* and Moustique stepped out of the trail, clinging to a sapling. *Scus'm,* a man's voice muttered. Two figures he could not make out completely, though he caught flashes of a white sleeve, white headcloth. When they had passed, he swung down into the groove of the trail and continued. The drumbeat quickened, drawing him up like a jerk on a leash tied around his neck. The trail made a sudden twist to the left and steepened sharply. Moustique helped himself up the rise with one hand furrowing the crumbling earth, then straightened in a clearing of packed clay. The brightness of the stars and moon amazed him as he came out of the tree cover. In the center a thick pole was wound around with a carved snake, and spiraled with a painted rainbow. There was a fire that cast no light, and the *hounsis,* swaying and singing, were turned blue-silver by the moon and stars—white shirts and headcloths glowing.

Kulèv-o
Damballah-wèdo, papa
Ou kulèv-o
Kulèv-o
Kulèv, kulèv-o
M'ap rélé kulèv-o
Damballah-papa, ou sé kulèv
Kulèv pa sa palé . . .

O Serpent
Damballah-wèdo
you are a serpent
Serpent, o serpent
I'm calling the serpent
Father Damballah, you are the serpent
The serpent does not speak . . .

The part of Moustique's mind that registered these images was shrinking, blinking as it fell away like a revolving coin. His body moved in perfect unison with the steady uprush of the drums, as he broke the line of *hounsis* and moved toward the *poteau mitan.* That otherworldly cry came from his own thick throat—he hardly knew it. His head threw back, the stars spun round and up and up like flecks of butter in a churn. The drumming sucked the stars into whirlpool, then everything went bright.

"Li konnen prié BonDyé?" A man's voice, with the rough-silk feel of a cat's tongue.

"Li kab chanté Latin, mêm." A girl, her voice bright with pride.

Moustique turned onto his shoulder and opened one eye upon the hard-packed dirt.

He knows how to pray to the white man's God?

He can even sing in Latin . . .

But now the voices had stopped. Moustique felt attention turn to him—he saw the man and the girl indistinctly through his half-closed gummy eyes. The flutter of their white garments sent his mind off-balance again. Nothing was clear, not where he was or how he had come there. Above the clearing, the sky was paling into dawn. Moustique heard cocks crowing down the gorges, and listened for the morning reveille of Toussaint's army at Habitation Thibodet, but then he remembered Marmelade, and Delahaye, and he sat up sharply, flinging out an arm.

"Dousman." Marie-Noelle supported his elbow, held his hand in hers, without the slightest pressure. Gently. His eyes yawed crazily around the clearing. He was still in the *hûnfor,* but the *hûngan,* with his cat's-tongue voice, had disappeared. He got to his feet; the movement dizzied him.

"Dousman . . ." Marie-Noelle was still supporting him, balancing him by his right arm. He looked at her, confused.

"Té gegne youn espri nan têt-ou," she said, quietly. Come with me.

She led him toward the trail head, guiding him with the pressureless contact of her hands. He felt the fragile clarity of someone waking from a fever. Everything was lucid, but nothing in his consciousness resolved into the elements of self.

There was a spirit in your head . . .

The dawn was damp, and agreeably cool. Moustique's knees were a little wobbly, but he felt his strength returning, along with his presence of mind, the farther they went down the trail. Marie-Noelle's light touch was pleasant, cool fingers just feathering his palm, and her demeanor was pleasant too—as if they'd always stood in this relation, whatever it might be.

Sunrise was baffled by the cover of the trees, but when they came out into the border of the town, the full light struck them and the church bell began to ring. Moustique, returning further to himself, felt a personal jab of panic.

"Oui," said Marie-Noelle, and thrust the priest's slop jar, emptied and rinsed, into his hands. "Yes—hurry."

A fold of her skirt brushed his leg as she turned away. Moustique scurried toward the church, pausing to set the jar down on the threshold of the priest's house. The congregation had already begun to assemble when he went in, but Delahaye paid him no mind—distracted perhaps by the party of *gens de couleur* who had already taken their positions in the front benches.

The priest stood before the altar, tall, lean, almost spectral in his best vestments, the ends of his purple stole twitching from a slight rotation of his hips. He spread his large hands over the people below him.

"*Dominus vobiscum . . .*"

As customary, Moustique led the mumbling response. "*Et vobiscum te . . .*" He took a darting glance over his shoulder. Marie-Noelle sat on one the rear benches, not far from the *hûngan*, a small, elderly man with a crown of white hair over a dark face wrinkled like a nut meat. The other back seats were filling with men and women dressed in white, many among them who last night had served the *loa*.

L'Abbé Delahaye collected herbs and flowers and kept large books in which he sketched the plants, pressed their leaves, and noted down their uses if there were any. A couple of afternoons each week he sent Moustique out to gather plants for him, and encouraged him to talk to people about their value. On this pretext Moustique returned to the *bitasyon* where the *hûnfor* was, seeking out the *hûngan* who, as was usual, doubled as a leaf doctor, *doktò-fèy.*

Moustique had some rudiments of herbal medicine from observation of Toussaint; also his own father had taken some interest in the subject, though less systematically than Delahaye. From the *hûngan* he learned more, though little enough that was new to the priest. To be sure, Moustique did not report to Delahaye that the *hûngan* had also begun to teach him the names and natures of the *loa*, particularly Damballah, the spirit which had chosen to possess him. But in two weeks' time, Moustique was assisting in the ceremonies at the *hûnfor*, wearing the white clothes and *mouchwa têt* of a *hounsi*, chanting an Ave Maria or a Pater Noster and perhaps some other fragments of memorized Latin scripture, before the African spirits were invoked.

The world of the church and its saints mirrored the world of the *hûnfor* and the African mysteries, just as (the *hûngan* explained) the surface world of living people was mirrored by the Island Below Sea, inhabited by souls who had left their bodies: *les Morts et les Mystères.* Flushed with this new understanding, Moustique felt as if he were empowered to walk on water. His life had come into a delicate balance, unlike anything he had ever known before. He was at peace within himself. Even Delahaye appeared satisfied with Moustique's newfound calm. If he returned belated, with the slop jar, blinking in the full light of day, the priest did not reprove him for his tardiness, but was pleased that the boy seemed to have finally got beyond his sense of shame. Of course, Delahaye had no idea where Moustique went at night.

*   *   *

Moustique began to understand that Marie-Noelle was, like himself, a doubled entity. Her daylight self—the priest's dutiful cook—was modestly, piously Christian. Her moonlit self was something other, engaged with the mysteries of the *hûnfor*. But with each encounter of those days and nights, Moustique felt her other image attached to her like a shadow. He felt the two images floating closer and closer until at last they would be one, and so it seemed inevitable to him when one night he woke in the small hours with that sense of being called, though this time there was no drumming. The priest's snores ran on as usual. The moonlight, shattered by the jalousies, spread in long, flat rays over the objects in the room. Moustique rose carefully, slipped through the door. His feet fell silently on puffs of powdery dust. No drumming but the beat of his own blood. The silence seemed perfect everywhere, and no one was about, but he felt that sense of expectation, almost choking in his throat, still leading him. He went counterclockwise around the corners of the priest's house. In a pool of moonlight near the cold ashes of the cook fire, Marie-Noelle stood still and calm. When he appeared, her balance broke, and she took a few steps away from him toward the shadows, her movement lilting, then paused, poised on the balls of her bare feet, looking back over her shoulder.

He overtook her just within the shade of the *ajoupa* where she had stayed before. Her right hand lay against his collarbone lightly, slightly cool, the barest touch. Their left hands were joined together, as if they were going to waltz. *Dousman*. Moustique did not know if one of them had said the word aloud. Gently, sweetly . . . *dousman*. Her taste was the sweetest experience that had ever graced his senses.

Then his days passed easily, as if in dream, for everything in the scripture and liturgy he was set to learn found its reflection in the knowledge of the *hûnfor*, while each time he entered the *ajoupa* with Marie-Noelle his dreams became actual: voluptuary visions embodied in real flesh. The moon kept waxing night by night, inflating its lopsided edges until it was a perfect circle, whitely blazing in the velvet sky.

Then one night there was no moon. When Moustique, having parted lingeringly from Marie-Noelle, reentered the house to collect the slop jar, there was no sound of the priest's snoring, though Delahaye lay in his usual position abed, his sharp nose jutting up like the fin of a shark. Moustique's senses registered the change, but his mind took no account of it. He walked to the river in the wandering starlight, cleaned the jar and then returned. When he turned the corner of the church, yawning lazily, turning the damp jar in his hands, he found the priest smashing the *ajoupa* to flinders with an ax.

Inevitable. Moustique could see that now. Why had he not seen it always? The empty jar had fallen from his numb hands, but had not broken. The relief he felt in this scrap of good fortune was meaningless now, he recognized. Delahaye lowered the ax and braced his hands on the haft, trembling slightly across his shoulders. On occasion Moustique had seen him preach dreadful, fiery sermons, but this was worse, much worse. The priest's thin lips were white from pressure, red spots flared in the hollow of his cheeks where the skin stretched taut over the the bone.

"The Devil," Delahaye said slowly, "will be driven from you, boy."

Moustique stayed rooted, as if fascinated by a snake. The priest caught his wrist, spun him around, and pushed him against the trunk of a tree. Automatically Moustique's arms rose to embrace the wood. His cheek was flattened against rough bark. The priest tore his shirt from collar to tail, ripped down his trousers to the ankles. A pause, a breath, then the first lash fell.

The instrument was a four-foot length of green liana, cut in advance for the purpose, as Moustique saw from his one squinted eye. The vine sizzled in the air before each strike, but it did not land as heavily as a leather whip, nor cut as a knotted cord would have done. Not that Moustique had ever been whipped before. He had felt the flat of his father's hand, but whipping was for slaves, for blacks, and not for him.

Delahaye had evidently some experience of the work to be done. He laid on neat horizontal stripes, accurately spaced and placed, across the back over the buttocks and the thighs. He paced himself, as for long endurance, and in the intervals of breath, before he struck again, he spoke.

"You have . . ." *snap!* ". . . sinned with the woman . . ." *snap!* ". . . but have you also . . ." *snap!* ". . . bowed to the Devil?" *snap!* "Have you invited . . ." *snap!* ". . . the great black Satan . . ." *snap!* ". . . into your heart?"

Each blow was painful, but superficially so, a sting and a welt rising from the skin. Soon enough Moustique understood that Delahaye did not mean to do him serious bodily damage, not of the sort that would cripple, maim and scar. Still the sting of the liana brought tears to his eyes, and an expulsion of breath he would not let become a cry.

"Christ our Lord . . ." *snap!* ". . . drove out the devils . . ." *snap!* "He sent those devils . . ." *snap!* ". . . into swine!" *snap!* "Casting out . . ." *snap!* "I cast out . . ." *snap!* ". . . beat the blood of black sin . . ." *snap!* ". . . out of your veins . . ."

Moustique's mind dislocated and began to travel. He had seen whippings aplenty, for under slavery they were common enough. And in the camps of the first rebellion, the black chiefs had whipped their men for various infractions, but not Toussaint. Toussaint had never ordered a man whipped, though if an offense were too grave for verbal rebuke, he might well command the offender to be shot. It was told that Toussaint had never been whipped himself, but many in his company had been, as well as ear-lopped, amputated, branded with hot iron . . . the scars were evident everywhere. Toussaint's fearsome subaltern, Dessalines, would sometimes remove his coat and shirt and shift his shoulders in a subtle manner which caused the bands of cicatrix all over his back to writhe like fat white worms.

Moustique's own father had once broken up a whipping. The slave had been pegged face down on the ground, blood from his stripes soaking into the dirt. Père Bonne-chance had hopped down from his donkey and traversed the field with his brown cassock flapping. The whip-handling overseer, he said later, was white *canaille* from a French prison, bandy-legged, troll-like, but with a long, muscular arm. Père Bonne-chance put his own body under the lash, letting the leather wrap around his stubby forearm. With a jerk he brought the overseer stumbling toward him and hit him with his free hand a short blow that stunned him and knocked out several of his teeth. He untied the thongs that bound the wrists and ankles of the injured slave and brought him to his own house to be treated and healed. The master of the plantation had been angry when he heard of the episode but had taken no action; the embarrassment of brawling with a priest would not do.

Now Moustique thought of the agony his father had suffered on the wheel before his death, and his own wish to whimper shamed him further. Nothing bound him to the tree, his whipping post, but he was fixed there, without the will to move. To close off the cry building in his throat, he bit down on his lip till his mouth filled with blood.

The beating stopped.

"Go into the house," Delahaye said.

After a moment, Moustique pushed himself up from the tree trunk and looked glazedly at the priest. A swirl of golden dots ran before his eyes.

"Go," Delahaye said, half breathless. He stood straight, though his voice was strained, and a beading of sweat stood on his forehead. Moustique went limping toward the house, holding his torn trousers up with one hand.

Delahaye came in a moment after him and got a fresh shirt and pair of cotton pantaloons from his own store.

"Put these on," he said. "Go on, dress yourself." He turned his back and looked out the window.

Moustique, delicately, put on the new clothing. He could not see the marks of the whipping on his back, but exploration with a fingertip let him know that the skin was welted but not broken. His worst injury was the bitten lip.

Delahaye turned to face him. "You may sit down."

Moustique swallowed a mouthful of blood and remained on his feet.

"Another preceptor might have beaten you more severely," Delahaye pointed out. "And afterward, rubbed salt and hot pepper seed into your wounds."

"I know it," Moustique said, thickly because of his swollen lip.

"Very well." Delahaye draped his stole over his shoulders and sat down at the table, looking up at Moustique with his clear gray eyes.

"Understand," the priest said. "It is not your African blood that I rebuke, but the sin which runs in the blood of all men, no matter what their color. The sin of your father, visited on you." He paused, eyes drifting, then returning to Moustique's face. "Saint Paul said, 'It is better to marry than to burn,' but a priest must not, may not marry, and fornication is a grievous sin."

Delahaye put his hand on the cover of the heavy Bible which lay on the table, but did not open it.

" 'Now if I do that I would not,' " he intoned. " 'it is not I that do it, but sin that dwelleth in me. I find then a law, that when I would do good, evil is present with me. For I delight in the law of God, after the inward man, but I see another law in my members, warring against the law of my mind, and bringing me to captivity to the law of sin which is in my members.' "

Delahaye paused to clear his throat.

" 'O wretched man that I am!' " he went on. " 'Who shall deliver me from the body of this death?' "

Delahaye looked hard at Moustique, who swallowed more blood and kept his silence.

"The words of Saint Paul," the priest said. "But it is Christ only, who delivers. Kneel down, my son, and make a true confession. Repent and your sins will be washed away, even if you have bent your head before the Devil."

Moustique licked at his cut lip and knelt down carefully. The movement hurt him less than he had expected. He rocked back on his heels and looked up at the priest.

"Saint Paul said also," Moustique pronounced slowly, " 'If you live in the Spirit, you are not under the law.' "

It seemed to him that Delahaye quailed.

"My God," the priest said. "What have I done?" He covered his face briefly with his large hands. When he took them away, his eyes went wandering, over the window and the furnishings of the room.

"From what tree were you grafted, after all?" he said at last. "Well, boy, I have no will to beat you any more today . . ." He got up heavily, went into the bedroom and shut the door.

Moustique stretched out gingerly on his pallet. The bleeding of his lip had slowed, so he didn't have to swallow as often as before. In less than two minutes he was unconscious. His double life had robbed him of sleep for many days. Now he slept dreamless through the heat of the day until evening.

The priest had gone out when Moustique awoke, leaving the bedroom door ajar. Moustique went to the river and washed, then returned slowly, greeting no one that he passed. His mind was a near-perfect blank. There was no sign anywhere of Marie-Noelle. He knew that most likely she would have fled to her home *bitasyon* in the mountains.

Behind the priest's house, the embers of the cook fire were dark. Shattered wood from the smashed *ajoupa* had been heaped across it. Moustique wondered if someone else would be engaged to cook. As for himself, he was only slightly hungry and could think of nothing to eat that would not aggravate his torn lip. Delahaye had not yet returned. Moustique went indoors, lay down and slept again.

When next he woke, the lightless room reverberated with the snoring of the priest. The bleeding of his lip had stopped completely though it was raw and very swollen. His appetite had not yet returned. His mind was clearer than it had been before. He understood that he might regain the priest's esteem, which was of value, but that to do so he must renounce both woman and the *hûnfor*. There must be other ways to God.

He got up cautiously, the weals stinging his legs and back. He listened to the rhythm of the snores. The straw *macoute* he used to gather herbs hung on the wall. Moustique put into it half a loaf of bread, the silver chalice, and the priest's stole. His shoulder was too sore for the strap, so he slipped from the house with the mouth of the straw bag clutched in one hand.

Dark of the moon. Moustique felt his way to the corral. The little jenny came to him of her own accord, whiskering over his palm. Moustique improvised a rope hackamore, then dropped the top rail and led her out. Wincing slightly, he swung onto her bare back, and rode from the town into the mountains, not knowing where he meant to go.

I2

South from Le Cap across the mountains, past Plaisance toward Gonaives, the road was more theoretical than actual, and Jean-Michel, known since childhood by the stable name of Choufleur but now officially addressed as *le colonel Maltrot,* had known as much before he decided to travel with the carriage from his white father's plantation in the Plaine du Nord. The ridiculous difficulties of crossing the mountains with such a vehicle were no surprise to him, and yet he cursed roundly and loudly whenever it was necessary to dismount and order the wheels unshipped from the carriage so that it could be carried piecemeal by the twelve men of his escort, over rockslides and mudslides, or across sections of crumbling ledge too narrow for the wheel span. Sometimes he cursed the men directly to their black African faces. Most of them had been slaves on his white father's plantation, though now they were French Republican soldiers (in theory, as the road was theoretically a road and not a near-impassable goat track); at any rate they were accustomed to obeying him, whether because of his military rank or his proprietorship, Choufleur did not know, or care.

At last they came down from Morne Pilboreau, descending the whipsnake turns on the dry mountain faces above Gonaives. They did not continue toward the coastal town, but turned westward, through another notch in the mountains which led into the canton of Ennery. Four men carried a wheel apiece, and six men hefted the carriage itself by its axles and tongue, while the remaining two went unburdened except for their weapons, and were prepared to respond in case of attack, though none seemed likely. The passage was quiet, sunny and humid. Choufleur rode bareback on one of the matched pair of gray carriage horses, his seat so assured that the lack of a saddle did not detract at all from the dignity of his bearing. Little clusters of wattled huts had sprung up on either side of the road. When Choufleur sent a man to inquire the way to Habitation Thibodet, he learned they were already almost upon it.

Here where they'd paused to ask directions, the road was muddy and rutted but wide and level enough now. Choufleur ordered his men to pin the the carriage wheels back on the axles. While they worked, he paced, fastidiously lifting his polished boots clear of the muck. A little brown goat by the roadside bleated at him and ran to the opposite end of its fraying rope tether. When the horses were hitched, Choufleur climbed into the carriage, which went jouncing forward amid the foot soldiers, who smiled covertly at each other now they'd been relieved of their extra loads. The road surface varied from sucking mudholes to patches of raw rock that pounded Choufleur's tailbone painfully. He would have been far more comfortable astride the bare back of either gray, but the impression to be made by his arrival mattered more.

The entrance to Habitation Thibodet was marked by two delicate brickwork columns, fixed with hinges, though there was no gate. A sentry emerged from the shadow of each column and the two men barred the way, symbolically, by crossing the bayonets fixed to their muskets. Choufleur leaned out the carriage window, displaying his uniform coat and the left epaulette.

"I am looking for General Toussaint Louverture."

"He isn't here," one of the sentries replied, and exchanged a glance with the the other. Both men were barefoot and shirtless, and wore identical cartridge boxes strapped across the shoulder. The one who had spoken had the letter *V* branded on the smooth, flat muscle above his left nipple.

"You may pass anyway," he said. The two men lowered their bayonets and the carriage rolled unevenly past them.

The drive to the *grand'case* was wet without being boggy; looking down from the carriage window Choufleur saw that it had been seeded with many small stones to keep it from turning into a swamp. On either side the fields were cultivated, mostly in beans, and the plantings all

looked in good order. There were only a few *carrés* of cane, but Choufleur grudgingly admitted to himself that the *pwa rouj* were more practical just now—efficient provision for the troops.

The carriage wheeled in front of the *grand'case* and halted by the
cane mill. Choufleur beckoned one of his men to open the door for
him, then climbed out and straightened his back gingerly. He adjusted
his coat and shot his cuffs. The artificial pool in front of the house made
a nice effect, with its stone borders planted with flowers and its surface afloat with water lilies. The house itself was nothing extraordinary,
a single story of whitewashed wood, but the carpentry was skilled, and
the building was well set off by tall coconut palms above and behind it,
and by channels of sparkling water that rippled down on either side to
join, gurgling, in the central pool. The railings of the gallery were trained
over with purple-flowering bougainvillea. A black house servant in a
plain cotton shift stood with her fingers grazing the rail, regarding the
arrival with some of the astonishment Choufleur had hoped for.

He nodded to her and cleared his throat. "You may announce the
Sieur Maltrot."

The girl hesitated, exhaling through her parted lips, then turned
abruptly and ran barefoot into the house.

Elise had been dozing under her mosquito net in the bedroom when she
heard Zabeth's voice calling, *"Le Sieur Maltrot, li fek rivé!"* She was some
few minutes organizing herself to greet the guest, all the more unexpected for the fact that the Sieur Maltrot had disappeared during the
first months of the insurrection and was generally assumed to be dead.
The French nobleman had been a peripheral member of the circle of
her friend Isabelle Cigny, as well as an acquaintance of her first husband, Thibodet, but his famous cruelty showed plainly enough through
his rather antique manners, and Elise had not liked him, had not in the
least regretted his loss, and was not overjoyed now to hear that he had
returned from the grave. Therefore she sighed as Zabeth helped her pin
up her hair and slip into a less revealing robe. She dallied over Sophie's
cot—the child was napping away the day's most suffocating heat, murmuring almost inaudibly in sleep, her face bright with a sheen of perspiration. Elise brushed an insect from the netting, and then, with a quick
glance at the mirror, went tripping toward the front door.

Nanon had preceded her onto the gallery, where she stood with her
long nails pressed to her wide lower lip—an attitude of perplexity, perhaps even dismay. Elise, standing in the doorway, looked past her and

saw that that the new arrival was not the Sieur Maltrot at all, but one of his bastard mulatto sons, the eldest she thought, who had been educated in France and returned with the airs of a white man—she took in also that *something* had already passed between him and Nanon, though it did not seem to have been speech. As Elise walked toward the gallery rail, Nanon turned abruptly and swept past her, eyes large and dark and her lip bitten red against the unusual paleness of her skin, into the shadows of the house.

"Ah, of course, Madame Thibodet," Choufleur said breezily, as he smirked and extended his limp hand toward her. He had already mounted to her level, with no encouragement from her.

"In fact it is Madame *Tocquet*," Elise corrected him, and smiled in a way that showed her top teeth only.

She felt a mixture of reaction which included outrage at his effrontery (presenting himself here under the name of his white father!), the desire to order him driven from the property by dogs, with cudgels; while at the same time she scrutinized the good cloth of his uniform coat, the brocade and the buttons with the look of real gold, and in the middle distance the fancy carriage and the black soldiers of his escort, all of which inspired her with a vague uncertainty—and then there was that flash of uninterpretable *something* that had passed between him and her brother's concubine.

Choufleur was going on, assuming this and that with the same airy confidence, still limply holding the hand she had reluctantly offered him, while he pronounced the usual platitudes about the length of the road and the lateness of the hour (though in truth it was not very far past midday and the sun was broiling directly overhead). It was bewildering to look at those swirls of freckles on his face, as if two sets of different features were present there, but neither completely resolved. Elise found, however, that she had made up her mind.

"But of course," she said in her sweetest simper, and turned toward Zabeth, who waited a pace behind her, to her left. "Go and change the linen in the west room."

Well satisfied by the success of his entry to Habitation Thibodet, Choufleur passed the afternoon in a self-guided tour of the plantation and the encampment surrounding it. There was no more than a skeleton garrison in the military camp, for almost every ablebodied man had been drawn off to the fighting in the Artibonite Valley, but women and the half-grown children and a handful of old men were keeping up the cultivation creditably: the coffee trees on the upper slopes looked as prosperous as the red and brown beans in the low ground, and there would even be a small harvest of cane, to be processed into brown sugar at the mill. Choufleur was impressed, if grudgingly, and somewhat more disagreeably aware that things looked better managed here than on his own lands in the north.

The men of his escort had fanned out through the encampment to scrape up new acquaintances or in a couple of cases to renew old ones from the north, recovered here and now by hazard. Sifting their gossip, Choufleur learned that Toussaint had not been seen here for two weeks or more, though he might reappear at any time, and that the French doctor Hébert had been absent for as long, serving as medical aide in Toussaint's forces. The only white man on the place was Tocquet, the smuggler, husband of the French madame, and he came and went most unpredictably.

All this looked very satisfactory to Choufleur. He returned to the *grand'case* as the afternoon rain blew up, and rested in the room which had been prepared for him, letting rain sounds soothe him till Zabeth knocked lightly on the doorframe to summon him to dine.

The meal was served on the gallery to a small round table of four. "We have sometimes a more various company," Elise trilled, "but at present all our officers are absent, with their troops." She joked that they still made up the number for a card party.

Choufleur had been seated opposite Nanon; she was composed, but more than demurely silent, keeping her eyes downcast over her plate, and speaking only when spoken to. Choufleur did not address her directly, but let the conversation unfold as it would.

Elise rebuked Tocquet for cleaning his nails at table with the foot-long blade of his knife, but the gunrunner only smiled at her lazily and finished his manicure before hiding the knife away somewhere under the billow of his untucked white shirt. Choufleur had dealt with him, years earlier, during the first months of the insurrection when Tocquet had regularly brought guns from the Spanish over the border to the rebel slaves—he might well still be engaged in such traffic, for he was not one to be inhibited by shifts of political allegiance. The very notion of his marriage to the Frenchwoman seemed astonishing (Choufleur wondered if perhaps it were no more than a figure of speech), although the woman was certainly delectable. Choufleur had seen her a few years before, from a distance at Le Cap, and marked her as one of those European roses who would quickly droop and wither, in this climate. On the contrary, she had bloomed and flourished. Her blond hair was fuller and thicker than he remembered, her eyes a brighter blue, her cheeks plump and tasty-looking, like the skin of a well-ripened peach.

Frenchwomen did not truly interest Choufleur, however. He could appreciate his ambivalent hostess as he might a painting or a well-performed passage of music, but she did not stir his blood. He turned to Tocquet and began to quiz him on recent military movements in the area.

"One might compare Toussaint to a chess player," Tocquet said, after some hesitation. "A strategist—he has the long view." He forked up a bit of his grilled fish and considered while he chewed. "This accident when his hand was hurt on the heights above Saint Marc cost him a tempo, as in chess. For that, the Spanish and the English could combine to recover Verrettes. But when Toussaint was back in the field, he surprised them in the interior and took Hinche."

"An exchange of equal value, you would say?" Choufleur stroked his chin.

He knew much of this intelligence from dispatches, but was more interested in Tocquet's reading of the raw information. Tocquet was like a crow flying over a battlefield, all-seeing, but with no particular stake in the fortunes of any one army. Also, since Toussaint reported directly to Laveaux, information did not flow in Choufleur's direction as freely as it might, owing to a mood of tension which seemed to be growing between the French commander and the mulatto military administration at Le Cap.

Tocquet shrugged. "If we remain with the notion of chess, position can matter more than material."

"But do you imagine he can really out-general European officers?" Choufleur said, testing. "An old Negro, uneducated . . . he has seen nothing beyond the shores of this island."

He was aware that Elise had stiffened, just perceptibly at his choice of words.

Nanon, her head still tilted over her plate, rearranged her grated *vivres* and her *riz ak pwa*; it was not clear whether she were attending to the men's conversation or not.

Tocquet smiled out of one corner of his long, thin-lipped mouth. "Oh," he said, "to have lived to Toussaint's age in this country is proof of sagacity, is it not? How many 'old Negroes' have you seen here? Concerning his generalship, I myself do not believe he can be outmaneuvered in the interior. He knows the country too well, and can move his men very much more quickly than European troops will ever travel over such terrain, in such a climate. As for your European officers, not one of them has offered him any serious difficulty until Brisbane, and that in the Artibonite, where it is open country."

"Some say his sagacity may amount to deviousness," Choufleur said. "Do you suppose this allegiance he's sworn to the French is genuine?"

Tocquet looked at him, scanning his uniform coat from the brocaded cuff to the epaulettes, long and lingeringly enough for Choufleur to feel a beading sensation behind his eyes, like water just before the kettle boils. But Tocquet removed his gaze in time to break the tension, looking out over the gallery rail, where a little rainwater still dripped on the bougainvillea vines, and on into the dark.

"I have heard," he said, "and it may be true, that Toussaint invited Brisbane to parlay at Gonaives. To discuss, so to speak, a realignment of the forces he commands . . ."

Choufleur, who had known nothing of this, felt a prickle down his spine.

"It appears that Brisbane himself may be an exception to the rule, but by and large, as I'm sure you know, our British invaders prefer to purchase their enemies rather than to fight them."

"You interest me greatly," Choufleur admitted. "And what next?"

"Well, it seems in the end that Brisbane thought better of attending this meeting in person," Tocquet said. "He sent subordinates with his proffers and proposals. Whereupon Toussaint was outraged and arrested the lot of them—for attempting to suborn and corrupt the virtuous General Toussaint Louverture."

Tocquet slapped a palm on the table, hard enough to jingle the glasses, and broke into a sudden harsh laugh. Elise added her tinkling tone to his mirth. After a moment Choufleur forced himself to join their laughter, but Tocquet had already cut himself off. He pushed back his chair and bit the end from a black cheroot.

"You may call it deviousness, low cunning," he said. "Be damned to all soldiering, I say—honorable or not. But Toussaint is making war, not a chivalric tournament."

Choufleur nodded. Tocquet raised an eyebrow, then leaned forward to light his cheroot from the nearest candle.

"Brisbane had wit enough to avoid that one trap . . ." Tocquet settled his back in his chair and exhaled a wave of smoke toward the gallery ceiling. "And Toussaint, as you will mark by these tales, has recognized him as a serious opponent. If Brisbane takes him for a foolish old Negro, I believe he is likely to lose the game."

Toward the end of the dinner the children came scrambling out onto the gallery, Sophie begging for a sweet, Paul tugging at Nanon's skirt, asking to be let go to play at the borders of the pool. Elise watched Choufleur watching Nanon with Paul, until Nanon rose, murmuring, apparently glad of the excuse, and went with her son down the gallery steps into the fresh, damp night.

"*Maman, kite'm alé,*" Sophie whispered urgently, hauling on Elise's arm with all her strength.

"*Dis, 'laissez-moi aller,'*" Elise said absently, correcting the child's Creole into French, but Tocquet had already left the table to finish his cheroot while wandering in the darkness, as his habit was, and Choufleur had risen from his seat, was bowing to her, offering flowery thanks for the repast.

She released Sophie, sending Zabeth after her to make sure the child did not drench herself in the pool. Having completed his sequence of compliments, Choufleur also went down into the yard, but Elise lingered by the gallery rail.

The moon was waning from the full, the pale disk flattened on one side as if a thumb had pressed against it. Sophie and Paul crouched frog-like, splashing and giggling at the pool's edge. Sophie would certainly need to be dried and changed before bed. Elise felt a flash of irritation, for after all Zabeth had done nothing to restrain her charge, and Nanon meanwhile stood several paces back from the children, her arms folded as if to wrap her beauty closer to herself, her high cheekbones tilted toward the moon. Choufleur faced her across the pool and, despite the considerable amount of moonlight, Elise could not make out his features now, but he looked well in his uniform—he would have been, as she thought idly, a fine figure of a man.

Near the dark wall of the cane mill, the coal of Tocquet's cheroot flared and faded, flared again, rising and falling with the motion of his invisible hand. Choufleur strolled in that direction. That limberness, the fluidity of his movement, Elise thought, set him apart from a white man even in the dark. Nanon too had that same liquid grace, though now she was still as a caryatid in the moonlight. By the cane mill, a flash of light illuminated Tocquet's and Choufleur's faces leaning together, and then there were two cheroot coals, glowing and fading in the shadows.

Even through the fumes of strong tobacco, Choufleur caught a whiff of fresh-pressed syrup where he stood by the mill wall. He sniffed audibly, meaning Tocquet to hear.

"The mill has been working," he said. "Is there sugar here?"

"Some small quantity of the brown," Tocquet said carelessly. "But mostly it is crude molasses, sent away for the making of rum." In the moonlight he seemed to register Choufleur's expression of interest. "Well, you may look it over if you like."

Tocquet unlocked the mill door and groped through the dark opening for a stub of candle. Lighting it, he stepped inside. In the candle flame, the screws and cogwork of the mill threw long, imposing shadows. Choufleur followed the sap gutter to the series of kettles and troughs—all empty. The fires were cold and the ladles hung in horizontal racks on the wall. Choufleur ran a fingertip over a sticky edge and tasted it.

"You do not work the mill by night."

"Why, there are scarcely hands enough to run it by day." Tocquet shrugged. "With the war . . ."

"And yet, you are the proprietor, are you not?"

In the shadows, Tocquet raised an eyebrow.

"I mean," Choufleur said, "the question hardly seems to interest you."

"I am proprietor here by grace of my marriage," Tocquet said. "Come, I am no planter. No more than yourself. I don't believe we are pretending it's the first time we have met. My wife occupies herself with such affairs."

"A woman."

"Not to be underestimated." Tocquet produced his keyring from his loose trousers and unlocked another door. "Besides, she has capable advisers, including, sometimes, no less than Toussaint." He smiled absently as he entered the smaller room. "Toussaint's interests do extend to the production of sugar."

"Toussaint stops here?" Choufleur had followed Tocquet into the mill office.

"From time to time," Tocquet said, lighting a second candle in a bracket on the wall. "He is not the only guest."

Choufleur scanned the spartan furnishing—four straight chairs, a cot, a simple desk. Bundles of herbs hung on strings from the ceiling and on the wall were pinned some botanical sketches and a map of the colony with some obscure penciled markings.

"Why, it has quite the air of a military headquarters."

Tocquet sniffed. "Toussaint's headquarters is wherever he happens to dismount from his horse." He stooped and collected a bottle that had been unobtrusively placed between the writing desk and the wall.

"And is the rum Toussaint's?"

"You are inquisitive," Tocquet said. He uncorked the bottle, drank and extended it. "*Santé,*" he said, as Choufleur took the bottle. He sat down on one of the rough-cobbled chairs and Choufleur followed suit.

"I have a question of my own," said Tocquet, stretching out his legs and pulling on his cheroot. "If you doubt Toussaint's capacities in the field, where will you find a better officer?"

"Among the Republicans? In the south it would certainly be Rigaud," Choufleur said promptly. "Beauvais also. There is quite a capable officer corps both at Jacmel and at Les Cayes. At Le Cap there is Villatte, with whom I serve."

"All very excellent gentlemen of color," Tocquet said. He looked about for a place to tip his cheroot, and finally resorted to the cup of his palm. "Do you suppose they can rival Toussaint in the confidence of the new-freed slaves?"

Choufleur tilted the rum bottle to the light. "We have all of us our experience in the management of such people."

"As slaves, you mean. It is nothing to me—and I don't make predictions. But slavery is done with in this country, of that much I am sure."

"And Toussaint poses as the great liberator!" Choufleur burst out. "Can no one see it is all a fraud? He rides the wave, but he did not make it. And there are men more capable than he—as soldiers and as leaders."

"Do I hear the voice of your colleague Villatte?" Tocquet smiled, but his eyes had narrowed. "One hears that his ambitions are frustrated, in Le Cap. Or perhaps it is Rigaud who speaks with your tongue— he who has realized his ambition somewhat more completely, so far from Laveaux's command as he finds himself, on the Grande Anse—far from any French authority."

Choufleur felt a flush rising on his cheekbones. Aware that he had overspoken, he endeavored to grow colder. There was always an iciness inside him he could call on when he must.

"You and I have crossed paths in many places," Tocquet said, relaxing and crossing his legs. "From here to the north coast and to the Spanish border, in spots where many different flags were hoisted and different men or factions claimed command. I went unmolested everywhere, and by my observation, so did you. I am a friend of the world, you see!— that's what these times require." Toquet tapped his boot on the floor. "If French authority reaches the place where we sit, it does so by way of Toussaint Louverture . . . no other. If you would travel from Gonaives to Dondon all along the Cordon de l'Ouest, you must do so by his leave. Say what you will of his abilities, it is no mean achievement to have mastered that line. And if Toussaint should wish to close it, Rigaud would have to send his messengers to Villatte by sea."

Choufleur retained his composure despite this barb. "I am surprised to find you such a partisan," he said.

"You misunderstand me," Tocquet said. He stirred the ashes in his palm, and held his smudged forefinger to the candlelight. "My home is where I hitch my horse. Thus far I am in the same spirit with Toussaint."

"And no further?"

"For the moment, Toussaint guarantees our security here," Tocquet said. "For my own part, I have never been ambitious to possess anything which could be burned or murdered, but—"

"—there are domestic arrangements to consider," Choufleur said, with a deliberately unctuous smile. "The woman with her child—your brother-in-law and *his* woman—"

A shadow fell on him as Tocquet stood up, but Tocquet only turned to snuff the candle in the bracket above the desk. Automatically Choufleur got to his own feet. Holding the other candle nub, Tocquet approached, stopping just out of arm's reach. Choufleur felt his scrutiny exploring his face like the fingers of a blind man. He let his right hand drift toward the pocket pistol he kept tucked into the back of his waistband, under the flap of his coat. Many white men had examined him in such an assaying manner, studying the swirls of freckles and the degree of pigment in the skin beneath them, and there was always, along with the other elements, a tinge of contempt in their eyes. He felt none of that in Tocquet's regard, but instead a strange sort of sympathy, though it did not relax his wariness.

Tocquet blew out the candle and stepped past him. In the sudden dark, Choufleur touched his pistol grip, but Tocquet was moving through the doorway, muttering something about the lateness of the hour. In the main area of the mill a shaft of moonlight marked the patch to the outer door. Choufleur followed Tocquet outside. He dropped the stub of his cheroot on the floor and trod on it.

Tocquet raised his palm to his lips and blew the heap of accumulated ash away on the night breeze.

"You did not come here for no reason," he said, glancing quickly at Choufleur and then away. "I wish you an uneventful night."

Tocquet prepared for bed in five rapid motions: he shifted his knife from his waistband to underneath his pillow, then stripped off shirt and breeches and hung them on the two pegs above the bed which no effort of Elise's could persuade him to relinquish. He was asleep in thirty seconds if he wished, breathing with a light rasp just short of a snore, but tonight he did not wish it, though Elise dallied for a long time, washing her face and patting it dry and brushing out her hair before her mirror. A vague excitement covered her all over, like perspiration not quite breaking on her skin, but she did not want to be distracted by the man.

At last she snuffed her candle, raised the edge of the *moustiquaire* and slipped between the sheets. She was scarcely settled when Tocquet's hand spread over the soft skin around her navel, a light, inquisitive pressure. She murmured discouragingly and the hand lifted away from her, sliding beneath his pillow to curl, she knew, around the knife hilt.

In less than a minute, Tocquet breathed in sleep. Elise lay on her back, quite still, eyes open. The moonlight leaking into the room was striped by the jalousies, checked by the mosquito netting. At times the moonlight squares were set atremble by the movement of the breeze outside, and the palm leaves shivered above the rooftop. Wakeful, Elise focused her attention, beyond the leaf sound and the breathing of the man beside her. After her brother had diverted the water that threatened to rot out the whole floor of the house, many boards had been replaced, and since then the new planks grated against the old ones under shifts of weight, each with its own particular note.

It was a long time before she heard what she was listening for, and when it came it was very faint; he must be walking barefoot, and with the poised stealth of a cat. But the progress of the creaks was there, yes, quite unmistakable. From the west room to Nanon's he must pass her own, and when she thought by the sound that he must have arrived, she rose softly and opened her door the barest crack, to look out onto the corridor.

A spearhead of moonlight lay across the floorboards, and at its point, the opposite end of the hallway, was the door to Nanon's room. But he had not yet entered. Elise saw him against the door, part of him, rather: the back of his cocked head and one small ear, the swell of his milk-colored muscles from wrist to shoulder. He was shirtless as well as barefoot, and if his whole skin was freckled like his face and hands, these markings did not show under the moon.

He moved, the door yielding inward before him, and the jalousies of Nanon's window laid tiger stripes across his torso. Then darkness, as the door was shut. She heard a rustle, gasp, a muted hiss of complaint: *tu me fais mal.* Then silence. Elise cracked her door a little wider, listened harder. The gasps returned, more regular, rising to a different tone. With a secret smile she withdrew into her room and shut the door. She returned to her bed and covered the man with her hands and warm breath until he woke and rose to feed the appetite she felt so suddenly awakened.

*   *   *

Nanon had not been taken by surprise, not exactly; from the moment she had seen Choufleur standing between the mill and the newly engineered pool, she had grasped the nature of his errand well enough. Though they hardly spoke, the force of his intention bore down on her all through the evening, and increased when she retired to the room she normally shared with the doctor and Paul. There was no latch or interior fastener. She might have wedged a chair against the door, or balanced a cabinet that would topple when the door swung inward and perhaps make noise enough to wake the house. More than once in the recent past she had found herself barricaded in a room or a house with the doctor, who would use his pistols and rifle to defend the walls surrounding them. But the doctor was absent, and his weapons gone with him. Blocking the door would alarm Paul, who was tugging on her finger now, and pleading for a story. Nanon yielded to his desire, let him lie in her bed with her, and in the moonlight-spangled darkness she began the story of Tim Zwezo, crooning the songs in a low voice.

> *Tim Zwezo . . .*
> *Zwezo nan nich-o . . . Zwezo nan bwa . . .*
> *Tann-moin la . . .*

Paul was asleep well before the story finished, and she carried him to his small cot in the corner. Returning to her bed, she glanced at the unlockable door once more, but she would not block it, for the same reason she would not scream or struggle. If he came. She could not have named her reason, but she felt its power. *Kon Dyé vlé*, she said to herself. As God wills. With the matter disconnected from her own wishes, she slept soundly enough, though as soon as the door ticked open, she came instantly and completely awake.

His belly was barred by moonlight and shadow, his face completely in the dark, and one hand spread against the door, behind him, pressing it shut. Nanon stood up, bare feet on the floor, and moved sideways, thinking suddenly that after all the room was not a cage; if she lured him from the door, she might slip out and evade him—go to Zabeth's room in the rear? But Paul, she must not leave Paul alone with him . . . while she was distracted by that thought, Choufleur darted across the space between to catch her wrist, startling a gasp from her. She saw the rapacity of his expression when his face crossed the moonlight; the bones which pushed his features through the flesh were those of his father, and that frightened her more than the pain of her wrenched arm. His hand at the nape of her neck was hard and tight, fingertips digging bluntly into the tendons. She hissed a complaint, *you're hurting me,* and then went limp, went numb all over, unresisting. She had been forced before, and with some regularity, though not for a long time now, not since the doctor or since she'd borne her child. But she remembered that yielding was the better way; she'd be hurt less, perhaps not hurt at all. Also, it was most important not to wake the child.

Nanon became absent from herself, feeling no more than a muffled discomfort at his weight and his intrusion. She returned to the sticky folds of the bed, her nightgown rucked up above her breasts, Choufleur sprawling half across her.

"Enfin," he murmured in a breaking voice. "At last, at last . . ."

Salt water gathered in the hollows of her collarbones. She realized that Choufleur was weeping. This surprised her very much.

"I knew this time would come at last," Choufleur was saying. "I knew that we must come together. You have belonged to me, Nanon, from the beginning. Do you remember Vallière, the waterfall?"

Again, Nanon felt pricked with strangeness. She disengaged herself, but gently, sat up and pulled the sweaty wrinkles of the nightgown over her head. The breeze that ruffled the jalousies dried the sweat and tear stains on her bare skin. At Vallière, where they were children, there had been a falls, a small one, with a little grotto hollowed in the rock behind where the children played, and perhaps she did remember what Choufleur was now describing, how she stepped through the falling water from the cave into the light, revealing herself to him in her soaked chemise, her upturned face and waist-length hair sparkling with the water and the sunshine. *It was not that I first loved you then,* Choufleur was urgently whispering, *but then I first knew how I had always loved you . . .*

In spite of herself, Nanon was interested. She could indeed remember that green glade, the wet stone smell of the shallow cave behind the falls, the froth of the water falling through bright air. She had been, perhaps, thirteen; it was before the Sieur Maltrot had come to take her, to take her away, though probably not very long before. That younger self seemed to stand across a chasm from her now. Across the room, she saw that Paul slept calmly, undisturbed by anything that had happened so far. Choufleur's moistened fingertip circled her breast, and she felt the nipple swell and stiffen. The tingle of sensation expanded till its ripples rocked the weird emotion she was feeling too. She relaxed against her pillow and turned toward him and found his root, molding it with her thumb and fingers, or lightly teasing it with the nails, until it became its larger self. Best not to use the full extent of her professional expertise, she thought, for that would offend him . . . but this time there would be pleasure, and she would be present for the act.

"Do you still have it?" Choufleur said as she swung astride. "Give it me."

Nanon reached the silver snuffbox down from a bibelot shelf above the bed. Choufleur took it into his loose fingers, rocked and arched into her deeply.

"Ah . . ." he groaned. "I knew you'd know . . . I knew you'd keep it near . . ." He tightened his fist around the box, then dug his knuckles into the very small of her back. This was a seasoning of horror, Nanon knew, as a thread of nausea swirled into the vortex of sensation that sucked her deeper down, but it was very piquant, all the same.

Later, drifting in the afterglow, she revisited that other life across the chasm, and saw once more the girl she'd been at Vallière, before she'd been made a *fille de joie* at Cap Français. There was a trove of memories to match anything Choufleur had stored from those days, though it was a long time since she had opened the coffer where they were kept. She experienced them now almost as dreams: wistful, wishful, and finally distressing enough to keep her from real sleep. As she twisted and tossed for a resting place, her elbow knocked against the snuffbox, which reminded her that Choufleur, along with herself, had turned into something very much other than what they once might have been. He slept grimly beside her now, face down and unmoving, as if he were dead. But the moon had set, and the rising wind brought a damp breath of dawn. Nanon shook him by the shoulder, once, twice, until he grumbled.

"It's nearly morning," she hissed at him. "You must go."

"Hanh?" Choufleur muttered. "Let them discover us . . . What does it matter if they know?" He turned onto his back and flung his arm across his eyes.

"Not *now*." Nanon shook him again. "Not yet. Go now."

Choufleur sat up abruptly, swinging his feet to the floor, giving his head a sharp shake, left and right. He swiveled toward her fluidly, wrapped his hands around the back of her neck and the base of her skull, and drew her half-falling across the bed, into a long, deep kiss. With the release, he spoke, rather curtly. "You'll come with me. Tomorrow, to the north."

Nanon said what she had planned to say. "I will not leave my child."

His hesitation was informative. A moment of silence passed, then he stood up, paced to the door, turned back toward her.

"Then we will take him. Very well."

Nanon said nothing. A little blue light filtered into the room, so that she made out his silhouette but not his face. She heard Paul breathing in his cot.

"And if you remain here with him, what?" Choufleur's laugh was dry as ash. "He will live as the bastard son of a *blanc*."

Nanon, sitting upright with her hips swathed in a tangle of sheet, put her palms over her breasts and lowered her head. She did not know how much of this posture he could discern in the dim light.

"Believe me," Choufleur said, now with a pleading note, almost. "Come with me now, and we will wipe away everything that has been before."

Still she would not look at him. "How am I to know what to believe?"

"Make ready," Choufleur said, decidedly. "We leave tomorrow, before dawn." He moved to the door. She felt a change of air as it opened and shut, but he made no sound at all in going out.

Elise arose at her usual hour, dressed, ordered coffee, and awaited developments. When she heard Paul's voice, she put her head into the corridor and saw Nanon, groggy, her face puffed up with sleep, handing the boy over to Zabeth before falling back into her bedchamber. *Une nuit de délices*, Elise imagined, feeling herself well satisfied. She breakfasted with Sophie and Paul. Tocquet and Choufleur had already gone out, Choufleur pausing to make her an ornate little speech whose general drift had been that, owing to his carriage's need of some minor but time-consuming repair, he hoped to lay claim to her magnificent hospitality for one more night.

She passed the morning in the supervision of one household task or another, unable fully to fix her mind on any of these. Nanon did not appear till afternoon, floating dreamily onto the gallery as Tocquet and Elise were finishing a modest lunch of cold chicken and fruit. The day was still and suffocatingly hot, the sun swollen at the height of its arc. Pushing his plate away, Tocquet wiped his forehead and grimaced, then went to lie down till the heat should abate. Elise remained at the table, watching Nanon sip grapefruit juice. The colored woman did not seem to look at her, though perhaps she was spying, through her long black lashes.

"And how did you enjoy our Colonel Maltrot?" Elise said suddenly.

Carefully chosen, her words seemed effective. Nanon looked up involuntarily, her eyes widening for an instant before she regained her composure. Then her eyelids lowered, slowly. She did not speak.

"I find him interesting," Elise went on. "It's plain he is an educated man. Of talent, possibly, and certainly of strong will. Does he not look splendid in his uniform? One supposes also that he must be a man of means, judging from his manners, and the buttons on his coat."

"I did not suspect that *you* could admire such a man as he," Nanon said languidly.

Her emphasis was very slight, barely perceptible. That brown-syrup voice, her soft, brown, cow-like eyes . . . In a mad flash Elise wanted to rip the eyeballs from the other woman's skull . . . and yet she did not dislike Nanon. On the contrary, they had got on very well, more than amiably sometimes, during the months they had lived in this house together. There were moments, even hours at a stretch, when Elise had forgotten herself enough to fall into an easy intimacy with the colored woman. Nanon was intelligent, and well, if erratically, schooled in the arts of love and ways of men; she was naturally suited for the role of *cocotte*. Had the situation not been so clearly untenable, Elise would have preferred to keep her in the household.

"*Ma chère*," she began. Repressing a glance over her shoulder, toward the blinded window of the room where Tocquet had retired, she leaned across the table and trapped Nanon's hands in her own. "My dear, know that I think only of your welfare—of your future. Even if what I say seems cruel: with my brother you have none."

Nanon flinched and pulled away, but Elise clung to her hands and followed her, leaning in so near she scented the tang of sweat on the other woman's skin, and beneath it the faint perfume of sex.

"Of course, I don't know what he may have told you. He might promise anything, in his heat." Her voice was rising higher than she intended, and the lies came fully formed from her lips, without having ever entered her mind. "*Bon, sé youn cabrit li yé, konprann?* The man is a goat, my dear—imagine, such a one as he, a doctor and a brilliant scientist— why should he come out to this fire-blackened colony? Only that he had no choice, having left ruined girls and bastard offspring littered across half of France."

Nanon's hands went soft in Elise's grip. Not the least tension could be felt in her fingers, palms or wrists. All her body looked passively, vacantly relaxed, limp as fresh-killed meat. On other occasions, Elise had noticed this capacity of Nanon's to disappear within herself, and in an odd way she had envied it.

"As for the outcome of such relations in *this* country . . ." Elise gave the dead palms a little pressure. "*Ma chère.* I am sure you can bear witness much better than I."

Then she let go of Nanon's hands, and after studying her for a moment longer, adjusted herself against the chair back. Nanon's knuckles still lay against the surface of the table, her palms cupped together, as if she were trying to hold water. Her body was partly twisted away, so that Elise saw only the fall of her unbound hair, the smooth curve of her cheek, the shield-like corner where her wide lips pressed together. A carpenter bee hummed over the bougainvillea vines, working in and out of the hole it had drilled in the gallery rail. Elise waited a moment more, but as Nanon did not speak or shift or blink, she got up and went on about the business of her day.

That evening the four of them dined together as before, though conversation flowed less easily, since the military and political topics had been exhausted the previous night. Nanon remained subdued and withdrawn (Elise thought she avoided Choufleur's glances), and Tocquet had gone into one of his darkly silent moods, so he contributed little to the table talk. Choufleur, for his part, was more animated than when he'd first arrived, seeming exceptionally well pleased with himself and his visit to Habitation Thibodet. Elise rose to his repartee with all the vivacity she could muster. The effort left her weary, and on the verge of a headache.

Tocquet did not return from his postprandial cheroot, so Elise lay in their bed alone, skimming the surfaces of uneasy sleep. The man would pull away at times, go roving like a half-wild cat, and Elise had learned to tolerate that without complaint. Instinct told her, as much as experience, that Tocquet would not abide a clinging woman. But tonight his aloofness troubled her, and she was agitated by all the events of her day, and by her expectation.

When sleep did come, she slept leadenly, perspiring in the motionless air, and did not wake until late morning. Sophie's voice sounded on the gallery, breaking toward tears as she asked for Paul, and Elise heard Tocquet's voice murmuring some reply. His presence relieved her, at least temporarily, for sometimes the man might disappear for entire days or weeks, returning with gifts, most likely, but without explanation.

She collected herself and went out to the gallery. Tocquet held Sophie on his hip, supporting her back with one hand and brushing back dark curls from her face with the other.

"But when will he come *back*?" the child insisted.

Tocquet looked at her seriously, straight into her eyes, which resembled his own.

"He will not be coming back," Tocquet said. "He has gone away with his mother."

Sophie wailed, and pressed her damp face into the open throat of Tocquet's shirt. He patted her back, in rough rhythm with her sobs, and when she began to trail off into hiccups, he handed her over to Zabeth, who had been standing by. Frowning, he walked through the doorway into the house, passing Elise as if she were transparent and invisible.

Her heart contracted like a fist, went rigid and refused to relax. She knew instantly that he had heard all she'd said to Nanon, and that he judged her for it. A sick feeling swelled in the back of her throat. She followed him into the bedroom.

"But all I did I meant for the best . . ."

She could not keep that detestable whining tone from her own voice. Tocquet turned toward her, his belt knife naked in his hands. Elise knew well enough he had killed people with it. The knife never strayed more than a foot from his fingers, and sometimes its proximity had given her an illicit thrill. Now she felt only a miserable dullness when she looked at the grayed flat of the blade and the bright edge where it was honed.

Tocquet opened and tilted his hand and the knife poured from it, falling to lodge its point in a floorboard, its haft lightly trembling.

"Don't curse me," Elise said weakly.

"You'll curse yourself." He turned away from her, toward the mirror.

Elise's legs failed her. She sat down on the edge of the bed. She could not speak, or form a sentence in her mind. Tocquet squinted into the mirror, concentrating as he tied up his hair at the back with a leather thong. Then he swung round, scooped up the knife from the floor, and sheathed it under his shirt tail as he straightened.

"I will be going to Dajabón," he said, without looking at her, "to buy tobacco there."

He went out. Elise sank sideways onto the unmade bed, drawing her knees up toward her chin. Outside she heard his voice calling for Grosjean and Bazau. A chill pervaded her body and bones, though the day was swelteringly hot. She fingered the hem of the mussed top sheet, without the will to draw it over herself. From outside the house came the cries of birds, and presently the sound of hoofbeats as the three men rode away.

13

A rutted, muddy track ran toward Fort Dauphin and the Spanish border, across the coastal plain. Tocquet and his two retainers rode eastward. For the first several miles the road was screened by trees and shrubbery, wild bush or citrus hedges gone half wild, but then the undergrowth fell away, leaving a long unobscured view on either side. To the north, a flat, swampy, near-featureless plain stretched to the blue haze of ocean at the horizon line. Southward, the same flat land unrolled to the sudden steep eruption of the mountains of La Chaîne de Vallière.

With such wide, clear fields of view in all directions, they could have seen any sign of a threat long before it could reach them. At the same time, they could as easily be seen themselves, and there was nowhere for them to hide or flee. This point impressed itself on Tocquet without causing him any immediate discomfort, though he ordinarily preferred mountain country—terrain he well understood how to use to his advantage. But for the moment the plain was clear, deserted. All cultivation looked to have been abandoned, and although rumor had it, at Le Cap, that this whole area was roamed by large, fierce bands of insurgent blacks, there was no sign of any human presence, only a few horses and cattle grazing the plain between the road and the sea, the initials of their onetime owners carved in large, straggling characters across their flanks.

They rode without speaking, single file, the horses picking their way over trampled mud, among pools of brackish water on the roadbed. No sound but the creaking of saddle leather, or now and then the far-off calling of a crow. By midday it was very hot and bright and man-sweat mingled fragrantly with the sweat of the horses. From a cleft in the distant mountains came the sound of drumming, mallets rattling dry and sharp along the taut join of skin to wood; then the sound grew deeper, throatier, as the drummer worked toward the softer center of the head. Tocquet felt that Bazau and Gros-jean were lifting their attention to the drums, though he did not turn to look back at them. At such moments he became a creature of instinct, and as his hackles had not risen, he still felt safe enough.

They rode on without altering their pace; the drumming fell back out of earshot. Presently it grew cooler, as the afternoon rain cloud swept in from the sea to blot the sun. Tocquet squeezed his heels to his horse and urged their short column into a trot. Before the rain had begun in earnest, they were riding into the village of Trou de Nord.

The little town claimed but a single street: a few dozen houses built on either side of a curve in the road that continued across the river to Fort Dauphin. No sign of any white presence here, but the village was populous with blacks, and the arrival of Tocquet's party caused some small commotion. A market seemed to be just breaking up; in any case the moment had come for everyone to seek shelter from the rains; for the first fat drops were already pocking into the dust, and the wind had risen powerfully. Tocquet hailed an old man who had just scrambled up from under the hooves of his horse, and asked if he could purchase shelter for the night. The old man smiled with the two brown teeth left him, and spoke a muddy sentence too unclear to be understood. He took the bridle of Tocquet's horse and began leading it behind a house on the south side of the road. Bazau and Gros-jean came along on their own horses.

Behind the house was an open shed that served as stable. Toquet and his men tied their horses here and hurried toward the back door of the house. The rain unloosed everywhere in a rush, turning the packed earth of the yard to soup; Tocquet felt it lashing his shoulders, but his broad-brimmed hat kept his head dry.

The interior of the house was dim, musty. Some boards were broken in the raised plank floor. Against one of the walls stood a huge mahogany armoire, too heavy to be easily removed; one drawer was missing and the others were empty. There was a massive dining table of the same wood but no chairs, nor any other furniture. Pallets of straw and heaps of blankets were laid against the walls and in one corner a young woman sat nursing a newborn infant. The old man clucked and shooed at her and Tocquet saw he meant to drive her out into the rain.

"Kite'l resté," he said. Let her stay. He took out a silver coin and displayed it between thumb and forefinger; the old man looked at it dubiously, as if he did not comprehend what it might mean. It occurred to Tocquet that money might have fallen out of regular use in this region, now that all the *blancs* had fled. The girl looked at him round-eyed from her corner, covering the baby with the corner of a blanket.

"Can she cook?" Toquet asked.

The old man snatched the coin with a quick, flicking motion. *"M'pralé chaché vyé famn pou sa."* He darted out the front door, into the rain, paused and unfolded his hand to look at the coin, then went splashing on down the muddy road with his clenched fist tight against his thigh.

Bazau said something to the girl, who smiled shyly and lowered her eyes without speaking. Tocquet pulled off his muddy boots and walked sock-foot into the next room. There were only two rooms in the house, and this second smaller one held nothing but a bedstead with no slats or mattress. Off the rear was a lean-to kitchen. The roof was sound, at any rate. Tocquet went onto the gallery that fronted the road, where he sat down on a three-legged stool and took a cheroot from his pocket. He passed the cheroot under his nose, then put it in his mouth without lighting it. His supply was low. For the moment, he nibbled gently at the end of the cheroot; a fragrant tingle spread across his tongue. Gros-jean put his head out the door for a moment, and then withdrew into the interior again. Tocquet sat listening to the water streaming under the house, watching the wall of rainfall that dropped sheer from the edge of the gallery roof.

Presently the promised old woman arrived, carrying a loose cloth bag and a speckled hen under one arm. Tocquet showed her to the kitchen lean-to, where she set a fire beneath a huge iron kettle. With a practiced whirl of her wrist she snapped the head off the chicken and aimed the blood jet out into the rain. When the severed neck stopped spurting, she hung the chicken by its feet and went back to her cauldron.

Tocquet cleared his throat. *"Ki moun ki resté kouliyé-a nan Fort Dauphin, ou konnen sa?"*

"Sé Pagnol ki resté la." The woman grinned at him over her damp calico shoulder. It's the Spanish who are there.

Tocquet nodded. "Do they have black soldiers?"

"Yo gegne soldat noir anpil." The woman turned and faced him straight

on, holding a blackened wooden spoon in her left hand. "Also lots of French, they say. Lots of French have just come there in ships. *Anpil, anpil Fransé—grand blanc.*"

"*Vrai?*"

"*Yo di kon sa.*" The woman smiled. That's what they say. She turned, unfastened the bag and began pouring dry beans into the kettle.

Tocquet mused, unconsciously stroking the long ends of his mustache. He had heard in Le Cap that the Spanish occupied Fort Dauphin, and it was to be expected that most of their force should be black auxiliaries. Reportly most of Jean-François's men had fallen back into this area, after the clash with Toussaint. But the arrival of large numbers of Frenchmen in ships was a mystery . . . especially if these Frenchman belonged to the planter class—*grand blancs*, as the woman had said. Slave masters. He stooped toward the fire coals to light his cheroot, but then decided to restrain himself.

The rain had stopped by the time the food was ready, and it was a thick, velvety dark outside. As there were no chairs, they abandoned the table and sat on the floor with the plates on their knees. Urged by Bazau, the girl shared their food: chicken roasted on a spit and *maïs moulin*, a cornmeal mush mixed with red beans and seasoned with hot peppers. Tocquet produced a bottle of *clairin*, which he passed around the circle. The infant slept beside her in the drawer taken from the armoire, which had been lined with straw to serve as a cradle.

After eating, Tocquet went out with Bazau and Gros-jean. The two black men went into the town, while Tocquet strolled along the river bank. At last he made free to light his cheroot. It was clear and cool now, after the rain, and the sickle moon was sufficient to light his way. There were only a few mosquitoes, and the tobacco discouraged them.

By the time he had finished his smoke and returned to the house, the larger room had filled up with people, perhaps a dozen were camping there. In the smaller room, pallets were prepared for Tocquet and his men. He stretched out on the straw and dozed, rousing himself when Bazau and Gros-jean came in, considerably later. Their conversations had confirmed that the Spanish held Fort Dauphin with a large force of black soldiers under Jean-François. Rumors of a French presence in the town were generally persistent.

The old woman arrived to brew coffee for them just before dawn; they drank it standing and by first light were in the saddle. A high, eerie singing caught Tocquet's attention. He looked toward the mountains and saw a file of women coming down a path out of the morning; each balanced a basket of ripe red coffee beans on her head, and all of them were singing . . . So there was work still going on somewhere in the hills.

Tocquet clucked to his horse and rode toward the river. On the bank, they asked a woman washing clothes in the shallows where they might cross without swimming their horses. The river had gone down since the night before and came no higher than Tocquet's boot heel at the deepest point. They scrambled up a muddy bank on the eastern side, and rode on toward Fort Dauphin.

Now on either side of the road, spindly second-growth cane was coming back from the ashes of fields that had been burned. Some of it seemed to have been harvested, though in no very systematic manner. They rode on. Midmorning, the horizon ahead broke up and began to swarm. As they drew nearer, the spectacle resolved itself into a mass of men—the black auxiliaries. They had settled around an old fortified camp erected by a colonial governor on this plain. The works were a square of cabins connected by a palisade, but some years before the slave rebellion the camp had been abandoned by the whites and much of the wood had been pilfered for other constructions elsewhere. In any case there were far too many men here to be quartered within the old fortifications—they'd overflowed those boundaries and camped willy-nilly all around.

A party of black soldiers wandered down to the road to challenge them; from this encounter Tocquet confirmed that the auxiliaries were under the command of Jean-François. Though it was not long since he had traded guns to that black general, he did not choose to tarry now. There was an air of ill-discipline and disorder in all of this encampment— a far cry from Toussaint's camps around Ennery—and something in the feeling of the place made Tocquet's hackles prick. As one of the men who'd accosted them was a friend of Gros-jean, they were allowed to pass without hindrance or delay, and by afternoon they rode into the town of Fort Dauphin.

Tocquet left his horse with Gros-jean and Bazau, dispatching them to a tavern they knew. On foot, he entered the Place d'Armes, where a griz-zled, string-bearded Spanish officer was directing the movements of a few ratty troops with a broken umbrella. The men were all Spaniards of the Regiment de Contabre—no sign of the black auxiliaries here. On the road Tocquet had heard, from a friend of Gros-jean, that the men commanded by Jean-François were forbidden to enter the city.

He made a leftward circuit of the square, glancing into the church and the Maison du Roi. Although the Spanish seemed to be in posses-sion of all the official buildings, there were also many Frenchmen wan-dering in the square, dressed in the manner of *grand blancs*—expensive costumes, which, however, showed signs of harder, longer wear than intended. Some of these Frenchmen were promenading their wives, and others also had children in tow. Tocquet, who kept his hat brim low, saw no one he knew personally.

At last he came to the fountain at the center of the square and sat down on the edge of the basin. He trailed his fingers in the water, then removed his hat and dampened his temples. It was very hot, and his hair was stiff with sweat and the dust of the road; the streets of Fort Dauphin were all unpaved. He soaked a kerchief in the water, rolled it and wrapped it around his neck, before he replaced his hat. When the drilling soldiers next about-faced, he was able to catch the eye of the man he'd hoped to find—a supply sergeant named Guillermo Altamira. As soon as the drill ended and the men were dismissed, the sergeant tugged off his cap and came to join Tocquet at the fountain.

Altamira was a short, stout man, with smooth round cheeks and an olive complexion, his face bordered by glossy curls of hair and beard. Tocquet had always known him to be well informed, well supplied, and cheerfully enterprising. In the first days of the slave insurrection, the sergeant had sold him the guns he ran over the mountains to the black insurgents on the French side. As this project had certainly been sanctioned and encouraged by the Spanish high command, Tocquet felt that Altamira was better connected in the military hierarchy than his modest rank might betray. But for the moment he was only interested in cigars. He put his questions in Spanish, the language he always used with Altamira, though he was confident the sergeant also spoke French. The sergeant told him that none were to be found, but he could furnish a packload of cured leaf tobacco, and no later than the next morning.

"Let's drink to it, then," Tocquet said, readjusting his hat as he rose from the basin. The wind was rising and the sky had darkened and everyone was scattering out of the square to avoid the afternoon downpour. Tocquet and the sergeant hastened to a tavern two streets away, where Tocquet had told his men to take a room; however, their names were unknown when he asked at the door, and all the rooms were already full. Nonetheless, they went in and took a table. A black servant brought them rum and water flavored with lemon.

Outside, there was a crash of thunder, and the rain came down in sheets. A party of damp Frenchmen entered; the last of these turned back to shut the door behind him. Tocquet clicked glasses with the sergeant, they drank, leaned back, and sighed.

"Who're all these French who've filled the town?" Tocquet said. "They tell me here there are no rooms to let at all."

"Royalists," the sergeant said. "Landowners of the northern plain, so

I've been told. Come to seize back their property from the godless Jacobins—with the aid of the Spanish crown."

"How very interesting." Tocquet laughed shortly. "Who commands here?"

"Why, in principle it is Don García himself," said Altamira, "but just now, during his absence on campaign, the commander is Don Cassasola."

Tocquet camouflaged a smile by wiping the back of his hand over his mustache. Don Cassasola was that decrepit specimen who'd been drilling the troops with the umbrella. The door opened and he glanced over. Bazau came in from the rain and Tocquet hailed him. The news was the same, no room to be had anywhere.

"And the horses?"

Bazau cut his hand toward the floor and smiled; from this Tocquet understood that Gros-jean had managed to shelter the horses and saddles somewhere, somehow, for the duration of the rain. He nodded. Bazau strolled to the counter and began talking to one of the serving girls there.

"I myself am quartered at the citadel," the sergeant said, "where if you wish we might find you something . . ."

Tocquet shook his head, reaching automatically to pinch a mosquito that had just settled on his throat. He was not inclined to pass the night in a Spanish barracks.

"Or some of our officers, those who came here with their ladies, have taken houses in the Rue Bourdon," the sergeant said. "Perhaps if you find an acquaintance, you might ask for hospitality."

"Possibly," Tocquet said. "It's useful to know. In any case, I'll manage something."

The sergeant leaned closer to him. "Don't stay here long," he said, his tone carefully low. "Despite your manner of dress, you may be taken for French, and then—"

Tocquet glanced at him sharply, but Altamira had leaned back and was pouring himself a short measure of rum.

"I can have the tobacco loaded for you—tomorrow by the church, before morning mass. The load and the mule to carry as we said, and in time for you to make an early departure." He drained his glass. His olive face went blank as he stood up.

Tocquet passed him a gold piece: earnest money. "Till tomorrow then, and thanks," he said. The sergeant winked as he took the coin, but the rest of his face was grave, unsmiling.

As Altamira went out, Gros-jean came in. Through the door's gap Tocquet saw the rain was heavy as ever. He beckoned Gros-jean to sit at his table, offered him rum, then looked for Bazau, but he was still gossiping with the girl at the counter. Just to the left of them was a door that apparently led to the rented rooms, for sometimes a French lodger came in or out by that passage. In confidence that tomorrow he could restock his supply, Tocquet produced one of his cheroots and lit it straightaway. A mosquito bit the back of his hand as he did so. He crushed it, exhaling smoke and raising his eyebrows at Gros-jean.

From that rear doorway a figure emerged, a gaunt Frenchwoman who moved with a weird stateliness, as if she were crossing the hall of a church instead of a crowded, noisy tavern. Her head was uncovered, her hair tied tightly back, and her deep-set eyes were fixed on something no one else could see. Tocquet felt a twinge of familiarity which he could not quite place. The room grew quieter as she passed, and men scraped and shifted their chairs and attention, not for her beauty, for she was a harsh-looking woman, but for her strange intensity.

She stopped at a table in the center of the room and inclined her head toward a man seated there. A Frenchman, graying at the temples, wearing a *redingote* which had been at the height of colonial fashion perhaps three years previously. They conferred for a moment, then the woman withdrew, making a ghostly passage back toward the same corridor from which she'd appeared.

Tocquet returned his glance to the man she'd spoken to and felt again on the edge of recognition. A *grand blanc* of fallen fortunes, evidently. The striped coat was patched at the elbows, the left boot sole pulling loose from its upper . . . A curiously twisted cane leaned against his thigh, and his manner of toying with the pommel also said something to Tocquet. The other must have felt his regard, for he looked directly at Toquet with his dark eyes, a purse of his small, rather feminine mouth.

"Arnaud!" Tocquet got up and met the other man halfway. They clasped each other warmly by the arms, surprisingly, for they had never been close friends. The surprise of unexpected meetings could make for uninttended intimacies. Tocquet joined the other at his table. It was indeed Michel Arnaud, though thinner, and gone a little gray.

"I took you for a Spaniard, Xavier," Arnaud said. "But then, I took you for a Spaniard when we last met. But—have you dined?"

Tocquet glanced toward the door, which was closed, but he could hear the roar of the rain well enough on the roof; it would certainly rain for at least another hour. "Not yet," he said, "and I may as well, if you invite me."

"Of course," Arnaud said, and called to the servants to bring another plate.

Tocquet experienced a moment of awkwardness. To invite Gros-jean and Bazau to sit at table with such a man would cause more trouble than it was worth. He called across the room to them.

"Mezami!—alé manjé." The table where he'd sat with Altamira was now empty—he indicated this to the two blacks.

"Those are the same two men you had in the mountains then, no?" Arnaud asked.

"Yes," said Tocquet, mildly surprised. To a man like Arnaud one nigger would scarcely be distinguishable from another, he'd thought.

"They're faithful to you, then," Arnaud remarked. "While all of ours betray us utterly . . ." He waved a hand around the room, then let it fall back limply to the pommel of his cane.

Tocquet drew on his cheroot and unconsciously crushed another mosquito on his cheek, reviewing the many qualities he had disliked in Arnaud. His weakness for luxurious self-indulgence of all kinds, which was spread over him like a coating of butter . . . lubricating an inner frame of cruelty. His arrogance, his brutal cruelty with his slaves, his wanton wastefulness of life whether human or animal. His mistreatment of his wife . . . On the credit side, Arnaud was a fine horseman, he spoke his mind plainly and held to his decisions, and unlike many cruel men, he did not seem to be a coward. Though one might say his taste for danger was like his taste for wine.

"Was that Claudine who spoke to you just now?" Tocquet said.

"Yes." Arnaud's face shaded. "She is very much changed, as you see."

Tocquet said nothing. He had last seen Claudine Arnaud perhaps five years previously, but in that time she appeared to have aged twenty.

The serving girl arrived with a platter of pork slices, rice and beans, sliced peppers and onions. Arnaud served a plate and passed it to Tocquet, then gave himself a somewhat smaller serving.

"You've come a long road since we last met," Tocquet said.

Arnaud seemed to look through him. Truly, his face had changed. Where formerly it had been almost piggishly smooth, it was now carved into hollows in his cheeks, around his eyes. Some callow layer had been burned away; Tocquet wondered what might reveal itself beneath. He had last seen Arnaud in 1791, on the eve of the first slave rebellion in the north—it was quite likely that Arnaud would have blundered into that upheaval, returning across the Spanish border with a pack train of guns Tocquet had delivered to him. That had been Tocquet's first entry into the business of weapons supply.

"Yes." Arnaud cut a small bite of pork and tasted it, appearing to swallow with some difficulty. He took some wine and laid down his fork. "When I left you I fell into the hands of Candy, that mulatto general of whom you will have heard; he would certainly have killed me, after tortures such as I saw him visit upon other planters of that province, but I escaped with the help of a *prêtre savane*."

Arnaud crossed himself and closed his eyes for a moment. Flabbergasted at this gesture, Tocquet turned his attention to his plate.

"Afterward . . ." Arnaud resumed. "The plain was afire from one end to the other. My *habitation* was completely destroyed. Everything. And brigands roaming everywhere. I took to hiding in the hills for I don't know how long, until at last I met with a patrol which brought me to Le Cap."

"And Madame Arnaud, during your absence?"

"By whatever fortune she was visiting friends at Habitation Flaville, when the slaves attacked—it was one of the first. The men were killed but the women made their way to Le Cap in the end. Claudine was not so very much hurt in body, but in mind . . . for more than a year she seemed to have gone quite mad." He looked up. "Since we've left the colony, she has seemed to do better."

"How came you here, then?" Tocquet asked.

"Why, the Spanish have been circulating a broadside in Baltimore and Philadelphia and New York. They invited all the fugitive landowners of Saint Domingue to return to fight for the reclamation of their properties, under the Spanish flag." Arnaud shook his head. "If it means fighting Frenchmen, well, they are bloody regicide Jacobins—nor am I in any position to refuse. You understand, we sailed with the fleet when Le Cap was burned. I waded to a boat with my wife in my arms and nothing else but the clothes I was wearing." He plucked the frayed fabric of his *redingote*. "As you see. I came to Baltimore a pauper. Afterward we tried New York, but I found nothing for myself there either. Claudine was taken up by some holy sisters who instructed her as a nurse. She did so by the recommendation of that same *prêtre savane*, who had become her confessor in Le Cap and tried to help her in her madness . . ."

"He sounds an interesting fellow, this priest. Where is he now?"

"He was executed at Le Cap, for the crimes of another. I myself was present there, but could do nothing, though I knew him innocent. I pray for him now, Xavier, though I have small skill at prayer. The name he gave was Père Bonne-chance."

"Why, I knew that priest!—he had a little church near Ouanaminthe, by the Rivière Massacre. And I saw him later in the camps of the blacks . . . yes, it must be the same. He had a woman too, I think."

Arnaud nodded. "A *quarterrone* woman and a string of children, *sang-mêlés*. I would do something for those children now if I could find them—if I had anything to give."

Tocquet stroked his mustache. Arnaud was known to have sold his own half-breed children off his plantation simply to be rid of the sight of them. But that had been some time ago. Tocquet took a last bite of pork and pushed his plate back. "A decent fellow for a priest, I always thought," he said. "He had a sense of humor—seemed to. I didn't know him well."

"If God has any justice, he has no need of my prayers," Arnaud said. He crossed himself again, then cleared his throat. "Well, to finish my own story, I have been living in the North American Republic on charity and the labor of my wife—you may imagine. I have no better hope than to try to recover my resources here. And for yourself?"

"Oh, I could not rival such adventures," Tocquet said. "I've scrambled along as best I might—mostly over the border." In fact he had made handsome sums of money running guns into the camps of the insurgent slaves in the mountains, but Arnaud was unlikely to be pleased to hear this tale, and in any case Tocquet was close-mouthed about his business, as a matter of principle. "But tell me, how does it go since you've come here?"

Arnaud shrugged. "We're rusticating . . . and I'll confess to some impatience." He leaned across his mostly untouched plate, lowering his tone. "I would not like to say distrust. But I do not see any sign of an active campaign on the part of these Spaniards. They took care to disarm us when we arrived here—even to our knives!—on the pretext we would be issued regulation muskets later, but nothing of that kind has come about. We sit idly here while our stores dwindle. Don García gives us nothing but evasions. Meanwhile, a mob of *our renegade slaves* is encamped not a full day's march from here, I'm told, and all in Spanish uniform."

"True," Tocquet said thoughtfully, and crushed another mosquito on his forearm.

"So we wait," Arnaud said. "We wait, and we wonder."

Tocquet nodded. The warning he'd had from Altamira seemed too indefinite to pass on. In former days he would not have much troubled himself about what might happen to Arnaud for good or ill, though he'd always felt some sympathy for his wife—a pretty, brittle girl who'd come out from France completely unprepared for what she might find in the colony. Certainly she was no longer that. When she'd crossed the room a few moments before, she'd had the air of moving among a company invisible to all but her. Tocquet shook his hair back briskly, to rid himself of the thought.

They finished the meal in a thoughtful silence. Arnaud ate little, though he finished the clay pitcher of wine. Tocquet ate slowly, chewed thoroughly, and left nothing. When they were done he paid for both of them, over Arnaud's mild protest.

"Do you stop here for the night?"

"No rooms to be had," Tocquet said.

Arnaud nodded. "It's crowded here—there must be a thousand who've lately returned from North America, if you count the families with the men. We might find room for you with us, but for your men . . ."

"No matter," Tocquet said. He slapped another mosquito and grimaced at the splash of blood it left on the loose weave of his shirtsleeve. "Those gentlemen know how to manage—they'll find something for us all."

It proved that Bazau had already learned where to go from talking to the servants at the inn. When the rain had stopped, they found the horses and rode out from the eastern limits of the town, more or less in the direction of the Spanish frontier. In half an hour's time they were mounting a trail that wound up into the foothills. After the rain, the air was fresh, and cooler as they climbed, and the sky was perfectly clear, with a trail of stars hanging from the hook of the moon. A light breeze combing over the hills swept all the mosquitoes away. They passed through an old planting of coffee trees, neglected now and overgrown with vines, and soon a couple of dogs began to bark. They stopped; Gros-jean got down from his horse and waited. Presently someone challenged them from the shadows of the trees, and Gros-jean answered in a soft voice. Tocquet, who had also dismounted and stood mostly concealed by the shoulder of his horse, passed forward a coin from his purse. After a few minutes of negotiation, the dogs were quieted and taken away, and someone led them to a clay-walled *case* by the side of a still spring-fed pool.

They spread blankets on the dirt floor, and the two black men lay down at once, but Tocquet went out to smoke a cheroot by the wall of the *case*. Starlight spread on the quiet surface of the pool, and there was light enough for him to see other cabins in the trees beyond it. He knew the region well enough, but this *bitasyon* was newly sprung up, since the insurrection.

The insects of the forest erected a wall of sound on every side, but still there were no mosquitoes. When he was half done with his cheroot, he noticed a couple of women who had come to watch him quietly from the far side of the water, but they exchanged no word. Once the cigar was done, he went inside, stretched out on the blanket and slept until dawn without dreaming.

*   *   *

At first light the three of them rolled their blankets and rode out on the same path by which they'd entered. As they crossed a clearing, they were hailed by an old woman who was grinding coffee in a hollowed stump, using a wooden pestle taller than herself, but Tocquet did not want to wait for the coffee to be brewed, so they rode on without stopping. The sun was just risen when they came out on the brow of a hill above the town, where the view was clear all the way to the shallow jug-shaped harbor. Along the western road they saw the whole black army of Jean-François, flanked by horsemen, marching into the town.

By the time Tocquet and his men came to the church, Jean-François's black soldiery had filled the Place d'Armes. A thin line of Spanish troops stood before the church steps where they exchanged salutes with the black auxiliaries. As the men stood at ease, Tocquet rounded the church, and found Altamira waiting on the street behind it, holding a donkey loaded with two small bales of tobacco. The bales were strapped to a triangular wooden pack frame and covered with a blanket. Tocquet reached under the cover to crumble some leaf; he raised his palm to his face and sniffed, then nodded.

Altamira did not want to meet his eyes. He accepted the money they'd agreed on, and pointed farther along the street.

"Go that way," he said, "and turn to the right—you can reach the main road without crossing the square." Without waiting for an answer, he disappeared around the corner of the church.

They mounted again and went the way Altamira had indicated, Gros-jean leading the donkey ahead of the other two. At the next corner they turned and were soon crossing another street which led back again to the square. A number of the recently arrived French were walking to morning mass and among them Tocquet saw Arnaud, striding with a hint of his former arrogance and swinging the twisted cane lightly from his left hand. At his side, Claudine went gliding, her hands folded before her and her eyes fixed on some faraway horizon. She wore a white cambric dress with red embroidery like threads of blood; the hem of the dress trailed in the dust of the unpaved street, but she seemed completely unconscious of that. She walked in the same manner as she'd crossed the tavern floor yesterday—as if she were going to her execution amidst a mob of invisible mockers.

Neither of them had noticed Tocquet, and he did not call to greet them. When the Arnauds had passed, he and his two men went on toward the western road, but before they had reached the next corner, Tocquet pulled his horse up sharply.

"No, not this way," he said to Gros-jean. "Go to the hill where we were this morning and wait there till we come."

Gros-jean changed course without a word or hint of curiosity about the new direction. Tocquet motioned to Bazau, and the two of them rode back at a trot toward the Place d'Armes.

They did not overtake Arnaud and his wife. Tocquet imagined the couple must have gone into the church, because they were not to be seen among the other newly arrived French who stood around the edges of the square, peering uneasily at the black soldiers assembled in the center. Tocquet dismounted and led his horse to the foot of the church steps, where he handed his reins to Bazau. Before the doors of the church he turned and looked back over the square. No sign of anything untoward: the black men were quiet, and held their muskets carelessly, but there was something in their stillness that made the hair rise on Tocquet's arms and the back of his neck, and brought the taste of iron into his gullet.

He went into the church and stood in the rear, among a loose group of Spaniards loitering there, both soldiers and civilians. No one took notice of him, except Altamira, who simply shook his head, then turned his back. The service was already ending; a pair of horns sounded the recessional. The group around the doorway parted for the cross to pass, followed by the huge brass-bound Bible, held high by an acolyte. Next came the priest, Vasquez, huffing and wheezing under the bulk of his embroidered vestments, and after him the Spanish Colonel Montalvo, and finally Jean-François, resplendent in a dress uniform whose breast was jumbled with military decorations, ribbons and sacred medals. Once these had passed, the recession became general. Arnaud caught sight of Tocquet and began speaking to him, but Tocquet was too distracted to hear; he took hold of the other's sleeve and drew him out the doorway of the church. Claudine floated a pace ahead of them.

At the passage of Vasquez, Tocquet's skin had broken out in gooseflesh, though he did not know why. He knew Father Vasquez was vicar general to the troops of Santo Domingo and he also knew, from the many months he'd run guns to the black camps, that Vasquez had become the personal confessor of Jean-François. The presence of Montalvo also seemed to signal something, for he was a very different stamp of soldier than the enfeebled, indecisive Cassasola.

The cross bearer stopped halfway down the church steps. Jean-François and Vasquez stood beside him—to their right, the acolyte held the Holy Writ high. Montalvo gave an order and the Spanish troops below the steps separated into two wings and regrouped at the corners of the church, making way for Jean-François's standard bearers to come forward. Wheezily, but loudly enough to be heard in the square, Vasquez gave a full ceremonial blessing to the flags. Then he turned to Jean-François and said in a slightly lower tone, *Exterminez ces athées, mon fils, ces régicides, ces hébreux.*

Jean-François raised his plumed, argile helmet in both hands and settled it carefully on his head. He jerked his uniform coat straight by the tails, then raised his right palm over his men: the black troops straightened and lifted their guns. Jean-François gave a deep, explosive shout in Creole:

Touyé-yo kon kochon!

As he spoke his hand closed; the fist dropped like an iron hammer.

At first Arnaud could not grasp what had been said: the words entered his ears, but without their intelligence. First Vasquez: Exterminate these atheists, my son, these regicides, these Hebrews. Then Jean-François: Slaughter them like hogs! When the black general's hand fell, the whole Place d'Armes convulsed, and finally Arnaud understood what had been meant—what he'd feared since the Spanish had disarmed the members of his own party. He jerked involuntarily free of Tocquet's grip on his arm, then stilled himself and reached behind him for his wife's elbow, drawing her a step down to stand between him and Tocquet. Her head was high, chin forward, eyes surveying the scene below. If the spectacle impressed her, she did not show it. The black soldiers had exploded in all directions to kill the French who surrounded the square. They worked at first in a ghastly silence, butchering with bayonets and *coutelas* and musket stocks exactly as Jean-François had ordered (since their victims were unarmed, they could conserve their ammunition), but soon enough the air was torn with screaming, and grew thick with the fragrance of fresh blood.

Where they stood was an island of calm on the steps, directly behind the priest, cross, and Bible. Montalvo was already gone, and the Spanish troops were quietly withdrawing, filing into the alleys at either side of the church. As they retreated, the blacks began swarming up the steps to drag French men and women out of the church, slashing their throats or disemboweling them with bayonets. Just inside the narthex two women were being vigorously raped, their cries muffled by long skirts flung up over their heads.

Tocquet caught Arnaud's eye and jerked his head. With Claudine between them, they moved cautiously down the steps. At the foot, where the last of the Spanish troops were unwinding into the column of retreat, one of Tocquet's men stood holding two horses, his face impassive, apparently calm. Tocquet helped Arnaud boost Claudine onto the nearest horse; she sat sidesaddle, fingers of one hand twined loosely in the mane.

"*Doucement*," Tocquet said to Arnaud. "Don't hurry, don't show fear, and don't look directly at anything you see."

Slowly they moved behind the retreating Spanish column, down the alley beside the church. Arnaud walked beside his wife to steady her in the saddle. Bazau led the riderless horse ahead and Tocquet strolled beside him, his Spanish cattleman's hat pulled low over his eyes.

The Spanish column turned sharply to the left, marching down toward the harbor and its forts. Arnaud's every instinct summoned him to follow, but Tocquet shook his head. "They'll leave us locked outside the gate," he said. "Come on, this way."

There was gunfire now, sporadically audible from the square behind them, along with war cries of the blacks and screams of the slaughtered. Arnaud could not make out if these sounds were coming nearer. Then a hideous, desperate shriek erupted immediately behind him, as if from the ground over which he'd just passed. He made to look over his shoulder but stopped himself before he'd seen anything. He fastened his gaze on a sweat stain at the back of Tocquet's shirt. The ululating cry was suddenly cut off by a thunk and crunch, an exhalation. In its aftermath Arnaud thought he heard the sound of someone weeping. Claudine twisted her torso in the saddle and looked back at whatever was there to see, her eyes arid and crystalline, like two chips of salt. Arnaud's intestines went into a gelid knot. What Tocquet had said now seemed to Arnaud an article of faith—to look in the wrong direction meant certain death. He dug his fingers into his wife's thigh until she reacted and turned forward again.

They swung into the Rue Bourdon. It was calm here, no sign of any disturbance yet; there was even birdsong from the enclosed arbors around the houses. A man in the uniform of a Spanish lieutenant stood in the arched doorway of an eight-foot-high stone wall, looking in their direction. Tocquet approached him but in no great haste. The lieutenant made to shut the door, but Tocquet said something to him in Spanish. Arnaud made out only the phrase *por favor*, but spoken without urgency or pleading. Tocquet and the Spaniard conferred in the doorway, their voices low. Arnaud began helping Claudine down from her horse. At the far end of the street a mob of howling blood-stained blacks appeared. Arnaud's guts twisted again. He would not look at them.

He stared at the back of Tocquet's shirt, and over his shoulder saw the Spaniard shaking his head *no* (this word distinctly audible); he started to close the door again, but suddenly his whole manner changed.

He laid a friendly hand over Tocquet's shoulder, and his expression softened, slackened. The door swung inward and Tocquet crossed the
threshold, seeming to support the Spaniard, who leaned into him as if
overcome with dizziness or heatstroke . . . Arnaud led Claudine through
the doorway. He was watching the Spaniard's face over Tocquet's shoulder, the mouth open in a round of surprise. A little blood ran out from
the corners, then Tocquet disengaged himself and Arnaud saw that his
right sleeve was blood-soaked to the elbow, and then he saw the foot-
long dirk in his right hand. The Spaniard knelt, then stretched out face
down on the flagstones of the paved enclosure.

Around the edges of the wall were planted hibiscus and other flowering shrubs; there was even a fountain whose stream tinkled through a
couple of broken red-clay jugs. A cool shaded gallery ran lengthwise
toward the corner of the house's ell, where now a door popped open:
another Spanish officer came out, calling hoarsely and moving half at a
run. Tocquet had his back turned, closing the door, saying something to
Bazau, who still stood outside holding the horses, through a small iron
grille through which the black man's profile could be seen. Arnaud was
unable to react at first, though he took in that the Spaniard held a pistol.
Claudine confronted him, pulling herself up; her bones protruded
whitely from her face and her hands twitched on her dress front, as if
she meant to draw some terrible weapon out of herself . . . an instrument of complete annihilation. In the instant that the Spanish officer hesitated before her, Arnaud came unbound from whatever spell
held him and swung his cane as hard as he could at the back of the
Spaniard's head. The cane rebounded with a jolt that numbed his
palms, and the Spaniard fell forward, unconscious if not dead. His pistol went skittering across the flagstones.

Turning from the door, Tocquet looked at Arnaud and nodded solemnly.
A shrill, high scream came from the gallery, and Arnaud looked to see a
young woman standing with her fingers mashed tight across her lips,
supported by a black-clad duenna standing behind her. Tocquet grimaced at the bloody dirk still in his hand, then tucked it away under his
loose shirttail. With a bound he was on the gallery, holding the younger
woman by her hair, twisting it hard at the nape of the neck so that her
head rolled backward and her mouth opened soundlessly.

"Take the keys." Tocquet gestured with his chin; Arnaud lifted the
key ring from the duenna's belt. Together they herded the women into
the house. It was dim, disorienting at first, but Tocquet moved surely
through one room to the next and stopped at a pantry door. Arnaud tried
one key after another; it was the fourth that fit. The pantry was deep,

stone walls lined with shelves. Tocquet flung the women in and closed the door, then reopened it halfway.

"Take off your dress," he said.

The duenna spat at him, and in almost the same instant Tocquet had slapped her back against the wall. "I want the *dress*," he snapped. "No one means to attack your virtue." He banged the door shut and locked it with the key.

Two black servants, a man and woman in middle age, knelt in the corridor, their hands raised in attitudes of supplication. Arnaud ignored them, and went back out into the courtyard, where Claudine stood motionless between the two prone bodies, staring at the trickle of the fountain. There was a commotion outside the door, where the black marauders seemed to be interrogating Bazau.

"Were those French who came in here?"

"*Non, pa sa,*" Bazau said, disinterestedly. "They are Spanish."

Ice in his blood, Arnaud moved to a position where he could not be seen from the grille in the door. A black hand appeared at the top of the wall, groped, then yanked sharply away. The wall was crowned with broken bottles set in the masonry. Tocquet came hastily out of the house, calling to Bazau in Spanish to stop gossiping and bring the horses around to the back at once. A silence, then they heard the black mob moving onto the next house.

Tocquet opened another door in the rear of the wall, which led into a larger enclosure, with a kitchen garden and two stalls with a horse in each. Beside the stalls was a wider gate and Tocquet opened this to admit Bazau and the horses; as he did so, the two black servants bolted from the house, shot past him and escaped into the alley. Tocquet cursed, then bolted the gate.

"Saddle up," he said to Bazau, pointing to the horses in the stalls.

In the arbor, Arnaud was startled by a grunt and moan behind him. He turned to see the Spaniard he'd stunned with the cane pushing up to all fours, then sitting back woozily on his heels, gingerly palming the back of his head. Tocquet moved toward him deliberately, lifting his shirttail to draw a small pistol. The Spaniard's eyes cut to his own weapon, which lay on the flagstones a few feet from him, but Arnaud moved quickly to pick it up.

"Why?" Tocquet said. "I would like to know why . . . all this butchery and betrayal."

"I don't know," the Spaniard said.

Tocquet took a step closer, clicking back the hammer of his pistol.

"Jean-François took alarm at the return of the French slave masters," the Spaniard said hastily. "He demanded the sack of the town, and Vasquez took his part with Don García, so . . ." He raised his hands palm outward, with a queasy smile. "It's appalling, of course, but as for myself—"

Arnaud shot him in the right temple; his head jerked to the side and he plumped over backward with his legs still twisted under him. Tocquet looked at Arnaud and then at the body, as if he would measure it, and then at Arnaud again.

"*Bien fait,*" he said. "Take his uniform."

Having said this, Tocquet stripped off his shirt, revealing the handle of the dirk and the butts of two pistols in the waistband of his trousers. He used the shirt to wipe blood from the knife blade and his right forearm. Then he stooped over the fountain and washed himself further, rinsed out the shirt and rolled it into a damp bundle. He drank a little water from his cupped palm and then splashed more on his face and hair.

Arnaud watched his ablutions, standing with the discharged pistol hanging at the length of his arm. From a nearby house, or from the street, a man's hoarse voice cried out twice; the third shout was abruptly cut off. Tocquet went to the man he had stabbed, tumbled him over onto his back, and with some awkwardness dragged off his uniform coat. Then he glanced up at Arnaud.

"*Anou alé, monchè,*" he said. Let's go.

Arnaud raised the spent pistol to his face and sniffed the powder smell of the barrel. "I never killed anyone before," he said.

Tocquet looked at him with pure disbelief, then smiled crookedly and shook his head. He began wiping blood from the Spanish coat with his wet shirt and, when he was satisfied, put it on. The sleeves were rather too short for him, but otherwise it fit well enough. He walked to Claudine, who still stood mute and unmoving between the two bodies, touched her respectfully on the elbow and piloted her into the house, as one might guide a blind person.

Arnaud crouched over the body of the man he had shot, laying the pistol to one side. He unfastened the uniform coat and pushed it down over the man's dead shoulders. It was a clumsy business getting the sleeves off the arms, for the corpse gave him no help at all; though entirely limp, it was much less cooperative than the body of a sleeper or a drunk would have been. But when at last he succeeded in freeing the coat, he was relieved to find that it was free of bloodstains. He put it on and did the buttons up the front. A chill passed over him, but then he felt steadier. He had never killed a *white man*—that was what he had meant. What did it mean to do away with a slave? Arnaud's labor gangs had been so cursed with sloth and rebellion that he had occasionally been forced to make an example (perhaps he could not number those occasions), or to eliminate a bad seed from his *atelier*. There were times when lesser punishments had inadvertently led to death, and also there were other times, when Arnaud was drunk and with his friends . . . well, but Tocquet had always had queer notions on such subjects.

Arnaud dismissed the thought. He took the Spaniard's belt and put it on, recharged the pistol and settled it into the holster. When that was done he felt much calmer, though he still did not like to look at the two bodies in their blood pools on the pavement. Bazau came to stand in the doorway to the rear enclosure, and Arnaud, following the direction of the black man's glance, saw a tiny hummingbird suspended before the trumpet blossom of a hibiscus flower.

Tocquet came out of the house, conducting Claudine, who now wore the duenna's black dress. Her hair was covered with a black shawl and a black veil concealed her face to the chin, so that Arnaud could only recognize her by the way she walked. She also wore a pair of black gloves, with the empty ring finger pinned back to the left palm, as was her custom.

Claudine's momentum expended itself and left her standing just under the corner of the overhanging gallery roof. Tocquet kept walking to Arnaud. He took out a flat wooden box and opened it to show.

"Smoke?"

The box was full of slim black Spanish cigars. Arnaud declined. Tocquet chose a cigar and bit the end off it.

"Steadies the nerves, I find." He lit his cigar and tucked the box into an inside pocket of the lieutenant's coat.

"We'd best be off," he said.

"Have you gone mad?" Arnaud hissed at him. "It's a slaughterhouse out there."

"*Faute de mieux.*" Tocquet exhaled smoke and smiled. "I don't think much of our chances here. If we aren't disemboweled by the blacks, we're quite likely be hanged by the Spanish—we *have* killed two of the bastards, you'll recall. And that pair of servants will certainly give us up, wherever they stop running."

Bazau had found a proper sidesaddle to strap on the Spanish mare—perhaps it belonged to the young woman who was now locked in the pantry of the house. Thus Claudine was more comfortably mounted; Tocquet took care to adjust her stirrups. She was a poor rider, but fortunately the mare seemed gentle and steady, and Arnaud and Tocquet rode close on either side of her, with Bazau bringing up their rear.

Once they had turned off the Rue Bourdon, they passed a block strewn with bodies of men and women and children of all ages. On the next block they overtook a party of black men loading corpses on a cart—a man with epaulettes on his coat was collecting money and watches and rings in a sack. The general slaughter in the streets seemed to be finished, but the blacks were still breaking into the houses to ferret the French survivors from their hiding places. There was no fire. Near the edge of town they passed an impassioned warrior on the point of putting a torch to a roof, but a black cavalryman broke away from a patrol and knocked the torch out of his hands with a gun stock.

Tocquet fumed out smoke as he rode, and sternly returned the looks of whomever they passed. Twice he saluted black patrols on horseback, and each time his salute was dutifully returned. No Spanish soldiery was evident anywhere—they must have all locked themselves into the forts. Arnaud kept his eyes fixed on whatever appeared between his horse's ears. In fact his horse, the gelding they'd taken from the house on the Rue Bourdon, was skittish, perhaps unnerved by the stench of blood, but the work of managing the animal helped Arnaud keep calm himself. Sometimes he glanced across at his wife, whose veil hung motionless but for the tremble of her respiration. A crust of white dust formed on the cloth below her nostrils. Where was she? Arnaud knew her haunted by phantasma still more awful than his own. Sometimes he was moved to believe that the mind could not produce such things from its interior—that the demons must be external, real.

They rode at a brisk, businesslike trot and stopped for nothing. No one attempted to hinder them, or paid them much attention at all. When they came out of the town they could see Gros-jean holding the laden donkey and waiting for them at the head of the trail on the hill. Once they had come up with him, he fell into their train without a word and they rode on, toward Ouanaminthe and into the hills beyond.

14

All the north country had grown smaller since I, Riau, had last been there. Toussaint had threaded the mountains with his posts of the Cordon de l'Ouest, which pulled all the land up tight like the drawstring of a bag. At Marmelade and Plaisance and Dondon were soldiers who answered always to Toussaint, and also at other smaller posts in the mountains in between. Not so many soldiers at each post, because Toussaint had taken most of them to fight the English in the Artibonite. But those there were had eyes and ears and memory.

In the mountains I shot a goat with my pistol and cured the meat at the *boucan*. I rode to the market of Marmelade to trade a part of the smoked meat for a straw saddle. At the market were women who wove straw saddles very well. But before I had this saddle strapped to the back of Ti Bonhomme, there came a soldier of the post to ask who was Riau? What was his business there at Marmelade? Worse, this soldier looked at the horse as if he knew him from another time, and a different rider.

For that, Riau did not pass one night in Marmelade. At Plaisance, it was the same, and at Dondon. Beyond Dondon was Jean-François, still serving the Spanish whitemen with his camps around Grande Rivière, or in the other direction the colored men held Le Cap in the name of the French whitemen Toussaint now served. In the mountains were still *bitasyons* from the time of *marronage,* and new villages had sprung up as well, but the people were mistrustful of a stranger, because the whole country was at war.

I rode into the mountains north of Dondon, and when I could not ride any higher, I tied Ti Bonhomme to a tree with the rope reins and went on with my own legs, until I climbed Bonnet d'Evêque. It was a peak we had passed many times before, when Riau had belonged to the maroon band Achille led, who had been killed in the first fighting on the plain down there. They called it so because the mountain was pointed and split at the top, like a bishop's hat, and to climb it to the highest place I had to use my hands. From the top of it I could see very far in each direction. Behind was Morne La Ferrière, with a new *bitasyon* sprouting below the cliff, and smoke from charcoal burning. Below, Dondon, and Limonade, and the Plaine du Nord rolling out to the sea, and far to the west was Morne du Cap above the town, and the mountains near Limbé. Some of the plain was still fire-blackened from when we burned the plantations with Boukman, but parts of it were growing green again. Beyond the plain the line where the sea met the sky was curving to become a circle, so that I, Riau, must see and understand that wherever I went anymore I would meet myself coming again, out of all that had been done before. At every *kalfou* I would meet my own past actions, even if I went back to Bahoruco.

When I had climbed down from the top of the Bishop's Hat, I took the straw saddle off Ti Bonhomme and fastened it to a tree branch where the leaves would hide it. I untied the bridle I had made so it became a rope again, and with the rope's end I drove the horse away into the bush. When I could not hear him moving anymore, I took up the *macoute* with the smoked meat which was left, my pistols and watch and the bundle of letters, and with the rope coil on my other shoulder, I began walking to Dondon, where Moyse commanded for Toussaint.

There was a long climb to make up the twist of the reddish mud road to the notch in the mountains where Dondon was, in the pass to the plateau and the high savannah. Market women were coming down the road with baskets carried on their heads, and children leading goats or cows to forage. When the sun and heat were highest, I rested with my back against a tree, eyes half closed, my *ti-bon-ange* half out of my body. Then I climbed some more and came into the town near the end of the day. The road leveled off and I walked the curve of it among the houses and then the road rose again, only a little, to an open hump of clear land by the church. On the other side of the cleared bare earth Moyse sat beneath a canvas, with a pen and paper on the table before him.

When Moyse saw me coming toward the table, a smile came out on his face like a flower. Moyse and Riau had crept together into the camps of whitemen in these same mountains, to cut their throats by night along with Dessalines and Charles Belair, and also we had known each other at Bréda when each of us had Toussaint as his *parrain*. It was long since Riau had seen him, and in that time Moyse had lost one of his eyes in fighting with the *blancs*. Now Moyse passed his hand between his face and me, and when the hand fell to the table again, the smile was gone.

Moyse wore a uniform coat and tight trousers tucked into high boots like a *blanc* horse soldier. He looked at the paper on his table, and touched the quill pen with his fingertips.

"*Sa ou vlé?*" he said, and frowned at the paper like a whiteman. What do you want?

"*M'vlé sevi,*" I said. I want to serve. He would know how my meaning was twinned because Moyse also served the *loa*.

"Mmmmmm." Moyse made a long, low sound he must have imitated from Toussaint. He looked at me all over with his eyes narrowing. "Where are your boots, my Captain? and your coat? your cartridges?"

Well, it was true that I had left all these things behind when first I ran from Toussaint's army to go to Bahoruco. True also that I had no shoes now and no shirt either, only a straw hat and the *macoute* strapped on my shoulder and canvas breeches torn in rags almost to the hip. I knew where the thought in Moyse's head was leading him, toward the crime of deserting and the punishment. I had no thought inside my head, but my hands went into the *macoute* to hold one pistol by the barrel and the other by the grip. I held the pistols toward Moyse that way.

Moyse pushed back in his chair, and his hands fell below the table. I did not know what he would do, but just then something pushed me softly in the back and when I turned it was the horse Ti Bonhomme, now nosing at the *macoute* where he knew the bag of salt was hidden.

"*Sé chaval-ou?*" Moyse said. It's your horse? But I thought Moyse must know Ti Bonhomme from Bréda anyway.

"*Li égaré,*" I said. He has strayed.

Moyse began to laugh, his hands rising open into my sight again, and I was laughing with him then.

"Well, keep him," Moyse said. "Ride him." This time, when he stopped laughing, the smile stayed.

Then I felt foolish to have left the saddle at Bonnet d'Evêque, if the horse meant to follow me so far anyway. But Jean-François was at Grande Rivière and we at Dondon had many little fights with his people, so in one of these I took a leather saddle, and another horse too. Moyse found a coat for me to wear and I put the watch in a coat pocket where it ticked beneath the cloth, and people began to call me *Captain* again as they had done before I went away to Bahoruco. Soon Captain Riau had a little troop of men to order in the way the whiteman Maillart had taught him before.

All during this time Toussaint was fighting with most of his men in the Artibonite plain, or back and forth across the river all the way to Mirebalais. He had made a strong camp at the plantation of Marchand where Dessalines was born, in the pass of the Cahos mountains, and from there he attacked Saint Marc many times, but could not take it, or hold it if he did. He did cross the river to take Verrettes, but the Spanish came from the east to help the British take it back again. The British whiteman Brisbane was also a clever general, so for a long time it did not seem that either he or Toussaint could beat the other one completely, there in the Artibonite.

All this we knew from letters which passed from Toussaint to Moyse and back again, because Toussaint's fighting was far away to the south then. To the north and the east was Jean-François, who had more men than Moyse at Dondon, but not so well ordered or wisely led. Jean-François had money, gold from the Spanish to pay anyone who would come over into his army, and some people from the camps Toussaint had around Dondon did go over to Jean-François, or they would change sides daily, depending. Anyway, the French whitemen with Laveaux, who was Toussaint's commander and *parrain* now, had not money to pay anyone, or even enough of powder and bullets, so we had to take those things from our enemies whenever we could take them.

One day, Toussaint rode into Dondon with more than three thousand of his men, and no letter coming before to say that he would be there. That was Toussaint's way, and Moyse and everyone at Dondon was happy to be surprised by him like that, except Riau was not so happy because when Toussaint saw that I was there, he had six men arrest me and lock me into a room with no windows, in the strongest house of all Dondon. I did not have any time to look for Moyse or anyone else I knew, and no one spoke to me when they were chasing me to the guard house in front of the bayonets, but I heard myself called *the deserter Riau,* so I thought I would probably be shot the next day.

Every one must die, we know. Riau knew this, and told it to himself, but was frightened still, and did not want to do it. Better to have been

killed in the middle of one of the big fights I had been in with Halaou, or
Boukman even, long before. The storeroom had been used for coffee,
and there was still the smell of coffee there, but it was empty, only bare
shelves and hooks with nothing hanging from them, and no one brought
any food or water. Rats were gnawing and walking down under the wood
floor, and outside the door the guard sometimes coughed or thumped
his musket stock on the sill. I wondered about Merbillay's other man,
who had probably come to Dondon with the rest of Toussaint's soldiers,
if he was still alive. It was funny to think that we might pass each other
or speak to each other without knowing it. He might even be the man
standing guard outside the storeroom, or the man who would be ordered
to shoot Riau, whenever Toussaint ordered it.

I felt sad then because I remembered I would not see Merbillay or
Caco anymore when I was dead, but there was nothing I could do to
change what was going to happen. I heard the watch ticking in the coat
pocket and I took it out to look. The metal point moved in little jerks
around the circle. It seemed terrible for time to be shut up in the watch,
the way Riau was shut into the storeroom. Whitemen appeared to live
that way always, jerking with the pointer. Then I knew what it was I
must do, to try to keep living after all, so I banged on the door and called
out in my Captain's ordering voice that they must bring me pen and
paper.

At first, they did not answer me on the other side, but I kept shouting, with silences in between the shouts. Each time the long point of
the watch had traveled a quarter of the circle, I would begin to shout
again. At last I heard the voice of Moyse beyond the door, and though I
could not see him when the door opened, out of the ring of bayonets
and gun barrels, hands appeared to pass me pen and paper and ink,
and a stub of candle too, because there was no light for writing in the
storeroom.

I took a shelf board down from the wall and sat with it balanced on
my knees, to hold the paper. The words had been made already in my
head, but I wrote them very slowly in the handwriting I had learned to
copy from that dead Frenchman's letters, careful to think just how each
word must be drawn on the sheet of paper.

To General Toussaint Louverture
from his Captain, Riau

My General it is true that for desertion the punishment is Death. Your
Captain Riau does not have fear to Die. But a Dead Man cannot

serve his People and I have come back of my free will to serve. I pray
you let my life and my death also if it be on a field of battle serve my
people and their Cause.

  I am your servant
  Captain Riau

When the letter was finished and the ink was dry, I folded it two
times and dripped candlewax to hold it shut and wrote Toussaint's name
on the other side. Then I beat on the door until someone grunted on the
other side, and I slipped the letter through the crack beneath the door.
Outside it was night, or must have been. When I pinched the candle
out, there was no light at all and I lay on the floorboards and slept like I
had been shot already.

They came for me with muskets and bayonets, and Moyse was not
there nor anyone I knew, so I thought I would be shot anyway, maybe. It
was just dawn, with the mist rising from the square before the church. I
would go beneath the waters maybe without meeting Toussaint again, I
thought, but then I saw him sitting beneath the canvas where Moyse
had been before.

Toussaint wore his yellow *mouchwa têt* like always and his general's
hat was on the table beside the letter of Captain Riau. Now he wore the
French uniform, and he had a big red plume above the white feathers in
his hat, but everything else about him was the same as it had been.
Riau's thumbprint in the wax seal of the letter had been broken all the
way across, and when I saw that I felt fear, as if Riau's head would be
taken from his body after all, his feet torn off the earth forever.

"You do credit to your tutors," Toussaint said at last, with a tick in his
voice as if he might laugh, but he did not. He looked up and down from
me to the letter, with one of his eyebrows moving. Then he folded the
letter and put it away inside his coat.

"Well, my captain," he said, and his voice made a bark. "Return to
your troops!"

Behind me the bayonets came down. I saluted Toussaint and walked
away as stiff and straight-backed as I could, though for some little time
my legs were weak, as if they were full of water instead of bone.

I had thought Toussaint would put me to writing his letters again,
because he always had need of others to write for him, and that was why
I had made Captain Riau's letter in that way which it was. But instead
we all went out of Dondon that day, more than four thousand men altogether, to fight the Spanish whitemen in the high plain to the east. I
believe that Toussaint might have been thinking that those Spanish

would have left their towns unguarded from the north since they had sent their soldiers to help the English at Verrettes. But they had left soldiers enough along the way we went, and they had made ready for a big fight.

Above Saint Michel and Saint Raphael the Spanish whitemen had made a strong place dug into a mountain where the road had a sharp turn, and they had also dug a ditch to bring water across the road to block it, with many cannons aimed over the road from behind this ditch. If they were surprised to see Toussaint coming from that direction, they did not look like it.

If Halaou or Boukman had led that fight, our people would have been killed by thousands, running at the cannons behind that ditch. This time was not like fighting for a *hûngan,* though. It was to be in an army of ants.

Toussaint divided the men into three. One line of foot soldiers went around the back side of the mountain to wait for the Spanish on the road behind. Another line of foot soldiers climbed up the side of that mountain out of sight of the Spanish so to come down on their fort from above. Toussaint himself stayed on the road in front of the cannons, with some hundreds of horse soldiers.

The horse Riau had taken from the men of Jean-François had been given to another man by Moyse before Toussaint had come, and someone else had taken Ti Bonhomme while Riau was in the guard house waiting to be shot, so I was sent with the foot soldiers who climbed the mountain above the Spanish fort. I was happy enough not to be riding with Toussaint that day anyway, when I saw what was going to happen. For a little time it was quiet, with our men climbing under the sun, and Toussaint with the horsemen waiting below on the road just out of reach of the cannons, and the two lines of foot soldiers going around and over that mountain like ants on a sugar hill. But then as we came out on the heights above the fort where the Spanish could see us, Toussaint's horsemen stirred, and his long sword flashed, no bigger than a pin as it looked from the mountain. Then they charged.

Toussaint had to do this thing so the Spanish could not turn their cannons to shoot at us as we came down. I, Riau, could understand the need inside my head, but it was very bad to watch it. The cannons were loaded with *mitraille* instead of the big round balls, and when they fired, these little pieces of metal flew everywhere and hurt a lot of people. Toussaint charged two times and was turned back, and both times many of his men were shot down from their horses. I saw the horses were being torn to pieces also, which almost was worse, and some few of them broke their legs trying to cross the ditch that was filled with water.

When we came down from the mountainside, we found that the Spanish had dug a ditch all the way around their fort, so we could not come in so easily. But Toussaint led another charge, spurring up the stallion Bel Argent, who jumped all the way over the ditch this time, and then the Spanish broke where they were fighting us, so we all came among them together. Since it was too close for shooting, I began to cut them down with my *coutelas,* but there was no spirit in my head this time. It was more like I was cutting cane in the field at Bréda.

When the Spanish starting running back down the road toward Santo Domingo, the other line of our foot soldiers caught them as they tried to run away. A very great many of them were killed, and left their bodies lying everywhere in the road, so we passed a lot of dead men that way as we went on to the towns beyond. In the fort there were men who would not surrender, and Toussaint ordered them killed with swords. I had seen his mood to be softer when he won a fight, but he was hard and tight today, after losing so many men and horses to *mitraille.*

Both Saint Raphael and Saint Michel we burned to the ground. Toussaint ordered this because he had not enough men to hold those places, and he did not want our enemies to use them. Here on the high plain the Spanish pastured their mules and their cows, and Toussaint sent these herds across the mountains to the west. We had captured a lot of guns also, and powder which we needed even worse, and the cannons from the forts, and those too he sent back over the mountains. After we burned the towns, and when the ashes cooled enough, we broke up the parts that would not burn until not one stone or brick was still stuck to another. Also we burned whatever herdsman's huts that we found scattered on the plain.

To see those houses burning brought pleasure to Riau, but it was not the same blind, blood-drunk joy as when we first rose to burn all the plantations of the northern plain. At night were celebrations and dancing and the *loa* came down to many but not to me. I felt the loosening in my head, but I held to myself and would not let go—it seemed I wanted my own head for thinking but what I wanted to think about I could not say. In the night I dreamed I was a *zombi* working in a *zombi* crew, cutting cane like a slave again and loading it onto wagons. When the cane was cut, the stalk ran blood instead of sugar juice, and when I had put cane on the wagon, I saw it become the bodies of dead men. I looked over my left shoulder and saw Chacha who Riau and Biassou had made a *zombi,* doing the same work with Riau who was a *zombi* too . . .

Toussaint did not go to the ceremonies either. When the Spanish towns were all destroyed, we went very fast across the high plain and into the mountains above Mirebalais, where Toussaint had the last fort of his line, and then back along the inside bank of the river, toward the sea. All the time we went very fast. At one post or another Toussaint would leave a few men or exchange them. On the other side of the river the British were still in Verrettes, but on the side where we were, above Petite Rivière, Toussaint's colored officer Blanc Cassenave was finishing that fort which the English had begun. After we had passed that place, Toussaint went on to Gonaives, but Riau was sent with a small party to Ennery and to Habitation Thibodet.

When we had come there, I wanted to go right away to the *ajoupa* where Merbillay and Caco stayed, but then there came a thought which held me back. Maybe the new man had come to her again, already, either with our party now or at some other time. So I stayed away, helping to fire the forge down by the stable, because many horses had thrown shoes in all that hard fast riding. When night came, I did not go to eat with the others, but took a mango and a soursop away to eat in the dark below the coffee trees. Later on when I came back toward the camp, I watched from outside the fire circles. I saw Merbillay get up from one fire, with her *mouchwa tét* wrapped high and tight. The new child in her belly showed very much now, and her face was full and round and sleek. The man who put his hand on her far shoulder to walk by her was the one with the scars. They went together toward the *ajoupa* with Caco skipping behind them as if all this was usual to him.

What Riau had wondered about before was now true, because this new man had been with us all the time at the burning of the Spanish towns. I even knew his name, which was Guiaou. His scars were terrible, all around his trunk and on his head, like a big *djab* had bitten into him and chewed and spat him out because after all he did not like the taste. Guiaou had been in the fighting with Riau at the Spanish fort too, among Toussaint's foot soldiers, who climbed part of the mountain to come down from behind. He had fought well, half outside of himself, as if he was in a dream or underwater.

Now he had put the new baby into Merbillay, and he would lie beside her in the *ajoupa* all night. And my Caco, Pierre Toussaint who I had named, was with them in the *ajoupa* like he was their child and not Riau's. Riau felt angry at this, but the sadness which came after was more great. I might slip into the *ajoupa* and kill the new man while he slept, as I had crept many times into the camps of whitemen in the hills to kill them with my knife. Or I might fight him when he woke, fight with the *baton,* to the death. That way it would be less sure what would happen, and Toussaint would be angry if he heard of it because he did not want his soldiers to waste themselves in fighting each other with the *baton.*

All these ideas I saw from a little distance, outside the head of Riau. They were not part of me at all, only things which might or might not happen. I did not know at all what I wanted to do.

I went away to look for Bouquart. When I found him, he was with the housemaid Zabeth, under the hedge of oranges in the dark. Zabeth was shy to see me come, and she pulled away and went back to the *grand'-case*. Bouquart did not seem to mind this very much. He smiled and took my hand. Bouquart was admired by many women here at Ennery because he was a big, fine man who could run faster and jump higher than other big, fine men, now his *nabots* had been struck off. I thought, while we were walking, after all it would not be a bad life for Riau, to go about as a blacksmith cutting iron off people. To be free was a great thing, but to free someone was greater.

I was thinking of this when we passed near the fires and Bouquart looked surprised to see my captain's coat, because he was only an ordinary soldier. Guiaou did not have any captain's coat either, I thought, or captain's power to tell men what to do. Guiaou did not even have a shirt, it seemed. But that was a whiteman way of thinking.

Bouquart knew all the talk of the camp, because so many different women liked him, and from Zabeth he knew the talk of the *grand'case*, too. A quarrel had happened among the white people, he told me, after the colored woman Nanon had gone away with her child. A colored officer had come from Le Cap after Nanon, and the white mistress of the house had made her go away with him, or so Zabeth had told Bouquart. But afterward Tocquet had become very angry with his woman, and had gone away himself, and her own child Sophie was always sad, because she and Nanon's boy Paul had been like brother and sister. Now the white mistress was sorry for what she had done, and she lay in bed until afternoon some days, Zabeth said, or even until dark, crying and calling her little girl to her. So the happiness had left that house and misery lay on it like a sickness.

That night I stayed in the *ajoupa* Bouquart had made, and for many nights. Sometimes I was alone there, if Bouquart went with a woman. There was not any fighting near Ennery then, and with Toussaint away there was not very much training or drilling either. The French whiteman officers Riau had known at this camp before had all gone to the fighting it seemed, if they had not been killed.

I stayed with Bouquart at night. By day I would sometimes see Merbillay, but I did not try to speak to her. I knew that she knew that Riau was there in the camp with her and Guiaou—let her think of that whatever she would. One day when she had gone off to the provision grounds, I went to that *ajoupa* and took down the *banza* I had made from the ridgepole where it hung. I struck one note softly with my thumb and bent the string to make it cry. Then I saw Caco looking at me shyly from the *ajoupa* doorway. I curled my fingers to him, and he came to me.

I took the *banza* to Bouquart's *ajoupa* and played it there in the darkness after night came, bending the strings and beating my palm on the skin head. I knew that she and Guiaou could hear it where they lay. In the days Caco would come to me and we did many things together, inside the camp or going outside of it into the bush. I thought that sometimes Guiaou was watching us together too, though I did not see him. There were plenty of other women around that camp, but I did not want any of them.

In front of the *grand'case* the yard had been made soft with grasses, and flowers floating in a pool, and the ordinary soldiers were kept from walking there, but as an officer Riau came and went as he would, on his soldier business. So it was when the doctor had come back to Habitation Thibodet, I saw him on the gallery of the house. At first I was not sure that it was he, but when he had taken off his hat I knew—there was the bald, rust-colored head with its peeling skin, the small beard coming to a point. He had come from Gonaives, and was still dusty from the road, and he was quarreling with the white mistress of the house who was his sister. I stood below the bougainvillea vines that hung down from the gallery rail and heard the ending of their talk.

"*Madame ma sœur,*" the doctor said. They must have been arguing a long time for such an anger to come into his tone. "When I first came to this country I searched it from one end to the other, looking for you. Now you move me to wonder if it would not have been better for all of us if I had never found you."

The face of the whitewoman crunched up like wadded cloth. There were red spots all over the pale skin of her face now, because she did not keep herself clean anymore—Zabeth said, she almost could not live without the man. Inside the house the little girl began to cry. She was often unhappy now, infected with the mother's misery. The whitewoman turned away from the doctor, pressing one hand across her bare throat, and went limping into the shadows of the house.

Barefoot, I went up the stairs, hesitating at each step. I had my coat of a French soldier but I had not yet got any boots, so my feet did not make any noise as I climbed. Still I had not grown used to entering a big plantation house by the front door. Riau would never have done so, not as a slave at Bréda, and not as a maroon either unless perhaps he came to kill and burn. Captain Riau of the French army could come to the door like a *blanc*. I stood at last on the gallery floor, but the doctor did not see me.

He had sat down at the table, and over his shoulder I saw him looking into his *ouanga*, the piece of mirror he cupped in his palm, small so that it only reflected his eye. He gripped the edges of it so hard it cut into the creases of his hand. After a time he put it down and passed his blunt fingers over his face, then took from his pocket a small silver snuffbox and set this on the table near the mirror shard. He looked at both of these things as if he did not know at all what they were.

I thought of everything I knew about the doctor. He was a very strange whiteman. Sometimes Riau had even wondered if he were not a man of Guinée who by witchcraft was poured into the skin of a *blanc*. Some few other whitemen were a little bit this way, but all of them were priests of Jesus, and this doctor was no priest. Riau had known Doctor Hébert since Toussaint first captured him in raiding the plantations of the north. Toussaint had set him to be my writing master for a time, and had taught him how to be a *doktè-fey*. And whatever the doctor could see with his eye, he could reach with a bullet from his gun as easily as if he was touching it with his finger, but he did not care anything for this gift, and would rather heal than kill if he had the choice. He seemed smooth inside where whitemen always were jagged, and for that, Riau was glad to see him now, although he was in trouble.

When he saw me, the knots all over his face went calm, and he stood up, smiling as he spoke my name, and put his hands on my shoulders. I touched him gently on the elbows with my hands, and followed him to the chair he drew back for me to sit. But when he looked at the things on the table, the trouble came back into his eyes.

I saw his one eye floating in that piece of mirror, and I thought that it must be watching me too. I thought how shadows and reflections in a mirror may return the movements of the men who walk on the earth. Riau had his own trouble also, and what if Caco had vanished away to an unknown place, like Nanon's boy, Paul? I did not know what to do about my trouble, but now I thought maybe I could reach across the mirror and work on the other side.

"*Kouté, monchè,*" I said, and he looked up. "Listen, man, maybe I can help you find this woman."

The doctor's face came quick and alert. He heard, and he was interested, but he did not yet know if he ought to believe.

15

The color of day was just beginning to fade from the sky as Governor-General Laveaux's party of inspection rode out of the mountains from Marmelade onto the plain called Haut de Trou. As they reached level ground, the men urged their horses into a trot. Captain Maillart rode in the van, between Laveaux and his *ordonnateur,* Henri Perroud. They were all just sufficiently saddle weary that conversation had stopped among them some time before, but at the same time they were all reasonably content.

Trotting briskly, they soon overtook a file of four black women coming from the Rivière Espagnole, each balancing a jug of water on her head. Maillart reined up to ask them the way to Habitation Cigny. The second woman in the line grinned up at him and said that they were already in the outlying *carrés* of that plantation. The ox cart up the road she pointed to would lead them to the main compound, the *grand'case* and the mill.

Maillart spurred and caught up with his companions. The ox cart, which carried a half-dozen men with their hoes, slowed their pace to a walk, but there was no need for haste anymore, as they were assured of reaching shelter before night. Besides, the whole region covered by the

Cordon de l'Ouest had been more or less at peace ever since Toussaint had joined forces with the Republican French.

Rolling his head back to loosen his stiff neck, Maillart caught a glimpse of two crows winging across the paling sky to a fringe of trees at the field's edge. One called out liquidly and the other carried something writhing in its beak. Below the crows' path of flight the field was sparsely grown up in spindly cane stalks, or cleared in patches for fresh planting. Maillart noticed now that the men in the ox cart were seated on small bundles of fresh-cut cane.

The cart rumbled over the bare ground of the main compound, passing the *grand'case* to go on toward the small stone cane mill beyond it. The big house hardly lived up to that name, being no more than a single-story plank building, raised a few feet off the ground, with a porch in front of thatched palm leaves. Beneath this shelter two white women and a man in French uniform sat around a table. As Laveaux's party rode in, one of the women moved out from the roof of the porch and stopped, shading her eyes with one hand to watch their arrival. She was small, dark-haired, dressed in white. Maillart felt his heart rise up to greet her, but he wheeled his horse to the side and dismounted behind Perroud and Laveaux, so that the Governor-General might be the first to greet their hostess. Laveaux bent over her hand, murmuring.

"Madame Cigny, I am absolutely enchanted . . ."

"*Mais Monsieur Général,* the pleasure is mine . . ."

Then Isabelle swung lightly around to kiss her fingers toward Maillart, her dark eyes gleaming. He smiled and bowed to her from where he stood. The uniformed man had come out from the shade of the thatched porch, and Maillart saw that he was a black officer, a fine specimen too, tall and lithe, with glossy skin as black as oil, and features proudly chiseled.

"Joseph Flaville," Isabelle pronounced, and beckoned him nearer to her side. Flaville acknowledged Laveaux with a salute, but he did not offer this courtesy to Maillart. The captain drew back, searching Flaville's face for intentional insolence, but when he looked at the epaulettes he took in that the black man's rank was higher than his own. He inclined his head in a movement which was not quite a bow, and to cover his confusion led his horse away toward the stables, following a couple of barefoot grooms who had just come out.

The others were already at table when Maillart, after a contrived delay, returned to the *grand'case.* Isabelle motioned him toward an empty seat opposite Claudine Arnaud, then turned to continue what she had been saying to Laveaux. Maillart registered Claudine's presence with a start.

". . . you find us very rustic here of course—this plantation was not meant for a real residence—but as our town house is for the moment *unavailable* . . ." Isabelle looked pointedly from Laveaux to Perroud and back. "One can do no better." She threw up her little hands gaily and laughed.

"But I find it perfectly charming here," Laveaux said. "Of course, a lady of your grace would bring charm to the very worst desolation. But here it is absolutely . . ."

Laveaux looked across the yard, where a trio of brown hens were flying up to roost in the branches of a lone mango tree. Maillart studied his manner, knowing the compliments were formulaic, empty of intention. No romantic adventurer he, though women liked him.

". . . flourishing," Laveaux concluded, and turned his smile to meet Isabelle's.

"Well, you exaggerate in all particulars," Isabelle said, tapping the back of Laveaux's hand with her forefinger, "though you are kind." She grew serious as she looked out over the darkening fields. The hens clucked in the lower branches of the mango tree.

"And yet," she said thoughtfully, "things do go better here than one would have expected . . . Well, my husband could tell you more of the matter, but regrettably he is absent, *au Cap*—that business of our town house, you know."

Again she looked significantly from Laveaux to Perroud. Maillart shifted restively in his chair, wishing she would not press the point so. Of a sudden an electric thrill ran up his leg, for a slippered foot had pressed against his calf. He looked across the table at Madame Arnaud, but no, it was impossible; she was in a reverie so deep and dismal she had no notion of the company surrounding her. Again he felt the subtle pressure. Isabelle was turned from him, concentrating on Laveaux, but that meant nothing. He could remember a dinner at the oft-mentioned Cigny town house when Isabelle had kicked off her little shoe and let her foot walk over his lap and trouser buttons, her toes working dextrously as fingers, and yet all the while she kept up her banter with her husband and his guests . . .

"But truly," she was saying now. "All credit is due to your General Toussaint and to his officers—such as our most excellent Major Flaville."

Isabelle looked toward the black officer, who inclined his head without speaking.

"Since the good General Toussaint has covered us with his protection," she said, "there have been no outrages. Under his authority some cultivators have returned to the fields, and even to the mill. Oh, I know little of these matters, but I can say that my husband was able to take two wagons of brown sugar to Le Cap when he went there."

Maillart tensed, but she did not mention the town house a third time.

"For the moment we have not the skilled hands to refine the white," she said. "But we have peace, at least for the moment—*grâce à vos officiers.* And with peace, prosperity may return."

"Madame, you gratify my hopes, even as you do me honor," Laveaux said. He shifted his attention to Claudine. "But tell me, Madame Arnaud, how is it with your properties?"

All this while Madame Arnaud had been looking through and beyond the other parties to the conversation, holding herself peculiarly erect. She turned to Laveaux when he addressed her, her head moving smoothly but with a strange fixity—like an owl's head revolving, Maillart thought with some discomfiture. Her eyes too suggested some bird of prey.

"God has said that this land must lie fallow," she said. Her voice was husky, and surprisingly sweet. "This earth has given birth to monsters, yet they must be slain and sacrificed and the earth be watered with their blood, be nourished by the ashes of their bones. So for seven days and seven hours and for four hundred years. Four hundred years! *Babylon tonbé . . .* This has been written on the sky with fire."

Laveaux sat arrested, leaning slightly forward with his lips parted and one empty hand hanging in the air. Maillart glanced over at Flaville, who was listening to Claudine's speech with evident interest but no sign of surprise or dismay. Claudine turned her gloved hands up on the table and looked down at them with her glittering eyes. Everyone else's gaze was drawn to the left hand with its empty glove finger pinned to the palm.

"One may be maimed in the body and pass on the right side of the throne," she said intently, as if reciting, or reading from her palms. "They who are maimed in the spirit will be hurled into the pit with the goats—there they will be burned to cinders, but the fire does not consume."

Isabelle leaned sideways to cover Claudine's hands with her own. She turned them palm down and stroked their backs lightly with her fingertips. Claudine's stiff neck and back suddenly collapsed, and her head lolled. A handful of her lank and lusterless hair detached itself from her careless coiffure and hung partway across her face.

"*Ma pauvre,*" Isabelle murmured, and glanced up at Laveaux. "My poor Claudine insists on carrying water to the fields at midday . . . to serve the men who work the cane."

"What, herself?" Laveaux relaxed against his chair back.

"Yes, she says that God has ordained it. Or some priest, in her memory. Of course, the sun is quite too much for her at that hour and so at evening her thoughts become disordered for a time."

A black woman in a cotton smock had appeared behind Claudine's chair, where she stood impassively waiting.

"Her husband's plantation is on the Plaine du Nord—" Isabelle said, still stroking Claudine's hands. She had leaned across Maillart to do so, and he could smell the tang of her perspiration under a trace of perfume.

"Not so very far from here," Isabelle went on, "but still it was more completely devastated. Not a stick left standing, as I understand. But Monsieur Arnaud is there as we speak, and he may make a restoration— thanks to your protection." This time she looked meaningfully from Laveaux to Flaville. Then, at Isabelle's nod, the black woman pulled back Claudine's chair, and Claudine rose and mutely allowed herself to be led into the house.

"Her suffering has been very great," Isabelle told Laveaux. "I shall not enter into the particulars—"

"No, of course." Laveaux waved a hand.

"—but she finds it unbearable to return to her husband's plantation, at least in its present state, so I have offered her my roof."

The black woman returned carrying a plate of roasted goat meat ringed with peppers. Another house servant followed with a platter of sweet potatoes.

"Our nourishment may be coarse but at least it is plentiful," Isabelle said. "Thanks be to God. And this particular goat has not been hurled into the fires of hell but only into the *boucan*," she smiled thinly, "or so we may hope. *Bon appetit.*"

For the remainder of the meal, Isabelle was comparatively subdued, while Laveaux quizzed Flaville on local military dispositions and the state of supply. The black officer's replies were courteous, with no hint of servility. Maillart was aware of his intelligence, as well as a rather unmartial air of inner calm that had disconcerted him before among the black military colleagues recently thrust upon him. Flaville's French was adequate, and his manner of speaking lost no dignity when some- times he lapsed into Creole. Isabelle watched and listened to him with an uncharacteristically quiet attention. No more sallies of her toe beneath the table. . . . Maillart reflected that he had never understood her, and that he never would. He took this thought to bed with him, and found that he slept poorly.

The sound of a door closing somewhere in the house woke him completely. Across the dark room, Perroud snored tranquilly enough. Maillart turned over and pounded the shucks in his mattress tick, but could not settle. Isabelle had not exaggerated the rusticity of the situation, he reflected, so far as these accommodations were concerned. He put on his trousers and shirt and went outside.

Moonlight washed over the compound, and the air was fresh and surprisingly cool. A white-robed figure was moving away from the house and around the corner, toward the cane mill. Whoever it was walked in an oddly stiff way, arms fixed to the sides as if bound there. Curious, Maillart moved to follow. Behind him, another voice spoke.

"So, you too are restless . . ."

He turned to see Isabelle Cigny stepping out from the thatched roof of the porch. She wore a peignoir light enough to catch the moonlight, with a darker shawl about her shoulders, against the mountain chill. A kerchief was bound over her head.

"Walk with me," she said, and moved nearer to take Maillart's arm. The captain moved with her automatically, letting himself be led. A tingle moved from his elbow to his spine, a sensation foreign to him, unlike the usual desire. In the jungled hills above the plantation began the hollow tap of a drum. Ahead, the person in the white robe disappeared behind a rise of ground. Maillart and Isabelle followed the same path.

Beyond the cane mill, the rise crested and on the other side gave way to a long, gentle slope. Maillart halted and caught his breath.

"Did you not say this place had never been meant for a residence?"

Isabelle sighed. "But this side of the hill is not Habitation Cigny. Here was Habitation Reynaud, my father's seat."

Maillart pressed his tongue to the roof of his mouth. Near the top of the knoll where they stood was the scorched foundation of a magnificent house, overgrown now with vines and wild shrubbery. The white-clad figure of Claudine Arnaud had passed this point, and wandered on to the generous oval drive, in whose center was a dark, oily pool with a toppled fountain. The drive let into a long boulevard, arrow-straight between the stumps of palms. The trees must have been very tall, but they had all been hacked down, and partly consumed by fire.

"My God," Maillart said. "What losses."

"Oh," said Isabelle, "I took it all for granted when I was a girl—while my father lived. And after . . . it was the life of the town I thought I wanted. And of course Cigny is more a man of affairs than a planter. I meant to bring my children here one day, but then . . . it is as you see."

He felt her shiver. Her hand tightened on the hollow of his elbow, then eased its hold. In the cleft of the hills above, that single wandering drum they had been hearing gathered itself in a more urgent rhythm and was joined by another. The fine hairs prickled on the back of the captain's neck. He had come to associate night drumming with dawn attacks.

"Major Flaville has them all well in hand," Isabelle said, as if responding to his thoughts.

"You seem on very close terms with that officer," Maillart replied, and at once regretted the sullenness he heard in his own tone.

"Some allies are chosen of necessity," Isabelle said. "A military principle, is it not? For the nonce Flaville is the chief authority in these parts, and without him no one would come to the fields . . . they would only work in their own gardens—if they worked at all." She shook her head above the ruins below. "We must recover some life for ourselves here, especially so long as the house in town is—"

Maillart turned to face her, inadvertently breaking her light grasp on his elbow. "I meant to tell you, you mustn't press Laveaux about the house," he said. "The situation at Le Cap is very difficult just now."

"Oh," said Isabelle, "I would not abuse your kindness. If not for you—"

"Never mind that," Maillart said, and placed his hand palm-out against the moist air between them. It was true that he had spent much of his credit with Laveaux on arranging the Cignys' safe return to their properties in the northern province. This credit had been considerable, given Laveaux's astonished gratitude at Toussaint's shift of allegiance to the French Republicans. Of course, the prize was not a mean one either, for in the ordinary course of things, *émigrés* and other partisans of the *ancien régime* were liable to be executed.

"Only listen," he said now. The drums shifted rhythm and intensified, forcing an urgency into his words he did not fully intend. "It is this very question of the houses at Le Cap which is causing so much unrest among *les gens de couleur* there. Governor-General Laveaux was so long immured at Port-de-Paix that the mulattoes erected their own little kingdom in Le Cap, under Villatte (who I admit to be a capable officer) and a few others."

"I have heard of Villatte." Isabelle nodded. "Joseph is in correspondence with him from time to time."

Maillart noted this "Joseph" with a certain pique, and remembered that when they'd arrived that afternoon she'd presented Flaville by his first name rather than his rank. Perhaps it was only the Creole dame's familiarity with her servant. He told himself it was unimportant, and went on.

"Understand that the mulattoes have rebuilt most of those houses at their own cost, when the town was burned in ninety-four. And unfortunately they have since made themselves very much at home. More recently, since Laveaux has shifted the seat of government from Port-de-Paix, Perroud has been taxing them to pay rent on those houses."

"Indeed," said Isabelle.

"As for myself, I share your sentiments entirely," Maillart said. "But from the governmental standpoint these are sequestered properties, and the financial situation is near desperation too. But in any case the mulattoes have been most unwilling to pay. I would not speak of revolt, exactly, but I tell you I was happy enough to leave the town for this tour of the Cordon de l'Ouest . . . so I must urge you, do not press Laveaux . . ."

"Or I might find myself hanged for an *émigrée*." Isabelle's ironic smile flashed, then faded. "I suppose I must congratulate myself that the guillotine was not successful here—owing to the tender sensibilities of our blacks." She laid her hand across the hollow of her throat.

Maillart looked at the fragile gold chain that crossed her collarbone, and thought involuntarily of the stone member of the carved pendant which must now be concealed beneath her hand and the fabric of her gown.

"Don't think me ungrateful," Isabelle said gravely. "I understand very well how much you've done for us." Surprisingly, she reached for his free hand, and held his fingertips lightly in her own.

"But tell me," she said. "Do you know who occupies our house?"

Maillart hesitated. "That freckled mulatto they call Choufleur," he said. "The 'Sieur de Maltrot,' as he styles himself. Who has lately been promoted to a colonelcy."

Isabelle's lips contorted in the moonlight. "I confess I find that news distasteful."

"Yes," Maillart said. "I did not like to tell you." He paused. "I don't know why he chose your house. For his father, the actual Sieur de Maltrot, had as fine a house in the town, which he might have taken without challenge."

"I think I may imagine his reasons," Isabelle said, seeming to smile to herself.

"At the worst, the work of restoration which he ordered has been well completed," Maillart told her, turning his head toward the scorched and overgrown foundation. "And it began with little more than what you see here now."

Isabelle swung their joined hands, looking pensively down at the wreck of her father's house. "Did you know, there used to be peacocks here? Almost a dozen of them. The blacks say they still see one some-times, in the jungle."

She shook her head. The drums rolled to a crescendo and then cut off, so abruptly that Maillart had a sensation of falling. Below, the revenant figure of Claudine Arnaud looked frozen. From the cleft of the mountains came an ungodly shriek.

"Ah," said Isabelle, releasing the sound with a shudder. "It comes." Again she put her hand to her throat. The drums recommenced, on a different beat.

"Savage as it may be, it draws one," she said. "Sometimes I feel drawn to go."

"Please," said Maillart. "You mustn't think of it."

Isabelle shook herself. "Of course, I do *not* go," she said, looking down the slope. "Claudine has been."

"You amaze me," Maillart said. "She must be quite mad."

"Oh, the peasants would not harm her," Isabelle said. "They respect her. Fear her, even. Perhaps in some way they worship her. They believe her enchanted, raised from the dead—a *zombi*, Joseph told me. Or some believe she is only possessed."

" 'Only,' " Maillart repeated. "Perhaps they are right."

The wind lifted, and Isabelle seemed to shiver again, so that Maillart was moved to put his arm about her shoulders, but instead he only tightened his grip on her hand. This reaction against his first impulse annoyed him. It was a puzzle, the idea of friendship with a woman, a business he had small competence to conduct. Among the palm stumps, Claudine Arnaud leaned slightly forward into the wind, the sleeves and hem of her pale garment fluttering like sails.

"Is it true what you told Laveaux," he asked, "about the water?"

"Oh yes," Isabelle said. "Very much so. She carries buckets on a wooden yoke across her shoulders like a slave woman, and serves the field workers with her own hands. Nothing will restrain her from it—it ought to kill her, in that midday heat, but she is not easily killed. She conceives it as some sort of penance, I believe."

"Has she not already suffered?"

"Amply," said Isabelle.

For some minutes there had been silence in the cleft of the hills, but now a guttural grumbling began, a half-human-sounding voice that rose toward a melody, chanting, singing in an unknown tongue, perhaps some African language. The drums began. Maillart became aware of a darker figure, standing still as a tree some thirty yards from Madame Arnaud, farther down the boulevard of stumps.

"It is only Joseph," Isabelle said. "He follows her sometimes, when she walks at night. To see that she comes to no harm."

"Strange."

"Perhaps."

With a sudden impatient movement, Isabelle pulled her kerchief off and held it in her free hand; the cloth went flagging in the wind. She shook her head back so that her dark hair loosened and flowed freely off her shoulders. The gesture seemed almost a signal to the man below, but that was a ludicrous notion, Maillart thought. When she tossed her head, the gold chain came tight against the tendons of her neck, and he thought of the stone phallus nudging the space between her little breasts. The idea was erotic, but abstract.

"He witnessed it," Isabelle said. "When Claudine chopped off her finger."

"Who?" Maillart shifted his weight from one foot to the other.

"Joseph Flaville," Isabelle said. "That was in the first rising of ninety-one—Claudine was in a wagon with some few survivors of the *gérant's* family . . . from Habitation Flaville, you know, where she had been a guest. They were trying to make their way out of the plain to Le Cap, through the bands of renegades roaming the roads and the fields. Joseph was not as you see him now. Oh, he would not tell me so much, but he must have been fresh and hot from murdering his own master, or something of that sort. He was among the band that intercepted their wagon."

"I've heard the tale, at second hand," Maillart said.

"One of them wanted to take her wedding ring, but it would not come over the knuckle of her finger. So she snatched a knife and hacked it off and gave them the ring as a price of passage. But Joseph said that she spoke to them in a devil's voice like what we just heard there." Isabelle tilted her chin toward the cleft in the hills where the drums still rolled. "All those marauders were much impressed, because they had not known a white woman could be taken by a spirit so."

You seem very much in the confidence of your Joseph, Maillart thought again, but it seemed unfriendly, petulant even, to say as much aloud.

"She escaped by a hair's breadth, at any rate," Isabelle said. "And again, more recently, that massacre at Fort Dauphin . . ." She shook her head thoughtfully. "Perhaps there is something about her."

The drums went silent. Below, the white woman and the black man seemed hung in a balance, under the oblong of the waning moon, with the damp wind sighing all around them.

"What?" Maillart said. "Do you believe it? All this talk of possession or whatever it may be."

"Possibly it is only a matter of the words one chooses. 'Something came over her,' one might say." She shook her head slowly. "I did not know her before that time, but they say there was no love lost between her and her husband in those days. She saw no one—he kept her shut up in the country while he pursued his . . . profligacies. So perhaps her action was that of an animal which chews itself free of a snare." Isabelle wadded the kerchief in her hand, fist clenching over it and relaxing.

"Certainly Arnaud's reputation was of the very worst," Maillart said. "On every account—except his horsemanship. He was once brought to law, or near it, for torturing his slaves. And it takes something out of the ordinary to become notorious for cruelty in this place."

"Yes, there was something of that sort," Isabelle said. "Whatever it may be, that plantation holds a horror for Claudine, so that she is loath to return there."

"It is good of you to keep her here."

"Oh," said Isabelle, "I do not call it goodness. She fascinates me . . . I mean, her power."

"I don't understand you," Maillart said.

" 'If thy right hand offend thee . . . ?' " Isabelle flashed her coquette's smile, her fingers pulsed against his palm. "Power to act on such a precept?"

"But surely that was only her derangement."

"I don't know." Isabelle gazed down over the ruins. "At times she is more than lucid enough. Perhaps not in the company of her peers . . . but when she teaches the little children she is as well reasoned as any convent nun."

"The children?"

"Yes, she has been catechising the little *négrillons* hereabouts. She lectures them about BonDyé, and she has the fancy of teaching them their letters, which she acquired, apparently, from that rebel priest who was executed at Le Cap."

"A harmless fancy, I suppose."

"Harmless?" Isabelle sniffed. She unfolded her kerchief and snapped it toward the ruins of the house and drive and fountain. "Look for yourself at the harm it has done. Blacks reading books—reading the newspapers. Taking on notions of Liberty. Equality." Her lips twisted over each word. "Fraternity. Your Toussaint, for example—they say now that he has read Raynal, and Epictetus, and so come to picture himself a black Spartacus come to lead his people to their liberation. A black Moses, possibly." She let go his hand and hugged herself. "There is madness, if you like." She stared moodily down at Claudine. "Of course, her

black brats pay her little mind. They listen so long as they are amused
and then they run away . . ."

"Will she stay dreaming there the whole night through?"

"She is free to do so if she wishes. Let her exercise her freedom. But I
am cold, and tired. And irritable, I confess it." This time the smile she
sent him seemed apologetic. "Let us go in."

Maillart offered his arm once more. They returned to the *grand'case*
with the night breeze blowing through the space between them. She
bade him good night with a press of her fingers against his forearm, and
he let her go with no more than an inward protest. A puzzle, friendship
with a woman. He began to think he might master it. But when he lay
down on the shuck mattress, his blood ran around in all directions without settling, so that he wanted to get drunk, or spend himself upon a
woman, any woman, white or black or yellow, who might be willing or
who even might be forced. He lay wakeful, smothered in the filth of his
imaginings. There was a moment when he thought he heard the love
cries of Isabelle elsewhere in the house, but when he woke to find Perroud pulling him onto the floor by his heels, he knew it must have been
a dream.

Dawn swept tendrils of gray mist around the house like ghostly
fingers. Maillart's horse had already been saddled by the grooms. He
gulped half a cup of coffee, groggily kissed his fingers to Isabelle as he
went out. Laveaux and Perroud and the others were mounted, waiting,
having already made their adieux to the ladies. He checked the girth
automatically with the ball of his thumb, then swung astride his animal.
They rode out of the compound and up through the green gorges,
through the brightening sun dapples and among the little roosters who
crowed from the cover of the trees. Before the day was done, they had
reached Dondon.

At evening Toussaint and his troops swept in from the central plateau,
where they had lately overrun the town of Hinche. That night Laveaux
and his French officers dined with Toussaint and the pick of his subordinates. Maillart watched, with an astonished sense of the inevitable, as
Laveaux rose from his place at the head of the table and took each platter away from the waiter and held it in his own hands so that Toussaint
might serve himself. And still Toussaint, as was his habit, ate sparingly,
no more than bread and water.

Yet by his conversation and the respectful manner of his address, he
showed his sensibility of the extraordinary courtesy Laveaux had offered
him, so that the Governor-General did not seem to notice how he

stirred his rice and meat around his plate without actually tasting them. Maillart watched how agreeably the white man and black engaged with one another. Around the table, the others seemed to follow suit. Someone had foraged a barrel of more than passable red wine and Maillart, given the sleeplessness and manifold confusions of the previous night, found that it struck him forcefully. By the end of the meal he was awash in euphoria and joined in the toasts—*Liberté! Egalité! Fraternité!*—with no sense of irony or resentment or reservation.

The wine proved good enough to have no consequences next day, so that Maillart rose fresh and well rested to attend Laveaux's review of Toussaint's troops. The black officers were presented one by one— Dessalines, Moyse, Christophe Mornet, Desrouleaux, Dumenil, Clervaux, Maurepas and Bonaventure—to receive their official promotions from the Governor-General. Laveaux took care to compliment each one of them in detail, when such details were known to him. Each of those officers sank onto one knee before him, as if he were being knighted, then rose and walked back to his troops with that proud rolling gait which Maillart, during his service with Toussaint, had come half reluctantly to admire and even somewhat envy. Behind their officers the four thousand men stood holding their odd assortment of weaponry absolutely still, impassive, half starved and more than half naked most of them, but rooted like a forest with each man steadfast as a tree.

"You are moved," Laveaux said, as column by column the men wheeled and began marching out of the square.

"My general, I have led these men from time to time." Maillart cleared his throat. "Never have I had better men to lead."

Laveaux nodded and looked away and then was struck by something he saw in that other direction. "But tell me, who is he?"

Maillart followed his gaze. Toussaint seemed also stricken with amazement, watching the elderly, stooping white man who was making his way toward him with the aid of a black cane. Toussaint swept off his bicorne hat and held it twitching against his knee.

"By God, it is Bayon de Libertat," Maillart declared. "His former master from Haut du Cap—how did he come here?"

The two men were embracing now, exchanging kisses on each cheek. De Libertat's cane slipped from his grasp and fell away from him, raising a pale puff of dust when it struck the ground. Toussaint stooped and lifted the cane, and gave it back to him.

16

Surely today must be a better day—Elise had been telling herself this insistently now, for something more than a week. At waking she repeated it to herself like a prayer, clenching and unclenching her hands and muttering the sentence over till the words lost their sense. The weather was hot and oppressive, even at dawn. Still muttering silently, but moving her lips, she forced herself to lower her feet to the floor and take her light robe down from its peg and go out to the gallery to order her morning coffee. *Surely today must be a better day.* Her brother had already risen, and sat at the gallery table, holding Sophie's hands and joggling her vigorously on the instep of his riding boot. The little girl laughed and shouted in high excitement and dropped her head back so low that her long, dark curls swept the boards of the floor.

"*Bonjour ma fille, mon frère.*"

But both of them quietened, almost apprehensively, at this greeting. "*Bonjour Maman,*" Sophie said, but with an air of caution. She slipped off the doctor's foot and went unbidden into the house, so that Zabeth might bathe and change her. In the doorway she turned back with a toss of her ringlets and a smile on her plump red lips for the doctor, then skipped into the shadows of the hallway. How naturally the gestures of flirtation came to her, Elise thought—*Ai,* in a few short years the child ought to be sent to school in France, but could she bear to part with her? And yet she knew too well the wantonness fostered by a Creole upbringing . . .

Surely today must be a better day. The doctor had turned his injured eyes from her. He set his relics on the table—the shard of mirror and the silver snuffbox—and gazed down at them as moodily as a Negro contemplating his fetish. Elise reached across and tapped the snuffbox with her fingernail.

"What in this article fascinates you so?" she asked him, flinching at the harshness of her tone.

The doctor's eyes passed over her and away. "It was a souvenir Nanon kept by her," he said, and looked out beyond the pool to the yard where men were leading out saddled horses. "I suppose it puzzles me that she would go away without it."

"I found it in her bedclothes," Elise said, with a studied carelessness. "Of course, she left in haste. . . . I never knew her to take snuff, did you? But whatever was in it I couldn't make out. A mushroom maybe, but with the smell of corruption. Some witchery, I'd imagine."

As she spoke, she felt perturbed again by the sharp and sour flavor of her voice. Inside herself she felt hard and dry, desiccated as if by a desert sun. The doctor sighed and pocketed the snuffbox, then, after a moment, the shard of mirror too.

"Today I must take my leave of you," he said.

"Oh?"

"With Toussaint's troops."

"Where is he bound?"

"As to that, he has kept his own counsel." The doctor smiled distantly, and not for her benefit. "But today he is moving large numbers of men—across the whole cordon as far as Dondon, I believe."

Someone among the uniformed blacks in the yard called out his name. He stood, looking diffidently at the floorboards.

"Well, my horse is ready."

Elise felt her hardness cracking out into anger. Was she not justified, after all? But she did not want to parch and crack, as Madame Arnaud had done. Of a sudden she felt terrified by his departure.

"My brother," she said, softly as she could manage. "Believe this much: I never meant to wound you."

"No," the doctor said abstractedly. "No, I don't believe you intended any harm to me."

Cold comfort. He stooped, taking her hands limply, leaning forward far enough to brush the dry outer scales of his lips across her cheek.

Then he straightened, pulled back the skirt of his coat to check his pistols, and walked down the gallery steps toward the horses.

Elise sat stirring the dregs of her coffee. A crow flew ragged-winged across the pool. She looked up at the geckos which clung upside down to the gallery ceiling. Sometime after the horses and men had moved out of earshot, Sophie reappeared, fresh-washed and dressed.

"*Ki bo tonton Antoine?*"

"*Français, Sophie,*" Elise said. " 'Where is my Uncle Antoine,' you should say."

"*M'rinmin li,*" Sophie said. I love him.

"*Dis, 'Je l'aime,' *" Elise said, drawing the child to her. "I am very happy that you love your uncle. But today he has gone off with the soldiers."

Sophie, petulant, pulled away. "Well? Then when is Papa coming back?"

Elise cracked and began crying into her cupped hands. *Surely, surely today must be better.* Yet she knew very well that Xavier might never return. Now she must keep crying uncontrollably, frightening the child, until Zabeth came out of the house to pat her shoulder, whispering *non, non, madame, maîtresse-moin, non, pa kon sa. . . .* Zabeth must lead her faltering back to the bedroom, where she would lie weeping bitterly or staring at the ceiling. She would call Sophie to her bedside, hoping for cheer, and infect the girl with her own sadness, until perhaps they would quarrel and weep to have done so, then, all emotion exhausted, fall into a wretched, uneasy sleep. So it must go on. She thought, as she tried to stuff her sobs back into her mouth with both hands, that perhaps she might go herself with the child to France. That future was open to her still. Just now it would be winter, bitter cold with the taste of snow. There she might live properly, decorously, without love.

In the middle of Toussaint's cavalry column, the doctor rode to Marmelade that day, and passed many hours of the night in the company of Riau—both of them taking dictation from Toussaint. The import of his message was simple enough: he wished his colleague Villatte to order three of his junior officers—Pénel, Thomas André, and Noël Arthaud— to attack Jean-François from the the area of Limonade and Trou de Nord. But, as always, Toussaint picked over his phrasing and kept them late into the night. When at last the letter was sealed and the scribes were released, the doctor rolled out his blanket beside Riau and fell into a sleep too deep for dreaming. Next morning he dozed in the saddle, all the way from Marmelade to Dondon.

When Riau had offered to help in his search for Nanon and the boy, the doctor had been touched by this gesture of friendship, but without thinking much about what form this assistance might take. Well, perhaps it might be no more than an exercise in superstition. He knew Riau believed that his shard of mirror was a supernatural eye, connected to his gift of marksmanship and to an ability to see at even more improbable distances, and Riau had since told him that the silver snuffbox, somehow special to Nanon, might have a sympathetic power to lead him to her. All this might be called mere African simplicity, or worse, and yet the doctor felt it was not so simple as it seemed. For he too regarded those objects as talismans. The mirror he'd found years before, when the courtesan's rooms Nanon had kept, or been kept in, near the Place d'Armes at Le Cap had been sacked and vandalized and looted in the rioting there. That was the first time she had disappeared from his life and well before he had been brought to recognize the depth of his feeling for her—nevertheless he picked up the broken mirror and had kept it ever since. As for the snuffbox, he could analyze its contents well enough by scientific method, but its meaning was not to be interpreted so readily.

He carried each of these items in opposite pockets of his coat, so that they seemed to balance him somehow, keeping him centered in the saddle during those moments when he slipped away into dream on the rough, winding track to Dondon. The mirror was fitted to the palm of his right hand, the snuffbox to his left. It was as if they were magnetized.

The village of Dondon was buzzing with preparations for the attack which was planned to begin in two days' time, in coordination with the movements Toussaint had requested from the northern plain. Riau, Captain Riau, went off to organize ammunition and supplies for the troops in his command. As yet there were no wounded in the camp, so the doctor was left to his own devices. He unrolled his blanket and lay upon the ground. His secretarial exploits of the night before had left him weary, but he could not quite sleep. The absence of the little boy Paul nagged at him like an itch in an amputated limb, and as for Nanon . . . His first instinct would have been to search at Le Cap, since he knew Choufleur was posted to Villatte's command there, but since Toussaint was marching to Dondon, the doctor had been drawn along with him.

To be drawn in that way, as if by gravity or magnetic attraction, was a relief from the labor of planning one's own actions. Riau was very much gifted with this ability, and when the doctor was in his company, he found it much easier and more natural to act without forethought. Thus they might both arrive where they meant to go, without developing their intentions. All the same, the doctor was surprised to learn, when Riau returned to him an hour before sundown, that he had been asking questions and obtaining answers, and that he had heard how Choufleur's mother, a Madame Fortier, lived not very far away on a coffee plantation on the slopes of Morne à Chapelet.

"It is just there," Riau said, leading him up to the top of a knoll behind the Dondon church, "You see?"

Just there looked an intimidating height, even at long distance, and the doctor knew from his experience that it would unfold further complications when they got nearer to it.

"I'd better find a mule," he said, shading his eyes to look at the sun-struck mountain.

"*Pou ki sa ou besoin mulet? Monchè,* I don't think you need a mule for that." Riau laughed, then looked uneasy. "We don't go anyway, until after the fighting."

"No, let us go at once," the doctor said. "I mean tomorrow, early." If there was to be fighting all over these mountains, he very much preferred to overtake the woman and the child, if he were so lucky, before it began.

Riau still looked uncharacteristically fretful. "I can't run away like that," he muttered, and looked down at the gorge between them and the mountains of their destination. "*Monchè,* if I go with you tomorrow I will be shot."

"Ah," said the doctor. "I didn't think—forgive me, but I will ask leave for both of us to go."

Toussaint, though much occupied, heard out his request—heard it at much greater length than the doctor had intended. By simply holding his silence, rubbing his rather delicate fingers down the edge of his long jaw and looking at him with his slightly red-rimmed eyes, the black general seemed to compel him to keep talking, until the doctor found himself going far more deeply into the circumstances of Nanon's departure from Habitation Thibodet—and even into the history of his own relations with her and the boy—than he had ever thought of doing. A group of the junior officers, Moyse and Dessalines and Paparel, had stepped out from under the canvas sheet where Toussaint was holding his councils; the doctor did not know whether they were within earshot, or if they'd care to listen to his tale, but by the end of his speech, he felt that he was flushed all over.

"You are free to go on this errand," Toussaint finally said, reaching one hand to the back of his head to adjust the knot of his yellow headcloth. "For one night only—both must return the next day."

The doctor bowed his acknowledgment.

"Take note, as you go, of what people may be moving in the region of Morne à Chapelet," Toussaint said as the doctor began to withdraw, and then, suddenly projecting his voice, "And pay attention to that one." He pointed to Riau. "*Sé grand marron li yé.*"

At this the junior officers all grinned and chuckled among themselves and agreed loudly that Riau was an incorrigible runaway. But there seemed to be no menace in all of this, and Riau made a good-humored retort over his shoulder, as the two of them went off to make ready for the journey.

Next morning, the doctor left his saddle horse in camp, having requisitioned a black mule with a blue cross over its shoulders. If the animal's high, pointed back made for a precarious seat, its surefootedness was well worth the exchange. Their way was difficult and, as the doctor had suspected, sometimes traversed ledges scarcely two palms wide. And as he had also anticipated, the distance expanded as they went, so that they spent hours laboring up the dizzy peaks and sharp defiles without drawing appreciably nearer to their destination. Now and again they passed across plantations fallen into desuetude since the revolt, and often little villages had sprung up among the coffee trees. Riau, whose sense of the Fortiers' location turned out to be extremely vague, stopped at each of these *bitasyons* to ask the way, and also to gather the intelligence Toussaint had requested. But they did not meet any men under arms, and by report of those they spoke to it seemed that the troops of Jean-François had not penetrated this area for some time.

By late afternoon the doctor had begun to despair of reaching the Fortier place at all—if it still existed. They must look for a place to camp for the night, then hope to find their way back to Dondon next day in time to comply with Toussaint's order. He lost himself in this gloomy prospect as they rode around a bend in a stream bed they had been following for a mile or more. As the stream turned sharply uphill, the gorge around it widened into a gently sloping valley, sheltered by cliffs on either side, and terraced with well-tended coffee trees. Here the day's work was just ending, and a line of black women was filing toward a wooden barn, with baskets of red berries balanced on their heads.

"*Nou la,*" Riau said. We're here. He called to one of the women to confirm his intuition; this was indeed Habitation Fortier.

"It is admirably placed," the doctor said, looking up toward the house, an unassuming structure of weathered gray board, seated at the top of the valley above the coffee trees. The mule went zigzagging up the terraces, Riau's horse following with only slightly less agility. The doctor found himself saddle-sore in a whole new way when he climbed down and hitched his mount. For a moment he stood admiring the expanse of the green terraces rippling down from the house, listening to the purl of the stream that ran beside them. Then he turned and walked with Riau up a pair of wooden steps to the narrow porch.

Riau knocked on the door frame. Silence, a creak of floor boards, voices muttering low. A sort of curtain hung before the door, made of reeds broken into short lengths and gathered in star-like clusters on knots of closely hanging threads. Behind the reed curtain, the door opened, but no more than an inch. They waited, but there was no further sign.

"This one is looking for him they call Choufleur," Riau said. "Also the woman Nanon, with her child."

"They are not here." A woman's voice, rusty but melodious beneath the rust. "Go away."

"But, I beg you," the doctor said, and the door stopped closing. Riau looked at him solemnly, but the doctor did not know what else to say. He took the snuffbox from his pocket and held it with his two cupped hands containing it like water. Behind them the wind breathed through the trees. The whole house seemed to take a deep inhalation, and the door swung inward. Through the suspended bundles of reed the doctor could discern a tall and slender silhouette.

"Wait where you are," the voice said, and the figure turned and faded into the interior.

The doctor exchanged a glance with Riau. He put the snuffbox back in his pocket. From deep in the house came a murmuring too low to be understood. Then the silhouette reappeared.

"My husband wishes to know if you will sit at our table, *blanc,* and call us by our proper names."

"Of course—it would be my honor."

"Very well," the voice said. "*Vous êtes le bienvenu.* Welcome to Habitation Fortier."

The doctor hesitated a moment more, then parted the reed curtain with both hands and went inside.

For the long duration of the evening meal the doctor did not in any way allude to Nanon or Choufleur or for his real reason for being there, but instead affected to be paying a social call. The conversation was rigid with politeness, couched in formal, antique French. The doctor was careful to address his hosts as "Monsieur," or "Madame Fortier," whenever he spoke to either of them. They talked mostly of nonpolitical news

from France: art, the theater, scientific and medical developments—
quite as if the colony were not shredded by war all around them. Riau
followed the conversation, alert but without saying much himself. He
ate diligently, though not too fast. The cooking was unusually good. No
wine, but their water glasses were fragile balloons of crystal.

Monsieur Fortier was considerably darker than his wife: a *griffe, sacatra, marabou?*—the doctor had not perfectly mastered the complex colonial categories for mixed blood. Fortier was also younger than his wife,
though prematurely bald. He spoke little, in short, clipped phrases, and
ate sparingly, without pleasure. Sometimes his whole face would seem
to swell and he would lean forward over his plate as if he would burst
into some violent reaction. But instead he would always maintain his
silence, the tension draining from his face by slow degrees.

Madame Fortier seemed perfectly at ease, untroubled by her husband's peculiarly noticeable discomfort. She was a graceful and nimble
conversationalist—skilled in that art as any Frenchwoman, though without the slightest tinge of frivolity. Partly because of her great height and
her regal posture, she cut a striking figure at the foot of the dark wooden
table; also, though she was past the middle fifties, she was still a handsome woman, and must certainly have been a splendid beauty in her
youth. In the light of the guttering candles, her complexion was the
color of pale honey. Her hair was iron-gray laced with white, like moon-
rays pouring out from her face, then swept back and captured by the
complex turban which rose from the back of her head.

"Take your chair out onto the porch," she told the doctor, once the
meal had concluded. "Someone will serve you a glass of rum."

The doctor did as he was bidden. With a brief word of thanks to
the Fortiers, Riau went to the room they'd been assigned to share. Outside, the doctor placed his chair against the house wall, and sat looking
out over the starlit terraces below. His mule, tethered on a long cord,
looked up at him, snuffled and went back to grazing. Behind the reed
curtain the doctor seemed to hear the same sort of muttering as he had
that afternoon before they'd been admitted to the house.

Presently Madame Fortier came out alone, carrying a tray loaded
with two glasses, a calabash bottle, a clay jug, and a cut lemon. From
the calabash she poured a measure of rum and passed it to the doctor,
then indicated the water jug with a tilt of her head. The doctor declined.
He squeezed a few drops from the lemon into his drink while she filled
her own glass. They drank.

"*Santé,*" Madame Fortier said. She sighed, then busied herself filling
and lighting a small black pipe.

"Monsieur Fortier has retired?"

"Monsieur Fortier has gone to the *ajoupa* he keeps on the other side of this hill," she said. "Sometimes he likes to sleep on a straw mat on the ground and listen to the night song of the *siffleur montagne*. Perhaps it is romantic, but my bones are too old for it. I hear the night birds very well from my own bedroom. Also, my husband is discontented by your presence here, *blanc*. He is no lover of white people. He would have had me send you away, but I told him that as you wished to show us courtesy, you deserved our courtesy in return."

"*Merci pour ça,*" the doctor said. The hot burst of rum in his throat reassured him.

"*De rien,*" said Madame Fortier. "Regarding your purpose here, I can also offer you exactly nothing, except my advice that you abandon it."

"Have they been here?"

Madame Fortier's lips tightened on her pipe stem. "Yes, but briefly." She blew out a wreath of smoke. "But they are not here now, and I do not know where they have gone. I tell you, *blanc,* if the woman has left you, let her go. What does it matter?"

"I think of the boy, if nothing else."

"What can this boy be to you, this little *sang-mêlé?*"

"He is my son," the doctor said. The sentence rang between his ears. Perhaps he had never made this statement aloud in the presence of another person.

"Give me the snuffbox," Madame Fortier said.

The doctor complied. Madame Fortier lifted the box near to her face and examined the fleur-de-lys stamped on the lid. She turned it this way and that in the vague starlight, and ran her finger around its scalloped edge.

"I can tell you something of such sons," she said. "For example, there is my son Jean-Michel, whom you more probably know as Choufleur— this matter of naming is something to be discussed. His father is a *blanc* like you, the Sieur de Maltrot—perhaps you knew him also."

"By reputation only," the doctor said. "Well, by sight. He disappeared during the first months of the insurrection."

"He is dead," Madame Fortier said, still turning the snuffbox in her hands. "As you may be also, *blanc,* if you persist. I have for my son the feeling of any mother. I also recognize that he is vicious as a poisonous snake or a mad dog. He would certainly kill you, *blanc,* if you put yourself in his way, and perhaps he is even hoping you will do so. I tell you this for your own benefit—it is nothing to me if you live or die. I do not love you. Take more rum whenever you are ready."

"Thank you," the doctor said. He reached for the calabash. "*Permettez-moi.*"

"But you are too kind." Madame Fortier dropped the snuffbox into the lap of her skirts and held out her glass for him to replenish. *"Santé,"* she said. They drank.

"You have not the manner of a *colon,"* she told him. "Perhaps you have not been long in Saint Domingue?"

"I came in the summer of ninety-one," the doctor said. "About two months before the risings."

"Ah," she said. "You chose an interesting moment, no?" She took a moment to refill and light her pipe. "But let us consider this matter of names. Possibly you do not know that before the commissioners brought the new laws from France, we who are of mixed blood were not allowed the use of our own names—not if they derived from the names of white people. But no, it must be *le-dit Maltrot,* the *so-called Fortier* . . . Thus you may comprehend the sensitivity of my husband on this point."

"It is very understandable," the doctor said.

"For similar reasons, my son has seized the name of his white father and even his title and now calls himself the Sieur de Maltrot. Whereas his stable name Choufleur was first coined by his father, as a mockery of his freckled skin, as if the child were a speckled cauliflower. Maltrot invented it for spite, and still it was taken up by friends and family, and I used it myself with no thought of harm, and yet my son cannot hear this name without humiliation. Still, why must he rush to claim his father's name? Maltrot was cruel, even for a white man."

"That was an aspect of his reputation," the doctor said. Madame Fortier had fallen silent. He heard the whistling of a night bird somewhere above the cliffs that embraced the valley.

"Of course, cruelty is the first quality of any and all *blancs,"* she said. "Cruelty and greed, no matter how you may hide it. The Church was the first and best disguise. But whatever God created white people must be sharp-beaked as a hawk, or better yet, a vulture. Now we see *blancs* coming out of France blathering of equality and brotherhood, but underneath it is the same, I tell you—cruelty and greed. I challenge you, find me one Indian on this island—here or on the Spanish side. Three hundred years ago Ayiti held five kingdoms under five *caciques*—there were half a million of them. One finds their tools and relics everywhere, but not an Indian, not one. All of them destroyed by the whites. And now the *blancs* are doing the same work in Africa. Will they rest until the last children of Guinée have been stamped out of existence altogether?"

As this question appeared to be rhetorical, the doctor kept his silence, reaching unobtrusively for the calabash of rum.

"Bien," she said. "You may imagine the difficulty for those of us who

have mixed blood. If one has a mind to think or a heart to feel. One is neither one thing nor the other. Well, should I wish myself out of existence? No, instead I wish the white people to the devil, while I myself remain at peace. My husband too has reached his own accommodation. But so we return to the subject of my son."

Madame Fortier applied fire to the bowl of her little pipe. Discreetly, the doctor trickled rum into his glass. He did not bother with the lemon.

"You will understand that my son Jean-Michel was, according to the laws of *blancs,* the chattel and property of his father. As was I—for I was born into the *atelier* of slaves at Maltrot's plantation on the slopes by Vallière. Now, Maltrot used me with tremendous cruelty, as he did all women whom he carnally knew. His delight was to take the pleasures of love by force and to make the act itself and everything surrounding it as painful and humiliating to his partner as he might. In all such things he was very ingenious. Perhaps by reason of this predilection, he never made a marriage with a *blanche* and so produced no heirs or descendants other than colored persons like my son Jean-Michel. Although indeed the other children I bore to him did not live long, all instead falling victim in infancy to illnesses such as *mal de mâchoire."*

Madame Fortier turned and looked at him penetratingly. "As you are a medical man, perhaps you know something of this sickness."

"Only a little," said the doctor. He knew that lockjaw was a very common reason of death among the newborns of slave women, and although there were many theories as to its cause, none had been definitely proven. "I myself have witnessed few cases, for since the insurrections began here, the illness appears to have greatly decreased."

"Well," Madame Fortier said, smiling a little. *"Monsieur le médecin,* you are not without intelligence. Perhaps, with patience, you may learn something. If, for example, you were to gain the confidence of one of those old African crones who minister to women brought to bed in childbirth, you might discover that, if someone drives a long needle or pin through the soft place at the top of the skull of a newborn child, the wound is next to invisible, or no more than an insect bite—yet the child's jaws freeze and lock completely so that, unable to take nourishment, it will soon perish."

The doctor felt a chill which began at the extremity of his fingers and rapidly advanced along his arms toward his vital center. He felt his heart and lungs shrinking on themselves. "You speak of murder," he said.

"By no means," said Madame Fortier. "You have misunderstood me altogether. And in any case, supposing you were to gain the confidence of the proper old *paysanne,* she might very well tell you that it is better

for a child born into a world of hellish torments to be released and go straightaway home to Africa, *Guinée en bas de l'eau.*"

The mountain breeze, which was more than cool, again swept over the valley, shivering the branches of the coffee trees. The doctor gulped at his rum, which failed to warm him.

"But forgive me," said Madame Fortier, "I wander from my subject. Maltrot took a peculiar interest in his surviving son. Oh, he did not acknowledge his parentage, not openly. But he sent the boy to the priest of Vallière to be taught to write and cipher. And Maltrot himself taught him to play chess and dice and cards, and to drink rum, and wine and brandy when these were to be had—laughing at his inebriation, to be sure. He set the boy to learn the general workings of both a sugar and a coffee plantation, so that in time he gained some competence as an overseer and even as a manager. He saw that my son learned horsemanship and even (this at first surprised me) permitted him to acquire some skill with sword and pistol. Afterward he put him into the *maréchaussée* to be a catcher of runaway slaves. Choufleur grew most adept at this— so that he soon became the leader of that cavalry. He became an expert hunter of wild men, and he also learned especially to savor—for he has that same strain of cruelty inherited from the father—the whippings and amputations and other tortures visited on the recaptured runaways.

"You may call it kindness, all this education proffered him by his father, if of a strange variety. But it was not. No, there was a more sophisticated cruelty at the bottom of it, long in the planning and slow to bear its poisoned fruit. Choufleur learned the tastes and the prerogatives of *blancs* only so that he might more keenly feel his privation of them. Feel with the cut and burn of a whiplash how, although he had the desires and capabilities of a *blanc*, in reality he must always be only the puppet or servant of *blancs*. That his joys would always come only on sufferance of a master and that he himself had right to nothing, not even to his name.

"Now I must tell you how cunningly the father applied salt to the wounds of the son, once the moment was right. At the time of which I speak, Jean-Michel had lately entered his young manhood, while Nanon, whom you are seeking, was a girl of perhaps fifteen. Now, my son knew something of women already, as Maltrot had introduced him to brothels in the towns on the coast. But he knew nothing of love. Nonetheless, he had some capacity for love, as I saw when he and Nanon began to walk together." Her voice caught slightly. "I may say that if they had been left to their own devices, you might be hearing a different story now, or more likely you would not be hearing it at all."

"*Permettez-moi,*" the doctor said, and raised the calabash. Madame Fortier held out her glass to be refilled.

"Thank you," she said. "Useless to ponder what might have been. The reality of what occurred is that the Sieur de Maltrot had also observed the awakening of interest and affection between my son and the girl Nanon. Perhaps he had already taken note of her beauty, which was then in its first flower. So when the moment seemed most propitious to his purposes, he exercised his seigneurial right—also of course his right of property—to ravish the girl away from my son and make her his own concubine. He used her after his ordinary custom for some weeks at Vallière, very much in our presence though not absolutely before our eyes. Afterward he took her to Le Cap, where he established her as a *fille de joie,* and where one imagines that you, sir, must have first made her acquaintance."

"It is true that we first met one another at Le Cap, Madame," the doctor said.

Madame Fortier had put her head to one side and was looking at him curiously.

"I would argue that we came to one another freely," the doctor said. "And that her choice in the encounter was still more powerful than my own. Though perhaps you would not believe me, and it may be that I am mistaken, too. But please continue—your story is more than interesting to me."

"Ah," said Madame Fortier, and turned her face to the starlit valley. "Well, having carried out these actions, Maltrot perceived that perhaps he had gone too far for his own security, and that Choufleur might murder him outright without regard for the consequence, which consequence would of course have been very dreadful. Whereupon he freed both me and my son. This step surprised both of us very much. You may know that it was the habit of many libidinous *blancs* to free their slave mistresses and their bastard progeny, often from the moment of their birth, but Maltrot had never given the least sign of any such intention. However, he did free us both. I went away with Fortier, but Maltrot sent Choufleur to France, there to further his education for two years at the expense of his father."

Madame Fortier took up the snuffbox from her lap and turned it so that it glittered in the light. "Of all I loathed about that man," she said, "I most detested his manner of taking snuff. For he always used it as a seasoning for some abomination he had devised, before or after, if not both. But he has taken his last pinch." She opened her knees in a gesture that seemed almost lewd, letting the box fall back into the hollow of her skirts. "His precautions, canny as they were, were not sufficient."

She closed her thighs to hide the box, and rolled her weight toward the doctor. "Tell me, have you looked inside?" Her eyes shone on him strangely. "Do you know what it contains?"

The doctor swallowed. "The amputated sexual member, evidently mummified, of a human male."

"Why, you are absolutely correct!" Madame Fortier snapped her knees apart so sharply that the tightening skirt fabric catapulted the box into the air. She reached to catch it in one hand and, laughing gaily as a girl, offered it to the doctor. "Your prize, sir, it is yours to keep—so far as I am concerned. My son, who returned from France a nicely finished article, presented it as a compliment to me. Tangible proof he had severed the organ that planted the seed of him in my womb. Oh, he lured his father into the mountains during the insurrections of ninety-one, and he had a whole roster of details to tell me of the revenge he took when once he'd trapped him there—but I would not hear it, and I would not accept the box. Though I am more than happy to know the man is dead. I might have predicted that my son would next offer the box with its contents as a sentimental keepsake to Nanon . . . though not that it would pass into your hands. I would not have predicted any part of you."

"Madame, you flatter me." The doctor felt the negligible weight of the snuffbox dragging his knuckles down to the back of his knee.

"Oh, I do not mean to. A delicate love offering, is it not?" said Madame Fortier. "Do you think my son a savage? You may be correct on that score also. But his is the savagery of a *blanc*. Oh, he is not yet done with killing his father, for the father lives on in his own blood, and owns him still."

"I am sorry for your trouble," the doctor said.

"Save your pity for yourself," Madame Fortier said. "I have other sons, with Fortier, and I am free, though Choufleur is not." She rose to her full, astonishing height, her skirts falling to her ankles. "For that young woman I do feel sympathy," she said absently. "There was sorrow in her eyes when they were here—yes, they have been here, but I do not know where they have gone. To Le Cap or more likely to Vallière."

"But Vallière is in the hands of the Spanish, or of Jean-François."

"Oh, I do not think my son will be at risk. He knows Jean-François very well, and it is not so long since he was fighting on that side. You may yourself have difficulty in going to Vallière, but in any case, I advise you not to follow. I do not hate you, *blanc*—but what can this woman be to you save a piece of your property stolen by another? I fear that my son has come to regard her in much the same way. If you would be sensible, let her go."

Madame Fortier swung and parted the curtain of reeds with one hand as if she would reenter the house. Then she walked back to stand over the doctor, reaching her right hand down to him. He took the hand, which was square-cut and seemed strong to him, though its fingers applied no pressure to his own.

"*Bonne route, blanc,*" she said. "I wish you no harm, but I will not see you tomorrow."

Madame Fortier was true to her word, though next morning a house-maid did appear to present the guests with a tray of coffee and a flat round of sugared cassava bread. The doctor's head hammered from a surfeit of rum, and coffee seemed only to add the symptom of queasiness. His spirit was unquiet as well. But he and Riau saddled up and rode out before the sun had cleared the ridges of Morne à Chapelet. All day they labored to retrace their path to Dondon, stopping only for the doctor to harvest certain herbs for the composition of wound salves. And once he halted above a gurgling ravine to empty out the snuffbox over the rocks and the rushing water below. He had meant to toss the box itself away after its contents but at the last moment changed his mind and put it back empty into his pocket.

They rode on. By the time they rejoined Toussaint's force, the doctor had sweated away all the effects of the rum and felt nothing but a dense fatigue, in which no vestige of a thought could form itself.

Next morning Toussaint's army, divided into five columns, poured out of Dondon. The doctor, riding with Toussaint's own column, was so situated as to have the long-range view of the other four lines of troops, wrapping themselves into the mountains above Grande Rivière. With the addition of the three columns which Villatte was supposed to have dispatched from the north, the entire attack would whip around the valley of Grande Rivière like the tentacles of an octopus.

But for the next several days the doctor was able only to confront what came immediately into his hands. With Toussaint's vanguard he rode in the attack on Camp Flamen. The first fort barring their way to this camp was overrun with slight resistance. Toussaint paused long enough to learn that posts on the neighboring heights of the chain had been taken as easily by his other columns and sent an order to Dessalines to join him at Camp Flamen.

But here the defense was more determined, so the doctor was soon submerged in poulticing and bandaging or amputating hopelessly shattered limbs. The hideously scarred Guiaou, whose touch had a strange gentleness, as well as strength enough to hold a man still while the doctor sawed off his arm or leg, assisted him. Once the battle was over, Riau came to help him too, so that all three of them worked together, seamlessly, communicating by gesture more than speech. Camp Flamen fell to them that afternoon and Toussaint began a foray toward Cambion, but dropped back at nightfall because of ambushes.

The surgery went on through the night, and the doctor threw himself down to sleep just as Dessalines and Médor were marching their troops out for predawn attacks on Camp Roque and several other posts. An hour later Riau shook him awake and he clambered into the mule saddle (he had never found time to reclaim his horse) and rode with Toussaint's column on the fort of Saint Malo. Here Toussaint subdivided his men again so as to attack from two directions, while his other columns reduced and burned a number of smaller surrounding posts: Cormine, Bense, Salenave, Dupuis. . . .

The doctor saw to the priming of his pistols and long gun, but Toussaint had no intention of risking his surgeon near the front line, and the campaign was so very well organized that the doctor had no need of his weapons, and soon forgot he was carrying them. He installed his surgery at Saint Malo and worked through the night again with his assistants, the howling of the wounded under his saw sometimes punctuated by gunfire and shouts from ambushes in the forests all around. Toussaint also stayed up the whole night through, receiving and sending reports and orders from the adjacent columns; occasionally he would fold his arms, inhale deeply and let his eyes roll back in his head for perhaps as long as forty-five seconds. When he exhaled and refocused his eyes, he would seem as lucid and refreshed as if he had slept for several hours.

The doctor stole another hour of sleep and jerked like an automaton back into the mule saddle. That day the columns marched closer together to support one another in case of ambush, but the doctor took the precaution to lash his knees to the saddle so that if he fell asleep, he would not fall off the mule.

They rode on for several days more, with the accompanying reduction of more camps and forts: Cardinau, Pistaud, Tannache, Ducasse. Toussaint was taking a great many prisoners, whom he dispatched along with his own wounded back to the security of Dondon. But the doctor remained near the fighting lines, dazedly carrying on his sawing and bandaging, a blood-soaked *zombi* carpenter of shredded flesh and bone. He seemed to slip in and out of awareness, a dark-feathered wing passing over his vision.

Sometimes the wing lifted on astonishing spectacles: the troops of

Moyse climbing the cruel heights toward Fort Bamby, under constant cannonfire but so disciplined they never fired a shot in reply and never hesitated in their advance till they forced the wall and did in their opponents with fixed bayonets. On the heights all around, the camps of the enemy were burning, and then Riau came through the smoke of the fires to tell the doctor that soon indeed they would advance to Vallière, next day or the day after. At this the doctor's heart quickened, as for almost the first time since the campaign began, his recollections of Nanon and Paul came fully through to him.

Next day Toussaint took his main force to the attack of Camp Charles-Sec, believing that Noël Arthaud, dispatched by Villatte, had cut the road to Vallière to prevent any reinforcement coming to the enemy. But in the midst of the fighting at Charles-Sec it was discovered that Arthaud had failed in this maneuver—the eighth tentacle had been severed or at least had missed its mark, for Jean-François rushed out from Vallière with twenty-five hundred men to join the battle. At risk of being surrounded himself, Toussaint cut his way out of the trap and withdrew behind the cordon he had now extended as far as Montagne Noire. Then, having secured the outlying posts, he took his exhausted army to Marmelade, where the men could rest and he would compose his report of the campaign to Laveaux.

"All the valley of Grande Rivière is ours," Toussaint claimed in the letter which Doctor Hébert, among others, helped to copy out fair.

But, in truth, the region had become a no-man's-land which would be contested for many more weeks. The doctor hurled himself into fifteen solid hours of impenetrable pitch-black sleep, and finally woke to the dull apprehension that for his private purpose the campaign had been a failure—for the time being he had no hope at all of reaching Vallière.

17

Midmorning, Toussaint left Gonaives and rode, amid a half-dozen of his cavalry, toward the dry-bony mountains north of the town. But before beginning the scaly, lizard-backed ascent, he abruptly dismissed his escort and turned off toward Ennery. The other riders were puzzled, he could see—except for Riau, who straightaway suspected him of *marronage*. Toussaint smiled at the the thought of Riau's lightly masked expression, and with a light pressure of his knee urged Bel Argent into a canter. It was flat and easy going here, and the white stallion could stretch his legs with small risk.

These sudden reversals of direction were common enough—a constant rupture of his pattern of movement, so that he always arrived without warning where he was least expected, so that his ways from crossroads to crossroads were unpredictable and unknown. But for months Toussaint had hardly gone anywhere unescorted; he must have a few of his best riders round him, trusted men who were gradually being shaped into a sort of personal guard of honor, as well as his surgeon, his secretaries . . . Well, let them wonder. He smiled again at the thought of Riau—as if he, the general Toussaint Louverture, would desert the army of thousands he had created.

He leaned forward in the saddle, the reins curling upward through his lightly closed hands, which hovered above the white mane of Bel Argent. A pleasant breeze stroked his face and pulled at the corners of his hat. Within the grip of his lean thighs, the muscles of the horse's back flowed like water, a wave rolling ceaselessly forward without breaking. There was no need for any thought.

Such moments had become rare for him. Soon his mind began to work again. He reined in Bel Argent before the stallion could overheat himself, leaning forward to gently stroke the warm and slightly sweaty neck, and walked him slowly down the road. Already they had reached the gate of Habitation Thibodet, and Toussaint might have been tempted to enter to check on the progress of the cultivation and the status of the garrison there—but he did not. He would press on to Marmelade, which had been his original destination that morning, though he'd arrive there by a different route.

Beyond the gateposts, as the road began to rise, he turned from it and pressed the stallion up the steeper slopes toward the ridge, skirting the outermost coffee trees. He could hear the voices of women singing as they gathered the red berries—that was good—but he kept out of their sight behind a screen of trees, leaning still farther forward now as Bel Argent mounted the difficult grades. Then he felt himself brushed, along his right profile, by someone's regard, and turned to lock eyes with that scarred one, he who had come out of the Savane Désolée with his tale of what had happened to the "Swiss." An instant of recognition, and Toussaint was gone behind the trees, leaving the cultivated land altogether now, climbing around a thicket of bamboo. What was his name, that scarred one? Now he would report that he had seen the General Toussaint, passing in ghostly silence on the back of his white horse.

Or perhaps he would not speak of it. The name came to him: Guiaou. Toussaint remembered now that there was some trouble between him and Riau. Something to do with a woman, certainly . . . he did not exactly remember, but whatever it was had moved him to post Riau away from Ennery. Perhaps no more than an inkling . . . But Riau could not be too tightly constrained or he might bolt again altogether, or try to. Riau had several useful skills, and Toussaint did not want to be obliged to order him shot. Besides, he was fond of Riau, whom he'd adopted long ago when the boy was first brought out of Guinée as a *bossale* to Habitation Bréda. Of course, he had been *parrain* to many others in those days of slavery. And to be the General Toussaint Louverture was to be father of sorts to four or five or six thousand men.

He took off his general's hat, as if it were to blame for the direction of his thoughts, and fastened it to his stirrup leather. The hat rode by his left knee, its red and white plumes flexing with the motion of the horse. Bel Argent, shoulders straining slightly, broke out of the bamboo onto the trail at the top of the ridge. The mountain air was distinctly cooler, and Toussaint's headcloth, sweat-soaked under the hat, began to dry.

He was deep inside his own lines here, and safe as safe could possibly be, in this country at this time. He let the white stallion choose the pace: a brisk, spring-loaded walk. Today for the first time in many days, there was no particular reason for haste. And solitude was most welcome to him. His mind ran empty, clear and light. There was nothing, only a global awareness of the damp smells of the jungle, shifting of shadows and ticking of insects in the leaves.

But here was a new *bitasyon* sprung up since he had last passed this way. A new clutch of wattled cabins half completed, corn plantings spiraling among boulders up the hillside to his right. And there above him on the trail, a naked boy of three or four stood gaping down at him, slack-jawed, eyes as round and white as hens' eggs, then plunged into the bush. Toussaint heard his voice calling to the others. He followed the curve of the trail around the clustered houses. A young woman in a blue headcloth stood watching him from a doorway as he went by. His mind began to work again. This too was *marronage*, this sprouting of villages and gardens all through the hills, as if the liberated people had indeed gone back to Guinée, or invented their own Africa, here and now. At this he felt a twinge, almost of envy. A creole born in Saint Domingue, Toussaint had never seen Guinée.

Again he thought of Riau's wandering spirit . . . which was far from unique. Then the jungle closed behind the horse's tail, and the voices of the children died away, and his thought left him. He rode on. No, he would not go to Marmelade today, though the town was easily within his range. He clucked to Bel Argent and turned him down from the road, crossing a narrow rivulet at the bottom of a shallow gorge, then climbing to strike the red groove of another trail beyond.

The cactus fence had grown taller around the small square *case*, but this time the two little dogs did not bark. One came to the door and sniffed the air, then turned around and lay down with its tail hanging over the sill. The old woman stood in the bare-earth yard, pounding a pestle taller than herself into a mortar hollowed from a stump.

"*Bonsoir, grann,*" he said to her.

The old woman turned and bared her gums, her whole face wrinkling in pleasure, though she seemed unsurprised.

"*Ou pa sezi,*" Toussaint remarked.

"It was my spirit who told me you might come."

Toussaint nodded as he swung down from the saddle and moved to tether Bel Argent to a tree. No doubt the spirit which informed her of his arrival was the same spirit that had moved him to come. He took off the saddlebags and undid the buckles of the girth. The corners of his portable writing desk pressed his ribs through the leather as he carried his load toward the house. Notes for letters yet to be written, copies of letters already sent . . . but tonight he would not write, or dictate.

The dog got up whimpering as Toussaint stooped to lay his load within the sill. The tip of his long sword's scabbard had dragged a trail in the dust from where his horse was tied. He unbuckled the sword and leaned the hilt against the outside wall.

"I will go and wash," he said. The old woman nodded as she stooped to turn a golden mound of cornmeal out of the mortar onto a large clay dish.

Unbuttoning his coat, Toussaint walked around the plantings of yams and beans toward the tinkling sound of the spring. He laid his clothing and his pistols on a rock and waded into the spring-fed pool, watching his reflection disappear as it joined with his corporeal self: the slightly bowed legs and wiry arms and tightly knotted torso. The water was cold, clarifying; he could feel it in his back teeth. He went completely underneath the water. When he came up, snapping his head back with a gasp, he saw a gaggle of children assembled on the rocks, gazing at him and whispering.

The General Toussaint Louverture! The horse, the plumed hat, the big sword had conspired to give him away. In the beginning he had been invisible, a little leaf doctor in the service of Jean-François and Biassou, merely an old black man wandering the mountains with a sack of herbs, a simple *doktè-fey*. Then, the movement of his hand had been invisible, as his hands moved round him now, beneath the mirror surface of the water. He had that still, his secret hands, but now at the same time he must also be the General Toussaint Louverture with his uniform and insignia and big warhorse, at the head of his troops with his long sword flashing in the light. This, too, was necessary.

One of the bigger girls shoved a smaller boy down from a boulder; he yelped and slapped at her calf in protest. The children all scattered as Toussaint came out of the water. As he dried himself he thought of Brisbane—one Englishman who liked a fight, and who had been highly visible at long distances, in his red coat. The square line of his jaw, with the bulge of beef-eating muscle below each ear . . . though in fact Toussaint was imagining those details. If he had been close enough to Brisbane to see him so well, he would have killed him or made him prisoner.

Brisbane was dangerous. The other British commanders much preferred to keep their troops in the coast towns, where they would be safely away from the hazards of combat, though distinctly more vulnerable to dysentery and the various fevers, which Toussaint knew were now making terrible inroads among the garrisons at both Saint Marc and Port-au-Prince. Whitelocke and his other subordinates would rather have the colonial and *émigré* militias, such as the Chasseurs of Dessources, do their front-line fighting for them—troops which far from causing Toussaint any serious concern, furnished him rather with amusement. Brisbane was very much another matter, more than willing to commit his troops to battle on the open flats of the Artibonite, where Toussaint was somewhat hesitant to commit his own. He had triumphed over his English enemy with a spectacular cavalry charge at Grande Saline, but still the risk of such flourishes was greater than he liked. At the same time, he did not enjoy the thought of British troops establishing themselves in the mountains of the interior for long enough to acclimate themselves. A body of European soldiery which had developed immunity to the tropical illnesses and had also learned something about the terrain would be a more serious threat than he wanted to contend with, and Brisbane seemed more capable than anyone else of taking his men to that level . . . Wary of a full-scale engagement, Toussaint had been tiring Brisbane's force with constant skirmishing all over the Artibonite plain, relying on swift and swerving movements and on superior knowledge of the countryside. Then Brisbane, conspicuous at the head of the British troops as Toussaint was at the head of his—Brisbane, according to the will of BonDyé (here Toussaint crossed himself, half consciously, as he walked back toward the old woman's cabin), had been picked off by a sharpshooter, ambushed in fact, not far from the Artibonite dam. Not killed outright, but wounded so gravely that he was carried from the field. Since then, the British campaign in the Artibonite had stalled.

There was a hazard in visibility, Toussaint thought, to have made oneself remarkable . . . he respected Brisbane, though naturally he also hoped that he would die. Regaining the *case*, he sat down for a moment on the sill, nudging one of the feisty little dogs aside so as to open his saddlebag. He took out a clean yellow square of madras and tied it over his head. The smell from the cook fire was enticing. Of course, the old woman was not really his grandmother, though he addressed her so and trusted her as if she were. He had other such honorary *grann* scattered over the country in whose huts he would sometimes award himself a short period of seclusion—no one else quite knowing where he was. With the grandmothers he could also eat without stint or suspicion; theirs was the only food he fully trusted, save what came from the hands of his own wife.

He found some fodder for Bel Argent, then walked barefoot over the packed dirt to the rear of the *case* and stood inhaling the aromas. The old woman was stirring her iron cauldron while the girl chopped up wrinkled green and orange peppers on a chip of wood—she looked up and smiled shyly to greet him and then looked away. The wind rose up to lift the leaves, and it grew cooler as the clouds rolled in, but it did not really rain; only a few fat drops smacked down before the clouds passed over. They ate outside, crosslegged round the cook fire, using fresh, broad banana leaves as plates. *Maïs moulin:* cornmeal mush with beans and a little meat with its juices, raised to a high piquancy by the peppers.

They ate seriously and talked little. The old woman did ask after Moustique, though when Toussaint told her he had absconded from Delahaye's care, she seemed to know about it already.

"Oui, li kouri nan tou morne isit," she said smiling with evident approval. *"Li pale ak tou lespri sa yo epi ak BonDyé tou."*

Toussaint set his banana leaf aside and drew up his knees, responding to inner twinges of annoyance. The *marronage* of Moustique bothered him more than most, mainly because it embarrassed him before l'Abbé Delahaye. The idea of the boy—running all over these mountains, as the old woman had put it, talking with all the spirits of Africa and also with the Catholic God. He'd heard elsewhere that the boy had left the area and gone north in the direction of Le Cap, but who on earth knew where he might really be? Delahaye would be especially piqued to learn that his charge had carried his smattering of Catholic doctrine to the *hûnfors*.

He emptied his mind by carefully combing out Bel Argent's mane and tail and brushing the animal's white coat till it gleamed obscurely in the light of the crescent moon. This had been his work at Bréda, so long ago, and it soothed him still, as it calmed the horse. But now this agreeable task was almost always done by others.

Sleep came the instant he stretched himself out, resting his head on the supple leather of a saddlebag. Dreams whirled over him like filaments of spider web crossing and recrossing: trails and roads and *kalfou* and his constant movement, reversing itself like a whiplash cracking back along its braided length, or a snake coiling, striking, recoiling. Here yield, here retreat, feint, parry, flank. Here, make a stand, on the height above Petite Rivière, which Blanc Cassenave had fortified. Below, the brown river folded around the cliff, winding and constricting and, off to the southwest, a blue haze hung over the ocean and Saint Marc.

Toussaint woke, immediately lucid, aware of the writing desk's hard edges through the saddlebag under the back of his head. A second later he knew where he was and how he'd come there. The old woman and the girl breathed softly on their pallets against the opposite wall of the small, square room. One of the feisty dogs got up to look him over, even though he had not moved. Then the dog grunted, turned and lay down. Toussaint could smell horse sweat from his saddle blanket on the floor nearby. And Blanc Cassenave was dead . . . Toussaint had written his epitaph in a letter to Laveaux, drafted by some odd coincidence the same day Brisbane had been shot.

> *During his detention Blanc Cassenave was struck with apoplexy, which had every appearance of an unbridled rage; he died of suffocation; may he rest in peace. He is out of this world; we must give thanks to God accordingly. The death of Blanc Cassenave abolishes any sort of procedure against him, as his crime had no accomplices.*

A copy of this letter, among others, was shut up in the writing desk beneath his head. Now Toussaint had taken all the sleep he needed, though it would be hours yet before dawn. He was ready to compose and dictate, but there was no secretary. He lay still.

REQUIESCAT IN PACE—Blanc Cassenave had died in prison, arrested by Toussaint following what had practically amounted to a rebellion, a mutiny, or so it could be argued; the story might be told in more than one way. Was the man suffocated by his own rage as Toussaint had reported, or was it the weight of the chains laid on him? Toussaint had been elsewhere at the time of his death and did not know the answer for certain. It was no small thing to put a man in chains. He felt that Blanc Cassenave had himself to blame for his demise, though he had been among the most brave and capable of the colored officers to begin with. Indeed, he had made himself remarkable. But there was the matter of the four hundred pounds of gunpowder that he had failed to forward to Toussaint. Blanc Cassenave had shot forty men whom he claimed were traitors but whom Toussaint believed to be simply his personal enemies. Well, and he had openly defied Toussaint's authority when reproached about the gunpowder, and had fomented dissension all through the posts along the Artibonite River (allowing the English to capitalize on the confusion). He had spread a rumor that putting the plantations back to work was only a masked design on the part of Toussaint, and even Laveaux, to restore slavery. His diversion not only of the gunpowder but also of munitions and other booty captured from the enemy suggested a scheme to set up his own private force—Toussaint understood very well what that signified since he had done the same himself while nominally under command of Jean-François and Biassou.

Beyond this individual rebellion, it smelled as if Blanc Cassenave had been conspiring with Villatte, and perhaps there was even some larger conspiracy afoot among the mulattoes, for so many of them seemed to feel themselves racially superior to their black brothers in arms.

But now Blanc Cassenave was dead, and Brisbane, perhaps, would soon die. The Cordon of the Artibonite was in order, and the whole Artibonite plain seemed within Toussaint's grasp, though he could not close his hand upon it until he had rooted the British out of Saint Marc.

The corner of the writing desk dug into the hollow at the back of his neck; it made his mind a hive of swarming words. Outside, Bel Argent lifted his head from grazing and whickered softly, then, as if the warhorse had anticipated it, the drumming began beneath the *mapou* tree beyond the next ridge. The idea of Moustique resurfaced in Toussaint's awareness, and as quickly he wiped it away. Words rose up through the leather of the saddlebag, fuming into his head like smoke.

Some of those drifting phrases gave him pleasure; for instance, his report to Laveaux on the ambush of Dessources's Chasseurs on the Artibonite, in which Toussaint had captured seven supply wagons, slain sixty of the enemy and scattered the rest. As for Dessources himself, *he owed his escape only to the speed of his horse*—yes, that had been felicitously put. The prisoners reported that Dessources had also been wounded in the thigh, but Toussaint certainly hoped he would survive and return to the field—he found Dessources an amusing opponent, courageous certainly but weakened by contempt for the enemy and an excess of pride, two qualities which made him easy to draw. His immediate subordinates, whether colored or white, were similarly self-willed and volatile, to the point that they were barely capable of acting in concert. As for the black soldiers that made up their numbers, these were distinctly undercommitted to the proslavery struggle and so collapsed easily under pressure, though many of these same men fought bravely and stubbornly once incorporated into Toussaint's own troops.

The texture of the drumming changed and intensified, and Toussaint, slipping again partway toward dream, felt his limbs moving lightly on the mat, as if in water, but he did not wish to give way, and then, with the harsh cry of the *loa* descending, the drumming stopped. He was conscious of his cool detachment, as if he had become a *blanc*. The boiling of language in his head subsided and the words flattened out again on their papers, inside the desk sheathed by the leather bag. There were others skilled in the art of marshaling words on paper, most dangerously the mulatto Pinchinat, who was involved in some obscure machination which connected Villate on the north coast with Rigaud in the Southern Department (but Toussaint did not want to think about that just now . . .); meanwhile even Jean-François, in his angry letter rejecting an invitation to join the French Republicans, had managed a fine flourish:

> *Equality, Liberty, &c &c &c . . . I will only believe in that when I see that Monsieur Laveaux and other French gentlemen of his quality giving their daughters in marriage to Negroes. Then I will be able to believe in this pretended equality.*

That letter had been written quite some ago, and quite likely someone else had furnished Jean-François with the phrasing, but still this shard of rhetoric was difficult either to bypass or digest, and similar arguments continued to gain sway among the people of the Grande Rivière valley. Even some of Moyse's men at Dondon had been moved to defect to Jean-François, and though Toussaint imagined they had been more persuaded by proffers of Spanish gold than by any words spoken or written, the problem was serious and must be addressed. He had already countered by accusing Jean-François of slave trading *You ask if a republican is free? It takes a slave to ask such a question. Do you really dare you, Jean-François, who has sold his brothers to the Spanish, brothers who are actually digging in the mines of that detestable nation, to supply the ostentation of its king* and Jean-François was truly guilty of this charge, as Biassou had been guilty of the same action before him. Toussaint could well have wished that Jean-François had disappeared from the scene instead of Biassou (who according to rumor had gone to Spanish Florida and perhaps been killed there in a brawl), for Biassou was the weaker general, as Dessources was weaker than Brisbane, though not by so great a measure. Jean-François could be defeated, though not without effort and difficulty. There was no one who could not somehow be defeated.

But when Jean-François had been dispatched, the question he had raised might linger and attach itself to another and another after that, for all black men and women in the colony would be most loyal to whoever they believed would protect their freedom. And freedom to do what? There must be work to feed the struggle—Laveaux's French faction had no gold, nor sufficient supplies nor ammunition, so that Toussaint must take most of what he required from the enemy. This he had so far managed to do, but still there must be money to purchase weapons and supplies for the future, and so there must be work which produced something exchangeable for money—thus, plantation work, but that resembled slavery.

Here was another problem Toussaint did not wish to think about, for he could not immediately solve it. Here the circle closed upon itself. As he had proclaimed to the former cultivators in the area of Verrettes:

Work is necessary, it is a virtue; it serves the general benefit of the State. Any slothful wandering person will be arrested and punished by the law. But labor also takes place under the condition that it is only through compensation, a justly paid salary, that one can encourage it and carry it to the highest level.

It was well enough to speak of working for a proportion of one's own benefit measured against the common good, and Toussaint himself believed in this principle, but for the great majority, this was not liberty. Freedom was here, in this mountain village with a few animals and gardens on which the people might easily live; freedom was what he himself had come here, for the space of a few hours, to enjoy.

The drumming had begun again, under the mapou tree. Toussaint shut down his mind. Only so much could be gained from thinking, reasoning like a *blanc;* problems which did not yield to reason might be dissolved in other ways. He calmed himself by silently reciting, against the driving of the drums, a chaplet of the names of camps that surrounded and protected his positions: Grande Saline, Rossignol, Poinci Desdunes, Latapie, Laporte, Théard, Chatelain, Pothenot, Donache, Boudet, Remousin . . . Then it was dawn.

Midmorning, he came riding down the zigzag path out of the *mornes* above Marmelade. Women swinging empty baskets as they climbed to the provision grounds stepped aside and smiled at him as he passed. Toussaint touched his hat to the prettiest, and also to the oldest among them. Now and then Bel Argent's hooves dislodged a shower of pebbles which rattled down to startle the quick brown lizards that flicked this way and that across the trail.

Skirting the square with its church and the building he'd adopted for his headquarters, he rode to the house at the edge of town where he had installed his family. Suzanne was just returning from the river as he dismounted—she stopped dead and hugged her bundle of clothes. Behind her, the hugely pregnant Marie-Noelle was startled enough to drop the bundle she was carrying. The girl covered the O of her mouth with one hand and crouched awkwardly, knees splaying around her swollen belly, to collect the spilled garments and brush off the dust.

Suzanne set her bundle inside the door and stretched out her hands to her husband; Toussaint leaned in and pressed his cheek to hers. He was content that he had surprised her even a little, though she did not show a great deal of surprise.

"Where are my sons?" Toussaint said, but Saint-Jean, the youngest, was already running from the house to wrap his arms fiercely around Toussaint's thigh above the boot top. Toussaint took a step back to regain his balance. Suzanne smiled at them from the doorway, hands on her hips, as Toussaint swung the boy onto his hip and kissed his forehead.

"The others are at their studies with the priest," Suzanne said.

Toussaint lowered the boy to the ground; Saint-Jean scampered toward the white warhorse, then hesitated and looked back.

"But this one must study and learn also," Toussaint said. "Eh?"

"Oh, the priest receives him later in the day," Suzanne said, cocking up one hip. "He takes him alone and the other two together."

She went into the house and, a moment later, set a chair outside the door. Toussaint removed his hat and coat and handed them to her. He carried the chair to the shade of a mango tree and sat down, pulling off his boots and stockings and working his bare toes in the loose dirt.

Marie-Noelle had sorted out her washing and was carrying part of it away toward the main square. Toussaint raised his arms slightly from his sides, allowing the breeze to run through his shirt sleeves and comb over the madras cloth tied around his head. A speckled hen plopped down in a sunny spot of the yard and began a luxurious dust bath. Saint-Jean came around the back of Toussaint's chair and threw both arms over his shoulders, pressing his hands on his father's shirt front and laying his cheek on the back of his neck.

Briefly, Toussaint closed his eyes. When he reopened them, Suzanne had appeared with a calabash full of cool water. He took it from her hands and drank. For some time longer he sat quite still, only his toes flexing a little, his mind deliciously empty and clear. When the shade of the mango tree began to move away from him, he put on his boots with the ghost of a sigh and crossed the yard to knock on the frame of the door.

"Will Saint-Jean go now to the priest?"

"He will go later," Suzanne called from within. "After the heat."

Toussaint went down across the square before the church. Indeed, it was very hot already, the sun vertical above the plumes of his hat, and the dust stirring white around his boots. When he came near the house behind the church, he could hear the drone of the boys' recitation from the priest's study. Occasionally, there would be the slap of a hand on the table to punctuate a correction l'Abbé Delahaye had made. Then the drone began again. Toussaint stood outside, half smiling as he listened.

When the lesson had ended the boys tumbled out, knocking into each other in the doorway: Placide the taller, scrawnier, serious-looking, with his high forehead. His skin had that coppery Arada tone, while Isaac was darker and more compact—somehow denser, it seemed. From his first years he had weighed as much or more than his brother, as if his bones were made of stone.

Both boys brightened when they saw him waiting. Toussaint hugged them, touching the backs of their heads, and sent them home to their mother.

"If you like, we can sit outdoors," Delahaye said. "In the house it it is rather close, at this hour."

He led the way to a little arbor, upwind of the cook fire ring, where three chairs had been arranged around a wicker table. Delahaye motioned for him to sit.

"They are applying themselves to their work?" Toussaint said. "They study with concentration?"

"Oh, they are assiduous enough," Delahaye said. "They progress, in small steps." He sat down with a whoosh of his cassock. "And certainly they are more faithful acolytes than some."

"*M'regrette sa,*" Toussaint said hastily, for he was already sensitive on the point of Moustique. I'm sorry for that. He looked away. "I have heard the rumor," he muttered, "that he has been running the hills hereabout, but my own men find no sign of him."

"I've seen nothing of him either," Delahaye said, "nor yet of my stole and chalice, or my donkey." With a quick, irritable movement he brushed an insect from the back of his neck. "However, he did leave us some remembrance of himself," he said, "As you may now very plainly see."

The priest looked significantly toward Marie-Noelle, who was waddling out of the house with a tray of refreshments. On the table between them she laid out cold bread and whole bananas, large glasses of water and small ones of rum. Toussaint kept silent till she had withdrawn.

"Suzanne will come to her, when it is time," he said.

"Yes," said Delahaye, "I knew that had been so arranged. And it must be soon, no? She looks ready to burst. But no matter."

Toussaint picked up a banana and inspected the peel. Satisfied, he slit it open with thumbnail and took a small bite.

"There is news," Delahaye said, a slightly rising note in his voice. Toussaint lifted his head.

"Brisbane has died, from the effects of his wound," Delahaye said.

"*Ah.*" Toussaint set the banana back down on the table and spread his hand out flat beside it. Delahaye looked at him narrowly.

"No Latin phrases?" the priest said.

"*Tout grâce à Dieu,*" Toussaint murmured. "You are certain?"

"Oh, quite," said Delahaye. "Infection. He had been shot through the throat apparently, and in this climate . . ."

"Yes," Toussaint said, rocking almost imperceptibly in the chair. "Yes."

Delahaye was still looking at him, with an edged curiosity. "You prosper very well in Caesar's world, my son," the priest said.

Toussaint, eyes lidded, swayed slightly in his seat but said nothing. He folded both arms across his chest and breathed deeply in.

"Blanc Cassenave is also dead," said Delahaye. "It seems impossible that anyone can raise himself to oppose you."

Toussaint let his eyes fall completely shut. Against the closed lids floated up the face of Joseph Flaville and, a little behind him, Moyse. He exhaled, opened his eyes and looked at Delahaye.

"If God is with me," he pronounced, "then who can stand against me?"

18

In the green and gilded light of morning, Captain Maillart rode down from La Soufrière, through Bas-Limbé and out onto the great level expanse of the northern plain. He was flanked by two black riders, assigned to him by Toussaint at Marmelade: Quamba and Guiaou. Of these the former was an able horseman and useful groom. Toussaint had told Maillart, with his hint of a smile that never quite flowered, that he believed Guiaou might one day make a horseman also, if he should gain confidence and overcome his fear. And today when they came down from the last slopes of the mountains onto the flat land of the plain, Guiaou, riding on the captain's left, seemed to be much at his ease. Maillart glanced at him, half covertly, from time to time. Guiaou's seat was sufficiently solid, and he held the reins above the saddle bow in relaxed hands. A loose chemise of off-white cotton covered the patterns of his dreadful scars, save those on his head and forearm. As he rode, he seemed to look about himself with pleasure.

"*Riziè marron,*" Quamba remarked, to Maillart's right. The captain looked over. There was a sizable, irregular rice planting—gone mostly wild, as Quamba had suggested. *Bwa dlo* with its pale white and violet blossoms sprang up among the rice shoots. White egrets stood spectrally about the shallows, and in a deeper slough was a long-horned cow submerged to her neck, blissful, now and then stretching her head to take another mouthful of green shoots. As they passed, two nearly naked men came out of the surrounding jungle and began to swing broad-bladed hoes at the border of the planting.

They rode on. Another cluster of horsemen seemed to be in sight ahead of them, at that point just below the horizon where mirages were wont to appear. Maillart shaded his eyes for a better view; he could not make out if they were three or five. The figures did not shimmer as mirages do, but presently he did not see them anymore; the road ahead was empty.

By now the heat was rising and the air around their little party ripened with the smell of horse and human sweat. Silence, heavy as the air, was broken by the occasional chink of harness rings, or someone's voice at a distance, urging cattle or goats out into the pastures. At a crossroads a small crowd of women had gathered with their wares: green oranges and bananas of several kinds, some coconuts and mangos. Maillart reined up and arched an eyebrow at his companions.

"*Ki bo Bitasyon Arnaud?*" Quamba addressed the question at large. Where is Habitation Arnaud? The oldest woman among the *marchandes* raised a toothless face as shriveled as a peach pit.

"*Ki sa ou vlé?*" she said. What do you want?

"*Koté blan k'ap fé travay anko—l'ap fé sik.*" Maillart said. Where the white man has the work going again—where he is making sugar.

The woman's eyes whitened. "*Blan ki fé sik mêm?*"

A white man making sugar again? There was a general buzz among the women. Presently the old woman nodded with a seeming satisfaction and pointed a leathery finger to the road which led inland. Maillart pricked up his horse but, on a second thought, stopped again and purchased a stalk of bananas, which he fastened to his saddle knee with a bit of thong.

Then they went on. With the sun mounting toward the meridian, the heat was wet and smothering. Maillart moved as little as possible, giving his horse its head, only sometimes turning his face, like a sail, to receive the intermittent, feeble hints of breeze. He left the chore of inquiring the way to Quamba, for even the effort of moving his lips made him pour sweat.

They turned southwest and rode along a narrow muddy lane, pitted with deep sloughs which the horses must pick their way around with care; in one was an abandoned wagon, buried to the hubs in sucking mud. There were other tracks, some fresh, and Maillart noticed a pile of warm horse manure that put him in mind of the party of horsemen he thought he'd seen earlier in the morning. But no one was in view. Jungle pressed in on the roadway, the interlocking leaves of trees so tall they blocked the view of any landmark. With the sun at the center of the sky, all sense of direction was lost. But Quamba kept inquiring at the crossroads, and presently they came to a pair of blackened gateposts at the entrance to an *allée* of palms. The gates had been wrenched down from the masonry, and most of the spearheaded iron bars removed— perhaps for use as lances, Maillart speculated. A palm trunk had been laid across the gateway as a barrier, and Quamba began to dismount to shift it, but Maillart shook his head and jumped his horse over the obstacle. His companions followed suit. Maillart saw that Guiaou leaned forward and knotted his hands in the mane of his horse, with an air of desperation, but at any rate he was not unseated.

Some of the palms bordering the *allée* had been hacked down, and through the gaps one could see patches of undertended cane. The citrus hedges of the main enclosure had been set afire but incompletely burned, so that now they greened again, pushing through the ash and the charred stems. Maillart leaned sideways, plucked a lime and sucked the juice to freshen the taste of warm, stale water in his canteen.

But for a single small shed near the blackened square that might have been a stable, all the buildings of the main compound had been razed by fire. On the opposite edge of the clearing, rope had been strung from tree to tree to mark off makeshift stalls for horses, and here, Maillart took in at once, a party of black cavalrymen had recently hitched their mounts. The black men wore French uniforms, and as Maillart slipped gratefully down from his own horse, he found himself beneath the cool regard of Major Joseph Flaville.

The captain suffered a conflict of impulses. He might toss the reins of his horse to the other, as if he were a stablehand, then turn his back. They might continue to fence in this manner, trading slights indefinitely, until one of them found a way to betray the other, perhaps even on the field of battle. All that was a great stupidity. Maillart felt so, even through the wave of unreasoning resentment which resembled the blind rages he had formerly felt against O'Farrel of the Dillon regiment— strangely, for Flaville had done nothing to offend him, or even to compete with him. Had he?

Maillart saluted. "Good morning, Major. I had not looked to find you here."

Flaville returned his salute. "Nor I you, Captain."

Maillart broke two bunches of bananas from the stalk he had purchased, and held them out to the black officer.

"For yourself and your men, if you like them."

"With pleasure, and my thanks." Flaville smiled naturally, accepting the fruit, and whistled for one of his men to come on the double and see to the captain's horse.

Unaccompanied (for Quamba and Guiaou were conversing with Flaville's subordinates), Maillart strolled down toward the cane mill, where Flaville had told him he would find the proprietor. On the way he paused by that solitary shed—so odd to find it standing still, where everything else had been destroyed. The door was chained and fastened with a padlock, but there was a knothole. Maillart peeped in, then recoiled. The sun glared down on him more fiercely and the air now seemed too dense to breathe. Someone was watching him from the cane mill, a man in a loosely woven, conical straw hat with fringed brim. Only by the walking stick he held in both hands across his thighs did the captain recognize Michel Arnaud. The stick was unusual, grooved like a corkscrew—reputedly it was not wood at all, but a dried and hardened bull's pizzle. Maillart wanted to look into the shed again, to verify what he had seen or (much better) discover it an illusion, but would not do so under Arnaud's observation.

He caught his breath, then went to greet the master of the land.

"Welcome," Arnaud pronounced, letting his cane swing free as he took the captain's hand. "Come in and see the work, for what it's worth."

Maillart followed him through the doorway, which at present lacked a lintel. The roof was gone too, so the area of the mill was open to the sky. The masonry walls were jaggedly shattered, battered down to ankle height in places, and fire-blackened to the top.

Arnaud was following the captain's glance. "Yes," he said. "They were very thorough in their destruction, but had not the patience to smash down *all* the walls." He snorted. "I may call that my good fortune. The press itself they were careful to knock down, but the iron—that was less damaged than I feared and, as you see, we have raised it up again."

Maillart followed the cane tip to the fresh masonry, more sloppily done than the older stonework, which supported the two vertical iron cylinders of the cane press. A system of gears ran through the wall to a spoked wheel outside. Through the gaps in the broken wall, Maillart could see two bullocks and a single mule, turning the central hub which ran the press. A boy urged the animals along with soft speech and light flicks of a green switch.

"*Ouais, ça roule encore.*" Arnaud fanned himself with his hat, a near-shapeless, hastily crafted object of the sort a slave might have worn. "It works—after a fashion."

The captain stared at the crushed cane stalks emerging from the interlocked grooves of the press. Below, the syrup flowed into the slant of a dug-out log.

"Come." Arnaud gestured with his cane.

Maillart followed him to the lower level, where the sap was boiled and reduced to sugar. The roof had disappeared here too, and the posts which had supported it burnt back to foot-high stumps. Two men worked the syrup with long-handled ladles. Flies covered the viscous surface of the tanks.

"We have not the means to refine white sugar now," Arnaud said. "And I regret to say there are impurities even in the brown. Still, it is something. He raised his voice. "Finished for the morning! Go rest!"

The men at once laid down their tools, and Maillart heard the gears of the mill clank to a halt. He followed Arnaud around the outer edges of the broken walls, and they walked up through the compound. A chill clutched at the captain as they passed the shed, and then the heat returned, like fever.

"It was not so in better days," Arnaud reported, "this business of the noon hiatus. But now they will not work without it. He slashed at the air before him with his cane. "Free labor." The cane whistled and sang alarmingly. "I give you *that* for free labor!" He let the cane drop against his side. "Well, it's what we've got."

Maillart had seen no sign of a residence, but now they were mounting a twisted trail that passed through the citrus hedge and climbed through a stand of bamboo that covered the lower slopes of the *morne* behind the plantation. The path gave onto an apron of cleared ground, which opened out before a low rectangular dwelling, backed against the raw face of mountain. Flaville was waiting for them there, seated at a roughly carpentered table on the porch.

"*Anou bwé rhum,*" Arnaud said, directing the captain toward a stool, as he went into the house. Maillart sat down and looked about. Though the climb had not seemed so very arduous, he now could now see over the compound from a considerable height. To the left was the sound of running water, and he saw that a ditch dug in the clay channeled the runoff around the border of the little yard—away from the house floor, which consisted of splintery puncheon embedded in the earth.

Arnaud returned, carrying two bottles pinched together in one hand, and three cups fashioned from calabash in the other.

"We are not very elegant," he said, setting down these accouterments. He sat and poured a measure of raw, clear rum into each gourd, and pushed the cups across the table to his guests.

"*A l'aise, messieurs,*" he said. "The other bottle is water."

The captain drained his cup of *clairin,* and refilled the gourd from the water bottle. Flaville, meanwhile, sipped his measure more slowly. Arnaud drank about half his cup, then pushed back his stool to stand again.

"Well, I will look for something for us to eat."

"Allow me to help you," Maillart said, having come to the conclusion that there must be no servant on hand.

"If you will." Arnaud shrugged.

The captain followed him indoors. The house was an alley of four rooms, two on each side of a corridor and open at either end. The roof was palm thatch and the walls were lattice, plaited from sticks. Arnaud turned to the right and Maillart followed, parting a hanging curtain made of strings of red seeds from the bean trees. He found himself in a bedchamber, furnished with a wardrobe, a chest of drawers and a heavy bedstead. Without pausing, Arnaud passed through to the room behind, which was empty except for several padlocked chests and a pallet on the floor.

Taking a bunch of keys from his pocket, Arnaud unlocked one of the chests and took out a platter covered with a cloth, and a small clay jug. Atop another chest was a dish with a bunch of bananas, two mangos and some limes. Arnaud nodded at Maillart, who picked it up.

In the bedchamber he hesitated, catching the captain's eye in the mirror propped on the chest of drawers. It must have been a fine mirror, once, though now the surface was smoke-stained and the gilt wood frame much damaged by fire.

"I have prepared this room for the return of my wife."

Maillart inclined his head toward Arnaud's reflection. He noticed that in this room alone the puncheon floor was sanded fine. Arnaud turned his face from the mirror and led the way back onto the porch.

"A woman comes to cook at night," he said, unveiling a plate of cold corn cakes. "But I don't trouble myself for the midday meal, we are so . . . short-handed." He took off his ragged-brimmed hat and ran his hands back through his graying hair. "The work will recommence at three."

"Ah," said Flaville, with the air of making a pleasantry. "One might say that the Code Noir is respected here, nowadays. Concerning the treatment of the . . . cultivators."

Arnaud gazed into space without replying.

Far below, behind the mill, men were loading sacks from a lean-to onto the pack saddles of a train of donkeys. "I see that something is already begun," Maillart said.

"Yes," said Arnaud, pouring molasses from the clay jug over his cornbread, "that convoy must leave in good time, to reach Le Cap before darkness."

Maillart contained a restive movement and said nothing, though he was perturbed. Toussaint had sent him on this exploration to discover not only to what extent the production of sugar had been restored but also where the product was being sent—for Toussaint wished for all such exports to pass through his own hands at Gonaives. As Laveaux, Toussaint's commanding officer, was in charge at Le Cap, the black general could have no reasonable objection to sugar being shipped in that direction. But Maillart felt uneasy, and the silence round the table weighed upon him. Flaville chewed methodically at the hard corn cake.

"This house," the captain said, groping for a subject. "You did not choose to rebuild on the old site."

"No," Arnaud said. Thumbing the underside of his jaw, he looked down with the captain at the train of donkeys filing out, past the burnt black square of earth where the old *grand'case* had stood, and past that solitary standing shed.

"Here one takes the air more easily," Arnaud said. "It is better for the health. Also there are considerations of security. Besides, the old site is accursed."

Again the silence bore down on the three of them. The last donkey had left the compound, which was empty, motionless, except for that shed, which seemed to waver in the shimmering heat. The captain swallowed and swallowed at his bite of cornbread; only with the greatest difficulty could he get it down. When he had finally succeeded, he reached for the rum bottle served himself and drank.

"Why," he said. "Why was that one shed left standing?"

"Yes," said Arnaud. "*C'est ça la question.* It has stood there since ninety-one—three years, man, since this place was sacked and burned. There is something inside it which I do not know how to remove, and yet it must be taken away before my Claudine can return here."

Maillart drank rum, then poured himself a water chaser. Arnaud's eyes were distant, glassy; he seemed unaware of his company. The captain was puzzled as to why he had chosen to speak so openly before Flaville; it did not seem to be unconsciousness.

"How shall I explain myself?" Arnaud pressed his palms on the table as if to rise. "You did not know me in those days, but I tell you, in the last three years I have aged twenty. Before the rising of ninety-one my hair was black as a crow's wing, friends, and I had no thought but for my pleasure, or sometimes rage against the failure of my enterprises—my barren wife, my plantation foundered in debt and made barren too by the sloth and mortality of my slaves."

Maillart considered. He had not known Arnaud personally, true, but his reputation—for extraordinary and ingenious cruelty to his slaves—had spread far and wide. Caradeux, Lejeune, Arnaud—those were names of terror. Flaville, the captain noticed, had stopped eating, and now sat upright on his stool with his arms folded across his chest.

"Though my wife is taken with a religous mania," Arnaud pronounced, "I am myself no great believer." He looked directly at Maillart. "When you found me, sir, wandering in the bush after the sack of the northern plain, I had ceased to know if I were a man or an ape. But I have been taught to believe in these years that the evil which one does returns. If that is true, so also may the good.

"It must be said that my wife did a very great evil, whose blot still lies across this land," Arnaud continued. "She did so only following my example." He drew a breath, looking away from Maillart. "You know what you have seen, down there."

The captain's eyes slid shut, against his will. Imprinted on their lids he saw, as through the knothole, the human skull and heap of bones littered on the shed floor, and the pair of skeletal hands still lashed to a hook on the wall above.

"*Bruf*," said Arnaud "It was there my wife murdered her lady's maid, a *bossale* fresh from Africa, who, as it happened, was carrying my child. You will understand, in my heat I had sowed the whole *atelier* with half-breed bastards, but this was the first and only time my wife showed how bitterly she was offended. As you have seen, the very bones still hang in bondage, and my wife is bound to them, and so am I.

"As for myself, I have undertaken many like actions. I cannot remember all those horrors, nor even half of them. My poor wife, misled by me, committed such a horror only once; it is that which has unseated her reason, I believe. I would take away the stain from her if I might, even take it upon myself. But I do not know how. There was a priest who might have advised me, but he is dead"—Arnaud's voice broke into an eerie laugh—"tortured to death, my captain, by our *concitoyens* at Le Cap." He made a half-turn to include Flaville in his discourse. "So, gentlemen, as you see, I am without hope or help."

Maillart massaged his eyelids with his fingertips, then opened them. The clearing and the jungle swam before him for a moment and gradually grew still. Somewhere a cock was crowing. The captain had always thought it odd how the cocks of the colony gave voice at any hour, never restricting themselves to the dawn. Flaville tightened the fold of his arms across his chest and breathed in three times, deeply, with short, sharp exhalations through his nose. Then he relaxed his arms and raised his head.

"Perhaps I can arrange the matter," he said to Arnaud.

"If you should even attempt it," Arnaud said, "I am forever in your debt."

After the meal the three of them retired to rest in the shade through the worst heat of the day. Maillart found he was to share his room with Flaville; two pallets were prepared on the floor in the first room opposite Arnaud's personal chambers. Flaville stripped off his garments, folded them neatly and lay down without saying anything. At first the captain was uneasy at the quiet presence of the black man across the floor from him. But soon the singing of the insects and the dancing of the sunlight through the chinks in the latticed walls began to lull him. His breathing slowed; he did not wake till twilight.

The room was empty, but someone had brought a basin of a water and a jagged scrap of soap. Maillart washed his face and torso, combed his wet hair back with his fingers and went out onto the porch. There was a pleasant smell of stewing chicken. Arnaud had come in from the fields and changed his clothes; Flaville sat near him, at the table.

Maillart walked down the path to see that Quamba and Guiaou were settled for the night. He claimed two more bunches of the bananas for the master's table, and leaving the rest to be shared among the men, he climbed back up. During the meal Arnaud replied to Flaville's occasional questions, or volunteered descriptions of the difficulties, the failures and small successes, of his effort to bring the cane fields back from ruin. It seemed he was not alone in all this; the northern region was spotted all over with French colonists lately returned from exile, although at least as many properties were under the management of black or mulatto tenants now.

Maillart listened, keeping his silence for the most part. He could not help thinking of that donkey caravan, now unloading sugar at Le Cap if all had gone well with the journey, and of Toussaint's likely displeasure. But he would play the simple soldier; his only part was to observe and report.

The woman who had cooked cleared away the plates and brought the rum. It was dark by then, but the moon was high above the plain, so that every detail of the compound was plainly etched in silver. As Maillart reached for his gourd of rum, he heard a drum beat slowly, four deep, throbbing beats. Then the hush resumed. From the trees came a procession of men and women, who moved toward the shed with rhythmic, swaying steps. It seemed that Guiaou was among them, or at least the captain recognized his shirt, but Guiaou had a different gait, a different manner, as if he'd been transfigured. When the singing began, that deep-throated voice made of many joined together, the fine hairs stood to attention on Maillart's forearms and the back of his neck. Drawing near the shed, the procession broke up into those bewildering spiral patterns that had so often terrified the captain in ambush situations, yet now the movement was graceful, delicate and gentle, like ink diffusing into water.

An old man held up a candle flame to each of the cardinal points of the compass, then set it aside and saluted the same four directions with a bottle which must have held strong spirits, for it burned gaily when he poured it on the ground and set it alight. Someone (was that Guiaou?) rushed forward and danced jerkily, barefoot on the bluish flames. Someone stove in the shed door with a maul. Three women entered, then came back out, bearing the bones gently on a litter woven of green branches. Led by a gaunt figure in a tall black hat, the procession snaked away into the trees.

The door of the empty shed hung lopsided from the frame like a broken tongue. Maillart glanced sidelong at Arnaud. Though he made no sound, a flow of tears ran from his eye sockets and branched along the angles of his jaw, and his throat worked steadily, as if he were swallowing blood. Presently he stood up, collected the rum from the table and disappeared onto the descending trail.

The captain glanced at Flaville, who seemed alert, poised as if ready to leap from his chair in any direction, though there was no hostility, no menace about him. Maillart felt something similar himself, as though his body and bones were made of air.

When Arnaud emerged on the ground below, he was carrying a lighted torch. He splashed the rum from the bottle on the walls of the shed on either side of the door, then thrust the torch against the liquid stain and quickly sprang back. There could not have been enough rum to justify the effect, but the whole shed went up all at once like fire from a volcano.

Next day they rode to Haut de Trou, Arnaud accompanied by Maillart and Flaville and the men they'd brought with them: a strong party, for the state of the countryside was uncertain. Bands of unorganized rebels and fugitives still roved about, and the blacks who'd returned to work the fields were restless, chafing under the new labor laws proclaimed by both Laveaux and Toussaint. Maillart had time to reflect on the matter during the day's journey, for there was little conversation among the leaders of the group.

Toussaint's edicts had been especially stern. He forbade any independent clearing of new land by the new-free slaves (Toussaint had no desire to see more maroon villages sprouting in the hills), indeed there should be no work of any sort for independent gain or sustenance—all efforts must be combined for plantation work and the restoration of export crops. Reasonable, Maillart knew well, given the troops' constant need for munitions and other supplies which must be imported, but the strictness of the edict was sufficient to start murmurs of its resemblance to slavery . . . According to Laveaux's parallel proclamations, this labor was not slavery because it was paid: the cultivators were meant to receive the fourth part of all they produced. Yet Toussaint himself was pleading that this clause of the program was unworkable, for the time being at least, with all the Plaisance Valley laid waste. Under such sharecropping the Cordon de l'Ouest might sustain itself, at best, but could bring in no money for guns or soldiers' pay. And even on the Plaine du Nord, where the land itself recovered more easily from the devastation, Laveaux's policy was honored most often in the breach.

"It is a lovely principle," Isabelle Cigny jingled across her supper table that evening, "but in practice—well, my friends . . ." She spread her hands above the different platters. "For example, our repast. Perhaps I parrot my husband's views—he will be desolate to have missed you yet again!" She inclined her head to Maillart and Arnaud in turn.

"Likewise," said Arnaud.

"My regret is sharpened," said the captain, "by the thought that we dine at the grace of his markmanship." For the meat was wild dove, shot in the cornfields by Monsieur Cigny. The birds were sweet and tender . . . and worth about two bites apiece; Maillart could happily have eaten twice the number available for his consumption.

"Precisely," said Isabelle. "One may imagine that wild game is free for the taking, yet as *mon bonhomme* would put it, game costs something in powder and shot—precious commodities in this difficult time, to be sequestered with difficulty—and with some small risk—from military requisitioning."

This time she fired her glances at Maillart and Flaville. "Gentlemen, I presume we speak in confidence."

"But of course," said Maillart, while Flaville stretched in his chair, smiling with apparent pleasure at her performance.

"Well," she went on, "as for the corn and the yams and the greens, they too have their price in labor. Labor diverted from the coffee and the cane. How is that 'fourth share' to be extracted from such a situation? Why, our cultivators do well to feed themselves twice daily! Am I unjust?" She fluttered her fingers at Arnaud.

"By no means, Madame."

"And that is not all," Isabelle said. "The gravity of the predicament is just this—oh, my husband would certainly say the same if he were present." She smiled around the table, her eyes skimming their faces, all attentive but for Claudine, who maintained her customary air of trance.

"All very well for our . . . *cultivators,* that they should be free," she said. "Oh, let me applaud their freedom . . . *Vive la liberté!*" She raised her arm dramatically, but the toast fell flat, as she had doubtless intended it should. "Yet those people did not come to us free of charge, and the merchants and brokers of the Bord de Mer, whether here or in France, do not forgive *our* debts for their revolution."

"Well said," Arnaud pronounced, then went on to develop the theme in bitter detail, using his own examples.

Maillart went to bed, early, for he did not want to give the fact of Monsieur Cigny's absence any time to work upon his mind—not that it should make any difference, for Cigny had always been an absentee husband, in all the time Maillart had known his wife. He lay down awaiting insomnia and did not know how deeply he had slept until he woke, all of a start, his ears vibrating with the fierce cry of a woman's joy.

He knew that voice, oh so well . . . but now it had a more abandoned note than he had ever heard. For Isabelle had always been the mistress of their pleasure, riding him like a pony bridled to her desire. Who would enjoy her favor now?—he and Arnaud were the only white men on the premises, and the captain recalled how gently Arnaud had taken the maimed hand of his poor mad wife between his own two palms, how patiently he'd coaxed her to their chamber. However vigorous his infidelity, it seemed unlikely he would stray tonight, and anyway he had by his own account a taste for darker delicacies.

It was not inconceivable that Isabelle might have adopted the practice of Lesbos, but again there was the lack of a candidate. Surely not Claudine—that *was* unthinkable. Once Isabelle had recounted to him certain adventures undertaken with a mulattress, companion of her unmarried youth, in colonial slang her *cocotte.* At the time he'd been both excited and repulsed, and now the strain of his arousal was positively painful, so that he was tempted to relieve it by himself—but he put the thought away from him, and it subsided. Perhaps he had only dreamed that voice, he thought, as he yawned backward into sleep, or again, it might have been Isabelle who dreamed.

Major Flaville, though he left them his men as an escort, did not accompany them on their return to Habitation Arnaud, but rode to inspect camps farther to the east. Maillart regretted this circumstance soon enough, for there were great disturbances in the fields all along the way. On several occasions his company found itself menaced by blacks shouting across the hedgerows, *A bas blanc! A bas l'esclavage!* Sometimes more particular epithets were directed to Arnaud, whose past reputation seemed to be quite generally known.

The women, Claudine and Isabelle (who had elected to see her friend installed in her husband's home), rode in sedan chairs supported by poles, each carried by a pair of retainers of the Cigny plantation. This antique mode of transport solved, in rather a bumpy fashion, the problem of roads impassable for carriages, but in the present situation, the captain thought, it might also give the wrong impression. *Down with white people! Down with slavery!* There were moments when Maillart suspected that the Cigny litter bearers might drop their loads and flee, but when he loosened his pistols in their holsters, the action seemed to calm them. He thought Quamba and Guiaou would hold firm, and at the worst they could abandon the chairs and take the ladies pillion. But the worst did not come to pass, and in the late afternoon they reached Habitation Arnaud in good order, having endured no worse than shouted maledictions.

Work in the fields and in the cane mill had altogether ceased. Arnaud, his face darkening, went to demand an explanation of his *commandeur*. He left Isabelle to help settle Claudine in the house, while Maillart dropped onto a stool on the porch, washing the dust from his throat with water, beginning to think of a glass of rum.

The buzz of angry voices reached him from the compound below. He saw Arnaud surrounded as if by a swarm of ants, at bay with his back to the mill's broken wall, a hundred-odd blacks half circling him. Seeing nothing else to be done, Maillart jumped up and dashed down the trail, thumbing his pistol butts as he ran.

He found Quamba and Guiaou lingering by the horses, and was relieved to have their support; both carried good muskets, and Maillart had heard of Guiaou's wonderful efficiency at close quarters with a *coutelas*.

"*Ki problém yo?*" he asked shortly as they strode toward the irritable crowd. What is their problem?

"*Yo pa vlé travay.*" Quamba shrugged. They don't want to work.

Arnaud stood with his cane cocked in his right hand, as if he would strike the *commandeur,* who faced him, just a step or two out of reach. Arnaud's concentration was so narrow that he seemed unaware of the others' approach. Maillart could not make out what the black man was saying—there were too many voices grumbling at once—but he saw

Arnaud toss the cane deftly from right hand to left and with the same motion draw a double-barreled pistol from beneath his shirttail. In the abrupt silence, his voice rang clear.

"Pull me down if you have the heart for it," he declared. "You may tear me limb from limb, but first, I tell you, some of you will die."

The silence held, and after a moment Maillart was moved to shout out, *"Kité nou pasé!"* Let us pass . . . Several of the blacks at the rear of the throng turned to take note of Quamba and Guiaou, who held their muskets at the present-arms position. A corridor opened in the crowd, and Maillart beckoned to Arnaud, who walked slowly to join them, his cane trailing and his pistol pointed to the sky.

"Doucement," the captain advised. "We must not look like running."

"Of course," Arnaud answered. They were backing up, with maximal dignity, weapons still at the ready. The crowd of blacks was scattering into smaller knots, which moved as if to flank them. When the moment seemed right for them to turn, the captain was astounded to find himself facing Claudine Arnaud, upright and rigid and staring like an angry hawk, with Isabelle a pace behind her, holding onto her elbow.

"What the devil are you doing here?" the captain snapped.

"I could not restrain her," Isabelle said, with an ill-tempered flush of her own. "I could not let her come alone."

Maillart sniffed. But he had noticed that those little knots of angry blacks approached no nearer, and perhaps it was the figure of Claudine which held them back.

Unmolested, the little party reached the lower mouth of the trail to the house, and began climbing, with Maillart, Quamba and Guiaou bringing up the rear. Flaville's men, the captain noticed, had vanished altogether.

"Give me a whip and the right to use it," Arnaud puffed as they gained the porch. He laid down his pistol and propped his cane against the table edge—both hands gripped emptiness as he spoke. "I would peg out that insolent black bastard and flog him till the bones showed through—I'd put a stop to this rebellion—"

"Sir, you would be dismembered after," said the captain, with a significant glance at Quamba and Guiaou. "As you yourself so recently described."

"True enough," said Arnaud, looking at his own palms with a certain bewilderment. His shoulders sagged. "The times have changed."

He beckoned the captain into the house. Isabelle had persuaded Claudine to stretch out on the bed; she had taken off the other woman's shoes and loosened her clothing and was alternately fanning her, or dabbing at her temples and throat with a damp cloth. Oblivious to this activity, Arnaud passed through to the second room, where he knelt, unlocked one of the chests, and began unpacking arms and ammunition.

Maillart felt his spirits lift a little. "You anticipated this," he said.

"I would have been a fool if I had not," Arnaud said. "Come." He hoisted a stand of weapons and motioned for Maillart to the same.

Arnaud led the way behind the house and up another trail that climbed against the cliff face, to a cleft in the rocks, within convenient reach of the spring. There he set down the guns he carried. Obeying his gesture, Maillart looked out from the cover of a chin-high boulder and saw that he commanded not only the house with the clearing and trail head before it, but also, at a greater distance, the whole compound below. He let his breath out with the hint of a whistle.

"So *that* is why you moved the house site."

"One reason among several," Arnaud said. "We have our arms, plenty of powder and shot. There is water as you see, cornmeal and a few other provisions. If your men are reliable, we may maintain a watch both here and below and so hold the house. In case of serious attack we may fall back here to these rocks, where we shall not be easily dislodged."

"It is well conceived," the captain said. "If things continue to go amiss with your plantation, you might consider the military."

Unsurprisingly, Arnaud's cook did not report for duty. Isabelle busied her pretty hands to cook some cornbread. A few bananas remained of the captain's stalk, and Arnaud had a little store of tasteless, leathery dried meat. Isabelle chattered throughout the meal, with no more and no less than her usual vivacity. She drank a glass of rum and water, and now and then, when Claudine seemed agitated, reached out to take her hand and soothe her. Maillart, who knew her easy manner was not unconsciousness but courage, admired her speechlessly.

The drums began at moonrise. Maillart was on watch, behind that high boulder, but there was nothing to see. The compound was empty except for pools of moonlight. In the low ground, hidden by the trees, the drums muttered and grumbled, starting and stopping without resolution, then began again more confidently, the interlocked rhythms gathering, swelling. At their peak, when Maillart's whole nervous system waited for a scream, Claudine came out of the house, pursued by both Isabelle and Arnaud. From his height, the captain watched their dumb show: Claudine darting this way and that in her long white gown, nimbly eluding the hands that would confine her. Quamba and Guiaou had moved to bar her way from the trail head, but Claudine flung herself directly into the bush, where she was lost for a few minutes to Maillart's view.

Guiaou produced his *coutelas* and hacked a path in for Arnaud. Claudine must have caught herself in strangler vine and shake-hands briars, for Arnaud soon led her out onto the open ground before the house, a long swath of fabric torn from the hem of her dress and trailing on the ground. Isabelle took her other elbow, and the two of them conveyed her indoors.

Within fifteen minutes, Arnaud had come up to relieve the captain's watch. Maillart protested that he was before the hour, but Arnaud said that as he could not sleep or rest, it was better for him to take the next watch, and be replaced at midnight. He did not seem to want to talk of what had just passed with his wife, or anything else either, so the captain left him and went down to the house.

It had been arranged that one white man and one black would keep watch at all times. Quamba stood erect, posted at the trail head, while Guiaou lay on a grass mat nearby, his head pillowed on his hands. Maillart could not make out if he was sleeping or gazing at the moon. He went into the house without saying anything to them.

Through the bean-seed curtain he heard Claudine's voice complaining as in fever, and Isabelle's, calm and soothing. He parted the curtain with one hand. Claudine twisted on the bed, turning her face to the wall. Her shoulders stiffened, then relaxed. Isabelle watched her, stroking her back, for a few minutes, then raised her head. She stood up and came to meet the captain in the doorway.

"I gave her rum," she said. "She did not want it, but I made her take it. It will help her to rest."

"I feel I might benefit from a similar treatment," the captain said.

Isabelle smiled distantly. "Wait on the porch."

Maillart went out and took a seat. His hackles rose and fell involuntarily with the rhythm of the drums. Dogs must feel this way, he thought. Then Isabelle came with the rum and the water.

"*Ah, merci,*" said the captain, drinking deep. *Mais, ma belle,* he thought, *it is your touch that cures, far better than rum.* He did not say it. Isabelle took a seat beside him and gazed in the direction of the sentries at the trail head.

"Sometimes I think one ought to let her go."

"She would never return from such an expedition," the captain said.

"You don't know that."

"I have a strong suspicion."

Isabelle did not reply. Maillart looked at her moonlit face, a sad expression, or perhaps only wistful—or possibily it was only some trick of the light. He drained off his rum and stood up.

"I must go and sleep if I can, before my next watch." He bowed to her and went into the house.

What a curiosity, friendship with a woman . . . Maillart lay down expecting the white fog of insomnia to settle over him, detailed by frustrated lust. But he was asleep as soon as his head touched the pallet, and woke to find Arnaud shaking his shoulder. "Your watch, *mon cher.*"

In the shadows by the trail head, Guiaou had replaced Quamba. Maillart nodded to him, then splashed some water on his face from a pail on the porch floor. Refreshed, he climbed to the post among the rocks and turned his face to the fields below. The drums had stopped; it was two hours until dawn. The thought of the sleeping celebrants made Maillart's own head heavy. But he stayed sufficiently alert until first light, when Arnaud climbed up to join him.

"Look there, would you? Just over there."

Maillart shaded his eyes, searching. He saw a smudge of smoke, then began to pick out ant-like forms beneath it. With a skirling of conchs, the image resolved into a mob of men with torches.

"They're going to the mill." Arnaud cursed, then dashed down toward the house and passed it without a halt, rushing down the trail toward the compound. Maillart followed more slowly, for fear of falling and breaking a leg. Arnaud was galloping toward the mill; he had not paused at the house even to collect his cane.

Maillart took a moment before he followed, for he must organize Quamba and Guiaou, and check the priming of his own pistols. Isabelle appeared in the doorway of the house, fingers pressed to her lower lip. The captain shook his head at her, then went down with his men.

Arnaud had interposed his body between the mob and his precious mill machinery. He might be a fool, the captain thought ruefully, or he might be a monster of cruelty, but no one could call him a coward. Maillart had been in the country long enough for his instinct to gauge the state of crowds, and this one was very near the point of explosion, though the appearance of himself and his men with their muskets balked them for a moment longer.

Through the silence of that reprieve came the thumping of hoofbeats on hard earth, and all attention turned to the mouth of the *allée.* Joseph Flaville rode into the compound, in the midst of a party of five other horsemen, their mounts all in a lather. Flaville, his face sweat-stained, his uniform collar rucked up in the back, looked as if he had been in the saddle all night.

His eyes slipped over the two white men without acknowledgment, then fixed on the crowd of blacks. Each man had armed himself in some fashion, with a *coutelas* or hoe or long pointed stave. Some of them merely carried lumps of stone, but the men in the front rank had a few rickety-looking old muskets among them.

Flaville caught his breath, drew himself up in the saddle, and raised his right palm like a priest giving absolution.

"Pa brulé champs. Pa touyé blan."

He waited, then his hand began to descend, light as a feather, finger-tips combing the humid air. As the hand came down, all tension began to drain from the crowd, and the men began to disperse, mumbling.

Don't burn the fields. Don't kill the whites.

Flaville and his men wheeled their horses and galloped out of the compound the same way they had come. Maillart let his breath out with nearly enough force to scatter the dust at his feet. He and Arnaud exchanged a speechless, wide-eyed glance, then began trudging back up to the house.

For the next two nights they kept watch as before, but there was no drumming and nothing to see. On the second day Arnaud and Maillart made a sortie as far as the deserted mill. The spoon heads of the long syrup ladles had been dismounted and lay scattered by the troughs, their staves expropriated for spear shafts. Arnaud fanned his hat despairingly before the troughs. The syrup was covered from end to end with a humming carpet of flies.

When they came out of the mill, they saw Claudine standing and staring down at the scorched square where the shed had been until the week before. She was formally attired in a dress of striped silk, and Maillart thought that at that moment she looked no more deranged than any other colonial dame one might find in such circumstances. Guiaou stood at an angle, watching her.

Arnaud came to her side, and she turned and scrutinized him fiercely, as if her sight had been restored, after blindness. When he offered his arm, she took it lightly and allowed him to escort her back toward the house. Her step was graceful, Maillart noticed as he brought up the rear. When they'd gained the porch, Claudine sat down and adjusted her skirts and folded her hands with an air of composure quite unusual for her. The captain caught Isabelle's eye. She arched her brow, but did not speak, as though there were some bubble which a word might puncture.

On the morning of the third day, all the men returned to work. At breakfast the whites in the house on the hill could hear the singing in

the cane fields. Afterward, when Maillart and Arnaud walked down to
the mill, they found the animals harnessed to the spokes of the turning
wheel, the spoons refastened to their handles, the *commandeur*, head
lowered and eyes averted, awaiting Arnaud's direction.

About midday, one hundred of Toussaint's infantry marched into
Habitation Arnaud, led by Captain Riau and accompanied by Doctor
Antoine Hébert. The doctor looked exhausted. His long rifle tilted
crazily across his saddlebow. His legs were rubber when he slid down
from the saddle. His shirt was streaked with sweat and dirt, his odor was
high, and his face was stubbled out all over, above and beyond the chin
beard he always wore, but Maillart ran to him anyway, and kissed him
on both cheeks.

"What news, Antoine?"

"Rebellion," said the doctor. "I thought you'd know." Seeing the captain's face, he added, "Well, it is finished now."

"Tell me," Maillart said. He led the doctor to the shade of a tree
which arched over the well, and drew up fresh water for him to drink. A
few paces distant, Riau was calling orders, disposing the foot soldiers
about the compound.

"Flaville," the doctor said. He drank and dumped water over his head,
and combed back his wet hair with his fingers. "He raised his troops
against Toussaint—a very poor plan, in my estimation. But he set off
rioting among the cultivators, and even turned the troops of Moyse at
Bas-Limbé to his part."

"But surely Moyse has not betrayed Toussaint?"

"No," said the doctor. "It does not look so—Moyse was at Dondon,
where order was kept throughout this whole disturbance. Those troops
of his who rebelled were detached from his immediate command . . .
but you know the suspicious mind of our general. It appears, however,
that Villatte was the engine of this affair."

"Yes," said Maillart. He thought of the sugar which had been sent to
the north coast. "He would hope to expand his influence from his center
at Le Cap."

"Quite so," said the doctor. "Though he has been frustrated, this
time, I believe. But still at the bottom of it all there is a great discontent
with the labor policy. And there I believe that Moyse is no better contented than anyone . . ." He pulled a bandanna from his pocket and
mopped off his face.

"I am happy to see you safe," he said. "It has been an inauspicious
time to travel these parts, without the escort of an army in force."

"It has been quiet enough here," the captain said. "But the result?"

"Oh, there was a little skirmish at Marmelade. I believe that certain rascals were shot in the fighting, and others hanged immediately after, while Major Flaville has taken shelter at Le Cap, to await the disposition of his case."

"I should report that he showed us every courtesy here," Maillart said. "And especially to our ladies. It may be that we even owe him our lives."

"Well, that is something to know," said the doctor. "I do not think he will suffer so much. That will be for Laveaux to decide. It is all being handled according to form—a case of insubordination. And last night Toussaint received a letter of submission and apology from Major Flaville. All quite correct." He smiled thinly. "As you see, I have been riding all day and writing all night . . . You may imagine, such letters. But what in the world is going on here?"

While they were talking, Claudine, still dressed in her striped silk, had begun to approach the well, a wooden yoke across her shoulders, balancing two large wooden pails. Guiaou trailed a little distance behind her.

"Surely you know Claudine Arnaud," said the captain. He took the doctor's forearm and drew him to the other side of the tree.

Claudine came to the well, lowered a bucket and began with great effort to draw it up. Guiaou moved to help her, but she thrust him away and went on straining at the winch alone.

"She takes water to the men in the cane fields," the captain explained. "I have heard of this, but never before seen it. In her derangement, she fancies it a penance."

The doctor stroked a thumb along his jawline. "I don't know if I call it so deranged," he said musingly. "Why should we not help her?"

"But as you see, she will accept no help."

Indeed, Claudine had rejected Guiaou's overtures once again. She took up the loaded yoke with no assistance and, the tendons straining from her neck and her face pouring sweat, began to stagger forward.

"Well, but let me try," the doctor said.

Cat-footed, he slipped to her left side and hooked his fingers round the handle of the bucket, lifting only enough to take half the weight. Claudine corrected her balance, but otherwise seemed to take no notice. The doctor looked over his shoulder at Maillart, who hurried to follow his example on her opposite side. Harnessed together in this way, and still with Guiaou following behind them, they went to offer water to the workers in the fields.

19

All that time that I, Riau, traveled with the doctor looking for Nanon, I could not stop thinking of Merbillay. The reason was the doctor, himself, and how the thought of the woman who had gone away from him was always large and heavy in his mind. The thought of his lost son came into his head each day to grieve him, too. He did not speak about it, but Riau could feel his thoughts whenever I was near him. And we were always together then, not only in the searching, but in the fighting too.

Sometimes Riau wondered what would happen if we found Nanon and Choufleur together, because the mother of Choufleur was right. Choufleur would have happily killed the doctor as soon as he saw him coming up the road toward the house where they stayed. Or maybe he would wait and kill him more slowly, so that the doctor would be made to know just who was killing him, and why. Choufleur was that kind of man, I knew. Sometimes I wondered how that might be. The doctor himself was as skilled with pistol or long gun as any white man I had ever seen. His skill was like a sorcery sometimes, but his spirit was not attached to killing men.

But if Choufleur was really at Vallière, then he was safe from us, because the doctor and Riau became knotted up in all the fighting before we found any way to go to that place. There in the valley of Grande Rivière was the biggest fighting Riau had ever seen, and for more days. Each day was to rise before dawn and go out climbing the hills and shooting and hacking at enemy men until it was night, like a long day of cutting down cane in the fields of some plantation.

In the first days of that fighting it was Captain Riau leading his men to each fight, mostly the taking of little camps on the peaks or the notches of the mountains above the big river. Some of these camps were easily taken, but as the days went on the fighting was more bitter, and Captain Riau began to see his men shot down to death on either side of him. This gave me another sadness, because I, their captain, could not save them from this death. Baron took them, though they stood at my right hand, and they went down beneath the waters.

Most of us had forgotten what the fighting was about by then. It was not killing whitemen now. These were the men of Jean-François who stood against us, our brothers of Guinée, and some months before we had been fighting on the same side as them. It was true that Jean-François served the Spanish *blancs* who still kept slaves across the border. Also, Toussaint tried to win the men of Jean-François over with words, and some of them did come, but most did not, and so it was our work to fight and kill them. Toussaint wanted to drive the men of Jean François all the way back across the Rivière Massacre and into the Spanish country.

But after many days of this fighting all around the banks and the mountains of Grande Rivière, Toussaint took Captain Riau away from his troops and sent him to work with the doctor. Riau was tired of the fighting by then anyway, but even when doctoring I was in man's blood to my armpits, whether sopping or bandaging or sawing arms and legs. It was the doctor who had called me to this work, because we had done so together before, but he had also called Guiaou, who was the new man of Merbillay.

So we were kept together, Riau and Guiaou; only when the wounded were coming back quickly from the fights there was no time to think. In the mornings before the fighting had well begun, I and the doctor, or I and Guiaou, would go searching for leaves to make poultices that stopped torn flesh from rotting, and kept maggots from feeding on the wounds. But someone must always stay to care for the wounded. Riau saw that Guiaou was natural for this nursing. Although his scars were frightening to see, his voice was gentle and his hands had a gentle touch. Even his eyes were soft and warm if one looked past the scars to see them.

Sometimes when I lay down at night, I thought how Guiaou would bring this gentleness to a woman, and then my head would turn ugly inside. But I could not hate him. Sometimes at night we both awoke together when the wounded cried out in their fever, and we talked across the bodies of the men we nursed in the light of a little dry-wood fire. That way I learned the story of the Swiss, and of the sharks who tried to eat Guiaou. I learned how Guiaou was afraid of water, though his *maît'têt* was Agwé. I knew that he was afraid of horses too. He did not say so, but I could see him working to master the fear whenever he had to ride a horse or groom one. Giaou knew something of Riau also from those talks at night, but we did not ever talk about the woman.

Then Toussaint came near to losing a battle, and had to take his men away to keep them from being killed. That was at Camp Charles-Sec. Toussaint had expected men to come out from Le Cap, where the mulatto Villatte commanded, to help his side, but the men did not come. For two days afterward the air all around Toussaint was trembling like thunder, because he thought Villatte had held those men back on purpose to betray him.

Guiaou was sent back to Ennery after that. My heart went dark against him, because he was going to Merbillay, while Captain Riau must stay at Marmelade with the doctor and Toussaint. Even then the doctor was always thinking about Nanon and scheming ways to get to Vallière to look for her, but there was not any way for him to go there. Toussaint had taken many towns and camps round Grande Rivière, but he had not taken all that he meant to.

But still there was peace all across the mountains and the valleys, as far as Dondon and beyond, and so work began again on the plantations. In those days Toussaint and Laveaux spoke out new laws, that all must work, and men began tending the cane again, but many of us did not like it. Those men who were soldiers of the gun despised those men who worked with hoes, and so the men of the hoe became unhappy. Then too, Joseph Flaville was mistrustful, and Moyse, but Riau spoke only with Moyse, because we had known each other at Bréda, before the first rising. Moyse did not like it that Bayon de Libertat, who was master of Bréda, had come back to be with Toussaint, or any whites like him either, who were making work on their lands again.

But they were always almost like brothers, I said to Moyse, Bayon and Toussaint. It was not like man and master between them.

No, said Moyse, with bitterness and suspicion. It was more like two masters.

This was a very bad thought, but once it had come into my head, I could not get it to go out again.

In those days too the doctor kept on brooding over the woman he had lost. He did not say so, but when he took out the empty snuffbox and the piece of mirror which was the magic eye his gun saw with, I knew which way his thoughts were going. Then my own bad thoughts would come to me, of Guiaou with Merbillay, and what might be happening for Caco. It seemed a long time I had not seen my boy . . . Maybe if I had not been near the doctor, these thoughts would not have troubled me so. I would not be thinking of Merbillay unless perhaps I saw her. But I was not sure anymore of that either.

Then Joseph Flaville tried to make a rising against Toussaint, with the men of the hoe who were not contented, but he was knocked down double quick. Maybe Flaville had hoped that Moyse would rise up with him, but he did not. It might have been that Moyse was waiting and watching from Dondon to see how things would go, but things did not go well for Flaville, and he had to run off to hide at Le Cap, or else Toussaint would have killed him, surely. But after Flaville had reached Le Cap, General Laveaux the Frenchman settled the thing between them, like they were two sons of his who quarreled without cause.

When that business was getting finished, I met Guiaou, again by chance, at the plantation of the *blanc* Arnaud on the northern plain. But soon after, Toussaint called us both down to Gonaives, because he wanted to send us on a mission.

At Gonaives the headquarters was a happy place, because they had all found out that the Spanish whitemen had made a new peace with the French ones on the other side of the sea, where their home was. So there would be no more fighting between the Spanish and the French in Saint Domingue, and we would not have to fight the men of Jean-François anymore. The news said that Jean-François had taken his top officers onto a ship at Fort Dauphin to go and live in the country of *blancs,* away from Saint Domingue. At Gonaives everyone was happy for this news, and only Toussaint was solemn because Toussaint never thought of battles won already but only of those which were still to fight.

Toussaint was thinking of Dieudonné, who was now leading that big band which Halaou had led, in the west. Dieudonné was now in the mountains of Charbonnier, not so far above Léogane, where the colored Generals Rigaud and Beauvais were watching the English, at Port-au-Prince, and sometimes fighting them. Dieudonné had three thousand men, maybe more, but he would not go down to help Rigaud or Beauvais, even though the English were still keeping slaves, and they had old *colon* French slave masters in their camp as well. But Dieudonné did not trust any mulattoes. So Rigaud had written to Toussaint to complain about this and to ask his help. Rigaud was afraid too that Dieudonné might even take all those men over to fight for the English against him.

Maybe it was all because Sonthonax had warned Dieudonné against the mulattoes, when he gave him the commissioner medal before he went out of the country. Toussaint thought this, but I, Riau, had seen with my own eyes how everything Sonthonax had warned about had happened, and also before the eyes of Dieudonné. Because Dieudonné was there too when Halaou was killed, in the room of Beauvais, while Beauvais watched, and Dieudonné believed Beauvais had planned it all before it was done. Riau could not know if Beauvais had done so or if he had not, but I saw his face when the shooting started, and he did not look frightened or surprised.

After that, Riau would not have taken orders from Beauvais either or put himself in his power in any other way.

Dieudonné had a *blanc* writing letters for him now, like Toussaint, only I do not think he could read the letters after they were written, as Toussaint could do. One of those letters said that everywhere he looked among the French, he saw mulatto officers, or white, but no black officers, and so he would not join such an army. So Toussaint thought that if Dieudonné knew that he was a general himself along with so many of his own black officers like Dessalines and Maurepas and Charles Belair and even Henri Christophe, who had been promoted by Laveaux before Toussaint came into Laveaux's camp—then Dieudonné would see that he should join with the French. Riau and Guiaou were to go into the west to tell him so.

I knew why Toussaint would choose Riau to go on this errand. After Riau returned to his duty of captain, Toussaint had picked all the story of Riau and Halaou and Dieudonné out of my head like a whiteman picking the meat out of a nut. Why he would send Guiaou was not so clear. Maybe he wanted to send us together, somewhere. Anywhere. I did not know if Toussaint knew about Riau and Merbillay and Guiaou, but it was possible that he did know, because he always looked into such affairs among his men as if he was their father.

But maybe it was the story of the Swiss that made him think of sending Guiaou. All that story began in the west, so Dieudonné would know of it already. After all that had happened, it meant something for Guiaou to trust anyone again, and Guiaou did trust Toussaint. And Dieudonné had known Riau from past time, so Toussaint hoped there was trust between us already.

He had already written a letter for us to carry and read to Dieudonné, and to his seconds and his men. It was a long letter, and it said what was usual for Toussaint to say in his letters then, that only he and Laveaux were fighting for freedom (or anyone who was on the side of those French whitemen), and that Laveaux could be believed in like a father, that the English were keeping and selling slaves still, as the Spanish were too. All of those things which I had heard before. I did not pay so much attention to the letter for Dieudonné because I could always read it later on. It was Guiaou who must take it into his memory from Toussaint's mouth, because Guiaou did not know how to read.

We were supposed to persuade Dieudonné to join with Rigaud, because Rigaud was fighting for the French himself. He was even under the command of Laveaux, like Toussaint, although Laveaux was very far away, and I do not think they had ever met each other, except through letters. I saw that Toussaint had something else behind his head, all the time, but I did not see what it was because I was thinking of the journey and of going with Guiaou. The journey would be over water.

Toussaint had got a boat at Gonaives and had put cannons on it. This boat was meant to keep corsairs away from the harbor, and from the salt flats to the south. It would not have been any good against a real English warship, but it could frighten away the little sloops of pirates. The name of this boat was *Liberté*. Guiaou and Riau were supposed to get on this boat to cross the water of the bay to get to the place below Port-au-Prince where Dieudonné was.

Of course Guiaou did not want to get onto the boat at first. I had seen him hesitate before a horse, then master himself and mount. But before the boat, his fear was stronger. I, Riau, must take his hand and lead him, while his eyes were shut, and he stumbled like a blind man over the plank that went from the dock's edge over the edge of the boat. Guiaou's hand was trembling in mine. I thought how gentle this hand could be with the wounded men in Grande Rivière and thought too how the same hand had touched Merbillay in all her soft and secret places, and how the hand must have sometimes even touched Caco, whether in kindness or anger I could not know. Not all these thoughts were bad ones, but I was glad to let go of Guiaou once we were on the boat, and I did not feel sorry for his misery to be going over the water.

La Liberté slipped out across the surface of the sea. I, Riau, had traveled farther in Saint Domingue than we would go this day. To the south as far as Bahoruco, and all along the north coast, and many times over the mountains of the Spanish border—but all that was over land. I had not traveled over water since the whitemen brought me out of Dahomey, with a chain around my neck. That was not such a good thing to be thinking either.

I had not thought to sacrifice to Agwé. One must prepare Agwé's meal, his meat and drink and his cake, and put it on a little boat and sail it away on the ocean, with no one tending it. When no one is looking, Agwé will take the boat down under the waves and eat his food in his palace beneath the sea. But I had not made this sacrifice, and now I thought, what if Agwé takes *La Liberté* to be his own boatload of food? On land I did not think so very much about Agwé, unless he came to a ceremony. Now I was sorry I had not paid more attention.

Behind my closed lips and teeth I sang the song of Agwé.

Maît' Agwé, koté ou yé?
Ou pa wé moin nan récif?
Maît' Agwé, koté ou yé?
Ou pa wé moin nan lamè?

Master Agwé, where are you?
Don't you see me on the reef?
Master Agwé, where are you?
Don't you see me on the sea?

The men sailing the ship and arming the cannons did not hear, but Agwé must have heard, beneath the sea.

M'gagne zaviro nan main moin
Moin pa kab tounen déyé . . . .

I have the rudder in my hand
I am not able to turn back . . .

Guiaou, who had been huddled on the floor of the boat, jumped up to his feet and stretched out his arms toward the two horizons. Then his eyes turned white and he fell backward, with his heels kicking the boards of the deck.

I put my body across his till he was quiet. My chest against his chest, holding him down. When he was calm enough to sit up, Agwé was in his head. I let go, but watched him carefully, because sometimes Agwé will jump into the water from a boat, and take the body of the one who carries him.

The sailors and gunners were looking at us out of the sides of their heads. They had despised us a little before because we were not sailors, the way our men with muskets and pistols, who were soldiers, despised the men who only worked in the fields with their hoes. The men behind the cannons were especially proud and haughty when we first got onto the boat, but now none of them wanted to offend Agwé.

Agwé spoke aloud only once, in words no one could understand. The voice was like water running over rocks, or water in a pot just as it boils. His face was grave and beautiful, and a little sad. The whole way, he sat very still in the front of the boat and looked down at the prow dividing the waters. All the way that we had to go the ocean was calm and still.

Along the Côte des Arcadins the water was pale bluish-green above the reef, and so clear that we could see the fish darting over the white sand. Men came out from the shore in dugout canoes to catch the fish on spears. Toward the ocean side was the island, La Gonave, coming up from the water like La Balène, the back-hump of a giant whale. At first we could see the white flashes of sail from the small *voiliers* of those people who lived there. Then nothing. La Gonave disappeared. The sailors said it was a mist, but Riau could not see any mist. It was like the sky or the sea had eaten the land and everything that had been on it.

We passed near enough to Port-au-Prince to see the low rooflines of buildings on the shore, and the tall masts of English ships, stripped of their sails, at anchor. None of those ships came after us, *Grâce à BonDyé*. As we went by Port-au-Prince, the sky came clear and the sun was yellow and warm again and the air all around was sparkling.

Dolphin were jumping on both sides of the boat, and Riau remembered seeing that before, at dawn when the ship of slaves from Dahomey sailed into the harbor at Le Cap. It was just sunrise, and the dolphins seemed to be bringing the ship in like pilots, while Riau stood watching, fingering the sore places the iron collar had worn around his neck. Some said the spirits of men were in the dolphins.

Then the ship docked, and they took Riau to the barracoons among the other slaves out of Guinée, and after a few days Bayon de Libertat came from Bréda to look at Riau where he stood on the block. I could not understand anything he said because I had not yet learned any French or Creole. But Bayon showed me how to turn and move by touching me here and there with the tip of his cane. He clucked his tongue over the sores which the irons had left, and he pulled out my lower lip to look at my teeth and gums, and he leaned close to smell my breath. All these things he did with the gentleness one uses with an animal. Then he paid my price in money and took me away to Bréda, where I found Toussaint waiting.

I had not thought of any of those things for a long time.

At the end of the day, *La Liberté* came to shore south of Port-au-Prince. A little before, Agwé had lain down and closed his eyes, and when Guiaou sat up, he was himself again, except he did not seem to be afraid. Some of Rigaud's men had come out to meet us, in case the English would try to capture us from Port-au-Prince. They took us up toward the mountains where Dieudonné stayed, but when they had come a little way into the hills, they turned back to Léogane, saying that Dieudonné would not want to see them with us. This did not matter, because Riau already knew the way.

We came into the camp by moonlight. Riau could even calm the dogs, because I knew their names. People came out to greet us in friendship. I saw many that I knew from before, and even the one called Bienvenu, who had run away from the plantation of Arnaud, before the first risings. Guiaou also found certain people that he knew from other times, though he had never traveled this country with Halaou or Dieudonné.

Dieudonné was not there that night, but his second men, Pompey and Laplume, said that he would come next day. I lay in an *ajoupa* near Bienvenu, and in the darkness we talked of a long-ago time, when Bienvenu had run from Arnaud and had got the horns of the headstall he was forced to wear all tangled in the vines and bush of the jungle, so that he would have been caught by the *maréchaussée*. But Riau came and cut away the headstall with his *coutelas,* so that Bienvenu was free to keep running until he reached the maroons in the mountains. I thought of this and I thought of Bouquart and his *nabots,* and I was pleased to remember what Riau had done. And then I slept.

In the morning Dieudonné was there, smiling and pulling on my biggest toe, shaking my foot and leg to wake me. I got up and we went together to bathe in the cold stream of the mountain, so that our heads would be bright and clear. From my memory, I told him what was in the letter of Toussaint to him, and Dieudonné agreed to call his people together to hear the letter read, as Toussaint had wished.

After we had eaten something, the people all came to where they could listen. Dieudonné explained to them what it was about, and I, Riau, began reading in a big, proud voice, and slowly so that everyone could understand.

Could it be possible, my dear friend, that at the very moment when France has triumphed over all the royalists and has recognized us for her children by her wonderworking decree of 9th Thermidor, when she has granted us all the rights for which we have been fighting, that you would allow yourself to be deceived by our former tyrants, who are only using part of our unfortunate brothers to load the others with chains? The Spanish, for a while, had hypnotized me in the same way, but I was not slow to recognize their rascality; I abandoned them, and beat them well; I returned to my own fatherland, which received me with open arms and was more than willing to reward my services. I advise you, my dear brother, to follow my example . . .

All these words were sent from Toussaint to Dieudonné, but they were meant to be heard by all—Toussaint had said so. Dieudonné pulled himself up very tall and filled up his whole chest with air, out of pride that such words were sent to him from the black general in the north. But his face did not show what he was thinking.

If some special reason should prevent you from trusting the brigadier generals Rigaud and Beauvais, Governor Laveaux, who is a good father to all of us, and with whom our motherland has placed all her confidence, should deserve your own. I also think that you will not withhold that confidence from me, who am a black man like yourself, and who assure you that I want nothing else in the world than to see you happy—you and all our brothers. For myself, I believe that we can only be happy in serving the French Republic; only under her flags are we truly free and equal. That's the way I see it, my dear friend, and I don't believe I am fooling myself . . .

Each time I stopped to take my breaths, I looked about. There was Guiaou, standing between Pompey and Laplume. At the other side of the circle was Bienvenu. The faces of the women were quiet and sober beneath their colored headcloths, and even the little children without clothes were still and listening, though they would not understand the meaning of French words.

In spite of everything I have been told about you, I do not doubt that you would be a good republican: and so you must join with Generals Rigaud and Beauvais, who are good republicans, since our fatherland has recognized their services. And even if you have some trivial troubles between you, you ought not to be fighting, because the Republic, who is mother to us all, does not want us to fight our brothers. Furthermore, it is always the unfortunate people who suffer the most in such cases . . .

When it was finished, the circle scattered. I went with Dieudonné, but we did not speak of what the letter had said. I ate a meal together with his woman and his children, and I saw a new girl baby who was born to him during that year.

After we had eaten, we slept through the heat of the day. When we woke, Dieudonné asked me many questions about how it was in the north, under Toussaint. All that he asked I answered truthfully, even when the truth was not pleasing. True that the French of France had made a stronger freedom paper than any other whitemen. True that the governor Laveaux seemed to respect what this paper said. True that Toussaint fought everywhere for black people to be free, and that, although there were some white officers serving him, there were many more black, and the white officers were not set over them. At the same time it was also true that men were made to work in the fields by the word of Toussaint and Laveaux, and that when Joseph Flaville rose up against this, he was beaten down.

I told Dieudonné what I had heard Toussaint say many times, in his close councils when the letters were written—that there must be cane, and sugar to sell for money, for only money would buy guns, and only guns would win and keep our freedom. But saying this was not enough to take the cloud from Dieudonné's face, or from the mind of Riau, either.

That night was a *bamboche,* but Dieudonné did not go for long. He was there to show himself, and stayed to dance only one dance, and then he went away. I, Riau, went with him. Dieudonné did not want to speak anymore then. He lay down to sleep, saying that he would look at his dream to learn what he would do.

I lay down also, but it seemed a long time before I slept. I did not think that Dieudonné would find it in his dream to join with Rigaud, or even with Toussaint. He did not want to be under a colored officer, and he did not want to leave his own country to go be with Toussaint in the north, though I did not think he wanted to join with the English either.

But I must have slept at the end, and heavily, because when I woke I was confused and frightened and at first I did not know where I was— shouting was everywhere and muskets firing like the whole camp was under attack, and Dieudonné's woman was screaming and crying, as if she had already seen what would happen. Before anyone else could think, the men rushed into the *ajoupa* and fell on Dieudonné. They pointed their guns at him and pricked him with their bayonets, and they tied him up like a chicken for the *boucan.*

All this while Riau kept still. I tried to make myself invisible so that none of those men would think of me. It was then that I remembered Guiaou. I had not thought of what he had been doing during the day and the night, after Toussaint's letter was read. Later I learned that Toussaint had spoken to Guiaou alone to tell him that he must speak to

Dieudonné's second men, and persuade them apart from Dieudonné, in case Dieudonné was already sold to the English.

And so Laplume, when he heard this, got the men to rise against Dieudonné to make him prisoner. This was not so hard to do because Toussaint's letter had already worked on the heads of the men who had listened to it that day. Laplume said he did so because Dieudonné meant all along to go with the English, but I did not think that was true, but that maybe Laplume saw this chance to throw down Dieudonné and take his place.

Laplume gave Dieudonné to Rigaud, but afterward he gave himself and those three thousand men to Toussaint, never to Rigaud or Beauvais. Of course Rigaud was very angry about this, but he had no one to punish except Dieudonné. I did not see it, but I heard that Rigaud loaded Dieudonné with so many chains that the weight of the iron crushed the breath out of him, and so he died. This happened at the prison of Saint Louis.

I, Riau, said nothing when all this began to happen. There was nothing I could say or do to make it different. And when Guiaou and I went back to the north, Toussaint was very pleased when he heard what we had done.

One could not blame Guiaou, because he had only done what Toussaint asked of him, and he believed in Toussaint with his whole heart. One could not even blame Toussaint, even though it had been very tricky, because Toussaint was right that we must all fight together as one to hold our freedom. Also it would have been a bad thing if all those men had gone with the English. But I could never forget the eyes of Dieudonné fastened on me while they were taking him away, even though BonDyé and all the spirits knew that Riau had not meant to betray him.

20

In the central courtyard of the Governor's House was a rectangular stone tank which was home to a dozen turtles, one of which had climbed up out of the murky green water onto a stone and balanced there, turning its long, snake-like neck one way and another. When Laveaux's shadow fell across the tank, the turtle became very still for a moment but did not plunge. Presently it relaxed and began to probe the air again with the soft, fleshy bulb of its head.

Laveaux smiled absently down into the tank, turning a cup of coffee in his hands. He was drowsy and was still wearing slippers, though otherwise he was dressed for the day. Last night he had stayed late in his cabinet, working on correspondence with the Minister of Marine in France—so much to report, so much to request. Hostilities with the Spanish along the interior border had ceased. Indeed, by the terms of a treaty between France and Spain, signed in Europe the previous July, the entire Spanish side of the island was ceded to French rule, though Laveaux did not have men enough even to think of occupying that territory. The British invasion on the coasts remained a serious threat, despite Toussaint's campaigns in the Artibonite and Rigaud's efforts in the Southern Department. Laveaux still had next to no European troops to oppose to the British and their renegade French cohorts, and due in part to the power of the British navy, the reinforcements he asked for were unlikely to arrive.

This morning he had risen early to continue his clerical chores, before the heat became too paralyzing, before the outer rooms of his office were crowded with petitioners and plaintiffs. He yawned.

The turtle turned its head, aiming the flat black dots of its near-sighted eyes at him. Its damp shell was drying, patchily, to a lighter shade of gray; the shell was about the size of a dinner plate. Laveaux smiled sleepily, beneficently. When he had first taken up residence in Governor's House, the turtles had all ducked underwater whenever he leaned over the tank—or whenever his foot fell in the courtyard, for that matter. But now they were not afraid to look at him. Indeed, several other turtles besides the one sunning on the rock had craned their necks out of the water as if to greet him. Their confidence was perhaps misplaced, for in theory all the turtles were destined for soup. On the other hand, Laveaux had become rather fond of observing them, and did not order turtle soup.

He sipped his coffee, then turned from the tank and left the court-yard. There was the splash of the turtle falling from the rock, and he smiled again as he mounted the steps, his slippers shuffling slightly at the heels. In the antechamber were half a dozen colored men appar-ently waiting for an audience; he nodded to them as he passed through, but no one responded. The feeling of uneasiness passed when he closed the door.

Suppressing a sigh, Laveaux sat down at his writing table, put the dregs of his coffee aside, and began to sort through his various papers. It was close in the small room, and a veil of sweat had already covered his forehead. Where to begin? To request: more men, more money. To report, the spreading tension in the town, which had constituted itself a little mulatto principality (in effect) during the months Laveaux had been sealed up at Port-de-Paix. Since then, he had enjoyed small suc-cess in collecting the rents owed on the houses of French colonists now restored and occupied by the more prominent colored families, yet he must press them, for there must be revenue from somewhere. He had not been so gladly received when he had established his administration at Le Cap. Villatte, the highest-ranking officer of the colored contin-gency, had not been pleased to be superseded in the town, and indeed seemed to disregard Laveaux's authority, though he stopped short of outright insubordination.

Or perhaps Laveaux might try to tally up the small exportations of brown sugar that had lately been achieved—into what gaping financial cavity should those tiny profits best be dribbled? He dipped a pen. 30 *Ventose,* he inscribed at the top left corner of his sheet, and paused, tilting his head toward a hubbub coming from the antechamber.

The door of the cabinet flung open, rebounding from the wall, and six or eight colored men crushed into the little room, all in a state of high excitement, all talking at once in loud conflicting voices, so that Laveaux could not make out what any one of them was saying.

"Citizens, what do you want?" Laveaux was on his feet, conscious that without his boots he lacked authoritative height, and that the worn slippers doubtless looked silly and weak.

Someone swung a fist at him by way of reply, but Laveaux reflexively slipped under the blow, caught and twisted his assailant's arm and threw him back among his fellows. No one had presented a firearm or blade, but Laveaux now took in that all of them carried canes, or else peeled sticks which they brandished like clubs.

"Assassins!" he shouted, hoping to be heard elsewhere in the building (where was the guard?). "I am unarmed."

He thought he heard the voice of his aide-de-camp, calling in another room, but soon cut off—there were only more mulattoes swarming in at the door and surging toward him. Laveaux kicked over the writing table to tangle their feet, and made for the other door, which gave onto a large salon. In this direction he might reach his sword and pistols. The inkwell toppled with the table, and rolled, spoiling his papers. Let them be ruined, Laveaux thought; it was all futile anyway.

In the salon he encountered a hundred-odd more colored men, enough to fill the room to the walls, moving to encircle him. The smaller group pressed out of the cabinet, cutting off all retreat. Laveaux brushed at his weaponless belt, then raised his hands and cocked them. He turned in the circle like a bear at bay. No one seemed quite prepared to strike across the space dividing him from the crowd.

"In the name of the people," said the man who had missed his first blow, "we arrest you."

"But you are not the people," Laveaux spat, turning and searching among their faces. "I see no black citizens, no white citizens—no, you are assassins."

There was no one he recognized by sight. Villatte himself was conspicuously (deliberately?) absent at this moment, and no one was in uniform. But he did notice, in the shifting rear, the smirking, freckled face of that colored officer, Maltrot . . . but he was in civilian attire, foppish, swinging a gold-headed cane. Laveaux mistrusted him still more than Villatte, if that were possible. He had no help, but also felt no fear, only an odd relief, as at the lancing of a boil. He turned, silent now, daring all approaches, but from behind someone came down on his shoulder with a stick. The blow itself was nothing, a painless tap, but it released the crowd to rush upon him. Laveaux crouched, parrying sticks and fists, his hands high to protect his face, and his elbows protecting his midsection, at least partially.

It was critical to keep his feet, he thought. But someone caught the back of his hair and snatched him off balance and down to the floor. He felt his slippers falling off as he was dragged over the threshold. Shiny boots kicked at him, though with no great accuracy; the faces swirling above him were nothing but teeth. When they had hauled him out into the dust of the street, the blows began to land more frequently, and harder, and he felt the visceral responses of an animal confronting its own death. But he was not killed, only tossed into a cell of the town prison, the door slammed tight and locked behind him.

He was hurt, but not mortally. His face was bruised, bleeding from the nose and from superficial scrapes. He threw his head back, swallowing blood, inhaling. Real pain, sharp, from his battered rib cage, came with the breath. That much was serious. There was a small square grille in the left wall and Laveaux approached it, meaning to call out in protest, to summon help, a doctor. But the aperture gave onto another cell, in which he recognized the *ordonnateur*, Perroud, who seemed to have been similarly mistreated and whose face was pale with terror.

Near sunset, Toussaint Louverture and the captains Riau and Maillart were concluding their own secretarial work. Toussaint had sent for sealing wax and, a few minutes later, for rum to offer his subalterns; he himself would take only a glass of water. Maillart softened the wax above a candle flame, then turned his hand to drip it onto the closure of the first letter. There was a scuffling outside the door. Maillart expected the refreshments, but intead Henri Christophe was announced, with an urgent message from Le Cap.

Christophe entered, his hat in his hands. His coat and boots were caked with dust from hard riding, but he was perfectly composed, his movements slow and dignified. ("Manners of a head waiter," someone had said, to mock him, for Christophe, a free black before the Revolution, had formerly served in such a capacity at a hotel in Le Cap.)

Now Christophe saluted Toussaint, waited permission and then began to speak. Laveaux had been arrested, he said, at the instigation of a cabal of mulattoes. Villatte had effectively proclaimed himself governor . . .

Toussaint listened, stooped forward in his chair, chin tucked in and head inclined so that he seemed to be studying the floor. Christophe's voice was even, rounded, as if he had planned and memorized his speech during the journey and was now delivering it from a podium in an assembly hall. As he spoke, he looked at Toussaint for some reaction and, finding none, continued.

The mulatto officers had all thrown in with Villatte, he said, but two of the black officers had not been corrupted. One of these had undertaken to rally all the blacks of the plain, with their chiefs, to Laveaux's support. He had also intercepted a messenger from Villatte who proved to be carrying a list of certain persons at Marmelade, Gros Morne and Gonaives.

"Kite'm oué sa." Toussaint lifted his head and stretched out his hand. Let me see that. Christophe produced the paper from his breast pocket. Toussaint scanned it for a moment, his free hand covering his mouth, then turned to Riau and gave him the paper.

"Deliver these . . . persons to me."

Riau snapped to attention, clicking his heels smartly (Maillart had painstakingly taught him this gesture). He took the paper and left the room without a word. A woman carrying the tray of rum and water stepped out of his way, then entered through the open door and set the tray down on the table.

Toussaint gave Christophe a contemplative look and unfolded his long fingers toward the empty chair at his right.

"Well done, *mon fils,*" he murmured.

Christophe sat down. Toussaint poured some rum into the glass meant for Riau and passed it to Christophe. With a glance he indicated that Maillart might serve himself. The captain did so, but the flush of warmth in his gullet only increased his agitation. He watched Toussaint pour two fingers of rum into a glass and take a conservative sip. This was strange. It was almost unknown for Toussaint to take spirits.

Maillart could not stop his pacing, he could not, at last, stop his own tongue. Toussaint and Christophe sat motionless as figures in a painting. The captain thought his head would burst.

"My general," he said. "Shall I call for the horses? Make ready the cavalry?"

Toussaint stirred from his reverie and looked up at him interrogatively.

"Will we not ride at once?"

Laboriously, Toussaint drew out his watch and opened the case, took note of the time and put the watch away again.

"It will soon be night," Toussaint said.

"Yes, but—" Maillart spluttered. Save for his most insouciant enemies, the whole colony knew by now Toussaint's capacity for moving his forces long distances at great speed by either day or night.

"Control yourself!" Toussaint said, the sharpness of his tone a rebuke. "I know of your affection for the Governor-General. He has not been harmed—he will not be."

Maillart stood rigid with embarrassed anger. From the corner of his eye he saw, through the window, the reddened sun lowering over the sea. Toussaint pushed his left palm toward the floor.

"Doucement," he said, nearly a whisper. *"Doucement alé loin."*

Toussaint's favorite proverb. The softest way goes farthest. Maillart had heard it many times. He watched Toussaint's hovering hand. The fingers flexed, drifting like feathers over the humid air. The captain exhaled and felt part of the pressure drain from him.

"Before we strike with the sword," Toussaint said, "let us see what the pen may accomplish." He glanced from Maillart's face to the writing implements. The captain sat down heavily and picked up a pen.

"We write," Toussaint pronounced carefully, "to the municipality *au Cap.*" He tilted back, lacing his fingers behind his cloth-wrapped head, and drew in his breath to begin dictation. But of a sudden he rocked forward and looked at Maillart keenly.

"La patience," he said. "If you have patience, my captain, you will deliver this letter yourself."

Reclining on the litter of thatch palm that covered the floor of his cell, Laveaux listened to the rasp and whistle of his breathing. Each inhalation was a shaft of pain. When he had his wind back, he went to the slot in the door and demanded to see his doctor, but no one responded. He had had no contact with anyone except when a single, surly presentation of stale water, cold ham and dried-out cornbread was brought to him.

Through the grille which communicated with the next cell, there was only Perroud, transfixed with fear. Even in his fitful sleep he moaned and pled with phantom executioners. Laveaux, whose own mental clarity was disrupted by pain and the initial symptoms of a fever, began to consider that the other man's terror might be rationally founded. False charges had been bruited about, that Laveaux, in his favor toward the newly freed blacks of the colony, had turned against all the *gens de couleur* and perhaps even planned their extermination. All this was untrue, a very tissue of lies, but if he should be brought before a mulatto court . . . To perfect his usurpation of power, Villatte must do away with

Laveaux altogether, with anyone who might contradict his version of events. That much was logical.

Laveaux ought perhaps to have seen it all coming. Perhaps in a way he had. He had known Villatte's ambition, seen his resentment of Toussaint's advancement. Indeed, Villatte and the rest of the colored officer corps of the Le Cap contingent had borne the supervision by their French superiors with difficulty and distaste. In the days when Laveaux had been pinned down at Port-de-Paix, Le Cap and its environs had been their principality. No one in that mulatto faction had been overjoyed by Laveaux's return. For that reason, in part, Laveaux had preferred Toussaint. In truth, he liked the black general better, and trusted him more. But where was Toussaint now?

Laveaux's stomach made a queasy revolution. This was not fear, but impending dysentery. A consequence of tainted food, impure water. Coupled with fever, or even on its own, this illness might bring him death if he remained here for many more days. Such an outcome would be more convenient to his captors than a mock trial followed by an all-too-genuine execution.

Though he had managed to retain his watch throughout the struggles of his capture, the case had been dented, the crystal shattered, the works stopped by a boot or the blow of a baton. He could not divine the hour, for his touch of fever kept him from counting the bells of the church correctly. His cell had no window to the outdoors, but the wedge of daylight on the corridor floor had long since faded, so he knew that it was night.

Noise came to him indistinctly from the streets surrounding the prison, a batter of running feet and a crying out of voices. *Force à la loi! Force à la loi!* In his confusion Laveaux was not sure that he heard this right. And what law did the voices invoke? The just law of the French Republic, or something trumped up by Villatte's faction for the occasion? From their timbre the voices seemed to be those of the blacks to whom he had sometimes referred as his own adopted children. At this thought, Laveaux was moved almost to tears.

The bells of the town were tolling eleven when Maillart rode through the gate into the Rue Espagnole, in the midst of his escort of twenty black cavalrymen. Crossing the mountains had molded his agitation into a grim-edged determination. He had been obliged to restrain his mount—it would have been idiotic to kill horses in the desperation of the ride—and also, as Toussaint had counseled him, to rein in his own responses.

It had taken no more than an hour to draft Toussaint's letter to the municipal authorities and to make a fair copy. During that time Riau had returned with the Gonaives conspirators in his custody—those who were named on Villatte's intercepted list. Riau was off again immediately to complete the same mission at Marmelade, while the arrested men went into the guard house, from which the captain doubted they would ever emerge. He was very much encouraged by the speed and efficiency of these measures. And Toussaint's letter put it in absolute terms that if Governor-General Laveaux were not immediately released and restored to his normal functions, the most dire consequences would follow.

The moon hung over the sea like a scythe. Maillart admired it, his jaws tight. The stiff breeze sweeping in from the water dried the sweat his riding across the plain had raised. As he and his escort advanced toward the town center, they heard the sounds of a general disturbance and presently they were surrounded by many blacks who milled about shouting *Force à la loi*. These demonstrators recognized the men with Maillart as coming from Toussaint, and they were glad. Still chanting, they swirled around the captain's mounted group all the way to the municipality.

Maillart had thought to roust the municipal authorities from their beds, but he found them already assembled, though it was near midnight when he entered the building, banging his bootheels deliberately on the stone floors. There was more than enough to keep them from sleep, for although Villatte's faction held the town, they were surrounded by forces loyal to Laveaux—not only Pierre Michel's trained soldiers but also the larger and less organized bands which still roamed on the plain, and which once unleashed could not easily be restrained again. It was these latter who in ninety-three had burned Le Cap to its foundations. Pierre Michel had promised to repeat such scenes if Laveaux were not swiftly released. Moreover, as the captain had learned when he paused at Haut du Cap to confer with Michel, Pierre Léveillé was not in the custody of Villatte's conspirators after all, but instead had occupied the town arsenal, from which he defied them. . . .

Maillart flung the letter down on the table, and stood haughtily to watch as one of the group reached to take it up and crack the seal with the nail of a slightly tremorous finger. He watched them crane their heads together to read, and wanted to grin as he saw their faces pale to whey, but he merely pressed his lips to a tighter, straighter line. Out of all that cluster only one man seemed aloof, indifferent; he sat relaxed in a corner, outside the sphere of candlelight, so that the captain had not noticed him at first. It was Choufleur, the *Colonel* Maltrot, though in civilian dress and dandling a gold-topped cane in his freckled yellow fingers. Pleased that in these circumstances he need not acknowledge Choufleur's rank, the captain let his eyes slide over the freckled face as if it were another stone in the wall.

"We await your answer," Maillart said in his most imperious tone, then spun about and left the room, banging the door against the wall with a thrust of his arm as he went out. This episode had played very much to his satisfaction. But as he mounted his horse again, perplexity overtook him. Villatte had been nowhere in evidence, only the civil authorities, but might Choufleur be Villatte's representative, or his spy? For the first time he remembered Nanon's desertion, or abduction, or whatever it had been, and Doctor Hébert's distress. But after all there was nothing he could have done just then; it was not the moment for any such personal inquiry. Still, he must hold the thought for later, if a better opportunity should offer itself.

Motioning his men to follow, he spurred his horse to a brisk trot and rode toward the arsenal. That would be the safest, most advantageous place.

In fact Léveillé's force, though small, was encouragingly determined, and was supported by the throngs of people milling through the town. According to Léveillé, it was Pierre Michel who had inspired the popular movement—not so difficult to achieve since so many of the newly freed blacks looked upon Laveaux as heir to Sonthonax, and hence the father of their freedom.

Maillart was given coffee and rum with which to lace it. Why not, he suggested after his first swallow, dare a dawn attack to reduce the prison where Laveaux was held? But the others present did not agree, and Toussaint's orders went explicitly against it. Maillart was to deliver his missive, watch and wait. He knew himself that it would be unsound to risk the counterattack on the arsenal which such a sortie might provoke. No one seemed to know exactly where Villatte was at this moment but presumably he was in the *casernes* with the troops he had successfully corrupted, and theirs was still the largest force within the town.

Hold your position, watch and wait. The admonition ran looping throughout Maillart's mind throughout the night, whenever he woke, which was often, and even during his periods of fitful sleep. Temperamentally, he was ill-suited for such a role, but he had studied it during his service with Toussaint. If he asked himself what Toussaint would do in any given situation, the answer, most often, was nothing.

The next day passed in a cloud of rumor and indecision. Maillart would have liked to go out and look for signs of Nanon or Choufleur or both of them, but this project was also unfeasible, under the circumstances. Léveillé's little force kept to its stronghold, awaiting developments; the noisy crowds continued to circulate throughout the town. Sometime after midnight Maillart lay down to another extremely uneasy sleep. At four-thirty he was roused by the news that Villatte had fled the town, taking the now very small number of troops still loyal to him to the refuge of a fortified camp on the plantation Lamartinière. The coup, such as it had been, was over. The colored soldiers still in the *casernes* were ready to renew their obedience to Laveaux, and even now the civil servants were on their way, among a large crowd of the townspeople, to release Laveaux from his cell.

Maillart jerked on his coat and boots and, with Léveillé and a few others, reached the prison in time to see Laveaux coming out of the gate. He was haggard and filthy from his days in the cell; Perroud, a pace or two behind him, looked even worse. But Laveaux raised his right hand over the people who met him, like a priest giving absolution.

It was dawn, though the sun's face would be hidden for some time more behind the hulk of Morne du Cap; the light was coming up quickly. The crowd swept Laveaux directly to the main audience room of the municipal building, where he turned to face the men who had imprisoned him. Once more he raised his right hand, which trembled only slightly from his ague. He announced that, *for the love of the Good,* he would not seek to punish the guilty parties.

Eighth man back in the column, Doctor Hébert rode up the south face of Morne Pilboreau. Riau was ahead of him, Guiaou behind; leading the file was Toussaint Louverture. Still stronger forces, led by Dessalines and Charles Belair, had gone before them to Le Cap. They would not be called upon to fight this time. Nor would the troop with which the doctor rode. Toussaint's word alone had been sufficient, his finger wagged in warning more than enough. Villatte's conspiracy was foiled without a shot.

The doctor's mule picked a delicate way up the switchbacks of the mountain trail. It was the same mule which had carried him to Habitation Fortier and through Toussaint's campaign around Grande Rivière. He had come to prefer the mule's surefootedness for mountain rides. With a *paysan* straw saddle the comparative discomfort of a seat on the mule's bony back was not worth considering. He had even come to appreciate the mule's self-interested intelligence, which was far greater than that of a horse, though not always placed at the service of the rider.

A balloon of hope seemed to lift him toward the peak. They would reach Le Cap before night. There he might find traces of Choufleur, if not Nanon herself . . . and Paul. Choufleur had been billeted there before he had come to ravish Nanon away from Habitation Thibodet. His involvement in *l'affaire Villatte* was to be suspected. And Nanon, if left to her own resources, might have returned there. She knew how to manage in the town; it was where she and the doctor had first met.

Lost in these images, he floated up the trail. His American long rifle tilted across the saddlebow like an outrigger. The weapon was too long to be side-slung in its scabbard; the barrel would have furrowed the ground.

Farther back in the column some hoof or boot or horny bare foot dislodged a stone which fell over the trail's edge and went skittering down the dry, dusty slopes, gathering smaller pebbles and clods as it went down. Lizards sidestepped away from the miniature avalanche. The doctor twisted in his saddle and looked back. The switchbacks of the descent behind them were giddily steep. Scrub pine and cedar ran down the gorges, to the sparse *raquette* trees on the dry mud flats. Dry wind had withered a corn planting on a terraced face of the hill opposite. Far below, the chalky plain fanned out toward Gonaives. A blue haze at the horizon marked the coast.

Automatically the doctor touched the mirror shard in his right pocket, then, switching the reins from hand to hand, the empty snuff-box in his left. In this way he recentered himself. In the crushing heat, it dizzied him to screw his head around, but he thought there was no danger of sunstroke. He reached to check the brim of his straw hat. Beneath it he also wore a head cloth, as many of the soldiers did. He had learned that in full sun his bald scalp was apt to blister even through the weave of a hat. The rest of his exposed skin had been fired the color of a chimney brick, and only the bleached hairs on his forearms and in his beard betrayed that his blood was purely European.

As in a mirror, an image appeared to him. Toussaint as he had first seen him years ago, before he had taken the name Louverture, on muleback and unarmed but for the sack of medicinal herbs he held against the pommel of his saddle. In those days Toussaint's sole title had been "Médecin du Roi," which meant in effect that he was camp doctor for Jean-François and Biassou. Dreamily it came to the doctor that he himself had now inherited a similar position.

The men ahead of him were disappearing over the summit of Pilboreau, and in a moment more the doctor's mule crossed over. He found himself in the midst of the crossroads market. Toussaint had called a halt, to rest the horses from the climb. Those men with means to buy or barter were trading with the *marchandes* for fruit, while others sipped warmish water from the canteens or gourds they carried with them.

Carefully, the horses were given a very little water. Riau untied the neck of his salt bag and let his horse lick granules from his palm.

"Pinchinat has gone back to Les Cayes."

Toussaint's voice. The doctor looked up. Toussaint did not seem to be addressing anyone in particular, but a loose circle had formed around him, including the white officer Vaublanc, Riau, Quamba and Guiaou. The doctor could not imagine why he should have chosen this moment to begin discoursing on Pinchinat, though he knew the old colored gentleman was a rhetorician to reckon with, and an active intriguer on the part of the mulatto faction for the last ten years at least.

"Do you know?" Toussaint continued musingly. "Some say the words of Pinchinat are more dangerous than bullets."

The doctor considered. Toussaint must have been chewing on the subject all during their ascent. He would not raise it now without cause, though the doctor could not divine what his reasons might be. There was an endless fascination in pondering Toussaint's motives. Why, for example, had he delayed so long in coming to Laveaux's aid in person? One reason, the doctor had already thought, was that he would not shift from his position of greatest strength until the business at Le Cap had been concluded . . . favorably. Another, as he now reflected, was that Gonaives was a better post from which to gather intelligence from the interior and the south.

"He is old now, Pinchinat," Toussaint continued, "but still more cunning than a spider. Well, a spider can weave all day and still a man knocks down the web with one stroke of a green switch. So Pinchinat has run back to Rigaud in the south. When we come to Le Cap, we will not find him there . . . but it was he who brought the spirit of disobedience to Villatte, I think. And from where, *mes amis?* where did that spirit come from?"

Toussaint, who seemed to have been looking out over the treetops in the direction of Marmelade, now focused on Riau.

"One must not forget the Swiss," he said. "We have heard that it was Pinchinat who sent those soldiers to be murdered on the ship. All that web was of his weaving."

Riau remained impassive, still as a tree. Only his eyes shifted for a moment to Guiaou, then back to some invisible inner space.

"Yes," Toussaint said. Now his glance included them all. "As many times as the web is knocked down, the little spider returns to weave again." He laughed and covered his mouth with his hand for a moment. When he uncovered it, the smile was gone.

"Mount up!" he said, in a loud voice. All down the line the cavalrymen obeyed him. Within ten minutes the column was strung out over the ridge above the Plaisance Valley, the leaders already descending into the verdant jungle shade.

Captain Maillart happened to be standing near the gate of the *casernes,* chatting with one of the men on post, when Doctor Hébert's mule turned in from the Rue Espagnole. It was just sundown, and clouds boiled above Morne du Cap; the wind rose and the leaves shivered on the trees, though it would not rain. Captain Maillart offered a hand to help his friend down from the mule saddle. The doctor slipped to the ground and wobbled on his rubbery legs, bracing himself on the captain's shoulder.

"Well met," said Maillart. "Has Toussaint come at last?"

"Yes," said the doctor, turning to unship his long rifle. "Or nearly— he has stopped at Haut du Cap, at the Bréda great house. For council with Pierre Michel and some others. He will enter the town tomorrow morning."

Maillart nodded. The troops who had marched with Charles Belair and Dessalines had already overflowed the *casernes.* The colored officers who had so recently returned to obedience navigated warily among their black counterparts; so far a proper courtesy had been observed on all sides. With the men Toussaint had brought, the influx of black troops would approach ten thousand, and this was more, much more, than a show of mere brute force.

The last time such a number of blacks had descended on Le Cap (admitted to enter by Sonthonax in one of his most desperate moments), they had had come to rape, kill, loot and burn, and had left nothing but smoking foundations when they departed. Now Toussaint's trained men had filled the town, in a state of perfect discipline and good order. The great majority of them were nearly naked but for their arms which they kept so carefully, and lived and marched on next to nothing—a yam or an ear of corn or a piece of fruit twice daily. And yet they carried themselves upright with a fierce pride. They held themselves in: there had been no looting, no foraging, no forced requisitioning, no drunkenness, no insults offered to the women of the town. A boatload of European troops would not have conducted themselves half so well if landed in this situation, as Maillart knew from more than one experience. Toussaint's men were healthier, cleaner, better disciplined, and as reliable in the field, perhaps more so. The captain had come to feel more pride in them than in any other men he'd led.

"Have you toured the town?" he asked the doctor.

"I came straight here from the gate." The doctor took down his saddlebags. "And you—what news?"

"Oh, I've been everywhere." The captain turned his face away, looking out onto the street. "She isn't here, Antoine."

"You're sure of that."

"What knowledge is wholly certain?" the captain said wearily. "I have not turned over every stone, but I've looked in all the likely places. I did discover Fleur—do you remember her from the theater, the *promenade du gouvernement*? Her beauty has suffered, sad to say. Such tropical roses are fast to fade—" Seeing the doctor's face, he cut himself short.

"Fleur would have known, if anyone," he resumed in a subdued tone, "had Nanon appeared here. One must suppose that she did not. Choufleur *was* here, and up to his neck in all this affair, as anyone might have imagined. By my best intelligence he has fled the city with Villatte, to the camp they made ready for such an eventuality."

The doctor nodded, hefting his baggage; his eyes were lowered to the ground.

"Well, brace up, then," Maillart said, his heartiness ringing a little false on his own ear. "*Courage*—that camp can be reduced in fifteen minutes whenever Toussaint chooses—Villatte could hardly muster fifty men to defend it now. We'll get to the bottom of it all in time. But now let us stable this beast of yours and look to your own nourishment."

Next day the doctor undertook his own search, with the help of Riau, who had come into town from Habitation Bréda with Toussaint. Maillart had been over much of the same ground, and the doctor found no better answers, even with Riau inquiring at back stairs and in the servants' quarters. No one had seen her at the Cigny house, which Choufleur had occupied up till his abrupt departure, nor at the late Sieur de Maltrot's town house, which Choufleur had begun to restore. No trace of Nanon in any of the haunts she had frequented before her liaison with the doctor. Nor was there any sign of Paul.

At last he called at the apartment near the Place d'Armes where he and Nanon had lived for some weeks together before the town was burned. The place was now occupied by a staid mulatto family, whose matriarch was most unwilling to admit them. She feared the black face as much as the white, no doubt, for while a white *colon* might have come to reclaim the dwelling, a black officer might arrive simply to seize it . . . She answered their questions through a two-inch crack in the door. No, she had not seen such a woman. No, she'd seen no *sang-mêlé* boy.

When the door had shut, the doctor stood with his head bowed, staring down at the pitch apple tree beside the portal. On one of the fat green leaves Nanon had scratched the child's name *Paul,* above the date of his birth. The inscription was there yet, the letters yellowed but still clear. They said pitch apple leaves held up as well as wooden tablets, maybe even stone. After a moment the doctor took out his penknife and added the family name to the leaf. *Paul Hébert.* He trimmed a corner from another leaf and put it into the snuffbox, but the gesture felt hollow to him even he performed it. And what if the pitch apple tree should be a tombstone? As he put away the knife his hand met the shard of mirror and he gripped it so hard the edges hurt his palm. He'd found it here, after a riot in the town, when Nanon's rooms had been vandalized, her mirror smashed. So many times it had held her image . . . if only the fragment could function as a magic eye (as Riau believed it did) to show her to him now.

He felt that Riau had been watching him intently all this time, but still was surprised at the sadness—compassion, it was better said—in the other man's face when he turned to meet it. Riau was also offering something in his right palm, a heap of the coarse salt crystals he'd gathered at the pans near Gonaives.

"Faut goûter sel, mon cher," he said. "You must taste the salt, and wake—she will not come back to you."

All the streets were flowing toward the Place d'Armes, and Riau and the doctor let themselves be carried by that stream. In the center of the square, Governor-General Laveaux was revealed on a platform, presenting Toussaint Louverture to the throng of his own soldiers and the multicolored citizens of the town. In all the colony, Laveaux announced, no one was closer to him than Toussaint. No one had served himself, and France, as loyally, as skillfully; there was no one whom he trusted more. Therefore from this day forward Toussaint was proclaimed Lieutenant-Governor of Saint Domingue, and would be not only General-in-Chief but also Laveaux's second in command in all aspects of government.

"Here is the savior of constitutional authority," Laveaux announced in his peroration, "a Black Spartacus!—come to avenge all the outrages carried out against his race."

At that a shout went up from the people, but throughout Laveaux's speech Toussaint stood with his head humbly lowered. At times it seemed he might even kneel to embrace the Frenchman's boots. But when Laveaux had concluded and the popular shout had faded to an echo, Toussaint pulled his shoulders back and grasped Laveaux's hand and raised it high, together with his own, calling out in his most forceful voice, "After God, Laveaux!"

Sometime in the later watches of that night, Maillart woke to the noise of terrible cries. The doctor, with whom he'd shared his room, was suffering some nightmare as if he were under attack. The captain called his name and groped to wake him with his touch. Because the sky was overcast, there was no hint of light in the room, and no breeze, so the space was suffocatingly close. Maillart could see nothing, nothing at all, but the doctor, moaning, flailed an arm at him, then somehow hooked it over his neck. They were wrestling against the edge of the cot, then among the folding legs when it overturned. Maillart clawed at the doctor's forearm, fighting for breath. He'd known his friend was stronger than he might appear, but this force seemed almost supernatural.

"Antoine," he choked. "Antoine!"

"Annghh," said the doctor. His grip relaxed. "What is it?"

The captain pulled free of him and delicately probed his half-crushed windpipe. "How should I know?" he said.

"Annh," said the doctor. "What?—forgive me."

"It's nothing," said the captain. As he spoke, a fresh wind carried the cloud off the moon, and a tendril of breeze came into the room with the new light. Maillart felt the anxious sweat beginning to dry and cool on his skin. The doctor righted the cot and stretched out on his back. The captain returned to his own bedding.

"Such a dream . . ." the doctor murmured. "I was in the river. You can't imagine how deep, the water. And the trees on the bank were so huge, so ancient—they must have been there when Adam and Eve were in the garden."

Gooseflesh broke out all over the captain's exposed skin. The moonlight held steady and bright in the room. He turned his face to look at the doctor, who lay with his head gathered in his palm, his short beard jutting toward the ceiling.

"I was swimming," he went on. "But it seemed my strokes did not break the water. There was moonlight everywhere as there is now. It was very cool, and calm, and leaves were floating all around me. Leaves and lilies. Then I went under. I don't remember if I dived. But I went down, through planes and currents of leaves below, and when I passed through each of these layers, there would be more of them still further below. So very deep . . . the light of the moon followed me all the way down, because the water was wonderfully clear. It was like swimming down through time . . . Eons and eons of it.

"And then, at last, I did reach the bottom. There was a lot of silt, soft and cloudy. It didn't seem dirty or unpleasant. The moonlight was still there and by feeling in the silt I found something made out of silver. Some instrument, a spade perhaps." The doctor frowned. "Once I had found it, it seemed I had been looking for it all the time.

"I took it by the handle and began to rise. All that time I had been weightless, as if I were flying—have you ever flown in dreams? But the spade was heavy, and held me down."

The doctor sat up on the edge of his cot. "For the first time, I knew I needed air," he said. "I had not seemed to breathe before. So many of those currents of leaves were still above me."

He held his open hands one above the other, several inches apart, and made some queer, mesmeric passes to show what he was talking about. Maillart saw the shifting currents of leaves as if they'd appeared between his fingers, so clear and sharp in the crystalline water.

"It was so beautiful," the doctor said. "But with the weight of the spade I could not keep rising. The weight pulled me back down, knee deep in the silt."

The doctor paused. Maillart could see his bare chest lifting with his breath. A gloss of sweat on his cheekbones. His eyes dark hoods.

"If I let the spade go, then I might float again," he said. "I understood that, though I regretted it. I let the spade sink into the silt, and I kicked myself free of the bottom. I was coming up easily now, and it was all as beautiful as before . . ." He shook his head, letting his hands drop to his knees. "But too late. I would not have time enough to reach the surface. My lungs must open and I must breathe the water in."

"But that was *my* dream," Maillart blurted.

The doctor swung his legs up onto the cot and lay on his back as before.

"I mean," the captain said, "I dreamed the same as you."

"Yes," said the doctor, with no sign of surprise. He was quiet for a moment, except that the captain could hear his breathing.

"But why did you wake me?" the doctor said. "I was happy."

"You were screaming," Maillart said.

"Yes," said the doctor. "I suppose that's true."

He said no more, and presently they slept.

Fort de Joux, France

September 1802

A step behind the anxious jailer, Caffarelli picked and splashed his way through the flooded third corridor, lifting his polished boots high before setting them back down in the wet, clicking his tongue with distaste. Boards had been laid to bridge the flood, but they had warped and bowed beneath the water and were useless, already rotting at the edges. It was very cold. Caffarelli held himself tight so as not to shiver, standing in the ankle-deep water while Baille took an interminable time to find the right key on his huge ring.

The door groaned inward. The next corridor, the last one, had a higher floor which was mercifully dry. Two iron-bound doors were set deeply into the wall, toward the far end of the corridor.

"Laquelle?" Caffarelli's voice rebounded in the narrow vault, louder than he'd intended.

Baille pointed, and swung forward the heavy ring of keys.

"Laissez-moi." Caffarelli closed his hand over the shank of the key Baille had selected.

The jailer, his plump face damp with anxiety, began to splutter a protest. Caffarelli silenced him with a raised forefinger.

"Yes!" he hissed. "I will enter alone, I will remain with him, alone. You will leave us so. My orders."

Baille subsided, and let the key ring slip. Turning his shoulder to exclude the jailer, Caffarelli fit the key to the lock and with a grinding effort turned it. The sound of the lock disengaging would certainly be audible within the cell, but Caffarelli waited. Suspense. He could practically feel Baille's noisy, moist breathing on the back of his neck. He adjusted his cuffs and collar, pushed the door open and stepped in.

Side-lit by the red embers of his fire, the old Negro who called himself *Louverture* sat with his left arm propped on his chair back, looking up toward the door with an imperious expectancy. Caffarelli had studied him at second hand. He had pored over Toussaint's letters, cross-examined the military officers and civilian officials who had dealt with him in the past . . . those who had survived to report the experience. He knew in advance that Toussaint was physically small, but he was still unprepared for his diminutive stature. This? Why, the man's legs were so short his heels did not quite touch the floor. At the same time he was disconcerted by something in Toussaint's expression which made him feel that the old Negro had overheard his muttered colloquy with Baille (although this was hardly likely, given the thickness of the door) . . . that the effect of his entrance was spoiled and the advantage had somehow shifted away from him altogether.

But Caffarelli was already proceeding according to plan, having brought his feet together neatly when he entered and made a movement of his hips and neck which faintly suggested a bow. He had already begun to speak, in his most unctuous tones: "Sir, you can surely imagine the great pleasure I feel to find myself in the presence of a man whose name is so celebrated, who has accomplished such extraordinary things . . ."

All the while these honeyed droplets purled off his tongue, Caffarelli was aware of the tumblers turning in the lock behind him as Baille muscled the key around, and around again, for the double lock. In another part of his mind, Napoleon's instructions came back to him: . . . *you will see Toussaint, who has caused the Minister of War to write to me that he has important things to communicate. In speaking with him, you will make him understand the enormity of the crime of which he has made himself guilty by bearing arms against the Republic, and that we have considered him a rebel from the moment he published his constitution, and that furthermore his treaty with Jamaica and England was made known to us by the court of London; you will strive to gather everything he can tell you of these different subjects, and also about the existence of his treasures, and whatever political news he may have to tell you . . .* He observed Toussaint closely for any sign of reaction to the words he continued to utter, without, himself, really listening to them: ". . . and so I would be charmed to be instructed by such a man as I describe, should he be willing to honor me with his conversation . . ."

Toussaint was watching him with what seemed an indulgent smile. A yellow cloth was tied around his head, for what might have been a comic effect, if not for the man's strange, compelling dignity. The fingers of one hand were splayed along the right side of his long jaw, pressing hard enough to indent the flesh. When Caffarelli had stopped talking, Toussaint turned to the table at his left and lit the single candle. Then he swung back in a leisurely manner toward his visitor, passing a hand across the lower part of his face as if to wipe away anything his expression might reveal.

"Of course," he said. The voice was low, but resonant, larger than the man. "It is you who do me honor. Please sit down."

That night Caffarelli sat in the room provided for him, composing his notes by the light of a sputtering oil lamp. At his left hand was a glass of extraordinarily sour red wine. He wished for brandy; there was none. Perhaps sugar. He sipped the wine, grimacing. Baille had told him that Toussaint sugared not only his wine but everything else he put into his mouth; the prisoner's consumption of sugar was ruinous.

He licked the vinegarish residue from his teeth, and sighed. This mission would detain him here longer than he had anticipated. Toussaint was a maze not easily negotiated. The first interview had taken nearly all the day. Well, Caffarelli had expected the isolated captive to be eager to talk. But not that his discourse would travel in such smooth, impenetrably interlocked circles. In five hours of questioning he had learned practically nothing of use.

The wick of the lamp was of the poorest quality, so that the flame and the light fluttered constantly. Caffarelli scratched with his pen. He must unreel all the secrets from Toussaint's mind and set them down on the paper. But for the first day, little enough to report. Toussaint had talked all around him (and Caffarelli was proud of his skill as an interrogator). His rich, low voice was pleasant to hear and, after a couple of hours, it had begun to make Caffarelli feel sleepy, in spite of the cold.

What a wretched place it was, this Fort de Joux. Though it was only September, the mountains were already heavy with snow. Probably the snowcaps never melted even in high summer. How long he must remain here only God knew.

The wick fizzled, releasing a great burst of darkness. Caffarelli froze in place, but it was absurd, absurd—he could not be frightened by the dark. A tiara of red sparks crowned the wick's end, nothing more. Outdoors the wind was whistling.

This misfortunate castle. Set in an exterior wall was another barred cell—no more than a niche, really: three feet by three by four. Here some feudal lord had shut up his wife at the age of seventeen, having discovered her unfaithful when he returned from a Crusade or some such adventure. Baille had dutifully conducted him to this point of interest, when Caffarelli had first arrived. According to the tale, the cell was so placed as to force the girl to look out upon her lover's corpse, which swung from a cliff on the mountain opposite. Some spikes and grommets could still be discerned with a spyglass, Baille said, but Caffarelli had not had the heart to look.

The sparks swelled and joined, a red rim on the end of the wick. Caffarelli found it difficult not to hold his breath. In that tiny cell, the unlucky wife could never have straightened her legs. The thought of her constantly curled limbs especially disturbed him. Of course people were smaller then—but certainly she could not have stood erect beneath the three-foot ceiling. Berthe de Joux had been her name. He pictured her curled like a fox in a cage, gnawing at crusts, pushing her own ordures out through the bars with her fingers. Watching the bones of her lover drop from the cliffside as gradually the ligaments gave way to rot. She had died an old woman in this confinement, but how long would it have taken for her to grow old?

The red rim yellowed, the flame expanded on the wick. As the light returned, Caffarelli forced the stale air from his lungs and drew in fresh. He concentrated on each exhalation, sweeping the morbidity from his mind. Dipping the pen into the inkwell, he continued his notations on Toussaint. *He tells the truth,* Caffarelli wrote grudgingly, *but he does not tell all.*

Next day when he entered the cell, he found Toussaint feverish, scarcely able to speak. He kept massaging the yellow kerchief tightly bound around his head, or alternately pressed another wadded yellow cloth along the line of his jaw. His imperial courtesy, already sufficiently bizarre under such circumstances, was still further distorted by his fever. Toussaint excused himself from conversation, until his illness should abate. Perhaps—no, certainly—tomorrow. Under his left hand was a hefty manuscript of his own composition, which, he declared, would answer any and all questions until he should again be able to speak for himself. Let Caffarelli take this document and read it at his leisure; for the time being, Toussaint begged to be excused.

But Caffarelli lingered. He had the thought that the fever must weaken Toussaint's reserve. But although the old Negro babbled a few phrases, he let nothing slip. He said nothing of any import at all, other than his repeated proffer of the manuscript. After three-quarters of an hour, Caffarelli felt the touch of shame; he did not regard himself as a torturer. Besides, the manuscript tempted him. He picked it up, wished Toussaint a swift recovery, bowed and took his leave.

Throughout that day and well into the evening, he read and reread, with mounting frustration. One could not call Toussaint's memorandum a tissue of lies. On the contrary, it was an assemblage of literal truths, artfully arranged to give false impressions. Each fact was just, and each was delicately balanced against the others to create this inverse image: Toussaint had never, not for one instant even in a thought, placed himself in rebellion against France. A good revolutionary citizen, he had never sought to be anything other than a humble and dutiful conservator of the colony for the nation he in his heart regarded as his own. The Captain-General Leclerc had presented himself in the guise of an invader. He had not troubled to properly present his orders from Napoleon to General Toussaint, who was after all in chief command of Saint Domingue at the time of Leclerc's arrival. It was Leclerc who had forced his landing and commenced hostilities. And so on   and on

As one kept reading, one was required to believe that Toussaint had resisted Leclerc's arrival with all the forces at his disposal, had burnt towns and plantations, had poisoned wells, had fought desperate battles in which thousands were slain—without ever intending a bit of it! It was all a regrettable misunderstanding.

Preposterous. And yet, it was so seamlessly wrought. The more time Caffarelli spent among the loops and circles of Toussaint's words, the more he seemed to hear the man's compelling voice, pouring the concoction into his ears . . . At moments he came so close to believing that he had to leave the room and walk outside to brace himself with the bitter cold, the clear vision of sharp mountain peaks and the rectilinear walls of the castle.

What was most genuine in the memorandum was the outrage. It came in flashes, in response to the undeniable treachery of Toussaint's arrest and to the rough, humiliating treatment he and his family had endured ever since. In this regard, there were passages which inspired Caffarelli to fellow-feeling. The outrage was perfectly sincere, and yet it was and must be founded on Toussaint's contention that he had always been the loyal servant of France, for otherwise it would be unjustified.

This link, Caffarelli suddenly perceived, was what gave the whole document its improbable credibility.

They sent me to France as naked as a worm, Toussaint had written. *My properties and my papers were seized; the most atrocious slanders were broadcast about me, far and wide. Is this not to cut off someone's legs and then order him to walk? Is it not to cut out someone's tongue and tell him to speak? Is it not to bury a man alive?*

All this was outrage, with no hint of self-pity. There was the point of attack. If moved to outrage, Toussaint might speak freely. More freely than otherwise. There was the opportunity . . . Caffarelli looked up at the wheels of brilliant stars in the frozen sky, then across at the cliff opposite, its dark descent from the pale snow-covered slope above it. It came to him that he was standing directly above the cell of Berthe de Joux. He shrugged the thought away; his course for the morrow was set.

In the morning he found Toussaint recovered from the worst of his fever, though he still pressed the kerchief against his jaw as though it pained him gravely. His eyes were hollow, but clear; the febrile glitter of the day before was gone.

After the opening round of courtesies, Caffarelli began as he'd planned, theatrically. He slammed the manuscript on the table. It is all nonsense, he declaimed, raising his voice to resound in the close space. All deception—and useless too. For the evident truth is that you expelled from Saint Domingue all agents of the French government save those who might furnish you with the external façade of continued obedience. That you raised a great army of soldiers who were all devoutly loyal to yourself alone, and flocks of civil servants who owed their devotion only to you.

All the while he was speaking, Caffarelli looked forcefully into Toussaint's eyes, meaning to stare him down, but the black man did not quail or recoil or react in any way at all. In a perfectly balanced stillness, Toussaint merely observed. Caffarelli was obliged to shift his gaze to the drizzling stone wall behind him. You put the entire island in a state of defense; you dealt secretly with the English; finally you proclaimed a constitution and put it into effect before you sent it to the French government for approval—a constitution which names you governor for life! And this—he bashed the manuscript with the flat of his hand—has no bearing whatsoever on any of those facts I have just mentioned. But these are the facts which we must discuss. I ask you, what have you to say?

Caffarelli sat down and composed himself to wait. The tick of a watch was just barely audible, somewhere in the other man's clothes. For a long time, Toussaint did not speak.

Part Three

GOUTÉ SEL

1796–1798

Never make a politician
Grant you a favor
They will always want to
Control you forever . . .
So with a fire make it burn,
and with blood, make it run . . .

—Bob Marley,
"Revolution"

In July of 1795, the European war between the French Republic and Spain was ended by the signing of a treaty in the city of Basel. By the terms of this treaty, the conflict between French Saint Domingue and Spanish Santo Domingo was also concluded, and the heretofore Spanish portion of Hispaniola was formally ceded to France. However, the French Republican Army (with its mostly black or colored troops) was still preoccupied with the English invasion and had no men to spare to occupy the ceded territory, though Spanish-sponsored warfare along the border ceased for the most part. Jean-François and Biassou, the two black generals still in Spanish service, departed from the island, leaving many of their men to be absorbed into the force of Toussaint Louverture.

Named Lieutenant-Governor by Laveaux, Toussaint had risen higher in the colonial hierarchy than any nonwhite person had ever done before. Although his official military rank, général de division, was not the highest in the land, he was effectively the commander-in-chief of the French army in the Northern and Western Departments of Saint Domingue. He continued to prosecute the war against the British in the Western Department. The colored general André Rigaud was fighting the British in the Southern Department on behalf of the French Republic, but with much *less frequent communication with Laveaux than Toussaint (who wrote dozens of letters to his superior during this period, reporting all his operations in detail). The British invasion had faltered, unable to establish itself securely beyond the coastal towns, where huge numbers of soldiers fell prey to fever, but it had not yet failed, and the British were still rotating new commanders.*

In France, meanwhile, Léger Félicité Sonthonax confronted accusations leveled against him by the land- and slave-owning colonists of Saint Domingue who had brought their case to Paris. Skilled in debate and in the law, Sonthonax now faced a much more conservative French government than the one under which he had proclaimed the abolition of slavery in 1793. His accusers sought to blame him for many offenses, including the surrender of Port-au-Prince to the British invasion and the burning of Cap Français in 1793. In October 1795, Sonthonax was completely vindicated. In the spring of 1796, he was placed at the head of a new Commission, including two other white men, Leblanc and Giraud, and one mulatto, Julien Raimond—and thus began his second tour of duty in war-torn Saint Domingue.

21

In the mornings the mountain air was almost cool enough to sting, and cool, blue breezes shivered the leaves on the trees that surrounded the house. Since Paul had gone, Nanon had begun to wake near dawn; though such early rising was far from her habit, she could sleep again in the child's absence. She did not fret, but rose, brushed her hair and caught it up in a madras cloth, belted a cotton robe over one of the diaphanous fancies Choufleur had given her to wear to their bed, and went to take coffee on the gallery, with perhaps a little fruit, like the great lady of some lonely manor.

There were few people about the place, since Choufleur had gone to Le Cap with Paul: only the cook and a couple of house servants, and four armed men for her protection, led by a *sacatra* named Salomon. It was true, perhaps, that there was still some danger, for the whole canton of Vallière was a wild and remote place, and near the Spanish border too. When she was a girl, the area had been the resort of maroons, and the *maréchaussée* came through constantly in pursuit of them. Also there were sometimes incursions of Spanish from across the border, for the boundary line was in constant dispute. The difficult slopes of these mountains were no great temptation as farmland to the slothful

Spaniards, but there was supposed to be gold around the headwaters of Grande Rivière, so sometimes the Spanish crossed and burned the French plantations. More recently it had been black men in Spanish pay—Jean-François and the troops he commanded, who had fallen back into these mountains after the winter battles in the valley of Grande Rivière. These bands were ill-disciplined, nothing like Toussaint's troops which Nanon had grown used to seeing camped round Habitation Thibodet, but as Choufleur seemed to have a special understanding with Jean-François, his establishment was never molested. But the war between the Spanish and French was officially ended, and Jean-François had sailed to another country, leaving his men scattered in small roving bands, living as maroons once more. Sometimes they raided the provision grounds here, but there had been no threat to the main compound. In any case Choufleur had assured her that four well-armed and determined men would be more than sufficient to defend the house successfully.

Nanon was not fearful, only freighted with ennui. She sipped her coffee and nibbled uninterestedly at a small sweet *banane-figue,* watching the garden below the gallery, which had gone half wild, the jungle encroaching at the edges of the circular clearing. The breeze came up and the leaves lifted and swirled together, then flowed toward her. At the bottom of the garden she saw Salomon pass between the brick gateposts, and look up at her coolly for a moment before he disappeared. The garden was empty except for the little finches sitting in the trees.

The housemaid came out on the gallery and shook out a tablecloth over the railing. *"Ba'm jis chadek,"* Nanon called, imperiously. The maid lowered her head and went to do her bidding, returning a moment later with the grapefruit juice she had requested. Nanon tasted it, but the juice was bitter following the coffee; after all, she did not want it. The commanding airs of a mistress had diverted her for a time, but as there was little to order to be done, the novelty had soon faded.

And yet her first weeks here had been deep delight. Here was her home, her own true country; she had not known how much she cared for it till her return. She had never thought to return to Vallière, but now she was here—and free. Then too, there were the pleasures of love. The release of Choufleur's long-bottled passions excited her; he had convinced her with his body that they had truly been waiting all their lives to be joined. He was a fiercer lover than the doctor, and if he sometimes frightened her a little, the fear was no more than the shivering edge of the thrill. The doctor had been tentative at first, seemed inexperienced; she had had to teach him a great many things, though she had enjoyed the project. He was a willing student too, and in the end he had learned to please her very well. It was also true that his was the first man's touch that she had come to enjoy. She did not think of the doctor when she was with Choufleur, but Choufleur had been away for some weeks now, and so sometimes she remembered the doctor's gentleness with her, though she did not miss him as much as she did her son.

She watched the little birds flickering from tree to tree among the heavy leaves, and thought of Paul, pressing her fingers against the hollow of her throat. In their first days here she had taken the boy to the places where she had played herself as a little girl; it gave her joy to teach him her childhood games. And Paul was happy, happy enough, though at first he cried for Zabeth and Sophie, and he asked many questions about the doctor, whom he had called *Papi*. Nanon twisted her head restively, pressing the join of her collarbones. She pictured the doctor holding Paul by both hands and joggling him on his raised instep, both of them grinning and laughing wildly at each other. But Paul was so young; he could forget.

There was nothing in this image, nor in any image she had of the doctor, which agreed with the story Elise had told of him. Nanon had returned to this inconsistency many times since she had come to Val lière, and all the more in Choufleur's absence, which left her too much to her thoughts. Particularly, the doctor's first ineptitude as a lover did not fit with Elise's proposition that he was a careless and callous seducer. Well, perhaps a man might falsely play the ingenue the same as a girl (though in her considerable experience Nanon had never encountered such a thing). But the doctor's affection for Paul had seemed so genuine! Yes, but with a child so young, she told herself, there was no difficulty. Love of the bastard infant diminished as the child grew taller and began to occupy a larger space in the world. Nanon had seen it many times. Her own father was a white man, and she had a few bright, furry memories of him dandling and petting her when she was very small, giving her special chocolates from Europe whose remembered scent and taste still made her salivate. But after she was three or four years old, she did not see him anymore.

A tiny spider climbed the juice glass, no more than a moving crimson dot. She watched it cross over the rim and fall into the liquid it contained. The spider was too light to sink. Nanon imagined its struggles, which she could not see because the spider's legs were too small for her to discern. She went indoors and dressed and walked barefoot down from the gallery through the garden to the gateposts. Hinges had been set in the masonry, but the metal gates had never been delivered or hung. All such enterprises had been suspended when the Sieur de

Maltrot had disappeared into the mountains of Grande Rivière five years before.

Nanon worked her toes in the fine dust which lay between the posts. Choufleur did not like her to go barefoot—it made her feet hard and horny, and he claimed that it would also make them splay out like the flat, ugly feet of some market woman. But he was not here to prevent her, and she liked to feel the earth and the plants with her feet. To walk barefoot made her feel independent, free, though she knew this notion was ridiculous.

To the left of the gateposts, deteriorating terraces of coffee trees ran down a partially cleared slope. Infrequently tended, the trees were in a poor state, tangled with parasitic vines, taken over by the strangler fig. Still they did produce some beans. Beyond, the mountains rose to pierce the swagging wet bellies of the clouds that always overhung the highest peaks.

To the right was the deep green slash of Trou Vilain, and the trail running down the near side of that gorge toward Fort Dauphin and the coast. Nanon shaded her eyes, for she thought she'd seen some movement on the trail. But nothing. She looked to her left and saw the *sacatra* Salomon passing between the coffee trees, a fowling piece balanced in one hand. The trail was still empty when she looked again. The knowledge had risen in her mind, however, that Choufleur would come back this day, and that all would not be well when he returned.

One of the little hawks called *malfini* came gliding over the deep slash of Trou Vilain and turned and folded its wings to stoop. It rushed down toward the earth like a bullet and disappeared behind the foliage and then in a moment labored up into the air again with a large, long-tailed something wriggling in its talons. Rat. Trou Vilain was full of rats. They had come from ships in the harbors below and now lived in their own *marronage* on the jungle floor.

Nanon turned through the gateposts and walked clockwise around the hedges that enclosed the house, glancing up at the fret-sawed boards that ornamented the upper stories. She put the house between herself and Salomon, who might still be watching her from down in the coffee. At the rear was a gap in the hedge where the house servants came and went, and from it a trail ran around the brow of the hill behind the house and off among the trees. She walked, swinging her hands and humming, but the sense of foreboding clung to her. She had been astonished, even dismayed, when Choufleur announced that he intended to take Paul with him to Le Cap—and without her, for it was some tricky political errand that took him there. At once she had controlled herself and tried to think better of the plan, for Choufleur, as if he had expected her consternation, explained gently that he wanted time alone with the boy, that they could come to know each other better, as was desirable if (but here Choufleur, who had been dressing for his journey, turned from her and spoke into a corner of the bedroom walls)—if Paul were to be as his own son. And besides, he went on, adjusting his cuffs as he turned toward her again, the boy ought to see his birthplace, and learn something of the town.

Nanon gave her consent, for what it was worth. Had she withheld it, there would have been a great quarrel and the outcome would most likely have been the same. She brought herself to hope that what Choufleur said of the shared journey might prove true, but at the same time his manner with the boy up to that time gave her little encouragement. From the beginning Choufleur had treated Paul with the sort of studied calm one uses with an untrustworthy animal, a dog known to bite. He made no sudden movements, he was *not unkind*. As for Paul, he kept well away from Choufleur whenever Nanon did not urge him to approach. The situation never promised intimacy, but perhaps the two of them had attained some closeness on their excursion to Le Cap.

As she climbed the trail, it grew cooler, damp. She was ascending into a cloud. The black trunks of the trees around her were slick with condensed water. In a cut she sat on a felled tree and listened to water rushing in an invisible stream nearby. She had plucked a green orange as she came up, and now she peeled it with her nails and ate it, spitting the seeds accurately at the center of an elephant's ear leaf a few feet from her. She felt that Salomon was somewhere near, though she did not see him. When her mind had emptied, she got up and went on.

These days she often went on long rambling walks which sometimes lasted all the day. There was little to do in the house or around the compound—supervise the cook, or the laundress . . . With more attentive management, something more might have been made of the coffee, but Choufleur did not like her to interfere in such matters, and she had little disposition to do so anyway. When she had first arrived on the arm of Choufleur, she had played the great lady before the house servants to such an extent that she could not now descend to a more ordinary level of companionship with them. She now regretted this a little; it left her walking, solitary. She had lost weight, as she ate less than usual and exercised more, and so regained the girlish slenderness which she had lost after childbirth. Choufleur was pleased at this result. Nanon did not particularly enjoy the walks herself, but they did calm her.

Now she circled to the right, climbing a steep path cut in the stone, her bare toes working on the wet rock surface. The trail leveled and curved outward and began to descend. A spur ran further up the hill toward palm-leaf panels enclosing a *hûnfor*. There were no drums at this hour, no sign that anyone was present; still Nanon took care not to look in that direction as she passed. In the cleft of a tree she found a wild orchid and picked a bloom, carrying it in her right hand as she went down through scattered banana trees into a clearing gilded by the sun. It was past noon, and the warmth was agreeable after the chill of the rainforest. She took a ripe banana from a stalk, and walked toward the tombs at the far side of the clearing. The larger one was a great rectangular stone covered on all four sides with hieroglyphs, thought to be the grave of a great Indian *cacique*. A smaller stone, less ornamented, more completely covered with vines, was supposed to cover the grave of a child.

She sat on a stump with the tombs at her back. The clearing spilled downward, banana leaves tilting crazily around the borders, and gave her a long, clear view across the next gorge to the cloud-covered peaks beyond. She ate the banana. As she tossed away the peel, she saw Salomon passing, half hidden by the trees at the edge where the jungle resumed. He still carried the fowling piece and, if challenged, would claim to have been hunting, though he would return to the house without game, and though Nanon knew he had not fired his gun even once, for she had not heard it. Salomon followed her on her ramblings. He was never far from her, just barely out of sight. He was acting on Choufleur's orders, or on his own interpretation of what Choufleur's wishes would be. All for her safety, but Nanon did not like it. Salomon had motives all his own mixed in, she thought, suspecting that he looked at her lasciviously. She did not like to be spied on, although for the time being she had nothing to hide.

She sat for a while longer, trying the pale blue orchid against her wrist, or tucked into her bodice. She lifted it to her nose, but there was no scent. Presently she got up and went on, still carrying the flower.

It was not yet sundown when she returned to the coffee terraces below the house, but the quality of the light was tempered, changed. She looked at the empty trail, then up into the sky, where the *malfini* circled again, its claws empty. Or perhaps it was another hawk. When she looked again, Choufleur was riding slowly up the difficult trail, leading a second, riderless horse behind him by the reins.

Paul was nowhere to be seen. Nanon looked for him, twice and again. At first she felt a numbness from her skull to her heels, then nausea, then she controlled herself more tightly. Digging her nails into her palms, she slipped off through the coffee trees. Choufleur must not see her yet. She hurried through the garden and into the house, calling orders: *The master has returned! Heat water for the bath*, and so on. By the time Choufleur had stabled his horses and climbed the gallery steps, Nanon had put on shoes and a finer dress. With the orchid pinned in her hair, she sat behind a tray of cool limeade, wearing a tremulous, insincere smile of welcome.

She had never seen him look so haggard, his expression so very dark. The black glare in his eyes struck her first, and then she began to take in the details. A coating of dust from the road covered his hair like powder on a wig, and was caked all over his face too, which was streaked with sweat. He was out of uniform, and his light riding trousers were dirty and covered with horsehair and sweat-stained at the crotch. No evidence of his usual fastidiousness. For several days he had not shaved, and the effect was unfortunate, for his beard was sparse and came in patchily among the freckles. He stopped with his hand on a chair back and looked past her.

Nanon poured a glass of the limeade and offered it. "What news from Le Cap?" she asked. The question seemed neutral enough to be safe.

Choufleur accepted the drink, sipped and grimaced. He turned toward the door of the house and, though no servant was in evidence, shouted loudly, *"Bay nou rhum!"* He dragged the chair back and dropped heavily into it, passing his hands across his face. When he uncovered his eyes, they looked more weary than enraged.

"The news is bad enough," he said. "Villatte has bungled it all. Or he was misled by Pinchinat—the weasel! Or—what does it matter? Toussaint and his black rabble are too many. And now Laveaux embraces him, calls him the Black Spartacus—Faugh!" He turned and spat over the railing.

The housemaid brought the bottle of rum. Choufleur slung away his lime concoction in the same direction he had spat, poured three fingers of rum in the glass and drank it down. He coughed and cleared his throat.

"Laveaux," he said. "A weak man, I tell you. For all his honor and his airs. It is *weakness* that makes him set those Africans above us. Well, Villatte said, as I left him, that he would like to see Laveaux's throat slit by those very Negroes he embraces. And I confess, I feel the same."

"Where is Villatte?" Nanon said, having grasped the essentials of the situation.

"At Habitation Martellière. 'Camp Villatte,' as he has christened it. His little empire—there is the height of his ambition now. He will give himself up soon enough—or be killed. But I know him, he will surrender."

"And for yourself?" Nanon reached her hand partway toward his, then stopped.

Choufleur's eyes grazed over her face. "I'll bide my time." He poured a mixture of limeade and rum and sipped it more conservatively. "Word is that Laveaux has claimed there will be no reprisals, but we shall see. Villatte will certainly be arrested, but I tried not to show myself too close to him in all this affair . . ."

"That is well," Nanon told him. "My dear, I have ordered you a bath."

Choufleur nodded absently, as if he had not grasped the sense of what she said, but he rose and followed her into the house. As they passed through the bedroom, he caught her shoulder and whirled her around, then seized and crushed her to him. Nanon had a confused impression of bristles and dirt and horse and human odors intermingled. The rum was a veneer on the sourness of his breath.

"Stop!" she said. "Wash yourself first—oh . . ." She changed her tone. "Oh, stop it," she snapped. Irritation was what had most discouraged the Sieur Maltrot. Any note of pain or fear excited him. She had not thought Choufleur to be the same, but his grip loosened and she twisted away.

Choufleur stood with his hands quivering at his sides. Under the dust his face had paled; the freckles stood out sharp and dark, while his lip trembled. As often before, Nanon was moved by the helplessness of his need.

"Only be gentle," she said. "Don't rush me so." Forcing a smile, she loosened her hair, and with the same movement tossed the orchid onto the bed. Choufleur relaxed; his eyes tracked the arc of the falling flower. Nanon began to put off her clothes to accommodate him.

Afterward, she lay abed in a daze, while Choufleur went to his bath and soaked. Her fingers toyed with the crushed and tattered petals of the orchid. In spite of it all, he had carried her with him, however roughly; for a time she was all body. But with her thought, the question of Paul returned. She rose and gave herself a cat bath, standing before the bedroom washstand, then went to meet Choufleur as he rose from the tub.

She took the towel from his hands and began to dry him. It was an act of worship. His body was as strong and supple as the body of an animal that hunts its food. As she knelt to massage the towel around his calves and ankles, she was reminded of the woman who washed the feet of Jesus with her hair.

Choufleur furled the towel around his hips and arranged himself in a straight-backed chair. Nanon stood behind him, her left hand lightly massaging the cords of his neck, a long straight razor in her right. With smooth assured strokes she began to shave him. This too they had adopted as a ritual.

"Where is Paul?" she said.

"At school in Le Cap. I thought it better."

"You did not tell me."

Choufleur turned his head to the right, though not quite far enough to look at her. The razor indented the skin of his cheek. "You would not have agreed. But it is best, because—"

"What school?"

"The Filles Sainte Marie."

Nanon probed her left thumb into the recess at the base of his skull, feeling for the lie if one were hidden in his head.

"Ah . . ." Choufleur sighed gratefully, rolling his head back against the pressure.

"I will go to Le Cap to visit him and see that he is well."

"No," Choufleur said quickly. Then, in a reasoning tone. "This political trouble, you see. It would be unwise for you—for us. After a month, perhaps six weeks . . ."

The razor stroked backward along his jawbone. Nanon stopped it, rinsed the blade. She shaved upward along the side of his neck, stopping the razor at the same point, under the jawbone, beneath the ear. The blade pulsed lightly, with his heartbeat. She held it there. After a moment, Choufleur's hand lifted stealthily and closed about her wrist. When the grip was secure, he tightened it. His hand was cold, hard as a manacle, but somehow she did not feel the pressure. With a thrust Choufleur moved the razor from his throat, and turned in his seat to look up at her with eyes as vacant as the moon.

During the night they made love once more, and again it was an eruption of anger from Choufleur. He had invested too much of himself in Villatte's attempted *coup d'état*, and now the rush of his disappointment broke on her like surf. It exhausted her, and when he rolled away she fell into a dense and heavy sleep. The dream which came to her was so lucidly clear and vivid that it remained in her memory for a long time afterward as if it had been a real experience.

Choufleur rode down the streets of Le Cap carrying the boy before him in the saddle, holding him with the delicacy one would devote to a breakable object like a wine glass or a china cup, a care devoid of tenderness. At the gate of a great house he stopped and dismounted and lifted Paul down. Some little *négrillons* were playing in the enclosure and Choufleur nudged Paul in their direction. He tied up his horse and knocked on the house door and after a moment was admitted.

Through the crystal lens of the dream, Nanon watched Paul playing with the black children, two little boys, brothers perhaps, one with his loins swaddled in a scrap of cloth, the other entirely naked. They were unclean, and flies gathered at the corners of their eyes. But their teeth were good and their smiles were bright, and they were friendly. They had between them a pair of wheels on a stick for a toy and they were quite willing to share it with Paul, who pushed it around and around in the dirt, the three of them laughing and crowing together.

"What will you give me for the boy?"

Choufleur stood in the shadows of the house door, speaking to a burly white man dressed in a striped vest over a white shirt, loose canvas pantaloons. A cloth was knotted over his head; he wore a single earring.

"Give?" the white man said. "But slavery is finished in this country, my friend. You cannot sell. I cannot buy."

At this Choufleur shifted his weight and murmured, "Well, but there is slavery in Jamaica, and over the mountains in Santo Domingo . . . other places too."

The white man turned to look at Paul more closely. "The boy looks white."

"The father was a white man," Choufleur said. "The mother, a *métive*."

"He is too young," the white man said. "What can he do?"

"Whatever anyone wishes him to do," Choufleur said.

The white man looked at the boy again, stroking his thumb beneath his lower lip. "And you will not return for him?"

"Never," said Choufleur. "No one will return."

The white man turned on him eyes a startling bright blue. "All right then. You may leave him."

"But give me something." Choufleur's voice turned wheedling, obsequious—a note Nanon had never heard from him.

The white man took a leather drawstring bag from his trouser pocket and probed in it with a stubby finger, his lips puckered. He selected one gold portugaise and placed it on Choufleur's extended palm. Choufleur shrugged and closed his fingers. The white man clapped him on the back.

"*Arrangé.*"

"*Ça.*"

Choufleur swing into the saddle and rode out the gate without looking back. Nor did Paul take any note of his departure. But the eye of the dream followed Choufleur instead of remaining with the boy. The gold piece was still closed in his hand, but as he turned into the Rue Espagnole, he flung the coin away without looking to see where it landed.

Nanon came up from the dream gasping and choking like someone barely saved from drowning. She covered her mouth with both hands to suppress the urge to vomit. For some minutes the dream still seemed to her a fact—more real to her than her actual surroundings. Slowly the world replaced the dream. Striped by moonlight slanting through the slats of the jalousies, Choufleur lay against her hip, sleeping silently, motionless. Even his breathing was completely inaudible. He always slept so, as if in ambush. Nanon took her hands away from her mouth. The story he had told her about the school might well have been true, in whole or in part. At the same time the dream was not *only* a dream. All she knew for certain was that Paul was not dead, for had he been she would have known it in her bones.

In the days that followed, Choufleur busied himself about the plantation with a fervor she had not seen in him before. Apparently he had a pressing need for money, and there was coffee on the trees, and much work to be done very rapidly in order to convert it into cash. Choufleur was gone each morning when she woke, and usually did not come back to the house until it was fully dark. In his absence Nanon busied herself by ordering elaborate meals to tempt his palate. She sent Salomon on a long excursion after wild mushrooms to be sautéed with game birds. She herself went into the woods to gather wild flowers to decorate the house. In bed she deployed her most subtle wiles to please him.

All the while, Paul lay between them, the bulging presence of the subject neither of them raised again in words. Each night Nanon opened her legs and felt Choufleur rush against her, through her and beyond. He had held her image in his head for the many years of their separation, and now he thrust himself through her, toward that image, which was elsewhere. She saw it would come to no good end. But she would not leave, for it was not yet finished.

One morning she woke to a startling bright, warm light. Choufleur had rolled the jalousies, which usually stayed down throughout the day. The sunlight played over her honey-colored skin—she had slept nude, and he must have pulled the sheet from her. She stretched and lifted her face toward him, but he was looking at her coldly.

"Where is the snuffbox?"

A chill crawled over her bare skin. She looked at Choufleur's narrowed eyes. The freckles swam across his face. The snuffbox had not been mentioned between them since he had brought her to Vallière. *We will wipe out everything which has been before*, Choufleur had told her.

"Why do you ask?"

The box with what it contained had been left in the snarl of bed-clothes when they had eloped from Habitation Thibodet. At the time Nanon had thought no more of the matter than that she did not wish to touch it again. And yet she'd retained that grisly souvenir all the way from the fire at Le Cap to Ennery, as if it were precious to her. As if her relations with the doctor were insufficient to wash her clean and free of it. After she had come to Vallière, she began to realize that the doctor must have found the snuffbox, if not his sister (but she felt sure the doctor had it), and taken it as a clue to her abrupt disappearance with the child.

Choufleur had turned from her toward the window. The light was so bright it seemed to burn the features from his face. He looked back at her with his eyes full of sunspots.

"See?" he said, pointing a finger. "See how he marked you?"

Nanon glanced at herself. The streaming sun had picked out the faint white scars here and there on her skin—they were scarcely notice-able in dimmer light. Sometimes the Sieur Maltrot had burned her with the coal of his cheroot, all the while appraising her for a response. Sometimes he would make a shallow cut on her belly or buttock or on the soft skin inside her upper arm or thigh, then press his thin lips to the wound and batten on her blood. *We will wipe out everything that has been before*—she aimed the thought at Choufleur, but did not speak it. She had not remembered those pale scars since coming here, nor had he seemed to notice them.

"Jean-Michel," she said, calmly as she could manage. "You are not yourself."

Choufleur looked down at her with the frosty detachment she knew from his father. At this moment all his features belonged to the Sieur Maltrot. Only his eyes and the freckles were his own.

"Am I not?" he said.

Nanon reached for the hem of the sheet and drew it up to cover herself, but her movement seemed to release him from his stasis. He pounced, snatching the sheet from her hand, catching one wrist and pinning it down in the bedding. *Not this.* She fought him, flailing and clawing with the free hand and kicking her legs out in all directions, but he trapped the other hand soon enough, so that she could not help herself. Her heels were drumming on his back, her struggles merged with his excitement. In the lull that followed, it was her own response that angered her as much as his mistreatment. She pushed him away sharply.

"You want your snuffbox, do you?" she shrilled. "What have you done

with my son? You have not killed him—you would not dare to kill him!
And as he lives, so will I go to find him—"

Choufleur, his face swollen, was tearing a strip from the sheet.
Alarmed, Nanon caught her robe from the bedpost and darted for the
door, but he was too quick and strong for her to escape him. He gagged
her with one piece of the sheet and tied her hands behind her with
another. He threw her face down on the bed, stood panting, and jerked
on his clothes.

Outside the room she heard him berating the house servants who
were offering him coffee, an omelette—*Get out! Why are you loitering
here! Leave us our peace and our privacy!* Then silence. Nanon lay numb.
She did not stir from the position where he'd left her. Her hands
throbbed in the binding. The sheet was damp and frothy in her mouth.

After a time Choufleur came into the room again, kicking the door
shut behind him. There was a clatter of metal falling on the floor. Something in that sound made Nanon turn over and wriggle up against the
headboard. Choufleur was coming toward her with an iron collar open
in his hands; the chain attached to it rattled over the floor. Nanon shook
her head wildly, and squirmed away into the corner, but there was
nowhere to go. He shut the collar around her neck, and pounded a fat
rivet into the rings to close it, the two metals melding together. The
blows of the hammer bruised her shoulders. She closed her eyes and bit
into her lip. There was more rattling, as Choufleur locked the free end
of the chain around a bedpost.

She opened her eyes. He stood at a little distance, studying her with
apparent satisfaction. His left hand lazily unbuttoned his trousers and
let them fall. He did not touch himself or move toward her, but Nanon
watched him rising, like a bird fascinated by a snake. Then he strode to
the bed and caught her hair above the collar and twisted it until she
gasped. He made her kneel, and forced her face down to the mattress,
and used her as brutally as his father ever had.

For three days it was the same. When Choufleur had finished, he went
out, leaving her water and a slop bucket. On the gallery she heard him
telling the servants that Madame was still ill and not to be disturbed;
they were not even to enter the house, much less the bedroom. He had
removed the rags of sheet so that she could drink and care for herself.
When he returned he sometimes tied her hands again, or sometimes
left them free. Always he came in the heat of the day, and both of them
would be swimming in sweat when he battered her body with his. At

evening he brought her a meal. Sometimes he left the plate for her to feed herself or, if her hands were bound, he spooned the food into her mouth. He slept elsewhere, but returned to use her at different hours in the night, and always in the morning.

What was most humiliating, frightening, was her own response. Nothing in her had risen to meet the cruelties of the Sieur Maltrot, ingenious as they often were. She had made her body a piece of wet rope for him, held her essential self remote and untouched. But with Choufleur there was love braided into the torment. That was different, much more powerful, much worse.

The chain was exactly long enough for her to reach the bedroom door, not long enough for her to cross the sill. As the bed was a massive affair of solid mahogany, no effort of hers could have budged it so much as an inch. If the grating of the chain across the floor ennerved her, she might carry it in her arms to stop the sound. There was a full-length mirror near the bed, and sometimes she wept herself dry before it, then stood there looking curiously at the ugly spectacle created by her swollen nose and reddened eyes. Sometimes she stood naked before the mirror, posing and draping herself in the chain. Sometimes she dressed herself and covered the iron collar with an arrangement of scarves. Then Choufleur would have to strip away all this fabric before he raped her senseless.

He did not wound her with fire or steel, only twisted her limbs this way and that, and forced himself in wherever it pleased him. He had the Sieur de Maltrot's gold-headed sword-stick, and sometimes he threatened her with this, but never cut or struck her. On the morning of the fourth day he pounded the rivet out of the collar with the hammer and a spike, and left her free.

Nanon said nothing. She sat on the bed's edge, touching the band round her neck where the collar had been, looking down at the floor without a thought.

"If you had left me," Choufleur said in a low voice, "I would surely die."

She did not answer, but raised her eyes when she heard his feet moving on the floor. With a practiced twist of the wrist, Choufleur unlatched the sword-stick and pulled free the blade. He braced the pommel against the door jamb and set the point under his left nipple. Nanon had leaped across the room before she knew she meant to move, knocking his weight away from the blade, which flexed and sprang free, then clattered off the wall. The point had raked a shallow red line across his ribs, and somehow there was a deeper bloodier cut in the butt of his palm, but both of them ignored it. Choufleur was crying uncontrollably. Babbling how he loved her, hated himself, he washed the chafe marks of the collar with his tears. Nanon whispered the soothing nothings suitable to an hysterical child. Soon she was weeping with him. They clung to each other like two drowning people, and in the end, they slept.

Afterward everything returned to normal, or as nearly as it could after what had passed before. The collar lay on its chain underneath the bed, hidden by the fringes of the coverlet. The servants returned to the house to cook and clean and wait upon them. Choufleur went out to work in the coffee every day, and Nanon directed the servants in his absence. But she did not go walking in the woods anymore. In those vacant hours of the day she sat motionless on the gallery, her mind a blank. She did not, could not, think of Paul, or anyone, or anything.

When he riveted the collar around her neck again, Nanon did not try to run or resist. She sat demurely on the edge of the bed with her head lowered and her hands folded in her lap. Choufleur did not assault her afterward. He seemed abashed, ashamed. He stood up without looking at her directly and said that he must take the coffee down to Fort Dauphin and that he did not know for certain when he could return.

When he had left the room, Nanon lowered herself down to lie curled on her side. Distantly she heard the sounds of the donkey train receding down the trail on the brink of Trou Vilain. Then nothing, only the chittering of insects, the short harsh cry of the *malfini*. The jalousies were shut and the lines of light climbed around the walls with the passing of the hours of the day. Her mouth was dry and her tongue swollen, but though she could see the pitcher of water he had left on the armoire, she did not have the will to get up and fetch it.

When the knocking began on the bedroom door, she ignored it. It stopped, began again, stopped again. A voice called, then left off calling. Silence. Then the door swung open.

Salomon. The *sacatra* was tall and gangly, with a long, bony jaw and great hollow eye sockets that stood out like spectacles. He carried his head at a strange stiff angle, as if his neck were frozen. Nanon had always thought him exquisitely ugly. She was dressed, but he could see that she was chained to the bed. Like any man, he would be drawn to molest and abuse the helpless thing. She did not think she would be much affected.

His whole face worked with some strange emotion. She saw his jaw muscles knot and slacken, as if he were chewing something he could not swallow. He came to the bed as she had expected, but he did not touch her, except to take her two hands in his own.

"*Ma chère,*" he began, then stopped, coughed, and shook his awkward head. "My dear, slavery is finished in this country."

Nanon did not reply to this, though she recognized that his words came from her dream.

"Wait here," Salomon said.

Where would I go? Nanon thought when he had gone out. The idea came near to amusing her.

Salomon came back with the hammer and spike. Cursing steadily in a low voice, he knocked the rivet out of its joints. Then he opened the collar and lifted it away.

Nanon stood up and walked toward the open doorway, arresting herself where the chain's limit had taught her to stop. Her fingers trailed around the chafings of the collar on her throat.

"No," she said. "It is not finished."

Then she turned from the door and came back to the bed. She took up the collar and held it for a moment, then closed it around her neck and signaled Salomon with her eyes that he must fasten it back as it had been before.

22

There were three little black boys close to Paul's own age at the house where Choufleur had left him, and two older colored girls of twelve or thirteen. All six of them slept in a little shed in the enclosure opposite the house, in the same room, in the same pile, like puppies. Paul whimpered a little, in the dark. His first night camping on the road with Choufleur, he had cried outright for his mother, for he'd never slept apart from her, but Choufleur pinched him till he stopped. Each night afterward he swallowed the tears when he felt them coming, as quietly as ever he could. But tonight he must have snuffled audibly, for Angelique, the twelve-year-old *griffone*, arched an arm across the heap of sleeping children and ran her fingers lightly up and down his back until he relaxed and slept with the rest.

In the daytime the two girls worked in the house, but the little boys were mostly left to themselves. Sometimes they might be assigned a chore, but no one seemed to monitor how dutifully they performed it. They were not meant to leave the enclosure of the house, but sometimes they did. The little black boys were familiar with such escapes, and they led Paul a few blocks down the street to the open marshy ground of La Fossette, where the dead people were buried, and tried to frighten him with tales of the cemetery and its gloomy president, the grim and skeletal Baron de la Croix. When they came back, they were whipped about the legs with a green switch by one of the older colored girls who stayed in the great house at night. The black boys squinched up their eyes and opened their mouths to howl full bore, but Paul could see they were mocking their punishment. He tried to take his own whipping in the same spirit, though the switch stung his legs terribly. At home with Mami and Papi he had never been punished so.

He did not understand what had happened to him, or why he was made to go with Choufleur (Mami had been sad and yet she told him he must go). That Choufleur had left him here and gone away did not worry him. He was relieved to be quit of Choufleur, but he wanted his mother. His longing passed over the whole situation at Vallière and returned to Ennery, where Mami and Papi had been together. But no one at this great house was unkind to him. In this house there was no wife or mother, only the burly white man with the earring, and a lot of colored girls a few years older than the pair who slept with the little boys in the shed; they were pretty, and wore scent and bright-colored clothes. The sweet smell of the girl who had thrashed him made the whipping all the more painful, for she was pretty and he would have liked to be near her if she were not beating him.

At night men came and there were parties until late, with singing and shouting and the tinkling laughter of the girls. Sometimes men's voices rose in anger, and sometimes bottles flew out the windows to shatter in the courtyard near the shed where the smaller children slept. Angelique and the other young colored girls were obliged to go into the house each morning to clean it after the parties late at night.

One morning when Paul came out from the shed, setting his bare feet down carefully between the chunks of bottle glass from last night's celebration, he felt that he was being watched, felt himself shrink up inside. From Choufleur he had learned not to seek the attention he had craved from Mami and Papi and Zabeth and Sophie and Tante Elise and really almost anyone at Habitation Thibodet . . . but it was better not to be noticed by Choufleur. The man in the earring stood in the doorway of the great house, muttering with a tall bearded Spaniard who wore a big hat. They were talking about him; Paul felt this. When Choufleur and Mami had spoken about him, when he had had to go away from her, it had felt the same, though he had not heard what they were saying any more than he heard it now.

Angélique came out from the shed and unconsciously pulled off her shift and began washing herself beneath the pump. Paul felt the men's attention move to her, and found himself looking at her in a different way, at the buds of her breasts and her hips' swell, with an excitement which was strange to him, uncomfortable too, but magnetic. Angélique felt it, and pushed the pump handle down. Turning her back, she returned to the shed, leaving the men grinning at each other with their yellow teeth in the shadows of the doorway.

"You must not hesitate," said the man with the earring. "For the pair of them, or even only for the girl—it must be soon, because of the commissioners . . ." He lowered his voice. Paul moved a little closer, though he looked elsewhere, at the flies which had begun to hum over the sticky bottle shards now that the morning sun had grown warmer.

"Yes, you are right," the Spaniard said, thumbing his short beard. He glanced at Paul, then raised his hand to shield his mouth as he went on talking. Dressed for the day, Angélique brought a crook-neck broom from the shed and began sweeping the enclosure, her face sullenly downturned. The men still watched her, whispering, as the flies collected over the heap of her glass sweepings.

In the middle of the night Paul awoke with Angélique shaking his leg. The other girl was listening at the door of the shed. The three little boys who had been his companions lay still—too still and breathing too quietly for them to be truly asleep. Paul did not try to speak to them, but followed the two girls outside. The big house was dark and silent above them, which meant that it must be very late.

Using the other girl's joined hands as a stirrup, Angélique hoisted herself up the wall beside the gate. She slung a saddle blanket over the spikes of bottle glass cemented into the top of the wall, and then dropped down out of sight. The other girl drew back the blanket and folded it under her arm. Angélique hissed to Paul from without the gate, and the other girl pushed him toward her. The gate was chained shut as always at night, but Paul had already learned from the other boys that he was small enough to slip through the bars.

Angélique took his hand; in her other she carried a small rag bundle. They trotted down the street through the cool, moist air of the predawn. At the edge of the town, Angélique stopped, looking out over the mists that hung low over the marsh, blanketing the cemetery wall. She pressed her fingers over her mouth. With a prickle, Paul remembered the ghoul tales he'd been told. Perhaps Angélique was also frightened at the thought of Baron, for she turned back and led him scurrying through the streets of the town.

Dawn discovered them hastening along the quay, dodging the porters who were already setting out their ropes and slings and barrels. Paul was beginning to tire. He wanted to find out where Angélique was going, but he did not ask, because he did not want to learn that she did not know.

Three ships with high masts and white sails were coming in at the mouth of the harbor, crossing over the steel-colored peaks of the steady waves. Down by the Customs House a crowd was gathering. Paul and Angélique were drawn down into it. The sun was bright now, warm on their backs. Someone nearby was eating fresh, warm bread, and Paul's mouth stung with a run of saliva. The first ship had docked and they were letting down the gangplank onto the quay. At the top of the gangway, a little white man appeared, and all of the crowd sucked in its breath and cheered.

Sonthonax! Sonthonax! Papa Libeté nou!

All the crowd was black men and women, next to no whites and few mulattoes. The men threw their straw hats in the air, and the women stretched out trembling hands as if they were receiving holy spirits.

Sonthonax! Sonthonax! Father of our liberty!

A corridor opened in the crowd, and Paul and Angélique were pushed back. Angélique arched onto the balls of her feet, craning her neck to see, but Paul had only to let go her hand and he could worm forward through the legs of the adults as easily as he'd slipped through the bars of the gate. He saw the little white man come down the gangway, turning his raised hands to either side to salute the crowd. He was plump and not very tall. He wore a sash and a shining medal and had long reddish-brown hair that hung over his coat collar. There were other white men coming behind him, wearing the same sashes and medals, but the crowd did not pay much attention to them.

Sonthonax! Sonthonax! Papa Libeté nou!

On the far side of the corridor that had opened for the arriving Frenchmen, Paul suddenly noticed a group of men on horses, wearing bright, silvery helmets with plumes. In their midst, looking down with an air of calm solemnity, was the General Toussaint Louverture. Toussaint meant Ennery and Mami and Papi—Paul broke toward him, into the open space, and was at once knocked down. Laughter. The commissioner had stooped to set him on his feet again. His eyes were glistening, and he seemed transported. He gave Paul a pat on the head and then a thump on the back to send him along. As he stood straight, the cheering grew even more furious than before.

The crowd closed behind the commissioners as they made their way toward Government House, and began to press along after them. Caught in a back eddy, Paul could still see the plumed helmets bobbing ahead of him, but he could come no nearer. The crowd carried him to the gate before Government House. Paul clambered up on a cistern for a better view. Sonthonax took a musket from a grenadier of his escort and whirled it high above his head.

"Gadé," he cried in a breaking voice. *"Gadé sa—sa sé libeté-ou!"*

He handed the musket to the nearest man in the crowd and turned to walk within the gate. Paul caught a glimpse of the disarmed grenadier's perplexed expression before the crowd closed over him. The last plumed helmet passed the gateway, and then the gate was swinging shut. That musket was still passing from hand to hand, exalted in the air above the crowd, with the commissioner's words repeated: "Look! Look! This— this is your liberty!"

When Paul realized that he had no idea what had become of Angélique, he began to feel afraid. From the height of the cistern he looked all around but caught no sign of her. He jumped down and tried to make his way to the gate where Toussaint had entered with the commissioners, but the crowd carried him in the opposite direction as it dispersed.

Someone trampled on his toes, and as Paul flinched away, he remembered his shoes, and the change of clothes Mami had sent with him— these articles had been left behind at the house they'd left that morning. He had not thought of them, not even the shoes, when Angélique woke him in the night. Now he kept a more careful eye on whatever booted feet came near him as he trotted along with the scattering crowd. It also occurred to him that he could not have found the house he'd fled with Angélique even if he had wanted to.

The current of foot traffic carried him as far as the *marché des nègres* at the Place Clugny. He swirled around the square among the marketers, letting them jostle him along. It was very crowded. There were fruit and vegetables and coffee from the mountains, fish and butter and cheese and dressed meat and live animals all for sale. A good number of small black children were begging: *Ba'm manjé.* Give me food. Paul was more parched than hungry but all the comestibles on sale around him awakened his appetite. Standing near one of the begging black boys, he lifted his own hands for charity, but the other, jealous of his place, wheeled on him and shoved him away with both hands and knocked him down into the dirt.

As he scrambled to his feet, he heard a cry he recognized. Angélique appeared above the crowd, her face bruised and tear-stained. The Spaniard of the morning was dragging her up into a wagon bed. She opened her mouth to shriek another protest, but the Spaniard slapped it shut. A few people glanced up briefly at the scene, and as quickly turned their eyes away. The Spaniard pushed her down against the side rails, and as the wagon wheels began to turn, they disappeared from Paul's view.

He ran. His throat was swollen, so that he breathed with difficulty.

He was running downhill from the market square, full tilt and blind till a stitch in his side halted him and he doubled over, sucking wind. He staggered another block and a half and emerged onto the waterfront. A porter narrowly missed his head with a swinging hook and cursed him as he passed. Paul ducked under the belly of a passing oxcart, dodged the rear wheel, and came up on the breakwater. A broken hogshead was wedged among the stones and he crawled into it to hide himself. Although his throat was choking with tears, he was too tired to cry; instead he slept.

Red light was bleeding through the broken barrel staves when he awoke. He limped the length of the quay and came at last to the fountain beyond the Customs House. There he drank, and washed his face and wet his hair. For a little time he felt calm, and empty. Then a knot of hunger struck his stomach like a rope's end. He walked into the town through the gathering dark, drawn forward by the smell of roasting corn. In the darkness beside a lighted doorway a woman was turning ears over a small brazier.

"Ou gringou?" The woman looked up at him curiously. *"Eh, ti blan, ou gringou, oui?"* Are you hungry? Paul's eyes must have answered for him, because the woman lifted an ear from the grate and handed to him. Hot. Sweet milk from the kernels burst into his mouth when he bit down—he scorched his lips and fingers but did not care. The woman was calling into the house, and presently a man appeared in the doorway, looking at him while the woman muttered. *Ti blan,* she had called him, little white. Paul saw his pale fingers wrapped around the corn. A hazard—his light skin made him noticeable. The man beckoned him toward the doorway, but instead Paul began to run. The woman called after him, but there was no pursuit.

He finished the corn in the barrel where he had lain throughout the day. During the night he was roused by rats scrabbling over the cob, but when he threw it out, the rats went after it and did not come back. He adjusted himself against the barrel's curve and let the waves rushing against the rocks carry him off to sleep again.

For the next several days he lurked in the barrel through most of the daylight hours. It gave him only partial shelter against the evening rains, and soon he caught cold from the constant damp. His grimy shirt sleeves stiffened with snot and his nose was red and raw from rubbing. His cough echoed within the barrel. Sometimes he returned to the Place Clugny to try his hand at begging, and now and then was rewarded with a piece of fruit, or coins enough to buy a roll from a stall.

But when the black beggar boys noticed him, they drove him away. Also his light skin attracted a peculiar attention from adults, and he was wary.

At night he scavenged the garbage piles among the stray dogs of the town. From the dogs he learned to crack discarded bones for their marrow. He could also gnaw the rinds and seeds of fruit, which did not interest the dogs. Sometimes he was sick from spoiled food, or because an unexpectedly large find obliged him to overeat. Because of the rats he could not keep any sort of food in the barrel.

Then one morning as he cautiously crept into the Place Clugny, he heard his name called and cowered away by reflex.

"Paul!" A colored girl, perhaps fourteen, dressed in a plain brown smock. Her face was honey-colored, her brown eyes kind. Her calloused fingers against his face, turning it up to the light. "Do you remember me? It is Paulette! But no . . . you were too small."

She looked over her shoulder, continuing to speak, "I knew him, cared for him, in the camps of Grande Rivière." Behind her stood a mammoth black woman, solid as a mountain.

"I too," the black woman said. "Yes, I know him." She lowered herself by degrees until she balanced in a hunker. Her huge hand cradled the back of his head. Paul felt a strange calm spreading through him from the soft center of her palm.

"Zoray li," the black woman said. "His ears—such ears! they were the same when he was born."

Paulette took his hand and he walked from the square beside her, the black woman at his other side. Paul did not exactly remember Paulette, but it seemed natural for her to have charge of him. From her opposite arm hung a basket full of greens and yams and manioc from the mountains. The black woman walked with her hands swinging free, a great basket of charcoal balanced on her head.

They reached the northern limit of the town, where the last houses were tucked among the claws of the mountain where they were fixed into the earth. Above was a little white church on a round hillock, but Paul lost sight of it as they stepped into a courtyard. Several pails of water were waiting by a stairway. Paulette let go of his hand to pick up one of them and indicated that he should do the same. To balance himself Paul took a pail in each hand, though they were very heavy. Following her, he struggled up the steps that twisted among the plastered houses and then became a dirt path corkscrewing still farther up. The black woman came behind them with her charcoal.

At last they emerged onto an area of packed earth surrounded by *ajoupas* of straw and sticks and wattle. Paulette set down her burdens and Paul did the same, a little water splashing on his feet. She panted, smiling at him. He returned the smile. A bright breeze coming in from the harbor cooled and dried the sweat of their effort. If he looked in that direction, he saw the ships in the harbor and the red tile roofs of the town, even Government House and the open spaces of the Place d'Armes and the Place Clugny. They were a little below the level of the rear of the white church. When he looked in the other direction, Paul saw more *ajoupas* scattered up the slope, and higher, where the cliff was nearly sheer, black children his own age were gamboling among the goats.

Sophie did not ask after Paul any longer. She had given up asking for her father as well. Tocquet had abandoned them, perhaps permanently— Elise had no way of knowing. He did send money, from time to time. Every six weeks or so either Gros-jean or Bazau appeared to give her a little bag of coins, gold and silver, struck by several different nations like a pirate treasure.

After the first weeks of Tocquet's desertion, Elise had pulled herself up from her initial collapse. She walked through her days, although with a bitter, shriveling heart. As for Sophie, once the first flood of her sorrow had passed, she seemed the same as before, yet Elise knew that her losses were too great to have had no effect on her at all.

What was the man waiting for? She knew that Bazau and Gros-jean would be bringing him reports. Perhaps Tocquet was waiting to hear that she had given up and gone to France, in which case he might swoop down to reclaim Sophie and the plantation which was hers through her first marriage, and now his. But maybe he cared only for the land, for she would take Sophie with her if she did go to France. Did he not know it? If she were to go . . . Once her pride had returned, it prevented her from cross-examining Gros-jean or Bazau as to Tocquet's whereabouts or his activities. But the men gossiped enough around the military camp that the news came back to her eventually, through Zabeth or Guiaou or Riau, sometimes even from one of the French offi- cers, Maillart or Vaublanc. She knew that Tocquet was based in his cat- tle corral on the central plateau, that he was selling beef to the French Jacobin army, and trading tobacco along the smuggler's run from Daja- bón to Ouanaminthe to Fort Liberté.

Elise's humors ran from sorrow and regret to indifference to anger, day by day. If she had not done what she had done! . . . or if, somehow, she could undo it. In one of her irritable moods, she began taking Tocquet's things out of the wardrobe, with the idea of discarding them or throwing them away. On the floor of the wardrobe, under a pile of folded trousers, was a long wooden box with a sliding cover. Its weight was surprising. Elise heaved it onto the bed and wrestled the lid back. The groove was warped and sticky from the damp. Inside, two long dragoon pistols and a short, broad-bladed sword. There was powder and lead and a bullet mold and a roll of papers in oilskin which seemed to be maps, though she did not look at them closely.

Elise picked up one of the pistols and aimed it wobbling around the room. The thing was monstrously heavy. Only by bracing the barrel across her forearm could she hold it steadily level. She sighted into the mirror, her own eyes hard above the hollow eye of the gun barrel.

From the gallery, she caught sight of Guiaou crossing the yard below the doctor's lily pool. She hailed him: *"Vini moin!"*

Guiaou reversed his direction, glancing toward her, and climbed the steps.

"What must I do to shoot this thing?" Elise said, carelessly waving at the pistol on the table. "Show me, if you please."

Guiaou shook his head, but he was accustomed to obedience, first by slavery and then by military discipline. He showed her how to prime the pistol and patch a ball. Elise lifted the weapon and pointed it at a palm trunk below the gallery. When she pulled the trigger, the barrel flew up with a great red whoosh and all the crows lifted, cawing, from the trees. She reloaded the pistol by herself. Guiaou showed her how to close one eye and sight along the barrel. When she fired this time, a long frond came away from the palm and feathered down slowly to the surface of the pool.

Zabeth stood in the doorway with her mouth a wide round of amazement. Sophie was behind her, clutching her skirts, but she was excited, laughing. Elise passed the two of them with a mysterious smile. In the bedroom she cleaned the pistol with a rag and a stick as Guiaou had recommended, then laid it aside, unloaded. She took off her dress and bound down her breasts with several winds of a long cloth. Then she put on a man's shirt and a pair of Tocquet's Spanish breeches, belting them low around her hips. Standing before the mirror, she swept her hair up to the top of her head and fixed it there with one of his broad-brimmed hats.

Not quite. Her face was still too round, too soft, too feminine. She found a blue kerchief and tied it across her mouth and nose—it was not uncommon for riders to mask themselves so against the dust of the road. With the kerchief in place she felt she might pass for a youthful *caballero*. When she picked up the pistol for confidence, she found that it made her reflected eyes steelier and more resolved, even if she held the pistol below the mirror frame.

Swinging a feather duster, Zabeth walked into the room and caught sight of her costume. *"Non, Maîtresse,"* she gasped. She seemed to have read all Elise's intentions. *"Non, pa vré. Non."* But Elise only smiled as she pulled off the kerchief.

"It is a masquerade," she said. "It is nothing."

Zabeth lowered her eyes and went about her dusting, though Elise could see that she did not believe her. Perhaps it was for the better if she did not.

That evening Elise let Sophie stay up as late as she liked, told her stories and gave her sweets until the child was, in fact, a little ill. Then when she had fallen asleep, Elise lay stretched beside her, listening to the intake of her breath, a long, dark, curly clump of hair tickling her nose and cheek. The great temptation was to take Sophie along on this adventure, but she must not. With luck her errand would not keep her away so very long. And Zabeth, with whatever she had surmised, would be here to care and to comfort.

She slept for a few hours beside her little girl, then woke and rose and went to her own room and put on the man's garb, belting the short sword to her waist. Carrying her riding boots in one hand and loaded saddlebags in the other, she went out of the house and to the barn, where she saddled her roan mare and led her out. It was Tocquet who had taught her to ride astride like a man—first when they had eloped from Thibodet and later when they had returned here, with Sophie, across the mountains of the interior from the Spanish side of the island.

At sunrise she was on the heights of Pilboreau, and beginning to descend, her good light-footed mare overtaking the market women as they walked down toward Plaisance with their wares balanced in baskets on their heads. The loaded pistols rode in scabbards before her knees, but there was no incident. Small squads of Toussaint's soldiers seemed to be posted everywhere, and some of them she recognized, though she was relieved that they did not know her. The roads were peaceful all the way. In the late afternoon she rode into Limbé and decided to pass the night at an inn there, as she did not want to risk being caught on the road after dark.

She gave the innkeeper a gold piece from one of the little purses Tocquet had sent. He whistled at the coin, and cut it with a knife before he rang it into his pocket, then gave her an appraising look. Elise's stomach fluttered, but all he did was offer to find a woman for her pleasure . . .

She declined, in the gruffest tone she could conjure. She ate cold chicken alone in her room, and slept as if she had been laid out by a maul. Next morning she was stiff and saddle-sore when she left the bed, and longed for a slow hot bath, though she knew that was impossible. An hour in the saddle limbered her. At midday she entered the gate of Cap Français.

Her brother ought to have been here somewhere, if he was still in the retinue of Toussaint. But she went first to the Cigny town house, for she had learned during Choufleur's visit that he had established himself there. She gave the door knocker a few noisy, masculine slams, then put her hand on the sword hilt for courage. The person who opened the door was not Choufleur at all, nor any of his retainers either, but her old friend Isabelle Cigny.

Isabelle smiled, swayed and stooped in her half-mocking curtsey— her manner with any strange man. She did not know her, Elise saw, with satisfaction. But in the next instant she saw that Isabelle felt or suspected something. With a flourish she swept off the hat and shook her long blond hair down on her shoulders. Isabelle stood back, gaping, then seized her with both hands and drew her into the house and into a warm embrace.

"We are to thank that half-breed son of the Sieur Maltrot for all this restoration," Isabelle said, sweeping her hand around her parlor. "The house was burned to its foundation in ninety-three, you know. I cannot complain of the construction, though as for his taste in décor—suffice it to say it is not my own."

Elise brushed a quantity of dust from her breeches and sat gingerly down on a garishly striped sofa. It was true that the whole room was a gaudy blaze of clashing colors, though the materials were opulent. "Choufleur," she said. "I had expected to find him installed here . . . though of course I am far happier to find you."

"My dear," said Isabelle. "It seems so long ago, that man tried to force his *entrée* here. He thought to carry on his *amours* beneath my roof!— and may have done so later on, when the wheel of Destiny raised him up to take possession of this house. But now that wheel has cast him down again."

"Where has he gone?"

"Of that I know nothing, and care even less. He was supposed to have been here during the mulatto rebellion—up to his neck in it too, I dare say."

"And with his woman and her child?"

"I could not say. They had all been routed before our return, you understand."

Elise reached across the coffee table and took hold of Isabelle's hands. "Listen," she said, and she began to explain all that she had done and all that she finally hoped to undo. When she had finished, Isabelle disengaged her fingers and sat back.

"But you do not know if Nanon would return," she said. "And would your brother have her, now?"

"I think he would," Elise said. "Oh, I don't know—I understand nothing anymore, except that I have paid too high a price for this propriety. Why did I prize it so? It has cost me my husband's love, my brother's good regard, my own child's happiness. If I could only find that boy—I did not understand the depth of my brother's attachment to him. I was wrong. To the devil with propriety, I say now—and up with libertinage, if it must be. I don't know what Nanon would do, or what she ought to do. Only I would unsay the lies I told her, if I could."

She stopped talking, and both women listened to the tramp of the squad of Toussaint's soldiers on the street beyond the round-arched, floor-length windows. A voice called an order, and the footsteps passed by and receded.

"Nanon," Isabelle said softly. "She is far from transparent, I must say."

"But you speak as if you know her," Elise said.

"She is not easy for a woman to know," Isabelle said, "as you might testify yourself, my dear. She has made it her business to suit herself perfectly to the company of men. But she stayed here until the town was burned. Your brother brought her here for shelter. The child you seek was born here, even. Oh my dear, there is so very much you have not been told."

"Is my brother in the town?"

"I believe so," Isabelle said. "We have seen little of him. He is closeted with Toussaint and the commissioners. It is still quite uneasy here between the blacks and the mulattoes and, of course, ourselves. With Villatte and his confederates still at large—he has still a great many sympathizers, though they are silent now. One must suppose that every colored man would take his part."

"Commissioners?"

"Why yes—has the news not reached you yet at Ennery? A new agency has just arrived from France: Sonthonax, Raimond, Leblanc, Giraud and Roume. But of course it is Sonthonax above all."

As she pronounced the final name, Isabelle's lips made a sour pucker.

Elise recalled that the Cigny family had identified Sonthonax as a dangerous lunatic well before he'd proclaimed the abolition of slavery. "And what is expected of Sonthonax?" she said.

"Who can predict?" Isabelle tossed her head. "The man is volatile. Though we whom he denounced as *aristocrats of the skin* when he first came here can scarcely hope to find his favor now. They say he is turning even from the mulattoes, wholeheartedly to the blacks."

That might be understandable, Elise thought, given Villatte's rebellion, but since she did not wish to cross her friend, she did not speak. During the pause in their conversation they heard the sound of marching feet again, and then a voice called a halt. There was some rustling within the house, the creak of a hinge, and then a housemaid knocked on the parlor door frame to announce Major Joseph Flaville.

"A moment," Isabelle said. "Ask him to wait." As the maid went out, she rushed to Elise. "Let us preserve your incognito."

"But—"

"Here, let me." Suppressing her laughter, Isabelle twisted up her friend's hair and tucked it down the back of her shirt, then tied the kerchief over her head to hide it. Then she cocked her head back for a look.

"It's as well you hadn't time to wash your face," she said. "You look quite the adventurer." She called to the housemaid, "Send him in!"

Flaville strode into the room, carrying the belt of scabbarded pistols from Elise's mare. The pistols dragged on the carpet as he bowed.

"With the unrest," he said, "it is perhaps unwise to leave these arms unattended on the street."

Remembering her role, Elise scrambled up and returned his bow. She did not speak, but with a twisted smile she accepted the pistols. A prickle of half-hostile wariness passed from Flaville's hands to hers.

"Major Flaville, I present to you," Isabelle sang gaily, "the Chevalier . . . Thibodet."

Flaville looked at her narrowly. Stroking a pistol butt, Elise did her best to harden her eyes. The officer did look well in his uniform, whatever his color. His bearing was absolutely correct. He had a bull's neck, and his whole body was powerful beneath the cloth. His skin was a shining bluish black, like gun metal; she was tempted to touch it.

"There was a Thibodet at Ennery," Flaville said. "But . . . an older man?"

Elise's tongue clove to the roof of her mouth.

"It's his nephew you see now," Isabelle said hastily. "But do sit down."

"I cannot stay," Major Flaville said. "My duty calls—I only came to restore the pistols to their owner."

Elise bowed deeply, hiding her face. When at length she straightened, Isabelle was walking Flaville from the room. After two minutes she returned, choking on her giggles.

"Oh, we took him in to perfection," she said. "He is even *jealous.*" She flared her nostrils in imitation. " 'Who is that boy? Why do you have him here?' " And she collapsed into laughter on the sofa beside Elise.

"Jealous?" Elise said. Her curiosity was piqued by the word, though she herself was bubbly with amusement and relief.

Isabelle stopped laughing for a moment and flicked the subject away with the fingers of both hands. "Oh, it is nothing—all foolishness, a game," she said gaily. "He has been helpful to us—indeed a real friend in time of need. It makes a difference, for our position is delicate, with Sonthonax, especially, so lusty for the blood of *émigrés* . . ." She sighed, looking out the tall, narrow window. "One comes almost to prefer Toussaint."

At last Elise could give herself over to the luxury of a long, hot soak. She emerged with her skin shriveling, and began to put on clothes she'd borrowed from Isabelle. But before she was half dressed she decided to stretch out on the bed, only to rest her eyes for just a moment . . . and did not wake till she was called to supper. There were guests—Michel Arnaud and his wife Claudine, notorious for having hacked off her own ring finger during the horrors of ninety-one. Elise knew the legend well enough, though she had not previously met its subject. Madame Arnaud was still and reserved, contributing little to the table talk, which mostly concerned the maneuvers of Sonthonax since his arrival, and the delicacy of the situation with the mulatto population of the town, suddenly invested by such a large, and largely black, army with Toussaint at its head.

After the meal Elise was glad enough to retire and take off the confining clothes that Isabelle had lent her, for Isabelle was considerably smaller than she. For the same reason she was willing to fall in with Isabelle's scheme for the following day—that they would go out together with Elise in her man's disguise. Arnaud and Monsieur Cigny had gone together to a waterfront broker, concerning the sugar Arnaud had brought in from the plain, and Claudine was visiting the Ursuline sisters, so there was no one to observe or interfere with their project. At ten o'clock they left the house, Elise sporting Tocquet's shirt and trousers, and Isabelle leaning delicately on her arm. Isabelle did the talking, when talk was required, so that Elise's voice might not betray her.

All that day and the next and the day after that they tried to learn Choufleur's whereabouts, so as to discover Nanon or Paul. At first, luck seemed to run in their favor, for when they called at the house of the late Sieur Maltrot, the servants there recalled that Choufleur had been there, without any woman companion but with a small boy who could have passed for white; they had stayed one night and gone out together the next morning. Choufleur had returned to the house, but without the boy.

But there the trail grew very cold. Elise and Isabelle quartered the town all day, only returning to the Cigny house to wait out the worst of the midday heat. They spent another period of searching during the late afternoon, taking care to return to the house before the others, so that Elise could resume the clothing prescribed for her sex. Isabelle had left word for a couple of her dresses to be altered during their absence, so that Elise might wear them more comfortably. But even with the better fit, the skirts had begun to feel odd to her.

On the second night Arnaud came back in a state of high excitement—it seemed he'd discovered the mulatto family of a French priest, the Père Bonne-chance, who had been of service to him in the past. Elise was puzzled by his elation. She had not known him before this meeting, but he had had a very hard reputation which preceded him wherever he went; for example, he was thought to have sold his own colored children into slavery. Therefore he seemed the last person on earth to be so transported by the discovery of a priest's concubine and her pack of colored brats. Though it was just such a colored brat that Elise herself was hoping to find, and if she failed she would not recover her own happiness either.

At the end of the second day of fruitless search, Elise realized that she had not really considered the possibility of failure. The mission itself had given her such new heart that she had not thought of what might happen if it did not succeed. She could scarcely think of Xavier, and how was she to face her brother? For the moment she did not have to face him, for he was out at Haut du Cap, with Toussaint, at Habitation Bréda. Toussaint was holding himself aloof from Sonthonax and the Commission, as if he were an independent potentate whom the French agent must flatter and court. This subject was discussed, with some rancor, by Messieurs Arnaud and Cigny over each evening meal.

On the morning of the third day, Elise and Isabelle happened to be passing the house of the Sieur Maltrot again, though without intending to stop, when one of the servant girls came running after them in the dusty street. A slip of a thing, no more than ten, she whispered to them behind her hand that she thought that Paul might have been taken to a certain house in the town whose very mention made Isabelle turn silent and grave.

They could not investigate in person, Isabelle said, when the girl had scurried back to the house. *Pas question*. No decent woman could be seen even on the same block as *that* establishment. But she would make inquiry; there were other ways. Indeed word came to them that night, by way of Major Joseph Flaville, that Paul had been in that house for several days, but that he had run away.

The thrill with which Elise received this news was soon replaced by discouragement. If Paul was alone and adrift on the streets of Le Cap, they ought already to have run across him. And if not, what hope was there? At supper she could scarcely follow the talk, and that night she slept poorly.

Next day she and Isabelle sallied out as before, this time to search the poorer quarters of the town where indigents fetched up. They explored the huts on the marshland near the cemetery ground of La Fossette, and then the *marché des nègres* at the Place Clugny. Elise sensed Isabelle's interest flagging. The excursions on the arm of her disguised friend were losing their novelty, as the likelihood of finding Paul declined.

But as they were leaving by one of the byways running out of the Place Clugny, Isabelle snatched at Elise's sleeve and pulled her back the way they had come. The street was crowded with market stalls and market women, so that Elise could not make out what her friend had seen.

"What?" she said, "What is it?" But Isabelle did not hear her, Elise realized. A handcart loaded with flour inched past, and a string of four mules went by in the opposite direction.

"Maman Maig'," Isabelle said. "I am sure it is she!"

On the opposite side of the street a gigantic black woman sat on a block of stone, eating fish and rice with her fingers from a halved calabash.

"Who is it?" said Elise.

"The midwife," Isabelle hissed. "She attended Nanon when the boy was born."

They stood before the black woman, who did not look up. With an unaccustomed diffidence, Isabelle explained whom they were looking for, mentioning his connection to Maman Maig'. All the while the black woman went on eating. Her fingers were shiny with oil from the food. It was not clear if she were listening or not.

"*Pa konnen,*" she said, when Isabelle had stopped talking. I don't know. The denial seemed universal, as if Maman Maig' knew nothing on any topic at all, or nothing she would tell these questioners. But she did look up, not at Isabelle, but at Elise, who felt a ring of sweat breaking out where the band of Tocquet's hat compressed her skull. The black woman's eyes were narrow, squeezed slantwise by rolls of fat. Elise felt that her disguise was penetrated, not only that but all her being. The cloth binding her breasts cut into her ribs, hindering her breath. The energy that had animated her drained away and was replaced by unbounded hopelessness. Then Maman Maig' was not looking at her anymore, and Isabelle was leading her away, toward the Cigny house for shelter from the sun.

She lay on a low daybed still in the same shirt and trousers (Isabelle had ordered them washed and pressed the night before), having only removed her boots and loosened the shirt at the throat. Above her the attic walls slanted to a peak. At one end of the room a round window like a porthole cast a magnified round of sunlight across her hips and legs. She occupied this little room because Arnaud and his wife were installed in the larger guest room on the floor below. Nanon had stayed here, Isabelle had told her, in the last weeks of her *grossesse*.

She could not sleep, nor truly rest. The room was too warm, close under the roof, at that hour. Isabelle had urged her to lie down in her own bedchamber, or on a divan in the parlor on a lower floor, but Elise had very much preferred to be alone. She flattened her hands over a point below her navel, pressing against a curious pain where the light had concentrated. The pressure seemed to bring an image, in no way like a dream, of the black woman they had met this afternoon, her face lowered and intent, her hands maneuvering out of sight. A woman cried out terribly; there was a flash of intense white light. She saw the infant Paul, scarcely recognizable, suspended upside down between black hands, like a flayed rabbit, his skin purple, blood-streaked, his head a cone-shaped, clay-like mass. He mewed, and the image faded.

Nothing. The room throbbed. Elise sat up. She was streaming sweat, but did not feel it. With the hat and boots in her hands she crept down through the dozing house to the front hall. A footman watched her curiously as she put on her boots, but he said nothing when she let herself out.

Now she walked very much like a dreamer, and with a dreamer's clarity of intention, though she herself could not have said what that intention was. It led her toward the Negro market where they had been that morning. Elsewhere, the streets had emptied of pedestrians, due to the midday heat, but the Place Clugny still buzzed and swarmed. Elise grew dizzy. Her intention failed her. Bewildered, she began to retreat.

Like a marionette with its strings abandoned, she wanted to fall in a jangling heap. At one of the corners of the market square she sank down onto a block of stone. There was a swelling pain in all her joints as if they were ill fit together. A dreadful weight pressed down on her head, so that all the bones of her spine were crushed against one another and twisted into discord. A black circle rimmed with gold appeared before her eyes, and whether she opened or closed them, it pulsed at the same rate. *Sunstroke,* she thought, but the word had no import. She saw no way out of the blaze of heat and light.

But then a shadow interposed itself between her and the sun. Elise was washed in a water-cool draft like the shade of an ancient tree.

"Levé."

She opened her eyes and saw Maman Maig' filling the sky above her, the black face neutral, vatic, like the face of an Egyptian statue.

"Rise," the woman repeated. She held the palm of her hand several inches above the crown of Elise's head, then arched her wrist and raised it. Elise felt all the knots in her body unraveling as she came floating to her feet.

With her dream-certainty restored, she followed Maman Maig' across the town. The black woman never once turned back to look at her, but an invisible filament connected them like a leash. They went diagonally across the Place d'Armes and thence into a northbound street. At its end, on a knoll below the mountain, Elise saw a small white church whose name she did not know. It seemed that the church was their destination. But when they came nearer, Maman Maig' turned away toward the waterfront, and a wall of housefronts blocked the church from view.

Here the four-square order of the town disintegrated, disrupted by the roots of the mountain clawing into the edge of the grid. The church was hidden, somewhere above. Maman Maig' went in through a rusty iron gateway, then somehow fit herself through a crack in the opposite wall of the small, square courtyard they had entered. Elise followed devotedly. The path was so narrow she could not understand how Maman Maig' could maneuver so easily. But they went up and up, a tight spiral twisting between house walls made at first of plaster, then baked mud, finally of sticks and straw, unwattled. There was a dark beat at Elise's temples; her sense of direction was lost. Finally they came out into a wide open space, like a ballroom Elise thought for some reason, though it was only an area of packed earth surrounded by little huts, with a pole in the center painted in a spiral pattern like the path they had just climbed.

A deliciously refreshing breeze blew on the back of her head and her shoulders, and she turned her face into it. The sweat dried quickly. She took off her hat. The wind was coming off the water, and down below, beyond the red-tiled roofs, she saw the sail-less masts of ships bare and skeletal as winter trees in France. When she turned back, Maman Maig' was no longer there, but the disappearance did not worry her.

There were other onlookers. Even on the cliff above the village the little black children had stopped their play to gaze down at her. Among the *ajoupas*, Claudine and Michel Arnaud were mysteriously present— Arnaud raised a hand to the back of his head and stared at her with frank astonishment (she realized that her hair had come unpinned and fallen down her back). But Claudine, who never seemed surprised at anything, seemed no more startled now. Between the white couple stood a tall mulatto woman wearing a high turban, and an even taller, gangly colored youth with a priest's purple stole incongruously draped over his bare, boney shoulders.

There were others too who watched her from their doorways, but Elise had eyes only for the little boy coming toward her, hand in hand with an older colored girl. Of a sudden it seemed to her that *he* was the person she had most injured and offended—that it was Paul whom she did not know how to face. But he kept coming toward her as though unaware of any wrong between them, tugging at the colored girl's hand. When he was near enough, he reached out and caught the seam of Elise's trousers and folded it in his fingers as he looked up into her face. The wind was still blowing at her back, fluttering her hair forward across her shoulders.

"*Matant mwen,*" Paul said. My aunt. And Elise was so delighted at the recognition that she did not think to reprove him for speaking Creole instead of French.

"Of course," Arnaud said, "I did not know the boy was yours—I took him for another of Fontelle's family, which is numerous. And to be sure," he added, with a faint smile, "a great many other things, Madame, were not entirely as they seemed."

Elise felt a slight warmth in her cheeks. She brought her knees more primly together beneath her skirt; she had resumed wearing dresses for all occasions. Tocquet's shirt and trousers were packed away now in the saddlebags.

"You seem very intimate with this Fontelle," she said.

Now it was Arnaud's turn to flush. "In no improper manner," he said. "She was, after all—"

"—the wife of a priest," Elise supplied, with a downturn of her eyes which partly masked her irony.

Arnaud flicked his eyes toward his wife, who perched stiffly on the edge of one of Isabelle's parlor divans, her hands crawling slowly over each other in her lap. "Though he failed in his vows of chastity, he was a priest who saved my life," he said. "Possibly, in another sense, the life of my wife also."

Claudine had been staring fixedly through the high arched doorway which gave onto the second-floor balcony above the street. At Arnaud's words she rose like a marionette lifted by invisible threads and floated to the balcony rail. Arnaud pushed himself up and followed. He set a hand lightly on her shoulder, whispered persuasively in her ear. But Claudine's body gave a tremor from her heels to her head; both her hands curled around the railing and would not be loosened. With a murmur Arnaud left her there and resumed the chair where he had sat before.

"Although," he said, in a lower voice, "sometimes I find it better not to mention the Père Bonne-chance in her hearing, for it causes her mind in its vagary to revisit the scene of his execution, for which she was unfortunately present in the flesh."

Elise followed Arnaud's gaze to his wife's rigid back. She did not seem to pay any attention to talk.

"Not far from here," he muttered, "in the Place Clugny." He shook his head. "But on that day in ninety-one—it was the Père Bonne-chance who brought me safe away from the rebels at Ouanaminthe, when they were killing the white men one by one with such awful tortures as I will not describe to you. He had been priest among the rebels too and had some credit with them. I came to the house he shared with Fontelle with my feet blistered and bloody from the long road, and she washed my feet and dressed them with oil." He turned his head toward the current of air that flowed in from the balcony door. "Later when he was prisoner here, he confessed my wife and eased her of her torments to some degree . . . For those things I owe a debt of gratitude which I would repay to his survivors. Though for the moment my means are slight."

"And what of the girl?" Elise asked. "Paulette."

"She was acquainted with your brother when he was prisoner of the rebels at the camps of Grande Rivière. Père Bonne-chance had brought all his family there. He did what he could to ease the lot of the white captives and to preserve their lives. But afterward he was taken for a conspirator and jailed here at Le Cap, and in those days your brother and his woman took Paulette in to care for their child."

"I will take her now, if she is willing," Elise offered. "She has kind ways with Paul, and I would welcome her at Habitation Thibodet, if her mother should agree."

"That would be a place well found for her," Arnaud said. "I think that Fontelle might be brought to agree. I suppose you would certainly improve the girl's French, and train her in other accomplishments in return for her work. I don't know how they have bumped along in those hilltop huts, but Fontelle is a woman of some pride."

"Of the seven sins, pride is the most wicked." Claudine had turned from her place at the balcony rail and stood looking down on them from the doorway with a hard glitter in her eyes. "Pride is the sow that devours her young." Her left hand with its missing finger rose stiffly from the shoulder, accusing a vacant space in the room. "See how she comes riding on the scarlet beast! see her seven heads and her ten horns!"

Arnaud stood by her, murmuring again, massaging her stiff arm until the elbow flexed and he was able to lead her to a seat. Claudine sat rocking slightly, her eyes closed, her lips working without sound now. Her long, dark lashes were bright with unshed tears.

"You must pardon her distraction," Arnaud said, with a forbearance Elise was surprised to find in him. "In any case," he said, as he sank back into his chair, "I think your idea for Paulette is a very good one."

In the event, Fontelle was persuaded to Elise's plan without much difficulty. However, Elise stayed on in Le Cap until Toussaint returned, in the hope of meeting her brother, to give him the news of Paul's recovery face to face. There was a reasonable chance that Doctor Hébert was still in Toussaint's entourage, though she did not know for certain.

On the morning that she heard that Toussaint had arrived from Haut du Cap, Elise set out toward Government House, holding Paul by one hand while Paulette held the other. The boy had recently had a haircut and a new suit of clothes, and Paulette was shyly pretty in a new dress Elise had bought for her. Elise herself was more carefully coiffed and groomed than she had recently been, and she felt that the three of them looked very well together.

There was excitement in the streets, and a general flow down toward the harbor. Villatte had been lured in from his armed camp to parlay with the commissioners—then Toussaint and Sonthonax had arrested him. Today, it appeared, he would be taken aboard a ship to be sent to France for trial and judgment. Curious, Elise let the children lead her along with the crowd.

On the quay, Toussaint's honor guard, a group of tall and handsome-looking black cavalrymen, had pulled their horses into a double cordon, defining a pathway from Government House. Elise craned her neck, but did not see Toussaint himself anywhere. She did catch a glimpse of her brother's bald head; he sat his horse somewhere beyond the second rank of the honor guard, looking about himself sleepily. Then the helmets of the guardsmen moved together and obscured her view. She could just make out the inscription on the silver plate: *Qui pourra en venir à bout?*

A buzz ran through the close-packed onlookers, for the deportees were being marched down to the ship. From where she stood Elise could see no more than the tops of their heads as they went by. As they went up the gangplank, though, they were more clearly visible to all the crowd. An armed guard went before and after them, but they had not been charged with chains. Perhaps the tall one who looked back briefly from the deck was Villatte himself. Then they all disappeared below.

The crowd began to scatter and diffuse, and Elise, though she peered for another sight of the doctor, had no luck. Toussaint's honor guard—some ninety men, after all—was in the way. They formed in ranks of three abreast and went trotting back toward Government House. For the moment they seemed to have answered the question their own helmets raised: *Who will be able to come through to the end?*

23

When the sister of the doctor, who was Tocquet's woman, ran away, the news came to our camp through Bouquart, who had it from Zabeth in the *grand'case.* Although we might have heard Zabeth's voice for ourselves, as loud as she cried. No one in the camp cared very much one way or another, but Zabeth was in great trouble because she believed that her mistress would die. The whitewoman had taken pistols and man's clothes and a horse to ride away to no one knew where. In the camp the men spoke of it carelessly—who knew what such a whitewoman would do, or why. But I, Riau, smiled to myself when I thought of the doctor's sister going off into *marronage* that way, and I hoped that all the spirits would go with her and watch for her safety.

Soon afterward the little girl became sick with a fever. Zabeth was still deeper in terror for that, because she loved Sophie as much as she would love the child Bouquart had put into her belly, who was still waiting to come out. Zabeth's voice brought all the old women down from the hills around Ennery to the *grand'case,* and she even sent for Riau too, because she knew that Toussaint had taught me some of what a *doktè-fey* knows, and she believed that I knew whiteman's medicine from the doctor too, which was not true, except for bonesetting and cutting off ruined arms and legs. When I came to Sophie, I saw at once that she did not have a fever that would take her away from this life. Her spirit was weakened because her father had not come back or sent any word for so long, and then the mother vanished also, even if Sophie cared as much for Zabeth as for those other two. But she would not die. When I came, the old women had already chosen the right leaves to send that fever away from her. And in a few days Sophie had left her bed and was not really sick anymore, though she was pale, and quieter than before.

I did not think so much about Sophie or any troubles of the *grand'case* because at that time I had a trouble all my own. This was because Guiaou and Riau had come to be at Ennery at the same time. We each must go where orders sent us and they had not sent us to Ennery together, not for a long while. But after all the men of Dieudonné came to join his army, Toussaint was so very pleased that he let Riau and Guiaou choose where they would be sent next. I chose Ennery, and it seemed Guiaou must have said the same, and that was how it happened. There was not so much fighting just then anyway. Even when Villatte tried to make his rising, Toussaint left Riau and Guiaou at Ennery, though he took a lot of men north to take care of that trouble.

That was the first time I saw the new child born to Merbillay. A girl child, and Guiaou had planted the seed of her. Her name was Sanschagrin, but Merbillay and everyone called her Yoyo.

So many babies and small children were in the camp with us now. It seemed I had not noticed them until I saw Merbillay holding this new baby in her arms. In slavery time we did not see so many children because women did not want to bring them into the world to be slaves, and many women found one way or another to stop the children coming. It was different now, and women were glad when the babies came, and I was glad to see Merbillay and this new girl baby smiling at each other, though I had no voice in her naming.

I saw those smiles from a distance, though. It was Guiaou who stayed in the *ajoupa* with Merbillay, and Caco, and the new child Sanschagrin. Since Riau had been there last, Merbillay had coated the stick walls with layers and layers of clay to make thick walls that passed no light, so it was a real *case* now and not an *ajoupa*. There was no wooden door, only a pale blue cloth hanging over the doorway, which in the day was tied like a woman's waist so light and air could come inside, but those clay walls would keep a man out still.

Once, when I knew Guiaou had gone down to the river, I went to that clay *case*. Merbillay was lying on her mat because it was the hot time of the day, and the baby was asleep beside her. It took some little time for my eyes to see because I was not used to the darkness the clay walls made. At last I could see my *banza* still hanging from the rooftree like always. Merbillay saw it too, and she got up slowly from the mat—I watched her moving, and her face and arms were shining and slick with sweat, but she was not smiling now. She took down the *banza* and gave it to me, and even our hands did not touch as I took the *banza* by the neck. When I went out with the *banza* in my hand, I thought that I would not be going back to that *case* any more.

Much higher on the hill I had an *ajoupa* which was made only of sticks and leaves, not clay, so it was cool and full of wind and sunlight. I hung my *banza* there, and there I kept my coat of a captain hung on crossed sticks to keep its shape—if I was not wearing it, for every day I went with other officers and the white captains Maillart or Vaublanc to train new men, and keep the old men ready. But in early morning or at evening the officer coat would hang on the crossed sticks, with the watch ticking in the pocket where I could not hear it. I would not wear even a shirt, and the air would run all over my skin, and I would be playing the *banza*. I played sad tunes that had no words to them, the same few notes repeating. Sometimes Caco came up to my *ajoupa* by himself as if the tunes had called him—we would listen, or I would hang the *banza* from the roof and we would go and do some other thing together.

I did not go to look for Caco at that clay *case* anymore, but only waited for him to come to me. Sometimes for days he would not come. I would walk near the clay *case*, but it seemed whenever Guiaou was not there then Couachy was somewhere nearby, watching. Guiaou and Couachy had fought against the English together in the Artibonite and after that they walked like brothers together.

And I, Riau, had walked in the same spirit with Guiaou, especially in the fighting around Grande Rivière, when both of us had tried to help the whiteman doctor heal the wounded men. Since then, since Dieudonné was sold, a crack had opened up between us like a crack in the earth opens when it has been too dry. Yet I thought I must not blame Guiaou for Dieudonné when really I was angry about the woman. If I thought more deeply, I knew also that it had been Toussaint's hidden hand which moved Guiaou in the taking of Dieudonné, but in those weeks at Ennery I did not usually let my thinking go so far in that direction.

Bouquart asked why I did not start with some other woman, and he named women who were ready to come to me. I knew them anyway, there was more than one and some of them were beautiful. One liked me for the captain's coat, and others for different reasons. I saw their smiles, but my spirit did not draw me to them.

So on an evening I sat alone inside the *ajoupa,* playing to myself as I would do at that hour, following the voices of the birds outside. I sat on the ground in a corner with my back against a post, but through the space of the doorway I saw the clouds rushing across the sky and all the birds were hurrying too, because of the rain, except the rain would not really come, because the season was past. When I heard footsteps, I thought maybe Caco was coming, but the feet were heavier than his, and I saw through the woven walls of the *ajoupa* the figure of a woman on the path. Between the cracks and sticks of the wall her face and her form were broken up, though I saw she was wearing a long red cloth wound many times around her head. Maybe it was one of those women Bouquart had spoken of. I began folding away into myself to hide from her. But when she stepped into the doorway, it was Merbillay. Guiaou was not away with the army then. He was somewhere on Habitation Thibodet, but Riau was not thinking of him then, and neither was Merbillay.

A few raindrops spattered into the dust behind us as she came in, and a few more flattened on the palm thatch of the roof. She was a long time unwinding that red spangled cloth from her head. We did not speak of anything at all. With the heaviness of rain, the air between us was like water, so that each of her movements made a swirl that touched my body, though we were not yet near enough to touch.

After, a shaft of sun came through the scattering sounds and made the shape of a flattened circle all in green and gold over a few small *carrés* of cane field in the valley. Merbillay and I looked down at this together, feeling a calm and a stillness between us. All the time she kept inside the doorway though, and I felt how she did not want to be seen by anyone, and a little seed of anger was somewhere in my head, though not yet opened.

After this day, Merbillay came to me sometimes, without warning and without a word. I would not know when she was coming, and still I could not go to her. Each time she came, the hot, sharp sweetness was stronger than the time before.

In the next days the doctor's sister returned. She had gone away in the darkness riding in man's trousers and all alone, but when she came back, she was riding sidesaddle like a regular white lady and escorted by five of Toussaint's ninety new guardsmen with the tall, shiny helmets, and with her was the boy, Paul. Then there was a lot of happiness in the *grand'case,* and Zabeth shouted and cried in joy, and soon the story of all that happened came out to us in the camp through Bouquart—how Elise was in harmony with her brother again because she had found the child (though they had not found Nanon at all) and how Choufleur had wanted to sell the boy, to make him disappear.

I, Riau, was glad for the people in the *grand'case,* because I was in friendship with the doctor since a long time. Also I had watched Sophie with a different eye since Zabeth had called me to her treatment. Even after the fever left her, she had been pale and sad, like a ghost, but now the light returned to her eye, when she saw her mother and Paul again. Pauline, who was the daughter of that *marron* priest and Fontelle, had come with them too, to help Zabeth with the little children . . . but they were more like three or four small children, laughing and playing together.

But it was not finished yet, because they had not found Nanon any-where. That doctor did not have the proud ways or the manner of other *blancs*—he was so much another way that you might fail to see him when he was there, but when he had once set his teeth into something, he would not let go very easily, no more than a big *caïman* from the river. I knew this, and I pictured him with the mirror *ouanga* he kept in one pocket and the snuffbox *ouanga* he kept in another pocket far away as if it would be like gunpowder and fire if he and Choufleur ever met, and I saw that in the end they must come together. Their story was not fin-ished yet, and neither was mine.

I saw before my eyes a newborn baby stuck on a long spear, with arms and legs still wriggling, though it must soon die. By the force of pity you wished for it to die soon to end its suffering and end the suffering you felt when you had to look at it that way. And yet I, Riau, had looked at sights like that with another feeling. In the time of the first risings, Riau had done certain things, or certain things had been done with his body which I did not now remember, either because he was ridden by a *lwa* or . . .

Choufleur must have wanted to wipe out that boy, Paul. To make it like he had never been born. I felt that this must be the truth. But the *blancs* had been the first to put babies on spears, before the risings, when they rode against the colored people of the west.

Then I walked down to where the clay *case* was. I felt a purpose in my head without knowing what it was. Only it was many days since Merbil-lay had come to my *ajoupa* on the hill. That whole part of Habitation

Thibodet was like a little town now because people had been living there so long. Most of the other *ajoupas* had been finished with clay walls too and the paths were packed down hard between them. There was a chicken, here was a goat, there was a donkey nuzzling stubble by a housewall. Merbillay sat on the low clay sill of the doorway with the new baby at her breast.

The sun was exactly on top of my head and burned down through my body and legs and on into the ground hot enough to boil the water that pools beneath. Merbillay looked up at me with a still, stone face, and I looked at her without knowing what to say or do.

Couachy came from the corner of another *case*, walking quickly and speaking in a loud voice. *"Ki problèm ou?"* The wrong words, too loud. What is your problem? Riau had no quarrel with Couachy, but when he spoke, the seed of anger bloomed in my head and filled it up with its stinging red flower.

For a moment I did not know exactly what was happening, only I heard Merbillay's voice, high and shrill with anger, but not the words. Only the surge and pull of blood and muscle, jolt of bone. Then I saw that Guiaou had come from somewhere to stand with Couachy, and Bouquart was by me, holding my elbow. Merbillay stood in the doorway with Yoyo held high on her shoulder and beginning to complain for the loss of the breast, and Merbillay was still cutting at all of us with her tongue, but at the same time her eyes darted everywhere to be sure it would not be safer for her to run inside the house with the baby. I saw Caco's face too, looking around her hip at us.

Bouquart and Guiaou were shouting also, and maybe Riau was saying something too, but Couachy was silent; his tongue came out of his mouth only to touch the blood that seeped where his lip was swollen. Seeing the blood, I thought that fighting might really begin among all of us. But Bouquart pulled me back very hard with his hand on my elbow, and then Quamba came.

Quamba walked to us in that quiet and slow way he would have walked toward horses who were fighting or frightened, rearing or tossing their heads or struggling against a tether or trying to break out of some stall or corral. Every one stopped shouting when Quamba came, even Merbillay. She stood with her mouth still open, but no words came out anymore, and Yoyo stopped and whimpered and turned her head on her shoulder, to look. Quamba came between us all with his soft, gentle step, and he spoke in a voice so calm and soothing that we did not need to hear the words, no more than a horse would have needed to understand them. Quamba had worked upon Guiaou's fear of horses, and

Riau knew him even before that. Also Quamba had taken the *asson*, at the *hûnfor* above Ennery, and this too gave him respect with all of us.

My head was still all hot inside so that I could not understand what he was saying. But his words were calming, and his hands moved smoothly on the air between us, as if he were testing whether he might touch Guiaou or Riau without being stung or burned.

"*La paix*," said Quamba, to Guiaou and then to me. Bouquart drew on my arm and I let myself go back with him. Then we turned together, Bouquart and I, and were walking away from them all and away from the clay *case*, and after a few steps I shook my arm free of Bouquart's hand.

"*La paix*," Quamba called in a slightly stronger voice, though not really loud. I looked back and met his eye to show that I had heard him. But there was no peace in me anywhere.

The next day Merbillay came again to the *ajoupa* on the hill. And after ward she came even more often than before. There was hardly a day when she did not come. I was glad, but part of this gladness was mixed with anger, and I knew there would be some more trouble.

Then, after some days, the *blanc* captains Maillart and Vaublanc came up the path to my *ajoupa*. I was so much surprised to see them there, I wondered if maybe they did not have an order to arrest Riau. But they only stood outside the *ajoupa*, breathing hard as whitemen do when they have had to climb a hill. They spoke about the weather and the fineness of the view. It was true that you could see a long way from that hilltop, all over the deep valley and around the *mornes* which closed it in. The white captains asked my leave to come inside the *ajoupa*. There was not a lot for them to look at in there, but Maillart asked that I take down the *banza* and play a little, and afterwards they took it up and turned it over and passed it between them, comparing it to instruments they knew from France, though it seemed it was not very much like any of those.

Then the two white captains left the *ajoupa* and made ready to start down the path, only Maillart turned back to me suddenly and placed one hand carefully on my chest and took in a deep, important breath.

"You must not fight Guiaou," he said. "Riau, I tell you as—as your brother officer."

So that was what it had been about, from the beginning. I said nothing, though I had the angry thought that Maillart, even if he had been my *parrain* to teach me the whiteman ways of fighting, Maillart was not my father. The words of the Creole song came in my head. *We have no mother. We have no father. We come from Guinée* . . . but we did not come out of Guinée because we wanted to.

Maillart would not have understood any of that. I saw that he had come out of friendship, perhaps brotherhood, even if he could not say the word without some difficulty. Another *blanc* would not have come at all. I had not even known that Maillart bothered himself to know where Riau stayed at night. He was shaking his head now, smiling a little, in the manner he might have had with another white officer.

"Women," he said. "They are to admire, to serve, to enjoy, perhaps . . . but not to die for."

"But if you were in my case, you would fight a duel," I said.

The Captain Maillart turned some of those colors that rise so easily in a whiteman's skin. He could not very well say that it was not the same for me. I did not know if he thought this either.

Vaublanc, who had been watching us, spoke then. "You are an officer, and Guiaou is not," he said. "You cannot challenge an enlisted man. No more can you accept his challenge, or even notice it."

Blanc rules. Maillart was nodding to agree. I thought, yes, if I wore my officer's coat, I might order Guiaou what to do, and Couachy too (but neither of them was in my company), and yet this would not make the problem of the woman go away. What would Maillart do if his woman went with a man not an officer? I did not ask him this, though, because I could not think of any time when a *blanche* had done such a thing, so maybe it was not possible.

The white captains must have thought they had said enough, because they made ready to go down the trail again. When Maillart had taken a few steps, he stopped and looked at me again.

"There was a time when I *was* in your place," he said. "And I did not fight the other man." He looked at me to know if I thought that fear had prevented him, but I did not think so, and then he went after Vaublanc, down the trail.

I took leave for one night and one day and went to another higher mountain where there was *bwa danno*. I cut a *danno* from the ground, measuring it to be longer by two hand's lengths than Guiaou's *coutelas*. I had thought a lot about that *coutelas*, because Guiaou was very quick and skillful with it, and he preferred it to a gun.

With my own *coutelas* I peeled the *danno*, all the way to one end of it, but on the other end I left enough of the smooth, gray shiny bark to cover the place where my hand would grip. Beneath the bark the wood was pale and slightly supple, like a whipstock, but also very, very hard. I liked it better than the longer heavy clubs which some men fought with, like Bienvenu. Those heavy clubs would strike a killing blow, but they moved slower than a knife.

If Maillart had not come to speak to me, though, I might have chosen something else than a *danno*. I might have made ready to fight with a pistol or some other weapon more certain to kill. But that thought did not come to my head until later.

I carried the *danno* to the *ajoupa* and kept it leaning just inside the door. I did not take it down to the compound or carry it at any time I must wear my officer coat, but shirtless, high on the *morne*, I worked and worked until the *danno* spun around my hand like the wing of a hummingbird, so fast you could see only the blur of it, whirling forward and then back with scarcely a hitch between the two directions. I worked the *danno* with both hands, and changing from one hand to the other, until striking from any direction I could cut a green branch big around as my thumb.

When I first returned from the mountain where *bwa danno* grew, Merbillay had been there and left one of her *mouchwa têt* spread over my sleeping mat, not the red cloth but a blue one. I put it across my face and breathed the scent of her. She came soon again, and often. All the time she was in that *ajoupa* with me, the *danno* leaned against the woven wall inside the doorway, but if she noticed, she did not say anything about it.

Once in the late morning of a day when there was no drilling of the soldiers down below, Merbillay and I lay naked on the mat side by side, dozing as the sweat dried on us in the breeze that blew through the sticks of the wall. What woke me was the sound of many voices, and when I woke, Merbillay had jumped up with a frightened look on her face and was winding her cloth to cover herself.

I picked up the *danno* as I stepped through the door. A shout went up from all those people, but when Merbillay came out they cried even louder. Bouquart came to me and when I saw his troubled face, I knew that he had wanted to come to me to warn me when he saw it begin—he wanted to tell me this now, but I stopped him from talking. Already the *danno* was twitching in my hand like the stiffened tail of an angry cat.

Guiaou stood forth, the baby Yoyo cradled in his left arm, and he was shouting, pointing at Merbillay, then at the baby, then at Merbillay again. The hum inside my head was too loud for me to understand his words. Caco was not anywhere, and I was glad for that. Guiaou's *coute-las* was strapped to his right hip, and I saw only his hand passing above it, forward and back as he moved his arm to point. Then Merbillay was holding the baby somehow and the crowd had closed behind us, between us and the *ajoupa* and Merbillay was sucked away into the crowd. The crowd had made a circle around only Giaou and Riau. Down the hill I heard Maillart's voice shouting angrily, but the crowd had blocked the trail head and would not let him come up.

Only once did I look into Guiaou's face with the deep scar tearing it open so near to one of his eyes, and after that I looked only at his hip and shoulder and the space between, which the *coutelas* would come out of. But my good *danno* was longer and already it was whirling in my hand. I struck first, high, overhand, drew his parry and reversed the strike almost before the metal touched the wood. With this I hit him on the leg but not as hard as I should have because I was too excited. Still he stumbled and fell back, the crowd opening a pocket to receive him, and I charged, but he laid himself long and low and took the wood across his back while lashing the knife at my forward leg. The *danno* made a red welt on his skin, but the cut toward my legs drove me back-ward to the center of the circle.

We stepped around each other, left, left left, feinting. No advantage for either. I rushed him with two underhand cuts flowing one into the other without a break, but he skipped back and the crowd gave way and he found space to escape. I cut backward, up in a curve from his right foot to his left shoulder, and met the blade halfway. If I had thought sooner, I could have ridden the blade down to smash his knuckles so I tried the same stroke again, but the blade was not where I expected it, because he had flipped it under to lie along the outside of his forearm. He struck up with his elbow as the *danno* went by and the blade hooked out to bite deeply into the underside of my right arm.

The crowd sucked in a moaning sigh. I parried, parried, could not strike. I could do no more than stop his cuts. The blade rolled forward in his hand, quivering, sniffing for Riau. I stepped in, slashing the pat-tern of an 8, but Guiaou somehow escaped this without parrying and then the *coutelas* made three tiny weak flicks forward that cut a circle around my wrist.

That was Riau's own blood on the ground, sticky between my bare toes as I circled, stepping, left left left . . . The blood was leaving my head to fall into the dirt through the cuts in my arm, and I felt cold in my head and a ring of darkness was all around my eyes.

Espri mwen, I said in my head. *Ogûn. Ogûn Feraille vini mwen!*

Guiaou must have felt that I had weakened, for he came in hard with the *coutelas*. I did not know what I did then, only afterward I knew it as if someone else had seen and told me about it all. My hand turned upside down in a reverse parry, and Guiaou flipped the blade toward his left side because he expected the swallow strike to come whipping all the way round Riau's head to hit him there, but instead I caught the low end of the *danno* with my left hand and spun it up and around to his collarbone. With my right arm I would have broken the bone altogether, but the left-hand blow was hard enough that his hand with the *coutelas* dropped back against his knee. Already I had reversed the *danno* into my right hand, and as the *coutelas* came up wavering, I caught his wrist with a wheeling underhand strike and the *coutelas* flew up high, away, flapping like a bat's wings against the sky.

The crowd made that same moaning of the breath. I looked again into Guiaou's face and saw he had given himself up to Baron Cimetière. Death was not so much to him anyway—he had already died at least one time before, beneath the waters with the sharks. The *danno* in my hand began to turn. I could have struck him anywhere, but the *danno* left my hand and went flying off wherever the *coutelas* had gone. I don't know why, but the same spirit that had given me the strokes that took away his knife gave me this action, and the spirit left me standing there, holding my empty hands out to Guiaou.

In the night the drums began at the *hûnfor* which was on a high, rounded hill behind the valley where the houses were and beyond the slopes of coffee trees. Riau walked to the drumming, alone at first, then with Bouquart, then with some others. I did not carry the *danno* or any other weapon, though we had found the *danno*, lying near Guiaou's *coutelas* in the stones beside the streambed. My hands swung light and empty beside me, checked by a dull pain from the cut on my right arm, which was bandaged and poulticed with leaves. After the fighting Guiaou and I had dressed each other's wounds, waving away the old women who came to do it for us.

Now we came up through the circle of torches onto the round, cleared top of the hill, and I turned to the left, circling the *poteau mitan*. The drums were strong already, and the *hounsis* swayed and sang, all dressed in white. On the far side of the circle the trees were cut, and I saw a long way out over the valley, under the sharp starlight.

There was Guiaou circling the other way from me, his arm in a cloth sling from the hurt to his collarbone. He wore a new shirt for the ceremony, and the poultice Riau had put over the *danno* slash on his back stuck here and there to the fresh cloth. Our eyes met for a moment, and we turned away from one another and looped back, moving among the others whose steps were shifting, lightening toward dance, our pathways swooping like the trails of swallows in the sky. As I turned and looked out over the valley, the stars began to run and bleed so that I saw the trails of them. Turning into the circle, I searched for a still point with my eye. Near the *poteau mitan* Quamba sat very still, cross-legged on the ground with the *asson* before him between his knees, the bead strings drooping over the gourd. Later, much later, he would call his spirit. His spirit would not be the first to come. On the far side of the clearing a woman in a high red turban stood up swaying behind the drums to lead the singing, and this was Merbillay.

> *Mèt Agwé, koté ou yé?*
> *Ou pa wé mwen sou lanmè?*
> *Gegne zaviro nan main mwen . . .*
> *M' pa kab tounen déyé . . .*

Guiaou was shocked backward, his legs stuttering—I saw his eyes go white, but the *hounsis* caught him before he'd fallen to the ground, made a hammock of their arms where he lay with his arms and eyelids twitching.

> *Master Agwé, where are you?*
> *Don't you see I'm on the sea?*
> *I have the rudder in my hand. . . .*
> *There is no turning back for me . . .*

Then he rose up smoothly from among them, and Agwé was in his head. Agwé rising like a cresting wave, a dolphin breaching out of the crest. Like water Agwé rippled toward Riau and caught his left arm which was not hurt and pulled him into the wave's curl . . . smooth and glassy, collapsing on itself. The stars whirled and bled together white as milk and Riau was no more, but there was Ogûn.

In the next days, Riau was very calm within himself, and floating like a burned-out log floats as a boat on top of the water. There was the peace Quamba had wished me, though it had not come all at once. Riau was not moved to do anything, only to follow whatever would come. In those days Merbillay did not come at all, but Caco came and we did many things together. I saw there was no trouble in Caco's head, which made me glad.

One day Guiaou himself came up the trail. He was not wearing the sling anymore. He had his *coutelas* and his musket on his shoulder, but I knew he had not brought those weapons against me. When he came in front of the *ajoupa,* he set down the musket against a sapling and told me that some men were moving to Mirebalais and that he would be going with them.

"Yes," I said, because I had heard that there would be a movement of some troops, only Captain Riau was not going with them now, and would still be posted here at Ennery. I had not known that Guiaou's company was ordered out, and I wondered why he would come to tell me.

Guiaou stretched his back and breathed deeply and worked his bare feet around in the dirt where the chickens scratched. At last he told me that Merbillay's blood had stopped, which meant another child was coming.

"*Ti-moun sa-a gegne dé pè,*" I said. I don't know why I had not thought till then that there must be another child. The words came from my mouth before I thought of them. That child will have two fathers.

"*Sa!*" Guiaou said, as if he had been searching all over the world for the words I had said and was very excited to find them. We looked at each other strangely for an instant, then turned and looked all around the hills and the sky in opposite directions. But then it seemed that my left hand was touching his right, palm to palm. The two hands held each other gently for a moment, then released, and Guiaou had shouldered his musket and was going down the hill again.

The same day the soldiers marched out of Ennery, I helped Merbillay move her things to the *ajoupa* on the hill. There were not so many things, but she made herself a great trouble arranging them in there. She would have made me the same trouble too, but seeing that Yoyo was restless and whimpering, I carried her outside. Caco had gone off in the woods alone somewhere. I thought he was happy to move to the hill for a time, because there were less people than down below who might catch him to do work.

Yoyo could crawl very well by then, and she could stand if someone held her by both hands. I lifted her to her feet that way and coaxed her to take a step or two, but she curled up her legs beneath her until I let her down again. She crawled in the dust, bubbling and humming. When she came to my legs and began playing with my toes, I caught her up into my arms. She smiled at me with her red gums and then she turned and nuzzled her damp mouth against my skin. She had a warm, important weight, like bread. This was the first day that I had held her, and I felt that every other thing I had to carry had been lifted from me.

24

Though he normally used his cane only to swagger, Arnaud found himself depending on it, leaning into it, on the last twists and turns of the path up the hill. Dark faces peered out curiously from the huts that lined the path. Rare for a *blanc* to pass this way. He was sweating when he reached the rim of the hill below the church, but a stiff breeze came off the water, which quickly cooled him.

The hill was a dome, smooth as a skull. On the brow, three wooden crosses tilted into the wind; the center cross stood somewhat higher than the others. Arnaud turned in a circle, pivoting on his planted cane. Between the crosses and the church, his wife sat on a low wooden stool with her skirts spread all about her, catechizing a gaggle of black and colored children who sat in the dust at her feet under the shade of a scraggly flamboyant. Thin and reedy, her voice reached him against the wind.

Ki moun ki fé latè?

BonDyé! The children's chorus swelled in answer.

Ki moun ki fils-li?

Jisit!

Claudine leaned forward to sketch the letters for *Bon Dieu* and *Jésus*

Christ on a panel of dust one of the older girls had smoothed for her, using a pointed stick for a stylus. There was no paper for such a project—one of many shortages. She gave the stick to one of the colored girls, who crouched to begin copying the words, her tongue pushing out her cheek in her dense concentration. As Claudine straightened up on the stool, she caught Arnaud's eye and smiled at him and perhaps even colored a little as she lowered her head. There was something in her movement that recalled for him an early meeting, though not their first, in France, when he had first desired her. The feeling confused him, but he continued to approach.

"You may go," Claudine said, and as the dismissed children scattered she erased the dust slate with the sole of her worn shoe. Arnaud held out his hand to her and she took hold of it to rise.

"Well, my wife," Arnaud said, with an ease of manner only partly forced. "Are your students attentive?"

"As you see them," Claudine replied.

As she spoke, her eyes connected with his own. They were not rapt upon some hollow, holding phantoms only she could see—she was present with him now. At such moments he was wont to believe that her mind was healed, though he knew from experience that at some later time her thought would fail again into disorder, her eyes haze over on the void, her speech shatter into chants of Revelation, garbled with her private visions.

"That one has some natural quickness," Claudine said, pointing to the colored girl who had copied the phrases in the dust and now ran laughing from teasing boys around the church steps.

"As well as a natural lightness of mind," Arnaud said, watching the child scream and flee.

Claudine frowned to reprove him, and Arnaud repressed any further remark. There was a part of him that responded with frothing indignation to the notion of teaching blacks their letters—it was this sort of practice that led to rebellion, was it not? What could be more obvious? But her stints of teaching, which had been recommended to her by the Père Bonne-chance, seemed to clear and calm Claudine's mind as nothing else could. Therefore, when Arnaud's rage rose up at her fancies, he did his best to swallow it. When he was able (no more than half the time), he even sought to imitate her gentle, unassuming way with the blacks who served them still or whom they chanced to meet. The patience required for this effort was not natural to him. In former times he'd had no patience even for his wife, and now there were a great many moments when his patience failed him altogether.

Below, the red tile roofs of the houses spread to fill the pocket of level

ground between the mountains and the sea. The sun was setting behind
Morne du Cap and the blood-red waves rushed against the pilings of
the harbor front. Doctor Hébert was laboring up the same path Arnaud
had climbed. With a little resentment, Arnaud noticed that the doctor
not only required no cane, but was even able to lend some assistance to
the white-haired old gentleman in his company. It was, Arnaud was startled to recognize, Bayon de Libertat.

Reaching the hilltop, the old man stopped and gasped and pressed
his clawed arthritic hand against his heart. The wind whipped his long
white hair out from his head. Arnaud waited for him to catch his breath
before he spoke.

"I am astonished to see you here," he said, releasing his wife to move
toward the newcomer. "Delighted too, of course."

The two men embraced, then held each other at arm's length. De
Libertat's crippled hand flopped ineffectually against Arnaud's coat
sleeve. Then the old man turned and bowed to Claudine, who curtsied
in reply.

"And when did you return?" Claudine inquired. Her period of lucidity
was sustaining itself, Arnaud noted.

"Oh, I have been here for quite some time—but quietly, you know, at
Bréda." De Libertat looked about with his pale blue eyes. "At first it
seemed unwise to appear in the town." His expression clouded slightly.
"Perhaps it is still unwise."

"Would that Commissioner Sonthonax were such a friend to ourselves as he is to the blacks." What Arnaud really wanted know was
whether Bréda was again producing sugar—such rich land, far better
than his own—but he hesitated to ask directly. Commending himself to
patience, he took his wife's hand back on his arm.

Doctor Hébert was looking up at the three crosses, hands on his hips
and his short beard jutting.

"How came this church here?" Arnaud said, turning to De Libertat.

The old man turned his working hand palm upward. "Abandoned by
the Jesuits," he said.

They looked at the church, a white board rectangle, raised on a stone
foundation high enough to require five wooden steps to the door. On the
peaked roof was balanced a small square belfry. As they watched, the
bell began to ring.

"Vespers," the doctor said. "*Allons-y?*"

They strolled together toward the church steps, Arnaud in the rear,
Claudine depending on his arm, her head demurely lowered. To their
left, the long seed pods of the flame tree shivered in the wind. Together
they mounted the steps to the church. Arnaud felt a certain heaviness;

regularity of religious observance was not natural to him. He glanced down at the curve of her cheek—pleased to remind himself how the little weight she had recently gained had partly erased the harsh lines that had marked her gaunt face these last years. She looked younger. Confused by his fugitive emotion, Arnaud caressed the back of the hand which lay so lightly on his inner forearm.

The congregation was small: only the children Claudine had been instructing, the woman Fontelle, who was mother to the older colored girls, and a few blacks from the *bitasyon* on the knoll behind the church. Though the room was half empty, the white party settled on a puncheon bench to the rear. Near the sanctuary, a waist-high drum spoke in a slow, guttural tone. Arnaud started. In his experience, the drums portended unrest, sometimes attack. But this drum's voice was slow and sonorous as a processional phrase from a pipe organ.

Moustique walked into the sanctuary from a side door, bearing a silver chalice before him like a grail. He wore a long, off-white vestment fashioned roughly from a sheet, but the stole round his neck looked authentic.

"See how she beams," the doctor whispered, aiming his beard's point at Fontelle. "The mother of a priest."

Arnaud nodded, glancing at the turbaned mulattress, who did indeed have a very large smile spread over her long jaw. That twinge of feeling touched him again. He recalled again how, when his feet were torn and bloody from walking the roads barefoot from Ouanaminthe, Fontelle had poulticed and bandaged them, so that they could carry him farther from the mortal danger. He took his wife's right hand, the whole one, in his left and pressed it.

Moustique set the chalice on a wooden table covered with a bluish cloth. He stepped in front of this makeshift altar to address the congregation.

"*Que l'Esprit Saint soit avec vous.*"

The children answered him in Creole, and then, following a few notes from the drum, began singing portions of the liturgy. Bayon de Libertat's white hackles were rising; he stirred restively on the bench.

"But this is no true priest," he complained.

"*C'est un prêtre savane,*" the doctor replied, tranquilly. "A bush priest."

Arnaud made an effort to concentrate his mind on the service. Like most Creole colonists, he had honored his religion mostly in the breach, except during the period of his education in France, which had been supervised by priests. He looked at Claudine somewhat uneasily, for sometimes the church ritual would fling her into one of her transports. But for the moment she seemed calm enough. Arnaud fell to turning his cane, its corkscrew involution passing the curls of his fingers like a screw in well-worn threads. His own character, he mused idly, as Moustique intoned the passages of scripture, was twisted in like manner—his short temper, greedy self-regard, and zest for certain cruelties braided and coiled together with the gentler, more forebearing self which, when he remembered the Père Bonne-chance and the debt of atonement he owed to Claudine, he sometimes tried to be.

What if there were really a Hell, he thought suddenly, as Moustique's voice hummed on. If so, he was certainly destined for that place. The poisoned, corrupted parts of his soul would surely drag down those other elements of himself with which they were entwined. Images boiled over him—his own hands nailing the hands of a rebellious Negro to a post, severing the leg of a runaway, lopping off nostrils, grinding a branding iron into charred flesh. He had compelled one slave to eat his own amputated ears, had ordered another to be ground to bloody pulp in the cane mill he had tended . . . All these actions seemed those of some other person, as if demons had entered his body to accomplish them, and yet they were his very own. Arnaud began to sweat heavily, as if stricken by a sudden fever. Sweat-slick, his fingers lost Claudine's hand.

Moustique was reaching the climax of his sermon, to which Arnaud had not much attended, but now he was caught by the flourish with which the boy produced a small stone carving from his long, loose sleeve.

"Just so, the Holy Spirit descends upon us on the earth . . ." Moustique swept his hand, cupping the carving, down toward the chalice. It was a stone relic of the *caciques,* a bird with wings folded, like a stooping hawk. The stone bird vanished as if into the chalice, but reappeared suddenly in Moustique's other hand, whirling high above his head. Bayon de Libertat grunted in irritation at this sleight of hand.

"In the First Beginning," Moustique announced, "the Holy Spirit moved so upon the waters, to create the world." The bird disappeared into his sleeve. He turned to genuflect before the cross.

Now they were singing the Sanctus in Creole, while Moustique chanted a hodgepodge of Latin phrases (Arnaud would not have known the difference except for Bayon de Libertat's sniff). Moustique elevated a round of cassava bread, and then was pouring from a gourd into the chalice, not wine, Arnaud could see, but water. His words too were unorthodox, from the marriage at Cana instead of the liturgy, ending with the phrase *you have kept back the best wine until now.*

Bayon de Libertat was embracing the doctor, giving him God's Peace. The old man turned and gave Arnaud the same quick hug, muttering *la paix* into his ear. Then he made his way to the center, crossed himself before the altar, and left the church. Arnaud was facing his wife, then holding her so hard and close he felt her heartbeat. *La paix*. His eyes spilled over. They released each other. Arnaud was still sweating terribly, the residue of his fear.

Now they were filing toward the altar, the white people following the black. Arnaud did not want to go to the rail, but by a force like gravity he was drawn to follow Claudine. As he knelt beside her, he recalled that if he received the Host in a state of sin, there would be no forgiveness. But it was too late; Moustique had slipped the sweet cassava into his jaws and he had shut his teeth on it. When Moustique made a second pass, he stopped and gave Arnaud a perplexing look and with a finger wet from the chalice sketched the cross upon his forehead. Arnaud's lips met the silver rim. He nearly choked, for after all it was only water.

Outside the church considerably more people were gathering than had attended the service. Bayon de Libertat was nowhere to be seen.

"I believe he was in a hurry to return to Bréda," the doctor said to Arnaud's question. "This issue of the *émigrés* has become very thorny, even though Bayon enjoys the best of Toussaint's protection and goodwill."

"How well I know it," muttered Arnaud, who would himself be counted as an *émigré*. The ocean breeze had dried his sweat again, and he felt very much more himself. His former self. "But all this comes from Sonthonax," he burst out irritably, twitching his cane against his thigh. "One does not encounter such prejudice from Laveaux, nor even from Toussaint." The familiar fabric of his fears and interests and resentments closed around him like a cloak.

The doctor turned his face toward the water. It was dark, the moon just rising from the waves. Arnaud subsided. He knew that the doctor was privy to the councils of Toussaint with Sonthonax, and also that he served as intermediary between them when they chanced to disagree. It piqued him, sometimes, that his own hopes were strongest with Toussaint, that this former slave tricked out as a general should be in better sympathy with the old plantation owners, whom Sonthonax had damned as aristocrats and *émigrés*. At other times he saw more plainly that he must accept Toussaint's favor, and even court it, if he and Claudine were to survive in this land.

But now the drummer was coming down the steps from the church door, with the great drum hoisted on his shoulder, gripped by one of the heavy pegs which tuned the head. A current in the gathering on the hilltop moved Arnaud to follow him around the rear of the building. Claudine was in the van of this procession, walking between Moustique and

Fontelle. Also near her was the black major, Joseph Flaville, though, as he was not wearing his uniform, it took Arnaud a moment to recognize him. He followed, but the others had closed the gap between them; he could not reach his wife.

They were walking down over broken ground, stepping over ditches slashed by runoff from the mountain. The *ajoupas* on either side of their way seemed to be empty now, but there was a hum of voices from an enclosure further ahead: an oval shut off by flat shield-shaped panels woven of palm fronds. Torchlight from the interior pushed up against the bluish light of the moon.

Crossing a ditch, Arnaud slipped on a stone and fell but caught himself on a fist and scrambled up the other side, his stick trailing uselessly. Claudine had already crossed into the peristyle, but when Arnaud reached the opening in the palm panels, two black women crossed a pair of lances, draped with flags, to bar his way.

"*W pa kab pasé,*" said one, her eyes remote beneath the crease of her red headcloth. "*Sé pa pou blanc.*"

"But—" Arnaud began. The doctor was plucking at his elbow. He let himself be led away. You cannot pass, the woman had said, it is not for whites. But Claudine had entered there. A path led around the outside of the frail palm-paneled wall, through which the torchlight flickered, and then more roughly to a ledge that ascended to higher ground above the peristyle.

"Here," the doctor muttered, coming to a halt. "They will not mind us."

Craning forward, Arnaud nearly toppled into a brushy ravine below the narrow ledge. He braced his stick on the crumbling dirt and pushed himself back. They were looking into that pagan temple as if into a bowl. Arnaud could make small sense of what he saw. A throng of blacks milled about inconsequentially under the light of burning splints of *bwa chandel.* Disorder in all directions, so far as he could see. The big drum from the church had been placed between two smaller ones that played a rhythm full of dismaying shifts and dislocations, and someone was chanting words he could not understand. Divested of his priestly robe, Moustique capered about like some lord of misrule, circling backward round a central post, a cutlass wheeling, shimmering in his hand. From a distance, Fontelle and Joseph Flaville watched soberly, shifting from foot to foot. Arnaud looked everywhere but could not find Claudine.

The beat of the drumming changed, and a new hub of interest began turning in the crowd, a circle opening round a huge black woman, whose face was a mask of caked white clay. Eyes slitted, she rolled her hips in a billowing motion, her skirts held high and tight against her buttocks and her thighs. Arnaud was riveted to her movement, just as all those who stood encircling her were, but it was something deeper than sex, a still more primal power.

"Maman Maig'," the doctor breathed, as if confirming something to himself, and at his words Arnaud recognized the midwife in this undulant figure who both was and was not her. The circle stretched into an oval and another dancer was admitted, dressed all in white with a white headcloth. By comparison her movement was pale and ghostly, like the tossing of an empty sheet in the wind. Her skin was white also—Claudine, Arnaud realized, in different clothes . . .

At the very moment of his recognition, she shrieked and tore at her head with both hands. Her cry was that of a damned soul or someone being flayed alive. The thought came to Arnaud that all he saw—the thrust of torch flames and insistent drums and guttural chanting and the grotesquely seductive dance—was part and parcel of the Hell he had imagined in the church and which, in her episodes of madness, he imagined Claudine to inhabit. Hell made immanent. All that these same people had performed in the church was sham, and what it covered up was this. He lunged in Claudine's direction, but the doctor caught him up and he let himself be detained, mouth agape, watching: Claudine had toppled backward and lay in the crook of Maman Maig's great fleshy elbow as if floating on a wave of the night sea, while certain congregants stroked her hands ("They will not harm her," the doctor was saying) and still others whispered in her ears to calm her or inspire her. In Maman Maig's free hand a gourd wrapped in bead strands rattled— once, twice, again, and Claudine rolled forward on her heels, regained her balance and took a stiff step forward as the people scattered away from her.

"They will not harm her," the doctor repeated. "You see how they respect her."

"But what can this be?" Arnaud hissed. He had seen her so before in her fits of madness: stiff angular posture and glittering eye and movements trembling with a terrible rigor. He felt now that the doctor was correct. They had not harmed her. Rather they were helping her, in ways he'd not been able to divine.

"What can it mean?" he said, as his breath sighed out of him.

"I do not know," the doctor murmured. "Only that, by their belief, Claudine is herself no longer—one of their gods has entered in her place."

"The Devil!" Arnaud said, cold to the core despite his words' heat. The echo of her scream still pierced him like a frozen blade. "You mean she is possessed by a demon." In his confusion he remembered the story of Christ driving demons from the man they rode into a herd of pigs, and at the same moment wondered if he'd damned himself to the same end by taking the sacrament unshriven. Over the cliff with the swine into the pit . . . Hair stood up on his neck and arms, but he felt the doctor touching his forearm and calming. He watched his wife, moving with a step unlike her own, addressing the congregants who swirled about her with a fierce authority.

"I would not say as much as that," he heard the doctor saying. "It may be that they do not imagine angels and demons in the way that we do. I know that when one of their spirits descends, they don't imagine it comes for ill."

Some few days later, riding south to Gonaives, the doctor revisited the scene in his reflections—Moustique had given him some introduction to those African mysteries; had shown him where he might stand to watch without, himself, being observed by the celebrants . . . but he hardly knew what to make of what he saw. Perhaps it was Mesmerism . . . some African strain of Magnetism—how would they have come by it? According to rumor, some European mountebank had introduced a corrupted version of Mesmer's practice among the colonists of Le Cap, shortly before the insurrection, and so the blacks might have absorbed it from their masters . . . yet the doctor felt it was not so. Unconsciously he touched the shard of mirror in his pocket. After these observances, if not because of them, Claudine was calm and lucid, seemed perfectly sane and even almost contented, as if she had been cured. If that were so, what did it matter if he understood?—though certainly Michel Arnaud would be less easily persuaded. The doctor let the rumination go. They had passed Plaisance and the crossroads for Marmelade and were descending toward the coast and the port town. On either side of him, the helmet plumes of Toussaint's guardsmen tossed in the dry wind.

At the foot of Pilboreau the road inland to Ennery attracted him, but though he would very much have liked to see Paul and Sophie and his sister again, he could not stop. Perhaps on the return. His mission to Gonaives was too urgent, too delicate. The wax seal of Sonthonax's letter chafed against the inner lining of his coat.

From the moment of Sonthonax's return to Saint Domingue, there had been a certain prickliness between him and Toussaint. Nothing overt, no open conflict. On the face of it there was scarcely any difference of opinion between the two. Sonthonax had not quarreled with Laveaux's appointment of Toussaint as Lieutenant-Governor of all the

colony; on the contrary it agreed very well with his own policy to promote black men to posts of high leadership. Early in June, Sonthonax
had declared it a crime for anyone even to say aloud that the freedom of
the blacks was not irrevocable, or that one man might own another. And
yet the doctor sometimes felt that Toussaint was not entirely overjoyed
to see the commissioner acclaimed by the freed men as author of their
liberty.

He struggled to put these thoughts from him. A short way south of
the Ennery crossroads, he called a halt and dismounted to buy a pannier
of mangoes from the market women gathered in the shade between the
river and the road. He shared out some fruit among the men of his
escort, and took a piece to eat himself—the mangoes were too ripe for
slicing, so eating them involved one's whole face. The guardsmen
grinned at each other, sucking the pulp of the seeds; the doctor's beard
got sticky from the juice. He washed his hands and face in the river
stream before they mounted and rode on. The balance of the mangoes
he'd present to Toussaint and his family.

In the midafternoon they came to the *caserne* at Gonaives, where the
doctor found Captain Maillart, attached to the headquarters as an aide-
de-camp. Toussaint was away, but was expected before evening.

"What news?" the captain cried, holding the doctor's horse as he
dismounted.

"Dispatches," the doctor said, "and mangoes." He opened his coat to
show the commissioner's seal on the letter he carried.

"I'll leave you that delivery," the captain said.

"As bad as that?" the doctor said, letting his coat fall shut as he unfastened the pannier of fruit from his saddlebow.

"I don't say so," the captain said, looking about uneasily, and lowering
his voice, "only the commissioner never got on so well with our general
as when they were passing out those muskets to the cultivators."

"But of course," the doctor, said, ruminating as they walked toward
the building.

He had witnessed a few of those scenes—products of Sonthonax's
first exuberance at returning to the colony. Under Toussaint's escort, he
had convoyed out onto the northern plain or into the mountains round
Limbé, with wagonloads of muskets shipped from France. With his own
hands Sonthonax had distributed the weapons, sometimes brandishing
a firearm before delivering it into eager hands, and constantly repeating
the phrase which had become the motto of such occasions: "Whoever
would take this weapon from you would take away your freedom!" Wild
cheering greeted all such demonstrations, while Toussaint smiled behind
his hand, or moved to loosen the canvas from the wagon beds, no doubt

calculating all the while that all those guns would sooner return to his own command than to that of the Commission . . . which had sailed into port with thirty thousand muskets, four hundred thousand pounds of powder, but only nine hundred European soldiers.

The doctor had discussed the implications of that situation with the captain before, but now was not the moment to revisit the topic—there were too many of Toussaint's black subalterns standing about within earshot as they stepped beneath the door lintel to enter the shadows within the building. In the inner courtyard, the doctor drank the glass of rum that Maillart offered him, then pulled off his boots and stretched out on a borrowed cot. For a time the cot seemed to sway with the same motion as his horse. He thought how those muskets had seeded the hills. Thirty thousand former slaves equipped with muskets—did Sonthonax imagine that he ruled them? In case of conflict, those men would much more likely respond to the discipline of Toussaint—if to any rule at all. Toussaint of the opening. Strange numinosity in the phrase he'd chosen for his name. He of the aperture, the gap, the tear in the fabric of the world that had been before. With that the doctor fell unconscious and slept until dark, when someone came to let him know that Toussaint had arrived and was ready to receive him.

In a small private office Toussaint waited for him, alone; he had asked for a service of coffee but sent the orderly away. Now he motioned the doctor to serve himself. It was close and warm in the little room, though outdoors the evening breeze stirred litter on the street. Doctor Hébert produced the letter, and Toussaint set down his coffee cup to accept it. He cut the wax seal with his thumbnail and sat back, crossing his leg and pursing his lips as he held the document high toward the light.

> *In one of my last letters, dear General, I let you know that your children would be able to leave for France on the battleship* Wattigny; *as we must order this ship to depart very soon, I beg you to send them to me at once; they will stay with me, and I will offer them every friendly attention up until their departure . . .*

The doctor stirred sugar into his coffee and drank. He was still woozy, from having slept in the daylight and awakened after dark, but the strong brew returned him some lucidity. Toussaint held out the letter toward him, indicating he should read.

> *You can count on all my solicitude, and that of General Laveaux, that your children will be brought up in France in a fashion which corresponds to your views. Rest assured that the Minister of Marine,*

who is my close friend, will offer them all the protection of the Republic.

Doctor Hébert set the letter on the desktop and reached again for his coffee.

"The *Wattigny*," Toussaint said, "is the same ship in which Villatte and his partners in crime were deported."

"A warship sufficiently well armed to force the British blockade," the doctor said carefully. "This passage has been arranged to ensure the safety of your sons."

Tousaint folded the letter so that the edges of the wax seal were rejoined, and spread his fingers out across the paper, leaning forward. The back of his hand was netted with pale spiderweb creases in which the white dust of the roads round Gonaives was permanently engrained. His son would be safe on the *Wattigny*, the doctor reflected, and also safeguarded, and also under guard.

"The commissioner has established schools at Le Cap," Toussaint said. "For the sons of the colored men, and equally for the sons of the blacks. He has made it known that in the future no man will be promoted officer who cannot read and write his name."

"It is so," the doctor said.

"I have taught my sons to read and write," Toussaint said. "Their names, and more. They have read Holy Scripture, and something of natural philosophy as well."

The doctor nodded.

Toussaint lifted his hand from the letter and leaned back in his seat. "You may know," he said, "that under slavery, only the *gens de couleur* might send their sons for education in France. Sons of black men, even if free—even if born in freedom—had no such opportunity. For that one had to have a white father, a white grandfather. But now—it is well for my sons to see the French Republic with their own eyes and be instructed in the duty of French citizens."

But they will be hostages! the doctor thought. Don't you see that? Of course, he knew that Toussaint had seen that point but had also somehow seen beyond it. It was not easy to plumb his thinking, and in such a project instinct often served one better than reason. When Sonthonax had ordered the arrest of Bayon de Libertat, the doctor's instincts shouted that it was most impolitic to interfere with Toussaint's personal loyalties in any such way. Many had so advised Sonthonax, even Pascal who had come out from France as secretary to the New Commission, but Sonthonax, the great abstractionist, saw nothing but the principle. Though soon enough Bayon de Libertat had gone free.

"Perhaps my sons will even learn Latin," Toussaint was saying.

"No doubt they will," the doctor said. "Mathematics, too." It occurred to him that if his sons were to be surrendered as hostages, Toussaint might well hold the entire colony hostage against their safe return.

"You will find them ready to depart," Toussaint said. "Placide and Isaac. Saint-Jean will not make the voyage at this time. He is too young— his mother is against it."

"Very well," the doctor said. His mission was accomplished and with much less trouble than he had expected, so why did he feel consternation where relief ought to have been?

"You will not find them here," Toussaint continued. "They are with their mother at Ennery—a property I purchased there as a retreat." He smiled, raising his hand to cover his mouth momentarily. "It is convenient to Habitation Thibodet, should you wish to pay a visit to your sister."

"Very much so." The doctor stood, feeling himself dismissed. "But I brought mangoes, for your family—" He recalled that he had left the pannier underneath the cot where he had slept.

"Then take them with you to Ennery," said Toussaint. "Or no—They need no more mangoes at Ennery. The officers here may enjoy them."

"Accept a couple for yourself as well." But the doctor remembered as he bowed out that Toussaint's front teeth had been loosened by the spent cannonball that had struck him in the face outside Saint Marc, and since then he did not gnaw fruit.

The journey from Gonaives to Ennery was brief, but the doctor made an early start so as to have the greater part of the day with the children. Paul was older now, and bolder. He rambled all over the plantation on his own, and was a frequent visitor to the black encampment, where he had struck up a friendship with Caco who was Riau's child. The two boys were constantly together, wandering between the *ajoupas* and the *grand'case,* but Sophie was still included in their games.

He and Elise supped early, with the children at table, and afterward he put Paul to bed himself. When the boy had fallen asleep, Doctor Hébert rejoined his sister on the gallery. As he sat down, she pinched out the candle with her fingers, leaving them alone in the moonlight and the faint scent of jasmine that grew below the railing.

"You find Paul well, I trust," Elise said.

"I do," the doctor said.

"He still asks for his mother sometimes," Elise said. "Not so very often, but when he wakes at night."

To this the doctor found nothing to say. He had no word or inkling of Nanon. Vallière was still cut off. The scattered bands of Jean-François had accepted Sonthonax's guns but had at once turned them against the Republican troops, swarming over the valley of Grande Rivière and harassing Moyse at Dondon. It was rumored they were also being armed and incited by the English.

"I have heard nothing from Xavier," Elise said. "No personal word, that is, for sometimes he sends money. And gathers intelligence too, I imagine."

"So far we are in the same case," the doctor said, though it occurred to him that he had no such way of knowing that Nanon was even still alive.

"Yes," said Elise, and turned to face him, the moon shining in the dark hollows of her eyes. "One must have faith, and hope. I have done what I can to make things right." She bowed her head for a moment and then raised it. "So as to be at peace with myself, at least. No matter what may come from another."

Her hand crept across the table toward him. The doctor took it in his own.

"*La paix,*" he said, as if in church. He pressed her hand, and went on holding it. Linked thus, they faced the cool light of the moon.

The Desfourneaux plantation, which Toussaint had acquired, abutted upon Habitation Thibodet, just as the black general had said. The doctor arrived there early the next morning to collect the boys, having sent word of his coming in advance. They were ready for him, their small valises packed. Suzanne waited with them on the gallery of the Desfourneaux *grand'case*, now her own house. Madame Louverture!—consort to the great and terrible black general. But she gave herself no airs at this elevation, dressed in no higher style than a country woman on market day: a clean, pressed cotton dress with an apron, a blue *mouchwa têt* bound tight to her brow. Her face was wonderfully calm, expressionless, as the doctor bowed over her hand. She embraced the boys quickly, Isaac and Placide, and with a little shove sent each of them from her, toward the gallery steps.

The lads had their own horses—good ones too—and were quick and confident in the saddle, as one would expect of Toussaint's sons. Both kept their eyes on the road ahead as they rode out. Only the doctor looked back once, to see Suzanne standing mute in the doorway of the house, her hands hidden in her clothing, while Saint-Jean peeped from behind her skirts.

Doctor Hébert had a liking for both boys, especially Placide, whom he took to be the more intelligent. Isaac clowned all the way up the mountain to Plaisance and beyond. He persuaded one of Toussaint's guardsmen to lend him a plumed helmet, so much too large for him that it kept slipping down over his face. Whenever this happened, the boy's blind movements would make his horse shy and threaten to buck, and though Isaac could easily bring his mount under control, he would not give up the helmet, so that the same scene kept repeating itself through-out the journey. Placide, meanwhile, asked constant questions, about the ocean voyage, about life in France, about the Collège de la Marche where he and his brother would be enrolled, at such a level of detail that finally the doctor could no longer answer them.

Sonthonax received the boys in his house as he had said he would, treating them with the greatest consideration. Laveaux also, whom they had been taught to regard as a distinguished uncle, called on them, and gave them many hours of his time during the two days prior to their departure. The doctor turned out on the waterfront to see them board the *Wattigny,* and as they stepped down onto the deck of the ship and disappeared from his view, the notion struck him: *What if they do not return? What if I never see them again?* But this was one of those wandering, unattached thoughts that sometimes brushed him in the colony—it was not properly his own.

Then, at the height of the fever season, the doctor had all the practice he could desire among the newly shipped soldiers, who were all suf-fering the usual maladies of acclimatization. Enlisted as messenger and liaison between Sonthonax and Toussaint, he was too often on the road to bother renting a room at Le Cap. At first he slept in the *casernes,* among his military patients, but when Isabelle Cigny learned of this, she insisted that he come to her. Arnaud and his wife were semi-permanently installed in the Cigny house, if Arnaud were not away tending his cane fields on the plain, and as the house was also fre-quented by military and civil servants both black and white, it was a good place to capture gossip from all quarters. At night the doctor retired to the small attic room Nanon had once occupied. This floor of the house had been burnt completely in the sack of the town in ninety-three, but Choufleur had restored the room just as it had been, com-plete with the small round window under the eaves.

Throughout the summer the English kept Toussaint occupied with inconclusive skirmishing along the Artibonite. Rumors from the south, where the mulatto general Rigaud commanded, ran to scandal and catastrophe. Sonthonax had sent three delegates—Kerverseau, Leborgne, and Rey—with instructions to undermine the mulatto oligarchy as they found it possible, to investigate the role the southern *gens de couleur* might have played in the Villatte rebellion, and particularly to ship the notorious Pinchinat to Le Cap in order that he might explain his conduct to the commissioners. The delegates proved adept at stirring up trouble, but Leborgne outdid the others by seducing Marie Villeneuve, a colored beauty of Les Cayes who happened to be engaged to General Rigaud. To put a razor edge on the insult (Isabelle Cigny found this detail peculiarly delicious), Leborgne invited Rigaud to his rooms "to see the most beautiful woman in town," then drew back his bed curtain to reveal to the general's dismayed sight his own debauched and ravished fiancée—Rigaud would have strangled Leborgne on the spot and was well on his way to doing just that, the story ran, when the household servants intervened.

A short while later, Les Cayes erupted in a riot, and a good many whites were slaughtered while Rigaud stood by, wondering aloud, *Why are the people in such a rage?* This time there was no black army standing by to quash the mulatto rebellion, as Toussaint's men had done in the case of Villatte. Sonthonax's delegates escaped the massacre by scurrying to different boats which eventually returned them all to Le Cap. Upon their departure, Pinchinat came out of hiding to reoccupy the house he'd abandoned at Les Cayes, and the whole Southern Department moved into open rebellion against the authority of the Commission. When Sonthonax issued a proclamation outlawing Rigaud, the mulatto officer tied it to a donkey's tail and had it dragged through the streets of the town.

Whenever the doctor visited him, Toussaint was close-mouthed on that whole subject; he had advised Sonthonax to conciliate Rigaud rather than interrogate him, but once the delegation had achieved its disaster, he said no more about it. His mind was fixed on other matters: the campaign he was organizing against the British at Mirebalais, and the election of deputies to the French legislature. *"My General, My Father, My Good Friend—"* he wrote to Laveaux in August,

> *As I foresee (and with chagrin) what unpleasantness is likely to happen to you in this unfortunate country, for whose inhabitants you have sacrificed your life, your wife, and your children, and as I would not like to be witness to such unhappiness, I wish for you to be named deputy, so that you can have the satisfaction to see your own country once again, and be safe from the factions that are gestating in Saint Domingue . . .*

Sonthonax himself stood for election to the Council of Five Hundred at the same time as Laveaux. His motive for this move was hotly debated in the Cigny parlor and around the dinner table. Monsieur Cigny posited that Toussaint himself would engineer the election to rid himself of Laveaux and Sonthonax, whose authority was an obstacle to his ambition, while Arnaud maintained that Sonthonax, seeing his support eroding on all sides and having made as great a hash of his second mission as of his first, sought election as proof of his popularity and as cover for his eventual return to France, where it had taken all his lawyerly dexterity to escape the guillotine, when he had been recalled the first time. Then again, Laveaux's election might have been engineered by Sonthonax and Toussaint in concert, as both had something to gain, potentially, from the Governor-General's departure. It was Isabelle Cigny (strikingly well informed for a woman, the doctor took note) who argued that since the assemblies in France were taking a markedly conservative turn, it must be in the interests of the abolitionists, both Toussaint and Sonthonax, to have their voices heard in the capital and in the legislature.

Whatever his reasons, Sonthonax ordered Toussaint to march on Mirebalais just before the election—to get him out of the way, some said. At the same time he sent the French General Desfourneaux, with whom his understanding was very poor, to attack the rebels around Vallière. The doctor tried and failed to attach himself to the latter expedition, and so was present at Le Cap during the elections, where he observed that the officers in attendance were among Toussaint's best-trusted subordinates. But practically no black officer could be found who was *not* personally loyal to Toussaint (that, Sonthonax had been heard to mutter, was the problem). And so, when Pierre Michel appeared before the electoral assembly, with both his sword and his pistol drawn, and advised everyone that he would destroy the town if Sonthonax and his preferred candidates were not elected, was he acting for Sonthonax, or for Toussaint, or for both of them together?

In the event, both Sonthonax and Laveaux were elected deputies that day. Upon this news, the area around Port de Paix went up in flames, with the field workers burning the plantations and slaughtering the remaining whites, all the while shouting *"Vive Sonthonax!"*—a curious war cry in such circumstances. When the French General Pageot had failed to subdue this insurrection (for want of reliable troops, as he later excused himself), Sonthonax dispatched Toussaint to the scene. Captain Maillart, who was familiar with the region, remained attached to Toussaint's staff during this mission to the northwest peninsula and brought back the report that everything had been settled with no fighting. Though Toussaint had appeared in force, he had stayed his hand—his mere presence was sufficiently calming to the rioters. With a few private conversations and one public oration, he had put an end to the trouble.

You have liberty, Maillairt quoted Toussaint, *What more do you desire? What do you think the French people will say when they see the use you make of the gift they have so recently given you—drenching your hands in the blood of their children?*

How can you believe the lies of those who claim that France would return you to slavery? Do you not know all that France has sacrificed for liberty, happiness, the rights of man?

And remember always, my brothers, that there are many more blacks in the colony than white and colored men combined. So it is for us, the blacks, to maintain order, and by our example to keep the peace.

Thus Maillart recounted the scene from memory, over rum in the barracks, where the doctor had joined him. Toussaint had delivered the speech from the saddle of his warhorse, with his troops drawn up behind him, their arms at rest. Certainly there had been threat behind his persuasions, but the persuasion evidently had sufficed. The cultivators had carried their implements back to the fields; once again all was calm.

"Of course," Maillart said, pausing to suck smoke from his cheroot, "he had suborned all the leaders beforehand. Or rather, he'd brought them back to the fold of the Republic, for they'd first been suborned by the English at Le Môle."

"But," said the doctor, "was it not the election of Sonthonax that set off all this clamor?"

The captain raised his legs onto his cot and leaned back against the plastered wall. Alarmed by this movement, a gecko retreated higher on the wall, farther from the orb of candlelight englobing the two men.

"True, he said very little about Sonthonax," the captain mused, "but I think he managed to give the impression that the blacks could get along as well without him as with him."

On October 16, 1796, Governor-General Laveaux boarded a ship for France, where he would take up his legislative duties. With him he bore the strongest testimonials of Toussaint's filial devotion, and also many messages for Toussaint's sons in France. His departure left Toussaint without a military superior in the colony, and only one man equal to him in rank: the Frenchman Desfourneaux, who was also a general of division.

By then, Commissioner Giraud had returned to France, while Commissioner Leblanc had died (in circumstances which gave rise to suspicion of poisoning). Raimond, the sole mulatto member of the Third Commission, was keeping his profile discreetly low, while Roume was more or less incommunicado in Spanish Santo Domingo. The French General Rochambeau had failed to take possession of the Spanish half of the island, which a clause of the Treaty of Basel had ceded to France. Subsequently Rochambeau had been deported by Sonthonax, for this failure and an air of insubordination surrounding it. Meanwhile the Spanish continued to violate the treaty in various covert ways, supporting the English invaders as they might, especially on the border around Mirebalais.

Now thoroughly detested by the mulatto factions, and generally mistrusted by most of the whites, Léger Félicité Sonthonax was still very popular among the vast majority of the newly freed blacks, and he remained the highest civil authority in Saint Domingue. Though he'd been elected to the French Assembly at the same time as Laveaux (and though his enemies in that increasingly reactionary body had engineered an order for his recall), he seemed to have no plans to leave the colony.

25

"Mesdames, messieurs, les jeux sont faits," Maillart said gaily.

In fact the only lady present was Elise, looking on benignly though she did not play. Across the table from her sat Doctor Hébert, nursing a glass of rum and sugared lime juice; he had not taken a hand in the card game either. Maillart and Vaublanc displayed their cards, and at once Maillart grimaced and sighed and pushed his chair back. With both hands, Captain Vaublanc scooped in the mound of paper scraps from the center of the table.

They'd been at this game for two years or better, and though at first Maillart had been the heavy winner, in the last six months Vaublanc had won back more than half of the highly theoretical property he'd originally staked and lost. Now he arranged the paper slips in ranks, picking up one and then another and squinting at it in the candle light.

"Azor . . . Rosalie . . . Acinte . . . Levieux . . . Lafleur . . . Petit Paul, called by the blacks Bouquart—" Vaublanc halted and brandished the last slip at Maillart. "You'd palm off this one on me, would you?—the beast is worthless, an incorrigible runaway. In ninety-one he was still at large. Give me another."

"As you like." Maillart reached into his waistcoat pocket and produced his own store of paper slips, fanning them between thumb and fingers. He selected one and proffered it and then, as Vaublanc reached for it, drew it back.

"Consider," he said, grinning and twisting a point of his mustache. "This Bouquart is here even now, out there . . ." He gestured beyond the gallery rail into the damp, fragrant darkness, beyond the purling sound of the rivulet feeding the pool before the Thibodet *grand'case*. "This Bouquart has been serving in Riau's command, but were he mine, I would not give him up. He is fearless. He stands when the others run away, and inspires them all to turn and fight again. And the strength of him—what a specimen you have there."

"A Mondongue," Vaublanc grumbled. "Useless in the fields . . . a *bossale* who would never bow to the yoke."

"You do not surprise me," Maillart said.

The talk stopped, while in the outer darkness the wind rose and rushed through the leaves and then subsided. The doctor tasted his rum and rolled the glass between his palms. He pondered. In France, that other Vaublanc of the National Assembly, who was the captain's distant kinsman, was demanding that Sonthonax be brought to account for all the losses of property he was supposed to have occasioned in Saint Domingue, and behind him was arrayed the whole faction of dispossessed, exiled colonists, whose influence seemed to be waxing. If by some chance slavery were to be restored, would the card game suddenly turn serious? For Maillart, the doctor thought, it was no more than sport, but Vaublanc had actually once owned those people whose names were written on the slips.

Elise bid them good night and went into the house. Maillart leaned forward to light a cigar stub at the candle flame.

"Where is your famous brother-in-law?" he said. "The tobacco here is nearly exhausted."

To this the doctor said nothing. Maillart blew smoke toward the overhead fan, stilled for the want of a servant to pull the rope, its blades festooned in spiderweb.

"Simcoe," Maillart said.

Vaublanc looked up at him cannily. "A fighter, that one. They say he's landed thirty thousand troops."

"A fighter indeed," said Maillart, "and the first the British have fielded—since Brisbane."

"*Exactement.*" Vaublanc picked up the cards and shuffled and bridged and let them flutter into a single deck. The pasteboards were sticky from heat and damp and the touch of many sweating hands. "One does not like to be unpatriotic," he said, "but men like Dessources, or the Vicomte de Bruges—"

"We have already learned their caliber," Maillart said.

"Quite so," said Vaublanc. "I think that General Simcoe may provide us with a more interesting experience."

Doctor Hébert drained his glass and set it on the table; nodding to the officers, he got up and went into the house. Zabeth was just leaving Paul's room for Sophie's. When he went in, the doctor found the boy lying quietly under the sheet in the light of a candle, looking up at the shadows of the ceiling. Paul turned his eyes to him gravely, then looked away and up once more. The doctor sat down at the bedside and began telling him a story, interspersed with snatches of song in Creole, though he was no singer. He knew that at this time of night the boy missed his mother most, although, determined in his small stoicism, he did not speak of her. Later in the night there would sometimes be bad dreams.

Pauline came in, dressed in a shift for bed, and stooped to kiss the boy's forehead. Smiling shyly at the doctor, she left for Sophie's room where she now slept—still near enough to hear Paul when he cried out with his nightmares. The doctor went on singing softly, the words tumbling and scraping low in his throat, until the boy's hand relaxed in his and his eyes closed and his breathing slowed in sleep.

He carried Paul's candle into his own room, and by its light took off his clothes and hung them on pegs on the wall. He pocketed the silver snuffbox and the mirror shard and set those articles on the bedside stand beside the candlestick. Kneeling, he examined the sacks of herbs and salves and rolled bandages which would be packed into his saddlebags next day. Then he sat down naked on the edge of the bed and meticulously cleaned his pistols and checked the firing mechanisms and reloaded and reprimed them. As he handled the pistols, he thought of Choufleur in quick bright flashes which he tried to repel as quickly as they came to him. His long gun had been seen to earlier and hung ready on its nails above the door.

A mosquito whined around the room, and the doctor stalked it carefully, his shadow looming huge and dark in the candlelight. At last he crushed it against the door jamb, then slipped his legs between the sheets and snuffed the candle. By touch he found the snuffbox and thumbed up the lid. Of late he'd been filling it with sweet-smelling leaves, citrus or jasmine or lavender, as if to mask the faint tinge of rot which in truth had long since evaporated . . . to purge even the memory of corruption.

Dark of the moon: no light came through the jalousies, but the breath of air was fresh and cool. The doctor's bare legs twitched under the sheet. Nanon had shared this bed with him, then briefly with Choufleur (he'd extorted the latter scrap of information from Zabeth). It would not do to think of that. He had been with other women, only once or twice, since Nanon's disappearance, but it was joyless (though the girls were beautiful), dull and distant even at the moment of release. He'd noticed that Maillart, surprisingly, also seemed to have lost his well-established taste for whoring. The doctor turned on his stomach, then on his back . . . he began to think he would not sleep at all, but next he was awakened by the crowing of the cocks.

The muster had begun before dawn and just as the sunlight began to yellow, they were riding out. Morriset, who commanded the dragoons of Toussaint's honor guard, led off the column, with Toussaint back by several ranks, riding among his aides and pocketed by the helmeted dragoons. He sat smoothly, easily erect on his huge charger, the white plume waving gaily in his hat. The women and children were lining their way, watching, calling out to certain men and applauding all of them. The children capered about and ran at the heels of the horses. The doctor saw Paul and Sophie come running from the *grand'case*, pursued by Pauline who was shouting remonstrances, but when she overtook them, she did not make them go back; instead all three joined the other spectators. The doctor pulled his horse out of the line and stood on the bank on the other side of the road, his horse prancing restlessly beneath him. Across the stream of marching men he caught Paul's eye and smiled and saluted the boy with a touch of his finger on the brim of his straw hat. Paul had found Caco, and the two boys were running up and down the line of the march, taking turns rolling a wooden hoop with a stick. The girls, Pauline and Sophie, stood hand in hand watching more quietly; Zabeth had also come out to join them, though Elise was nowhere to be seen.

Maillart's troops passed, the captain winking, grinning at the doctor, then Vaublanc, then Riau, who pulled his horse up to stand where the doctor had halted. Sober, expressionless, Riau reviewed his foot soldiers as they passed. Caco jumped and whooped on the far side of the line, but Riau gave him no notice. He was studying the men in their motley: uniform coats over torn canvas trousers or ragged relics of the tricolor, horizontally striped breeches brought into the colony by republican *sans-culottes*. These breeches were sometimes trimmed down to shorts, sometimes simply shredded to the hip. Many wore straw replicas of European military hats, and some had remnants of the originals in felt, and many wore tricolor cockades pinned to their headgear and were

further ornamented by tribal scarification out of Guinée or brands
inflicted by their erstwhile masters on breast or cheek or shoulder, along
with punitive mutilations: lopped ears and slit nostrils, and some lack-
ing fingers, a hand, an arm, and a few went along one-legged managing a
crutch with one hand and a musket with the other, and some had no
garment whatsover but a binding round the genitals and a belt bearing a
knife and cartridge box, musket in hand and ready. It was this Riau surveyed (the doctor knew): the condition of their weapons.

They passed, and finally Riau raised his head and whirled his hat at
Caco, whereupon Paul and Caco both leapt in the air in the ecstasy
of this recognition and came down clutching one another. The next
squadrons were still marching up, but the doctor fell into the ranks and
rode beside Riau.

That day they came to Petite Rivière and camped around the fort: La
Crête à Pierrot, raised on a peak above the town, with the slow curl of
the Artibonite winding around it. Next day they rode the river valley to
Verrettes, where Toussaint had garrisoned another fort, and there they
crossed the river and pressed on into the mountains to the south. Before
night they came to the crossing of the road that ran from Mirebalais in
the interior to Port-au-Prince, where the English were. They camped
that night at the fort of Gros Figuier. No cart nor anything on wheels
could pass the road to Mirebalais, so during the night the men unshipped
the cannon and took the carriages apart. Next day when they marched
on, Christophe Mornet remained behind with a small detachment to
bar any British coming up that road from the coast. The doctor watched
agape as the men, six or eight to each cannon bore, went loping up the
mountain ledges as if those loads of ironmongery were no more than
bags of feathers.

The valley of Mirebalais and the hills around it were green and fertile, fed by many rivers, large and small; the source of the Artibonite was
not far off, across the Spanish border. The pastures were rich, and there
were many corrals and herds of livestock roving, also prosperous coffee
plantations, most operated by colored men but some also by whites. As
Toussaint's army passed, the field workers laid down their tools and
their baskets and came to the bordering hedges to watch, and sometimes the landowners appeared, raising a hand in neutral greeting.
When Toussaint had occupied Mirebalais two years before, he'd taken
care to put no plantations to the torch; he had kept order, and though
afterward the slave-holding planters had invited the British into the
region, and though they might fear Sonthonax and the Republicans,

they were not hostile to Toussaint (and some of them, indeed, had had secret notice from him of his arrival).

The army did not march directly on the town of Mirebalais, which was strongly fortified and garrisoned by a force of two thousand men under the Vicomte de Bruges. Toussaint contented himself with overrunning the camps on the surrounding heights: Grand Bois, Trou d'Eau and others. The enemy survivors of those skirmishes were driven down into the plain of Cul de Sac, whence they might make their way to Port-au-Prince, perhaps. Toussaint ordered the gun carriages reassembled and began deploying his cannon on the heights above the town. At dusk word came that Christophe Mornet had successfully repelled a sortie from Port-au-Prince: seven hundred men led by the Baron de Montalembert had been driven back. De Bruges would not be reinforced from that quarter.

An hour before dawn of the next day, Riau roused the doctor by waggling his foot, then shushed him with a finger laid on his lips as the doctor jack-knifed from his pallet with a cry of alarm half out of his throat. There would be something interesting, Riau explained, if the doctor wished to accompany him.

They left the camp, a party of ten men on foot, on a path too steep and treacherous for horses, making their way by touch or memory or by the faint light of the setting half-moon. Full daylight found them high in the mountains with the birds just beginning to stir in the leaves, the fruit bats returning to their daytime hiding places, and sunlight spangling out over mountain after jungled mountain: great, green waves of them rolling away in all directions as far as the eye could see. They went on at a brisker pace. Riau had an advance runner who served as a guide. In less than one hour they began to hear dogs barking, and a hairy black hog burst out of the jungle and bolted grunting to the downhill side of the trail.

Riau's advance man pulled up sharply, pointing at a pile of dry leaves sifted across the trail. Another man stooped, lifted the mat beneath the leaves—below was a deadfall mantrap lined with sharpened stakes. A voice spoke from nowhere.

"*Ki moun ou yé?*"

"*Nou moun Toussaint,*" Riau said. We're Toussaint's people.

A wild man stepped from the bole of a tree, naked but for a bead string round his waist. He had such a great mass of matted hair, his head looked to be the size of a bull's.

"Riau?"

"Himself!" Riau smiled broadly and spread his empty hands, fanning them around his head like fluttering leaves.

"Then you may pass," the wild man said, and at that a great number of men like himself stood up from their hiding places above and below the trail, lowering the muskets they had aimed from ambush. The muskets were shiny, new-looking, the doctor noted. A tingle traveled up and down his spine.

The bull-headed wild man led them on a hidden path, his fellows falling in behind him. More dogs were barking and there was poultry clucking, and the doctor began to see corn tassels sticking up among the wild leaves. They came out into a spiral village of stick and mud *ajoupas*. Here a great number of men were already assembled in the open, each carrying a new musket with its light wood and bright metal, their women and children admiring them shyly from the doorways.

"Who are these people?" the doctor hissed.

"Mamzel and the Docko Maroons," Riau told him, glancing toward the leader of the band. "But today, they are our Twelfth Brigade. Toussaint organized them like that, when he was at Mirebalais before."

The doctor digested this information thoughtfully. "And their weapons?"

"The gifts of Sonthonax," Riau said, laughing cheerfully.

To call the Dockos a regular brigade was a stretch of credibility but, under the direction of Mamzel, they moved with a united purpose. They went loping out from their village in a single column, lacing through the mountains with a snake-like movement. Though the heat was mounting rapidly, they held a sharp pace and stopped only rarely for a scant mouthful of water. The doctor poured sweat. His long gun seemed the weight of several cannon—Riau had advised him not to carry it . . .

At last they made a full halt on a peak above a grassy savanna, while Riau undertook a signal with two flags. He scanned the hills beyond the plain with a little spyglass, and he must have seen the answer to his signal, for he told Mamzel they would press on, and quickly. They came down from the mountain and set off at a dead run across the savanna toward the town of Las Cahobas. The doctor jogged with his long gun clasped crossways in front of him, his pistols banging on his hips, his chest about to explode. A herdsman tending cattle on the plain was staring at them, frozen in astonished dismay. A little too late, he caught his horse to ride for the town, but the Dockos ran him down and dragged him from his horse, and one of them swung into the saddle where he had been and rode at the head of their charge. By that time they already heard the ragged sound of gunfire, for Toussaint had struck the town from the other side with his main force, so when the Dockos rushed into the street, the rout of the defenders had already begun, Spanish soldiers and British redcoats scattering in full flight. With a honking of conch shells and high, thready war cries, the Dockos ran after them into the western hills.

Las Cahobas was taken. Riau had rejoined his regular troops and was organizing a house-to-house search for any enemy soldiers who might have gone to earth. Gasping, the doctor limped through the settling dust to the town square, still crading his long gun, which he had not once fired. Below the overhanging roof of a tavern opposite the church, Captains Maillart and Vaublanc sat with a bottle of rum between them; with them was Xavier Tocquet.

Vaublanc half-rose to drag another chair to the table, into which the doctor collapsed with a sigh and a puff of dust from his trousers. He balanced the barrel of his long gun against the table's edge.

"*Hóla,*" Tocquet offered.

"*Bonsoir,*" said the doctor, looking about himself in a daze. Tocquet pushed the rum bottle in his direction.

"Is there water?" the doctor inquired.

In his racing march among the Dockos he had drained the quart canteen he carried, though Riau had counseled him to drink less. The more you drank, the more you sweated, was Riau's idea of the thing, and that was waste. True enough, the doctor had been able to observe that his maroon companions seemed to perspire a great deal less than he did.

"Look inside," said Maillart. "The servants seem to have run away."

The doctor pushed through the slatted door and stood blinking in the dull, dust-swirling light of the tavern's large common room. Five or six of the Dockos were tossing a sizable cask back and forth—each man who succeeded in catching it without letting it fall rewarded himself with a long draught direct from the bunghole. Their hair and faces and shoulders were streaked and shining with spilled rum. One of Toussaint's uniformed officers stuck his head in at the back door and called out a crisp order. Reluctantly the maroons quit their game and filed out, leaving the cask on its side, leaking slightly from the ill-fitted bung.

The doctor investigated behind the counter. Spillage was considerable; his blistered feet sucked in a swamp of rum and sour wine, and flies were coming in at every door and window and crack in the wall. Finally he found a waist-high clay vessel which had survived, upright and covered with damp banana leaves and mostly full of water still cool from river or a well. He dipped a cupful and drank, hiccuping in his haste to swallow. Then he filled a smaller jug with the water, and gathering four cups by their handles, he went back outdoors to the table facing the square.

"*Dlo,*" he announced, passing the cups, and began pouring a tot of rum into his own.

But the mood round the table had gone gelid in his absence.

Across the pack saddles of a string of mules, Jean-Jacques Dessalines was looking their way, immobilizing them in a glowering stare. Tocquet's man Bazau stood holding the lead animal of the pack train by its rope hackamore. Bazau was impassive, still as a tree, but at thirty yards distance the doctor felt his fear.

Dessalines whistled up a grenadier and unscrewed the bayonet from the man's musket barrel. With this implement he loosened a square of sailcloth and drew it back from the packsaddle; beneath the cloth were muskets stacked like firewood. Dessalines moved on to the next mule, and the next, his glare at the white men hardening as he unveiled each load. When he came to the lead mule, he reached around Bazau's shoulders from behind; the movement seemed gentle, almost affectionate, but it pulled Bazau up and back on his heels, with the bayonet point piercing the slack skin under his jaw. Collapsing away from the blade, Bazau gave up his weight to Dessalines. His arms made a trembling movement, but he did not call out. A little blood seeped down the runnel of the bayonet.

The doctor's eye was caught by another movement: Riau, with a couple of his men, crossing the far corner of the square. Riau stopped and studied the details of the scene, and, with no apparent reaction, walked on, behind the church and out of view. Dessalines began to drag Bazau away in the direction of the *caserne,* his eyes always on the white men at the table.

"*C'est moi le responsable.*" Tocquet's voice carried well as he stood up, though it was neither too loud nor especially strained. "The mules and muskets are mine."

At once Dessalines unwound his arm from Bazau and let him reel away. He walked toward the white men, unconsciously wiping the bayonet with his thumb, then licking his thumb clean. Tocquet had moved, clearing the corner of the table; his hands were hidden beneath the loose tail of his shirt. Cautiously the doctor glanced at the barrel of his long gun, in easy reach as it leaned against the table. His pistols too were still primed on his belt. He could smell the bitter, stinging sweat that pulsed from Vaublanc and Maillart. Raising a weapon against Dessalines would precipitate unimaginable disaster. And Dessalines was near enough for the doctor to hear his breathing. The bayonet was reversed in his hand, lying against his coat sleeve. With his free hand he absently touched the spot beside his neck, hidden beneath the gold braid on his coat, where the first raised band of scar tissue commenced, etched there by a stray curl of the whiplash. Tocquet stepped, very softly, to the right, and Dessalines's head tracked him like a beacon.

Dust and hoofbeats in the square. Abruptly Tocquet raised his voice. "General Toussaint?"

In fact Toussaint was just riding into the square, flanked by Morriset and two dragoons of his honor guard. He looked at Tocquet curiously, and more searchingly at Dessalines.

"Mon général, s'il vous pláit . . ." Tocquet performed the deepest of bows, both his hat and his hair sweeping the dust. As he rose up, he gestured at the mule train with his hat. "Accept these weapons as a gift to your soldiers. Victory to the French Republic!"

The cheer collapsed on its own echo. Toussaint said nothing. His mouth covered by his hand, he rode the length of the mule train, studying the loads. He signaled to Bazau, who'd remained standing by the lead mule, to loosen a musket and hand it up. Solid in the saddle, Toussaint aimed the musket toward the church door with both hands, pulled back the hammer and dry-fired the gun, then turned it around to squint into the bore. With half a smile, he gave the weapon back to Bazau.

"With pleasure," Toussaint said. "May these new guns lend us new strength."

Tocquet swallowed. "Allow my man to help you with unloading," he said. "Bazau knows all those pack mules as if they were his kin."

"But of course," said Toussaint. He signaled to his guardsman, and they rode out of the square at a slow trot. Dessalines was drawn after them like iron to a magnet. Leading the mule train, Bazau brought up the rear. As they all departed, Tocquet crossed himself, surreptitiously; the doctor was the only one to see.

"Nom du diable," Maillart said.

The doctor belted the rum he'd poured and served himself another measure.

"Of course you *were* selling guns to the British, one assumes," Vaublanc snapped. "And to the *émigrés,* of course."

"To the highest bidder," Tocquet said, without inflection, and resumed his seat behind the table.

"To be sure," Maillart noted. "I hope you are satisfied with your price today."

"Oh, absolutely." Tocquet pulled a square of yellow madras from beneath his shirt, dried his palms and assiduously wiped his forehead and temples. "And aside from that, there remains still hope of a better profit," he said. "I can furnish a large supply of beef, still on the hoof. Also tobacco—some rather nice Spanish cigars, which I can make available to you gentlemen at very friendly prices."

Maillart glanced at Vaublanc, one eyebrow cocked.

"Excellent," Vaublanc said, and Maillart added, with perhaps a whisper of irony, "Victory to the French Republic."

Next day Toussaint threw his entire force against the surrounded town of Mirebalais, beginning with a brisk cannonade from the heights he had occupied. By noon the town was on fire in four different places, and the Vicomte de Bruges began evacuating his men along the line of retreat that Toussaint had thoughtfully left open, via the fortified camps of Grand Bois and Trou d'Eau. But the British and their *émigré* allies had no time to regroup, for Toussaint's men overran those camps as well, and quickly. De Bruges and his command were obliged to retreat, in great disorder, all the way to Croix des Bouquets, leaving Toussaint in control of the interior. In their flight they abandoned several cannon and other munitions which Toussaint was more than happy to appropriate.

On the day of the battle Toussaint had detached enough men to douse the fires in Mirebalais before very much damage was done. That evening he moved his headquarters into the house of the former colonial administrator—the same house he had taken the last time he'd occupied the town—and set about organizing his dispatches and composing his reports.

Casualties had been less than usual in this campaign so far, so the doctor was not medically occupied for more than a couple of days. He found Guiaou among the troops and put him in charge of the field hospital; Riau also took part in its supervision, and several old women with the status and knowledge of *doktè-fey* had come out of the hills to lend their aid. With those matters well in hand, the doctor was free to attend Toussaint, and to help in the constant review of his correspondence.

Headquarters house was an old building for the colony, mostly of mahogany, under the shade of ancient trees, enclosed by a wall of crumbling, rose-colored brick and surrounded by an elaborate garden which had managed to survive all the wars undamaged. The gallery wrapped around all four sides of the house and was a pleasant place to sit and await one's appointment within. Maillart and Vaublanc were often to be found there, sunk to a less than military posture in fan-backed, rattan chairs. They had abandoned their card game for the time being, as the black subalterns who were constantly in their company here would certainly not have been amused (and some of them were doubtless numbered among the assets staked in the game). Besides, gambling did not suit the mood of that oasis; it was better to sit quietly, not moving a hair, watching the hummingbirds suspended above the blooms of flowers, or listening to the once-tame parrots chattering in the trees. Those parrots spoke several languages: French, Spanish, Creole, English (mostly curses) and perhaps a smattering of Taino (though no one could verify the latter). It was always shady and cool on the gallery, even at the hottest hour of the day, and almost always calm except at evening, when the rains rolled in and the wind swelled up through the leaves of the garden to inspire everyone with the same delicious agitation.

In theory, Toussaint's offensive had been the lower half of a pincer movement; to the north, General Desfourneaux was expected to subdue all the rebellious factions in the valley of the Grande Rivière, occupy Vallière and then move south to the town of Banica, joining Toussaint either in that town or at Las Cahobas, which was not much farther south. Desfourneaux was to conduct these operations in concert with Moyse—perhaps an unfortunate arrangement, as the white and black officers had formed a relationship of mutual dislike, mistrust, and contempt. Whatever the cause, when Toussaint's men reached Banica, they learned that Desfourneaux's force had not managed to win its way so far. Perhaps the northern advance had been turned back outside Banica, or perhaps it had failed before Grande Rivière; the rumors all conflicted, and no one could say for certain what was true. Having nothing better to do and not much resistance to stop them, Toussaint's men took over Banica themselves, but the offensive would penetrate no farther.

Still the success was very considerable, so much so that Toussaint took the trouble to write a proud account to Laveaux in France—or perhaps it was his old habit of reporting always to Laveaux, rather than to Sonthonax, who was now his sole superior in the colony—*I'm letting you know of the happy success of my last enterprise in the region of Mirebalais, The Mountain of Grand Bois, Las Cahobas, Banica, Saint Jean and Niebel, which are all entirely in our possession . . .* And Mirebalais was a rich valley, scarcely damaged by half a decade of riot, war, and revolution. Plantations continued to prosper, mostly under mulatto proprietorship but with some white owners and managers who had hung on, producing mostly coffee, but also some sugar—cash crops for the war effort (though getting the harvests to a port remained a problem, while the British still occupied Port-au-Prince and Saint Marc). Better still, Toussaint had cut the line through which the Spanish had been covertly supplying the English on the coast, or rather he had diverted the supply line to himself. It might have looked odd (as Maillart and Vaublanc were still sometimes heard to mutter to their fellows on the gallery) that Toussaint had chosen to adopt Tocquet as his principal quartermaster rather than ordering him shot—but it was a practical decision, which guaranteed a steady flow of beef and grain and guns and powder and rum and even a little wine from the Spanish half of the island. More-over, everyone rather liked Tocquet, as well as being a little afraid of him; better yet, Tocquet was supplying all the Republican officers—black, white or colored—with a decent trickle of free cigars. . . .

Toussaint was almost always calm, wherever one found him, no mat-ter the circumstances—the same calm like the eye of a hurricane. But during those days at Mirebalais he seemed to have moved toward a deeper tranquillity. Most nights he dined with his staff officers, and he let them tell stories of past triumphs, even encouraged them ever so slightly (though usually he frowned on such anecdotes as boastful, and reproved them with scriptural pieties). Now he seemed to enjoy hearing some junior officer tell how, two years before at Mirebalais, he had astonished the Marquis d'Espinville by showing him the full courtesies of European warfare, d'Espinville who had intended to fight to the death, trapped in the fort with his last eight hundred men, believ-ing that if he surrendered they would all be slain with barbaric African tortures—another French nobleman humiliated not only by Toussaint's greater skill on the battlefield but by his magnaminity after he'd won—some of d'Espinville's men from that campaign were now serving under Toussaint in this one.

Still tastier: the tale of General Brandicourt, whom Toussaint and Moyse had trapped in a ravine in the north. Toussaint had spurred Bel Argent up shaley, near-vertical terrain that would have stopped a Norman knight, crossed the ridge and dropped into Brandicourt's neatly hemmed position—alone—so as to make the general his pris-oner, personally. He compelled Brandicourt, near tears or apoplexy from frustration, to write an order to his second officer commanding him to surrender the balance of his men. With this stratagem, Toussaint had captured a French force twice the size of his own at the time, and by sheer ingenuity of maneuver, without a shot being fired, as if it had all been a chess game. And then, that time at Petite Rivière, when Toussaint had marched his men across a hillside in view of the enemy, then around the back of the hill, and around again, and again until his apparent force was doubled, tripled, quintupled, and the false show of strength won him another improbable victory.

This idyll abruptly came to an end when word came from the west that General Simcoe was marching to Mirebalais with the better part of his thirty thousand fresh British troops. The doctor was present when the dispatch arrived, in council with Toussaint and other aides and scribes in the salon of the headquarters house. There was no ripple in Toussaint's outward composure, yet the quality of his calm altered instantly, returning to that storm-center concentration. No movement, only a slight flaring of the nostrils. Minutes passed, ticked off by the pendulum clock in the hall, while the parrots swore at one another outside in the garden.

"Gentleman, strike the camp," Toussaint said, raising his head as he laid his palms on the table in a smooth gliding movement. "We depart Mirebalais in one hour."

Riau and Vaublanc and the other officers left immediately to execute the order, but Maillart lingered for a moment.

"But General—"

Toussaint, who was gathering his papers and arranging them in his portable writing desk, did not give any sign of having heard.

"Will we not give him any battle?"

"Sir, we will not," Toussaint said brusquely, and then he did look up, with that weirdly ingratiating smile which uncovered only his bottom teeth. "We will march to the coast and capture Saint Marc."

Maillart's eyes widened for just half a second. He snapped a salute and left the house at a run.

Half an hour was more than sufficient for the doctor to roll up his little hospital. Most patients had already taken up their bedding and departed, and the few who remained were fit to travel. There was hardly work enough to be distracting. His mind buzzed annoyingly: would Vallière ever be taken? would he ever see Nanon again? and what did Tocquet mean to do about Elise and Sophie? His saddlebags packed and loaded, his guns in good order, the doctor rode back to headquarters and hitched his horse outside the wall, meaning to spend his last few minutes in Mirebalais overlooking the pleasant garden.

Outside the pale and dusty brick wall came hoofbeats and boot thumps and voices crying orders or complaints. The inside of the house was all abustle too. The doctor sat on the gallery. It was midafternoon and very hot, but if he did not move at all, his sweat would cool him as it dried. Stillness, perfect stillness. He watched faint currents of air stir the leaves, almost imperceptibly, feeling his self move out of his body toward them.

Fey-yo, sauvé lavi mwen . . . That was the herb doctor's sacred song. Leaves o Leaves Oh save my life. . . .

Xavier Tocquet came out of the house with a distracted look, adjusting something on his belt beneath his shirt tail. When he noticed the doctor, he stopped and clicked his tongue.

"Nice while it lasted, no?" With a sigh he fell into the adjacent fan-backed chair.

The parrots quarreled—*Son of a whore! Va t'en faire foutre!* The doctor drew out one of his pistols and laid it on the table between himself and Tocquet and withdrew his hand. This action came from the stillness he had attained; he had not consciously intended to perform it.

Tocquet narrowed one eye at the pistol barrel, which was pointed his way. The doctor produced the other pistol and set it symmetrically alongside the first, its grip presented to his companion. He put his hands in his coat pockets. Mirror. Snuffbox.

"You can't be serious." Tocquet bugged his eyes at the weapons. "This? From you?"

"I should like to know your intentions," the doctor heard himself say.

"My—" Tocquet twisted his hair over his shoulder. "My intentions regarding exactly what?"

The doctor gripped the talismans in his pockets and thought, in silence, of his forlorn sister, while Tocquet looked across the garden, massaging his brows with one hand as if he'd taken a headache.

"I don't suppose I *had* any intentions," Tocquet finally said. "Only there was such a stench of propriety round that place of a sudden, one could not breathe. So I got out of it." He looked at the doctor. "You do understand what she had done?"

The doctor nodded without turning his head, his eyes still on the leaves.

"One might even say I acted on your behalf, my friend," Tocquet said. "It was your arrangements she destroyed, was it not?"

"One might," the doctor said. "But that was then, and now . . . I should like to know your intentions."

Tocquet made a wry face, rocked in his seat. "Things have changed, I know," he said. "I've had word the boy has been brought back to Ennery. One supposes the mother would also be accepted, at this point?"

He looked at the doctor, who said nothing.

"By Christ," Tocquet said, turning his head toward the garden once more. "All the world thinks me an outlandish fellow, but I'll swear that you are still stranger than I. They say you can pick up any man's pistol and hit a skylark on the wing. I don't doubt it. But you must know, there's more than one man who has worked for my death, and I am still walking, while some of them are not. You do not care for killing, you. I would wager you disapprove of dueling—as a matter of principle, no?"

"I should simply like to—"

Tocquet threw up the flat of his hand. *"Assez—m'emmerde plus."* He twisted in his chair, looked out at the leaves, then back at the doctor. "Tell me, if I were to return, would I be received at Habitation Thibodet?"

"Enthusiastically," the doctor said. "By both your wife and your daughter." He paused. "By the entire household, certainly."

"Ah," said Tocquet. "In that case, if you should happen to arrive there before I do, please tell them to expect me very soon."

"That will be my pleasure," the doctor said.

For some minutes neither of them said anything more. Indoors, the clock chimed the quarter-hour. Riau and Maillart came in at the gate of the enclosure and trotted up the steps into the house.

"You did not think you could force me to return," Tocquet said, glancing at the doctor. "No, and you did not mean to fight me either."

"Oh, I don't quite know what I meant," the doctor said. "I only wanted to—"

Tocquet stopped him with a hand on his forearm. "Don't say it, my friend." He leaned a little closer and kissed the doctor on the cheek.

Flanked by Maillart and Riau, Toussaint came quickly out of the house, his hat in one hand, the writing desk clasped under his elbow, a red *mouchwa têt* tied over his head. The red cloth gave the doctor a blunt jab of foreboding. On the gallery Toussaint stopped, laid down his burdens for a moment, and fumbled with something else in his hands. Sparks and the smell of smoke. He was holding up three torches, handing one each to Maillart and Riau. The doctor was up and out of his chair, his jaw clicking down. Toussaint turned and with a ceremonious sweep of his arm flung the torch into the foyer.

"But yes," he said, as he collected the desk and put his hat upon his head. "Burn it." His voice was suddenly loud enough to be heard beyond the wall and all the way to the town square. *Boulé tout kay yo!* Burn down the town.

Riau moved at once, using his torch to set fire to the house at several promising places. Maillart was not so quick to follow suit, but he did obey. The wood, well seasoned, went up quickly.

"Alors, quoi faire?" Tocquet asked rhetorically. He stood up, struck a light, set fire to the chair he'd been sitting in and hurled it through the nearest window into the house. Standing back, he pointed to the pistols still on the table—the doctor hurried to snatch them up.

The heat was sudden and immense, parching the pores on the doctor's face. He and Tocquet left the enclosure quickly. Outside, the troops were all drawn up for their departure. The doctor went at once to quiet his horse; alarmed at the fire, the animal was fighting its tether. Tocquet touched the doctor on the shoulder; they embraced. Already the flames were shooting high above the brick wall, and the parrots were circling out of the smoke.

"I won't go on this adventure to Saint Marc," Tocquet said. "I still have four hundred head of cattle grazing on the central plateau. It's finished here, as I needn't tell you—I'll drive my beef to Dajabón, and then we'll see. Give all my love if you're there before me."

"That I shall." The doctor swung his leg over the saddle and caught up the reins. Looking after Tocquet, he waved and touched his hat brim. But Tocquet had not looked back; he was just breaking into a jog as he turned the corner of the wall.

They rode out, Toussaint at the head of his troops, holding high another torch which was by then mostly symbolic, since the town was well ablaze in all its quarters and the inhabitants had evacuated with much cursing and wailing. Toussaint had made reasonably sure that no human life was sacrificed to the flames, but the householders had had little time to salvage their belongings. As they went westward along the Artibonite Valley, the doctor pictured the old garden of the headquarters house, its leaves and blossoms withering in the heat. Finally the mortar must crack in the outer wall, and all the bricks come toppling down. Two hours yet till the evening rain, and by then Mirebalais would be a field of charcoal.

When the rain did come, the river swelled brown with earth washed out from the cultivated fields, but Toussaint's army marched on, scarcely slackening its pace, the men and horses slip-sliding in the mud. Those with blankets shrouded themselves against the downpour. The doctor was equipped with a long oilcloth duster and the tight weave of his straw hat shed water for the first half hour, but after that everything soaked through and he was as wet as any man among them. When the rain stopped, they halted for two hours, building fires to dry their clothes and blankets, eating light rations, resting as they might, while the rainforest continued to shed water all around them. Then by moonlight or through the dense darkness under the trees, they pressed on in the direction of Saint Marc.

Toussaint had damaged no plantations on the way to Mirebalais—such had never been his policy, and on this occasion his haste was great. But the destruction of the town was sufficient warning to the surrounding planters that it might be better not to become too cozy with the British, with the result that Simcoe found the locals surprisingly aloof when he marched through en route to the pit of sodden ashes which had been Mirebalais, and it took him longer than it otherwise might to gather the intelligence that Toussaint had spiraled around his advance and would soon be threatening Saint Marc, which Simcoe had left mostly exposed, lightly defended by Dessources and his colonial Chasseurs.

By then, Toussaint had already put Dessources to flight any number of times, and probably could have killed or captured him more than once, but it was becoming apparent to some observers (Maillart and the doctor, for example) that Toussaint preferred to leave incompetent enemy commanders in the field, that they might fight and lose again another day. By the time Simcoe managed to reverse his advance and rush back to the defense of Saint Marc, Dessources and the Chasseurs had been cut to pieces one more time, their remnants holed up in the town. Once Simcoe had brought his army back, Toussaint faded his own troops toward Gonaives and the Cordon de l'Ouest; he did not mean to fight a full engagement with such a large force on the Artibonite plain. A chess player's victory of position: Simcoe would not risk another sally toward the interior, and all his fresh men would remain pinned down on the coast. Let fever take them.

In the wake of his uncertain campaign in the valley of Grande Rivière, General Desfourneaux (who got on with Sonthonax no better than with Moyse) was arrested and relieved of his command. Soon after, Toussaint Louverture was notified of his promotion to General-in-Chief of the French army in Saint Domingue. At Le Cap, Sonthonax arranged an elaborate ceremony for the promotion, at which Toussaint was presented with a pair of beautifully chased pistols and, also a gift from the French Directoire, an ornate saber whose blade was engraved with a statement of thanks for the part he'd played in saving Laveaux from the schemes of Villatte.

Throughout this affair, Toussaint was courteous, humble, and curiously withdrawn. There was none of the exaltation he had displayed when Laveaux proclaimed him Lieutenant-Governor. With his new rank conferred upon him, he addressed the crowd in a low tone, saying only that his elevation did him too much honor, that his sole desire was to drive the remaining enemies from the colony and work for the happiness of its true citizens. At the state dinner which followed, he was taciturn, ate nothing but bread and cheese and part of a piece of fruit, refused the wine in favor of cold water.

That night, on the veranda of the officers' quarters in the *casernes,* Toussaint sat late in the company of a few of the black subordinates to whom he was closest: Dessalines, Christophe, Moyse, Maurepas and a few others. The doctor, who'd heard from Maillart that Toussaint seemed indisposed to entertain his white officers that evening, would not have approached, but he was walking with Riau and found that they'd drifted in that direction before he knew it. The chairs were all occupied, so Riau remained standing, while Doctor Hébert sat down on the stone coping at the edge of the veranda with his heels stretched out in the dirt of the yard and his face gazing out into the darkness. If he turned his head, he could see the high, shiny boots of the black officers under the table, shining faintly in refracted candlelight. Though Toussaint still abstained, the rest of them were drinking rum, and when Moyse passed him down a glassful, the doctor accepted it gratefully.

A sputter of conversation in Creole flared up and faded; the doctor paid little mind. He nursed his rum and looked into the dark. Presently a touch on his shoulder roused him; Moyse was showing him Toussaint's saber and pistols for his admiration. The doctor pulled the saber a few inches from its scabbard and glanced at the inscription, then resheathed it. He had no facility with any blade larger than a scalpel. The pistols were another matter. They were beautifully decorated but far from merely ornamental—Manufacture of Versailles, they would shoot true. The doctor aimed each one of them into the dark, held them both together in each hand and grunted in satisfaction at their balance and their weight.

Some further response was clearly called for. "These are handsome weapons," the doctor said, standing up to set the pistols on the table.

"They ought to be," Toussaint said, gathering the sheathed saber against his thigh, "if I have given my sons for them."

The doctor, who thought it best to construe this comment as addressed to the company at large, resumed his seat on the stone curb, recovering his glass which was now almost empty and withdrawing his face from the light.

"Have I not struggled unceasingly against the Spanish? and the English? against all enemies of the French Republic? I have brought victories, and brought order to the countryside, and I have even given my boys into the care of France. Is it possible, after I have offered so much, that my loyalty should be in doubt?"

This plaint ought to have seemed odd, on such a day, but somehow it did not. For no explicable reason, the doctor found himself thinking of how Toussaint had defeated Simcoe by refusing to engage him, so that the British general was constantly unbalanced because he found no resistance anywhere he threw his weight. He tilted his glass and waited for the last few drops of rum to trickle toward his tongue. Dessalines leaned forward to try his palm against the candle flame for a moment, then sat back. Toussaint's words still hung in the air without reply.

"*Nou pa konnen.*" Riau's voice, speaking from the shadow of the pillar where he stood. We don't know. Several of the black officers were murmuring softly, as if they found his words to be apt.

26

August, and the sweltering heat was so overpowering that even the dogs of Le Cap were faint with lassitude, lying under stationary wagons or stretched over baking curbs. Doctor Hébert glanced wearily down at the dogs as he passed them. He and Captain Maillart were climbing the grade from the port; they had tried a promenade along the waterfront, but at this moment no breath of air was stirring even from the sea. Crossing the Place d'Armes at a diagonal, they struggled for a few more sweaty blocks, then paused on the corner of the Rue Saint Louis to let their lather dry before they went on to the Cigny house, where both were invited to dine.

They had come before the appointed hour, but the doctor was still occupying a bedroom in that house, and Maillart seemed sure enough of his reception. As they approached, they saw Isabelle Cigny standing on the second-floor balcony, fluttering a handkerchief in their direction. When they'd reached the portal, she furled the handkerchief around a large brass key and let it drop to the captain's deft catch. Servants were in short supply, and those she had were busy in the kitchen; they must let themselves in, she explained, and she swung her skirts from the filigreed iron railing, through the double doors and into the house.

Maillart unlocked the door and held it for the doctor. Once they had entered, he laid the key in a slightly tarnished tray on the hall stand, retaining the handkerchief bunched in his left hand like a posy. The parlor was empty; they found Isabelle in the kitchen, bullying the cook. Claudine Arnaud sat at the center table, polishing silver knives and forks, with the help of a couple of *négrillons*. She smiled at the doctor's greeting, and went on with her task. One of the little boys went out for water, and on his way he paused to lay his cheek against Claudine's skirt, wrapping one arm around her waist for a moment before he skipped out.

"Remarkable," Isabelle said, turning from the stove to whisper to the doctor. "Her way with them?"

"Quite," the doctor said. He watched Claudine. The boy who had remained was offering a fork for her inspection. She turned it this way and that, peering between the tines, then smiled her approval and set it with the already polished pieces.

"This mania for teaching them to read—who knows where *that* will end, I wonder . . . but those little ones will do anything for her, do it patiently and well, when no one else can get them to do anything at all. And she is specially invited to their dances, you know, those Negro *calenda* —" Isabelle looked up at him, her lips parted and her face flushed from heat, which was still more intense in the kitchen. *Dances indeed,* the doctor thought; Isabelle probably knew or suspected something more than that. He felt probed, but said nothing, knowing she'd not let a silence linger.

"Eccentricity, one might call it," she said brightly, "but—" All at once she affected to notice, for the first time, the captain standing in the doorway. "My handkerchief, if you please," she said to him.

Maillart moved toward the middle of the room, flourishing his cloth posy. "Would I relinquish my lady's favor?" he said teasingly.

"Oh, give it me," Isabelle said, and reached, but Maillart held the pale drape of cloth just an inch or two above her grasping fingers. She stretched out prettily on tiptoe, but the doctor thought her smile was worn a little thin. He ducked his head, slipped out the door and went up the stairs to his garret.

Half a jug of tepid water was on the washstand. The doctor washed his face and hands and torso, then stood by the round porthole, letting the humid air do what it could to dry him as he peered down at the street. He put on a fresh shirt and went down to the second-floor balcony where Isabelle had been standing. Presently Captain Maillart came out through the double doors to join him.

"Well, who captured the handkerchief in the end?" the doctor said.

Maillart contrived a cough. "That game's not worth the candle," he said shortly. The doctor gave him a curious glance, but Maillart was looking the other way down the street.

"Why, here comes our host, I do believe," said the captain. "This affair must have a certain weight, if he's attending."

The doctor leaned out, the iron rail hot against his palms. The burly, bearded figure of Monsieur Cigny was just coming to his door, head lowered and features concealed by his hat brim. Cigny was known for avoiding his wife's entertainments as, in more halcyon days before the insurrection, he'd turned a blind eye to her *amours*.

"It is the commissioner, after all," the doctor said.

"And General Toussaint?"

"I saw him at Bréda, this morning."

Maillart was looking at him sharply.

"Well," said the doctor, "I cannot say if he will come."

Pale dust swirled up at either corner, from the horse and cart and foot traffic of the day's end. Farther off to the south, the noise of the market at the Place Clugny was a distant, monotonous hum. Now, gratefully, they felt a breeze, swiftly rising till it was truly a gust of wind. The clouds were boiling over from Morne du Cap, and people called urgently to one another as they scurried from the street. Maillart's hair whipped around his head. The doctor squinted, one eye tearing around a dust particle that had blown up from the street. The sky was bulging over the mountain, slate blue and gray and purple and black, scored here and there with a rake of lightning. Then it opened, and the rain came down.

Indoors, Monsieur Cigny sat by his lamp, intently reading a two-month-old newspaper from France. He grunted a greeting when the other two men came in. The ladies had withdrawn to dress for the evening; an agreeable brown, spicy smell drifted in from the kitchen. The doctor and the captain sat down opposite one another and, with small concentration, began a game of chess. The narrow arched doors had been closed against the rain, which rushed loudly against them. It was close in the room, but the air, though heavy, was growing somewhat cooler.

"Me voilà en bonne républicaine." Madame Cigny crossed the threshold and dropped into a curtsey, holding the pose for a moment, with a smile fixed on her face as though it were painted on china. Then she stood and turned in a supple circle with her arms stretched out.

"Marvelous," the doctor said dutifully, while Maillart fluttered his fingers against his palm. The dress was eye-filling: taffeta in French tricolor stripes of red, white and blue, with a full skirt and puffs of white muslin at the sleeves and bosom. Even the buttons had been carefully covered in tricolor fabric, in the manner of wee Republican cockades, to complete the effect of ardent patriotism.

"Ma chère," said Cigny, glancing up above his reading glasses, "I hope you do not go too far." He sniffed and lowered his head into the newspaper. Isabelle smirked in his direction and went out.

The rain had stopped. Maillart got up to open the doors; a current of cool moist air entered the room, guttering the lamp flames. The captain frowned over his position for a moment or more, then turned over his king with his thumb and stood up, giving Doctor Hébert a significant look. He left the room, and after a moment the doctor followed him onto the second-floor balcony.

It was full dark, but the moon had risen from the harbor, and poured clear light all over the street. Maillart slipped a hand into his inner coat pocket and produced a flask. The doctor accepted and turned it up.

"Why, it is real cognac!" he said.

Maillart nodded, and drank in his turn. "A stroke of luck," he said, "at the *casernes.*"

Below, lamps at the doorway cast a warm yellow apron against the paler shade of moonlight on the street. A coach had pulled up, and from it descended the Commissioner Julien Raimond. He handed his wife down, and the two of them went into the house; the doctor could hear Isabelle's voice tinkling for a moment before the door closed.

Maillart offered the flask again, and the doctor accepted. Two men were dismounting from their horses before the door: black officers, Moyse and Clervaux. They entered. The doctor returned the flask to Maillart, who drank and dried the neck and corked it, then put it away in his coat. They watched the passersby on the street below: for some few minutes no one stopped. Then a larger carriage, with two soldiers riding at the rear like footmen, pulled up sharply. A soldier moved smoothly to open the door, and out stepped Pascal, secretary to the Commission, then Sonthonax himself, bareheaded. A moment, then the gentlemen helped down from the coach Marie Bleigeat, the colored beauty Sonthonax had married the year before. She carried a bundle in her arms and was followed by a small black woman with a basket.

"We had better go down," the captain said. Again the doctor followed him, grateful for the cognac. The evening would not be naturally relaxing.

In the parlor was all the company they'd seen arrive, along with Major Joseph Flaville, who seemed to have been there for some time, much at his ease on a small spindly chair which his imposing figure covered so perfectly he seemed almost to be levitating there. Did the captain twitch when he noticed Flaville? But the doctor was distracted at once by the commotion surrounding Madame Sonthonax; all the women were exclaiming over the parcel she cradled: Jules-Pierre-Isidore Sonthonax.

"But sir," said Monsieur Cigny, bowing to the commissioner. "I am delighted to see, as we all must be, how firmly you have rooted yourself in this country."

Sonthonax was not a tall man, and the extravagant commissioner's sash round his midsection emphasized a certain portliness. His brown hair hung straight to his shoulders, unpowdered and unadorned. His head came directly out of his shoulders like a bullet, which gave him a formidable aspect despite his insignificant height. For a moment he said nothing and all the company had to wonder how Cigny's pleasantry would be taken. Sonthonax had fair skin which colored easily, but soon it appeared that his flush was only a new father's inarticulate pride.

Isabelle shook her fan at her husband in mock reproach. Marie Sonthonax dimpled, dropping her head, while the white men laughingly congratulated the commissioner; the black officers, meanwhile, retained a greater reserve. The baby was carried to the next room for further admiration among the women, and soon Doctor Hébert was called into service, to verify that Jules-Pierre-Isidore had all his features and fingers and toes and was an enviably perfect specimen of humanity. Bending his ear to the infant's heart, the doctor was pricked by a strange emotion; his own son Paul had been born in this house, and he had been in attendance. The ripple of feeling lent sincerity to his voice as he praised the qualities of the Sonthonax first-born.

There was a bustle round the door, and Isabelle turned expectantly as Monsieur Cigny opened it. The new guests were the black Colonel Maurepas and his wife. Madame Maurepas appeared quite frightened to find herself there; she stood stiff and mute while introductions were accomplished, but Maurepas himself seemed comfortable enough with the formalities. He bowed to Cigny, still lower to Isabelle, and balanced his hat in his hands.

"General Toussaint Louverture presents his compliments," he said, "with his regrets; he cannot join your company this evening."

At once the baby began to wail, as if on cue, though the doctor knew it was only that the women had teased him into a state of irritation. Marie Sonthonax squirmed in an unhappy confusion.

"Oh," she said. "I ought not to have brought him—"

"But my dear, it was I who insisted." Isabelle Cigny pressed Marie's ivory forearm. "Jules-Pierre-Isidore is our most important guest, and our evening certainly could not succeed without him."

With that, the moment was salvaged. The smallest Sonthonax was given into the hands of the little black woman with the basket—his wet-nurse, it appeared. A door was shut upon them, and soon all was quiet, while in the parlor the evening went on.

At dinner Sonthonax fully recovered his powers of speech (which very rarely deserted him) to shower the kitchen with compliments. He was known to appreciate the pleasures of the table, and Isabelle had put herself out to impress him. There was a proper fish soup, a lovely rich shade of brown and redolent with spices; it had taken the cook (Isabelle explained) four attempts to achieve the right shade of *roux* without scorching it. The next course was beef, with a garnish of mushrooms gathered from some moist cove near Haut du Cap. The conversation mostly revolved around the food, for each course and dish came trailing its anecdote, and Sonthonax was deft with his compliments and showed an almost professional interest in the procedures of the Cigny kitchen.

And no one was seeking to turn the talk in another direction. The table rather lacked for ladies. Madame Arnaud had dressed (or had been dressed by Isabelle) in a white revolutionary chemise, decorated with frills of tricolor ribbon; almost alarmingly form-fitting, the garment let the doctor see that Claudine had indeed regained some weight since her bouts of madness had abated. She seemed calm, even almost contented, but at table she spoke only when spoken too, and that briefly, leaving her costume to make the point that she was as thoroughly Republican as anyone could wish. Michel Arnaud was absent, supervising their plantation on the plain, which was probably for the better, as he could not have carried off such a masquerade.

Sonthonax's bride was a woman of some worldliness, at twenty-seven the widow of one Villevaleix, who'd been a very wealthy colored gentleman of the northern region. A beautiful woman, and gorgeously dressed, she observed the mock flirtation between Isabelle and Sonthonax with the mildest interest, now and then contributing a phrase or two in a languid, honeyed tone. Across the table, Madame Maurepas kept her eyes lowered, her head bowed; she was dressed as if for church, and looked as if she wished she were invisible.

Presiding, technically at least, at the table's head, Monsieur Cigny had lapsed from his scintillating moment at the doorway into the abstraction he usually displayed on such occasions. As for the black officers, they ate slowly and seriously and said next to nothing—their officers' mess was always a silent proceeding, though there might be garrulity

before and after the meal. Raimond and Pascal put in a word as necessary to keep the conversation from faltering, for at any complete silence
one could not help but notice the absence of Toussaint.

Isabelle had managed some unusually nice wine to accompany the
repast, but once the ladies had withdrawn, rum stood in the place of
brandy for the gentlemen. Monsieur Cigny offered round his cigars.
Sonthonax, who looked well satisfied, leaned back in his chair, stuck his
feet out and slipped a hand between the buttons of his white waistcoat
as if to stretch the fabric.

"Gentlemen," he said, reaching for his glass and raising it. "I give
you—an absent friend." He revolved the glass in his hand, looking at the
amber swirl of rum. "He who has united all our forces for the defense of
universal liberty, the General-in-Chief, Toussaint Louverture."

As they drank, Cigny choked and spluttered. Commissioner Raimond turned to him with great solicitude and thumped him rhythmically on the back until his cough subsided. The doctor looked all around
the the table, somewhat uncomfortably. The company was not designed
for easy after-dinner conversation, no matter how well steeped in smoke
and rum.

"I offer this glass to the Governor-General Laveaux," Maurepas
was saying, "who steadfastly defends our liberty against its enemies in
France."

They drank. Monsieur Cigny swallowed this toast more easily, the
doctor noticed. But for all the tricolor cockade Isabelle had pinned to
his lapel, he was a royalist at heart, more likely to have sided with
Vaublanc than Laveaux, and if slavery were to be restored tomorrow, he
would not be at all aggrieved. Then again it had probably required some
effort for Sonthonax to propose the first toast to Toussaint, who had
chosen to remain at Breda in the company of Bayon de Libertat—a
branded royalist and aristocrat, slave holder, minor nobleman . . .

"To our good friend among us now," Moyse declared. "The Commissioner Sonthonax. Let him remain with us always, to defend the Tree of
Liberty he was the first to plant in Saint Domingue."

The doctor drank, swallowed, left his head tilted back against the
top rail of his chair. On the ceiling, three geckos were cautiously converging on a single mosquito, its shadow spread ominously large by the
light from the candles. So far as the black officers were concerned,
Isabelle's invitations had been quite canny. Moyse, Clervaux and Maurepas were Sonthonax's staunchest supporters among Toussaint's cadre,
while Moyse and Flaville were close as brothers, and Moyse was Toussaint's nephew. There would have been a smooth liaison from Sonthonax to Toussaint across these men, who were Toussaint's own—if

only Toussaint had chosen to appear. Oh, the doctor, thought, it was a delicate game she played, and how gracefully she'd absorbed the disappointment, too. The widening rift between Toussaint and Sonthonax was well enough known to all, and if she'd facilitated a rapprochement between them, Isabelle's position would have been improved with both. She might even have felt secure enough to bring her children back to the colony, which was, as the doctor knew from Maillart, her heart's desire. He wished her well, but he'd served himself as message-bearer between commissioner and general for too long to be optimistic; he had not been surprised in the least that Toussaint kept away.

"Tomorrow's festival," Julien Raimond announced. "May every throne of tyranny be overturned, and all people rise to freedom."

They drank. Of course it was the Republican holiday that had inspired Isabelle's choice of dress for herself and Claudine—they'd wear the same costumes next day to salute the Tree of Liberty. But tonight the mood was something less than festive, despite the effort of all those toasts, and once the men had rejoined the ladies, the party was not much prolonged.

The doctor felt a little stuffy, after such an elaborate meal, and also he did not wish to linger for a post-mortem of the evening between Isabelle and her reluctant husband. He excused himself to walk Captain Maillart back to the *casernes*. The streets were quiet, sometimes a square or wedge of candlelight at windows which they passed, or someone standing silent in a doorway or under an eave. The captain walked with a wide swinging step, rolling his shoulders which had stiffened from too long sitting in a too-small chair. He nipped from his flask and offered it to the doctor, who took a small taste and handed it back.

"I am no great lover of Sonthonax," Maillart said, "but I wonder, what does Toussaint want in a French agent? No one could have shown himself more friendly to the blacks, and now Sonthonax has made Toussaint military master of this place."

"Governor-General, one might say," the doctor murmured, "in all but name. And there's the difficulty."

Maillart glanced at him in the moonlight. "I don't follow."

"Listen," said the doctor. "When Sonthonax was recalled to France in ninety-four, General Laveaux was the supreme French authority here— supreme over one starving fort at Port-de-Paix, I know, for it was you who told me that tale. Toussaint appeared and gave better than half the colony into his control again—then Laveaux made him Lieutenant-Governor. Now that Laveaux has gone, who succeeds him?"

"Ah," said the captain. "But Toussaint is General-in-Chief, not Governor."

"So Sonthonax would have it, certainly. But what does Toussaint think?"

"That," said the captain, "no one has ever been able to say."

"Yes, but you and I have both seen how closely he studies what has gone before. I'll wager he remembers Galbaud as well we do, even if he was up on the Spanish border when the whole fiasco took place. Galbaud was Governor-General when he went to war with Sonthonax and the Commission. It's hardly three years since they burned this very town to the paving stones."

The captain stopped in his tracks. "What do you mean?" They stood on the corner of the Rue Espagnole, with a wind blowing up toward them from the city gate.

"It is the posts themselves, as much as the men who occupy them," the doctor said. "In the old system, before the insurrection in ninety-one, it was the same. The civil authority set against the military. Intendant against Governor-General. In Paris they *designed* it so, to inhibit conspiracies for independence and the like. No one wanted to see another American Revolution break out in Saint Domingue."

"So . . ." the captain let out a whistling breath. "But surely in this case the particulars are different."

"But suppose they were not. Suppose Toussaint to be no different than any other French brigadier. Perhaps he really does see himself that way—he carries himself in the role. No different from the Generals Rochambeau and Desfourneaux, save for his African complection."

"Save that Desfourneaux is now in the guardhouse at Port de Paix, and Rochambeau has been shipped back to France to answer charges."

"Exactly," the doctor said. The captain offered the flask again, but he declined—the cognac seemed to mix poorly with the rum he had taken earlier. "Because they gainsaid Sonthonax. Perhaps also for lack of success in the field—or in diplomacy."

"Why, everyone knows he arrested them for protesting his favor of the blacks in the army."

"In other words, they gainsaid Sonthonax," the doctor said. "As much as to rebel against the civil authority here, do you see?"

"But with Toussaint? In confidence, of course, Antoine, but I know you carry their dispatches."

"Well." The doctor glanced over his shoulder. He nudged the captain; they both began walking again, toward the *casernes*. "You know most of their differences, great or small. Toussaint is eager to take over the Spanish side of the island, in accord with the Treaty of Basel, while Sonthonax prefers to delay. The whole business of the *émigrés* and the old landowners has been bitter—if it looks as if it's all about Bayon de

Libertat, you know well enough there are many more like him. Toussaint would have them all come back to manage their properties with free labor."

"Which is sensible, for that would raise revenue."

"And that revenue would furnish the army. Yes," said the doctor, "but Sonthonax, never mind his courtesies this evening, is obliged to regard those returning *colons* as traitors, enemies of the Republic. Strange as it may seem, our friend Isabelle and her family and her properties would likely fare better according to Toussaint's idea of things."

"You are right," said Maillart. "I have often thought so."

Their boots clopped on the empty street; the doctor's pace quickened as his thoughts ran more swiftly. "As for the rest of it, Toussaint has complained that Sonthonax is fomenting dissension in his ranks. I cannot judge that quarrel—there has been some trouble, indeed, and arrests to put it down, but for what cause I don't know. And the small differences—whether the coffee harvest of Plaisance and Marmelade should be shipped from Gonaives to support the army there, or be sold here at Le Cap for the benefit of the Commission . . ."

"But for an army in the field that question is not small," the captain said. They had come opposite the *casernes*, and here they stopped, lowering their voices so as not to be overheard by the sentry across the street.

"No, you are right," the doctor said. "And also, the whole catastrophe in the south. Toussaint warned the commissioners against it—sending such men, with such instructions. And he was right, for now we have Rigaud in open rebellion against the Commission."

"But not against Toussaint," the captain hissed.

The doctor looked at him intently.

"Rigaud sent an envoy directly to Gonaives," the captain said. He turned and spat into the street. "You were away and I did not tell you afterward—Choufleur was part of the delegation, you understand, so I didn't like to mention it."

"Let that pass. What did they say?"

"I was not admitted to their council," Maillart said, "though apparently it was successful. By the talk, there is a perfect understanding between General Toussaint and General Rigaud."

The doctor grinned wryly. "And there you have it."

"What?"

"When the powers are divided as they are, Rigaud can come to accord with one without the other. For example, he can tie Sonthonax's proclamation to the tail of his donkey and still have his perfect understanding with Toussaint."

"But in the end," said the captain, "the question remains, who shall be master?"

"Oh yes," said the doctor. "You're right about that too."

Maillart nodded and crossed the street; the sentry opened the postern door for him. The captain turned and raised his hand before he ducked inside. Alone, the doctor started back across the Rue Espagnole. There was an ominous feeling in his glands that had nothing directly to do with the conversation with Maillart. It had nothing to do with thought at all, but was more like some aching apprehension of bad weather to come.

A patrol passed, its leader greeting him. The doctor returned the signal. He turned down toward the harbor. There was an alley that would take him directly to the door of the Cigny house, but in the mouth of it a couple of dogs were sniffing over a garbage heap, and when the doctor approached they both raised their heads as if to challenge him. They did not bark or even growl; they were pitiful, half-starved dogs, inconsequential, and yet the doctor felt sure that they would attack him if he tried to pass through the alley. He walked farther down, suddenly, irrationally alarmed—what if his way was blocked so at every turning he wanted to make? But at the next corner there were no dogs. He reached the Cigny house and was admitted by the yawning cook and climbed the stairs to his attic bed.

Next day the national festival took place as anticipated, complete with a grand parade terminating on the Champ de Mars, with cannon salvos from all the forts and answering salutes from battleships in the harbor. The small, red-banded figure of Sonthonax was at the center of the occasion, the quick bright focus of all energy. As Monsieur Cigny muttered in the doctor's ear, no one could claim that the commissioner did not understand the value of circuses. The people of Le Cap had turned out in force to acclaim Sonthonax as founder of Liberty one more time and to listen to the oration he declaimed across their ranks.

"For five years," he remarked, near the end of the speech, "the armies of the Republic here have gloriously supported the first effort of an entire nation to break its chains—one would have supposed that they would have made haste to attend this commemoration of such a great day."

Isabelle, dressed once more in her tricolor taffeta, peered around the bulky figure of her husband to catch the doctor's eye for just a moment, before she resumed cheering and hurling flowers in the general direction of the podium and encouraging the more apathetic Claudine to do the same. Sonthonax had gone on to his next phrase. But the doctor had not missed that message—clearly a reproach, however light or brief. There were both black and white troops at parade rest on the Champ de Mars, the former commanded by Clervaux and Pierre Michel. But General-in-Chief Toussaint Louverture had not honored the event with his presence.

Much later, when all the panoply was concluded and the debris had been swept out of the streets, the doctor was roused from his mid-afternoon siesta by the sound of galloping cavalry. He got up, naked, and peered out the porthole, over the red tile roofs. In the next street, Toussaint was riding hard toward Government House, in the midst of twenty-five helmeted *cavaliers* of his honor guard. Though they'd missed the official parade by hours, a small crowd of children ran shouting in the cloud of swirling dust behind the horses.

The doctor dressed and went softly down through the dozing house and out the door. Guided by a premonition, he walked over to Government House. The thick, damp heat made him feel as if he were floating. In the courtyard the guardsmen had dismounted, taken off their helmets, and led their horses to patches of shade. One of them was walking Toussaint's charger, Bel Argent, to cool the stallion down. The doctor greeted them as he passed. No one challenged him at the door; he was well enough known in that place.

Julien Raimond and the secretary Pascal were in the anteroom of Sonthonax's offices. The door to the inner cabinet was shut. Pascal acknowledged the doctor with raised eyebrows and a cock of his head toward the door. Glancing at Raimond, who also said nothing, the doctor sat down in a chair against the wall.

In his haste he had worked up a sweat which now adhered stickily to his every crease. With a handkerchief, he sponged some wet dust from his face. No conversation. They might have been eavesdropping, but nothing could be heard through the inner door. After half an hour, Raimond took a large gold watch from his waistcoat pocket and looked at the dial, then wound the watch with a gold key attached to the other end of the chain. More silence followed, interrupted infrequently by a voice raised outside. A black fly flew in the open window, bumbled around the high corners of the ceiling, and finally found its way back out. Beyond the window the light was just beginning to fade and the air was thickening with rain.

Then Julien Raimond was on his feet, and the doctor registered that Toussaint had come into the room, though he had heard nothing, had not seen the inner door open. The general stood with his large bicorne hat in his hand. There was nothing particular about his expression, and yet he seemed extraordinarily compressed upon himself, like a tightened, swollen fist.

"When a hog has once eaten a chicken," Toussaint said, "you may put out one of its eyes, you may put out the other eye, but this hog will still try to eat chickens whenever it passes them."

Julien Raimond opened his mouth, then closed it. Toussaint had uttered this proverb in Creole—*parler nèg,* he called it. Black talk. His words seemed addressed to no one in particular, but now he focused on Doctor Hébert.

"I shall wait for you at Bréda," he said. He knocked his hat against his tight trouser leg a couple of times, then settled it on his head and marched out the door.

The atmosphere in the room relaxed slightly when he had gone, but the doctor felt foreboding. What had been the color of Toussaint's headcloth? He had seen the black general so densely concentrated a few times before, and killing had invariably started soon afterward, though not always or obviously at Toussaint's instigation. The door of the inner cabinet was slightly ajar. The three of them looked at each other; then Pascal, with a light push of his fingertips, swung it farther open.

Sonthonax was standing, behind his desk, with his hair sticking up in several directions, flexing his left hand on a ball of crumpled paper. He looked up at them all as though wakened from a dream.

"Oh," he said. "There has been a misunderstanding." He frowned at the desktop. "But no, perhaps it is nothing."

The doctor went down to the front steps of the building and stood watching the rain from the shelter of the portico. Toussaint and his men would have passed the city gate by this time, would be riding through sheets and curtains of rain, indifferent to the drenching, the horses splashing out mud and water to either side of the road to Haut du Cap. He stared into the rain, half mesmerized, listened to the rush of it over the roof. Presently Pascal came out to join him.

"Enlighten me," the doctor said. "What could he have meant by that parable about the pig?"

Pascal cleared his throat and glanced over his shoulder into the hallway of the building. "According to Commissioner Raimond," he said, dropping his voice, "Sonthonax proposed to Toussaint—and months ago, when he was promoted General-in-Chief—that the two of them should conspire to massacre all the whites here and make the colony independent of France."

The doctor felt air rushing out of his body through his open mouth.

Pascal was married to Julien Raimond's daughter, but always referred to Raimond with the greatest formality in conversation with third parties. Nevertheless one might assume that there was greater confidence between them than their official positions would require.

"Improbable, you say?" Pascal's mouth was wry. "Well, General Toussaint rejected this proposal, and he gave his word of honor to mention it to no one—still according to Commissioner Raimond, whom he did tell, so as to safeguard his reputation from being stained with this plot."

"But today," the doctor said. "This afternoon, what passed between them?"

"Today," Pascal said, "the general recommends that the commissioner should return to France to occupy his elected office in the Council of Five Hundred, where his eloquence may continue to serve the sacred cause of Liberty, et cetera, et cetera . . ."

"But the scheme of independence—"

"And massacre—one mustn't forget the massacre." Pascal frowned into the rain. "But the pig—yes, one supposes that like the pig who has eaten chickens, Sonthonax cannot help himself from returning to the notion of slaughtering the whites, when he has once conceived it. Or, that was the general's implication—of course Sonthonax said nothing of the kind either to me or to the Citizen Raimond."

The doctor looked at him. Pascal took a step nearer and lowered his voice. The doctor smelled stale coffee on his breath.

"Sonthonax is certainly popular among the great majority here," he said. "I mean of course all the new-freed blacks. Also there are some black officers who seem quite devoted to him. Clervaux, Maurepas, Moyse . . . perhaps Pierre Michel?"

There was more to the question than he had asked aloud. The doctor felt his center of gravity frost over and sink to the level of his heels. "If I understand you correctly," he said. "That notion is without a prayer."

"Ah," said Pascal. His eyes grew distant; he took a step back. "Well, with the changes in Paris—all the colonists gathered at Vaublanc's back and so on—perhaps it *would* be better for the commissioner to labor for liberty in France."

"They're calling for his head back there," the doctor said. "At least, that party which you have just mentioned."

"Perhaps, but as a lawyer, Sonthonax is not to be underestimated—whatever his qualifications as colonial administrator. Remember, he eluded those same charges, last time he was recalled to France." Pascal shrugged. "He may fall, but he seems to fall on his feet."

*   *   *

When the rain had stopped, the doctor walked back toward the Cigny house, picking his way round sloughs in the unpaved street. He did not enter at the front door, but instead went round to the square yard in back, and negotiated with one servant to borrow a donkey, and with another to discreetly fetch his writing implements and his pistols from the garret room. He was not disposed to answer any questions from his hosts at the moment. And though he might have gone out to Bréda with a military escort from the *casernes,* he much preferred to be alone this time. On donkeyback, his white face hidden beneath his hat, he'd likely be taken for a laborer returning from the field. The region was fairly quiet in any case, and at the worst he had his pistols. There was moonlight enough and the donkey seemed to know the way.

What a strange world it was, he thought, as the unshod donkey slipped almost silently through the posts of the city gateway. Puddles reflected moonlight from the road; to his left the cane fields bristled against the moonlit sky. When the Revolution had swept over France, the royalists had thought to make this colony a sanctuary for themselves (some of them were still struggling, feebly, in league with the English, to bring that about). Now that the Revolution looked to be faltering at home, perhaps it did make sense for a Jacobin of Sonthonax's type to try to make the colony a refuge for wandering revolutionaries. Although Pascal was right, of course: in answering for the excesses and failures of his first sojourn in Saint Domingue, Sonthonax had contrived his transformation into a good Thermidorean. Still, in the current climate, that might not be quite good enough.

The air was fresh and pleasant after the rain, and the road was mostly empty. Occasionally he overtook a file of women walking in the fragrant shadows with baskets on their heads, or was hailed by a donkey-riding peasant in a straw hat much like his own. Deeper in the trees to the right of the road, the flicker of firelight appeared at intervals, with the smell of roasting meat or beans boiling with peppers. The doctor took a lump of hard cheese from his pocket and gnawed it as he rode along. It was late when he came to Bréda, but the *grand'case* was ablaze with light, and he knew it would be a good deal later before his tasks were done.

Next morning the doctor rode back to Le Cap on an ordinary horse (the borrowed donkey had wound up somewhere in the train of Toussaint's entourage), swaying in the saddle and half hallucinating from fatigue. The letter which had been ground out all through the previous night, through numerous drafts by many secretaries, was in the form of con-

gratulations, praising the successes of Sonthonax in defeating the enemies of the colony, restoring peace and stability and the prosperity of
the plantations—in his dictation, Toussaint kept revisiting the phrasing
of those lines, which had apparently been discussed with the commissioner beforehand. But the rest of the document underlined the idea
that it was now essential for Sonthonax to return to France, in order to
present the truth of events of Saint Domingue to the Directoire, at this
time when so many others were trying so energetically to misrepresent
the situation here.

The letter was carried by a small detachment of Toussaint's honor
guard, along with the doctor and some other functionaries, but behind
them by perhaps a half-mile the army was also moving toward the town,
though with less than its usual sharp discipline. Toussaint's party rode
across the Rue Espagnole toward the *casernes;* midway along that route
the doctor doubled back and found the donkey, and leading it by its rope
behind his horse, he went down to the Cigny house to return it to its
owner. Already he could hear the clamor of the troops massing outside
the city gate.

Exhausted as he was, he rode back to the *casernes* at once; for one
thing, there was his horse to return, for this mount too had been borrowed out of Toussaint's cavalry. With that accomplished, he went into
the mess hall of the barracks, where the officers of Toussaint's Etat
Major had been summoned to add their signatures to the letter. Maillart, Vaublanc and Riau stood toward the end of the room, and the
doctor joined their company.

". . . *May you always be the defender of the cause which we have
embraced . . .*" Toussaint, standing at the front of the room, was intoning
the last phrases of the final draft. ". . . *of which we will be the eternal sol
diers. Vive la République! Salut et Respect.*" He reversed the paper and
laid it on the table, where it might be legible to the officers. His own signature, the characteristic three dots enclosed in the final loop, was
already affixed, but plenty of room had been left for the others.

After a moment of silence, a hubbub of discussion and argument
broke out. Many of the officers were admirers of Sonthonax, few were
prepared for this news of his departure, and some seemed downright
unwilling to sign the letter, though also reluctant to say so.

Toussaint sat down beside the table, adjusting the scabbard of his
ceremonial sword, and remained there, legs crossed, elbow on table, his
jaw supported by his hand. His eyes were somewhat heavy-lidded, but
that was his only sign of weariness, though he'd had no more sleep than
the rest of them, the doctor thought, as he swayed drowsily from foot to
foot. A long time seemed to pass very slowly. Riau was rapt, inexpressive

as a statue, and the doctor and Maillart restricted themselves to the exchange of a couple of anxious glances.

Toussaint stood up and raised his hand, palm out. Very quickly the room grew silent, but Toussaint's head was cocked, listening to a more distant commotion. The noise of the troops swirling outside the gate was just audible, like the rising hum of a hive of bees.

"What is that disorder?" Toussaint rapped out. "Go and settle it at once." He cocked a finger and aimed it toward the rear of the room. Vaublanc and Riau dashed out on the double. Toussaint relaxed, but only slightly. He remained standing, hitching up his sword belt with one hand. In a low voice he announced that Sonthonax himself had requested this letter of congratulations and that the officers had been gathered not to discuss the letter but to sign it.

Fifteen minutes later, the doctor, Maillart and Adjutant-General Henri Christophe were mounting the steps of Government House. Pascal waited outside the door, beneath the portico.

"What was that disturbance over at the gate?" he said. "One began to imagine a riot."

"Well, it is calm now," Maillart said shortly.

"So." Pascal mopped his forehead with a madras cloth. Christophe produced the letter, unsealed, its corners fluttering slightly, and Pascal took it. After the most cursory scan of the text he began to examine the signatures below Toussaint's: Moyse, Chevalier, Clervaux, Paparel, Dupuis . . .

"It's done then," Pascal said. No one contradicted him. He looked into their faces one after the other and then bowed and carried the letter into the building.

There were certain officers who had not signed the letter, though these, a short while afterward, came again to Toussaint and asked to be allowed to do so. Request denied. Toussaint now told them that no signatures had ever been needed beyond his own and that he was prepared to take sole responsibility for the message the letter bore. In any case it had already been delivered.

For three more days, Sonthonax writhed on the point of his departure. More letters were exchanged between him and Toussaint (who had withdrawn to Petite Anse), wreathed in compliments which smothered their veiled intent. There was no repetition of the disturbance at the gate; the considerable number of those soldiers who had entered the town maintained perfect discipline and a perfect obedience to Toussaint's orders; and it became increasingly clear that if there were to be any popular uprising, it would not be in favor of the commissioner.

Julien Raimond, Pascal, the young Colonel of Engineers Vincent, all encouraged Sonthonax to . . . accept his election to the Council of Five Hundred. Then, at four o'clock in the morning, the alarm cannon fired once at Petite Anse. Shortly afterward, the French General Agé arrived to bring the message from Toussaint to Raimond: if Sonthonax had not departed by sunrise, the next shot would have a much more definite target.

At eight o'clock, Sonthonax marched down from Government House to the port, where the frigate *Indien* was waiting to receive him. With him walked his wife, her face completely concealed by the opulent silk shawl wrapped over her head, the infant and the nurse and a few other retainers—also the black officers Mentor and Léveillé, and a couple of others who had missed their opportunity to sign that letter of congratulation. Their way was lined by Toussaint's troops (though Toussaint had not yet returned to the town) and by great throngs of the townspeople, no matter that it was barely dawn. Today there was no cheering; everyone stood drawn and solemn, like mourners at a wake.

Sonthonax was not to be underestimated, as Pascal had suggested, in any court of law, and by the time he had to answer for his conduct in Saint Domingue before the Directoire, his counterattack was thoroughly prepared. Toussaint was the mere puppet and tool, he maintained, of the royalists and priests and *émigrés* who surrounded him to this day; it was they who had first inspired him to lead the slaves to revolt, to lay waste to the colony with fire and sword, and murder so many landowners. It was they who had caused all the disasters, they who'd finally manipulated Toussaint to send Sonthonax away. As for Toussaint, his entire political career had been nothing but rebellion against France.

Meanwhile, Commissioner Raimond wrote letters of his own, denouncing Sonthonax for fomenting dissension and trying his best to set the white and black and colored people all at each other's throats, and Toussaint himself dictated a letter, in the form of a theatrical play (much labored over by the doctor and the other secretaries) which purported to reproduce verbatim those conversations wherein Sonthonax had tried to seduce Toussaint to join the scheme for independence, and Colonel Vincent, more credible than the others because he was white and French and had at first been one of Sonthonax's partisans, sailed to

France to contend that yes, Sonthonax had apparently intended to make the colony an asylum for revolutionary patriots, with himself its master . . .

Against all that, Sonthonax had his eloquence and one stroke of very good luck: by the time he stood to defend himself, his most dangerous enemies—Vaublanc and the colonial party—had been ejected from the legislature and sent into exile. His tongue was quick and agile as ever, and finally he not only eluded censure for his second tour of Saint Domingue, he was even commended for his work. But the master stroke of his speech was this: after denouncing Rigaud as a murderous insubordinate and Toussaint as a scheming rebel, he counseled against any military action against either one of them, recommending instead a general amnesty—Toussaint and Rigaud should be treated (if not courted) as legitimate representatives of France.

Toussaint did not know, till well after the fact, of Vaublanc's exile from influence. Therefore the doctor and Riau and the other scribes (now including Pascal, who had remained theoretically as Raimond's secretary but took more and more of his dictation directly from Toussaint) found themselves at work on a letter of reply to some of Vaublanc's most extreme vituperations before the French Assembly. Toussaint spent even more hours on this epistle than he had on the long dialogue between himself and Sonthonax—there was more of himself in it, Doctor Hébert thought, and perhaps more absolute truth.

He and Riau and Pascal sat at three sides of the same table, their pens scratching busily over fair copies.

I send you with this letter a declaration which will make you familiar with the unity existing among the slave owners of Saint Domingue presently in France, those in the United States, and those serving here under the English flag. You will see that their concern for success has led them to wrap themselves in the cloak of Liberty, but only in order to strike Liberty still more mortal blows. You will see that they definitely expect that I will be swayed to their perfidious opinions by fear for my children. It is not surprising that such men, who would sacrifice their country to their own interests, cannot conceive how many sacrifices a better father than they might bear for love of his nation, given that I found the happiness of my children on that of my nation, which they and they alone wish to destroy. I will never hesitate between the security of Saint Domingue and my personal happiness, but I have nothing to fear. It is to the care of the French government that I have entrusted my children. I would tremble with horror if I had sent them into the hands of the colonialists as hostages. But even if that were the case, let them know that in punishing the good faith of their father, they would do nothing but add to their barbarity, without the least hope of ever making me fail in my duty . . .

. . . but here a driblet of ink fell from the doctor's pen as he lifted it. It lay on the page, a black pearl shimmering on its surface. His hand halted in the air for a moment, then he replaced the pen in its stand and sat back gingerly. If he tried to blot the ink drop, he would spoil the whole sheet, and he was near the bottom. He turned his head to look out the window—they were in Government House today, for Toussaint now kept his offices there.

For some reason the picture came to him of Claudine Arnaud holding the child of Marie Bleigeat Villevaleix Sonthonax. Complete gentleness in the way that she cradled the infant, and yet her aspect had been somehow remote, shut away behind walls of grief and screaming, so that the image as it now appeared in his mind's eye was less Madonna with Child, more Pietà. At the same time he was revisiting the moment years ago at the Cigny house when he had lifted Paul for the first time. Isabelle Cigny had appeared at his side and had mentioned among other things how the infant's color would darken during the first few days of his life (though in fact the shade of his skin had not changed so very much, deepened only to the color of bone). Along with his softness the baby had had a large and important weight, and afterward whenever the doctor lifted Paul, he found him somewhat heavier than he had expected.

Riau and Pascal had also stopped writing and both were looking at him with large, curiously calm eyes. It could not be that they knew the thoughts that he was thinking, but for a moment it seemed that all three of them shared a feeling, as though they drank from the same cup. Then the moment passed, and Riau and Pascal lowered their heads and went back to their work. With his fingernail, Doctor Hébert detached the knob of dried ink from the page and blew the residue away. Then he lifted the pen and went on with his copying.

Do they suppose that men who have ever enjoyed the benefits of freedom would look on calmly as it was snatched away from them? They bore their chains as long as they did not know any condition of life happier than slavery. But today, when they have left it behind, if they had a thousand lives, they would sacrifice them rather than to be reduced to slavery again. But no, the hand which broke our chains

will not enslave us all over again. France will not deny her princi-
ples . . . But, even if that were to happen in order to reestablish slavery
in Saint Domingue, then I declare to you it would be to attempt the
impossible; we have known how to face many dangers to win our free-
dom, and we will know how to face death to keep it.

27

After the *blanc* Sonthonax had been sent away on the ship, Toussaint was happy in the way that he had been at Mirebalais for a short time, because we had all won a victory. There was no one over Toussaint any more, since Julien Raimond would not go against him, and the *blanc* Roume who was the other commissioner was far away in Santo Domingo on the other side of the Cibao Mountains. Toussaint moved into the House of the Governor of the time before the risings, where General Laveaux had stayed before him, because Toussaint was Governor-General now, with no one above him anywhere nearer to us than France.

I, Riau, stayed in the House of the Governor then as well, in rooms in the back along with some other officers of the staff, and the *blanc* Pascal. In the nights were grand dinners and entertainments, with the officers of Toussaint's army and the *hommes de couleur* who were important in the town, with their wives and also many beautiful colored women who did not have any husbands. The old *grand blancs* who had not been killed came also, and everyone treated Toussaint as if he was their father. He was master of the house then, and of the town and all the north except for Le Môle where the English were. And he gave himself to these parties of pleasure, more freely than he used to do, though it meant only that he might drink two glasses of wine or one of rum while he sat at the table or in the salon, instead of drinking only water as he usually did. Those evenings ended early anyway, and people who wanted to dance or go with the colored women went afterward to some other place, when the lamps and candles had been snuffed out at the Governor's House, and everything was quiet.

Suzanne Louverture came up from Ennery for a time, to be with Toussaint and keep his house for him, with the youngest son, Saint-Jean. Everyone treated her very nicely, even the *grand blancs* from before, because she was Toussaint's wife. But she did not like it very much. She did not know what to say to such people, and she went back to her plantation at Ennery as soon as she was able.

In those days, some said it happened that the old master of Bréda, Bayon de Libertat, came to the House of the Governor and moved to embrace Toussaint, but Toussaint pushed him away and said that he must not act so, for there was a greater distance between them now than before when Toussaint was a slave at Bréda. But I, Riau, I did not see this happen, and I did not really believe it either. I saw Bayon and Toussaint together many times, and they were not like that with one another, so I thought the story was invented by people who were against Toussaint in their secret hearts. Even at Bréda long ago, Bayon had not been so haughty like that when Toussaint was serving him, but instead he and Toussaint were easy with each other then, the same as now, so that it was hard to know even then that one was slave and the other master. But it was true also that Toussaint might have done this thing so that other people would see it and make a story travel which would stop people believing he was sold to the *grand blancs,* which some did whisper after Sonthonax had gone.

The House of the Governor was in the north end of the town, toward Fort Pinochet, and only a little way from the Customs House and the harbor. On the other side, the roots of the mountains were near. At night when all the noise and talk stopped and the Governor's House was still and dark, sometimes the drums would begin speaking from the dark round hill above. I, Riau, went to the drums sometimes, though it was not my *lakou,* but I felt my spirit call me to go. That was a strong place on the round hill, with the church before it where Jesus was killed, and on the other side, against the mountain, a place of the Indian mysteries. In the church that colored son of Père Bonne-chance preached Jesus, but at night he also served as *laplace* in the *hûnfor,* and Maman Maig' was *mambo* there. Through the eyes and tongue and the large hands of Maman Maig' the spirit worked to bring to that place on the hill the *blanche,* Claudine Arnaud.

Sometimes Riau's own spirit came to ride him at the drumming on that hill, so he could not say afterward what had happened or what the *loa* had done. Other times though, I stayed near to my head to look through my own eyes and see what happened with that *blanche,* when the drumming took her and her eyes rolled back and she collapsed into the linked arms of the *hounsis.* Then Erzulie-gé-Rouge rose up in the place of her body, red eyes afire in the pale drawn face, her hands made claws to tear at her clothes and flesh with anger and sorrow and bitterness for her losses. Or at other times it was Baron who rose, with his one eye bright and greedy on the world of living men, and other eye darkened, to look *anba dlo.* Many people came to that *hûnfor* because they had heard about this thing, and there were even a couple of white people who climbed to a spot above where they could see from a distance, since they could not enter the *hûnfor,* only Claudine.

When Erzulie-gé-Rouge entered the *blanche,* she asked many very hard services from the people there, and would not be pleased with any given her, but at other times it looked that Erzulie required of the *blanche* a service of gentleness. For that, Claudine was always kind and strangely humble. She took pains to be good to children and to teach them things, no matter what children they were, or if she knew them or not. With people who were grown she was quiet and spoke little, and held her eyes down—whether the people were black or colored or white like herself, her manner with them was always the same. The *serviteurs* had begun to say that she had her skin turned inside out, and that she did not have the spirit of a white person at all, even though Arnaud, who was her husband, was very well known for the cruel things he had done to his slaves, and some people claimed to know that the *blanche* had done still worse than he before slavery was finished, when a bad spirit was with her, but now that seemed to be forgotten (though there were some who would still have killed Arnaud for what he had done in that other time).

All this looked strange to me sometimes, but I did not think about so very much at all; when Riau went to the ceremonies, the drums carried every question away so that at last there was a harmony no matter what had gone into making it. Those were pleasant weeks in the town also and at Governor's House, and then Toussaint began planning a movement of his army, to secure the inner part of the country around Mirebalais which we had had to burn down when we left it the last time. As before, there would be some men moving inland along the Artibonite and others would go around the northern way up the valley of Grande Rivière and down through Banica. The doctor was ordered by Toussaint to go the southern way, to Gonaives and Pont d'Ester and east on the river—this made him unhappy since he was still hoping to get to Val-lière to find what became of his woman, maybe, but Toussaint himself was going the other way and wanted the doctor with him, for his writing and his doctoring and as a check on Pascal, perhaps, who would also be going with Toussaint this time.

While Toussaint stayed at Governor's House, the doctor had met some of the other colored women who came without men of their own and who had known Nanon well when she used to live among them at Le Cap, but none of them had any news of her—not since she had gone off to Ennery with the doctor himself. And though these women were beautiful themselves, he did not want them. He stayed by himself all the time, thinking about Nanon. Since everyone thought that Chou-fleur had gone to the south, maybe he had taken Nanon with him down there, so there was not so much reason to think she was at Vallière any-more. But as I, Riau, was to be sent on the northern route myself, I told the doctor I would look for her if I was able. At that time the army had even got some pay in money, so I could buy some things for Caco and Merbillay and send them with the doctor, who would be stopping at Ennery as that wing of the army moved through.

When Toussaint had gone south to Gonaives, other men went to Dondon with Moyse, and Captain Riau with his men among them. Our way went across the northern plain, and many of the plantations there were back at work, and there were a lot of people working in the cane. Some of our men, though, made mock of the cane workers as the army went past them, shouting that they were only men of the hoe, while we were all soldiers, men of the gun. I, Riau, thought it a bad thing to be saying, and I rode back down the line and made them stop. But after-ward I felt bad toward myself that I had done this, and for an hour the men were sulky because their captain had ordered them to silence.

By nightfall this feeling had gone away, and we reached Dondon and camped there, and the next day began marching with more of Moyse's men up the valley of Grande Rivière. There was no fighting, because Moyse had broken the last of Jean-François's old bands by that time, and the Spanish had left that part of the country. We saw other planta-tions working as we moved up the river valley, and lines of women with baskets on their heads, bringing coffee down out of the mountains to Le Cap.

But all this country was full of mountains and ravines where many people could hide. I, Riau, knew that very well from the time I had lived in these same hills with the band of Achille. Now we had to make all this place secure before we went to join Toussaint at Mirebalais, so that no attack would spring up out of the ground behind us. It was easy for Captain Riau to volunteer to cover Trou Vilain, since no else wanted that duty very much, but I wanted to go there because I knew the property of Maltrot was near the edge of it.

The little *malfini* were flying over Trou Vilain, hunting for rats in the vines at the bottom, and the road went up the side of the ravine. At the top, near the sky itself, a wagon moved on the road ahead of us, with a man and woman seated together on the box. The man must be a very good driver to bring a wagon over that path, when even the horse Riau was riding had to be urged to go. I seemed to know already who those people were although it was too far away to see them. The wagon turned off and disappeared, and we still had some time of climbing before we reached the place where it had gone out of sight. The driver had come down from the house and stood between the brick gateposts with his hands in his pockets. He had a beard that went all round his mouth and pointed from his chin, but without climbing his jaws to where his ears were. His skin was the color of mahogany and his eyes were hard, and he was standing up very straight watching us come, with interest but no fear. Although he had kept away from us when the doctor and Riau were at their place near Dondon, I knew that this was Fortier.

I got down from my horse and gave the reins to one of the other men to hold and went up toward the gateway on foot. When I was near to Fortier, I stopped and saluted him, for respect even though he was not dressed as a soldier. He had not moved, but something happened in the house behind him. Madame Fortier came out onto the gallery with a *sacatra* house servant bowing away from here, trying to explain something. She was a tall woman and we could feel the force of her anger all the way from the house to where we stood at the very bottom of the garden.

"Where is my son?" Her words were burning, and I thought that if I had been the son she asked for, I would have wanted to put myself a long way off. The *sacatra* was trying to say that Choufleur had not appeared there for many weeks, but Madame Fortier turned and whipped back into the house before he could finish. Fortier and I looked at each other and when he began walking up to the house, I followed a step or two behind.

I did not know it yet but the *sacatra* servant's name was Salomon. He went into the house after Madame Fortier, scuttling like a long-legged crab, as Fortier and I were walking up the steps. At the house door Fortier stopped and looked at me for a moment. Inside we could hear the voice of Madame Fortier cracking out like a whip-tongue and then curling back, but we could not make out what she was saying. Fortier nodded and entered the house, and I followed.

In a room at the back of the house was Nanon, and my heart jumped up, because now the doctor would be glad, maybe. *Si Dyé vlé*. For the first instant I did not know her; she was thinner, and lay on the bed with her hair flung over her face. Her hair was dirty and all stuck together and the whole room smelled as if she had not cleaned herself properly for a long time. A bowl of water was on the floor, and a plate with dried scraps and a broken chicken bone. Nanon rolled onto her back, drawing her knees up under the sheet which covered her to her chin. I knew her then, but her face was all hollow, as if from a fever. As she moved we heard the clink of chain links shifting, and the sheet slipped down. I felt the cold chafing weight on my own neck—this feeling was so strong that both my hands clutched at my throat. Nanon wore an iron collar such as slaves would carry on their necks, coffled together in a line when they were taken off the ship, and I, Riau, had been locked into a collar like this one, when they brought me out of Guinée into this country. In a line of other slaves so chained I was brought from the stinking ship's hold to the barracoons outside Le Cap, and afterward sold on the auction block, and then Bayon de Libertat took me to Bréda.

"That my son should be cursed for doing what he has done here," Madame Fortier was saying. "The evil will come back to him with the same weight. And you, child, to let it be done to yourself . . ."

There was more sadness than anger in her voice when she said this last part. But Nanon did not hear her—her eyes were the eyes of a *zombi* staring up at the spiderwebs in the corners of the ceiling. Madame Fortier lashed herself at Salomon.

"And you? What are you waiting for?—fetch the tools!"

Salomon lifted his arms, stuttering. He already had the hammer and the spike. My hands curved to take them, but Madame Fortier pointed to her man. She wanted him to do this work. I stood in the doorway, watching. Fortier took the tools and braced one knee on the bed, and I watched him set the spike to pound at the rivet, leaning awkwardly to tap with the hammer. He had less skill with the iron than I, but I would not cross Madame Fortier at that moment. She clucked her tongue, then stooped down to hold the edges of the iron ring so the hammer would not slam it so against Nanon's collarbones. All this time Nanon's eyes were still and empty like the eyes of a dead person.

Then I heard one of my men calling from outside the house, and I went to see what it was. A white man was coming up the path beside Trou Vilain, he told me. That was not an expected thing, just now in this place, so I went down to the gateway to see what was happening.

Three men were coming on horseback up the trail, leading two don-keys with pack saddles. The *blanc* in the lead had a broad hat in the Spanish style, so at first I thought he was some Spaniard sneaking across the border, maybe a gold miner. But there was something familiar in his way of riding, and then I recognized the horse, a speckled gray from Thibodet.

Tocquet, the gun runner. The two men with him would be Bazau and Gros-jean, then. I was sure of that, though they were not near enough yet for me to see their faces. When I understood who it was, I smiled inside my head, and I went down from the gateway to meet them.

Since the time he appeared in the camps of Jean-François and Bias-sou with the guns he brought from Santo Domingo, I liked this *blanc* Tocquet well enough. For the same reason others did not like him—he was only for himself, and he let you know it. That was simple. Also he treated the people who worked for him well enough, that Bazau had once told me it was no different between them under slavery than it was now.

Tocquet got down from the speckled gray horse and pressed his hands against his hips to stretch his back.

"So, my captain," he said. "What is your news, and have you got my friend Antoine with you here?"

I told him that the doctor was moving with Toussaint toward Mire-balais, but I had come here, on the army's way to Banica, because we had heard that this was one of Choufleur's places. I told them Nanon was staying here, as the doctor would have hoped. But it was hard to say to him, or to anyone, just how it was with her now.

Tocquet took his hat off and slapped it against his thigh, making the dust of the road fly up. The wind pulled at his hair and the ends of his mustache. He squinted at the sky, where the rain was gathering, then tossed the reins of his horse up to Gros-jean and told them to go and make a camp. There were some of my men who knew Bazau and Gros-jean from Habitation Thibodet, so I told them to follow them and make our camp with theirs. Those two were good foragers, as every-one knew.

Tocquet and I went up to the house and waited on the gallery, but no one came out, so we sat down. Salomon peeped out of the doorway, then pulled his head back inside without saying anything. We could hear Madame Fortier's voice calling directions from the back of the house, and from the kitchen fire they were carrying pans of hot water for a bath.

The rain began. After a while Tocquet stood up and stuck his cupped hands out from under the eave until they had gathered enough water for him to drink. He wiped his wet hands across his face and sat down again.

When the rain stopped, Fortier came out and sat in a chair near us on the gallery. He did not seem to need to say anything at all, as if he had known us both for so long there was no more to be said. But after a little time, Tocquet began speaking. He said some ordinary things, and then he told Fortier that both of us knew Nanon from before and so perhaps we could take her to people who cared for her. Fortier nodded at his words, folding his arms across his chest. It was quiet in the house now, except for sometimes a splash, and the sound of Madame Fortier's voice, murmuring. Fortier said that we should come back there the next day.

It was dark when we went out through the gateposts, and the stars were coming out above the mountain. The camp was not so very near, but Tocquet seemed to know which way to walk, and soon we had only to follow the good smell of roasted pork. When we came to where the camp was made, they had a good *boucan* started with a whole pig on the spit, and Gros-jean was stirring Ti-Malice sauce in a small iron kettle. All my men were happy because of this.

Tocquet found a small keg of rum in one of the donkey packs which had been unloaded, and he tapped it and everyone got a drink. A little while later the *sacatra* Salomon appeared at the edge of the firelight, with one of the women who served in the house; they joined our circle and told us what they knew of what had been happening in that place. Salomon was sore from Madame Fortier's tongue whipping him all that afternoon. He was glad to be able to tell someone that it was not he who kept Nanon on that chain, but first Choufleur and then Nanon herself. He told us how he would have set her free from that iron collar, but that she ordered him to fasten it around her neck again.

This seemed like a bad thing to me, and all the talk stopped once he had told it. In silence, like the others, I wondered what had come upon to her to make her feel this wish. But then the meat was ready, and the sauce with the hot peppers, and the rum went round again. There were some bananas too, from the trees that grew nearby. And soon after eating, everyone slept.

At first light I, Riau, awakened, as if someone had whispered in my ear, though there was no one, only the faint light moving over the hillside. I got up before anyone else had stirred and walked downhill through the stems of wild bananas. Across the clearing was a *hûnfor*, I saw now, though the drums had been silent the night before. And not far away, a place of the Indian mysteries—two stones carved all over with their signs. I looked at those signs which I could not read, remembering the language of my people in Guinée which I had forgotten since coming here. The same weight was on my neck as the day before and a sadness was on me, but when I looked up from the burial stones I saw the sadness was not mine but hers. Nanon was standing, on the other side of the stones. Her blood was beating in her throat, under the marks of chafing which the iron collar had left. As soon as our eyes met, she turned and began walking quickly away. As she picked up her bare feet, I saw that they were dirty, and torn in places. I followed her all the way to the *grand'case*.

The sun shone full yellow on the house and the wild garden by the time we reached it. Nanon went across the gallery and into the house, without turning her head, like a ghost walking. I waited at the bottom of the stairs. Madame Fortier sat at the gallery table with her coffee and a piece of bread. I did not see her man anywhere, but Tocquet came up from the gate to join me, and Madame Fortier gave us a hand wave to come up.

She ordered coffee for us to drink, and as we sat there sipping it, we told her what we knew of Nanon, and how we knew it. First I spoke, and then Tocquet.

"Bien," Madame Fortier said, when we were both done speaking. "She ought to go back to this *blanc* doctor, I suppose. Assuming he would still have her back. One does not know just what a *blanc* might do in such a case."

Tocquet and I looked at each other. Then Tocquet explained how the trouble had begun with the doctor's sister, how she had wanted to drive Nanon and her son away. Then I told her what had passed later, when Elise had changed her heart and gone herself to bring the boy back to Thibodet, where he was now, as a child of the house. All the time I was speaking, Madame Fortier drew herself up slightly and became more and more alert, like an animal hunting.

"Well, that is something," she said when I had finished. "It is the loss of that child that has hurt her as much as anything, I think. When I asked her if she would go back to this *blanc* doctor, she said that she would not. But if the child is there . . . She must not stay here, that much I know. Jean-Michel can bring her nothing but harm."

She stopped talking, and looked across the gallery rail. A humming-bird was in the air before a bloom, green feathers shining on his back.

"A thing once ruined cannot be brought back," Madame Fortier said. "As it is wrong to bring the flesh back from the grave, so the love that was once between this woman and my son has become a twisted thing."

She looked at me deeply, and I lowered my eyes, from respect for the pain which she was speaking. When I looked up again, Nanon had appeared in the doorway of the house, with her blank *zombi* eyes aimed down toward the gate.

"Vini moin, machè," Madame Fortier said, and Nanon did come and take a seat beside her. Madame Fortier laid her hand on Nanon's bare arm and she shifted, restlessly. Since the day before she was all clean, and her hair was washed and carefully arranged, and the bad smell replaced with a sweet one, but the wildness was still in her.

Madame Fortier began to tell her how Paul had been brought back to Thibodet, that the boy was well, and waiting for her there. As she spoke, Nanon's face began to twist and wrestle with itself. She seemed to be crying, but without tears or sound. At last she calmed herself and swallowed. The mark of the iron collar moved on her throat.

"I cannot go," she said. Her voice was empty and sweet. None of what had been in her face was in it. "I cannot go there now."

Madame Fortier took her hand away. There was a bad silence among us all.

Then Tocquet got up and went away behind the house. The silence remained. The watch ticked in the pocket of my captain's coat. After a while, Tocquet came back with a basin of warm water and crushed leaves. He got down on the floor in front of Nanon and began very gently to wash her feet. The leaves were *herbe charpentier,* I knew by their smell, and they had a healing power for the hurts on her skin.

Madame Fortier turned in her chair, breathing in sharply, and I felt something of her feeling pass to me. Tocquet was a proud man in his own way, which was not quite the usual way of a *blanc,* but I had never thought of him doing such a thing. It made me wonder how it might be between him and the doctor's sister when they were alone with one another.

Madame Fortier looked at me and we both got up and walked down through the garden and stood in the gateway. That same *malfini* hung in the air above the gorge, as on the day before. Madame Fortier clucked her tongue.

"I do not know if Jean-Michel will ever come back here anyway," she said. "He has gone to the south, to Rigaud, because the Commissioner Sonthonax would have sent him to France, a prisoner."

"But now it's Sonthonax who has been sent away," I said.

"What does it matter." Madame Fortier did not look toward me, and I did not feel that she was speaking to me either. Her voice rose up toward that little hawk. "There will be no peace between Rigaud and this black army of the north. Or if there was, my son would turn his back upon it. It is ten days since I dreamed his death. Not every dream brings the truth of what will be, but I know that Jean-Michel will not rest before he has destroyed either himself or the whole world."

There was nothing to be said to this, and I did not think she was speaking to me anyway, but into her own sorrows. After a time, Tocquet came to us and said that Nanon had agreed to go with him, not back to Thibodet, but to Le Cap, where she had lived independently, it seemed, before going down to Ennery with the doctor.

Since that was arranged as well as it might be, I took my men away from Trou Vilain. We joined Moyse and his people again to travel down to Banica and then on to Mirebalais. There was no hard fighting on this way, hardly any enemies for us to fight at all, for the English were not to be seen in that part of the country, and the Spanish had gone away across the Cibao Mountains.

When we came to Mirebalais again, Moyse began his attack from Las Cahobas. Christophe Mornet was at Grand Bois, and Dessalines in the plain just outside the town, so there was no way for the English to get away. After many days they tried to break out toward Arcahaye, and we killed a lot of them as they were running—more than half their people, it was reckoned later on. When we came into the town, we found plenty of powder and shot and some cannons, too, that the English had left behind when they ran.

Toussaint began at once to rebuild everything in Mirebalais that he had ordered to be burned down some while before. This was the first time our part of the army joined his, because he had come up from the other side. I was eager to bring my news to the doctor, but the doctor had gone back to the coast, with messages for the new British general whose name was Maitland. No one knew for certain what it was all about, but the whisper was that the English were going to give up all their posts to us, and without any more fighting.

28

"Pssst!"

Doctor Hébert, who had been walking uphill from the gate of the Port au Prince *casernes,* barely registered the signal. He had thought himself alone. A little while previously, General Maitland had called a hiatus in the conversation between himself and Huin, the French officer who was Toussaint's chief representative, and the doctor had decided to trace the course of the waterway that fed the *casernes'* fountain. A shallow channel ran diagonally across the provision grounds facing the row of square clay houses of the blacks formerly belonging to the King of France. The doctor had followed it a considerable way, studying how the water was used to irrigate the field he was traversing.

"Psst!"

He turned. The boxy black coat, speckled liberally with pale dust that adhered and caked on the sweat patches, was the first thing that seemed familiar, and then the pinched urgency of the features . . . Bruno Pinchon, looking nervously all about. Why he felt a need for stealth was not apparent. They were well away from the wall of the *casernes* and no other buildings were nearby. A couple of black men were slowly swinging hoes in their patches of beans and yams, but they were at least a hundred yards away.

"Ah," said the doctor, with small enthusiasm, as Pinchon scurried up to him. "I see no one has murdered you yet."

"Yes, that's all very well, but . . ." Bent on unnecessary confidentiality, Pinchon leaned in so close that the doctor must inhale the sour flavor of his breath.

"Oh yes, I knew you," Pinchon said. "I saw you go in this morning." He looked over his shoulder again. "But let us get on."

"What troubles you so?" the doctor said. "There is no danger."

He turned from Pinchon and continued walking beside the narrow waterway. Some distance ahead it crossed, still at the diagonal, the double row of trees planted to line the approach to Government House. Pinchon hovered at his elbow as he went on.

"You may say so," he said. "Oh yes, you may say so—but Maitland means to abandon us. Yes. He will leave us to the savages. It's true—I see it in your face."

The doctor trudged on, dark mud caking on the soles of his boots, weighting down his tread. It was late afternoon, still very hot. The others at the *casernes* had retired for a siesta, and now he rather wished he had done the same, instead of pursuing his curiosity about the waterworks. But when they reached the alley of trees, the shade brought some relief.

"Why won't you answer me?" Pinchon said petulantly, half dancing in his muddy shoes.

"You haven't put a question," the doctor said wearily.

He took off his straw hat and untied the headcloth he'd taken to wearing underneath it. He crouched down on his heels and rocked forward to rinse the sweat-sodden cloth in the stream of water, then used it to wipe down his face and the bald dome of his head. The water was somewhat cooler than he expected, which was pleasant. He wet the cloth a second time, rolled it and draped it around his neck. The coolness at the base of his head brought a measure of clarity with it.

"Your fears are unfounded," he said, looking at his own indistinct reflection, rippling in the water. "These are no savages as you fear, but as well-disciplined an army as I have ever seen. As you might know."

"They would have killed me at Gonaives!"

"In war, men kill their enemies," the doctor said. He squinted up. "Why ever did you come to this country, I wonder."

Pinchon looked away, sucking his thin lips in. "My wife has a property in the plain of Cul de Sac."

"Your wife is a Creole?" The doctor straightened up and shook out his cramped legs.

"No," said Pinchon. "The daughter of a *négociant* of Nantes, who took the land in payment of a debt—the miser! Neither he nor she had ever laid eyes on the property, but I was sent out to make it profitable."

"And?"

"Oh, it was all a field of ashes by the time I found it."

"Have you children?"

"One, a daughter." Pinchon continued to look thoughtful. "I have not seen her—she was born after I embarked."

The doctor was moved to a certain sympathy. He said nothing, and turned slightly, facing into a very faint breeze which barely lifted the leaves of the trees around them. At the end of the boulevard was Government House, a fairly handsome pile of stone, and the most significant building in Port-au-Prince.

"Don't give up hope," the doctor said, as the breeze faded.

He was thinking that Pinchon might really have a better chance of restoring his plantation under Toussaint's administration rather than that of the English. But before he could voice this idea, he was distracted by someone signaling him from the steps of Government House at the lower end of the boulevard.

The siesta had been interrupted—brusquely, though no one announced the reason why. With Maitland, Huin, and few others, the doctor was hurried to the port and into a longboat which rowed them out to a British warship in the harbor. Following Huin, he climbed the rope ladder to the deck of the warship. Maitland, however, remained in the boat and was conveyed to a smaller coastal vessel which was anchored nearby.

"What do you suppose?" the doctor began.

Huin turned up his empty palms. "They told me nothing."

"Well," said the doctor, "So long as we are not to have our throats slit, and be fed to the sharks . . ."

Huin let out a dry grating laugh. "Fortunately," he said, "we are dealing with English gentlemen . . . rather than our own colonial countrymen."

He reached under his coat and produced a small brass spyglass. After scanning the horizon for a few minutes, he offered it to the doctor. Resting his elbows on the rail, the doctor looked at the small adjacent island, with its half-moon battery protecting the harbor, or at the clouds gathering above the great mountain behind the town . . .

Huin plucked his elbow and reached for the glass, and when the doctor had given it over, trained it on the deck of the coaster where Maitland had gone. The doctor looked in the same direction—Maitland was recognizable to his naked eye, among several others he could not make out.

"That is Lapointe," Huin mused aloud. "But . . . now who is that by him? I have seen the face."

He passed the glass to the doctor. In the circle of the lens the tall figure of a mulatto in British uniform came clear. This must be Lapointe, who commanded for the invaders at Arcahaye, though the doctor did not know him by sight.

"The black, beside him." Huin gaved the doctor a nudge.

"Why, it is Capdebosque," said the doctor, having refocused the glass. "Of Toussaint's troop, and you do know him—he was sent out to Arcahaye before we came here."

"Now what does that suggest to you?" Huin said.

If the doctor was meant to know the answer, he did not. But Maitland had descended to the longboat and was being rowed to the warship. Soon enough he had climbed the ladder and swung his long legs onto the deck.

"Gentlemen," he said. "There is another of your party on that ship"— he gestured with his chin—"who says there are twenty-six thousand brigands—uh, revolutionary troops—prepared to fall upon Arcahaye. Of your own knowledge, can this be true?"

"It is the very truth," said Huin, without a beat of hesitation.

The doctor looked toward the bulk of the mountain above Port-au-Prince, thinking. The number was exaggerated by perhaps ten thousand. Still, if the British wished to believe themselves outnumbered, such was in fact the case. Also, the attack planned on Arcahaye was commanded by Dessalines and would likely turn into a massacre.

"This messenger's name is Capdebosque," said Maitland. "A Negro, but intelligent, and well spoken, I admit. If you know him, can you vouch for his fidelity?"

"Absolutely," said the doctor, sensing his role.

"This Capdebosque tells me there is a like number of bri— revolutionary troops, massing on the Cul de Sac plain to attack Port-au-Prince."

"Port Républicain," Huin corrected him smoothly. "Of a certainty, it is true."

Maitland looked from Huin to the doctor, then back at Huin. "Furthermore, this Capdebosque maintains that the population of the town is secretly in league with the republicans and will turn out as soon as the attack begins."

Huin nodded, with an air of sadness (for such a conspiracy would not be entirely creditable to his side), and made a slight gesture toward a bow. Maitland turned his face to the doctor. His forehead was high, with an upswept crest of graying hair. The complementary curve of his beard swept down toward the dimple of his chin. Slowly, solemnly, the doctor nodded his confirmation (though he knew nothing of any such conspiracy and was reasonably confident that it did not exist). Maitland's features seemed to take on extra weight.

Again they descended into the longboat and were rowed back to the town, the men laying on hard at the oars, for the clouds above the mountain were already forked with lightning. As they reached the shelter of the *casernes,* the rain began, and Maitland summoned a council of war to the neighboring government house. From this, the doctor and Huin were excluded. But by the time the rain had stopped and the moon showed its horns above the yard of the *casernes,* one of Maitland's staff came to tell them that next day they would sail to Toussaint at Gonaives, escorting a British emissary with the power to offer an immediate cease-fire and to arrange terms for the British evacuation of Arcahaye, Saint Marc, and Port-au-Prince.

They enjoyed a smooth sail up the coast to Gonaives and docked in the late afternoon, when the town was just beginning to stir from the midday retreat from the fire of the sun. Doctor Hébert fell to the rear of the party that landed, trudging up to headquarters in the center of the town. As he entered the shadowy foyer of the building, Captain Maillart got up from a stool near the door and drew him away from the rest of the group. Huin, after a brief conference with the sentry, took the British officer Nightingal directly in to meet Toussaint.

"Our general has taken an ill humor," Maillart said.

"Oh?" said the doctor. "I think we may have brought him better cheer. But what is the matter?"

"Another agent of the Directoire has landed, in Santo Domingo," Maillart told him. "But let that wait." He grinned. "There is someone else with news for you."

The doctor followed him through the building out into the bright, white-dusted square of the barracks behind. Maillart stopped and let out a short whistle. From an open doorway across the yard, Riau emerged, checking the buttons of his uniform coat; when he saw the doctor, his face split into a brilliant smile and his step doubled.

"She is found," Riau said as he joined them. "After all she was at Vallière just as we thought."

"Nanon?"

"Yes, of course Nanon, *monchè!*" Riau slammed the doctor on the back.

"She is . . . where is she now?" the doctor said. "At Ennery?"

"No," said Riau. "But she is with your brother. With Tocquet—she went with him from Vallière to Le Cap."

"She is not with Choufleur any longer, then?"

Riau's expression grew elusive. "No, she is at Le Cap now."

"But where did she mean to go in Le Cap?"

Riau frowned—it did not seem that he had thought to ascertain this information. Then he brightened. "But Tocquet will know."

Someone called his name from the doorway he'd come out of across the yard. Riau slapped the doctor on the shoulder once more and trotted away. The doctor stared after him, half stupefied.

"You had better sit down," said the captain.

"I had thought of going on to Ennery," the doctor muttered.

"You'll never get there before the rain. Don't be a fool, but come with me."

Maillart led the way into the cubicle he occupied. The doctor sat down on the edge of his cot. Maillart passed him a clay vase of water, and he sipped, set the vase on the floor and pulled off one of his boots. His mind was floundering . . . Nanon was found! yet not within his reach. Tocquet would know where she had gone. But Tocquet was as unfindable as Nanon. And she might be anywhere in Le Cap. It had been almost impossible to discover where Paul had got to. But Nanon would be easier to find than Paul, because he knew her ways, and knew a lot of her acquaintances.

He stretched out his leg and flexed his liberated toes. Maillart pretended to flinch from the odor. He poured some rum into a cracked cup and passed it to the doctor, who took a grateful draught, feeling the warmth explode within him. He took off his other boot and rubbed the arch of his foot. There was no use talking to Maillart about Nanon, for the captain did not really understand the extent of his attachment to someone he saw as only a colored harlot.

"Well, and the new agent," he said.

"It is General Hédouville," Maillart told him. "Pacifier of the Vendée, as he is now known."

"Indeed."

"So they describe him." Maillart rocked his head against the rough plaster wall. "But let us go outside, it will be cooler."

He stood and picked up his stool and gestured to the doctor to bring the other. Just outside the door they arranged their seats beneath the shade of the overhanging roof. A breeze was beginning to stir, and several other officers had come out from rooms down the way to take the air. The doctor returned their waves of greeting. His bare feet spread pleasantly on the flagstone floor. He sat down and leaned back against a post. The captain, who had thoughtfully brought out the rum bottle, splashed another measure into his cup.

"He has brought fresh troops, this Hédouville?"

Maillart turned his head to spit into the yard. "His honor guard, no more than that," he said with a flicker of disgust.

"What can they be thinking in Paris?"

"Apparently," said the captain, "they are thinking that Hédouville turned all the factions of the Vendée against each other, so that they defeated themselves."

"And thus Toussaint's displeasure, I suppose," the doctor said.

Maillart did not respond immediately. The doctor chewed over the thought in silence. For the time being, Rigaud and Toussaint were acting in concert, if not in perfect harmony, against the British. It was not exactly a relationship of trust. Outlawed by Sonthonax, Rigaud had been in open rebellion against the French agent, if not France itself, at the time of Sonthonax's departure, while Toussaint continued to profess his loyalty to the French government.

Maillart shifted and scratched his head. "But now it is the whole stupid dispute of the *grand blancs* and *émigrés* all over again. Hédouville has proclaimed—from Santo Domingo, of course—that they are not to be tolerated."

"Oh, I see," said the doctor. "While Maitland will certainly insist that they be amnestied."

"Maitland?" The captain sat up straight.

"Yes, he has sent this Nightingal to set terms for the British withdrawal—from all of the Western Department, my friend."

"The devil," Maillart said. "Why must we treat with them? Now, when we are finally in position to defeat them in battle, drive the lot of them into the sea."

"That might be an expensive pleasure," the doctor said. "The British are finished here, I agree. And Maitland is certainly commissioned to get them out with as little loss as possible. But he has still a few teeth in his jaw. If they fight, we will have losses on our side, and the British can leave every place they now occupy in ruins."

"Still they are in no position to dictate terms to us."

The wind quickened, skirling up dust all over the yard. The doctor looked across and saw the first fat raindrops beginning to pat down.

"Leave that to Toussaint," he said.

"Well, yes." Maillart leaned forward and reached down to collect the rum bottle from between his feet. "He is a wicked old fox, Toussaint, and no one knows for certain what is in his mind."

*   *   *

Next day, the doctor asked leave to travel to Le Cap, but when he was refused, he did not press the point. He did not give his personal reason, for Toussaint was in a humor to preach of duty, and the doctor did not want to hear the sermon. He got permission to go to Ennery for two days, which he passed agreeably enough with Paul and Sophie and Elise. Yet everything hung over them, still. Elise had recovered her morale, but if she had heard anything from Tocquet she did not say so, and for his part the doctor did not mean to upset her with news that the man might be as nearby as Le Cap. Nor did he know what to say to Paul about his mother. In fact the boy no longer asked for her, and yet the doctor felt the question in his look.

While at Ennery he got word that Hédouville was traveling from Santo Domingo to Le Cap, so he returned to Gonaives in the happy expectation that Toussaint would certainly be going north to pay his respects to the French agent. But it was not so. Instead, the doctor and the other available scribes were put to drafting a letter of apology (of sorts): Toussaint regretted that he must deny himself the pleasure of meeting General Hédouville, for the time being, as crucial military matters kept him at his post. Though the letter was infused with unction, the scribes were hard put to disguise the aloofness at the heart of the message. On the other hand, it was quite true that military matters were moving rapidly toward a crisis: Huin had gone south again to Port au Prince, where, aboard the British ship *Abergavenny*, he signed an accord with Nightingal which defined the terms of British withdrawal from all of the west coast . . . and by that time, as Huin reported back later, the sailors of the British fleet had already begun loading up supplies and ammunition from the town, under Maitland's orders to prepare for departure.

Generals Maitland and Toussaint Louverture both ratified the treaty, and only then did Toussaint notify Hédouville of what had taken place. In his reply, Hédouville warned Toussaint not to accept the submission of any *émigrés*, but by then the treaty had already gone into effect. By its terms, a three-month cease-fire would be observed between the British and the forces commanded by Toussaint, and during this period Toussaint engaged not to attack the posts that the British would still hold in the south at Jérémie, and at Môle Saint Nicolas on the northwest peninsula. In particular, he pledged, for the period of the cease-fire, *not* to support Rigaud, who was energetically besieging Jérémie (though Toussaint had grumbled over that clause, pointing out that no difference ought to be made between himself and Rigaud when both of them were loyal officers of the French Republic). The British would return the coast towns and their fortifications intact, and with the same armament they'd found when they first took possession of them. Toussaint, for his part, would guarantee the lives and the property of those colonists currently under British protection who chose to stay on when the British had left.

Captain Maillart shook his head gloomily over that last proposal, when the doctor had described it to him over another round of rum on the gallery of the house at Habitation Thibodet. "The agent will not like it," Maillart muttered. "How, indeed, can Hédouville accept it?"

He passed the bottle to the doctor, who served himself and handed it on to Riau, who was sitting with them in the moist dark. Elise and the children had long since gone to bed, but the mood of excitement that ran through the camp prevented the men from sleeping.

"As a *fait accompli*." The doctor shrugged. "He gains by it. France gains."

"What we gain," said Maillart, "is enemies snuggled to our bosom in the guise of friends. The British will withdraw their officers but leave us all our traitors who fought under their flag—transformed into *property holders* we are sworn to protect."

"Well," said the doctor, "I had not recognized you for such an inveterate Jacobin."

Maillart choked. "Never mind the politics, but it is too much—all I know is that we have been fighting these people for two or three years, and though we have defeated them—or might have—we are now required to embrace them." He looked at Riau. "They are slave masters too, these new *citizens* we are to gain. What will become of the slaves they have held all this while under British rule?"

"They will be freed," said the doctor, "according to French law."

Riau rolled his glass from one hand to the other, looking at the inch of amber rum in the bottom of it. He said nothing.

"Embracing one's enemies is a queer sensation," the doctor said. "The taste for it may be difficult to acquire." He drank, and glanced at Maillart's flushed face. "You yourself have crossed a border more than once, and worn the coat of more than one service—oh, it does you no dishonor. It was the ground itself that shifted beneath your feet."

"So." Maillart grunted and leaned back, withdrawing his face from the lamplight. Struggling to recover the thread of his thought, the doctor realized he was considerably more drunk than he'd given himself credit for.

"One loses the principle, I admit," he said, waving one hand slackly, "in all this, this . . ." The word would not come. "But consider the practice. At Le Cap, Agent Hédouville will certainly have learned that the treasury is quite empty. The army fights without pay for the most part." He looked at Riau. "The soldiers forage all their food." He hiccuped into the palm of his hand, then went on. "These enemies we are asked to receive—it's they who can make the plantations profitable again, and put some money back into the coffers of the government. Surely the agent will see that soon enough."

"As you like," Maillart said, "but I think there will be trouble."

"Oh," said the doctor. "When was there not?"

As General Maitland completed the withdrawal from Port-au-Prince, the Legion of the West, commanded by Laplume, moved up from Léogane to secure the town for the French Republicans. For some time, Laplume had been making forays over the Cul de Sac plain and attacking the heights above Port-au-Prince. Though Laplume reported to the mulatto General Pétion, and hence to Rigaud, his men were still mostly drawn from the wild bands Dieudonné had formerly led. They were the first to enter Port-au-Prince as the British departed. Toussaint had sent Christophe Mornet as his own representative. There were no outrages.

The last British sails slipped over the horizon, bound for the deep, capacious harbor of Môle Saint Nicolas. At Port-au-Prince, the French collaborators waited uneasily, for their situation could not be certainly known before Toussaint's arrival.

Though he might have covered the distance in a third of the time, Toussaint made a very slow progression to Port-au-Prince. With the officers of his staff, he made frequent stops on the Cul de Sac plain. Most of the plantations had fallen into ruin after so many years of war and marauding, but here and there a house or a mill was still intact. Toussaint halted, dismounted, crouched down to pick up earth and crumble it between his fingers, or broke off bits of the untended cane to try its quality.

Impatient, Captain Maillart squinted up at the sun, already well past its height in the sky. A cavalry troop and most of the staff sat their horses before a mule-powered cane mill. Bel Argent stood riderless, held by the captain of the honor guard. Toussaint had gone into the mill to check the mechanism for rust and breakage.

"Now why does he stop here?" Maillart muttered irritably to the doctor beside him. He looked over his shoulder at the dust cloud that marked the position of the infantry, marching half a mile behind them on the plain. "We shall pass another night in this wasteland before we reach the town."

"Because the land must not be wasted," the doctor said softly, and mostly to himself. "Because the land is more important than the town."

Maillart snorted, and his horse yawed sideways, as if it had caught his impatient mood. Toussaint came out of the mill, settling his hat down carefully over his yellow headcloth. He swung into the saddle and led them on.

The road across the plain was much deteriorated, but still gave room enough for three horses to go abreast. The doctor rode between Maillart and Riau, who wore for the occasion a tall hussar's hat he'd captured from the British cavalry, ornamented with a huge revolutionary cockade. Many of the officers and some of the men had tricked themselves out specially for this triumphal procession. But Toussaint wore only his plain uniform, with no decoration beyond the epaulettes. He had even forgone the plumes he usually wore in his hat, which was, today, a somewhat battered tricorne.

The sky was just beginning to redden before them when they finally came in sight of the bay. Sky joined the water on a curving, gilded line, broken by the low roofs of Port-au-Prince. Something lay on the road ahead, between them and the town. Toussaint pulled his horse up abruptly, one hand hovering between his sword hilt and pistol grip, before it froze, midair. For a suspended moment, he was as still as a startled snake.

Maillart stood up in his stirrups, craning his neck to see. "By God," he hissed to the doctor. "They have raised us a triumphal arch."

Toussaint relaxed, tucked in his jaw and lowered his head. He urged his horse forward on the road.

A cheer went up from the reception party, and a swirl of dust as they all began to stir about. It was indeed a makeshift arch, the doctor saw as they came nearer, rigged with boards and painted canvas. Half a length ahead of the others, Toussaint walked his horse toward it. Then, without troubling to stop his mount, he dropped to the ground and tossed the reins back over his shoulder; Riau caught them in his left hand. On foot, Toussaint continued to approach the arch, which was flanked by young white women with flowers in their hands, a prelate wearing white vestments and a gold-embroidered stole, a clutch of altar boys who held fuming censers by their chains, and four of the wealthiest planters of the region, each holding a pole which supported one corner of a fringed, royal purple dais.

Toussaint stopped and held up the flat of his right hand. The dais-bearers hesitated, their fat smiles withering.

"I am not God," Toussaint said in a low, clear voice. He removed his hat, revealing his dome of yellow madras, and held it in both hands as he bowed his head slightly. "It is only for God to be incensed so, and walk beneath a dais."

He flapped his hat at the dais-bearers, as if hazing cattle, at which they furled the fabric around the poles and stepped reluctantly out of his way. His long jaw set, Toussaint walked forward through a grisly silence and passed beneath the arch. As he emerged on the other side, the band struck up, the girls with their garlands burst into strained song, and everyone seemed to be throwing flowers.

Riau and Maillart and the doctor dismounted too, along with the rest of the staff officers, leaving the honor guard to lead their horses. They marched along behind Toussaint, who walked as if in the deepest trance, oblivious to everything before his eyes. To the doctor's right, Riau stood very tall, imitating Toussaint's fixed regard, the hussar's hat adding nearly a foot to his height. To his left, Maillart stumped along, shaking his head in mock disbelief, till an especially lovely girl managed to graze his cheek with a flung rose. At that the captain stooped to retrieve the flower, kissed the air and blew the kiss across the petals toward the blushing beauty who had thrown it, fixed the rose in his buttonhole and walked on in a much better humor.

The crowd closed around them, pressing nearer as the spectators grew more bold, some merely eager, curious, but also there were many petitioners, already vying for the notice of Toussaint. One young woman was so hugely pregnant that the doctor thought she might give birth there in the road, and yet she kept pace with Toussaint all the way, calling out desperately that her husband must either win or retain a post as inspector of customs, pointing at her great belly for emphasis—*the father of my child!* she cried over and over, her voice breaking from the effort and the urgency. Nearby Bruno Pinchon was scampering, jumping to raise his head above the others as he called—*Habitation Anlouis! Habitation Anlouis!*—and some other petitioner had snatched one of the rejected censers and was whirling smoke at Toussaint, despite his remonstrance, and begging for some favor the doctor could not quite hear. Toussaint took no notice of any of them.

In the days that followed, the doctor took the opportunity to finish his study of the irrigation system, broken off during his previous visit to Port-au-Prince. It was an ingenious arrangement in its way. One main canal was dug in an irregular course across the slopes above the town, and several tributary channels used the natural incline to feed water to the old Intendance, the *casernes*, the royal hospital, and the fountain on Government Square.

The doctor followed this latter channel to its terminus at the fountain in front of Government House. Toussaint's troops stood in quiet, orderly groups at the corners of the square, barefoot and shirtless for the most part, lean as greyhounds but just as fit. Some of them saluted the doctor as he walked toward the building. These were men who could march all day on one banana or a cupful of corn, sleep on their feet, fight on the morrow—they had been doing so for years. Small children circled them, wide-eyed and curious; a woman approached one of the squads with a covered basketful of bread. After a week of perfect discipline on the part of the black soldiers, and none of the pillaging or disorder that had been anticipated, the townspeople had begun to lose their fear.

Petitioners lined the hallways of Government House, waiting, hoping, to see Toussaint. The doctor felt envious eyes on his back as the sentries acknowledged him and let him pass through. In the anteroom, Bruno Pinchon sat next to a young woman cradling a newborn infant. The wife he had mentioned? the doctor wondered—but no, he'd said she was in France.

Seeing the doctor, Pinchon sprang up, his mouth already open to begin some plea, but just then the door of the inner office opened and the mayor of Port-au-Prince bowed his way out. Toussaint came after him through the doorway, telling him that Christophe Mornet would follow through on whatever business they had just settled. The young woman was instantly on her feet, thrusting the baby forward.

"*Habitation Anlouis,*" Pinchon interjected, but the woman stepped quickly in front of him, cutting off his approach. She made an accordion movement with her arms, gathering the infant to herself, then proffering it again.

"General," she said. Her voice was sweet, but a little shrill, and had a nagging familiarity to the doctor's ear. "General, I beg you—I beseech you! Be godfather to my child. We will name him, perhaps . . . Toussaint."

And now the doctor recognized her, from their first entrance to the town—she must have delivered this infant only the day, or two days, before. A pretty thing, he judged, with glossy black hair and large dark eyes and an appealing flush that spread across her face and also her bosom, which was very generously revealed by the cut of her gown. Held at arm's length, the baby did not cry or complain, but worked its little fingers at random, peering myopically from its button eyes.

Toussaint covered his mouth with his hand, and studied the woman and child without speaking. Then he reached to the back of his head, unfastened the knot of his yellow headcloth, and shook it out.

"Cover yourself, Madame, if you please."

As she absorbed his meaning, the young woman's color darkened to the shade of new-fired brick. Shifting the child to the crook of one arm, she accepted the square of cloth with her other hand. Pinchon, maybe a little too eager for the service, helped her to arrange it over her décolletage.

Toussaint indicated a chair, and she sat down and lowered her head. A fine high color, the doctor thought; it spread round the back of her neck like wine. Pinchon moved as if to renew his approach, then suddenly fell back into a seat, as if the force of Toussaint's look had flung him there.

It was a rare thing to see Toussaint completely bareheaded. The head was larger than it looked beneath his hat or headcloth, high and egg-shaped, with gray hair thinning at the dome. He covered his mouth with his hand. His eyes drifted half-shut, so that only the whites of them showed. The doctor knew he was very tired. The enthusiasm of his reception by the residents of Port-au-Prince had not been altogether feigned, but he had not fully anticipated its cause. The great majority of the whites who had remained believed that he would make the colony independent of France, and almost as many confidently expected him to solve the mulatto problem, permanently, by massacring them all.

"Madame," said Toussaint, "why should you wish me to name your son? Have you considered well what you are asking? I know you are seeking a post for your husband—I also know that all the white *colons* despise me in their hearts."

At this the young woman started up from her seat as if to protest, but Toussaint, who had seemed to be talking in his sleep, widened his eyes and stayed her with his hand.

"No, if I wore a skin like yours—but I am black, and I know the deep distaste the *colons* have for me and all my kind. It is true that Revolution has enlightened the French, so that we are well enough liked for the moment, but no work of man is truly durable. Only the work of God Himself can last forever. It may be that after my death, my brothers will pass into slavery again, and go under the whip of the white *colons*, who have always been our enemies. Then your son, when he has reached the age of reason, will reproach you for having given him a black to be his godfather."

Abruptly, Toussaint sat down himself, and leaned forward with his elbows on his knees. "No, Madame, I cannot accept this honor which you suggest to me. You wish a place for your husband in the Customs—it is his. Tell Commander Christophe Mornet what I have said, and it will be so arranged. You may also tell your husband that, while I cannot see all that he does, nothing is invisible to God. Let him serve honestly."

The young woman's blush had subsided considerably by the time Toussaint had done speaking. She stood up and curtsied gracefully. It was circumspect, the doctor thought, for her to say nothing, not even to risk a word of thanks. No fool she. Carrying the child, she went out, with Toussaint's yellow madras still half tucked into her bodice. They could hear the baby beginning to mew in the hall as she retreated.

"Monsieur Général," Pinchon began, once more rising to his feet. "You do not remember me, but—"

Toussaint looked up at him, his eyes red-rimmed. "Oh, I remember you very well," he said. "Better than you would perhaps prefer. Your name is Bruno Pinchon, and through your marriage to Marie-Céleste Latrobe you claim possession of Habitation Anlouis, a sugar plantation of eighty-six *carrés,* in the plain of Cul de Sac. This land was gambled away at cards by the son of the original Anlouis, now dead of his debaucheries, and so came into the hands of your father-in-law, who is a broker at Nantes. But neither he nor your wife nor you yourself have ever laid eyes on the property. You are no planter, and you know nothing of the work. I remember all these things, and I also recall our first meeting at Ennery, with everything that you said and did on that occasion."

Pinchon took a long step backward, his Adam's apple working.

"At Gonaïves too, when I claimed it for France, you barely escaped being shot for your involvement with the enemy," Toussaint said. "Now we meet for the third time." He exhaled, glancing toward the window, as if the sight of Pinchon pained him. "Well, you may enjoy your dowry. Make of it what you can. See Commander Paul Louverture at Croix des Bouquets and it will be arranged. Your life and property will be respected."

Pinchon also elected the virtue of silence—wisely, the doctor thought again. He bowed, stumbled, made his way to the door. In the hall outside there was a commotion among the others waiting for their audiences. The doctor stepped across and shoved the door closed on them all.

Toussaint was bowed in his seat, his shoulders shaking. The patchy baldness of his head looked oddly fragile. The doctor had never heard him speak with such a bitter pessimism as he'd used with that young woman—not, at least, of his own cause. But when he straightened and took his hand from his mouth, he revealed that his convulsions had been laughter, all along.

"Very well," he said, shaking his head and giving the doctor his cayman's smile as he pointed to the door. "Open! let the next one come in."

29

Captain Maillart did his best to swallow his irritation as he bowed his way into the Cigny parlor and found it full of the junior attachés of Agent Hédouville's suite, who were swift enough to discover the charms of his friend Isabelle. The Cigny house was enjoying a burst of popularity these days, for although the official policy with which Hédouville was invested must regard the family with a certain suspicion, a good many of the juniors seemed quite thoroughly *ancien régime* in their personal sentiments, and wore the black collars to show it.

He adjusted his frayed cuffs and sat down in the place Isabelle had indicated for him, a long, sturdy sofa, next to Joseph Flaville. The black-collared youths were looking at him, he felt, with slyly concealed amusement. That impudent puppy Paltre (not twenty-five years of age) was whispering with his companion Ciprien Cypré, similarly unlicked. They'd be sneering, Maillart was sure enough, at his worn coat with its stains of tropical campaigning (which they ought to regard as marks of honor) and still more at his subordination to the black officers, former slaves from whom he took his orders, whose rank was exaggerated so far past his own. Ten years in the colony and still a captain—that was due to his many changes of service, and Maillart had not wasted much thought on it either, until Hédouville's puppy pack had obliged him to. Paltre and Cypré were captains themselves, at the same age Maillart had been when he first came out to Saint Domingue, and perhaps no more feckless either, but he was not in a forgiving mood.

"*Sé fransé m'yé,*" he said to Flaville, but loudly enough to be heard everywhere in the room. "*Men, m'pa rinmin fransé tankou moun sa yo.*"

Flaville, who relaxed on the sofa with a serpentine ease, grinned and let a fluid movement flow through his whole long body, while Isabelle clicked her tongue and frowned to reprove them both. The two young captains drew themselves up a little, sensing they had been insulted but without knowing exactly how. I am French, but I don't like Frenchmen like these people. Maillart had learned that it distressed the new arrivals to hear patois, which sounded exactly like their own language but was incomprehensible to them.

Nanon raised her head from her embroidery hoop and gave him a quick, secret smile, then lowered her face again, indifferent to the blandishments of the two civilian clerks who were trying to engage her interest. Maillart felt distinctly better now. By God, she was a beauty—none of it had tarnished her, whatever she had been through. Say what you would about the wisdom of throwing one's whole heart at a colored courtesan, the captain could not dispute the doctor's taste. For himself, he was glad to have found her safe in the Cigny house, and that he would have this news for Antoine Hébert when they next met.

He accepted the coffee that was served him, and devoted about a quarter of his attention to flirting with Isabelle. The pattern of their banter was familiar as a waltz—he could sustain his steps without thinking about them. It meant little; he would not taste her honeyed chalice. So far as he knew, she'd given her full sweetness to no man at all, if not to her husband, since their odd quarrel at Môle Saint Nicolas. Friendship with a woman—ha. But his ease with her would annoy the little captains. It was childish to score off the puppies, Maillart knew, but he enjoyed it all the same.

And these were the officers meant to replace Toussaint's cadre!— for almost all Hédouville's suite was like these two: absurdly young, and arrogant in exact proportion to their inexperience. Maillart, who'd become for a time Toussaint's particular envoy to the new agent, had divined that much: Hédouville meant to assert control of the indigenous army by infiltrating his own officers, these cubs, ha. Hédouville himself was quite a different matter, clearly a capable officer, seasoned in battle and yet equally skillful in winning contests without battles. During his service under Toussaint, Maillart had developed a special appreciation of that latter capacity. And Hédouville would need all the guile at his command, since he'd been sent out with no force at all, to speak of.

The agent's original instructions were to arrest Rigaud for the flagrant insubordination he'd shown Sonthonax, but Toussaint had absolutely refused to carry out this order when Hédouville sent it on to him. Captain Maillart had had the dubious privilege of delivering Toussaint's letter of reply, which stated that since Rigaud was clearly a loyal servant of the Republic, as evidenced by the vigorous campaign he was then prosecuting against the British at Jérémie, why, to arrest Rigaud would be as if to arrest himself. Hédouville had received this response with equanimity, even with some appreciation (so it seemed to Maillart) for its pragmatism. Since then, he'd been evolving some quite different strategy, though the captain couldn't make out what it was. But Maillart rather liked Hédouville, thus far. And if he played his cards very close to his vest, one must also admit that he'd been dealt a difficult hand to play.

Isabelle was tittering at some remark he'd made, though Maillart himself could not remember his own witticism. He drained off the sugary swirl at the bottom of his coffee, set down the cup and stood to take his leave. Through the open doors that gave onto the balcony, he could see the masts of ships at dockside, over the rosy tile roofs of the houses down the slope. Flaville had also risen to go. Maillart stooped to brush Isabelle's hand with his lips, and went out.

In the stairwell, he paused to wait for Flaville, but it was Cyprè and Paltre who appeared instead, and Maillart quickly turned his back on them.

"Four grenadiers," one of them said. "No more." Maillart was not sure which. He did not bother distinguishing them. But he'd meant to be overheard; that was clear. Some clique among the puppy officers had declared that they'd want no more than four grenadiers to arrest "that old rag-headed Negro"—by which they meant Toussaint. The boast had become well known throughout Le Cap. Stiff-necked, Maillart walked across the foyer. A house servant was opening the door for him, and the light outside was a white-hot blaze. He spun, rage twirling him, but everything became strangely slow, so that while he watched his red fist floating toward the insolent face of Paltre, who was leading the pair, he was able to consider many things with apparent leisure. For some reason he was thinking of Xavier Tocquet and what he might do in such a situation—but he wouldn't have been in it at all, would not have let himself be drawn in so far. Flaville, who had been a slave, was coming down the steps behind the young French captains, and what insults he must have had to bear in silence in his time. If he struck Paltre, there must be a duel, and when he'd been their age Maillart would have fought, without thinking, to the death, borne the official reprimand, perhaps demotion, defended himself on the grounds of honor. This instant he could have killed Paltre without compunction, but the waste of it all repelled him. Paltre was flinching, showing his fear, and Maillart stopped his hand short of contact, opened it, let it come to rest on the younger man's shoulder. He smiled.

"If you speak of my commanding officer, the General-in-Chief Toussaint Louverture, let me advise you that he is a civilized man. But there are many *rag-headed old Negroes* in this country, and if you are so unfortunate as to meet with one of the less civilized variety, why, you may find your severed head stuffed into your slit belly, your own male member crammed inside your mouth. Now smile, my boy, and show your courage. I will not stop smiling, when I see you so. I have seen things in this country that have not appeared in your worst nightmares."

He gave Paltre's shoulder a little shake, released it, and strode out the door without waiting for any answer. But Flaville was in step with him as they turned to go find their horses.

"Ou bay blan-yo pè djab," Flaville said, as he unhitched his sorrel.

"As I meant to." Maillart returned his grin as he climbed aboard his mount. They saluted each other, then rode in opposite directions. You scared the devil out of those white people—an odd compliment for Flaville to have made to him, the captain thought as he rode across the Rue Espagnole toward the barracks, and yet its echo was most pleasing to his ear.

Under the lifting tendrils of morning mist, Doctor Hébert rode out from the gateway of Habitation Thibodet, his medicaments stored in his saddlebags and his long gun's stock thrusting up from a scabbard by his knee. His mount was a new mare Riau had procured for him—there'd been a lot of fresh horses coming over the Spanish border since the retaking of Mirebalais. The mare was a strong and handsome gray, but barely green-broke and skittish as a cat. She kept the doctor alert as he rode through the *bourg* of Ennery.

Beyond the village the road was flat and went beneath the shade of mango trees, with the warming sun striping down between their branches. By then the mist had burned away, and the doctor overtook a line of market women going to the crossroads, who smiled up at him from beneath the baskets on their heads. Coming in the opposite direction were three horseback men leading a pair of donkeys—and where had the doctor seen that particular broad-brimmed hat before?

But Tocquet recognized him first. When he swept off his outsized hat, the doctor's mare skated sideways, reared and went down almost all the way to her hindquarters. Rather than be thrown, the doctor slipped down from the saddle, sinking to his right boot top in the rutted slough. He caught the reins tight under the bit and brought the mare back down to earth.

"*Saluez,*" Tocquet said brightly as he rode up. Gros-jean and Bazau were also smiling as they halted their horses behind him.

"A magnificent animal you have there," Tocquet said. "She looks as if she could climb trees."

"She's willing to try," the doctor said, stroking the mare's soft nose, as she went on trying to toss her head. He looked at Tocquet. "You've been a long time on the road."

Tocquet looked off into the treetops. His face was shadowed with beard stubble over his lean jaw and the hollow of his throat. "Did you tell her to expect me?" he finally said.

"I didn't know when you would come." The doctor broke a stalk of bamboo from a cluster at the roadside and began pushing some of the swamp-smelling mud from the upper of his boot.

"You should find Nanon at the Cigny house," Tocquet said, shortening the focus of his eyes.

"My God, yes," the doctor said in a rush. "Riau told me she had come down to Le Cap with you but—is she well? . . . or not."

Tocquet looked into the treetops again. "Let us say, somewhere between the two. But you ought to go and see for yourself."

The doctor shook his head, irritably. "Yes, but Toussaint is most reluctant to spare me for the journey."

"I'll give you odds he'll be making that journey himself very soon, by the look of the messenger from Hédouville who passed me on the road."

"Oh?"

"If you're bound for Gonaives, you'll soon know more than I."

Tocquet squeezed his heels into the flanks of his horse. The mare shuddered as he put the big hat on his head again, but kept all four feet on the ground. The doctor tossed away his bamboo stalk, mounted, and rode on.

He had been shuttling between Gonaives and Ennery for the last few weeks, and knew that Toussaint was preoccupied with negotiations for the British withdrawal from Jérémie and the Grande Anse, which for the moment were going nowhere. Meanwhile, the luster of his triumph at Port-au-Prince had begun to fade, while Hédouville grew testy about concessions Toussaint had made to Maitland, and complained about the ease with which so many *grand blancs* proprietors had recovered their plantations in the Western Department.

By the time the doctor reached the Gonaives *casernes*, the message Tocquet mentioned had been delivered. Toussaint was requested, in terms he could not deny short of open insubordination, to present himself to Hédouville at Le Cap. And rumor carried the implication that the French agent was determined to assert control over any further negotiation with the British.

"I do not think he wants to go," Riau told the doctor with a shrug. "But if he goes, it is good for you, because . . ."

"Yes," said the doctor. "Yes, that is true." He felt an inner flutter at the thought of the attic room of the Cigny house, with its round window and low-angled walls, where he had been before Nanon, where she'd be now.

He passed that night in the *casernes*, his hammock strung next to Riau's. When he woke, the room was empty but for a small green lizard blowing out its throat contemplatively as it watched him from the windowsill. From the direction of the square he heard the hum of a commotion.

He got up and dressed and went out, already beginning to sweat from his exertions. It was later than he'd expected to wake, the sun already high. At the gate the sentries seemed uneasy, and when he asked them what was happening, they said only, *General Rigaud,* and pointed toward the headquarters building, where that officer apparently had gone.

Glancing once over his shoulder at the fading brick of the building, the doctor walked south, around the curve of the wide, white-dusty road, till he came to the square before the church. Some forty cavalrymen from the Southern Department stood holding their horses in the center of the square, ringed by many times their number of men from the Fourth Colonial Regiment, commanded by Jean-Jacques Dessalines.

Noticing Riau's tall hussar's hat protruding from the crowd, the doctor made his way over to him, excusing himself and apologizing all around as he shouldered his way through.

"What is it?" he said, but Riau was masked, no more expressive than a tree, though he shifted his weight slightly to acknowledge the doctor's arrival. The doctor looked to the center of the ring of men and felt a contraction of his viscera when he recognized Choufleur.

He wore the French uniform, though cut of a better cloth than that commonly used, with gold buttons to match the gold braid. Insignia of a colonel's rank. His face was pale, so that the swirl of freckles over it stood out like a dark mist, concealing his features with a veil of points which were almost black. The doctor remembered several of the things that Madame Fortier had said about her son. Choufleur was facing Dessalines.

"Your men are blocking our way," he said carelessly. "Move them out of the road, at once, if you please."

Choufleur and Dessalines were of a height, but Choufleur was much the slenderer, though by no means frail. He glanced over his shoulder at the man who was holding his horse.

"I do not take my orders from you." Dessalines's reply was uninflected; there was no anger in it but it was immovable, rooted like a tree. The black commander stood rooted, swinging slightly from the hips. When Choufleur turned to face him again, he seemed surprised to find Dessalines still standing there.

A pair of gulls came crying over the square, blown by the warm wind from the sea. The gulls banked into the wind and hovered, the wind pushing them slowly backward, then cried again and flew back toward the port. Choufleur's hand played over his sword hilt for a moment. Dessalines shifted his weight.

"I would not dirty my weapon on a Congo like you," Choufleur said. "Sooner a whip."

Dessalines said, nothing, but began to swell. Standing in place, he grew larger, heavier, darker. The doctor remembered the knot of scars that lay beneath his coat and thought of them moving, crawling like a nest of snakes. A murmur ran through the crowd surrounding the small mulatto troop, and the doctor's entrails twisted tighter. Riau placed a hand on his back, as if he'd felt his distress and wanted to steady him.

The ring of men opened, just to his left, and Toussaint Louverture stepped through the gap, accompanied by a taller, light-skinned general.

"Let them pass," Toussaint said.

Dessalines, who had been staring only at Choufleur, turned his head fractionally, just enough to take in the newcomers at the far edge of his view.

"Let the General Rigaud go to make his report to the agent, Hédouville," Toussaint said, in a reasonable tone, as if debating, though it was an order. "Why should I wish to prevent his going?"

Dessalines deflated. He turned fully toward Toussaint, saluted smartly, then called to his men, *Alé! Kité yo pasé.*

Toussaint's companion must be Rigaud, the doctor realized; he had not previously seen the colored general face to face, though he'd heard descriptions. He was taller than Toussaint, and quite a handsome man, with sharp European features. Only his hair looked somewhat unnatural; he was reported to wear a straight-hair wig. Now Rigaud had shaken Toussaint's hand with all appearance of friendliness and trust. He swung onto his horse, and Choufleur followed his example. At Dessalines's order, the men of the Fourth opened a corridor onto the road to the north, and Rigaud and his men rode through.

Perhaps two hours later, on the heights above Plaisance, Toussaint returned to the subject as if there had never been any pause in the conversation. "Let General Rigaud attend his meeting with Agent Hédouville. I have no wish to arrest him. I need Rigaud—to fight this war with the English."

Toussaint rode at the head of his own small party, flanked by Riau and the doctor; they had all left Gonaives about an hour behind the mulatto group, bound for Le Cap. Toussaint was looking straight down the road, sitting the trot of Bel Argent. He had the air of talking to himself, though he spoke loudly enough to be heard by those on either side of him.

"The class of the mulattoes believes itself superior to mine, and if I were to take Monsieur Rigaud away from them, they might find a leader more valuable than he. When he gallops, he lets his horse go. When he strikes, he shows his arm. As for myself, I know how to gallop, but I stop when and wherever I choose, exactly, and when I strike my force is felt, but no one sees my hand . . ."

Toussaint's face was set, his lower jaw thrusting out with his words. His companions, riding a half-length back, exchanged interested glances over the pumping hindquarters of Bel Argent. Their little column was atop a dizzy height with the Plaisance River valley winding below. Wet, gray clouds blanketed the peaks to the east. The doctor adjusted his hat and pulled his long duster closer about him. Though it was still hot, he knew it would be raining soon and that they would not stop for the rain. This peak, this range of mountains all the way east to the Spanish border, was the bedrock of the power of Toussaint Louverture. Perhaps it was their proximity that had unleashed the general's tongue, for it was unusual for him to speak so freely, especially of himself.

"Monsieur Rigaud can only make his people rise in blood and massacre," Toussaint went on. "Then he moans to see the fury of the mob he has excited. If I have put the people into movement, their fury never troubles me, for whenever I appear in person, everything must grow calm."

He fell silent. It was quiet all down the line, but for the sound of hoofbeats, the rattle of a stone kicked over the rim of the trail, the infrequent cry of hawks above the valley. Already the first drops of rain were slapping the rock and the flanks of the horses. At the damp touches the mare jibbed and began to skate sideways. The doctor reined her in and leaned to pat her withers. He pulled his hat brim down. When they reached Le Cap that night, they found they were in advance of Rigaud's men; they must have passed him on the way, whether because Toussaint knew a shorter route through the mountains, or that Rigaud was loath to ride through rain and darkness.

Doctor Hébert took the opportunity, while Generals Toussaint and Rigaud were closeted with Agent Hédouville, to visit the Cigny house, for Maillart had been quick to tell him that he would find Nanon there. The scene in Isabelle's salon was much as the captain had described it—a full complement of the supercilious youths in Hédouville's suite, paying their court to the ladies, except that Nanon was not present. The doctor forced his way through a few pleasantries and accepted the refreshment urged upon him. When after half an hour she had not appeared, it occurred to him that since he was familiar with the house, nothing prevented him from going directly up to the little room she and he had both occupied, at different times.

With this intention, he slipped out of the parlor, but Isabelle halted him before he had set his foot on the first step.

"I must tell you that your room is engaged by another," she said.

"Yes," he muttered, "I have heard so."

"Doctor Hébert," she said, as he turned reluctantly from the stairway. "I am sorry to say she will not receive you now."

His face must have expressed his astonishment. She caught his sleeve and drew him into a small windowless room across the hall and shut the door behind them. The cubicle was furnished with a round table, a lamp, a chair, most prominently a daybed draped with silk shawls. The doctor knew the place to be a theater for her seductions; indeed she'd once handed him a certain humiliation here.

"No," said Isabelle, as if she'd read his memory. "I only want to explain myself—as if I could." She fingered the light gold chain around her neck. Something attached to it stirred with the movement, but whatever it was lay hidden beneath the fabric of her dress.

"You must be puzzled," she went on, "when at first I was something less than enthusiastic to accept this colored courtesan whom you brought to shelter in my house, that I should now respect her wishes— even when they are perverse. And I do find them so. You are that unusual thing of value: a decent man."

The doctor inclined in her direction.

"I do not mean to flatter," said Isabelle, "but to give you your due. She would do well to remain with you for as long as you are willing to have her. But her relation with that bastard of the Sieur Maltrot was very powerful, it seems, whatever it has been—oh, she has told me nothing of it, I only suppose. You understand that *he* is certainly not welcome here, not to take one step across the threshold."

"Yes," said the doctor, "but—"

"She is uncertain as to your intentions," Isabelle said. "Or so I infer. That is not all. But perhaps your intentions are not perfectly clear even to yourself. I'd counsel you not to press your case at once, but leave her time. But do come often." Isabelle smiled, with a half-curtsey. "It always pleases *me* to see you."

Following this interview the doctor got his horse and went out herb-gathering along the roads east of Le Cap, hoping the exercise would settle his mind. He did not return to the city gate until dusk, and went directly to the *casernes,* where he shared Maillart's billet for the night. The captain inveighed against Nanon's peculiarity. *What does a woman want?* he kept saying, as the doctor rolled in his hammock, searching for sleep. *And I don't say such a woman, but any woman at all . . .* But the doctor did not want to talk about it.

The next morning he lingered in his hammock, his mood despondent, pretending to sleep till long after Captain Maillart had gone out. At last he rose and half-heartedly began sorting through the plants he had been collecting, using thread to tie up a few bundles for drying. But this project failed to engage him for long. He pulled on his boots and moped through the streets toward Government House.

There his interest was piqued by the sight of Toussaint emerging from the enclosure, on foot, surrounded by several of Hédouville's entourage. One might almost say he was being harassed by them, for the black general did not look at all pleased. The doctor came within earshot, as Fabre, captain of the little fleet that had brought Hédouville out from France, was gesturing toward the port.

"General," he said, "it would be my honor, as well as my pleasure, to convey you to France, and in that same vessel in which I carried General Hédouville hither."

The young officers at his back exchanged ironic smiles, fingering their black collars. Fabre's tone was mocking, and the doctor thought he detected hints of threat. Supplantation, deportation . . .

"Your ship is not large enough," Toussaint said darkly, "for a man like me."

The doctor hid a smile behind his hand, watching the white men's sour reaction to this rejoinder. That this African should rate himself higher than the representative of the French government . . . The gesture itself was something he must have absorbed from Toussaint. With that thought, he wiped the smile away and put his hand into his coat pocket, touching the shard of mirror.

"But, *mon général*," said one of the young men at the rear of the group. "How can you deny yourself the sight of France, the nation which has conferred such benefits on yourself and your people?"

"One day I do intend to go to France," Toussaint said. He took off his tricorne hat and revealed the yellow kerchief tightly knotted over his head.

The young Frenchmen standing out of his line of view smirked at each other. *Ce vieux magot coiffé de linge*—the doctor had heard the phrase, from Maillart and others, often enough. He'd also heard that two of the inexperienced officers who'd circulated the witticism had been killed in an ambush near Saint Marc; according to some whispers, Toussaint was behind their deaths.

Toussaint aimed the third corner of his hat at a sapling on the shady side of the street, no more than a green stick, and barely the diameter of his thumb.

"I will go," he said, "when that tree has grown large enough to build the ship to carry me."

To this the humorists found no reply at all. Toussaint stepped away from them, replacing his hat back on his head. He seemed to catch sight of the doctor for the first time.

"Ah—come with me, please," he said. "I want you."

At the *casernes* the doctor was set at once to transcribing, from Toussaint's dictation, a letter redolent with airs of loyalty and submission, which proffered to the Directoire Toussaint's resignation from his post as General-in-Chief and from the army altogether. In short, Toussaint requested his own retirement. As the doctor recognized this import, the quill began to dither in his hand.

"But," he began, dangling a blob of ink from the nib. "Can you really mean—"

He cut himself off, for Toussaint had begun to tremble, from his hands that gripped the table's edge through the cords of his neck to his temples throbbing beneath the yellow headcloth, where tufts of his iron hair showed under the sweat-stained fold of cloth. His eyes half closed, showing crescents of white. The feeling did not seem part of him but only to pass through him. This turbulence lasted for just a moment, then Toussaint smiled and wiped away the expression with one hand. He clapped and called the two sentries from outside the door: Guiaou and another whose name the doctor did not know. With his forefinger Toussaint indicated the stub of the second man's left ear (lopped off for some offense like theft or *marronage*) and the letter *R* branded on his cheek (which marked him as a rebel).

"Such benefits," Toussaint said. He lifted the tail of Guiaou's shirt (for Guiaou now possessed a shirt) and showed the patterns of his horrific scars. Guiaou stood erect, motionless, looking fixedly forward, whether proud or ashamed or indifferent the doctor could not have told.

"These too are graces of the French government," Toussaint said, his pointing hand vibrating slightly as he spoke, "along with whips and chains for every man and woman stolen out of Guinée, and when the final accounting is made before God, these will be reckoned with the other benefits. Yes, and if the French government had shown me one-half the honor offered by the English—" Toussaint's arm dropped. "Well, leave off," he said to the doctor. "I am done with you."

The doctor quailed, visibly it must have been.

"For the moment," Toussaint said, more equably. "You are at liberty. Only send in Riau as you go out."

Sweating, the doctor did as he was bid. Riau was lingering just outside the door and the doctor, having delivered his message, watched as he went in and took his position at the writing desk. As he scanned the draft of the letter, Riau's face, normally a rich and glossy black, dulled to slatish gray. Then Guiaou and the other sentry pulled the door shut and took up their positions before it.

The doctor wandered blindly down through the gate, toward the blaze of sun and the day-long commotion of the Rue Espagnole, imagining what would follow if Toussaint were to withdraw from the scene. He himself had better throw in his lot with Henri Christophe, or perhaps Maurepas. Ah Christ, it would all shatter and they'd fight among themselves. And who'd emerge the victor? Dessalines, or possibly Moyse. But more than likely, Dessalines—without a Toussaint to restrain him.

He walked across to Government House to find Pascal and ask him what possiby could have happened between Toussaint and Hédouville. "I've never seen him show such a humor as today," the doctor said. "Not in all the time I've spent in his company . . . and I've seen many things."

"I don't doubt that you have." Pascal tugged at the corner of his thumbnail with his teeth. "Well, I know this much of what has happened in the last few days. The Peacemaker of the Vendée has been

most frosty to Commissioner Raimond, and has shown rather more formal courtesy to General Rigaud than to Toussaint."

"But why—why would he want to offend Toussaint?"

Pascal gnawed at his thumbnail. "It's more that Rigaud wants
placating—he has long resented that Toussaint was promoted to a place
above his own."

"But General Hédouville came out with an order for Rigaud's arrest."

"Which Toussaint declined to execute." Pascal bit into his thumb,
then looked absently at the ragged flesh. "You know yourself the commissioners were much at fault in the whole debacle down south. The
envoys were ill chosen and they bungled the whole affair—else Rigaud
might never have been alienated."

"All right. But now?"

"*Now*, Toussaint is the highest military authority in all the colony, in
name. Also in fact—except in the Southern Department. Rigaud's command. Well, let us suppose that our Peacemaker has received Rigaud
more warmly than Toussaint, and has also given Rigaud to understand
that his policy will be to *withdraw* the supremacy of power that Toussaint now enjoys . . ."

The doctor experienced an inner recoil. "If Toussaint were to learn of
that, it would surely explain his distemper."

"Indeed, it was let slip to him intentionally." Pascal's teeth drew blood
from the corner of his tattered thumbnail. "It may be that he was even
placed so as to overhear the actual conversation with Rigaud."

"But why should General Hédouville—"

"Because he has no substantial force of his own," Pascal said, looking
somewhat unhappily at his wounded digit. "He must set the leaders
against one another, and hope to insinuate his own officers among the
cracks that open."

"I call that a very dangerous game."

"Agreed. But he played it to a victory in the Vendée, or so we are constantly told." Pascal said. "No doubt he hopes to do the same thing here."

"Give me your hand," the doctor said, taking it in his own as he
spoke. He squinted at the swollen area around the base of Pascal's
thumbnail.

"As for Toussaint," Pascal told him, "I think we may reassure ourselves that this idea of retirement is a similar ploy. Only observe your
own reaction—everyone else will feel the same. Even his enemies, or
those who feel that he has simply become too powerful. For the moment, there is no one else who can hold things together here."

"Let us take what comfort we can from that." The doctor shook his
head, wagging Pascal's hand in his. "But this nail biting is truly a vicious

habit, in a hot country. Look, you have already a bad spot here. You must let me poultice this."

When he had tended to Pascal's hand, the doctor parted from him and went on foot to the Cigny house, half dizzied by the heat and glare of the noonday sun. Arriving, he bypassed the front door without quite knowing his reason for doing so, and instead went round to the small crooked courtyard at the back, where a couple of servants whom he knew were resting in the shade. They smiled when they saw him, and at his indirect inquiry let him know that Madame Cigny was absent, having gone to call on a friend elsewhere in the town. When the conversation ended, they made no objection to the doctor's entering the house by the back door.

He went up the stairs, unpleasantly conscious of the noise of his boots and the creaking of the planks beneath them. But no one was about to notice. From the bedroom on the second floor, the snores of Monsieur Cigny resounded, as the master of the house slept away the worst of the day's heat. The doctor kept on climbing to the attic.

The door of the little room was slightly ajar; a nudge of his fingertips sufficed to send it floating inward. Nanon sat up on her cot with a gasp, and quickly pulled the sheet up to her collarbone. She'd been napping in the nude, as was her habit.

"Why have you come here?" she said.

"To let you know that our son is well."

Nanon flinched, turning her face to the wall, as if he'd slapped her. The doctor's pulse slammed at his temples. He had not considered before he spoke, but why was it the wrong thing to have said? Nanon drew the sheet higher over her shoulders, gripping the fabric from the end, tight as the hands of a corpse upon a shroud. She was thinner than before and there was a line of discoloration across her throat like an ugly necklace. Rust. The loss of weight brought a fragile edge to the beauty he remembered. So long since he had seen her at all, but she agreed very well with his memory. The heat bore down terribly here on the top floor, and the sheet clung humidly to the contours of her body. The doctor was aware of the grime caked on him, of an unpleasant taste in his mouth.

"I mean no harm," he said, squatting at her bedside, extending his hand. "Quite the opposite."

"Don't," Nanon said. "Don't, I beg you. *Je t'en prie.*"

The doctor's hand had stopped in the air. She would not turn her face to look at him. The atmosphere was so hot and close that he could scarcely breathe.

"But what is it?" he said. "Do you think I have come to bring some punishment, or even a reproach?" The plaintive grating of his voice was unpleasant even to himself. Why was he unable to strike a better note?

"Only come back with me to Ennery," he said. "Everything will be as it was before you went away. Whatever has passed in your absence will be forgotten, as if it never were."

Nanon did turn toward him then, chin trembling, her eyes large and gleaming under wells of tears. Her lips were parted, but instead of speaking she drew the sheet completely over her head and hunched down on the cot. As if what he'd last said were the very most wounding thing of all. Under the white shroud he saw her shuddering. Though he wanted to touch, to comfort, he withdrew his hovering hand, with a deliberate effort. He was resolved to do no harm.

"Perhaps I was wrong to have surprised you in this way." The whine was purged from his voice now; he spoke as gently as he might to a sick or wounded person in his care. "But I will come again tomorrow. Properly. I will call on Madame Cigny in the late afternoon. Do you understand?"

Under the sheet, Nanon made no reply. The doctor looked across the shape of her body, through the porthole window and down into the street below, where a man came laboring under the heavy shafts of a two-wheeled cart piled high with sacks of rice or grain. He strained forward at such a desperate angle that, without the cart to balance him, he would surely have fallen on his face. All the muscles of his bare back and arms stood out like harp strings under the black skin. Then he passed from view and the round glass was empty.

Still Nanon said nothing, but rolled away from him, on her side. The doctor suffered a spasm of dizziness as he stood up, and had to lean on the door jamb for a moment to recover himself before he went out.

At street level a hint of a breeze had begun from the port, just enough to cool the sweat that poured from every inch of his skin. On the Rue Espagnole he crossed paths with an open coach bound in the direction of the city gate. General Hédouville himself was the principal passenger. His graying hair stuck straight up like a brush, and a smile flickered across his smooth round cheeks as he spoke to his companions. On his right sat General Rigaud, listening attentively, and to his left, Choufleur.

The doctor stopped in his tracks, watching. He did not know what Choufleur had done, but felt that he radiated some evil intention. That gold-headed cane he affected lay across his knees—the doctor would have liked to snatch it and snap it over his head. Choufleur looked through him without appearing to see him at all, but as the coach passed his head came around like an owl's, as if an invisible filament connected his eyes to the doctor's face. This liaison sustained itself till the coach turned a corner out of sight.

"All women are whores," Captain Maillart announced in the later watches of that night. "Except of course your mother, and my mother." He hiccupped, then took another slug of rum and passed the calabash to the doctor. They were sitting just beyond the portico, on stools beneath the stars that shone all above the central courtyard of the *casernes.*

"Excepting nuns also," the captain belched, "who must be married to Our Lord Jesus Christ, to restrain them from the whoredom of their nature." He paused, considering. "I'd best except your sister too. My dear friend, your sister is not a whore."

"Oh, let her be one if you like." He was quite as drunk as the captain himself, and felt it every time he looked up at the stars wheeling over his head. "And what of your Isabelle Cigny?"

"A whore who has become a nun!" Maillart said triumphantly. "A Magdalen, I tell you. One may be fri-(urk) *-friends* with her. No more. Perhaps one might also be friends with a nun." Tilting dangerously on his stool, he gripped the doctor's shoulder. Their rum breaths mingled.

"Whores and nuns, my dear friend," he said. "There you have it. Make your choice between the two—you will have small joy from either in the end. What, then, are we to do? Can you tell me that?"

"No," said the doctor. He wondered where Riau had got to, and what he might be doing wherever he was. Riau had not appeared at the barracks all evening. For some reason he was thinking of the accommodation Riau had reached with Guiaou, and remembering that moment when Riau had offered him the salt with the prediction that Nanon would not come back to him. What had he meant by that offer of salt?

"We must GO WHORING!" Maillart shouted. From the opposite wing of the *casernes,* an invisible voice besought him to be quiet. Maillart pushed away from the doctor's shoulder. The legs of his stool clopped down on the stones.

"Your logic eludes me," the doctor said thickly.

"Yes, well," Maillart said. "It's true." His voice was glum. "The prettiest whores are all taken by those brats of Hédouville. We should have to fight for them." He brightened. "I don't mind that. Only afterward we'd be cashiered for it. Or shot. Or hung."

"It's hardly worth it," the doctor said. "Not for whores."

"Exactly." Maillart stood ponderously up and swayed in place. "And so, my very dear friend, to bed. Without any whores."

"Or nuns," the doctor said.

Maillart had gone into the room and crashed into something; the doctor heard him curse, scuffle, then gradually subside into silence. A few minutes later he followed the captain inside, but found he was too drunk to climb into his hammock. Drunk enough that the stone floor was not at all uncomfortable, except that if he lay at full length, the whole room went into a sickening whirl, so that he was obliged to sleep sitting up, his back wedged into a corner.

Overindulgence in strong spirits was a poor program for a tropical climate, the doctor had occasion to remind himself many times during the next morning. A long swim in cold water would have been the best prescription, but he had no time for it; Toussaint had let him know that they would be traveling back to Gonaives the day after, so there were preparations to make.

When he had done what was necessary, he went back to the *casernes* and managed with some difficulty to get into his hammock, where he lay swinging queasily, his tongue thick and swollen, his head a clot, his bowels uneasily astir. But in the end he must have slept, for when he returned to complete consciousness the light had changed in the stone-paved yard outside the room, and the heat had somewhat abated.

He rolled out of the hammock, found his feet, then stopped to pick up the calabash from the corner of the room where it had been abandoned. A little liquid gurgled when he lifted it. He removed the leaf plug and turned it up, grimacing at the bite of the rum in his throat. His stomach heaved, then stabilized, and the pain in his head faded. At the cistern he washed his face and rinsed his mouth with stale water, and with his fingers combed back his few strands of hair over his scaling skull. He found the gray mare in the stable and rode down to the Cigny house.

Isabelle intercepted him at the door. "Your room is free," she said.

"You are ever hospitable," said the doctor, "but I cannot accept until my next visit, for I am called to Gonaives tomorrow."

Isabelle gave him a meaningful look and laid her hand on his forearm. From the direction of the parlor he heard the clink of china and a rattle of male laughter.

"She's gone?" the doctor said. "Ah—what has happened?"

"She's gone with him—Choufleur," Isabelle hissed, her pale face breaking out in angry colors. "She went away with him this morning. My husband was about his affairs and I had gone out also—I daresay he watched for me to leave, the scoundrel! But she went freely, so the servants claim. He did not force her, or not with his hands. I mislike such a freedom."

"Oh," said the doctor. "Oh . . ."

"You are welcome to come in, of course," Isabelle said, smiling almost tremulously. "I did not like to keep you in suspense."

"No," said the doctor. "Perhaps I won't."

"As you know, he still keeps the house of the late Sieur de Maltrot," Isabelle told him. "That is, if he has not already taken her from the town altogether. Ah well, you must do what you can. I do not know how to advise you, but no good will come to her, with him."

He rode the gray mare down through bustling streets, reining her in and stroking her neck to soothe her as necessary; the mare was better used to country life and shied at every passing cart or swatch of fluttering fabric. At the waterfront, he turned and rode in the direction of Fort Picolet. Beyond the fountain and the battery was a little gravelly beach, and here he dismounted and hitched the mare and walked down to the water's lapping edge. He took a couple of steps into the light surf with his shod feet and crouched to thrust his arms into the ripples. The water was very cold on the pulse of his wrists, and he could feel the cold of it on his ankles through the leather of his boots.

The sun was tilting away over Morne du Cap when he turned from the water and started toward his horse. Great billows of sunset-colored cloud rose up from the ridges of the mountain. On the lower slopes he had a long view of the little church and behind it the *lakou* where Paul had taken shelter. Unseen, a drum tapped unevenly, rumbled, fell away to silence.

He rode in the opposite direction across town, along the Rue Vaudreuil. The Maltrot house stood at the corner of the Rue du Hasard, one block from the Place Clugny, where he and Nanon had had their first significant encounter years before. The house was shuttered, upstairs and down, unremarkable, pale paint flaking from the boards of the high-arched doors. An iron gate closing off access to the inner court was secured with a loop of rusted chain.

The doctor sat his horse and looked at the house. Far above the brick-colored roof tiles, a darker mass of clouds was gathering, and the wind freshened as it changed direction. Presently a tall colored woman wearing a dark blue dress came from the inner courtyard toward the gate, twirling a parasol of paler blue in both her hands. A servant raced ahead of her to open the gate, and bowed and scraped obsequiously as she came out. The mare shied at the movement of the parasol and the doctor got down and held her, stroking her mane and whispering.

"Monsieur le médecin." The tall woman was Madame Fortier, but more elaborately dressed than when he had last seen her. Her hair was wound up in a high cone shape, wrapped in silk kerchiefs and surmounted by a small, beribboned straw hat which was pinned at a jaunty angle. The gate hinges squealed as the servant closed the gate behind her, locked the chain and disappeared from view.

"How long did you say you have been in this country?"

"Since ninety-one," the doctor replied. "I believe it was June when I arrived."

"Ah," said Madame Fortier, watching him as he gentled the mare. "That is good."

"How so?"

"You are kind-hearted," she told him, "yet not so soft as you might seem, else you would not have survived so long."

The doctor nodded. "I am surprised to see you here," he said. "Pleased as well, of course."

"Well, it is nothing unusual," she said, lowering the parasol as she moved nearer. "Fortier has come down with the harvest of coffee from Dondon, and we must buy salt, and flour, and cloth."

"But of course," said the doctor.

Madame Fortier turned and stood beside him so that both of them were looking at the iron spears of the gate.

"Before, we were at Vallière," she told him. "There I found that woman you were seeking when we first met. I helped her to get away from that place, for my son had not used her very well, I am sorry to say. She went in the company of a *blanc* who claimed to be your friend."

"Yes," said the doctor. "He told you the truth."

Madame Fortier slapped the furled parasol against her skirt. The mare snapped her head back in response, eyes rolling. The doctor shortened his grip on the reins and stroked her.

"Now she falls again into the possession of Jean-Michel," said Madame Fortier. "How is this allowed to happen? This house is an evil place. I had not thought to enter it again for any reason."

The doctor flushed and looked away.

"That I should speak so, of the house where my own son is in residence," she said. "Well, if there is a Hell as the *blanc* priests say, then the father of Jean-Michel is there, and roasted to a crackling. But by another belief one might also say that the father's spirit works through the body of Jean-Michel, and so powerfully that I no longer recognize any quality in my son which belongs to me. Tell me, in all your medical art, is there found a cure for this situation?"

"None that I know," the doctor said. "Madame, you speak of a very great sorrow."

"It is so," Madame Fortier said, still looking at the gate. The wind rose, bearing a few plump drops of rain over the roof tiles and into their faces. A wagon rattled to a halt between them and the house. Fortier sat on the box; he beckoned to his wife.

"As for the woman, I judge that she is not beyond help," Madame Fortier said, "but I can help her no more." She nodded to the doctor and stepped toward the wagon, then abruptly turned back.

"Slavery is corruption," she said. "It rots the one who is owned and also the one who does the owning, like poison in the flesh. If this truth is not found already in your medical art, it remains a science you must master. Such corruption can only be washed out by blood."

Fortier took her hand and helped her up onto the box. As he clucked to his draft horse, she turned her face to the doctor once more.

"If you enter that house, have a care for your life."

The doctor saluted her with his hat, and remounted the gray mare. But he did not immediately ride away. As the deluge began he found his duster in a saddlebag and quickly put it on, then adjusted his hat brim to shed the rain. On the second floor of the house a shutter opened partially, and the doctor felt that someone was watching him from the darkness behind. He remained where he was. The mare stood stolidly for once, head lowered, as if the downpour had beaten the nervousness out of her. His pistols were primed and dry beneath the duster. Even if the steadiness of his hand was spoiled by rum, he never went anywhere, nowadays, without making sure of those weapons, though at this moment he had no idea what use they might be to him.

30

Toussaint invited General Rigaud to travel with him as far as Ennery and to break his journey to the south by dining and staying the night at Descahaux plantation. All during the day's ride the two generals were most affable with one another, and the mood of friendliness continued into the evening. Rigaud was extravagant in his praise of Suzanne Louverture (though he found her more receptive to compliments to her table than to her person). The youngest son, Saint-Jean, who had not gone with his elder brothers to France, was presented for inspection and admiration.

Otherwise the conversation mostly concerned the campaign against Jérémie, where the English were still quite firmly entrenched, though under heavy pressure from Rigaud's besieging force. Neither Toussaint nor Rigaud made any allusion at all to Agent Hédouville nor to any instructions that came from him. No doubt, the doctor privately thought, this subject remained a tender one. Captain Maillart was also present for this dinner, with a few other people from Toussaint's staff, and most of the party that had originally ridden up with Rigaud from the southern peninsula. But some few of this latter group had remained at Le Cap, including Colonel Maltrot: Choufleur.

When it was all over, the doctor rode over to Habitation Thibodet, only a short distance, though the road was lengthened by the skittish mare, jumping at shadows in the moonlight. A sleepy sentry admitted him at the plantation gate, and as he rode up the avenue he could hear chickens and guinea fowl clucking in their perches on the trees at either side. The *grand'case* was dark, as was the mill (since Toussaint had displaced his local headquarters to Descahaux). The doctor unsaddled the mare and turned her into the moonlit paddock. Saddlebags slung over his shoulder, he trudged up the steps to the house.

Elsie heard him entering and came to the door of her bedroom to give him a quick sleepy hug, her nightgown clinging damply to her, her body warm and heavy from the bed. The doctor thought he heard Tocquet's voice muttering somewhere in the dark behind her. He groped his way to his own room and dropped his saddlebags on the floor. The moist night breeze stirred the jalousies, and there was just enough moonlight slipping through the slits to help him find a candle stump. Cupping the yellow flame, he looked into Paul's room and for a moment watched the boy breathe in sleep. Then he snuffed the candle, pulled off his boots, and stretched out fully clothed on top of the covers of his own bed. Down the hall he heard Elise's voice, rising in the breathy excitement of love. At that he made a wry face in the moon-striped dark, but soon afterward he was asleep.

Next day he went up to the hillside camps to deliver various small articles Guiaou and Riau had separately commissioned him to bring for Merbillay and her children, Caco and the infant Sans-chagrin: white flour, a bag of peppercorns, dried beans, and a bolt of cloth. He satisfied himself that both children were healthy. With that accomplished, he had trouble finding anything to do with himself, and moped around the house for several days. Toussaint had gone down to Gonaives, but did not immediately send for him. He could not settle. Paul was happy enough, it seemed, and spent most of his days frolicking with Caco. Tocquet and Elise were almost ostentatiously blissful, and Sophie was so very glad to have her father home again—the doctor knew it was churlish for him to envy their reunion, but he still did feel rather like a beggar, peering through a pane of icy glass at the rich around their banquet table.

He could not bring himself to speak to his sister about anything that had happened with Nanon, but one night he did give Xavier Tocquet the barest account of the circumstances. Tocquet made no comment, only pulled on the ends of his mustache and looked elsewhere. But a day or so later Elise came to him where he sat at the gallery table, brooding over the snuffbox and his mirror shard.

"Brother," she said. "May I sit with you?"

He looked up curiously, for she did not usually address him in this formal fashion.

"Of course," he said. "After all, it is your house."

Elise took a chair, folded her arms and looked at him closely. "Are you angry with me still?"

"No," he told her. "You've done what you could to put it right."

"But not enough," said Elise, "for you have not regained your lover."

The doctor picked up the bit of mirror and used it to fire a reflected sunbeam out over the bougainvillea that climbed the gallery rail.

"What do those objects mean to you?" she asked.

"I don't know." The doctor considered. "Sometimes I think they are like chessmen, and if I only position them just so . . . Or sometimes I feel they are connected to other people in my life."

"I'll say that I do not quite understand her conduct," Elise said. "I would admit that I have wronged her. That I told her an untruth."

The doctor shrugged. "Perhaps she simply prefers the other man."

"You might make her an offer of marriage."

"You astonish me," he said. "Why, even your friend Isabelle Cigny warned me that if I did such a thing, I'd find myself transformed into a black."

"Antoine," said his sister. Her eyes welled up, magnified a larger paler blue. "I confess I've wronged you too. Can I not be released from my own error? In France it is one thing, but here another. I will make my own life here—I will not freeze my heart in France."

The doctor reached across the table to take her hand. "If my forgiveness will make you free, you have it."

He gave her fingers a gentle pressure and let them go. Elise sat back.

"When you next go to Le Cap, I think you ought to take Paul with you. Isabelle would keep him, I am sure."

"But why? To lure the mother? Her maternal sentiments don't seem to have been so very strong."

"You may not know the whole of it." Elise swallowed. "Take him—it might make a difference."

But then Toussaint did call him down to Gonaives. There was a flurry of correspondence with Maitland and the British, now nearly resigned to surrender Jérémie. That town was one of the strongest points in the whole Southern Department, but Rigaud had it tightly under siege; meanwhile Toussaint let Maitland know directly that he himself would blow up Jérémie's fortifications if it cost him two thousand men to do it . . . but would it not be better to avoid such bloodshed?

At the same time the surrender of Môle Saint Nicolas was also under discussion, but on this point Maitland had chosen to treat with Hédouville rather than with Toussaint. Indeed word came that Maitland had already come to an agreement with the agent on the rendition of Le Môle, and that the British general had posted a proclamation from Hédouville in the streets of the town, warning that all French royalists and *émigrés* under protection of the British would be expelled once the British had departed. Hédouville's proclamations were beginning to wear away whatever popularity he had hoped to enjoy, for another recent edict declared that all the cultivators must contract for no less than three years of labor on the plantations where they worked, and this news had started a rumor that the agent secretly meant to restore slavery.

If Toussaint was displeased at that latter development, he did not show it. On the contrary, the doctor thought that he might even be encouraging such whispers. But Toussaint was spending most of his energy, and that of the secretarial team, on letters to Maitland protesting the arrangement with Hédouville on the grounds that he, Toussaint, was the authority responsible for all military dispositions in the colony, and also reminding Maitland that whatever interest the British might retain in Saint Domingue would depend on sustaining the morale of the French colonists whose cause the British had intervened to support. Maitland must have been persuaded, for he declared his agreement with Hédouville to be null and void, had Hédouville's proclamation publicly ripped to shreds at Le Môle, and reopened negotiations directly with Toussaint.

So much the better, said Captain Maillart, who had seen the port on the Northwest Peninsula (as Doctor Hébert had not). True enough, Toussaint had kept Le Môle tightly surrounded with a cordon of his own land forces since July. But Le Môle was not known as the Gibraltar of the Americas for nothing—it was the best naval harbor on the island, now full of British ships of war, and garrisoned by eight thousand men: the best of those who had survived the fever season. If diplomacy failed, it would be a very difficult post to reduce.

Then, at Jérémie, diplomacy succeeded. Though Hédouville had wind of Toussaint's dealings with Maitland and sent many messages of reproach, it was nonetheless settled for the British to evacuate the southern town, on the condition that the French colonists remaining there would be protected. Maitland had evidently found it better to settle those terms with Toussaint, for Rigaud had shown himself severe against the former slave masters of the colony, and Hédouville still more so.

On the twenty-third of August, the doctor and Captain Maillart walked down to the harbor front at Gonaives and shaded their eyes to look out over the water. Sometime that day an English fleet would be passing, en route to Le Môle from Jérémie, but they were too far out to sea to be seen from the bay of Gonaives, their sails out of view below the horizon. News came by land, a day or so later, that all had gone according to plan, the British had embarked on schedule, and Rigaud was in possession of Jérémie.

Toussaint retired for a day to Descahaux, to see his family, and while there he directed the doctor and Captain Maillart to go up to Le Cap, bearing a circuitous and somewhat evasive reply to Hédouville's many letters. When he learned of this mission, Doctor Hebert made a quick decision to follow his sister's advice and take Paul along with him, though he was not absolutely sure what would be gained, and was a little worried that the child might somehow be hurt. Though Sophie was sorry to lose her playmate, and even Caco seemed a little downcast, Paul himself was all excitement over the trip. The boy had learned to ride a pony for short distances, but the doctor elected to carry him on his own saddle bow. He brought Paulette along as well, thinking he would need her help if he had to stay with Paul in the *casernes*. But as it turned out Elise was quite right, and Isabelle received them all into the Cigny house with great enthusiasm.

The morning following their arrival, Paul asked to go to the *lakou* behind the church on the hill, where he'd been given shelter, and Paulette seconded his wish, since she wanted to see her mother. The doctor decided to accompany them. Captain Maillart had already gone to deliver the letter to Government House, so his attendance there was not immediately necessary.

When they had gained the crown of the hill, a gaggle of children surrounded them, asking after Claudine Arnaud, their schoolmistress. For perhaps five minutes they competed to recite the bits of catechism they remembered, then ran off with Paul in tow. Paulette had run to Fontelle's arms, so the doctor and Moustique were left looking at one another somewhat diffidently. The doctor had always felt a sympathy for the youth, for many reasons, without ever quite knowing what to say to him. As the doctor approached him, Moustique turned his head, and as if by agreement, they walked around the rear of the church and toward the palm-paneled enclosure down the slope behind.

"*Antré,*" Moustique said, and shifted one of the woven panels. Four little cairns of stones had been placed in a square around the entryway. The doctor felt an odd tingle as he passed between them. He wandered toward the pole in the center of the enclosure. On closer inspection, the spiraling stripes represented a snake and a rainbow twined about one another, in balance, without touching.

"Damballah," Moustique said, indicating the inverted head of the snake. "Ayida Wédo."

The doctor said nothing, but let the question appear in his eyes.

"Damballah swims in the river of life," said Moustique, "and the rainbow of Ayida Wédo makes the sign of water. They join as man and woman do, to make a wholeness, and so they bring life down to earth out of the sky."

"Curious beliefs, for the son of a priest."

"A curious thing for a priest to have a son."

"Though encumbered with certain human weaknesses," the doctor said, "your father was as true a priest of God as I have ever met."

"Yes," said Moustique. "I have not departed from my father's belief. Above Damballah and Ayida Wédo, above all the spirits there is BonDyé still and always."

He turned his face up to the sky. The doctor felt a flash of irritation at his certainty.

"Did you know you are yourself a father?" he said. "Yes, you have a child at Marmelade—hardly an infant anymore—and rather to the dismay of your Christian preceptor, the Abbé Delahaye."

Moustique colored and raked one long hand at the tight curls of his close-cropped hair. Apart from the hair he might easily have been taken for a pure-blood Frenchman. On the nearly sheer hillside above the *lakou,* Paul appeared among the other children, capering with the goats who were grazing there.

"But I think you have come to discuss your own trouble, rather than mine," Moustique said silkily.

The doctor studied a number of broken eggshells arranged around the base of the pole.

"Damballah's food," said Moustique. Then, with an air of authority. "But for you it is rather to offer to Legba." He pointed to the low stone cairns. "Attibon Legba is standing in the gate," he said. "Legba waits at the gate and the crossroads and decides who shall pass, and by which turning. If you would work a change in your situation, you must ask his help."

"How?" said the doctor, in spite of himself.

"Sacrifice." Moustique turned his back and looked out over the sea.

The doctor snorted and made to leave the enclosure. All a lot of pagan nonsense. By daylight it was easy to think so. And maybe it was only her madness that had struck down Claudine Arnaud among the celebrants here, that night . . . As he passed among the cairns, he felt that same electric whir run over him. What would Riau have done in such a case? Without thinking he stooped, reaching into his pocket, and laid both the snuffbox and the mirror shard in the dusty center of the square the cairns defined. When he straightened, he saw Moustique looking his way with a faint air of approval. The doctor went out, and as he passed along the outside of the enclosure, he half-consciously made the sign of the cross above his chest.

Leaving the children on the hill for the time being (Fontelle would walk them back to the Cigny house, she'd said), he went down to Government House to take the measure of the situation there. Pascal was strolling in the courtyard when he entered. The doctor reached for his hand at once and declared that the swelling was greatly reduced.

"Oh yes," Pascal said. "That leaf pulp you insist on has such a vile taste it has quite broken me of nibbling it."

"And that is for the best," said the doctor. "But how does the agent find himself today?"

"What, after his missive from the General in Chief? He is in the humor one might expect in a man who sees his policy reduced to nothing, or nearly nothing. Toussaint has scarcely made a semblance of respecting his orders, so that Hédouville is brought to believe that Toussaint is the greater rebel than Rigaud was against Sonthonax, though more circumspect, more sly. His coziness with the old proprietors leads Hédouville to believe that the general is merely their dupe and tool—his words set into his mouth by his so-called secretaries   "

The doctor laughed. "You could tell him better than that yourself."

"But would he believe me?" Pascal cleared his throat. "Now the matter of the army—with the Treaty of Basel eliminating any Spanish threat, and the British clearly on their way out of the colony, Hédouville would reduce the indigenous troops to perhaps six thousand, excluding the gendarmerie, but whenever that subject is raised, up flares an outcry that slavery will be restored, and the agent suspects Toussaint has fed those rumors."

"Not necessarily," said the doctor. "What are the men to think—when the *blanc* soldiers seek to replace their guns with hoes, and contract them to the plantation for years at a time? That proverb of Sonthonax's is still in very recent memory, after all."

"Who would take *this* from you," Pascal quoted, raising a list above his head to brandish an imaginary musket, "would take your liberty." He opened his hand and let it fall. "A nice bit of theater, I give you that."

"And not without its kernel of truth."

"I'll give you that as well."

The doctor hopped up onto the heavy stone balustrade and sat there, lightly swinging his legs. "Once they have tasted the salt, they will not go back," he murmured. He looked across at a goat that had wandered into the yard of Government House and was busily eating the lower leaves of the shrubbery.

Pascal looked at him sharply. "What?"

"It's only something Riau once told me," the doctor said. "I don't entirely know what it means."

"Sounds like some witchery." Pascal propped himself on the opposite balustrade and crossed his ankles. "Well, grant that the love of liberty is paramount among the freedmen . . . Hédouville suspects that Toussaint has become the dupe of Maitland and the British."

"Whose final departure he is now engineering."

"Yes," said Pascal, "but if the British should coax him into independence?"

"I've seen no sign of it." The doctor swung his bootheels against the stone behind them. He thought of the time at Marmelade, when Toussaint had turned so abruptly and ruthlessly on the Spanish. He'd seen no sign of that either, before it happened, though perhaps there had been signs he had not recognized.

"Let me tell you something else," he said to Pascal. "What I know of leaves that heal in this land—all that I had from Toussaint himself in the beginning. If not for his knowledge, this day I should be taking that hand of yours off at the wrist, or possibly the elbow. I should know no better than to saw through the bone and cauterize the stump with a red-hot iron and hope that no corruption would spread into your vitals from the wound."

Pascal blanched and recovered himself. "Have you a larger point?"

"That Toussaint has worked for peace, in the main, and he has rendered justice wherever he was able. If he cannot heal the body politic, I do not know who can."

"Oh," said Pascal. "And so, he needs no one to direct him. Scarcely any liaison at all, really, with the government in France."

"There is that difficulty."

Pascal pursed his lips. "So Hédouville is left like an ant in a wine bottle. He can see everything, all around the circle, but he can touch nothing. No wonder that he grows a little agitated."

*   *   *

For some weeks there was nothing out of the ordinary, and scarcely any apparent tension in the town. Toussaint kept away from Le Cap. Hédouville busied himself with a light restructuring of the officer corps within his reach. Now and then he was able discreetly to replace some black officer with one of the Frenchmen he had brought out with him. If there were ripples of discontent, they ran too deep to mar the tranquil appearance of the surface.

The doctor had little, officially, to do. Of Nanon he could discover nothing more. For a time he haunted the Place Clugny and the Negro market which she'd frequented during their earliest acquaintance, but she did not appear there. It did not seem that she went marketing at all, or that she called on anyone, outside the Maltrot house. Unless Choufleur had spirited her off, as Isabelle had suggested, to one of his rural properties. But Choufleur himself was still in Le Cap. The doctor saw him more than once, coming out of the agent's suite of offices at Government House, haughtily erect in his gold-buttoned uniform, swinging his cane before him as if to make it known to anyone who might be in his path that he would certainly not give way. Rumor had it that Choufleur brokered messages between Hédouville and Rigaud, and that the agent meant to foment discord between Rigaud and Toussaint, a project perhaps more plausible now that Rigaud no longer had the British in the south to occupy him.

On more than one occasion, the doctor was obliged to step aside from the progress of Colonel Maltrot through the streets, and each time Choufleur strolled through the space he'd occupied as if he'd never seen him there at all. Once, the doctor was sufficiently piqued that he followed Choufleur, across the streets and squares of the town all the way to the gate of his house, where, waiting for the servant to open to him, Choufleur turned back with a supercilious smile. After he had gone in, the doctor remained standing on the far side of the street. The house was shuttered, as usual, though far from quiet. On the contrary it had the reputation of a bawdy place, the resort of gamblers and women of loose morals, some colored, and some in these latter days even white. He recognized a horse or two at the hitchrail. Some of the more debauched young men of Hédouville's suite were known to come here occasionally.

A pair of shutters opened on the second-floor balcony, and Nanon stepped through the rounded arch, and stood facing the doctor below, though without any indication that she saw him there. Rather she seemed to be looking across the roof tiles. Drunken laughter and the rattle of dice boiled out of the dark space behind her. Then Choufleur emerged. He grinned, over her shoulder, spitefully down into the doctor's face. With one hand he reached under her arm, cupped a breast and raised it so that the nipple pushed darkly at the fragile fabric of her dress. She gave way limply to his pressure, and Choufleur pulled her back inside.

Doctor Hébert was restrained from rushing the house only by the thought that Choufleur must mean to provoke him to do just that. He dragged himself away, though inwardly fulminating. Surely he could do something, find some way. Bitterly he thought of the "sacrifice" Moustique had put him up to—there'd been no change in his direction, no gate had magically opened for him. He was on the same doomed path as before . . . though in truth he was content to be rid of the snuffbox. Perhaps, by the next day, he would have conceived a better way to get into that house. But next morning he and Captain Maillart were both summoned to Môle Saint Nicolas.

Riding fast and hard with a small cavalry squad including Captains Riau and Maillart, the doctor came to Toussaint's encampment outside Le Môle, just as the black general was making ready to take formal possession of the town. He'd brought ten thousand men to the siege, which now would not take place—about half his effective troops—and every man of them marched into Le Môle at his back.

The British soldiers, in their finest dress uniforms, lined the hedges of the road into town. Again the local dignitaries brought out a dais, and this time Toussaint consented to walk beneath it, the town's priest bearing the sacraments ahead of him, while acolytes swung censers and women hurled themselves in his path to beg his blessing. Was it his apotheosis? the doctor thought half ironically, sneezing away sweet incense smoke, remembering how Toussaint had rejected this sort of panoply when they'd come to Port-au-Prince. Maillart looked at him narrowly, as if he'd detected the thought.

But now all the bells of the town began to ring, and cannons fired salutes from the batteries and the ships at anchor, as their procession came into the Place d'Armes, where General Maitland had erected a splendid tent for their reception. Two robust subalterns held back the flaps, but Toussaint stopped and turned and stood to attention, watching his infantrymen as they flooded the square and formed into ranks which pressed back into the surrounding streets for many blocks, so great was their number. When they were all properly drawn up, Toussaint saluted them and ordered them at ease, then stooped to go into the tent, with Maitland following him. For the next two hours the black soldiers stood at parade rest under the sun, looking neither left nor right, and amazing all onlookers with the force of their discipline.

A magnificent repast had been laid inside the tent, and the doctor and the captain fell to with real appetite. Maillart found himself seated next to Major O'Farrel, whom he complimented on surviving the wars.

"Thus far," O'Farrel said with an Irish twinkle, then rather more drily, "but am I promised tomorrow?"

Though Toussaint appeared to be in great good humor, he ate sparingly as was his custom on such occasions, taking only bread and water and whole fruit, with a few tastes of wine during the concluding toasts. At the end of the meal, Maitland offered Toussaint all the silver dishes from which it had been served, along with two brass cannon. The British troops turned out for his review, and he was taken to inspect the palace, whose furnishings would be turned over to him intact, in further token of the esteem of the Britannic Majesty. At evening, with all the ceremonies complete, Toussaint withdrew to Pointe Bourgeoise, with the greater part of his men (the town being rather too small for so many), leaving a small detachment to supervise the transfer of authority as the British embarked for their final departure from Saint Domingue.

Riau went with his men to the *casernes* in Le Môle, but the doctor and Captain Maillart, on the advice of Major O'Farrel, sought the hospitality of that old Acadian, Monot. There they took a light supper and exchanged their news. Monot had no other guests, only his lovely colored attendant, Agathe, sitting opposite his place at the table and pouring his water and wine. The old man grumbled over the British, still resentful of his ejection from Acadia thirty years before. "I am glad to see them go," he grated. "Though they did not misuse us, I shall be glad to see the last of them. Even if wild Africans come in their place."

"Oh," said Agathe, a hand pressed at her fluttering throat. "If Toussaint's soldiers look like savages, their discipline is very strong—supposing today a fair example."

"For those men," Maillart assured her, "today is no different from any other."

O'Farrel smoothed his sandy mustache against his lip. "If that is so," he said, "it is Toussaint's greatest triumph, to have made such soldiers of those men."

After supper they went into the garden, where Monot explained his irrigation system to the doctor, the thin channels of water glittering under the moonlight. O'Farrel drew Maillart a little aside.

"You may know," he said, "that of the eight thousand men collected here, only two thousand are British by origin, and the rest colonial troops, from the south and the west. They are seasoned men, but Rigaud would not have them."

"Shot through with royalists, no doubt," Maillart said. "And proscribed French *colons*."

O'Farrel squinted at him in the uneven light. "How long since you were a royalist yourself?" he said. "And in my estimation, you are still a Frenchman."

"Pardon," said Maillart, "I was considering the attitudes of Agent Hédouville more than my own."

"Those six thousand would come over to Toussaint," O'Farrel said. "They see no future with the British."

"Oh indeed? And yourself?"

"The same," O'Farrel told him. "If I would be accepted?"

"By Toussaint? Absolutely." Maillart reached to clasp his hand. "Well, I have not the authority to say so, but I think I can encourage you to put your mind at rest."

The events of the day had swept the doctor's personal troubles from him, but once he lay down on his bed, they all came flooding back. He could not sleep. Also there were mosquitoes. He'd left the door to the balcony ajar, in hope of a breath of sea air. Some noise roused him from his insomniac daze; was it Maillart at the balcony door? It seemed to be his voice, muttering in confusion. But whoever it was passed on and must have found a different reception at another door, for the doctor heard a female titter, a gasp, then panting breaths which gradually sawed into moans of joy.

"Do you not abuse the kindness of our host?" he muttered to the captain over their next morning's coffee.

"I shall only leave the old man's housekeeper better content than I found her," Maillart grinned, and, at the doctor's sour expression, "Oh come, Antoine, one is only human, and I've lived like a monk these last six months. Besides it's just a bit of unfinished business from my last visit to Le Môle."

The doctor's own privation had lasted a good deal longer. He did not desire Agathe himself, exactly, but he still begrudged the captain his conquest. When he identified this feeling, his own perversity displeased him, and he elected to go with O'Farrel and the six thousand colonial troops who would now in all likelihood join Toussaint's force outside the town.

A few days later, when the British embarcation was complete, General Maitland appeared as if from nowhere, outside Toussaint's tent at Pointe

Bourgeoise, escorted by Maillart and Riau and the merest handful of junior British officers. All the rest of the British troops had boarded their vessels, though the ships were still in the harbor. At Maitland's arrival the doctor felt a flutter of real uncertainty. If the British general had been expected, he had known nothing of it. What he did know was that Toussaint had just received a letter from Commissioner Roume, who was still residing in Spanish Santo Domingo, urging him to arrest General Maitland at any opportunity presented. Toussaint had rolled this very letter into his hand as he went out to greet his visitor.

"You do me honor, General," he said. "And here is something which may interest you."

Maitland leaned toward the paper which Toussaint had unfurled in his direction. "Treachery," hissed a British subaltern who was peering over his shoulder, but Maitland silenced him with a brush of his hand, then looked up at Toussaint with an expression just short of dismay.

"What should interest you still more is my reply." Toussaint passed him a second sheet. After a line or two, Maitland began to smile, and pivoted toward his companions to read a portion aloud to them, pausing between segments to translate:

> What? Have I not given my word to the English general? How could you suppose that I would cover myself with infamy in violating that promise? The confidence which he has in my good faith engages him to deliver himself to me, and I would be dishonored forever, were I to follow your advice. I am wholly devoted to the cause of the Republic, but I shall never serve it at the expense of my conscience and my honor.

As Maitland concluded wonderingly, Toussaint uncovered his own smile from behind his hand.

"Sir," Maitland told him. "Your sentiments are more than noble. One might call them . . . royal."

Toussaint's expression faded into watchfulness. He drew back the tent flap and beckoned Maitland within—alone. Before he went inside himself, he dismissed the sentry who'd been standing before the tent and called Riau to take his place.

"I'd give a good golden louis," Maillart yawned from his hammock, strung next to the doctor's, "to know what passed between them."

"You haven't got a gold louis," the doctor said.

"Who's to say I haven't?"

"Who in this army has been paid, in recent memory? Even so much as a copper?"

"Oh," said the captain, "but suppose the gentle Agathe should have given me a present . . ."

"You are intolerably smug."

"Well, she didn't," the captain acknowledged. "At least, not a present of money."

"Have your information for nothing then," the doctor said. "Maitland proposed that Toussaint should make the colony independent and that England would recognize and support him as its king."

Maillart sat up so suddenly that his hammock ejected him onto the dirt floor.

"How did you come by that piece of knowledge?"

"Riau," said the doctor. "His scavenging, during *marronage*, has sharpened his hearing very much. He can hear a louse walking on the hair of a wild goat."

"Listening at tent flaps is an excellent way to get shot." Maillart got up and dusted off his knees.

The doctor pushed his heels against his hammock to set it gently swaying. "Oh, but perhaps Toussaint wishes the proposal to be known, together with his reply to it."

"To wit?"

"He declined."

"In high dudgeon, one imagines." Maillart's shoulders brushed the canvas as he turned in the low space of the tent. "As the faithful servant of France, and so forth."

"No, it seems to have all been very cordial." The doctor paused. "You may recall, at Gonaives, Toussaint took a special interest in the news from Egypt—Bonaparte's landing there, I mean."

"Which all the power of the British navy could not prevent." Maillart ran his thumb down a seam of the tent. "I see. The point is well taken."

"All very cordial, as I say, though Toussaint refused the crown," said the doctor. "He and Maitland have signed a secret protocol—an addendum to the official accord for the withdrawal."

"Riau deduced this from the scratching of the pen?"

"The British navy will leave the ports of Saint Domingue open to merchant ships of all nations," the doctor went on, unperturbed. "England will have the right of trade, but not exclusively, in all ports of the colony controlled by Toussaint Louverture. Toussaint undertakes not to invade Jamaica and not to engage in subversion there. The English make the same undertaking with regard to Saint Domingue. Oh, and the lives and property of those French colonists lately allied with the British are to be fastidiously respected."

"In all areas of the colony controlled by Toussaint Louverture." Maillart exhaled, with a hint of a whistle. "Well, strike me dumb. Hédouville won't like it. Not the part about the trade, and not the part about the landowners. Why, the very existence of such an agreement must offend him."

"I don't think he's meant to know of it."

"Christ—he'll see it happening all around him." Maillart gripped the edge of his hammock with both hands and carefully levered himself into it, settling his weight with a grunt. "There will be trouble."

"Aye," said the doctor. "When was there not?"

As of October 10, 1798, there remained not one single foreign soldier on the soil of Saint Domingue—not in theory, at least, since the likes of Major O'Farrel had been integrated into the French forces under Toussaint Louverture. Toussaint sent an order throughout his entire command, that all his officers should call upon their men to pray twice daily, at evening and morn, wherever they might happen to find themselves—beginning with high mass, at which the Te Deum must be chanted in thanks to heaven for having facilitated the expulsion of the enemy without bloodshed, and with particular gratitude to Divine Providence for permitting several thousand persons of all colors to reenter the fold of French citizenship. Though these latter had been led astray, both the Lord and the state would receive them with open arms and without reproach or punishment. The religious rubric under which this formula unfolded would be difficult (the doctor reasoned with the captain) for Hédouville to reject.

Thanks to that same Divine Grace, some twenty thousand men would now be returned to labor in the coffee groves and cane fields. A good number of them would stand down from the army, turning in their muskets for hoes. If ever a new threat to liberty should arise, their weapons would be restored to them. Did Toussaint hope to placate Hédouville with this pronouncement? the doctor and Maillart asked one another. If so, he did not trouble himself to measure the success of his effort, but returned from Le Môle to Gonaives by way of Bombardopolis, with no detour to pay his respects to the French agent.

The doctor rode back to Le Cap with Captain Maillart and the cavalry troop in Riau's command. Toussaint's announcement of the labor program had cast a pall over the black soldiers, and Riau was silent and edgy throughout the trip. The doctor's mood was also dark. Even his reunion with Paul did not lighten it; on the contrary, the child's insouciance almost annoyed him, as did Isabelle's brilliant good cheer. Her family fortunes seemed certain to be improved by Toussaint's program, and she even talked of sending to Philadelphia for her own children, but the doctor was in no mood for other people's happiness.

In Hédouville's camp there was little rejoicing over the expulsion of the British. The sentiment seemed rather to be that Toussaint had stolen the credit for that event. Pascal had gone back to his nail-biting, poultice or no. The doctor stopped going to Government House. When he visited the *casernes,* he felt that Riau was avoiding him; Maillart said that Riau seemed to have gone off the white officers generally.

Then he met Riau as if by chance, behind the white church on the hill, where he had gone to collect Paul from his playmates of that *lakou.* Riau was out of uniform, barefoot, and seemed much more at his ease. He came to the doctor with his usual friendliness and a light touch on his arm.

"I see you have left your third eye in the *hûnfor.*"

He said no more, but the doctor felt his approval, and he felt lightened for the first time in three days. That night he dreamed of clouds passing over the mirror where it lay between the cairns of stone, cloud and blue sky flowing infinitely through that bright irregular window in the dust. This eye which remained open even while he slept, able always to learn and to know.

Next afternoon, he went, with a dreamer's certainty, first to the *casernes.* He had meant to find Maillart, but when he found that the captain had gone off with O'Farrel, that too seemed inevitable. Riau presented himself, as if by prior appointment. Together they walked across to the Maltrot house in the Rue Vaudreuil.

The doctor took the bars of the gate with both hands and shook it till the locking chain danced up and down. Whether because of his own urgency or Riau's uniformed presence, the servant scuttled up quickly and scraped the gate back for them to enter. Doctor Hébert walked through, slapping speckles of rust from his hands. The court was littered with broken glass, evidently from bottles flung out the windows, and some chunks of the glass were irregularly cemented along the tops of the surrounding wall.

The entryway was dark, and smelled of blood and vomit. A wizened old woman crouched in a corner, doing something with a bucket in a rag. The doctor pushed open a door to his left, comforted to feel Riau coming in behind him. The shuttered room they entered was a large salon, but dark and smoky and dense, with a few patches of candle or lamplight here and there. A stench of tallow and spilled liquor. Beyond an overturned upholstered loveseat toward the center of the room, a number of people sat gambling around a long, oval mahogany table. Nearer the door was another pool of light, over a low sofa where a woman lay face down with her knees drawn up under her and her dress rucked up to her shoulders. A tall sallow man crouched behind her, thrusting with an energy that fluttered her buttocks and imparted a serpentine movement to her spine. Several onlookers stood around, making low comments, maybe waiting their turns. One held a watch in his palm and there seemed to be a wager, though the doctor could not guess what was in gage. Among the spectators he recognized young Cypré, one of the newcome officers Maillart particularly detested; he seemed to be extremely drunk. The woman's face scrubbed against the velvet of the sofa, insensible from rapture or indifference it was hard to tell, her eyes showing rings of white and her lips slackly open on a stain of drool. The doctor did not know her.

Cypré drew himself up and said with a hiccup, "No niggers wanted here. This is a private establishment."

Riau walked past him as if he were invisible, toward the gambling table. The doctor followed.

Here Choufleur himself presided over the entertainment. There was a deck of cards by his left elbow, but these were not in play; instead he rattled a cup of dice above a mound of mismatched stakes: coins of several different mints, a watch, a bracelet, a jeweled stickpin . . . Six or seven men in the game, and one woman who looked white, with wispy blond hair and small pink pimples all over her cheeks—she wore a dull and dazed expression.

Choufleur glanced up at the doctor with no sign of surprise. He tipped the dice cup onto the table. Eight, numbered the black dots drilled into the bones.

"*Encore de la merde,*" complained the pimple-faced woman. She swayed against the mulatto beside her, nuzzling his uniformed shoulder, then pouting when he shrugged her off.

Choufleur glanced from Riau to the doctor. "I don't object to you," he said. "But in this house I don't like to see any face darker than a good *café au lait*—unless on a servant, of course."

The doctor barely registered this remark. His eyes were on Nanon, who sat to Choufleur's right. Her bodice was loosened and pushed down below her breasts, whose exposed nipples excited a feeling of sorrow in him. Around her neck was a riveted iron collar with a light chain running down her back from its ring. She did not seem aware of the doctor's presence, though she was looking in his general direction. Her eyes were dead.

"*Faites vos jeux,*" Choufleur said.

He cupped the dice and handed them to his left, then leaned down and collected the free end of the chain from the floor beside his chair. When he gave the chain a brisk tug, Nanon responded as woodenly as if that collar were locked around a post.

"Shall we cut the cards for her?" Choufleur proposed, widening his eyes at the doctor. He opened the deck with his left hand, turning up the ace of spades. "Ah well—hard luck," he said. "But never mind. To me, it is all one. You may have the use of her for an hour if you like."

He offered the doctor, who stood frozen, the chain's end.

"No?" Choufleur said. "But I can tell you, she is not quite sucked dry. There's still a drop or two of good juice to be wrung from her."

The doctor did not answer this either. A step behind him he was aware of the deep flow of Riau's respiration—this was not audible, exactly, but he seemed to draw inspiration from the other man's breathing. Choufleur shook the chain once again, then let it all fall to the floor.

"Perhaps another will be tempted," he said lightly. "*Putain c'est putain.* Am I right, my dear?—a whore is forever a whore." He turned his head toward Nanon, who remained as dull and lifeless as before. Then to the doctor. "Of course, it makes for a short career."

The doctor swiveled away from him and went to the floor-length window facing the street and wrenched the shutters open. The men at the nearer end of the table flinched from the last light of the day; one of them muttered a complaint. Round the sofa at the far end of the room there was laughter and a few handclaps—apparently that embrace had reached its goal.

Slowly the doctor walked back around the table. At the head, Choufleur sat very upright, his hands palm down before him, facing the fresh light from the arched window. Nanon had begun reeling the chain up from the floor and was gathering it into her lap with both hands. Without breaking his step, the doctor leaned across and slapped Choufleur on the side of his face, thrusting his weight into the heel of his palm to add as much injury to the insult as possible. A gasp from the other gamblers. Choufleur's head snapped sideways, then slowly revolved toward the doctor again. His freckles seemed to shrink and concentrate, hot and dark on the pale skin like stipples on the dice. His finger found a runnel of blood at the corner of his mouth.

Then he was up, slavering, "I'll kill you!" but two of his fellows were also on their feet, knocking their chairs backward in their haste to restrain him. The blade was half out of his sword-stick, but their grip on his wrists kept him from drawing it free. He spat, but the doctor turned sideways and the gobbet went past him.

"Excellent," he said. "I accept your challenge. If the choice of weapon is mine, let it be pistols."

"As you like," Choufleur sputtered. "You'll not get away with a saber cut. I'll blow your head off and piss in the hole."

He relaxed, and the men at his sides let him go. With a twist he reseated the slender blade in the sword-stick. The doctor looked at Nanon, who seemed oblivious to the entire episode. She had stood up, cradling the gathered chain below her breasts as if it were an infant. Making a trance-like turn, she moved slowly toward a staircase in the corner of the room.

"I propose we allow three days to settle our affairs," the doctor said, his eyes tracking Nanon as she began to mount the stairs.

"So long as you do not run away, *blanc,*" Choufleur said. "I won't be denied the pleasure of killing you. Of trampling your spilled brains into the dirt. Or maybe I will feed them to my dogs."

"After three days you may find me on the ground at La Fossette." The doctor returned his smile. "Bring whatever seconds you like."

"You may count on me, *blanc.*" Choufleur turned from him, and picked up the dice.

The doctor leaned forward and plucked a card from the scattered deck and tossed it up toward the ceiling. With the same hand he reached to his opposite hip, drew a pistol from under his coat flap and fired. As it crossed the shaft of fading daylight the card jerked sideways and planed toward the unshuttered window. One of the gamblers scrambled to retrieve it from the floor, and held it high with a bark of astonishment. The nine of clubs, with the numeral shot out of the top corner. Choufleur looked fixedly at the card, expressionless.

"I shall look forward to our meeting very much," the doctor said. He holstered his pistol as he turned away. Riau followed him out.

He was expected that evening to dine with the Cignys, but first accompanied Riau back to the *casernes,* with the thought of meeting Captain Maillart, who was also invited. He found Maillart shirtless, washing himself at the well; the captain looked bloodless beneath his sunburn, and sweat kept bursting out on his torso faster than he could rinse it away. The doctor thought at first he had taken fever, but it turned out the captain was simply shaken by what he had seen that day: an insurrection he'd been sent to investigate at Fort Liberté had proved to be much more than a rumor.

"I never saw anything quite so bad," Maillart said, mopping himself with his crumpled shirt. "Not since ninety-one, at least."

Riau quit the two white men, impassively, with just a flick of a finger at the brim of his hussar's hat. In ninety-one, as all three of them knew, he had been burning and looting and painting himself with blood of whites all over the northern plain. Riau was also close to Moyse, from their time in slavery at Bréda onward, and Moyse was certainly near the heart of the present unrest, though to blame him for it might be going too far, in Maillart's opinion. Moyse was not in any way fond of *blancs*. He had conspicuously failed to share Toussaint's pleasure at the return of Bayon de Libertat to Bréda (though De Libertat had not especially mistreated him in former times). He liked to say that he would learn to love whites only when they returned to him the eye he had lost in battle.

It had begun this way: Moyse commanded the Fifth Regiment, garrisoned in Fort Liberté, on the north coast near the Spanish border. He had been given an order to capture and return fugitive slaves from the Spanish territory, which had much displeased him and with which he did not comply. From this friction there evolved a rumor that the Fifth Regiment meant to massacre the whites of the region.

"Now," said Maillart, as he slipped into a fresh shirt. "Enter the Peacemaker of the Vendée."

Hédouville, it appeared, had seen in this situation the opportunity to relieve Moyse of his command, replace him with a white officer of his own choice, and perhaps disarm and disband the Fifth Regiment altogether. With the collaboration of the civilian officials of Fort Liberté, who were mostly white, Hédouville's agents had set about this project while Moyse was absent in Grande Rivière.

They might have succeeded, Maillart told the doctor as they left the gate of the *casernes* and began walking down through the blue darkness toward the Cigny house, and had in fact got so far as locking the Fifth Regiment out of the arsenal and obtaining a reluctant acquiescence of the junior officers to the change of command. But Moyse's wife ("a woman to reckon with," said the captain with a wag of his head) had won the soldiers back over, had inspired her husband's men to break into the arsenal and rearm themselves: she'd counted out cartridges for them with her own hands.

Moyse, for his part, raised revolt among the cultivators of Grande Rivière. This rising, now pouring down out of the mountains onto the Plaine du Nord, had turned Maillart back from his mission to Fort Liberté, and shaken him to his bootheels—perhaps it wasn't *quite* as bad as ninety-one (the sky was not yet blackened out by the smoke of burning cane fields) but some plantations had been sacked, bands of armed blacks drifted over the plain, and the white landowners, who'd returned to their holdings in significant numbers, were rushing to refuge at Le Cap—pursued by waves of armed blacks who shouted that Hédouville intended to restore slavery and constantly cried out for Toussaint.

By then they'd reached the Cigny house, which was in some turmoil due to the sudden and unexpected arrival of Michel and Claudine Arnaud in precipitous retreat from their plantation on the plain.

"But where *is* Toussaint?" said Isabelle.

"He is at Gonaives," Maillart said.

O'Farrel, who'd arrived separately, added, "Though the agent has ordered him to put down the disturbance at Fort Liberté immediately."

There was still another rumor—that Toussaint had already traveled to the north, encountered Moyse, and, having taken the measure of the situation, returned to Gonaives without doing anything to quell the rising. No one could say if this were true or not—Maillart could only testify that he had not seen him.

"Oh," said Isabelle, glancing at the window. "I wish Joseph would come—he was expected."

"Joseph?" said Maillart in a low tone, looking at her curiously.

"Flaville," said Isabelle. "He could certainly tell us more."

"Ah," said Maillart, "but to the best of my knowledge he is now with Moyse."

The doctor watched Claudine Arnaud, who had raised her chin alertly at the mention of Flaville . . . a man who had come a long way, in a short time, to be considered an ally by such whites as these. In ninety-one, as all of them could not help but remember, Flaville had contributed as much as anyone to the terror on the Plaine du Nord.

That night the doctor dreamed of Choufleur's salon of decadent delights, in such concrete and accurate detail that he might have been living those moments for a second time. But with one difference. In the floating eye of his dream he saw Riau take a loose cloth bag from his coat pocket and pour from it a small mound of salt on the table before the place where Nanon sat, wearing her fetter and chain. Her dead eyes flickered at his movement. Tentatively she reached forward and dipped a finger in the salt and brought it to her lips. As the salt spread on her tongue, she lifted her face and her eyes enlivened, but what she saw the doctor woke too soon to know. He wanted to ask Riau about it, but

laughed off the notion—that Riau should be accountable for what he
did in someone else's dream.

For two days the mood was so very tense that Doctor Hébert scarcely
thought of his appointment with Choufleur. Refugee planters kept coming into Le Cap, full of wild reports and rumors. The town was too
lightly garrisoned at the moment for any sortie to be risked—indeed it
was poorly defended against a landward assault from rebel blacks, if one
really came. The mood at Government House approached desperation.
Pascal had mutilated his thumb to the point that the doctor threatened
to tie his arm behind his back. In his effort to undo the disaster wrought
by Sonthonax, Hédouville had drifted more and more into alliance with
the remains of the mulatto faction in the north, but these were not sufficient to uphold him in the present crisis. And wherever Toussaint
might be, he was unresponsive.

Hand in hand with Paul, the doctor walked toward the village on the
hill. Paulette held the boy by his other hand, so he was happy, and the
doctor, glancing at their joined fingers, felt a bittersweet happiness of
his own. Thank God for this girl's durable feeling for his child, without which he might have been lost forever. She had borne her losses—
her martyred father, the Père Bonne-chance. Thank God, also, for
Fontelle . . . Paulette had something of her mother's grace; her step was
light, her back sinuously erect as she walked, though she balanced a
huge basket of laundry on her head. When they reached the steep,
twisting path which ran up the foot of the mountain to the church and
beyond, she did not break her stride, and neither did Paul, though the
doctor proceeded with much greater difficulty, sometimes obliged to
use a hand to balance himself as he slipped on the shale.

Paulette found her mother and the two of them began to lay out the
laundry, still slightly damp from the river, to finish drying in the wind
and the sun. Paul had joined his friends and headed for the cliffside.
The wind sprang up sharply off the harbor; the doctor caught his straw
hat as it peeled from his head, and carried it against his thigh as he
walked around toward the front of the church. Moustique was sitting on
the steps, dressed in his rough white vestment and the purple stole he
had taken from the Abbé Delahaye. The doctor went to join him, taking
a seat a step below.

The wind raised his remaining wisps of hair to stand straight up on
his peeling scalp, and this reminded him to jam his hat back on to protect himself against the sun. The sight of the stole made him think of
confession. Of a sudden he had the impulse to be shriven, before presenting his breast to Choufleur's pistol . . . though he had no doubt that
he could do away with Choufleur with his own first shot. Still, perhaps

it would be better to settle this question in advance, as he himself had suggested to his opponent. With a feeling of bewilderment, as if out of nowhere, he remembered that he ought also to give thanks for Maman Maig', who had delivered Paul first into the world and then for a second time into the arms of his relations . . .

"Do you pray?" Moustique looked at him significantly. The doctor realized his lips must have been moving to shape the thoughts in his mind.

"Rarely," he said.

Moustique nodded. "It is good to pray."

Irked by his assurance, the doctor said, "But you also bow to heathen gods. Do you not fear hell and damnation?" He jutted his beard toward the bell rope which hung just within the open door of the church.

"No," said Moustique. "There is no such difficulty." He leaned toward the doctor and looked at him with strangely clear eyes. "God is above all but He makes Himself manifest in the body of Christ. So too the *loa* are manifest when they mount the heads of their *serviteurs*. BonDyé cannot object to this, because He made it so."

The doctor's initial annoyance evaporated. He felt the seamlessness of Moustique's belief. Where had the boy got this absolute confidence? Certainly he had not possessed it when Toussaint delivered him to the Abbé Delahaye. Moustique had always seemed the opposite of his father, frail and nervous and too quick to emotion and confusion, despite—or perhaps because of—his intelligence. The Père Bonne-chance had been heavy, ursine, low to the ground and solidly settled there. The mosquito versus the *agouti* . . . But now Moustique had changed; he seemed inspired . . . inspirited. It was also true that the people of this place, whatever gods they venerated, had taken Paul in with unquestioning kindness. They had taken in Claudine Arnaud.

"Yes," said Moustique. "That is *lespri Ginen,* which is very much the same as Christian love and charity."

This time the doctor was quite certain that he had not mumbled the slightest whisper of his thought. The boy must be a mind reader if not a lip reader.

"If you live in the spirit," Moustique said, "you are not under the law."

The wind freshened from the bay. The doctor felt a shadow pass over him, though there was none.

"Father," he said, experimentally. No, it was too ridiculous, to address this stripling so, with his stolen garment and his patchwork of beliefs. Potent enough to get a child on a black maid—well, and what of it? But if it had been the Père Bonne-chance in his place, the doctor knew that he could have continued without hesitation.

"Bless me, Father, for I have sinned."

Moustique turned toward him, adjusting his stole, twisting his shoulders to block part of the wind. The doctor edged a little closer.

"It has been long since my last confession." Yes, years. The doctor was not especially devout, not usually, though lately he'd been moved to more frequent public observance by the dictates of Toussaint.

"I have fornicated, innumerable times, but with the same woman always. Almost always. But certainly outside the bond of marriage." But he did not feel this to be his sin. He closed his yes. "I have killed other men, in acts of war, out of a selfish concern for the preservation of my own life."

This was not his true sin either, though it saddened him to think about it. He felt the wind on his face and his closed eyelids, felt Moustique attentively waiting.

"I cherished resentment against my sister," he said, "who had done me wrong, it is true . . . but my forgiveness still was slow, even after she had done all she could to repair the harm."

Moustique murmured something not quite intelligible. The doctor felt a faint lightening, as if a pebble had been tweezed from the mountain which bore him down. The sun was red on the back of his eyelids. At the center, a whorl of darkness.

"I have been guilty of despair," he heard himself say. There, that was it. "In despair, I have conceived the intention to slay a man who believes himself my enemy."

He opened his eyes.

"*Ego te absolvo.*" Moustique pronounced the formula without tremendous conviction. "But if you would go in peace, you must free yourself of this intention. This, I think, you have not yet done. There is something which prevents you."

"No," said the doctor. He stood up, with the weight still upon him. "I mean, you are right."

But he felt embarrassed admitting this. He turned his shoulder to Moustique and shaded his eyes to look out over the roofs of the town. There was a roil of dust at the distant gate.

"Are they attacking?" The doctor looked briefly at Moustique, who was also squinting at the dust cloud. Nearer to them, a crowd of people was streaming onto the Champ de Mars.

"I'll go down to see," the doctor said.

"A moment." Pulling the white robe over his head, Moustique loped into the church, and emerged a moment later dressed in an ordinary shirt and trousers. Together they scrambled down the path.

Most of the white and colored townsfolk had gathered on the Champ de Mars, though few of the numerous blacks were in evidence. It appeared to be true that the insurgency begun at Fort Liberté had swept all the way to the gates of Le Cap, so that everyone was in deep terror of massacre and another destruction of the town. Ought they to send out their too-few troops to attack the rebels? or send a delegation to appease Toussaint? For it now was generally believed that Toussaint's own hands were invisibly stirring up this insurrection. But it also appeared that Hédouville would do nothing to conciliate the General-in-Chief, would not negotiate with him at all. Therefore the meeting dissolved without resolution.

The doctor remained in place as the parade ground gradually emptied out. He felt cold, though the sun was still high. He had seen Maillart and O'Farrel standing with their troops on the opposite side of the field, but Riau and the black officers had remained in the barracks with their men, and he suspected the garrison might split on similar lines if the insurgent blacks did penetrate the town. He'd seen it before. He'd seen Le Cap burnt to an ash heap and been lucky to escape with his own life on that occasion. Carrying the infant Paul, he and Nanon had somehow managed to make their way out of that holocaust and down to Habitation Thibodet at Ennery.

Now the field was entirely empty except for the figure of a solitary woman in a long yellow dress, standing down by the lower gate. The doctor felt that she was aware of him, though her face was a hidden by a parasol of the same fabric as her dress. He glanced to his right, but Moustique had vanished with the others. As the woman turned and passed slowly into the town, he followed, crossing the Rue Espagnole and keeping about half a block behind her. She could not have failed to notice him if she looked back, however, for there were far fewer people on the streets than usual for this hour. Everyone had gone in, either to barricade their homes as best they could or to pack their belongings in hope of making an escape on the ships in the harbor.

The woman crossed the Place d'Armes at a diagonal and continued into a side street. The doctor followed. He knew this block, and thought she must know it too, though he'd not yet had a glimpse of her face. He and Nanon had lived here in the first few months of Paul's life. Therefore he was not surprised when the woman stopped before the pitch apple tree, and after a moment shifted her parasol to the opposite shoulder to free a hand for lifting that leaf which was inscribed with the name Paul Hébert. The doctor waited on the far side of the street, slightly dizzy under the full sun. He saw her in profile as she bowed over the leaf, crumpling rather, as if with a sob, though she was still careful not to break it from the stem.

"But he is well," the doctor said, his voice ringing through the space between them. He took a tentative step into the dust of the street. Nanon looked up at him with swimming eyes.

"He is even here, at Le Cap, and you may see him."

She raised the green leaf cupped in her palm, the whole plant trembling with the movement.

"You have put your name with his."

"It is his name as well," the doctor said. "He is my son." He coughed. "I thought I was making his tombstone then. I wanted to write his name on something green, which would live on. As you and I together wrote his being in his body."

"How you must hate me," Nanon said.

"No." He was not quite within reach of her and did not dare come nearer. She did not wear the iron collar, he noticed, nor the chain, though the mark of the collar was visible on her throat, where he'd seen it earlier without knowing what it was.

"You can never understand," she said.

"But try me." Now he did take just one step closer. "Has he let you free?"

"Oh," said Nanon, as if in anger. "You see? You cannot grasp it. He leaves me, now, he leaves me always free. I may remove the chain whenever I like, and walk about the town. And no one cares if I return."

"Not so," the doctor said.

"Oh! he told me he'd send him to school—to school!—and I persuaded myself to believe . . . he'd as soon have sent him to the devil, he would. And your sister, she would send us both to the devil, she always hated me and wished me away . . ."

"Not true," the doctor said. "Not now."

Nanon released the leaf and shuddered, swaying from her ankles. With a quick step forward he caught her around the shoulders and stopped her fall.

"No matter," he said. "Only come with me now, to Isabelle's. Paul will be there and you shall see him, and afterward, we will find a remedy."

If she heard him, she gave no sign, but her head rolled insensible against his shoulder, the white crescents of her eyes showing under the lush dark lashes. As he took her weight, he found her dangerously hot. Her parasol had fallen beneath the bush, but he did not try to retrieve it. She could walk, a little, with his help, and fortunately it wasn't far. In twenty minutes he had bundled her over the threshold of the Cigny house. Isabelle was at home, and alone for a wonder, and she grasped the situation immediately, ordering Nanon to be taken at once to her own bed.

Paul was not there in fact, which was for the better, since Nanon was off her head and raving. The doctor prepared every leaf and herb he knew effective against fever, whether as compress or as tea. He was unnerved, underconfident, and wished very much for Toussaint—though Toussaint had little time for doctoring these days. None of his concoctions brought a good response. By dusk they'd changed her sweat-soaked sheets three times, and her fever was still climbing.

Riau appeared in the bedroom doorway. How had he known to come?—or had he?

"Salt," said the doctor, with sudden fervor.

The dream spilled out of him. Riau listened as if he were making perfect sense, then moved past him to the bed. He took Nanon's hand for a moment, peeled back her eyelid and stooped to look in. She moaned and flinched away from his touch.

"A supernatural malady," Riau murmured. "I must go for Maman Maig'."

"Yes, go," Isabelle said.

In the foyer Riau turned. "And Paul?"

"Let him stay with Fontelle," the doctor said, "if she will keep him." He hesitated a moment to see if the plan was sound, but yes, there was no safer place on earth for the boy that he knew. Riau was already out the door.

Within the hour he returned, floating in the wake of Maman Maig', who piloted her stately bulk along like a warship under full sail. She lit a candle, uncorked a rum bottle full of weeds, and shooed Isabelle and the doctor from the room. He sat with his back propped against the door jamb, listening. Maman Maig's voice sang or chanted words to songs he did not know. Her voice blended oddly with the sound of drums and moaning conch shells from the insurgent camps on the slopes around the town . . . as if Nanon had reshaped all the outside world to fit her fever.

He woke with a start, not knowing the time; the house was dark but the door was open to the bedroom where a lamp was burning low. Mamam Maig' sat cross-legged on the floor, snoring gently. She opened her eyes when he went in, but did not prevent his going to the bedside. Nanon lay still and gently sleeping, her flesh much cooled under the brush of his hand.

"Grâce à Dieu," he said, and kissed his fingers to Maman Maig', who simply closed her eyes and resumed snoring. Isabelle appeared in her night dress.

"Rest," she said. It was an order.

The doctor rolled himself on a sofa, with his feet hanging over the carved wooden arm. He woke a little after daybreak, to the smell of coffee and the sound of a spoon. Maman Maig' was eating pumpkin soup from a large bowl. He went in to Nanon and took her hand. She roused and looked at him with a weak smile, and her fingers fluttered against his for a moment before they slackened and she slept.

"The fever's broken," said Isabelle, handing him a cup of coffee. "Only let her sleep. Go out and get the news of the town."

"But—" the doctor begain.

Isabelle began straightening his clothes, which he'd slept in. "Leave us an hour—all is well here, but I do want the news. Something is happening."

"Has the attack begun from the plain?" But there were no drums just now, no *lambi* blowing.

"No," said Isabelle. "It's at the port."

He walked down to the harbor front. The wind was stiff and the day still cool, with whitecaps running in hard over the water. At the harbor's mouth, the masts of a sizable fleet broke the horizon, as the pilots led them out to open sea.

"Hédouville," said Pascal, appearing at the doctor's elbow near the Customs House. "He's gone. Also Commissioner Raimond . . . and a couple of thousand others who no longer like their chances here."

The doctor blinked at him slowly. "If Raimond has left, there is no French authority in all the island."

"There's always Roume, in Santo Domingo," Pascal reminded him. "And then, Rigaud."

"What do you mean, Rigaud?"

"Oh," said Pascal, cradling his suppurating thumb. "A parting stroke of diplomacy—Hédouville has placed Rigaud at the head of the colony and directed him to ignore Toussaint's authority."

The doctor gaped at him.

"I tell you I copied the letter myself, and saw it signed," Pascal said. "It is on the way to Rigaud even now, to be delivered by the shreds of the mulatto faction here—they've all bolted for the south, save those who are on those ships out there." He sniffed, uneasily. "Your duel may be cancelled, my friend—why yes, I know about it, everyone does. But I doubt even that bastard Maltrot will have lingered. Everyone is waiting for Toussaint to sack the town."

"But he won't," the doctor said. "It's over."

"You think so?" Pascal waved his arm toward the south gate, where the hubbub of the angry mob had recommenced.

"Believe me," the doctor said. "For now, it's finished."

*   *   *

He was right. By midmorning reports began trickling in that all along Toussaint's leisurely progress from Ennery to Plaisance through Limbé, the rebels had laid down their weapons and gone back to work in the cane fields. The crowd at the south gate quieted and dispersed. By the time Toussaint himself rode into town, flanked by his honor guard in their high plumed helmets, both Le Cap and the surrounding country-side were as eerily calm as a hurricane's eye.

In the course of that same day Nanon woke for long enough to see Paul briefly. The doctor would not let him stay long for fear of fatiguing her (and in fact he went out happily enough with Paulette after half an hour). Nanon slept through the day with brief intervals of waking; she was weak, but the fever did not return, and Maman Maig' left the house, saying there was nothing more to fear.

The doctor stayed by Nanon all day, sometimes dozing in his chair, because he'd slept poorly the previous night. On occasion Isabelle or Michel Arnaud came in with news of Toussaint's movements toward the town, to which the doctor barely attended. He watched Nanon, the light swell of her breathing under the sheet, the movement of her closed eyes in dream. In her waking moments she held his hand and looked at him affectionately, but she said very little and he did not try ask her any questions.

Isabelle bullied him to go to bed properly that night, and once he resigned himself to obey he fell into a dense, gluey sleep from which a servant unexpectedly roused him. It was still dark, and he could not understand what was the matter. Frightened for Nanon, he stumbled down the stairs, but the servant led him past her closed chamber to the doorway, where Maillart and Riau were waiting.

"Your engagement," said the captain, swinging out his watch on its silver chain. The doctor looked at him without comprehension.

"You forgot it?" Maillart looked at Riau. "He forgot about it!" But if Riau was equally astonished, he gave no sign.

The doctor's mare was saddled, waiting at the rail. He mounted and they rode along the dark street. On the slopes of Morne du Cap, the cocks had just begun to crow. A few kitchen fires had already been lit, and sometimes a woman's figure came looming out of the dark, leading a burro loaded with charcoal or bearing a basket on her head—bound from some distant mountain to the market at the Place Clugny.

As he came more completely awake, the doctor's mind began to flutter. The weight which had lain upon him like a boulder had been lifted away—he had felt nothing of it for the past thirty hours, and with it had gone the bitterness which had led him to provoke Choufleur. Ah, why would anyone choose despair over love? It seemed to him a sad thing that he must now be killed, just when he was beginning to comprehend the message which had come to him through Moustique. In a flash he understood that he had lost his capacity to kill Choufleur, but still he must face him and fire his pistol. There was no way out.

As they rode down into the low, swampy ground of La Fossette, the sky began to lighten behind a veil of fog. Mosquitoes whirled to the attack, out of the mist. Maillart cursed, slapping at his wrists and neck. The doctor kept still, bearing the bites so sudden movement would not spook his mare.

"*Là,*" Riau said, turning his horse toward a patch of flame in the fog.

"They're here," Maillart said, as if in resignation. Then there was no sound but the horses' hooves sucking in the mud.

Choufleur's seconds, two colored officers whose names the doctor did not know, had built a small fire and were feeding it green citrus leaves to discourage the mosquitoes. The seconds greeted each other cordially enough. Two pack mules were tethered with their horses; it appeared that Choufleur meant to join Rigaud's force in the Southern Department, supposing he survived the morning's encounter. When the doctor slid down from his horse, Choufleur pointedly turned his back, and stood facing the area of fog where the seaward horizon would eventually appear.

There was some some discussion about the pistols, in which Maillart participated. The doctor had gone numb. In the town, a church bell tolled the hour. The whole area had a foul, damp smell; he understood why Maillart did not like it. Unhealthy, at any rate. Riau was looking through tendrils of mist at the two low buildings which had once housed slaves off the ships from Guinée. Beyond, the border of the cemetery with its wet and shallow graves.

Maillart walked a distance from the fire with one of the colored officers. They stood back to back, then took five paces away from each other, then turned. Ceremoniously, each man drew his saber and planted it in the earth. Then they turned apart and paced off another ten steps. The doctor felt Riau's fingers brushed over the back of his hand. Riau leaned as if to whisper something, but instead only blew into his ear. This was strange, but not disagreeable, and it left the doctor with a curious feeling of warmth.

Maillart beckoned him over, handed him a pistol and walked back to the fire.

"The space between the swords constitutes the barrier." The captain's

voice came out ringing through the fog. "After the first shots, the pistols
are to be exchanged. Each man may approach the barrier and fire at
will. Doctor Hébert has the first shot, Colonel Maltrot the second, and
so following. Neither man may cross the barrier. Do you understand?"

"Yes," said Choufleur.

"I yield the first shot to my adversary." The doctor recognized his own
voice.

"Antoine, you can't do that!" Maillart snatched his hat off and hurled
it into the mud. Riau made a smoothing gesture with his palm and
moved toward Choufleur's seconds. After a moment's whispering it was
concluded that as Choufleur had given the formal challenge, the doctor
must fire first.

"But I struck him—I struck him in the mouth," the doctor said. "So
the challenge was mine. I intended it so."

"I don't accept this reasoning," Choufleur said. "Let him fire first."

The doctor looked at the four seconds. Maltrot, who stood disconsolately brushing vegetable matter from his hat, would not return his
glance. No appeal. His arm had already begun raising the pistol. The
light was still gray, but sufficiently clear. He had never known how it
was accomplished, but there was never any difficulty: if his weapon was
true, the bullet would go precisely wherever he had focused his eyes.
Now he was looking intently at the third button down from Choufleur's
collar, but as his finger compressed the trigger, he jerked the pistol up
and let the charge fly off into the sky.

There was a hiss from the cluster by the fire, and the doctor's mare
began rearing against her tether. Riau left the other seconds to calm her.

"I insist that he fire again, with a true aim," Choufleur said.

"He can't do that," said the doctor.

Another consultation: it was agreed that Choufleur must fire. He did
not seem particularly disappointed, but only shrugged and walked deliberately all the way to the sword his second had planted. It seemed to
the doctor that he took a long time arranging his shot. It was painful
for him to keep still and resist flapping at the mosquitoes who fed greed-
ily on his cheeks and ears. Finally the muzzle of Choufleur's pistol
flashed, and a moment later the doctor realized the shot had missed him
altogether.

Maillart brought him a freshly charged pistol. "For God's sake, will
you kill the bastard?" he snarled. "He won't hesitate to kill you."

The doctor took five steps forward, aimed at the empty space
between Choufleur's epaulette and his right ear, and fired into it. The
sigh from the group of seconds was like a moan.

Time passed. The mosquitoes went on feeding. The doctor was very,

very tired. When he saw the muzzle of Choufleur's pistol bloom out flame, he thought it was another clean miss at first, but then he felt the patch of moisture spreading over his left sleeve below his shoulder.

"A hit!" cried one of Choufleur's seconds.

"It's of no consequence," said the doctor. "I will continue."

He raised the left arm outward, flexing the elbow. The movement was normal. The bullet had certainly gone through without touching the bone, and perhaps it had only grazed him. The complete absence of pain would have worried him, under different circumstances. Maillart was giving him his first pistol, recharged. They did not meet each other's eyes.

The doctor took another step toward the barrier, and stopped to aim at the space in Choufleur's open collar, where his throat pulsed. Holding his pistol level, he began to walk forward again. It was much brighter now; the sun had risen and was spreading streaks of yellow over the gray-green vegetation of the marsh. Two steps from the barrier the doctor threw the pistol over his shoulder and heard it discharge as it struck the ground behind him. The mare lunged at her tether. The doctor continued moving very slowly toward the barrier with his open empty hands before him. With a bell-like clarity, he heard the seconds bickering.

"He fired."

"He did not."

"If the gun went off, in principle he fired. Colonel Maltrot has the right to his shot."

The doctor stopped beside Maillart's sword and let his hands drop to his sides. The bore of Choufleur's pistol seemed enormously large and dark. He was aware of many things at once: Riau, stroking the mare to calm her, a pair of white egrets bright and distant in the marsh beyond Choufleur, the movements of the clouds above, a triad of mosquitoes extracting blood from a soft spot behind his jawbone. With the sun behind him, Choufleur was bordered by a radiance in which the doctor seemed to feel his intelligence, talent, force of will, and frustrated capability for love. He raised his empty hands again and stepped into the space between the swords.

"He can't do that!" a second called.

Choufleur's aura darkened as he dropped his pistol and lunged, bowling the doctor over backward in the muck. He meant to strangle him, or simply drown him in the mud—the doctor was slow to recognize this intention, but finally it came clear. He began thrashing his limbs at random and accidentally kneed Choufleur in the groin. The pressure released, and he shouldered the other man off him and sat up with a pounding head, one hand on his bruised trachea. Choufleur was in a three-point crouch, his face green with pain; he seemed to be trying to say something but could not ejaculate the words.

Then the seconds laid hands on them and dragged them farther apart.

"This circus is at an end," Maillart spluttered. "Honor has been satisfied—after some fashion. They have faced each other's fire."

"Give thanks to God that you have survived," said the colored officer who had done most of the talking.

Then the doctor was somehow back on his own mare and riding toward the town. He had brushed off Maillart's effort to bandage his wound—let it wait till they got away from the swamp. Choufleur and his group had gone off in the opposite direction, according to their plan. As they came up out the marshland onto the more solid roadbed, the doctor felt a euphoria begin to spread over him. Till then he had not realized how little he'd expected to be alive at this moment.

Maillart looked at him over his shoulder, once, twice. His face was red, and his neck was red when he turned his back, and the cloth of his uniform coat trembled where it stretched between his shoulder blades. Then his laughter broke out of his control and spread to the other two. It seemed that no one of them could look at another without bursting out into fresh laughter.

Riau was the first to regain self-control, looking away toward the bank of the river as they approached the city gate. Following suit, the doctor began to regain his breath. There was some discomfort in his windpipe from Choufleur's try at throttling him; this troubled him rather more than the bullet wound, which also had begun to sting. The sun was now rising over the plain, and a flash of its warm light fell on his shoulders, on all three of them, spreading to include the single fisherman in his dugout flowing eastward on the calm surface of the river.

Fort de Joux, France

September 1802

Toussaint had breakfasted: stone-hard biscuit softened in his heavily sugared coffee, then sucked to mush among his unreliable teeth. The meagerness of the ration did not bother him. He had never had much interest in food, and needed little solid nourishment to get by—though he did wish the coffee were of better quality.

No great matter. His fever had passed, and today he felt rather well. Though surely he would never get accustomed to the cold of this place, so very different from the humid jungle peaks of Saint Domingue— these icy spines on the crown of the white man's world. But he had dressed warmly and built up his fire. Now he was waiting for his guest, with an almost cheerful anticipation. His interrogator, rather. But Toussaint had come very quickly to enjoy their interviews. He did not think about when they would end, though of course he knew they must end eventually, leaving Caffarelli unsatisfied.

He listened to the key turning in the frozen lock. In the doorway, the jowly, anxious face of Baille floated behind the figure of Napoleon's agent, muttering something not entirely audible across the cell. Caffarelli hovered on the threshold, his forward tilt not quite a bow. The door closed behind him.

"You are well?" Caffarelli looked at him narrowly.

"Oh," said Toussaint. "I am well enough. And yourself?"

"Exceedingly."

Unfolding his hand, Toussaint indicated the chair opposite his own. Caffarelli smiled and took his seat. With no apparent purpose, he looked into the corners where the barrel vault met the walls of the cell. Toussaint waited, motionless; not even his breath was perceptible.

"Your dealings with the English," Caffarelli began.

"I have already told you."

"But you had secret arrangements with them which you have not admitted."

"Sir, I did not. I made two treaties with the English, and strictly to arrange terms for their departure from Saint Domingue."

"The English suggested that you yourself might place the colony under protection of their crown."

Toussaint inclined his head.

"You entertained those proposals with a certain favor."

"Oh," said Toussaint. "There were some agents of the English who tried to place that idea in my head. I amused myself by making fun of them."

"And at the same time you accepted their gifts."

Toussaint let out a whispering laugh. "I had no gifts from the English." He considered. "I had some twenty barrels of powder from General Maitland, but nothing more."

Both men were silent while the castle clock tolled the hour.

"Yes," Toussaint said, "and once General Maitland presented me with a saddle and trappings for my horse, which I at first refused. But when pressed to accept it as a token from himself, rather than his government, I did so."

"Commendable," Caffarelli said drily, but Toussaint did not react to the prick.

"And your secret treaty, signed with Maitland. What were its terms?"

"I have already told you."

"You have not told all."

"I agreed not to attack the English at Jamaica," Toussaint said with an air of fatigue. "The English were to have the right to enter the ports at Le Cap and Port-au-Prince, but no other. They promised not to molest the ships of the French Republic in the coastal waters of Saint Domingue."

Caffarelli affected a sigh.

"Not all the English officers kept the bargain," Toussaint said irritably. "Their corsairs took four of our ships after it was signed. That was done by Admiral Farker and the governor of Jamaica, who complained that Maitland had let himself be deceived by a Negro."

"As perhaps he had," said Caffarelli.

Again Toussaint declined to react.

"And the other terms of the secret treaty?"

"I have already told you."

The castle bells rang two more times while the conversation continued to follow these same circular pathways. In the intervals, the ticking of Toussaint's watch buried in his clothes was just barely audible. The damp seeped glossily on the inner wall. Caffarelli veered to a new subject.

"And the treasure that you hid in Saint Domingue. Spirited away from the coffers of the French Republic."

Toussaint clicked his tongue. "The government treasury was reduced by the wars. I had no fortune, not in money. I spent what I had on the same cause, and the rest of my property was in land. There is Habitation d'Héricourt, near Le Cap, and at Ennery three plantations which I bought from the *colons* and joined together. Also Habitation Rousinière, which is the property of my wife. On the Spanish side of the island I had land where I raised livestock for the army."

"You sent a ship to the North American Republic, loaded with gold and precious things, and your aide-de-camp who conducted the cargo was shot when he returned."

Toussaint ran his tongue around the loose teeth at the front of his jaw. "It is true that I ordered the man shot, but that was because he had tried to debauch some young women of my household." He paused. "All you white men are always dreaming of gold in the mountains of Saint Domingue. There was gold once, but the Spaniards took it all away a very long time ago."

"Then what of the six men who went out from Le Cap to bury your treasure in the mountains, and who were shot on their return?"

Toussaint's heels cracked against the concrete floor, and his eyes grew round and white as he surged against the edge of the table. "That is a lie! A calumny, sir, which my enemies invented to dishonor me. They said I had killed men from my own guard on such a mission, but I called out my guard to prove the lie, and all were present. I would not put the shame of such an act upon my spirit."

"No," said Caffarelli softly. "No, perhaps you would not."

Toussaint subsided. Caffarelli produced his own watch and examined its face. The cry of a circling hawk came toward them distantly from the chasm opposite the cell of Berthe de Joux.

"I will leave you, for a time, to rest," Caffarelli said. "I will return this afternoon."

In Saint Domingue, Toussaint had never formed the habit of the midday siesta, which all who were able to do so practiced. But his secretaries could not work effectively during those hours; stunned by the heat, they spoiled their pages. Toussaint did not stop, but he slowed down, as a reptile might, his eyes half lidded, his body at rest, his mind in slow motion. Many notions and strategies unfolded in his head, and if something shifted in the terrain before his eye, he was aware of it.

Now, as he lay still, fully clothed under a blanket, with his arms folded across his breastbone, it was more difficult for him to enter this state, because of the cold. He could feel something in Caffarelli's intention reaching toward him, but he could not make out exactly what it was.

The cry of the mountain hawks around the castle had not given Caffarelli the idea itself so much as the language for it. It was, he thought, probably his best hope, if not his last.

He returned to Toussaint's cell in the afternoon, and for some two hours allowed the conversation to wander in the same circles as it had before. When he again raised the issue of the murdered men who were supposed to have hidden treasure, Toussaint's flicker of resentment was slighter than it had been earlier. But it was there, and Caffarelli pressed.

"General, you are not putting the truth of yourself into what you tell me. Does not that dishonor your spirit most of all? You give me the answers a slave would make, but you were no slave in Saint Domingue. Your constitution was a declaration of independence in everything but name. You were a rebel, and a proud one! You were an eagle—why pretend to be a duck? Tell me, tell the First Consul—tell the world *how it really was.*"

Toussaint rose up. He did so without moving, but the sudden ferocity of his concentration pressed Caffarelli back in his chair. For a moment he forgot that Toussaint was the prisoner and he was not. As he regained his sense of the true situation, he thought with a burst of excitement that he had won, but the moment passed. Toussaint shrank, his whole body slackened. He looked away as he began to speak, returning to that same circle of evasions he had always made before.

Part Four

THE WAR OF KNIVES

1799–1801

Si ou mouri, ou gen tò. . . .

—Haitian proverb

If you're dead, you're wrong. . . .

By the fall of 1798, Toussaint Louverture had seen the departures of three white representatives of the French Republic: Laveaux, Sonthonax, and Hédouville. His enemies claimed he had engineered these departures in order to extend his own power in the colony. Toussaint, however, always maintained his loyalty to France, where he had sent his two eldest sons for their education. He had certainly declined an offer of British support, tendered by General Maitland, in setting up Saint Domingue as an independent state, perhaps with himself as its king.

One official French agent still remained on the island, Roume, an elderly Creole from Grenada who had been part of various French commissions since the first slave rebellion in 1791, and who had represented the French interest in Spanish Santo Domingo since the signing of the Treaty of Basel. Toussaint now invited Roume to return to French Saint Domingue in the role of French commissioner, though his enemies claimed he did so only to give a shading of legitimacy to his own enterprise of setting up an essentially independent government.

By 1799, Toussaint's most powerful enemy on the island was a recent ally, General Antoine Rigaud. During the repulse of the British invasion,

Rigaud, a native of Les Cayes on the southern peninsula, had emerged as the principal leader of the colored minority, just as Toussaint emerged as the principal leader of the black majority. Rigaud and Toussaint might have come to blows eventually because of racial politics, but their conflict was accelerated and exacerbated by Agent Hédouville's parting gesture: he formally instructed Rigaud to disregard Toussaint's authority.

31

It was strange, because he was a *blanc,* while I, Riau, was *fils Ginen,*
how sometimes I would feel myself to be walking in the same spirit with
Doctor Antoine Hébert. I felt so very much that day at La Fossette,
when he would not kill Choufleur, although he could have killed him
easily, and with less danger to himself than it cost him not to do it. That
was not because I wanted Choufleur to keep his feet walking on our
earth, because he was a dangerous man who was sure to cause more
trouble. It would be for the better if someone did kill him, but the doctor chose not to do it, and Riau was glad, and even the Captain Maillart
felt that same harmony that was among all three of us as we came riding
out of the swamp with its rotting smell of graves, the sun shining down
on our backs in its rising out of the sea.

After this thing had happened I thought I would ask the doctor to be
parrain to the child who had two fathers, when that child would be
brought to the water of the whiteman's church. It seemed to me that
Guiaou would be for this idea as well because he had also worked with
the doctor in healing, and with Riau too, and I did not think Merbillay
would be against it. But none of us were able to go Ennery then, but
instead we were all sent here or there all over the northern plain.

Hédouville had been driven away, and Toussaint sent a long letter after him to the masters of France, saying he had not meant to chase their agent from the country, whatever Hédouville claimed himself, and still there was no one above Toussaint after Hédouville had left, except for Roume, across the Spanish border. Also there was Rigaud in the south, but no one yet knew what he would do, and there were many mountains between him and Toussaint. In the north was peace, but Toussaint made himself very busy getting ready for more war, and he seemed to think that this war would come in French ships from over the sea, no matter what letters he sent.

War wants guns, and guns want money, and money wanted sugar and coffee to be brought out of the trees and the cane fields. For that, more of the *grand blancs* were coming back all the time, after Hédouville had gone. They agreed with Toussaint, now, even better than with the French, and that hurt the confidence that some felt in Toussaint, especially with Moyse, and a few others. I, Riau, I was doubtful too, although I kept the doubt hidden behind my head. I saw many of Toussaint's letters and the letters which came to him, so I thought he was right that the war was not finished yet, and I knew we would need more guns, with powder and bullets to feed them.

For that, it happened that Captain Riau was sent with men to bring Michel Arnaud to his plantation on the plain again, with his wife who served the mysteries, because they had run away again from that place when the rising against Hédouville happened, and they did not know what they would find when they came back—if the place had been burned again or not, or if the people of the hoe there would have stayed. The doctor came with them also, to begin a hospital there for people who were sick or hurt. He had said to Arnaud that if he cared for the sick ones on his plantation, that would be a protection for himself, because people would return the good he did for them. Arnaud seemed to listen to this, although I thought it was against what was truly in him. No one was more savage to our people than Arnaud before the slaves broke off their chains.

But when we did come to Habitation Arnaud, the people had not burned the cane fields. The mill had been only partly rebuilt since they had knocked it down the first time, but they had not knocked down that part which had been raised again. And the people had stayed there instead of running away, in their *cases* around the borders of the cane pieces. The people seemed quiet to me, too quiet, and they turned their faces from us and lowered their heads when we came riding up that *allée* of stumps which led to the main compound.

Arnaud was happy—one could see his head lift up and his spine unkink itself—because he had expected it all to be destroyed. As for his woman, when she stepped down into the yard, she turned her head around and around like an owl, looking for that shed which was no longer there, and when her eyes found the burned patch where it had been, they rolled back white, and she fell away from herself toward the ground, but Arnaud came quickly and caught her up. The people of that place were watching from the hedges to see if the *loa* would rise up in her body, but she had only fainted, and Arnaud carried her into the house.

I, Riau, I had not seen the burning of the shed, but I had heard about it from the doctor and also from Flaville, and I knew what was in the shed before it had been burnt.

We stayed at Habitation Arnaud for eight days. As Captain, Riau might have slept in the *grand'case* with the doctor and the other *blancs*. Arnaud invited me to sleep there, but I did not want to stay in his house. Bouquart found a *case* down below the cane mill, and I went there at night to stay with him. In the day, I worked with the doctor and some of the men Arnaud had called in from the cane fields or the mill to help with raising the hospital. His woman Claudine came out then, and took an interest in what we would do; she asked for a brush arbor to be raised next to the room which would be for the hospital, where she might teach the children of those who worked the fields. Arnaud ordered this done to please her. All the time she walked high on her toes like a cat trying to cross water. It appeared that she was meant to stand over the leaf women who would tend the hospital, and the doctor taught her certain things to do. She was slow, but willing when she did these things, and she had a gentle touch. The children were drawn by this softness in her, so that they came willingly to the brush arbor when it was made to learn the letters in her book. Yet I wondered if this gentleness was really her own.

Arnaud thought it wasteful, this business of teaching the children. He said nothing, but his thought showed in the curl of his lip. He was suspicious of the hospital too, and so were the people who worked his fields. In the old days Arnaud had given himself to wounding, not healing. There was no great illness, and no one was badly hurt while we stayed there, but some of the men came to the hospital with the ordinary cuts on their hands and faces from the cane leaves. Claudine and the leaf women poulticed their cuts with *gueri trop vite,* so that they healed more quickly.

But one day there came to the hospital a runaway who had been caught by the *maréchaussée* and brought back to Arnaud during slavery time. She was an old woman now, or looked to be so. She did not come right into the hospital, but remained standing at the edge of the bush, with her breasts hanging slack against her ribs and the stumps where her hands were held up before her. Arnaud had cut off her hands as a punishment, when the *maréchaussée* brought her back to him. There was nothing to be done about it now, so the doctor turned his face to the wall, but Claudine did not look away, and the bolt of pain that passed between them was like thunder.

That handless woman stayed in her *case* all through her days because she could no longer do anything. Claudine persuaded Arnaud to take a girl out of the cane field to care for her in the daytime. Also she had made a wooden hook and a spoon to be fastened to those stumps, so that the woman could help herself a little. After Claudine had done those things, some of the other people began to meet her eyes more freely when she looked at them, and some of them would shyly touch her hands, although they were still fearful of her spirit.

On the fifth night that we stayed there one of my soldiers forced a woman from the plantation to open her legs for him, and I ordered him to be shot. There was nothing else to do about it. By dawn a great stir had begun among the woman's family and spread all through Arnaud's cultivators, and they would have risen against us if the man had not been punished. I shot him myself with my own pistol, but left it to others to bring his flesh to the cemetery. It was what Toussaint would have wanted and what he would have done, the same as if Toussaint himself were working through my hands, and in fact he told me so himself when I reported it to him. After this had been done, the people became calm again, and they went quietly back to work—too quietly.

I wondered if perhaps Arnaud practiced his old cruelties on them when no one else was there to see, but I learned from the people that this was not true. This I found out mostly from Bouquart, because he had taken up with a woman there, who gave herself to him freely, and that was a good way of getting the news. I teased him about Zabeth at Ennery, but there was not much heart in my teasing. Bouquart told me that the people were not downhearted for anything Arnaud had done to them, but because of Toussaint who had ordered that any man not in the army must work and stay on the land he worked for his whole life long, or else be punished by the soldiers with their guns. Also Toussaint had taken away many of the Sonthonax guns from the men who worked the land, saying he would return them if there was need to use them. No one said it was like slavery again, the way they had spoken about Hédouville, but I could feel them thinking so, although they would not say it to my face.

Bouquart was always away with his new woman at night, so I was alone in the *case*. I did not like this, and often I could not sleep. One night I rose as if a voice had called me and walked around the cane mill to the open yard before the *grand'case*. The moon was two days past the full, and in the light of it Claudine came drifting from the house and stopped in the burnt circle of the shed where Arnaud had once kept his slave-catching dog which the doctor had shot, and where later Claudine had murdered the maid named Mouche. She turned within the walls which were burned down, turning and turning under the moon.

From the shadow of the mill wall, I watched her. Arnaud was watching too, from a seat on the gallery of the *grand'case*. He sat very still— only the pommel of his twisted stick kept falling from one of his hands to the other. It made me uneasy to think that he probably saw me too, inside the shadow of the wall. Riau had more power than Arnaud then, but for that moment I did not quite believe it.

After a while I saw that someone else was watching too, a woman who stood inside a fringe of trees, across the clearing from the mill. I went to where she was standing, exposed to Arnaud's eyes under the moon, though he made no sign that he had noticed me. The woman was Cléo, a mulattress who had been housekeeper here. I had known her in the camps of Grande Riviere, where she had run after Claudine slashed the throat of Mouche in the shed. It was Cléo who told me all that story.

"*Zombi*," she said now, pointing her chin at Claudine where she turned, but I shook my head.

"No, she is waiting for Baron," I said.

Cléo turned to me with her mouth round in surprise, and I told her what I had seen at Le Cap, in the *hûnfor*, how Baron, or sometimes Erzulie-gé-Rouge, would mount the head of this whitewoman.

When Cléo had understood this, she stepped out of the cover of the trees and went to Claudine and took one of her hands in her own and put the other hand at the base of Claudine's head. A breath went out of Claudine like wind, and she let her head roll back against Cléo's hand. Cléo led her slowly to the house. All the time Arnaud was watching from the gallery, as if he had expected all these things to happen, though it had been years since Cléo set her foot on that plantation.

Two days later we were riding back to Le Cap, the doctor and Bouquart and I, and the other men in my command, to report to Toussaint that soon Arnaud would be sending brown sugar to the port, along with many other planters on the plain. That sugar would be loaded onto ships for England and America and would be traded for more guns and powder and shot. But the people were cutting the cane and milling it to

sugar under force from the army, and if they did not want to do it, perhaps there would be chains for them again, perhaps the whip. When
they saw us riding toward them, they lowered their heads and turned
away, because I, Riau, was a soldier of the gun, while they were only
workers of the hoe. It was like I had myself turned into a *blanc*. When I
thought this, I was cold all over, as though my spirit had gone away and
left me to become a *zombi,* dead flesh forked across the saddle, my arms
and legs answering to someone else's will.

The Commissioner Roume had come to Le Cap by the time that we
arrived there. Toussaint had sent for him across the mountains. I heard
the *blanc* secretary Pascal and some others who muttered that Toussaint
had done this only to hide the truth that it was really himself who did
and commanded everything now. Roume was an old man then, and frail,
but his heart was strong, and he spoke and acted by what he believed.
He was a believer in Toussaint. But also, Roume wanted to make peace
between Rigaud and Toussaint, or bring back the peace that Hédouville
had broken between those two.

For that, he called Rigaud and Toussaint to meet at Port au Prince,
and so Toussaint marched south, with a part of his army. We stopped for
a day and a night at Ennery, where Toussaint saw his family, and Riau
saw his. That child who had two fathers was born another girl child, and
we had agreed among the three of us to name her Marielle. When we
left Ennery for Port-au-Prince, Guiaou marched in my command, and I
had put him in charge of a squad of men, because he was respected for
his fighting and I knew the men would trust and follow him.

But there was not supposed to be any fighting on this march. Peace
covered the whole way to Port-au-Prince, and the plantations of the Artibonite Valley were back at work, and so were those of the Cul de Sac
plain. When we came to Port-au-Prince, Rigaud was there as expected,
and there was a great celebration of the end of slavery. Beside Rigaud
was Beauvais, and with Toussaint was Christophe Mornet and also
Laplume, who had been leading Dieudonné's men since Dieudonné
was taken and killed. All of these chiefs made a contest who could shout
the loudest—*Gloire à la République!* That night there was a big *bamboche* with drums and dancing, on the open ground above the town.

It seemed then that Rigaud and Toussaint might come back to the
good understanding which had been between them before, as the agent
Roume had wished it. Rigaud had a letter from Hédouville, which said
he did not have to obey Toussaint any more. I, Riau, knew of this letter

from Pascal and the doctor, but Rigaud had not showed it to the whole world yet. When he showed this letter to Roume, the old man told him that his own words were now stronger than the words of Hédouville, and that Rigaud must give obedience to Toussaint, even though in the south it was really Rigaud who commanded.

Rigaud did not like to hear this very much. Maybe he would have accepted it, though, if it had been a matter only of making words and a show of respect to the General-in-Chief. But Rigaud wanted Petit Goâve and Grand Goâve and Léogane to be a part of his command. These were the nearest towns to the south of Port-au-Prince, and they had all been places where Dieudonné was, before he was taken, and now Laplume commanded them in Toussaint's name, so there was the same old trouble which began when Laplume gave himself to Toussaint instead of to Rigaud. Roume did not agree that Rigaud should have those towns, and Rigaud grew angry when he was refused, because his temper was too quick and hot. In anger he rushed out of Port-au-Prince with the men he had brought with him, and perhaps before he had well thought of what would follow.

Then there was a lot of confusion in Port-au-Prince, because it seemed that the people there might take the part of Rigaud. Even Christophe Mornet, who commanded for Toussaint at Port-au-Prince and who had served under him for a long time and won battles for Toussaint against the Spanish and the English too—the whisper was that Christophe Mornet was with Rigaud in his heart and making ready to betray Toussaint at any moment. Maybe it was true, or at least Toussaint believed it, because later on Christophe Mornet was arrested and killed with bayonets at Gonaives.

During this time there had been a rising against Rigaud near Jérémie, which was very far out on the southern peninsula where Rigaud was supreme. Rigaud had been all around Jérémie with his soldiers and believed he had driven the English away from that town, although it was also because of Toussaint's talk with Maitland that the English sailed away. This rising was supposed to be in favor of Toussaint and some said it was begun by Toussaint's secret hand, but the colored men put it down soon enough, and afterward there were forty black men who were crushed into a prison cell so tightly that, for want of air to breathe, they died.

Toussaint was very angry at this, and he declared that it was always the blacks who ended up dying in such affairs. Most times until then, Toussaint had not been so strictly bound to his own color, but had been as friendly to whites and blacks, and to colored men also if he trusted them. But this thing that happened in the prison was very bad. It made me think of Dieudonné, with the air smashed out of him by his chains, and when Guiaou heard of it, though he said nothing, I saw that he was thinking of the Swiss.

It was all so uneasy at Port-au-Prince that Roume thought we must move the government to Le Cap, where it was safer. Toussaint agreed to do this, but before he took the army away from Port-au-Prince, he called all the colored people to the church so that he could speak to them. Toussaint climbed to the high place where the priest stands in the church. His eyes were red and he shook with anger from his bootheels up and when he took off his general's hat, he was wearing the red *mouchwa têt* beneath it, instead of the yellow one. I thought maybe war would begin that same day. I stood in the back of the church, with some of my men mixed with some of Laplume's. Guiaou was near me, and Bouquart, and also Bienvenu who was then one of Laplume's men, but Toussaint was speaking to the colored men and not to us.

"You colored people who have always betrayed the blacks from the beginning of the revolution—what is it that you want today? There is no one who does not know: you want to be masters of the colony, to exterminate the whites and enslave the blacks! But, perverse men that you are, you ought to consider that you are forever dishonored already by the deportation and the murder of the those black troops who were known as the Swiss. Did you for one instant hesitate to sacrifice, to the hatred of the whites, those unfortunate men who had spilled their blood for your cause? Why did you sacrifice them?—because they were black."

When Toussaint said that, I could feel Guiaou's thought—that at last the Swiss would be avenged, and with his help, because it was Guiaou who had brought the story of the Swiss to Toussaint. I felt the thought flow over him, and his body moved like a tree in the wind.

"Why," Toussaint shouted, *"does General Rigaud refuse to obey me? Because I am black! Why else should he refuse to obey a French general like himself, and one who has contributed more than anyone else to the expulsion of the English? You colored men, through your treachery and your insane pride, you have already lost the share of political power you once had. As for General Rigaud, he is utterly lost; I see him before my eyes in the depths of the abyss; rebel and traitor to his country, he will surely be devoured by the troops of liberty. You mulattos—"* Toussaint raised his right arm high and closed his hand into a fist. *"—I see to the bottom of your souls; you are ready to rise against me, but although my troops are leaving the west, I leave here my eye to watch you, and my arm, which will always know how to reach you."*

Then Toussaint brought his arm down like a sword cut and walked out of the church to his horse, which was held waiting for him while he spoke. We all of us rode north then, without stopping. Of course Toussaint's words came quickly enough to the ears of Rigaud, and not long after, Rigaud showed Hédouville's letter to everyone and laid claim to the powers that Hédouville had promised him. Then we all knew that the next war would not come from the whitemen over the sea, but that it would begin among ourselves.

32

In that close, blind, secret room of the Cigny house, Captain Maillart tumbled with Isabelle—*his* Isabelle again, or soon to be. It was midday, but no way to know in that windowless room with its shrouded lamps, except for the heat. Bathed in slicks of heavy sweat, they slithered against each other like eels. The thrill, so long deferred, bulged in the back of the captain's throat. It took him some time to realize that the excitement was not reaching the rest of his body and that the most salient part of him had declined to respond to this great occasion.

He sat up, more puzzled than distressed; he'd never, ever had such a difficulty—well, not since his first inexperienced fumbling which now seemed several lifetimes in the past. Isabelle plunged her face in her hands and began to cry, her fingers knotting in her black curls, her pale shoulders heaving.

"It's my fault, my fault," she choked. "I wanted to use you . . ."

"But what?" Maillart laid his hand on her back. "I don't understand you."

"Oh, it's all hopeless, I don't know—only I am in such trouble."

Maillart's hand kept dropping on her back in a slow, steady rhythm; some hollow within her answered, like a drum.

"But tell, my dear," he said. "What is your trouble?"

Isabelle straightened and turned to him her tear-streaked, distraught face. Her hips were caught in a pool of her skirt, her small bare breasts still alert from their unconsummated encounter.

"I'm with child." She collapsed on his neck.

"Well now," Maillart murmured. Their position was awkward. He sat on the edge of the divan where they'd struggled, with both his feet on the floor, his upper body twisted to support her. He glanced down at his numb and shriveled member. Could this portend some sudden vocation for the priesthood? He laughed, silently, at the absurdity. "Well, now," he repeated. "How terrible can that be?"

"Oh, you don't know." She snuffled against his collarbone. Maillart's fingers counted up the knobs of her spine. He rubbed her bowed neck. The chain was gone. He recalled the pendant that had shocked him before—that stone phallus more dependable than his own.

"Where did you get it?" he said absently. "That . . . thing, which you're not wearing now."

Isabelle pulled a little away from him. "I took it off for you," she said. "It was a gift, from Joseph."

Vomit squirted into the back of the captain's gullet. He clapped both hands over his mouth and forced himself to swallow it back. His mind went through a series of sickening swoops. Flaville's constant proximity, the quiet concentration of his power, like her shadow. Only because it was unthinkable had he failed to think of it before. An eruption of images fumed up at him like bats emerging from a cave: black limbs intertwined with white; her mouth on his, the red yawn of her nether lips. He gagged again, and with an effort calmed the convulsion of his belly.

"You see?" Isabelle was huddled in her own arms. "Even you reject me. The whole world will."

"No," said Maillart. "No." The sweat on his face and forehead had turned chilly. "I don't mean that . . . It's something of a shock."

He straightened his spine and looked at her carefully. She was still herself, still Isabelle. "You do have a difficulty," he admitted.

Isabelle rocked forward, with fresh sobs.

"And your husband?"

"He'll murder me," Isabelle said simply, cutting off her tears. "Oh, there is much he overlooks, but he has his limits, and I know them." She sat up, wiping her eyes on her forearm. "Incidentally, our children are his own."

"Well, then," Maillart looked away from her. "How far is it along? There are ways, I'm told . . ."

"No," Isabelle said. "I cannot. If I did so, even God would turn His face from me."

"I had not known you were so devout."

"No," she said. "But I too have my limits."

"Ah," said Maillart, rubbing his temples. "In that case, I don't quite see . . ." He was still looking at the opposite wall. "Does Flaville know?"

"I don't mean to tell him," she said. "It would make trouble."

"You've made your share of that, in any case." Maillart smoothed his mustache with his thumb. "Well, perhaps you're right."

"Oh," Isabelle wailed softly. "This time I am truly lost."

"Wait," said Maillart. "Don't despair. I'll get you out of it."

"Will you?"

"Yes," he said, though his mind had locked. But there *was* a way, some way. He could feel it, if he could not yet see it. "Yes, I will."

"Oh, my true friend, I knew only you would save me." Isabelle drove her small body against his again, and with the greatest abandon ever—as he felt how wholly she abandoned herself to him, his male vigor returned full force. But he shifted from her, even as she began to croon over his return.

"No," he said.

"But I want it!"

"No, we mustn't—"

"Oh, do I disgust you so?"

"Not in the slightest, my dear—the evidence to the contrary is in your hand." So saying Maillart disengaged himself cautiously from her hot grasp. "Only, as things are now, we mustn't chance spoiling our friendship."

The heat had begun to slacken a little by the time he left her. The captain walked down to the harbor front, to freshen himself in the sea breeze. Porters were laboring up the gangway of a cargo ship, bowed double under great sacks of sugar or coffee. A harbor pilot Maillart knew slightly hailed him from the bow of the ship. The captain responded with a nod and a flick of his hand and walked on, fidgeting unconsciously with the points of his mustache. When he had reached the Customs House he turned away from the water and began walking back into the town.

Bold as he'd been to say he'd solve her problem, no solution had come to him so far. Maillart was unaccustomed to worry, but he did worry now. He knew there must be some path out of the difficulty, but the route was far from evident to him. In a state of abstraction, unaware of anything around him, he walked all the way up the sloping streets to the *casernes,* where he found Doctor Hébert waiting for him. At that, it occurred to him that the doctor was probably the only white person in the colony to whom it would be safe to confide his quandary.

Maillart had a jug of rum in his quarters, and the doctor sat on the edge of a cot, sipping thoughtfully from a chipped glass, while the captain told as much of the story as he knew.

"Well, that *is* serious," he muttered, at the end. "Well, what to do . . . There are certain herbs, I have been told, though I have not tested their use myself . . ."

"She wouldn't," the captain said. "That is, she won't."

"Ah well, I don't much like the thought of it either." The doctor hugged his knees and squinted through the open door. The light in the yard of the *casernes* was turning an ominous purple-streaked color, and the thunder rose from behind Morne du Cap.

"But where does that leave her?" the doctor said. "She must put herself out of the way somehow, so no one is there at the time of the birth . . . Who else knows about it, did you say?"

"I'd wager no one but myself," the captain told him, and, thinking of the afternoon's aborted dalliance, "I can testify, it doesn't yet show."

"So much the better," the doctor said. "Hmmmm . . . You know, Nanon is in the same state."

"*Félicitations,*" said Maillart. But at the doctor's expression he bethought himself that this child too might have a somewhat irregular paternity.

"Yes," said the doctor. "I had meant to bring her down to Ennery, as soon as it was possible to go with her myself. But that wouldn't do for our Isabelle—she and my sister are great friends, but this would try their friendship sorely. Besides, there are too many visitors at Habitations Thibodet."

He stood up and padded to the doorway and peered for a moment up at the sky. The thunder pounded once again. The doctor turned back to face the room. "If we could get her up into the interior somehow . . ."

"On what pretext?"

"Health, perhaps. The fever season is coming on—it's healthier in the mountains, away from the swamps. Also there's trouble brewing around Le Cap, I think—Rigaud's partisans, you know. One of the reasons I'd like to get Nanon and Paul away." He stooped to pour himself another short measure of rum. "Isabelle could always visit her own plantation with no need for a pretext at all."

"Yes, but Cigny is there himself as often as not, now that the cane mills are working again," said the captain. He twisted up the end of his mustache. "Arnaud certainly owes her hospitality."

"But imagine his reaction when she presents the world with a

Negro baby," the doctor said. "You know, that child is apt to be black as your hat."

The captain said nothing. He felt that the predicament had impaled him with a barb which no effort could draw.

"Now then," the doctor mused. "Nanon has some connection in the mountains above Dondon, and at Vallière. I wouldn't so much mind it if she went in that direction—at least till all this dispute with Rigaud is settled. If it goes poorly, there will be fighting all up and down the coast, and Ennery isn't as far away as I should like."

"True enough," said the captain. "And it's not likely to go well."

"My thought, exactly," the doctor said. "Well, let us say that Nanon is to go as far as Dondon. With Paul, and perhaps with Paulette. Then leave it to Isabelle to devise her pretext to go with her. I expect that will be within the range of her imagination."

"Undoubtedly," the captain, feeling somewhat more at ease. The doctor drained his glass and set it on the floor beside the jug. As he did so, the thunder rolled again and the sky opened all over the town. Both men stretched out on their parallel cots and lay half dozing, listening to the roar of the rain.

On the morning of June fifteenth, the doctor, asleep in the narrow attic room of the Cigny house, was roused by a shudder of the bed beneath him. Nanon turned toward him, without waking, and held him for an anchor. His pistols, arranged beneath the bed where another man might have left his slippers, skittered and clacked together. In the parlor downstairs, Isabelle braced herself against a doorframe and watched as the china bibelots on the mantel danced and rattled against each other and the small rococo clock. The mirror frame slapped once against the wall. Then her reflection steadied and all was still.

Before nightfall a courier came up from Gonaives with the news that Rigaud had published Hédouville's letter generally, the letter which released him from Toussaint's authority and left him sole and supreme commander of the Department of the South. According to the whisper, which traveled with Pascal, Roume was drafting a proclamation which would declare Rigaud a rebel and outlaw . . . for the second time. Toussaint's reaction was unknown, as were his whereabouts.

The miniature earthquake was the first topic of discussion round the Cigny dining table that night. There had been more severe *tremblements de terre* in the region before now, strong enough to level buildings and start fires which consumed whole neighborhoods. Was the morning's convulsion truly finished or was it a harbinger of worse to come? Monsieur Cigny opined the former—it was nothing, he assured the company; there would be no sequel. But Isabelle laid down her spoon and folded her little hands together.

"You know," she said. "Although an earthquake is nothing to fear, I rather think that with all the other eruptions that seem likely to come our way, one might be well advised to retire from the town for a period."

"Other eruptions?" Cigny inquired.

"The, er, political instability," the doctor said rapidly, picking up the cue. "I think she may be right, at that." He shot a covert glance at Maillart.

"Unfortunately, yes," the captain added. "Even the loyalty of some of Toussaint's officers has been cast into doubt." He was thinking uneasily of Pierre Michel, though he did not say so. "And of course one must consider all the partisans of Villatte who have only been waiting for a favorable occasion."

Major O'Farrel, who'd so recently adjusted his own allegiance, let the conversational bubble drift past him.

"I don't call this occasion so favorable to the partisans of Villatte," Cigny grunted, still plying his soup spoon. "They can assemble no plausible force against Toussaint's black army." He held out an empty hand for bread. Isabelle hurried to supply him.

"Not in the north, certainly," Maillart agreed. "Nor in the Western Department. In the South, of course, Rigaud is master for the moment."

Cigny stared. "One wearies of these conflicts," he pronounced. "What profit is there in them—for anyone? It is a mere perversity of General Rigaud to refuse Toussaint's authority."

"It is the legacy of Agent Hédouville, and his cursed letter," O'Farrel said unexpectedly. "He would divide, where he could not conquer."

"But surely that must pass," Cigny said. "Rigaud may be strong in his own region, but he has no force to reach us here."

"Force of arms, no," Maillart said, "but Hédouville has formally released him from Toussaint's command. The letter gives him a position to promote dissension here, and have we not already heard the rumors he has loosed? Toussaint is in league with the proscribed émigrés—in thrall to them, I've heard it said. And Toussaint's policy of forced labor, on which your enterprises depend, Monsieur, is no more than a ruse to restore slavery . . ."

Cigny laid down his chunk of bread untasted. "And Toussaint?"

He was looking at the doctor, who covered himself for a moment by gulping from his glass of water. Because of his secretarial privileges, people were apt to assume that he knew Toussaint's mind, when nothing could be further from the truth. Toussaint's mind was like a mirror in a lightless room, and no one knew whence came the light that gave it clarity . . . Of course, the doctor could not say this, and everyone was waiting.

"If trouble comes it will not find him unprepared," he pronounced. "I believe in the end he will master this difficulty as he has mastered others."

" 'In the end,' you say. That is most comforting." Isabelle tracked back toward her original intention. "For the moment, I wonder if it offers sufficient comfort."

She glanced significantly at Captain Maillart, who narrowed his eyes and nodded his assent. With the corner of a napkin, Cigny meticulously cleaned a soup spill out of the curls of his beard. Isabelle rose from her place, circled the table, and laid her hands over Nanon's bare shoulders.

"My friend is in a delicate condition," Isabelle said. "I mean to care for her in her time of need. She ought to be taken away from the tremors and disruptions of the town, from whatever fresh disturbances may be in store, to some quiet place in the countryside."

Cigny's eyes widened slightly; he mashed the crumpled napkin under his pudgy hand. It was not so difficult for Maillart to read his thought: that his wife should make an issue of attending a mulatto trollop in her pregnancy? Perhaps she was laying it on a bit thick, at that.

Isabelle's hands tightened slightly on Nanon's shoulders, and Nanon raised her face, impassive, the heavy petals of her lips sealed together. My Christ, Maillart thought, has she told *her*? He was looking directly into the molasses swirl of Nanon's eyes, but there was no divining what she knew or did not know.

"Hmmmph," Cigny grunted, smoothing his beard down over his shirt front. "I mean to go tomorrow, in any event, to see about the mill at Haut de Trou. There is no reason why you should not accompany me if you so wish. Of course, you may invite anyone you choose."

He lifted his spoon again and lowered his eyes to his soup bowl. Isabelle clicked her tongue, parted her lips as if she would say something more, but then apparently decided against it. She gave Nanon's shoulders a parting squeeze, and went back to her own place at the table.

Bertrand Cigny went directly to his plantation on the following day— the place was reachable in a single long day's ride. But as the ladies were to travel in a carriage, it was decided that they would break the journey with an overnight visit to Habitation Arnaud. There was the boy Paul too, riding with them in the carriage, or sometimes, to humor him, taken before Maillart on the saddle. Paulette had been detached from the expedition, since Isabelle, for reasons only the captain knew in full, did not want anyone else's retainers to be part of her own entourage.

From the start their progress was painfully slow, since the roads were boggy from the rains. Every half-hour, it seemed, Maillart was obliged to dismount the black dragoons he'd brought along as an escort and help them cut brush to lay across some muddy slough so that the narrow wheels of the carriage might pass over without miring. Each delay fretted him; he was delighted to have been of use, but as eager for his own part in the affair to be finished. With Toussaint still unfindable, he'd left Le Cap on his own authority, and was uneasy about the situation in the town. The rumors of trouble had not been invented for the sake of Bertrand Cigny.

When they creaked into the Arnaud compound, late that afternoon, Maillart was somehow unsurprised to find Joseph Flaville already there, standing by his horse in a cluster of other riders, as if they too had just arrived or were departing. A tour of inspection, doubtless, to ensure that Arnaud's field hands were faithful in their service. The captain saluted and turned smartly to hand Isabelle down from the carriage. Flaville swept off his hat and bowed to the ladies. Maillart felt Isabelle's fingers flutter expressively over his palm. Flaville was offering his arm to help Nanon down the carriage step.

Claudine Arnaud had appeared on the low porch of the Arnaud *grand'case,* and Isabelle, with a contrived little cry of pleasure, went tripping across the yard toward her. Nanon followed; a footman lugging their portmanteaux brought up the rear.

Maillart turned to Flaville. He felt nothing of what he'd expected to feel. No trace of the nausea which had assailed him when he'd first learned the situation, no anger, no real resentment, but only curiosity. He knew that Flaville had attended that savage ceremony at Bois Cayman where the first revolt of the slaves was planned. He'd been a co-conspirator with Boukman, had presided over the sack and burning of plantations and massacre of their inhabitants, had no doubt painted his naked flanks with the blood of slaughtered whites. In the eight years since, he'd evolved into a capable, even an honorable officer, and if his dependability were ever in doubt, Maillart believed, that was only because his ferocity for the freedom of his people superseded every other loyalty. How all these qualities could coexist in the same individual was truly a subject for wonder.

"Have you got word?" Maillart said. "Rigaud's in rebellion."

Flaville folded his arms over his uniform tunic. "When?"

"We learned of it yesterday," said Maillart. "He's refused obedience to the General-in-Chief—no fighting yet, that I know of."

"And Toussaint?"

"Invisible." Maillart shrugged. "*Introuvable.* Or he was when I left Le Cap. Are you stopping here for the night?"

"I think not," said Flaville. "We were bound for Limbé, and by what you tell me, I think we ought to get there that much faster."

He swung his leg over the saddle and saluted. "Thank you for the news," he said, and led the other riders out.

Maillart was wearier than he'd recognized, his legs rubbery from the day's ride. He walked up the steps to the gallery and dropped onto a chair. The wind that came before the rain was shivering all the trees, and the guinea fowl pecking and scratching in the yard began to scatter. It made the captain feel hungry to look at them.

Isabelle came out of the house and handed him a glass of limeade laced with rum. He tasted gratefully, cleared his throat. She remained standing, near his side, looking out over the darkening compound. The captain was moved, by her grace and her fortitude. Isabelle was at her best in tight situations, he thought. Possibly that was why she'd been so fond of entertaining her lovers under her husband's nose. He wondered what she would have been like as a man.

"You said that an earthquake is nothing to fear," he reminded her. When she turned to him, he saw the thread of chain slip on her throat, and thought of Flaville with her, and dismissed the thought.

"Are *you* afraid of earthquakes?" she said.

Maillart reached for his drink. He had never admitted fear of anything to anyone, and certainly not to a woman. "There is no defense against an earthquake," he said finally.

"And for that, no reason to fear them," Isabelle said, with a click of her tongue, as if impatient at his lack of insight. But she stayed, her fingertips grazing the table, very near to his own hand which was curled around the glass. The air kept thickening, denser and denser, till the whole sky opened and the rain came down.

They stayed at Habitation Arnaud all through the next day and night, at the insistence of their hosts, who wished to make a token repayment of all the nights they'd spent under Isabelle's roof in town, and also wanted to display their projects. Maillart chafed as he was shown around the mill. He sensed that the whole country was drawing itself in for another violent explosion, while he was stuck in these doldrums. It would take two more days to get the women and Paul even as far as Dondon, with the planned stopover at Habitation Cigny.

At the lowest terrace of the mill, Arnaud dipped his hand into a large wooden basin, and lifted it, spilling white granules over the pale mound inside.

"Do you see?"

"It is sugar," the captain said, indifferently.

"*White sugar.*" Arnaud seethed with enthusiasm. "Do you know there are not five planters left on the plain who can refine it? All the skilled men have been killed, or disappeared into the hills."

Maillart examined the sugar again with slightly quickened interest. True enough, it was pretty stuff. And it would please Toussaint to know that it existed. Arnaud whistled up his refiners to be introduced. Both were smiling, and seemed pleased and proud of their positions. One, he noticed, lacked an arm, which had been severed near the shoulder.

As Arnaud must go on with the work in the mill, Maillart excused himself and went to find the ladies at the school which Claudine was managing for the smaller Negro children, in the lean to next to the new infirmary. He reached them at the moment of dismissal, for she let them go before it grew too hot—the heat muddied their attention, she had said. They were pressing around her now before they parted, and she gave them bits of hardened brown sugar to suck, and some of them kissed her fingers before they ran away. Maillart noticed that she carried her maimed hand without self-consciousness, and that it was less noticeable to him now than when she'd worn the glove.

"At eight years they must go to the fields," Claudine was explaining to Isabelle and Nanon. "That took some argument with Arnaud, who would send them at six. Still, it is something." She smiled, dimpling, and led them into the infirmary. In her renascent bloom, she even looked somewhat younger than before.

In the evening, Maillart was alone for a time with Isabelle on the gallery. Arnaud was detained at the mill, and Nanon and Claudine were with Cléo, the mulattress housekeeper, in the kitchen. Much as the delay annoyed him, the captain was looking forward to his supper; the night before Cléo had proved herself to be quite a remarkable cook.

"I must admit," he said to Isabelle, "I don't quite understand the situation here. One would take them for a pair of missionaries now. But in the old days there was no one in the colony with a worse reputation for cruelty to his slaves than Michel Arnaud. And the wife thought to be a gibbering lunatic . . ."

Isabelle nodded. "Some men improve under the pressure of necessity," she said. "Arnaud has a strong will, and formerly there was nothing to oppose it. Now he seems to take a certain pleasure in his work, but then there was nothing for him to do—all was done for him. It is the same case with many Creoles . . ." She laughed, with little mirth, and shook her head. "For that reason, I chose to marry a Frenchman."

Maillart could compose no reply to that. After a moment, Isabelle went on.

"Concerning Claudine, there was apparently a priest who assigned her the care of small children as a penance. As she has been faithful in the task, it seems that her sanity is restored."

"Indeed she is greatly changed, and for the better."

"And when one considers where she started—she was once a terrible figure."

"I know it," Maillart said. The tale in which Claudine hacked off her own ring finger to appease the bloodthirsty swarm of rebel slaves had been very widely told.

"Oh, I wonder if you do," Isabelle said. "I learned what I know of it myself only during this visit. It seems that Arnaud, like many men of his type, was in the habit of amusing himself with the Negro women here. Claudine, like many wives so situated, grew weary of seeing the product of his indiscretions scattered through her household. Also apparently he mocked her own lack of fecundity, or she felt that he did so by his actions. A housemaid he had given her was carrying his child. One day when Arnaud was absent on his affairs, Claudine dragged the maid out to that shed." Isabelle gestured toward the empty space, as if the structure she'd named were still standing. "She cut the infant out of the womb, and killed the maid with a razor. From this followed her insanity, and her carelessness of her own survival."

"My God," Maillart said. "She confessed this to you?"

"Hardly," Isabelle said. "Cléo was housekeeper at that time too. She did not tell me, but she told Nanon."

"So that's how it goes," Maillart said.

"They know everything, you see?" Isabelle said. "One has no secrets." She smiled ruefully, looking away from him. "In the old days, I never kept a personal servant long."

Maillart again had nothing to say.

"Cléo bore Arnaud's children herself," Isabelle told him, "and saw them sold away to other plantations, once they grew large enough to irk the master with the family resemblance."

"And after all that she came back here?"

"It is a little surprising," Isabelle said. "Of course, Cléo was something of a terror herself, in the camps of Grande Rivière. She took white women who had been so many times raped by the black chiefs that they had lost their attraction, and sent them into the river to do her washing. She had them beaten for small faults—like any Creole dame."

"I see," said Maillart. He had begun to feel a little chilly.

"An eye for an eye," Isabelle said. "They understand each other here. They've shared things. Claudine once said that it must all be washed away in blood. That was in her madness, but I begin to think it quite a reasonable remark."

"How did you come to know?" Maillart said. "About Cléo, in the camps, I mean."

"Joseph told me." As if unconsciously, Isabelle passed a hand over her abdomen. "Joseph knows that whole history of Claudine as well—I'm sure of it, although he never told me."

Next morning they set out at an early hour for Habitation Cigny. Paul became restless by the time the sun was high; whether he shared the carriage with the women or Maillart's saddle, he could not be still. When the opportunity presented itself, the captain bought a donkey from a drover who was bringing a string of them down to market, and set Paul astride, bareback, with an improvised rope bridle. The boy could manage his new mount well enough, and the work of it relieved his boredom. Since they still had the constant difficulty of negotiating the carriage across tricky places in the road, the donkey had no trouble keeping up with the rest of their caravan.

When they reached the Cigny plantation at Haut de Trou, Isabelle and her husband began to quarrel straightaway, though in muted voices and, as far as possible, out of earshot of their guests. Over dinner they continued to snipe obscurely at each other. The captain grasped that Isabelle had found undone a great deal of restoration she expected to have been accomplished at her father's house and gardens. Cigny's position seemed to be that every available hand was needed to produce cash crops. He had graver matters on his mind besides: the rumors Maillart had described had already reached his *atelier*. Cigny's field hands had been roused to rebellion during the disturbances leading to Hédouville's flight, and now they showed considerable discontent with Toussaint's still more stringent labor policy, though so far they'd remained at their hoes.

After everyone had retired for the night, the marital dispute continued, at a higher pitch. The partitions were thin, so Maillart could hear the querulous burr of their voices, though he was only able to distinguish a few words. Finally he heard Cigny raise his voice to a shrill and breaking pitch.

"You will not!"

"I will," said Isabelle.

Then silence, and the captain slept.

At first light he had gone to see to the state of the carriage, whose left rear wheel had developed a worrisome wobble in the course of the previous day, when he heard her voice behind him.

"We'll leave that thing for firewood. We shall ride."

"You can't mean it," he began.

"Come," said Isabelle. "Consider the road to Dondon. And beyond?"

The captain saw that a groom was already leading out a mare and a gelding, each improbably outfitted with a sidesaddle.

"But—" He was thinking of the danger, but Isabelle's expression told him, with unspeakable clarity, *And what if I did lose this child?* He swallowed, and turned around in a circle. Cigny was nowhere in sight, but Paul's donkey had also been brought out, along with his own saddle-horse. Isabelle mounted the gelding, brushing aside the assistance of the groom, and then Nanon got onto her mare with the ease of a countrywoman getting aboard a donkey.

They rode out, attended by the cries of the little cocks hidden beneath the hedges on either side. As they reached the road, Maillart bethought himself that Nanon was pregnant too, and wondered if she shared Isabelle's attitude. But after all, they'd not get a worse jolting horseback than they would have done in the carriage.

He rode on the inside of the black cavalrymen, flanking Isabelle and a few paces behind, where he could admire her slim, straight back, sprouting from the saddle like a green tree. He imagined her a man, a soldier. Brave to the point of recklessness, but without quite crossing that line. Some reckless men would crumble if the danger they courted responded to them, but Isabelle was of the type that grew more firm and steely in such circumstances. Through the thundering cloud of his other emotions, he could see that her affair with Flaville must have been her own most extreme means of daring the devil. Might he have done the same, in her place? But here his imagination failed him.

Dondon was boiling when they reached it, with soldiers rushing in all directions, preparing to move out.

"What are you doing here, Captain?" Moyse called harshly, fixing Maillart with his stubby finger. "No matter—take your men and report to Vaublanc."

Maillart told Isabelle and Nanon to wait where they were. He slipped to the ground and led his horse diagonally to the point where he saw Vaublanc assembling his troop.

"What the devil?" he inquired, though in truth he was not so very surprised.

"Rigaud has attacked Petit Goâve," Vaublanc told him. "Surprised Laplume and drove him back to Léogane."

"And now?"

Vaublanc swept his hand around the bustling square. "As you see. Toussaint has already crossed the Ester—we are to join him at Port-au-Prince. Dessalines is with him too, as best we know. How many men have you?"

"Six," said Maillart. "They are well mounted."

"Excellent," Vaublanc said. "I hope the horses are fresh—we'll be riding a long way in a short time."

"Allow me a moment," Maillart said. "I have these women . . ."

He turned and in a flash of panic realized he could no longer see Isabelle sitting her horse. But there was Nanon, Paul too. For some reason both of them had climbed into a wagon alongside a tall and rather elegant looking mulatto woman. Maillart handed the reins of his horse to one of his men and cut back across the square toward them. He felt himself raked by Moyse's regard, the good eye and the crater of the missing one. Moyse was wont to uncover the empty socket before riding into battle. A general superstition among the black rank-and-file held that the lost eye looked always into the underworld.

Distracted, the captain cannoned into Isabelle before he saw her. They clutched each other by the shoulders to keep from falling down.

"It's all right," she said. "We've found friends." She turned her chin toward the wagon. "Nanon knows this woman—so does Antoine. They will take us to Maltrot's old property at Vallière."

"But Choufleur!" Maillart blurted.

"You told me yourself he is with Rigaud—he will be otherwise engaged. And we will be protected. But you have orders—you must go."

She raised herself on her toes to embrace him, laying her cheek to his. There was a dampness through the dust. Then her sharp fingers pushed him back.

"Go quickly." She'd already turned away.

Maillart returned to his men and his horse. By the time he had mounted, the wagon had left the square. She was gone from him, into the unknown; he could not predict whether she'd emerge from it again. But it was no time for sentiment, and that, he reflected as Moyse led them down from Dondon, was doubtless a good thing.

33

Toussaint's sweep south to Port-au-Prince was so rapid and relentless that there was no thought of a stop at Ennery; the doctor, welded to his saddle after twelve hours' hard riding, congratulated himself on having sent Nanon and Paul out of the way . . . supposing they had safely arrived where they were meant to have gone. At any rate he was too exhausted to worry much when, in the train of Toussaint's cavalry, he rode into Port-au-Prince. Toussaint went directly into a war council, but the doctor was given leave to retire. He found a billet in the *casernes,* and despite his weariness went for clean water and changed the dressing on his left arm. The wound from Choufleur's pistol ball was slight, but slow to heal, and in this climate it could not be neglected. With the fresh bandage tightened, he stretched out and lay motionless as a plank. In the night he had fleeting dreams of Suzanne Louverture and her three sons, tucked safely away on the central plateau, across the Spanish border, during that period before Toussaint had entered French service; the lingering images of those dreams reassured him next morning when he woke to the rattle and clash of new arrivals.

Moyse had just brought in his regiment, and Captains Vaublanc and Maillart soon searched the doctor out. His question must have been plainly legible on his face, for Maillart was quick to tell him that all was well.

"They found a friend to take them to Vallière," he said. "A tall mulattress—she seemed a person of substance. I had not time to learn her name, but Isabelle told me that you'd know her."

"That would be Madame Fortier," the doctor said, considerably relieved. He squeezed Maillart on the shoulders. "I'm in your debt."

Maillart nodded dizzily, dragging the back of his wrist across his sweaty and dust-streaked face. He pulled off his boots and collapsed on the cot the doctor had just vacated.

At the well, where he went to wash his face, the doctor met Riau and got the news. Rigaud had attacked Laplume at Petit Goâve with a superior force and driven him back to Léogane—Laplume's men were mostly scattered and he'd barely missed being captured himself. The whites of Grand and Petit Goâve had been massacred, and the invaders had taken special care to slit the throats of landowners of whatever color who were known to have accepted the grace and favor of Toussaint for the restoration of their plantations. The mulatto Pétion, who served under Laplume but was believed by Toussaint to be a more valuable officer than his commander, had gone over to Rigaud's faction, whether out of loyalty to his caste or out of doubt that Toussaint would continue to trust him. Indeed Toussaint, as Riau whispered from a shadowed face, was already arresting certain of his black subordinates whose allegiance seemed dubious to him. But Pétion's defection galled him especially, for Pétion had been well placed to report on Toussaint's strength and disposition.

The colored General Beauvais, long Rigaud's second in the south, had gone to his post at Jacmel on the south coast immediately following Toussaint's tirade against the mulattoes from the cathedral pulpit at Port-au-Prince. He remained there, declining to announce himself in favor of either Toussaint or Rigaud, as if he hoped to conserve neutrality—and a doomed hope too, the doctor was certain. But Riau told him also, in a lowered tone, that Moyse seemed to be in a parallel frame of mind with Beauvais; Moyse felt small enthusiasm for what he saw as a war between brothers, though certainly he would do as Toussaint ordered him, being the next thing to Toussaint's blood kin.

Before noon their combined force pushed on to Léogane, twenty thousand strong or better. Numbers were firmly in their favor, but Toussaint was taking pains in his plan for a counterattack. He had a healthy respect for the talent in Rigaud's officer cadre and the motivation of his men—fresh from a victory and with much to fear from a defeat. But before he could mobilize further, word came from the north that mulatto rebellions had broken out all through the Artibonite to the north coast and west to Môle Saint Nicolas on the farthest tip of the peninsula.

There were rumors of trouble at Le Cap, and the agent, Roume, was horribly agitated. Even Gonaives was restless—the town which had been Toussaint's best bastion on the coast since he was serving under the Spanish. Toussaint called out his secretaries to inscribe his commands; the doctor was assigned the fair copy of a letter to the commander of Le Cap, Henri Christophe, which concluded thus:

> *The arrondissement of the east must still be the object of your solicitude in such critical circumstances. You know how volatile the inhabitants of that area are; set up camps which will keep order respected in that place, and you must even bring armed cultivators down from the mountains as you need them, to guarantee the security of the area; the colored men are as dangerous as they are vindictive; you must not take any half-measures with them, but have them arrested and even punished by death, whoever among them seems tempted to begin the least machination; Vallière should also be the object of your closest attention . . . I count more than ever on your imperturbable severity. Let nothing escape your vigilance.*

Toussaint put Dessalines in charge of the force facing Rigaud, demoting the defeated Laplume in his favor, and whipped north, bringing with him Moyse and all his men. There were revolts in favor of Rigaud at Arcahaye and all across the Artibonite Valley, but Toussaint smashed them to flinders as he galloped through, disarming all able-bodied mulattos not already a part of his own forces, and executing exemplary numbers of them, without the formality of trial; some were led in front of cannon and mowed down with grapeshot, while certain others simply were bayoneted, and others were taken out to sea and drowned.

When they arrived at Arcahaye, the doctor saw Toussaint shudder, groan, even seem to weep, at the discovery that his orders along these lines had been exceeded. *"Aii,"* he was heard to moan, before numerous auditors, "the people here are terrible. I told them to trim the tree, not to uproot it."

In fact a frightening number of colored men had been done away with before Toussaint reached the town; on whose authority was somewhat unclear. The doctor, moved by shock to make inquiry, was unable to discover if the orders came directly from Toussaint. "What does he want?" was all Riau would say. "When it rains, everyone gets wet."

So the doctor could not know if Toussaint was shedding crocodile tears or real ones—a mixture of both, he was inclined to think. In a strange contortion of their usual attitudes, mulattoes seeking clemency now found more compassion from Moyse than from Toussaint. On the other hand, Toussaint harmed no colored women or children, though Rigaud was quick to accuse him of doing so (and though the colored women were often found up to their necks in conspiracy).

What was one to expect, indeed? The doctor worried and gnawed on the question in his mind, dreamy with exhaustion as they rode farther north day after day. The mention of Vallière in Toussaint's letter had made him ill at ease, though he had a high regard for Christophe (who was also, fortunately, acquainted with Nanon). But what if the Fortiers were for Rigaud, or by some unhappy chance could falsely be connected to him? All over that region of the country, the Rigaudins were celebrating the fall of Toussaint, whose ruthlessless, when he reappeared, was meant to make them understand the extent of their prematurity. Wherever he advanced, Toussaint roused the field workers with the announcement that Rigaud and his partisans meant to restore slavery, and he gave them back the guns he'd promised to return whenever such an emergency arose. The whites of the areas Toussaint retook continued to be respected, and some were able to negotiate mercy for their colored children. But at the same time, all the white men fit to bear arms were drafted into the army on an emergency basis and sent south to report to Dessalines, while Toussaint continued his drive north.

Thus far, the campaign had presented itself to the doctor's view more as a police action than a real war. There'd been no battles, properly speaking, only arrests and executions, except at Pont d'Ester, where they'd met with some resistance when they crossed the river. But on the western peninsula it would be war indeed. The Rigaudins, who had raised the rebellion at Môle Saint Nicolas, had mounted a full-bore attack on Port-de-Paix, where Maurepas commanded for Toussaint. Word was that Maurepas was badly outnumbered, and hard pressed to hold on.

At night in the tent they usually shared, the doctor was kept awake by Maillart's uneasy fretting. The captain was not one to jump at shadows, but he was worried now that Toussaint might have made a strategic error in responding to the diversion in the north. The real threat, he proposed, came from Rigaud, who with sufficient resolve might break Dessalines's cordon at Léogane and attack Toussaint from the rear.

"But Dessalines has ten thousand men between Léogane and the mountains of Jacmel," the doctor objected. "Rigaud has not half that number."

"No, but consider their quality," the captain muttered. "Those are crack troops in Rigaud's command, and the smaller force is more mobile too. Think what Toussaint was able to accomplish in the old days with only four thousand men. And Rigaud has more reason to be bold—if he hesitates now, he *will* be crushed."

"I would not like the assignment of forcing a way through Dessalines," the doctor said. "Dessalines is not to be underestimated."

"That he certainly is not," the captain said. "Only I fear that, just now, Rigaud is more in danger of underestimation." He turned on his blanket, banged his elbow on a protruding root, cursed and went on grumbling while the doctor struggled to sleep. He was tired and ennervated by the constant state of alarm, and when he ought to have been sleeping, the ache and itch of his hurt arm annoyed him. He only hoped they would soon make their way to the seacoast, where he could bathe the wound in brine.

Often enough they moved at night. After the mass of the army had camped and cooked its provisions, Toussaint was apt to strike the tents of his immediate staff and move to some other location, away from the main bivouac. Sometimes he shifted his position more than once under cover of darkness; no one was ever quite sure where he slept—if he did sleep.

That night at Gros Morne, the doctor was unsurprised when Riau roused him by shaking his foot. He rose and poured himself into the habitual routines, saddling the mare, tying up the metal fittings of both saddle and bridle with rags to stop their jingling. Maillart was mutely furling up the tentcloth, then strapping the roll behind his saddle.

At this height, at this hour, it was rather chilly. A sliver of moon hung over the bowl where the army had camped, like a shaving of ice— but the men were gone. The main force had been filtered out earlier, in what direction the doctor did not know. Toussaint's little entourage was following a different route, apparently, for no one else was near them.

In silence, single file, they rode down a rocky defile in the general direction of Jean Rabel. The doctor stroked the withers of his mare. She had grown somewhat calmer, these last months, and was actually easier to manage by night, when less was visible to alarm her nervous eye. The doctor yawned, but quietly as a cat. At a turn of the descending path, he caught a glimpse of Toussaint. The size of his warhorse set him above the others, but he was not wearing his general's hat tonight, only the less conspicious madras headcloth.

At the bottom of the ravine, the trees closed over them; they moved on through thick, damp darkness, silent but for the whirring insects and the sigh of horses' breath. It was warmer here, and the road underfoot was damp and plashy, and there were a few mosquitoes, whose whine and sting would rouse the doctor from the doze into which he kept drifting. Just behind him in the dark, he thought he heard the rasp of Maillart's snore.

Then for some reason the horses bunched up, jostling each other as they clustered. The doctor raised his head from a nod, as someone at the head of the column struck a light, revealing for an instant the great bole of a tree knocked down across the trail. At Toussaint's hissed order the light was extinguished. But immediately there flared up a great silent bloom of red and orange light, and the doctor's mare let out a hideously human-sounding scream as she reared and bucked. He was airborne before he heard the roar of the cannon and explosion of the shell. He seemed to float for a long time, and in his trajectory he saw a man struck dead in the saddle, his horse falling with him as he went down. Then the earth struck him all across the back like a barn door, knocking the wind so completely from him that he was paralyzed, though hooves were lashing dangerously near him as the panicked horses reared and milled amid the blaze and racket and the reek of blood and smoke. When he heard more shrapnel tearing overhead, he managed a painful inhalation, rolled over and wormed his way to shelter in the flank of a downed horse, whose hindquarters were still twitching though the animal was dead.

Above the trail, the trees were full of fiery light, and the doctor caught a glimpse of his mare running full tilt into the middle distance— his long gun still scabbarded by the saddle, he recalled with sudden distress. But his pistols were in his belt, and his coat pocket was full of spare cartridges. He drew a pistol and crept up the bell of the horse's ribcage. His free hand, groping, came back to him sticky with warm blood. A dead man was flung backward over the horse's tail. All around them came isolated cracks of muskets, and the doctor trained his pistol on the firelight, but there was no target; the enemy was not visible. He seemed to feel a nudge at his side, perhaps a last expiring twitch of the dead horse. A shot would be useless, would only call attention to himself.

He slipped down to a better-covered position below the horse's belly. On the other side of him from that fresh cadaver was another living body, which exuded calm, like the form of a peaceful sleeper. The doctor turned on his hip and found himself looking into Toussaint's eyes, glittering with the red firelight, below the tight crease of his headcloth.

He remembered the warning nudge he had felt. Toussaint held a pistol in one hand and a dagger and the other, but he seemed to have drawn the same conclusion that at present these weapons were best left unused.

In the first dim light of the dawn they found only two men dead, though several others were lightly wounded by shell fragments. Three horses had been killed or crippled and two more run away. They doubled on the mounts that remained to them. The doctor took charge of Maillart's horse and let the captain ride behind him, for Maillart had been wounded slightly in the great muscle of his thigh.

"Now who's to be credited with that ambush?" Maillart said, grunting as the rough trail jostled his injury. "I suppose it's obvious enough. The Rigaudins have small hope of victory on the battlefield here."

"So they naturally turn to assassination." The doctor completed his thought.

"Naturally," Maillart agreed, and after a moment, "I suppose that won't be last of them either."

Toussaint, perhaps moved by similar reasoning, had changed the direction of his march. That day they set up a discreet command post in a cleft of the Cahos Mountains. He had divided his army in two. Moyse had gone to the relief of Maurepas at Port-de-Paix, while Clervaux, a mulatto officer still loyal to Toussaint, was taking the direct route to Môle Saint Nicolas. Both divisions were supported by throngs of field hands that Toussaint had hastily rearmed and brought along in his train.

Moyse, in a vigorous assault, relieved the siege of Port-de-Paix, and drove the Rigaudins back to Jean Rabel. In the aftermath of this engagement, Maurepas bound his prisoners across cannon mouths and blew them out to sea with grapeshot volleys; though the style of execution might seem savage, it had been introduced to the colony, a couple of years earlier, by the eminently civilized British General Maitland. Clervaux's advance, meanwhile, was delayed by the resistance of Bombarde, but artillery and assault reduced the post. Moyse broke the last Rigaudin bands at Jean Rabel, and their remnants went into hiding in the mountains. Moyse advanced westward along the Côtes de Fer, meeting little opposition now, meaning to converge with Clervaux at Le Môle.

Riau had been sent with Moyse, but after Port-de-Paix was retaken, he returned to Toussaint's headquarters in the Cahos. He had nothing to say about the battles he'd just fought, but he was leading the doctor's mare behind his own horse. The mare had the same trappings she'd worn when she bolted, and even the long gun was still in the scabbard, though its pouch of cartridges was empty. The rifle had been left out in the rain, so that its lock was stiff with rust, but the doctor took it apart and cleaned and oiled it until it moved smoothly once again. It seemed unlikely that in the present situation he would face attack, so long as Toussaint chose to direct the campaign from the Cahos, but still he felt more secure when the long gun was near at hand.

The Rigaudins at Le Môle held out for a week's time under a steady barrage from Moyse's cannon, but there was no hope for them against the reunited forces of Moyse and Clervaux—ten thousand regularly trained troops, plus an indeterminate number of freshly armed cultivators, completely surrounding the town (by land). Le Môle was also blockaded by a few French ships at sea, but the two chief officers loaded a canoe with as much of the local treasury as it would float, and on a night when clouds hid the moon they discreetly paddled out through the blockade and eventually made their way to the south. The day after their escape, Moyse and Clervaux took over Le Môle, putting to the sword all those who had obviously taken Rigaud's part. Toussaint's partisans, including the aged Monsieur Monot (who'd survived a month of very rough treatment), were set free from the prison

On September twenty-fifth, Toussaint came to Le Môle in person, and published a proclamation which denounced Rigaud for raising armed rebellion in the south and for sending his agents everywhere else to spread sedition. Rigaud's principle (according to Toussaint) was that the mulattoes were the only true natives of Saint Domingue (since France belonged to the whites and Africa to the blacks)—yet the blacks still ought to support Rigaud rather than Toussaint, for Toussaint had always favored the white masters who had long been the cruelest enemies of the blacks, and who certainly meant to restore slavery . . . To all this Toussaint rejoined that blacks and whites had been created to love one another—the very existence of mulattoes proved this point. No, it was Rigaud who despised the black race, believing his own to be superior; Rigaud's unwillingness to obey a black (Toussaint) had caused the whole rebellion! Did Rigaud accuse Toussaint of scheming to exterminate the mulattoes? One had only to look at the number of colored men and officers in Toussaint's own army to know this calumny was false.

Doctor Hébert, who took a peculiarly interested view of the situation, could confirm that Toussaint's reprisals on the western peninsula, while heavy, were not indiscriminate. No women or children were harmed at his order. When Monsieur Monot reclaimed his house and possessions, his delicious housekeeper Agathe was also returned to him, intact. Toussaint's proclamation was papered all over the town, and nailed to trees as the army progressed from Le Môle back eastward across the peninsula. It was true that a fair number of colored men and officers remained incorporated in Toussaint's force. It was equally true (as the doctor silently observed) that the colored prisoners of the northwest campaign had been handed over to the field hands who followed in Toussaint's train; barefoot, half naked, half starved and stumbling, they were subjected to all sorts of mistreatment from their captors, as the army moved down to Le Cap.

Michel Arnaud, who had come into Le Cap with a load of his sugar, rose early on a Sunday morning, meaning to escort his wife to morning mass. They had the use of the Cigny house in the absence of the owners, and it was not a very long walk from there to the white church on the hill. In the first yellowing light of the morning, it was still reasonably cool, with a salt breeze blowing in from the harbor, and gulls hanging on the wind overhead. Arnaud adjusted his step to that of Claudine, whose fingers rested lightly on the crook of his arm. There was a balance between them, something like contentment. Together they climbed the spiral path, but the white church at the top was empty, and no bell rang.

Claudine pressed his forearm and released it; he could sense her uneasiness, though she did not speak. Detached from each other, they walked down over the broken ground toward the cluster of houses behind the church. Arnaud's spine prickled as he passed the palm panels enclosing the *hûnfor*. The *lakou* was just beginning to stir as they reached it; all seemed as usual except that there was no sign of Fontelle or her children or any other paler face.

Maman Maig' sat on a low stool beside an open doorway of a *case*, her vast darkness absorbing all the sun that fell upon her. Arnaud approached, somewhat hesitantly, the woman was so imposing.

"*Salwé.*" That was Claudine's voice, speaking from behind him. Maman Maig' raised her head and returned the greeting. Excluded, Arnaud felt a flicker of irritation.

"*Koté Fontelle ak ti moun li?*" he asked brusquely. Where are Fontelle and her children?

"*Solda yo mené yo nan prison.*" Maman Maig's reply was ready enough, though not especially friendly. The soldiers have taken them to prison.

"*Ki bo prison sa yé?*" Claudine came up beside him as she spoke. What prison, where?

"*Nan La Fossette.*"

Maman Maig' tilted her head back against the whitewashed wall of the *case*. They'd hear no more from her, for the moment. Arnaud released his breath, and Claudine coaxed him back down the path they'd come by.

He might have thought it, thought of it sooner—why had he not thought of it? He knew that Christophe, in exercising the vigilance Toussaint had recommended to him, had incarcerated most of the colored people of Le Cap and the surrounding area, and that daily he executed a few who were thought to be tainted with conspiracy. Claudine had known too, or at any rate she had been exposed to the information, though often it was hard for Arnaud to tell just how far her attention penetrated.

She seemed to understand the situation, though they said little to one another as they returned to the Cigny house. Aided by the servants, Arnaud hitched one of the wagons he'd used to haul the sugar. With Claudine beside him on the box, he drove toward La Fossette. As they came in view of the barracoons, there was a rattling volley of gunfire, ripping unevenly like the tearing of cloth. A squad of soldiers broke out of their formation, shouldering their muskets. From a little distance a lone officer watched them from his horse.

Arnaud pulled up beside the barracoons, his face twisted in an expression of irony. In former times, he had arrived here in a much more elegant vehicle—to inspect fresh *bossale* slaves in whom he might be interested, before they were brought to the block. He would have them turn about at his order, and probe their features with the point of his cane. Now he set the cane's tip in the damp sod and used it to balance his descent from the wagon box, then turned to assist Claudine.

The members of the firing squad were dragging bodies over the soggy ground and tumbling them into a slow stream that bordered the swamp. Arnaud turned his face from them and walked toward the gate of the barracoons. From the buildings came the stench of human ordure and the musk of people too closely confined. A black sentry jumped up. Arnaud began speaking without breaking his stride.

"You have some of my people here—"

The guard stopped him with a bayonet—the point denting in the fabric of his coat. Arnaud's temples pulsed, he could feel the flush of anger darkening his face. Claudine caught up and restrained him with soothing motions of her hand along his back. Arnaud's hand was tight on the pommel of his cane; he wanted terribly to strike down the musket but knew he must not. Claudine drew him back, disengaging him from the point of the bayonet. The squad of soldiers had formed up to march back to the town. Arnaud called out and whirled his cane over his head.

At first this action had no result, but then the mounted officer turned his horse and jogged toward them.

Henri Christophe. An imposing figure, in the saddle as well as on foot. He had a natural air of dignity, which had served him well in former times, when he was headwaiter at the Hotel Couronne—an establishment which Arnaud had regularly patronized. He did his best now to keep any trace of that memory from showing in his expression. Christophe had been already a freeman when he used to show Arnaud to his table at the Couronne. He had been free since the 1770s, when he'd attended the American Revolution with the regiment of the Comte d'Estaing. Arnaud had been vehemently against the whole notion of including slaves or even black freemen (especially black freemen) on that mission. And now look at their trouble . . . but that was another thought he must not let betray itself on his face.

"*Ki sa ou vlé?*" Christophe said, with no sign he particularly recognized whom he was talking to. "*Blanc,* you have no business here."

"I'm told that some of my people have been wrongfully imprisoned," Arnaud said.

"*Your* people," Christophe said pointedly. "Yours?"

Christophe's horse snorted and tossed its head to shake off a fly. Arnaud took a step back from the burst of warm breath.

"Ours—as it were—of the same family." That was Claudine, moving up to stand beside him.

Christophe studied her for a moment, in silence, his expression grave. Arnaud wondered just what he might be thinking. Claudine had a general notoriety in Le Cap as Madame Skin-Inside-Out—the white woman who went to the African temples.

"Of your same family," Christophe repeated finally. "What people might these be?"

"The woman Fontelle, and her children."

"Who are also the children of Père Bonne-chance," Claudine added.

Christophe transferred the reins to his left hand and stroked his jawline with his right. The soldiers of the firing squad had formed in a wedge behind his horse, and waited with their musket butts resting on the ground. In the farther distance, Arnaud noticed three or four long-eared black swine exploring the stream bank where the bodies had been rolled. His stomach turned. There was nothing, he knew, a hog would not eat.

Christophe turned his head and called an order to the sentry at the gate. Presently Fontelle was brought out, with Paulette and her older sisters, Fanchette and Marie-Hélène. The older girls gave evidence of the charms which might move a priest to break his holy vows. In their present situation they would of course be targets of molestation, though there was no outward sign they had been harmed so far. From the second building, another guard produced Moustique. The boy was bruised around the mouth, and his hands were tied behind him with a straggling end of rope. The guard encouraged him forward with a couple of kicks to his rear.

"You claim kinship with these people?" Christophe inquired. There was a trace of sarcasm in his tone. Arnaud looked past him. The pigs at the stream bed had begun to squeal and lunge at each other, disputing the spoil they'd found. Nearby, a couple of white egrets stood motionless, bone-white, indifferent. Arnaud's tongue cleaved to the roof of his mouth.

"Yes," Claudine said clearly. "Yes, we do."

"They are suspect in the rebellion of Rigaud," Christophe announced. "If you are engaged with them, you too may be colored"—he smiled to underline his pun—"with the same suspicion. Ought I to let them go with you, or shut you up with them?"

At his words, the men of the firing squad raised their muskets. Arnaud, with a turn of his wrist, cocked his cane against his upper arm, as if to parry. He had no other weapon. It had become inadvisable for a civilian white man to go armed.

"Take them, then." Christophe seemed to lose interest in the whole question as he spoke. He turned his horse away and called an order to his men, who re-formed their ranks and began marching after him in the direction of the town.

With numb hands, Arnaud helped Fontelle and her daughters climb into the wagon. The boards of the floor were bare. The provisions they'd bought for their return to the plain had been left at the Cigny house, but after what had just occurred, he was not much inclined to go back for them.

"We must find some straw for the wagonbed," Claudine said, "when we go back for our other things." She was untying Moustique's wrists. Freed, the boy rubbed his hands together disconsolately.

"Eh? But no," Arnaud said, with a glance at Christophe's soldiers marching away toward the town gate. "I think it better not to return for anything, today."

"But we ought, if only for the straw." Claudine looked from him to the women in the wagon.

"Is their comfort so important?" Arnaud said. "I call them lucky to be alive."

"They can be hidden under the straw," Claudine said patiently. "In case we should meet any incident on the road."

Arnaud reflected, as he climbed after her onto the wagon box, that she had experience in such matters which he himself lacked. At the price of her ring finger she'd brought a wagonload of white women out of the burning plain in ninety-one . . . As usual his imagination failed him on the threshold of this scene.

"Perhaps you're right," he said, and, clucking to his horses, he started the wagon for the town. Claudine sat rigidly erect beside him, and now and then he stole a glance at her, in between scanning the road and the horizon for anything that might threaten their passengers in the rear. The usual questions flickered through his mind—how had she brought herself to do those dreadful things she'd done when they were separated? What power drew her to the African dances? How did she reconcile her actions there with her Christian devotion and the prescriptions of Père Bonne-chance? But he had never voiced these questions to her, and did not do so now, because he feared that to ask them when she was calm as she seemed might overset her reason, because they would be overheard by Fontelle and her family, because (as he'd admit to himself in his moments of greatest honesty) he was afraid of the answers she might offer.

Toussaint and his army passed Fort Picolet and entered Le Cap an hour after sundown drenched to the bone from the afternoon rain. The soldiers filled the *casernes* to overflowing, leaving the mulatto prisoners huddled in the cobbled court. Doctor Hébert and Captain Maillart slipped away to the Cigny house, where the servants were glad enough to admit them, though the owners were absent. From the servants they learned the curious story of Arnaud's rescue of Fontelle and her family. They dried themselves at the kitchen fire, ate a plain supper of chicken and yams, then fell into bed where they slept like two stones.

In the morning, the doctor changed the dressing on Maillart's wounded thigh, and, having admonished the captain to rest his leg, set out to learn the news of the town. From Pascal, he learned that Roume and Toussaint were at odds since last night's interview, not only over the war with Rigaud, which all Roume's influence could not seem to arrest, but also over Toussaint's dealings with the North American Republic.

For some months, Toussaint had had his own representative in Philadelphia, on some mission whose details had never quite come to light, and more recently the American president had sent Edward Stevens to Le Cap in the role of consul. Roume was especially piqued, by Pascal's account, that Stevens was delegated to wait upon Toussaint rather than himself, and that the trade agreement with the Americans had apparently been broken by General Maitland—when France and Britain were still at war!

By Pascal's account, there was no formal treaty—nothing for which Toussaint might later be called to account—but instead a discreet understanding that Toussaint would prevent French privateers from troubling American shipping in the waters of Saint Domingue. For their part, the Americans would let pass any French ship which carried Toussaint's safe-conduct.

"You may imagine, Roume was absolutely frothing," Pascal explained. "*Toussaint's* own safe-conduct—as if he were a king."

"I see," said the doctor. "Then again, such transactions are best judged by their results."

"You are right." Pascal drew out his watch and opened the lid. "But why should we not go down to the port? There is a ship just in from Philadelphia, which should be unloading still."

Indeed, when they turned the corner by the Customs House onto the waterfront, they found a great-bellied merchantman with the American colors snapping at the masthead. Gangs of porters were lugging long shallow packing cases down the gangplank—so heavy that two men were needed to heft each case.

"Muskets," said Pascal. "American made, of the first quality. Two thousand, six hundred and eighty of them—I saw the bill of lading myself. Of course there are casks of powder to match. And by way of a compliment, the ship will leave her ballast here."

"Oh?" said the doctor.

"The ballast is lead," said Pascal. "To be remolded into musket balls."

"Of course," said the doctor. "Why did I need to ask?" In fact the only aspect which mildly surprised him was the port of call. Since the withdrawal of the English there had been a steady stream of American ships delivering muskets, powder and shot to Gonaives.

In the afternoon, when the doctor waited upon Toussaint at the Governor's house, he found the general busy examining a group of white children, scions of the landowners on the northern plain, who were supposed to have been preparing for their first communion. Toussaint was not pleased with their performance, did not find their answers ready or confident enough. They must study their catechism much harder, he admonished them as he sent them out, for he meant to see them again, on Sunday at the church.

It struck the doctor that if Toussaint had leisure to preoccupy himself with devotional matters, the time might be right for him to ask leave to travel to Vallière. Approaching with his hat in his hand, he put the question.

"No," Toussaint said at once. "No, I shall want you here." He tilted his head to peer out the window at the angle of the sun. "It is already Friday, and you would be absent for four days at least— No, I cannot spare you, now."

The doctor bowed wordlessly and turned to depart.

"I may tell you that there has been no trouble in the region of Vallière." Toussaint passed a hand across his mouth and his lower jaw. "I have information which I trust—it is very calm there."

At the Cigny house the doctor learned that Maillart had gone out, against his instructions to rest his injured thigh. He found the captain at a tavern on the Rue Espagnole, counting up his winnings from a card game. His companions in play had already left, disgusted with their luck.

"Your leg," the doctor said, frowning.

"No more than a nuisance." Maillart stacked coins, happily.

"I want you to take a sea bath daily."

Maillart looked at him with total disbelief.

"Or fetch me my saw." The doctor grinned.

"And what of your arm, O my physician?"

The doctor pushed back his sleeve to show the pink pucker of healed flesh. "It has mended, thanks to the same treatment I recommend to you."

"Oh well, in that case . . ." Maillart muttered. "Well, where have you been all the day?"

The doctor told him.

"Have you any news of the south?"

"Little enough," the doctor said. "Some fighting around the Goâves, but there has been no important change of position—as far as anyone knows here."

"I do not understand Rigaud," said the captain. "It's all or nothing for him now—he ought to strike, and hang the risk! The risk has already been taken."

"Well, as we are fighting on the other side, we must profit from his error, if error it be," the doctor said. "Some say that Rigaud is waiting for help from France."

"A fantasy," said Maillart. "He has put too much trust in that letter of Hédouville's."

"Yes," said the doctor. "I think you are right."

"And meanwhile Toussaint passes his hours catechizing first communicants?"

The doctor shrugged. "He takes his religion seriously."

Although Toussaint would not give him permission to leave town, he also made no call on the doctor's services for the next two days. There was time enough for him to drag the captain to the sandy cove across the headland. Maillart, it turned out, did not know how to swim and was embarrassed by that failing, but the doctor pointed out that he would get the same benefit by standing waist-deep in the water, and after two days of this practice the wound did begin to improve.

On Sunday everyone was specially enjoined to attend the mass. Toussaint's soldiers lined the roadways, filled in all four sides of the Place d'Armes. In the middle of the square, all the mulatto prisoners of the northwest had been collected, and those from the Le Cap region had been brought up from La Fossette. Each group seemed further disheartened to meet the other—it looked as if they had been summoned to their own execution.

From the steps of the church, Toussaint Louverture presided over the square. When the little phalanx of first communicants arrived, all bearing lighted candles in their hands for the occasion, he stopped them before they could enter, and in a voice which carried to all four corners of the Place d'Armes, addressed them on the duties of mercy and the blessings of compassion. He expounded on these central Christian virtues for nearly twenty minutes, while the doctor and the captain exchanged glances of perplexity, and the priest and his acolytes looked out the door with barely suppressed impatience, and candle wax dripped down on the hands of the mystified children.

Finally, Toussaint let it be known, as an example of his general precept, that the colored people had now been punished enough. According to the duty of mercy and forgiveness, they would now be released. They were to be given a change of clothes (for the captives from the northwest were by then in a state of abject near-nakedness) and allowed to return to their homes, be it even as far as Môle Saint Nicolas, without interference from black soldier or black citizen. Still more, they must be treated as brothers by all who met them along their way.

They left Le Cap at dawn next day, Toussaint and the better part of his army, in urgent haste for the southern front. That night they spent at Gonaives, and left in good time the following morning. Toussaint chose to travel by coach across the Savane Désolée and the Artibonite lowlands, with the doctor seated across from him, listening to dictation. The doctor had Toussaint's portable writing desk shakily balanced on his knees, and was taking notes as best he could, though he knew his sheet would amount to no more than a maze of blots and illegible scrawling. He'd have been happier in the saddle, where he hoped to return; a couple of Toussaint's honor guard were leading their horses behind the coach.

At Saint Marc they stopped for a meal and to water the horses. Then Toussaint pressed on, ahead of his main force, escorted by twenty men of his honor guard and a few staff officers, including Maillart. The doctor and Toussaint had resumed their places in the coach. But on the outskirts of Arcahaye, Toussaint stopped speaking and let his head loll back on the hard leather cushion. For perhaps ten minutes he seemed to doze, or otherwise depart from consciousness (though his eyes stayed open just a crack). Then his head snapped forward and his eyes went wide.

"That mare of yours," he said to the doctor. "She still gives trouble?"

"What?" said the doctor. "Oh, it is hardly worth mentioning."

"But let me see if I can correct her." Toussaint grinned and called to the coachman to halt.

Stiffly, the doctor climbed down to the roadbed. One of the helmeted guardsmen brought up both the mare and Toussaint's white charger.

"Ou mèt alé," Toussaint advised his driver. The coach rolled off, following the group of horsemen at the head of the line.

With a smile, Toussaint indicated Bel Argent. The doctor swallowed, let out the stirrup as far as it would go, and swung himself up with more of a show of confidence than he really felt. The white stallion shifted under him like an earthquake. This was more horse than he was used to, but he nodded to the guardsman, who released his grip on Bel Argent's bridle.

Toussaint was whispering or breathing into the ear of the doctor's mare. He had left his general's hat in the coach, and without it he looked quite nondescript, except for his uniform coat, and even that was unornamented beyond the simplest insignia of his rank. He bestrode the mare and rode her forward. The coach had turned a bend in the road and was momentarily out of sight.

The doctor found that the best way to manage Bel Argent was to let himself be managed, as one allows oneself to be led by a superior dance partner. A case where the horse knew more than the rider. They were bringing up the very rear. Ahead, the mare spooked at something, maybe a glint of reflection from the stream beside the road, and commenced that skating sideways step, but Toussaint drooped forward over her mane, murmuring something which seemed to calm her. Then he came straight in the saddle again. Without the hat, in his red headcloth, he might have been some ordinary peasant, except of course for the quality of his horsemanship.

The light was slanting through the trees that lined the road as they came down into the area called Sources Puantes. The air was thick with the sulfur smell of the springs that gave the place its name. The doctor found himself unnerved, for no good reason he could think of. He stared glazedly at Toussaint's red *mouchwa têt*. The brimstone smell oppressed him; his skin began to crawl. Of a sudden he remembered that Maillart was at the head of the column, though he could not have said why this thought so alarmed him. A light squeeze of his calves was enough to bring Bel Argent into a smooth canter. They flowed forward, passing the coach.

Beyond the first riders in the column was a declivity in the road. The trees to the west were tall and thick-boled and regularly spaced. Red-gold sunlight spilled between them over the roadway, and the dark bars of the tree's shadows filled the doctor with a reasonless foreboding.

"Come to the rear," he called to the captain. Maillart looked at him, then curiously at the white stallion, then again at the doctor's face.

"Come quickly—you are wanted," the doctor said.

He turned Bel Argent and rode back down the line, passing the coach in the opposite direction; the coachman raised a hand to greet him. He looked back once and saw that Maillart was following. For seventy yards the road was empty, then came more guardsmen, and finally Toussaint, riding even slower than before, his eyes fixed forward as if upon some dream.

Captain Maillart fell in with the doctor, behind Toussaint. "What is it?" he said. "Who sent for me?"

But already they heard the snapping of gunfire and someone's out-raged shout. The rear guard was galloping forward toward the sound, and Maillart, grimacing, spurred his force to overtake them. Toussaint, however, kept on at the same leisurely trot, as if he had heard nothing and had no concern. The doctor drew abreast, then passed him.

Around the bend of the road, the two guardsmen were racing the runaway coach, while several others had dismounted and were firing on fleeing attackers through the trees at either side of the road. The doctor gave Bel Argent his head. The white stallion overtook the coach just as one of the guardsmen leaned down to catch the harness of the nearest horse and jerk the whole equipage to a halt.

The driver had fallen from the box and lay doubled over the left shaft of the coach, his fingers dragging furrows in the dirt. The coach doors were shot to splinters on either side. Toussaint's hat still lay on the seat, its red and white plumes broken by bullets, and the leather upholstery was perforated like a sieve.

Maillart reined up beside the doctor. "Antoine," he said. "Antoine."

But the doctor had no answer to the question in his eyes. He did not know himself how he had known.

Only the coachman had been killed. The guardsmen made their report to Toussaint in low voices: one of the assassins had been shot down but the rest had managed to escape into the surrounding brush.

Toussaint did not seem astonished by anything they told him. He listened gravely to the report, but made no reply. Retrieving his hat from the shattered coach, he plucked out the broken feathers, and settled it on his head. They rode on, speechless, into the gathering dark.

34

That first morning when she woke in the inn at Dondon, Isabelle was
seized with nausea the moment she sat up. Her throat bubbled up, and
she hunched over, spilling vomit onto a square of cloth she had just time
to snatch under her chin. She spat, swallowed, and regained partial
composure, though her eyes watered still and her gullet burned.

Nanon was asleep, or feigning to be, and without any servant at all,
Isabelle hardly knew what to do next. She felt ashamed. But she rolled
up the cloth into a damp, foul-smelling package, and, holding it away
from herself in her left hand, she tiptoed outdoors, barefoot and wearing only her shift.

It was still very early and quite cool. The town was unusually quiet,
since almost all the soldiers had poured out of it the day before. A few
chickens scratched in the dust of the main square and at the well several women were filling clay vessels and swinging them to a graceful balance atop their heads. Isabelle was ashamed to approach them, though
water was what she wanted. In the other direction she could hear the
sound of a stream and so she turned and walked toward it.

A few black women sitting on their doorsteps looked at her curiously.
The cloths that covered their doorways had been cinched in the mid-

dle, like a woman's waist, for light and ventilation indoors. After two blocks of low houses like these, a ravine bordered the edge of the town. Isabelle peered over the edge and decided she could manage to get down there, skipping from boulder to boulder and holding onto the hanging vines. The effort focused her, and by the time she reached the level spit of gravel by the water, the last traces of her nausea had receded. She knelt at the streambed and let the current wash clean her soiled cloth. The stain came out easily enough when she rubbed it over the stones. She washed her face in the cold water, and took a cautious sip—only enough to moisten her throat. She wanted next to nothing in her stomach, still.

With the damp cloth wrapped around her wrist, she walked downstream, looking for an easier way to climb back to the town. As she followed the stream around a bend, she came face to face with another woman, younger than herself and bare to the waist as she labored over her own washing. Startled, the other woman broke into a bright white smile. Isabelle curtsied, blushing at the absurdity of her gesture, which still somehow felt right. The black woman straightened, her hands on her hips, her full breasts trembling as she threw back her head to laugh.

Behind her, two small children played on a strip of fine sand. The infant boy was bare-naked, his polished skin a rich, iridescent black. Whenever he crawled for the water's edge, the older child retrieved him. It was a sweet moment, and the sun was warming on her back, but when she heard a bell begin to ring in the town, Isabelle knew she had better return.

"Koté m kab monté?" she asked, and the other woman smiled again, and turned to point farther down the stream, where Isabelle could see the foot of a much more feasible trail than the one she'd descended. She made her thanks and walked by. Halfway up the trail, she stopped and looked down through the hanging lianas, and waved the free end of the cloth at the woman and her children, but they were all unaware of her now. Nevertheless, her feeling of exhilaration sustained itself. At this instant she had nothing, was constrained by nothing but her body and the cloth that covered it, and there was no connection to her history here, except Nanon, who was herself such a mystery.

The feeling could not last forever, and already she began to feel oppressed as she walked back toward the tavern in the mounting heat. The others were eating a morning meal which she declined to share (though Madame Fortier cautioned her she'd see no more till nightfall): bananas and warm, runny eggs and pork dried on the *boucan*. Her stomach writhed at the odor. Monsieur Fortier seemed to be looking with disapproval at her bare, dusty feet. She went to the room she'd shared with Nanon and put on more confining clothing, along with her shoes and a bonnet which hid her hair and most of her face.

Madame Fortier sat on the wagon box beside her husband, while Nanon and Isabelle used the bed, which was three-quarters full with provisions purchased or bartered for in the town. There were various clay vessels packed in straw, and barrels of dried fish and peas and salt meat, and several rolls of calico against which they could recline, so they were not so terribly uncomfortable, though nothing could completely blunt the jouncing of the wagon over the worst parts of the road.

By midday, Isabelle's stomach had begun to turn, for all the pains she'd taken to leave it empty. The hollowness cramped upon itself, and the heat made everything worse. She found herself hanging over the edge of the wagon, coughing and retching up clots of burning foam. A line of Fortier retainers who were following the wagon with baskets balanced on their heads carefully sidestepped around the wet spots in the dust. Nanon rose to her knees and laid a gentle hand on Isabelle's shoulder.

Then the wagon lurched to a halt, so that Isabelle bruised her breastbone against the siderail. Presently she felt a hard grip on the back of her neck, thumb gouging, probing between the tendons at the base of her head. She was lifted, and the same grip dug harshly into the underside of her wrists. It was painful, but the nausea receded. Madame Fortier was holding her by the chin and peering at her face in the shade of the bonnet.

"How long has it been?"

"What do you mean?" Isabelle began weakly, but the evasion seemed pointless under Madame Fortier's firm hand and keen eye. She pulled back and covered her face with her forearm. "Between two months and three—I can't be certain."

She felt the tang of vinegar on her lips; Madame Fortier had moved her arm aside and was cleaning her face. The sharp smell of the vinegar brightened her.

"Eat this," the older women said, pressing a wedge of cassava into her hand. "Or only hold it in your mouth—it will do you good." She folded the fingers of Isabelle's other hand over the soaked rag. "And use the vinegar." She pointed to one of the stoppered clay jars.

"Yes," said Isabelle. "I'll do as you say. And thank you."

The firm hands squeezed her shoulders, then withdrew. Cautiously, Isabelle nibbled a corner of the cassava. Her stomach clenched, and she simply held the bread in her mouth, letting its faint sweetness dissolve. Monsieur Fortier muttered something to his mules, and the wagon wheels began to turn. Isabelle lay back, propped against one of the long bolts of cloth. They had stopped just short of a peak in the zig-zag trial, and as they passed into the descent, the wagon began to roll faster, with Monsieur Fortier grunting from time to time as he pulled back on the long bar of the brake. The barefoot women behind the wagon swung into a rhythmic trot to match the quicker pace, singing as they jogged along, words which Isabelle could not completely understand. If the nausea rose, a sniff of the vinegar rag seemed to quell it, and it was true that the cassava bread had put a more stable foundation beneath her stomach; without realizing it, she seemed to have eaten it all.

She became aware that Nanon was watching her with her usual air of self-enclosed composure, a moment before the other woman spoke.

"Is it always so with you?" she said. "When you are expecting a new child?"

"Not always," said Isabelle. "With the first, but not the second."

"Ah," said Nanon. "Robert." Her molasses tongue softened the name so wonderfully: *Wobè* . . . "I remember him well from the time when I first came to your house. And the second, Héloïse, was only a baby then."

"Let us not speak of it." Isabelle's eyes were pricking; she turned her face away and looked out blurrily over the precipitous fall of jungled escarpments, down into the basin of Grande Rivière. She could still hear the strange singing of the women who trotted behind the wagon. Some language of Africa; it was not ordinary Creole. She felt a terrible loneliness that seemed to come from her own hollow core. The moment she'd shared with the black woman and her children by the river returned to her. It seemed to her now that never in her whole life had she been so free as that woman was, unless in her earliest childhood. Perhaps even then her sense of liberty had been illusion.

Then a shadow blocked the sun, and she felt Nanon's warm weight settle against her side. The soft, rather heavy arm about her shoulders drew her in.

"When Paul was lost from me," Nanon murmured, "I was sad two times each day. In the morning when I woke, and at night, before sleeping."

"How terrible it is, sometimes." Isabelle heard her own whisper, as if from a long, echoing distance, returned to her from the vertiginous valley below.

"At night was worse," Nanon said. "But the morning was bad too."

Isabelle stirred against her, drowsily. She felt herself beginning to drift. Long ago, a lifetime it seemed, she had had an intense romantic friendship with a colored girl of her father's household in Haut de Trou. They had been permitted great intimacy, and had adventured considerably into one another's bodies, before either of them had ever known a man. Isabelle did not know what had become of the girl afterward.

This was not that. But it was pleasant. A kind of mother comfort—how long since she'd known that? She let herself be cuddled, like a little cat, feeling Nanon's fingers loosening her bonnet strings and walking the taut tendons of her neck. She let her head slip down to Nanon's shoulder. Before she knew it, she was sleeping, so soundly that she did not wake until that evening as the wagon began to climb the rim of Haut de Trou.

Madame Fortier claimed the front bedchamber, which Nanon had formerly occupied with Choufleur, for herself and her husband to share. Nanon had no objection, while Isabelle was in no position to object. Nanon sensed this, though she had no certain knowledge. The charade of Isabelle supervising *her* pregnancy had seemed rather thin from the beginning, and since Isabelle's own condition had been discovered, Nanon supposed there must be something irregular about it, though she did not give her notion any further thought.

On the evening of their arrival, Madame Fortier inspected the front bedchamber with her lips pursed and her nostrils flaring. She ordered all the bedding to be aired, and the mattress to be thoroughly beaten. With an air of distaste she fingered the collar of scars which Nanon's chain had left on the heavy mahogany bedpost during that time when she'd been left to circle the room like a dog tied to a tree and abandoned.

Next morning, Nanon found Salomon working round and round the the bedpost with a file made of sharkskin wrapped round a lathe. His eyes flashed white when he noticed her, and then he bent more closely over his work, giving her his shoulder. By the end of that day he'd ground down both posts at the bed's foot to the same degree, so that they remained symmetrical; he oiled them so carefully that scarcely any trace of the alteration could be seen.

Nanon had spied Madame Fortier, sitting on the gallery with a couple of mildewed ledgers under her hand; as she had no refreshment by her, Nanon went at once to the kitchen herself. The women were preparing coffee, but Nanon took the task out of their hands. She prepared a tray with two cups, a pot, a bowl of brown sugar, some wedges of cassava bread, and a sprig of bougainvillea in a vase.

Madame Fortier looked up abstractedly as Nanon placed the cup before her and poured. "My son, your particular friend, was not a great

hand with his accounting," she said. "All this is the work of his father."
She turned the pages fretfully. The paper was worm-holed through and
through, but still mostly legible; scrambling over the lace-like sheets
Nanon could recognize the pale, insectine script of the Sieur Maltrot.

"Jean-Michel never opened this book, I don't imagine," Madame
Fortier said. "It's been years since any note was made at all." Peevishly
she slammed the ledger shut and looked up. "Well?"

"*C'est pour Monsieur,*" Nanon said, glancing at the second cup.

"Oh," said Madame Fortier. "He has gone to the terraces, long ago.
The second coffee is yours, my dear. Sit down and drink it."

Nanon obeyed. After she had taken her first sip, Madame Fortier covered her hand with her own. "You are not to play the servant, child," she
said. "You are at home, as much as anyone here."

Nanon felt a warmth spread across her face. She lowered her head
and looked at the dark swirl of her coffee. Madame Fortier applied a
light pressure to the back of her hand. Then they both turned toward
the interior of the house, their hands slipping apart, as they heard the
distantly disagreeable sound of Isabelle retching.

In the next weeks, Monsieur Fortier labored mightily in the coffee terraces, which had fallen into desuetude once again, since Choufleur had
vanished from the scene. For her part Madame Fortier took inventory
of the *main-d'oeuvre,* comparing the slave lists of the Sieur Maltrot
(which were detailed and thorough) with the present population of
free blacks on the plantation. The discrepancy was less, she told Nanon
and Isabelle, than she might have expected. Toussaint's orders were
generally respected in this region, and most of the former field hands
remained on the property, though many of them, perhaps more than
half, seemed much more inclined to work their own gardens for their
own benefit, rather than trouble themselves with the coffee. Also there
had been more births, and more surviving children.

There was at first some difficulty in returning a sufficient work force
to the coffee groves, but after certain messages had been sent down the
mountain, a troop of Moyse's regiment appeared from Ouanaminthe,
and stayed long enough to remind the field hands that work was the
price of freedom. By the time Isabelle had passed through her phase
of morning sickness, the coffee trees had been carefully freed of parasitic vines and weeded round their trunks and returned to a state of
productivity.

Nanon's own pregnancy went more smoothly; she had no nausea to
contend with, and though she was further along than Isabelle, she car-

ried the child more easily. Of course, she was the larger woman, if not so clearly the stronger. Isabelle was more resilient, far less fragile than she looked; Nanon knew her toughness well. But this pregnancy looked as if it would try her strength severely. Even Madame Fortier whispered, privately to Nanon, that it had been inadvisable for the *blanche* to have come on horseback as far as Dondon.

For a month, six weeks, it did go badly with Isabelle. She could scarcely eat, so she lost her strength and grew spectrally thin, with the bones standing out on her face, as if the flesh were no more than a veil for her skull. She began to avoid the mirrors of the house for that reason—it was no aspect for a pregnant woman, though maybe not so inappropriate for her case. Maybe the child would starve in the womb, come rattling out like a dry, shriveled pea. But she could not quite bring herself to wish for that. Even the bitter remark she'd made from the saddle to Captain Maillart had only been half-intended. She could feel the child's life fully wrapped around her own, and she still clung to life herself, in spite of everything.

Then the period of illness passed, and she could eat again, and she did eat—like a tiger, to the frank amazement of Nanon and Madame Fortier. Even Monsieur Fortier, usually so inexpressive, would study her with interest at the table, stroking his beard with his long, graceful hand and humming to himself, as Isabelle demolished entire platters of food.

Her color came back, and so did her strength. Useless, for she had no future. The outcome of her situation was something which her thought rejected. Fortunately, this middle phase of pregnancy always made her stupid. She could feel, but could not think, and she embraced her feeling.

Nanon began to take her around the countryside. They might do whatever they liked all day, as the Fortiers required nothing of them at all, but indulged them like two spoiled children. For some few blissful weeks, Isabelle felt herself carried back to her own childhood, a time when no could gainsay her—her mother had died soon after her birth and her father had no will to oppose her. She had been the princess of Habitation Reynaud, admired and obeyed by all her father's six hundred slaves. The slaves had mostly been fond of her, for, though capricious, she had not been cruel. Now, as she went rambling with Nanon, she remembered with a strange emotion certain kindnesses they'd shown her, which she had not recalled for many years.

She and Nanon got the use of two little donkeys, and rode them all around the country in the style of two market women—sidesaddle but without stirrups, the forward knee hooked up over the animal's shoulder. Nanon showed her the tombs of the *caciques,* and the places where one could gather wild orchids or, better yet, wild mushrooms. She took Isabelle to a cavern full of Indian relics, now inhabited only by bats— which were reputed to smoke pipes of tobaccos, like ghosts of the old *caciques*. The two women giggled like girls over this tale, but afterwards were perhaps a little frightened by it.

Then one bright morning Nanon brought Isabelle to a new place. Isabelle had felt, from the moment they set out, that her friend had some particular plan. Nanon had packed an elaborate lunch in one of her donkey's panniers, and had put two blankets in the other. They rode an unfamiliar path, and soon Isabelle began to hear the sound of rushing water. They came out into a green glade in the center of which was a deep, foaming pool, fed by a twenty-foot waterfall.

"Oh," Isabelle said. "Oh . . ." She could say nothing more at all, the place was so very special, like a gift.

Nanon was tying up the donkeys, on long tethers so that they had space to graze. She spread one of the blankets over the grass, and set the basket of food and the other folded blanket on top of it. Then she took Isabelle by the hand.

"Come," she said, and Isabelle let herself be led. They climbed alongside the waterfall to about half its height, with the help of hands and footholds worn in the stone by long years of use. Ten feet up, they balanced on a ledge, and Nanon thrust her free arm to the elbow into the curtain of falling water.

"Come," she said, and she drew Isabelle forward into the current, before she could think of resisting. The cold drenched her, shocked her to the bone. Then she was through. She and Nanon stood in a little grotto behind the fall, hugging each other for warmth and laughing from excitement.

The sun, filtered through the falling water, covered them with a strange liquid light. Nanon pulled her dress over her head and balled it up and hurled it through the barrier. She turned to Isabelle and kissed her on the corner of the mouth.

"Don't be afraid," she said. Then she stepped through the veil, as she were herself translated into water, and disappeared into the tumbling light.

Isabelle stood poised a moment, with her finger laid on her open mouth where she had been touched. The waterfall made a weird window, through which everything appeared magnified, distorted, rearranged by the ropes of crystal fluid. She could not really see what lay beyond it.

She took off her own dress and jumped through the waterfall, holding the garment stretched out at arm's length like a flag. As she launched into the bright air, she shouted out a mixture of joy and fear and surprise at the chill water washing over her again. The water of the pool was warmer than she had expected when she went under, though it was very deep. She came up spluttering. Nanon reached out her hand to pull her up over the bank into the glow of the sunshine.

For a moment they stood side by side, studying each other's bodies, each pear-shaped from pregnancy. Nanon set her arm against Isabelle's; they were now almost the same honey shade, for in these last weeks Isabelle had abandoned all her usual precautions against the sun. Only her breasts and belly were still pallid, of course, and the parts of her limbs which were usually covered, and soon they were both giggling at the effect of this. Then they turned and stood side by side, looking into the pool, where their dresses floated like two great crumpled water lilies.

"The water is not so cold as I thought," Isabelle said "And it seems to get warmer the deeper you go."

"A warm spring feeds it from below," Nanon said. She wrinkled her nose, and Isabelle thought she caught a hint of sulfur in the air.

"But come," Nanon said, "you will burn."

She led Isabelle to the spread blanket and covered her with the folded one. They stretched out on their backs, side by side, with their fingers lightly laced and the sun red against their eyelids.

Later, when they roused from their doze, they were both very hungry. Isabelle busied herself laying out the cold chicken, bread and fruit, while Nanon hooked their dresses from the pool with a long stick and spread them on the grass to dry. Then she climbed again to the grotto behind the waterfall. When she came out this time, she was brandishing a bottle of white wine.

"*Miracle,*" Isabelle said, when she had tasted it. "But this is very good, it is certainly French. How is it possible?"

Nanon gave her only a sly smile. For a time they went on eating and drinking and silence.

"But it must be witchcraft," Isabelle said finally, as she drained her glass.

"No," said Nanon, a little sadly, it seemed. "No witchcraft. Choufleur kept his wine here, so it would not sour in the heat. Now I am the only one that knows." She smiled distantly. "There are still a great many bottles hidden there. I think I shall not tell the Fortiers."

"All this place must be your secret, then."

"It was one of the first secrets I shared with him. Later, after he had changed, it was all destroyed for me." Nanon turned to Isabelle, her heavy red lips curving. "But now I can love it again, because of you."

"Why, you touch my heart," Isabelle said. As she spoke, she felt a

shadow pass over her. She leaned back on her elbows. A hawk was circling the crown of the sky, but the hawk could not have cast such a
shadow.

"No," said Nanon, as if to answer the unspoken question. "I would
rather remember him as he was then."

"You speak of him as if he were dead."

"Yes," Nanon said slowly. "I suppose I do." She stood up and walked
over to her dress, which had dried by then, and slowly stooped to lift it,
like a burden she was reluctant to resume.

When Nanon's child was born, Isabelle assisted her as she had promised. The birth was uncomplicated, and Madame Fortier, though older
and more experienced in midwifery, stepped back at the last moment,
so it was Isabelle who received the bloody infant into her own hands. A
boy. She slapped his back to start him crying, as she'd seen others do,
then cleaned and dried him all over and swaddled him carefully in soft
white cloth. Nanon was insensible; Isabelle passed the baby to Madame
Fortier for a moment while she dried her own hands. When she looked
again, the older woman seemed to be in the grip of some interior struggle, her hands trembling, her face tightly drawn, so that Isabelle took
the infant back at once, and so quickly that she almost snatched him
away.

During the next three days, the newborn began to take on the face
he would wear through life. His features were very much those of his
father's, and it was plain enough to Isabelle that this father must be
Choufleur, rather than Antoine Hébert, though no one spoke openly of
the matter. Madame Fortier had none of the affection one might have
expected for a grandson. She handled the baby seldom, and whenever she did pick him up, Isabelle had the disturbing impression that
Madame Fortier could barely restrain herself from dashing his brains
out on the floor.

At the end of three days, Nanon was on her feet again, and Madame
Fortier announced her own departure. She and her husband must go,
she said, to see to their holdings near Dondon. Here at Vallière, all was
now in satisfactorily good order. Salomon had the field workers well
in hand and (Madame Fortier implied) the two younger women would
know well enough how to manage him.

At this announcement, Nanon merely lowered her head with her
usual self-obscuring modesty, but Isabelle found a moment alone with
Madame Fortier, just before they left.

"It is only a child," she said carefully, having chosen her words in advance. "Only a baby—and given to us to make the best we can of him."

"Is it so?" said Madame Fortier, drawing herself up to such a sharpness that Isabelle quailed, believing for an instant that the other woman had penetrated her own secret.

"A mother may fully give her love," Madame Fortier said, in a terrible voice. "But there is blood too, and nothing—nothing!—will wash blood away."

Then she softened ever so lightly. "But perhaps you are right," she said more quietly. "In any case, I admire your sentiment, though what this child will do for a father, I do not know. I do not say I am leaving forever, though it's best that I leave now, for a time."

She stood up, and with her usual stately grace went down from the gallery into the garden. Beyond the open gateway, Fortier was already waiting on the wagon seat. But Madame Fortier paused at the foot of the stairs, and beckoned Isabelle to come down within earshot of her whisper.

"For your sake too, it may be better that I leave now, young woman."

Inwardly, Isabelle wilted again, though she thought she kept her expression calm.

"You may find that Nanon has small enough experience in certain practical matters," Madame Fortier said, with a dubious smile. "If you are in trouble, when your time comes, you must send for a woman called Man Jouba."

"But where?" said Isabelle, who'd grasped her meaning well enough.

"Only say her name. They will bring her, out of the mountains." Without saying anything more, Madame Fortier glided across the garden, her back faultlessly erect, like a soldier's, as she stepped up into the wagon.

The management of the plantation now fell into the hands of the two women, which meant that it fell into Isabelle's. Madame Fortier had judged Nanon correctly, at least to this extent. But Isabelle took up the ledgers where Madame Fortier had laid them down. In the older woman's hand she found a meticulous record of all events on the plantation: the weather, positions of the stars and phases of the moon, progress of work in the coffee groves and drying sheds, a thorough record of illness, death and birth (not only among the people but for the animals too). Of the new child in the *grand'case* she had written this: "To the *quarteronée* woman, Nanon, was born, 6 January 1800, a male child, *quarteroné,* to be called François."

There were no more excursions, no larks in the countryside. Not only because of the burden of management, but because Isabelle felt the weight of her pregnancy much more heavily now. In fact she was ill, and full of foreboding. That halcyon day by the waterfall seemed eons away from her now.

One morning at the breakfast table, she felt herself give way, but not till she saw Nanon's startled face did she look down and see her skirts all stained with blood.

"Now let me die," she said.

"Oh, what can you mean?" said Nanon, shocked. But she bypassed her own question and called a housemaid to help Isabelle to her bed.

The contractions, convulsions rather, came quickly, then subsided, then came again in viciously stabbing sets. So it went all through the morning, afternoon, into the night and the next day. The child was not descending properly. Isabelle felt that her own body would crush it to a lifeless pulp, and take her with it too. She held the name of the midwife to her like a secret weapon she would not draw. At last she passed from consciousness into fevered dream. It was night again when she awoke, enough to be aware of Nanon dabbing her temples and her lips with a cool cloth. In the light of a candle behind her head, Nanon whispered to her to hold on.

"No," said Isabelle. "It is better I should die, and the child too."

"You can't mean that," Nanon said to her.

"Oh yes," said Isabelle. "If you knew the father."

"No father could merit such a wish. No matter who."

"It is Joseph Flaville."

She felt Nanon draw back. For a moment she knew herself abandoned, utterly alone, and she wished she had not spoken. Then Nanon took one of her hands in both of hers, and pressed and rubbed it till Isabelle began to feel a thread of energy returning to her through this contact.

"Even so," Nanon said. "Even so, we shall find some way."

"There is no way," said Isabelle. "From the day it happened I was ruined."

"There is. You will live for your children already born, Robert and Héloïse."

Isabelle felt the wetness of her tears against the pillow. "If I live," she said, "I will ruin them too."

"Do not say that!" Nanon hissed. "Listen to me. I will not let you go this way. When I was alone, and with child, and helpless, when the whites were killing women of my kind all through the streets of Le Cap, you took me in and saved my life and you saved Paul."

"But . . ." Isabelle was thinking that she had not taken Nanon in with her whole heart, but had done it at the doctor's insistence, and that at the time she had partly resented it. But there was no way for her to say such a thing, not now. So she did not, but let Nanon go on massaging her hand, until she began to feel that maybe Nanon was right about everything.

"Man Jouba," she muttered at last.

"What?" Nanon's breath was warm and sweet against her ear.

"Send for Man Jouba," Isabelle said. Then she slipped backward, toppling into the delirium of her pain, and for a long time she knew nothing more.

When she came to herself again, it was night and she was alone. All the house was very quiet. She did not know if it were the same night, but thought it must be at least the next. Nothing in her memory was clear. There had been dreadful pain, which had now abated. The memory of pain was never perfect.

Outdoors, the wind shivered the leaves and branches, and a cool current swirled through her room. Somewhere in the house nearby an infant voice began to wail, but was as quickly muffled by a breast.

She rose, but was stopped for a moment by a thrust of the pain she had forgotten. She bowed over, pressing both hands against the spot, gathering her flattened, slackened belly. It passed, and she straightened and reached for her robe. Fastening it around her, she crossed the hall to the opposite bedchamber. In the orb of light of a single candle, Nanon lay abed, suckling a tiny jet-black infant.

"You see," she said, as if she'd been expecting Isabelle's appearance at that moment. "He is already strong. Oh, he is like a little bull."

"*Li foncé anpil,*" Isabelle remarked.

"*C'est ça,*" Nanon agreed. "He is very dark." She looked up. "He has already needed his strength," she said. "The cord was wrapped two times around his neck. Without Man Jouba, you would both be dead."

"Yes," said Isabelle. "I shall certainly send her a present." She paused. "I must do it quickly, before my husband learns of this event, and I am murdered."

"This child will be mine," Nanon said calmly. "Brother to my François, but you shall name him."

"Gabriel," said Isabelle. "Let us call him Gabriel." She studied the black baby, who pummeled the breast with one hand as he sucked.

"But it is all impossible, this scheme," Isabelle said. "The servants know, and Madame Fortier . . ."

"Madame Fortier has taken good care to know nothing for certain," Nanon said. "What she may know, or suppose, she will not tell. I think no one at all understood your condition, before we had reached Dondon?—but if need be, we will say that your child was born dead." Nanon shook her glossy black hair back over her pillow. "That much is near enough to the truth, besides."

"But Man Jouba." Isabelle said. "The servants."

"Man Jouba has gone back to the mountains, where no one will find her if she does not want to be found. The servants will not speak of it, not to anyone who might harm you."

"Nanon," Isabelle said quietly. "What of yourself, and your own situation?"

If a shade crossed Nanon's face, it did not linger.

"Now that is a thought for another day," she said. "Tonight I am thinking only of you, and of these two children."

As if she had signaled him, François began to cry. When Nanon shifted to reach for him, the black infant lost his hold on the breast, slipped down and began to wail.

Isabelle lifted the crying baby and held him to her. He was not comforted by the movement, but howled louder than before. He felt much heavier than the other infant, denser, as if he were entirely carved from the cliff rock of the mountains. Tears were running down her face, and her own milk had started, seeping out through her robe.

"No," Nanon said. "You must give him up. Give him to me."

Isabelle obeyed her. She settled Gabriel at Nanon's other breast, so that he and François could nurse together.

"*Marassa yo,*" Nanon said with a crooked smile. "You see? They are my twins."

Isabelle saw. She knew she must not reach for what she saw. She must be grateful for her life and whatever it gave her, for the two children fastened to her friend's breasts, and the dark hand groping blindly toward the light one.

35

In the late morning, Doctor Hébert came riding up the tattered *allée* to Habitation Arnaud, yawning and half asleep in the saddle. These last weeks he had been whipsawed all over the country by Toussaint, who needed to be everywhere at once to discourage Rigaudin conspiracies; since the cluster of attempts on his life, Toussaint had also become still more chary than usual of staying too long (more than nine or ten hours) in any one place.

But today Toussaint was on his way to Port-au-Prince (or so he'd claimed, though he might just as well appear somewhere else) while the doctor had been detached from the immediate staff and was traveling now under escort of Joseph Flaville and a small cavalry squadron. They did not hurry. In the fields of the plantation, men were cutting cane and loading it onto ox-drawn wagons. Flaville took a detour and selected a stalk, peeled and tasted it with a critical expression. For the past year, Flaville had had the management of a couple of nearby plantations whose original owners had not made bold to reappear, and so had become a student of the quality of the crop. He chewed and after a moment smiled his approval. He sectioned out a length of cane to distribute among his men, who bit great sweet chunks from their shares and laughed as they rode on through the warm sunshine.

As they came clattering into the main compound, the doctor was roused from his doze and pulled his mare up sharply. A work of construction was afoot, exactly where that shed had been, and Moustique was busy directing it.

"*Ki sa y'ap fé?*" he inquired of the boy who came out from the stable to take charge of his mount. What are they doing?

"They are raising a church," the boy told him, with a brilliant grin. One of Claudine's catechumens, the doctor imagined.

He dismounted, took off his straw hat, and began unconsciously to scratch at his dry scalp as he considered the history of that square of ground. Once it had housed Arnaud's vicious slave-catching mastiff. Then Claudine had used it to martyr her maid. Now it looked as if Moustique meant to place the very sanctuary of his chapel exactly there. Perhaps it was fitting. Moustique noticed him and waved, with a smile. The doctor wondered how he'd hit on the spot, if someone had told him, or if he had simply been drawn to it somehow. There was a numinosity to places where blood had been shed.

Flaville had also noticed the construction and ridden in a wide ellipse around it, toward the cane mill. The doctor replaced his hat and followed him, on foot. He found Arnaud in the lower level of the mill, supervising the hands as they spooned with their long ladles from the tanks. The two skilled refiners had gone out to meet Flaville, almost as if they had expected him to come.

"What news?" said Arnaud, genially enough, as he wiped his hands on his shirttail.

"Beauvais has left Jacmel," the doctor said, after a moment's consideration. There was other news, in fact more urgent, but he was not eager to deliver it.

Arnaud stepped a little nearer, so he could lower his voice. "Has he come over to our side at last?"

"No," said the doctor. Interesting, he thought, that Arnaud should identify Toussaint's side as his own. "He's fled the country, since Roume declared him in rebellion. Apparently he means to go to plead his case in France."

"Ridiculous." Arnaud walked out from under the roof's overhang and spat on the ground. "He was a fool to think he could conserve his neutrality in such a situation."

"Oh, Beauvais is a man of honor," the doctor said. "One might say, meanwhile, that his conscience has given him a twisted path to follow."

He cleared his throat. "His men are very discontented with him, according to the spies."

"So Jacmel *will* come over."

"Unfortunately, no. Jacmel has declared for Rigaud and set in for a siege. I'm not sure who commands there now, perhaps Pétion."

Arnaud grimaced. "The man is capable."

"Yes," said the doctor. "But gravely outnumbered all the same. Dessalines has the town completely encircled by land, and Toussaint hopes for help from the Americans at sea."

"That's something," Arnaud said.

"It may be a great deal. Rigaud was ill advised to send his corsairs against the American merchantmen."

"Let's have a drink on it, then."

"Willingly."

Somewhat to the doctor's surprise, Arnaud began walking away from the *grand'case*. He followed, along a rocky trail, toward the invisible rippling of a spring. Yellow butterflies flickered around the shoots of red ginger at their feet. The doctor began to smell smoke, and fermentation. They turned a bend in the trail and came in view of a rectangular open shed covering a fire, a cauldron, hood and coil. An old women tended the cauldron, using wooden implements strapped to the stumps of her hands. She did not look at them.

Arnaud lifted a bottle from the coil's tip and in the same motion replaced it with a long-necked gourd. He drank and offered the bottle to the doctor. The rum was clear, thick, extremely strong.

"You have made great strides here since my last visit," the doctor said cheerfully. He glanced sidelong at the woman who keeled the great kettle over the fire.

"We make every effort," Arnaud said. They took another drink apiece and then they returned in the direction of the mill.

It was the hour of midday repose. Flaville had gone off, with his men, to one of the neighboring plantations. The doctor checked on his mare in the stable, drank a mouthful of water, and found himself a hammock strung in a grove beyond the *grand'case*.

The shadows were long when he awoke, and he could hear the voices of children singing at Claudine's little school. He rolled out of the hammock, pulled on his boots, and strolled idly toward the sound. A girl's voice called out a greeting; he turned, still groggy with his sleep, and saw Fontelle and Paulette under the roof of the kitchen *ajoupa*, turning a young pig on a spit.

During what remained of the day, he heard the recitation of Claudine's students, and inspected the infirmary, where all seemed to have gone smoothly since his last call there. Paulette, whose skills he knew, had taken over some of the duties of nursing, but under the gentler regime there was less injury and illness for her to see to. After darkness had fallen, they all gathered in the main room of the *grand'case* to eat. The assembly was sizable, including Cléo, Fontelle, Moustique and his three sisters; a long puncheon table had been knocked together to provide places for them all. Before falling to, they all joined hands while Moustique muttered a mostly inaudible prayer.

The food was good, and plentiful: rice and beans and fried plantain, a piquant sauce with soft green cashews to complement the pork. There was little conversation. At Fontelle's glance or the flick of her finger, one or another of her daughters would rise to refill platters or refresh drinks. In former times, the doctor reflected privately, Arnaud would not conceivably have allowed any colored person to sit down at his table—not even Cléo, though she had certainly shared his bed, in the bad old days. Now all of them, even Claudine, seemed entirely at ease in their positions. The doctor's only discomfort was that he had been sent to interrupt this harmony.

When the meal was done, Claudine and the other women set about cleaning up after it. Arnaud beckoned the doctor outdoors. A bottle glinted in the starlight. The doctor reached for it gladly.

"We are a little rough here, still," Arnaud said. "Concerning the amenities."

"Ah, but the rum is good," the doctor said. "Shall we go up?" He pointed to the path ascending behind the house. Arnaud gave him a startled look.

"Oh, there's no danger." The doctor slapped at the back of his neck. "Only, the mosquitoes down here."

They climbed single file up the trail to the pocket in the cliff which Arnaud had made his last line of defense, and sat down on the rocks, passing the bottle between them at slow intervals. The night was very quiet and clear. Under the starlight in the compound below, the doctor could see the progress made on Moustique's chapel. The sanctuary was now enclosed by three walls of woven palm leaf, and rows of benches had been placed before it, in the open air. Above, a bright, pale crescent rocked the darker orb of the old moon.

"Toussaint has declared a new distribution," the doctor said reluctantly.

"Oh?"

"Everything is to go into the government treasury," the doctor said, "save the quarter share of the cultivators, and the costs of production."

Arnaud's jaw clicked shut. "I shall have trouble with my people."

"It's for the war," the doctor said. "The soldiers must be paid . . . sometimes, something." He stood up and caught water from the spring in his cupped hands and sipped at it, to cut the rum. "You won't have to deal with it directly."

Arnaud stared at him. "And why is that?"

"You've been conscripted. I'm meant to bring you with me down to Port-au-Prince."

Arnaud exhaled heavily. As the air went out of him, he slumped forward, elbows digging into his knees. "The property will go to ruin," he said. "And after all our trouble."

"No, no," the doctor said. "Flaville will be here to manage it for you."

"Oh, undoubtedly." Arnaud jumped up, slapping the tight fabric of his breeches, and began to pace the narrow area. "I am certain that Flaville will manage very well—for himself, as so many of Toussaint's officers have begun to do. While I am sent away to be shot in their wars."

"Calm yourself," the doctor said.

"It is easy for you to recommend it."

"After all, you are not intended to be cannon fodder," the doctor said. "You'll be given a command, parallel to Captains Vaublanc and Maillart, for example. Toussaint wants to rally *all* the experienced officers."

"That means he must be expecting heavy losses," Arnaud snapped. "And I have had no part of the military in all my life."

"He knows that you served in the militia, and in the *maréchaussée*."

"And I know that *he* served as Bayon de Libertat's coachman," Arnaud said. "My Christ, but the world has turned upside down."

"So it has," the doctor said. "Which way do you like it better?"

"Which way do I— " Arnaud stopped in his tracks, and sat down on a boulder.

"You won't go unrepresented here," the doctor pointed out. "There is Claudine, and Fontelle." He paused. "And Cléo."

Arnaud thumbed his jawline, looking down over the compound. "I am to serve under Dessalines, then."

"Yes, under Dessalines," said the doctor. "Along with the others I mentioned."

Shifting his seat and stretching out his legs, Arnaud studied the half-built chapel where it lay bathed in starlight. "When must we go?"

"As soon as possible," the doctor said.

"Let it be Monday." Arnaud sniffed. "Our bush priest means to consecrate his church the day before."

"I had not known you to be so fervent in religion," the doctor said.

"Oh, I shall be like a medieval baron, it seems, with my own prelate, and a chapel within the walls," Arnaud said, with a dry laugh. "All this religiosity—it may be a little too much for me, but it appears to be healthful for Claudine."

"Yes," said the doctor, as he reached for the bottle. "She does seem to do much better now." Better than when the world was right side up, he thought, but did not say it.

Claudine rose, in the first thin light that leaked in through the jalousies, and slipped on a shift and a calico dress. She turned, facing the bed, and as the light began to grow in the room she watched her husband sleeping. Under his lids, Arnaud's eyes slipped and darted. His face assumed an aspect of ire, then shock. He flung up an arm as if to ward off an attack. Then his face drained into calm, and he rolled over onto his side and went on sleeping.

She left the bedchamber, closing the door delicately behind her. Arnaud had ordered a strong cabinet to be built of mahogany and fitted into a rear corner of the central room where they ate their meals. Claudine unlocked it with a small key from the ring at her waist. The cabinet was meant for the safekeeping of silver and fine china, but whatever such articles she'd once possessed had been stolen or smashed when the plantation was sacked in ninety-one. Now it held only some home-fired crockery, some utensils and cheap glassware.

She stooped and lifted the folded stole from the bottom shelf, and also gathered the gourd cup beside it. She'd got the cup by arrangement with a woman with a special skill in binding calabashes. There were two round protuberances at either end of a long neck. The gourd could be balanced on the smaller of these, and the larger one was cut across the hemisphere so that the whole resembled a large brown wineglass. Carrying these two items, she left the house.

Outdoors, Cléo was lighting the kitchen fire. She stood up as Claudine passed, and raised a hand in greeting. Claudine smiled her reply, and walked on. The dust on the path was loose and cool beneath her bare feet. As the mist lifted, the breeze set the fronds of the young coconut trees to trembling. Farther along, the dense expanse of the cane fields absorbed the tremor. She hesitated, closed her eyes and looked again. There was no smoke, no fire, but only the green cane standing, raising its leaves like the blades of spears.

She passed the cane mill and turned in the opposite direction from Arnaud's new distillery. The odor of burned sugar and rum gave her a momentary pang, but the breeze turned and carried the smell away from her. She went through a screen of mango and corrosol trees to the place where the rows of slave cabins had once stood. Most of them were now marked only by a few scraps of charred, decaying board amid squares of ash overgrown by new greenery. Small lizards were busy everywhere in these ruins. Those of the former slaves who still remained on the plantation had raised new *ajoupas* on the borders of gardens they'd cleared for their own benefit. Of the few little *cases* that had been rebuilt here, Fontelle and her children now occupied the nearest.

Moustique slept in the open air, apart from his sisters, on a pallet of leaves in the shelter of a lean-to roof against the rear wall of the *case*. Claudine inspected him for a moment, as she had studied the sleeping form of her husband. Moustique took his rest more calmly than Arnaud. His face was milk-colored, with the faintest tinge of coffee. There was but small trace of the blunt, rounded features of the Père Bonne-chance; he had the long nose and long jaw of his mother.

When she knelt to set the cup and stole beside the pallet, Moustique's eyes came quietly open. His gaze took in the objects, then expanded to include Claudine. He sat up and gathered his knees in his arms, leaning against the wattled wall of the *case*. If he'd been startled, he did not show it, but there was a question in his eyes.

"A gift for the church," Claudine began. She settled herself on the ground, crossing her legs under her calico skirt. She lifted the stole and unfolded the ribbon of fabric across her lap.

"This I sewed for you myself," she said, with a hint of shyness.

Moustique reached out his forefinger and touched the embroidered pattern of doves descending, scarlet on a white background.

"I am not a good seamstress," Claudine said. "Often I prick myself with the needle. I am sorry for those brown flecks, but they are marks of blood."

"Your work is very fine," Moustique said. He lifted the gourd cup and peered into the fibrous windings of its interior.

"When the spirit is present," Claudine said, "one has no need of precious metal."

Moustique set down the gourd and looked at her inquiringly.

"With these things you may replace the stole and the silver chalice, which ought to be returned to l'Abbé Delahaye."

Moustique cast his eyes down, looking at her bare feet and the pale film of dust which covered them. Claudine drew her legs in farther, so that her feet were hidden in the pool of her long skirt.

"How to begin . . ." she said. "What do you remember of your father?"

Moustique bowed his head, then raised it, his eyes full of pain.

"Yes," she told me. "I was there too. I saw how he suffered. But there was more."

Moustique lifted the gourd cup again and stared into the bottom of it. "He was kind," he said. "Indulgent, careless—even my mother complained of that. If something or someone outraged him, his anger could be terrible. But to us he was always kind."

"And to me as well," Claudine said. "He gave me absolution and brought the grace of the Holy Spirit to heal the disorder of my mind. You must understand, I had done the unforgivable. Wherever I looked, I saw burning."

With his two hands, Moustique drew the gourd cup against his breastbone and looked at her across the rim of it.

"You must know, *he* was an innocent," she went on. "When they broke him on the wheel, his blood washed away my agony." She raised her left thumb, pricked and swollen from her clumsiness with the needle. "Do you not see? Through bloodshed it is to be washed clean and through fire it will be purified."

Moustique's eyes narrowed. "When Baron mounts upon your head, he says that it must be for four hundred years."

"So many have told me," Claudine said. "But we do not know where in those years we live. The Angel of Apocalypse says there shall be no more time."

Inside the *case,* Fontelle's voice was faintly audible, and the answer of one of the girls. Presently Paulette came out of the house, a clay vessel smoothly riding on top of her head, going to fetch water from the stream. She glanced at them once and then away.

"Meanwhile," Claudine said, "we must live our days. Where there is sin there must be atonement. I am given to tell you that they suffer worse who are not permitted to atone. Your father gave me a penance, but this penance has become my joy. I cannot bring a child from my own body, but now I have many children here."

Moustique's face slipped and shifted in the glaze of tears that covered her eyes. She blinked them free.

"You yourself are father to a child," she told him. "A son, who has now four years."

Moustique colored and looked away. His blush was the rose shade of a white person's, she noticed. His lashes were long and delicate, like his sisters'.

"A priest is not meant to father children," Moustique muttered.

"That may be so," Claudine said, "but if all priests were faithful in that rule, you would not exist yourself."

Moustique set aside the gourd cup and stood up, dusting himself and looking about as if he could not choose a direction.

"Sit down," Claudine said. "From your own experience, you must know you would be wrong to leave your child without a father."

Moustique remained on his feet, arms folded over his chest.

"Return the articles which were stolen and accept these in their place—they are freely given," Claudine said. "Then you may claim your child, and the mother."

"You have been speaking to l'Abbé Delahaye, have you not?"

"I have seen him," Claudine said. "If you do as I suggest, he will not harm or prevent you."

"He will believe I am sold to the devil," Moustique muttered.

"Because you also serve the spirits?" Claudine raised her eyebrows. "But you should believe what you yourself teach: that one may serve Bon Dieu and the mysteries of Guinée together, without contradiction."

She stood up and shook out her long skirt. "Also," she said, "this is no scheme of l'Abbé Delahaye, but the motion of the Holy Spirit, which came through your father to me and which now moves through me to you."

Moustique gaped. She curtsied to him, smiled, and walked away.

That night the three women prepared the meal together as before, but when they had cleared away the dishes, all three of them disappeared, leaving their men with their rum on the dirt-floored porch. Arnaud and the doctor sat in silence, for a time, on three-legged stools against the wall. When the drums began, it felt to the doctor as if he had been hearing them all the while in the beat of his blood.

Below, the women entered the compound from the foot of the trail that led down through the stand of bamboo from the house. Cléo, Fontelle and Claudine, all dressed in white and wearing white headcloths. They walked together in a leftward loop around the rear of the church and joined a column of other white-clad women which was snaking its way up the far slope into the jungle.

Arnaud sat speechless, with a fixed regard, balancing his twisted cane on its point and letting it fall from one hand to the other. Now and then he tasted his rum. The doctor, who could think of no word to say to him, was silent also. When the first cry of the possessed rang down from the hill, Arnaud trembled as if he had himself received the shock. The doctor got up then, and laid a hand on his shoulder. Arnaud glanced up at him as if he might speak, but did not. After a moment he shifted just enough to break the contact. The doctor thanked him for his hospitality and went indoors to sleep.

At dawn the next morning they were summoned to the church by someone clanging on a pot lid. Claudine sat on the front bench, to Cléo's left, surrounded by the children she instructed. Arnaud took his seat beside her; the doctor settled across the aisle. Most of last night's celebrants were also present, still wearing their white garments. Claudine's face was haggard from her sleepless night, but she looked exalted.

"God is relation," Moustique preached. "God is others. God is love." He wore a different stole, the doctor noticed, embroidered with awkward, lumpy doves in red. The silver chalice was gone too; it had been replaced by a gourd.

The doctor bowed his head as the sermon went on. He felt the heaviness of his breathing, the darkness of his interrupted sleep. All through the night he had rolled on the wave of the distant drumming, but now he could not remember his dreams.

Moustique raised the circle of cassava above his head and tore it down the middle. He passed his hands over the gourd cup, singing the Latin words of the consecration. Behind him, to his left, a young boy thumped a drum to match his movements. Through the tingling haze of his drowsiness, the doctor moved forward and knelt at the rail to take communion. He glimpsed Claudine kneeling near him, her face shining and running with tears. Then the leathery bread was in his mouth, and Moustique brought the gourd chalice to his lips. The water was heavy, cool and sweet. Moustique put his hand on the doctor's forehead, applying a quick, firm pressure as he repeated the principal text of his sermon: *It is no longer I who live, but the Christ that lives in me.*

Next morning the doctor was witness to a scene of tenderness between Claudine and Arnaud as they parted on the wooden gallery of the *grand'case*. He sat his slightly restless mare and looked at them sidelong and reflected on the ties that bound them. The man's hand lingered on the woman's cheek. Then Arnaud turned quickly away and came with rapid steps to his own horse.

They rode out. Arnaud made no further complaint against his conscription; he did not mention it at all, though his face tightened as he surveyed the workers in his cane fields on their way down to the main road. In their earlier conversation the doctor had not found it necessary to make the point that Toussaint, amid all the current turmoil, had suffered a moment of mistrust in his alliances with the old *grand blancs*. While it was true that capable officers were always in acute demand, it was even more true that Toussaint did not want to leave any one of Arnaud's class in a position to engage in conspiracies or even raise open revolt behind his lines. The doctor imagined that Arnaud understood all this well enough and that there was no use speaking of it.

Three days later, the two of them had joined Dessalines's encampment surrounding Jacmel. Despite his first reaction, Arnaud fell into his service with a will. Toussaint had seconded him to Christophe rather than Dessalines, an arrangement he seemed to prefer. As for the doctor, he was kept thoroughly occupied in the hospital tents, for the resistance at Jacmel was desperate in proportion to its hopelessness, and there were many casualties, as Arnaud had predicted.

The morale of the black soldiers was not at its best. Moyse's notion, that this conflict was a misbegotten war of brother against brother, had caught on among them. Prior to his descent on Jacmel, Dessalines had rallied his troops by night on the plain of Léogane. While the supplies and ammunition were being distributed, stars had begun falling all over the sky, like a rain of burning fire. The men were thrown into terror by the starfall, which they took as an omen that their spirits had turned against them. Also, on the more practical side of the matter, Jacmel was one of the best-fortified towns of the colony, and Beauvais had prepared it well for a siege before he decamped.

Toussaint himself arrived to direct the early phase of the assault. Under heavy fire from the Jacmel forts, he built his own redoubts along the beach, to discourage any relief effort that might come by sea. Then he sent Christophe and Laplume on a night attack against Grand Fort and Fort Tavigne, which lay outside the entrenchments of the Rigaudins. In this engagement, Arnaud distinguished himself by successfully exhorting his men to hold Tavigne, continuing to face fire himself, though wounded in the shoulder. Grand Fort was also taken in the first rush, but a desperate effort of the defenders recovered it for Jacmel before the night was done.

No matter. Toussaint brought his heaviest artillery to Fort Tavigne, and from that height commenced to shell that town. The fiery rain, he pointed out to the troops under Dessalines, was now falling on their enemies.

The rumor that Pétion was commanding at Jacmel, which the doctor had reported to Arnaud, proved to be incorrect. Up until the taking of Fort Tavigne, another officer named Birot had been in charge of the town. After the fort was overrun and the bombardment began, Birot and his officers concluded it would be best to evacuate as best they might; however, the men in the ranks refused to follow them. With a handful of officers who shared his pessimistic view, Birot slipped out of Jacmel in a small boat and sailed west to Les Cayes, where he reported to Rigaud the parlous situation in the besieged town.

For months, Rigaud had done little enough to prosecute the war he had started. Above all he hoped for relief from France, if only in the form of an endorsement. While he waited for news, he could not settle on a course of action, but rather poured himself into his pleasures, which were various and exotic. But now he set out to relieve Jacmel, though with a contingent of only five hundred men. This mad sally was shattered by the regiments of Dessalines and Charles Belair. No matter how many were killed, the black soldiers of the north kept coming down, till finally Rigaud's troops broke under the wave and began to flee. Rigaud dismounted his horse and snatched at their shoulders or their coattails, trying to turn them back to the battle. When he failed, he began to scream at them: *Run then, you cowards, since honor is not enough to make you face death.* Finally Rigaud himself was dragged from the field by his own officers, lest he be killed or taken prisoner.

Following this catastrophe, Rigaud sent Pétion to Jacmel by sea; he managed to reach the town intact, paddling a canoe underneath the cannonfire from Toussaint's new batteries on the shore. The situation when Pétion arrived was still worse than what Birot had described. The soldiers were so weak from privation they had barely strength to hold up their weapons, and ammunition was so low they had to gather the missiles that rained down on them day and night to fire them back from their own guns.

All this news was vaguely known to the besiegers through several spies inside the town. And yet the resistance was still very stubborn. Christophe's best effort to take the Grand Fort a second time had been deflected, with heavy losses. Every day there were heavy losses, and the doctor labored hour after hour in the infirmary tent, up to his elbows and shoulders in blood. He had insisted that both Giaou and Riau be sent down from the front line to help him in these efforts.

Picking bullets out of Arnaud had become a regular activity for these three. Arnaud was hit half a dozen times, but never fatally, in spite of his enthusiasm for exposing himself to the enemy guns. "Creole courage," Captain Maillart muttered, at night under the tent he shared with the doctor. "You may call him cruel, call him foolhardy—call him a wastrel of the lives of his men. But the man *will* stand and fight."

The canvas of the tent flared red in the light of a shell bursting over the town. Maillart's face appeared, drawn and exhausted, in the crimson flash. The doctor knew he hated the siege, the spectacle of their opponents hemmed in to suffer and starve like rats in a trap. They might all hate it equally, but it made no difference—the doctor could barely register his own feeling, through the layers of his fatigue.

Arnaud would return to combat as soon as the doctor had him bandaged. No wound he took seemed to affect him, till finally, at the end of another terrible, interminable day, he came stumbling into camp with a look so deathly that the doctor thought he must have been hit in the vitals at last. But Arnaud protested that he was unhurt, and he didn't seem to be bleeding anywhere.

Both the doctor and captain offered to share their small portions of cornmeal mush. By that time rations were short even for the besiegers, whose numbers had picked the surrounding area nearly clean. In the shadows at the edge of the ring of firelight, Riau and Guiaou were probing goat bones for their marrow. From the infirmary shelter, a bit farther off, came cries of delirium and occasional groans of pain. Arnaud would accept no nourishment, but when rum was produced, he reached for it eagerly. Finally, in fragments, his story spilled out.

That afternoon, Pétion in his growing desperation had concluded to send the women and children out of Jacmel to throw themselves on the mercy of the enemy. Some three thousand of them had drifted toward Christophe's position. The order was given to fire on them with grapeshot.

"The *women?*" Maillart hissed, leaning forward.

"Indeed," said Arnaud, "and also the starving infants they had at the breast." But not all of them had been killed. For the survivors, Christophe had scattered some old bread on the ground. "They pecked it up like chickens," Arnaud said. He stopped, and stared into the fire as if it were alive with devils.

"And then?" the doctor asked unwillingly.

Arnaud pulled on the gourd of rum. "The surviving women were rounded up and herded to Habitation Ogé. There they were forced to descend into a dry well, covered with firewood and burned alive."

Captain Maillart was on his feet. "I cannot believe that Christophe ordered such a thing."

"Where the order came from, I can't say," Arnaud told him. "But you may believe that he carried it out. And what would you believe of me?"

Maillart lowered his eyes, looked this way and that. The doctor was frozen, cross-legged on the ground. Guiaou and Riau held their goat bones unconsciously in their tallow-streaked hands.

"What choice did you have?" Maillart muttered.

"What indeed?" Arnaud said, and rose himself. "I feel that I should have found some alternative. But perhaps I am best suited for such work." He turned and left the circle of firelight.

"Wait, man, wait," the captain called after him, but the doctor caught him before he could follow.

"Let him go," the doctor said, and with a bewildered shake of his head, Maillart subsided.

*   *   *

It had been six weeks since Pétion had come to the relief of Jacmel, and soon after the ill-fated exodus of the women, he concluded that the men must try to fight their way out. One of the garrison had told him of a little-used path which led out of Jacmel across Habitation Ogé on a short route to the mountains. Throughout the day, Pétion bombarded the road in the opposite direction, as a diversion, and after nightfall he led his men out by the other way suggested to him, under cover of a fort called the blockhouse.

One of the spies had escaped Jacmel the day before, and informed Dessalines of Pétion's escape route. So Dessalines's response to the diversion was itself no more than a pretense. Once the darkness was complete, Dessalines shifted the entire twenty thousand men of his command to block the retreat of the Jacmel garrison, now reduced to fourteen hundred. Against those odds, and with no hope of quarter, Pétion's men fought to the death and even, almost, beyond it. Tumbled in the mêlée, the doctor saw more than one man spurting blood from a severed arm and continuing to do battle with the other. Dessalines was impressed as well, enough to call a cease-fire. But the men of Jacmel used the respite to re-form themselves for one last desperate effort—they cut through Dessalines's lines to reach the mountains and the jungle.

Of the fourteen hundred who'd left Jacmel, only six hundred survived the battle. "What I could do," the doctor heard Dessalines remark, "if I had such men in my command."

For all his ruthlessness, his thorough mistrust of white blood, Dessalines respected courage wherever he found it. Before the campaign against Jacmel had begun, a young mulatto officer in Port-au-Prince had broken his own sword over his knee, to demonstrate his refusal to put his arms in the service of the invading army from the north. But Dessalines had adopted this youth into his command and made him a special protégé.

On March 13, 1800, the army of the north marched into Jacmel. The mood was less of triumph than of exhaustion, and the doctor had more work than ever before, for the acres of wounded soldiers surrounding him were compounded by hundreds of sick and starved civilians who had survived by a breath or two. The streets and squares were littered with the carcasses of mules and donkeys and draft horses which in the last days of the siege had been devoured to their ligaments. Vultures lined the rooftops, hungry for more death.

In a couple of days Toussaint rode in, to take formal possession of the town. Within the week he'd ordered Dessalines on the attack again, to press the advantage against Rigaud. Dessalines marched against Grand Goâve. Toussaint, meanwhile, summoned the doctor and some others of his staff, and told them to make ready for a fast gallop to Le Cap, where a new commission from France had recently arrived.

36

The *casernes* of Le Cap were not so crowded as usual, since so many men had been dispatched to the south, but there was still a strong garrison in the barracks, and the doctor, with Maillart and Arnaud, made a private retreat to the Cigny house, where accommodations would be more congenial. The house was dusty when they arrived, and the news was thin. Monsieur Cigny had been in town within the week, but according to the servants he had no recent word from his wife, nor any apparent concern about her silence. The indifference which covered her romantic adventures must cut two ways, the doctor reflected. Cigny had deposited a quantity of brown sugar with his broker and then, after two days, returned to his plantation.

"So *he* was not conscripted," Arnaud began to grumble.

"He is well past the age for military service," Maillart pointed out.

"Yes, and he can only produce brown sugar now, while I was sending out white."

"One could hardly imagine him absorbing even a single musket ball," the captain said. "Much less half a dozen, like yourself."

As Arnaud began to soften under the warmth of this flattery, the doctor followed the servants into the yard. There was one old woman who had a particular fondness for Isabelle, whom she'd known since childhood. And she did have news, but it had come by a long and crooked route. Someone in the harbor at Fort Liberté had spoken to someone who'd brought out a load of coffee from the mountains of Vallière, and that person had passed the word to another, and so it had traveled from mouth to ear until it reached the Place Clugny in Le Cap. All was calm enough at Vallière; there had been no raids, no disturbances or revolts, and that plantation which had passed from the late Sieur de Maltrot to Choufleur was even producing a good deal of coffee now. A woman in the *grand'case* there was supposed to have had great trouble in childbirth, so severe that they'd had to send for the wisest leaf woman in the hills.

"Did she live? What of the child?" the doctor blurted. "Tell me, *grann,* was it Nanon?"

Here the old woman's lips closed to a thin seam; she gave the doctor a canny look, but she would say no more.

That night the doctor slept uneasily, though exhausted from the last couple of days in the saddle; Toussaint had pushed them from Jacmel to Le Cap in half the time humanly possible. He kept starting awake in a flush of fear, for the child he knew (but Paul was safe at Habitation Thibodet) and for the child he might never know . . . At dawn he rose and washed and dressed and went to Government House to look for Pascal.

"There are three of them this time," Pascal advised him. They strolled the avenue by Government House, keeping their distance from others on the promenade. "General Michel, Julien Raimond whom you know, and Colonel Vincent."

"The engineer," the doctor said. "I know him too."

"They landed in Spanish Santo Domingo," Pascal said. "When they crossed the border they were arrested!—by Moyse, I believe. Michel is so overwrought at this treatment that I think he will return to France at the first opportunity."

"And Vincent?"

"He was dragged over the mountains at the end of a rope—made to run along behind Moyse's cavalry. Atrocious, you know." Pascal raised his thumb toward his teeth, then lowered it, at the doctor's glance. "He seems to have borne up very well," he went on. "Hardly even to have taken offense, if you can believe it."

"A resilient fellow," the doctor said. "I like that in him."

"Yes . . . he is with Toussaint even now."

"And what are his orders?" the doctor inquired. "Toussaint was concerned, as you know—and that rumor of a whole fleet on the way? Is there a regular military expedition following these people?"

They had just turned into the court of Government House, and Pascal lowered his voice as they approached the loiterers on the steps. "I don't know anything about a fleet. As for the orders, I haven't seen them. But Toussaint is to continue as General-in-Chief."

"So . . ." the doctor sighed as they climbed the stairs and entered the corridor. "Then Toussaint *is* justified. And Rigaud has waited for nothing."

"It would seem so," Pascal murmured. "There are other details, but I do not know them. Only there is some sort of new government in France—I don't understand exactly what."

As they walked into Toussaint's anteroom, Pascal stopped talking, for others were already waiting there. He and the doctor sat down in chairs along the wall, inclining their heads toward the heavy doors of the inner cabinet, through which they could hear nothing.

"My dear friend," Toussaint said, turning his kerchiefed head to one side and carefully looking at Vincent from the corner of his eye. "I am so very sorry for the accident of your reception. All a great misunderstanding— and Moyse is impetuous, as you know."

Vincent brushed down the front of his coat. "I know it better than ever before."

"I will speak to him," Toussaint said. "Yes . . . very seriously." He stroked his jaw. "But why did you land in Santo Domingo, instead of coming to Le Cap? It must have been this that provoked his suspicion."

For a moment, neither of them spoke; the voices of cart haulers came in from the street. They both knew that Hédouville had taken the same approach through Santo Domingo upon his first arrival in the colony.

"One did not quite know the state of things here," Vincent said carefully. "There were rumors of rebellion from Le Cap all the way to Môle Saint Nicolas."

"There is no reason for concern," Toussaint said. "Everything is in perfect order, as you see."

"Oh, you have my absolute confidence." Vincent rocked slightly in his chair, shifting the weight from his blistered heels. "As well as that of the First Consul."

Toussaint leaned sharply forward, like a jockey urging his horse on. "Then why does he send a fleet with soldiers?"

"Oh, that?" Vincent said. "General, I am surprised to find you taken in. That story was a rumor planted to deceive our enemies in Europe. In reality, that fleet is bound for Egypt, to carry reinforcements to our armies there."

"Ah," said Toussaint, leaning back. He spread his hand over the dispatch case which Vincent had set on the table before him, the moment he entered the room. "So he is cunning, your First Consul. *Rusé.*"

"He is a military man," Vincent, again with care. "Much like yourself."

Pursing his lips slightly, Toussaint lifted his hand from the dispatch case.

"I have seen your sons," Vincent said, in an easier tone. "They are healthy and prosperous, and thrive in their studies—especially Placide. Isaac is . . . rather the more volatile of the two."

"Well, I am pleased," Toussaint said. "You are kind to visit them."

"They are with the fleet."

Toussaint made a movement of surprise. Then he settled himself and said contemplatively, "So they will see Guinée."

"At least they will see Egypt, if only from shipboard," Vincent told him. "It will contribute to their education, certainly. And General Saguenat has been instructed to care for them like his own children. They are kept in the most perfect security."

"Yes," said Toussaint. "I know."

Absently he touched the knot which secured his headcloth at the nape of his neck. Vincent looked into his molasses-colored, red-rimmed eyes. From outside the door there was a scraping of chairs as other people found seats in the waiting room.

"But truly," Vincent said, with a gesture at the dispatch case. "France supports you absolutely, as it has always supported the cause of the blacks."

Toussaint masked the beginning of his smile with the usual movement of his hand. Sober, he opened the dispatch case and lifted out the documents. Raising the papers near to his eyes, he began to sort through them.

"You see," Vincent told him. "All is in order."

"Yes," said Toussaint. He laid down the sheaf of papers and stood up, moving around the desk. "I believe I ought to bring in our friends."

He drew the double doors inward, glanced around the anteroom, and beckoned to the doctor and Pascal, leaving the others to wait. Pascal pushed the doors shut behind him, while the doctor embrace Vincent with a genuine warmth. Tousaint, who had returned to his seat behind the desk, lifted a document from among the dispatches and began to read aloud.

Citizens, a constitution which has not been able to sustain itself against multiple violations is now replaced by a new pact designed to affirm liberty.

Article ninety-one carries the principle that the French colonies shall be ruled by special laws.

That disposition derives from the nature of things, and from the difference of climates.

Toussaint slid one sheet of paper beneath another and went on reading from the top of the next page. His voice was harsh and surprisingly loud.

The difference of habits, of morals, of interests, the diversity of soil, agriculture, production, requires various modifications.

One of the first acts of the new legislature will be the drafting of new laws designed to rule you.

Toussaint stopped, and turned back to the previous page.

"Special laws," he said. "This idea has been put forward before in Saint Domingue." He looked at Vincent. "Though of course, that was before you had ever visited our colony." He licked his tongue and leafed through the papers. "I see among the members of the new government names I recognize from former times," he said. He laid down the papers and covered them with his hand. "You assure me," he said, "that these gentlemen support the cause of the blacks, as they have always done."

The three white men shifted their feet and looked over each other's shoulders. All three of them knew perfectly well that the men Toussaint mentioned had been slave owners and ferocious defenders of their practice. The doctor wondered if Vincent knew (as Toussaint implied he did not) that the whole question of "special laws" had been a device to maintain slavery in the colonies at the same time that the French Revolution was proclaiming the universal rights of man.

"I have heard that the First Consul has a wife," Toussaint remarked.

"Josephine," Vincent said. "A lady worthy in every respect of her husband's great capabilities. Though I can attest that she is not only intelligent and perspicacious, but perfectly natural in her manner."

"Ah," Toussaint said, leaning back and stroking his jawline. "Then you are acquainted with her."

"That is my honor." Vincent coughed. "Only slightly, to be sure."

"She is herself a Creole, I have heard," Toussaint went on. "She has her substance from some great plantation in the colonies. And so she must have a particular understanding of the need for *special laws* to govern them."

"General, you are exceedingly well informed," Vincent said, while

Pascal and the doctor exchanged a private look of horror. "Of course, you also know that numerous such Creole whites serve loyally in your own armies, as we speak."

Toussaint stood stock still. His hand floated evenly, suspended a quarter-inch above the desktop. He had disappeared completely into his wide interior reservoir of stillness. Such moments always gave the doctor a combination of anticipation and fear.

"The First Consul's lady takes a particular interest in your sons," Vincent said, in a more moderate tone. "As does the First Consul himself, of course."

"Yes," said Toussaint. "I know."

"And General, you have only to observe . . ." Vincent leaned across the desk to indicate another passage in the document. Toussaint raised the sheet toward his nose and read.

> The following words: «Brave blacks, remember that only the French people recognize your liberty and the equality of your rights» shall be written in letters of gold on all the batallion flags of the national guard of the colony of Saint Domingue.' "

Toussaint laid the papers aside, face down. "Such an impressive sentiment," he said, and waited. "I wonder, if the First Consul considers me his equal, why does he not write directly to me."

Vincent colored slightly. "He sends *me* to assure you of the strength of his regard."

Toussaint studied him through lidded eyes. "Of course," he said finally, hand sweeping across the vestigial smile. "When such assurance comes from you, Colonel Vincent, I accept it, with all confidence."

Vincent smiled, with the hint of a bow. Toussaint picked up the papers and passed them to the doctor, his thumb anchoring the page from which he'd last read. "And your opinion?"

"An impressive sentiment," the doctor echoed. "Perhaps a little lengthy to be sewn upon a flag."

"You are correct," Toussaint said. "It will take some time to do so."

When the others had been dismissed, the doctor lingered, hovering at the side of the desk, trying to gauge if Toussaint's humor was auspicious for his request. But surely, on balance, Vincent's news had been good. And there might not be a better moment any time soon.

"General," he said. "If it is possible, I should very much like—"

"—to go to Vallière." Toussaint looked up sharply. "It is not possible. All is well at Vallière, but you must return to the south, no later than tomorrow. There will be more wounds for you to bind." He reached up for the doctor's right hand and held it without pressure, looking up into his eyes. "You are needed there," he said, "and no one knows it better than yourself."

By the time the doctor rejoined the army in the south, Dessalines had occupied the ashes of Grand Goâve, at the cost of six hundred of his own men dead and another four hundred wounded and waiting for care. As neither Guiaou nor Riau had been slain or hurt, the doctor engineered their reassignment from the battle lines to the medical service. With the number of injured so great and conditions so crowded, they lost nearly half of them to infection, dysentery and incidental fevers.

Despite the loss of his forward positions, and especially Jacmel, so crucial to defending the entry to the whole southern peninsula, Rigaud was not disposed to concede defeat. Whatever news he might have had of Vincent's mission had not swayed him toward submission to Toussaint. It was rumored he had sent his own agents to France and continued to hope for a better report from them.

Dessalines, meanwhile, pressed his advantage, via his usual tactic of moving his men at horrible speeds over terrain believed by the enemy to be impassable. Soon he had occupied the heights surrounding Petit Goâve, where the Rigaudins had retreated. They might also have been annihilated there, except that their commander sent two of his men to an outpost in the guise of messengers from Toussaint—Dessalines was to wait for reinforcement before he advanced. The ruse produced enough hesitation for the Rigaudins to slip out of the trap and regroup at the bridge of Miragoâne.

That was a strong position, especially after Pétion had cut the bridge and dug entrenchments on the bank he defended. The most suicidal determination of Dessalines's men could not carry them across the ford, under the constant barrage of grapeshot which refilled the hospitals every day and transformed the surrounding swamps into a cesspool of blood and putrefying corpses. A thousand men were lost in a single day. While continuing this frontal assault, Dessalines sent a part of his force across the inland mountains and down through a mangrove swamp to the rivershore. Rigaud had raised no defense in this area, but the swamp was not so impenetrable as he had believed. By night, Dessalines infiltrated more than half his army to the rear of the Rigaudins. At dawn, Pétion saw that he had been outflanked; he spiked his cannon and abandoned his position at the bridge. Rigaud, with a separate force directly under his own command, engaged his enemy on a field nearby, but by the end of the day was obliged to give up Miragoâne. Dessalines pursued the Rigaudins as far as Saint Michel and had soon taken this town as well.

There, Toussaint ordered him to halt, on the theory that Rigaud must now be ready to sue for peace. But Rigaud had no such intention. Wherever he was made to withdraw, he left the land a desert, burning the fields and fouling the wells with the carcasses of dead horses or cattle. *Leave the trees with their roots in the air* was always his parting order.

Toussaint had moved south to Port-au-Prince, where he was obliged to unravel another conspiracy to assassinate him. Furious at the latest attempt, he sent Dessalines back to the attack. Of the thirty thousand men that had composed the army of the north, less than half now remained effective, but still the Rigaudins were outnumbered by a factor of ten to one and were roundly defeated on the plain called Fond des Nègres.

"Is he mad, or drunk, or both at the same time?" Captain Maillart inquired at the end of the day. Seasoned soldier that he was, the carnage had made him miserable.

"Who can tell?" the doctor answered, as he scrubbed the blood of the wounded from his forearms. "Maybe he is insane with pride." He dried off, stretched out on his back and looked up at the night sky. "Or maybe Toussaint was right, that Rigaud truly believes his is the superior race. After all, there was a time when the French army and the colonial militia believed that one white man was the equal in battle of ten, or twenty, or fifty blacks . . ."

At that the captain bit his lip and glanced across the campfire at Arnaud, who volunteered no reaction; perhaps he had not heard.

Rigaud had fallen back to the town of Aquin, where he ranged the remnants of his men for another hopeless battle on the open field. Mounted at the head of his cavalry, he led charge after charge, breaking against the mass of Dessalines's troops like surf against the ironbound cliffs, till all his clothing was ragged with bullet holes. In the end all of his men were scattered, and Rigaud himself was driven to headlong flight, amid a general rout, all the way to the town of Les Cayes. Over the debris of the battle, Dessalines's men pursued the work of extermination against a few isolated pockets of Rigaudins who'd failed to find any escape route.

In the last hour of that day, Arnaud appeared at the hospital with a summons for the doctor. Dessalines wanted him on the battlefield. When the doctor asked his reason, Arnaud only shook his head. Somewhat ill at ease with this mystery, the doctor brought Riau along with him, leaving Guiaou to manage the wounded as best he might.

Flanked by Arnaud and Riau, he crossed the field of battle, which was littered everywhere with corpses and the carcasses of animals, and still adrift with clouds of smoke, though most of the shooting had stopped. Waste, waste was everywhere. How much Toussaint objected to such wantonness, the doctor thought, and touched the pistols on his belt. Here and there were tatters of musketry, shouts of rage and other cries. Amid a cluster of men ahead, the doctor saw the winking metal of Dessalines's plumed helmet.

Despite the brutal desperation of all that campaign, Dessalines's appearance had assumed a greater and greater magnificence throughout. But now he was divesting himself of his splendor. A lieutenant stood by, receiving his vestments: the helmet polished to a mirror sheen, the lavishly decorated uniform coat. Finally the shirt as well. Over the heavy muscles of his back, the net of ropy white whip scars contracted and released.

Some half a dozen Rigaudins stood by, surrounded by three times their number of the men of Dessalines. They had been disarmed but not otherwise restrained. One of them, a *sacatra* by his skin tone, sat cross-legged on the ground, eyes fixed dully on his lap, his right hand clasped over a seeping wound on his left arm. The doctor's attention was drawn to this. He did not know why he had been summoned. He did not want to look at Choufleur, who stood balanced forward on the balls of his feet, his coat removed and his shirt loosened, holding his cavalry sword with its point toward the ground.

Maillart was in charge of the guard party; the doctor shot him a questioning look, but the captain seemed unwilling to risk so much as a blink or a shrug. As the lieutenant handed Dessalines his sword, a sort of sigh ran round the men, and they shifted and widened the circle. With the swirling motion common among the black stick fighters, Dessalines rotated the blade one time around the outside of his arm. When the blade came up, it caught the red light of sun.

Darkness. The doctor coughed—smoke had got caught in his throat. The dark was only his exhaustion, rushing up behind his eyes. Why had he been called here? He did not want to be here. Choufleur's face was very pale, though streaked with smoke and dirt. He was looking only at Dessalines, not at the man's black visage but at the space between hip and shoulder, whence the blade would come. Choufleur's right foot advanced, sliding over blood-caked dirt. His blade was low. Against the pallor of his face the freckles were compressed as husks of burned-out stars.

Dessalines stepped in screaming, the blade whipping around like a tornado, but Choufleur stopped it with a more economical parry, and slashed down on Dessalines's blade at his hand, his teeth showing a tight white line with the movement, but Dessalines's hilt held. They separated. Choufleur circled to the right. Dessalines's expression clouded, compressed. He closed, the force of the rush pressing Choufleur against the ring of onlookers, which gave way to give him room. Again the thrust was parried, and Choufleur slipped under the blade with a back slash against Dessalines's calf, which cut into his boot leather.

It was clear enough that Choufleur was the better fencer. Dessalines, though heavier, was certainly as quick on his feet, but Choufleur had the more practiced arm and hand. Dessalines's men had begun to clap and sway, humming to their rhythm. The Rigaudins dared make no such demonstration in favor of their champion. The wounded man had been excluded from the circle, and between the legs of the others the doctor caught just a glimpse of him. He had lain or fallen on his side, with the wounded arm uppermost.

Dessalines rushed, with a complex under-and-over attack. Choufleur was inside the pattern of his sword, a little ahead of it even, for as Dessalines's blade came down, the point of Choufleur's sword opened a red line on his inner forearm from the elbow to the wrist, then caught the hilt of Dessalines's weapon and twirled it out of his hand.

Amid the excited shouts of the Rigaudins, the doctor thought he heard Maillart's cry of approbation—the sheer skill of the maneuver— but when he looked that way the captain had stifled his approval, his eyes lowered. Choufleur's blade was centered upon Dessalines's navel. The insolent smile. Perhaps a yard's distance between them. Dessalines stood with his wounded arm forward. If he was concerned at the shift of position, he did not show it. When he flexed the fingers of his right hand, blood came running into his palm. Unarmed, he moved to close.

Choufleur stepped back and dropped his own sword on the ground.

After an instant of shocked silence, the black soldiers began to clap and sway again. The doctor glanced at Riau, who wore his most masked expression. Riau's body swayed with the others around him, bending with the wind that moved them all, though he had not taken up the clapping or the chanting. Dessalines and Choufleur moved around each other. A rush and they were joined, struggling at each other's shoulders, bowed legs straining. Dessalines's wounded forearm smeared an arc of blood all over the back of Choufleur's shirt.

Then the two men were on the ground, tumbling over each other, and somehow a knife had come into play, in Choufleur's hand; it hummed slightly, shallowly, over Dessalines's back, unrolling a new hammock of red lines over the white lines of the whip scars. Dessalines did not seem to be much affected by the deft cuts. He got an arm around Choufleur's back, lifted and dropped, driving his shoulder into Choufleur's midsection. Choufleur's mouth came open, tongue thrusting out. When they separated, Dessalines held the knife.

Darkness. Once the doctor's eyes had cleared, he saw Dessalines and Choufleur both on their feet, circling, Choufleur breathing painfully by the look on his face, bruised from the deep blow to his chest. His movement had become a little dull. Dessalines feinted with the knife, then grinned and threw it up and away, out of the ring. Gone. Beads of blood stood out all over his back, on the fresh lines which had just been cut. He ran his left thumb along his inner forearm, tasted his own blood and charged.

Choufleur's abdomen was caught between Dessalines's scissoring legs, so that he writhed and strained for breath. Twisting, he got his hip engaged against Dessalines's thigh, caught a breath—his arms were useless, pinned in a bear hug against his sides. He sank his teeth into the black man's throat.

The clapping and chanting stopped. There was a horrible, motionless moment. The witnesses closed tighter around the men who struggled on the ground. Dessalines strained and squeezed with arms and legs, but Choufleur's jaws did not loosen. The doctor wondered with an astral detachment whether the teeth might not actually find an important blood vessel.

Dessalines took one hand out of his octopus grip and caught hold of Choufleur's ear. He wrenched, lifting, twisting; the pain must have been unimaginable, but Choufleur kept working with his teeth, a rime of blood running around his jaws. When the ear tore loose, flowering blood, Choufleur lost his jawhold for just a second, enough for Dessalines to push his chin up, wrap an arm snake-like around his neck. He turned on his hip, cradling Choufleur's purpling face with a strange air of gentleness. Squeeze and relax. The clapping and chanting had resumed. With each relaxation Choufleur sucked for air while his ear poured blood down Dessalines's forearm. With each squeeze, Choufleur's face turned scarlet. The impulsion of the black man's movement seemed to come from the net of scars, with blood flowing over them, the scars binding and loosening, more than the man. The scars refused to release the pressure, and Choufleur's face went from purple to black. His boot heels drummed a tattoo on the ground. Dessalines shifted his grip, catching Choufleur's chin and the back of his head, and with an unwinding movement of both arms rotated the head around until, following a dreadful ripping, crunching sound, it hung flaccid from the broken neck. With a sigh, he rolled away from the body.

Silence. Dessalines was up on his knees, the hollow of his chest pumping. They could all hear him breathe, like a saw on a log. The doctor began to consider his wounds. The cuts on his back were probably inconsequential, though of course one must treat them against infection. Was this the task for which he had been summoned? The sword cut on the inner forearm might very well be more serious, though from appearances it had severed no important ligament or tendon. Unless Dessalines had gone on using his hurt arm and hand by the sheer implacable force of his will alone. But the bite would be the worst of all, undoubtedly a very nasty thing.

The sun threw a red stain over the ground, darkening as the rain clouds began to blow up. Buzzards came flopping down out of the sky like stinking ragbags, hopping from one corpse to the next. Dessalines was on his feet, retrieving Choufleur's sword. He stopped and lifted one of Choufleur's limp, dead legs, and inserted the sword point into the seam between his buttocks. With a quick, muscular thrust, pulling back on the leg he held at the same time, he impaled the body all the way up to the throat. The slack head rolled sideways and disgorged a little blood.

The doctor gulped. He could not seem to close his eyes or move his head. Riau stood by him, neither more nor less expressive than a tree. Dessalines levered the sword upward with the sound of breaking bone, cutting through Choufleur's sex and his trunk all the way to the join of his rib cage. With a twist of the sword point, he spun the guts out over the ground.

Silence. Dessalines held the sword horizontally between both hands and snapped up his knee to break it. He dropped the pieces on the body. The ring of men watching slackened, began to dissolve. That same lieutenant came forward and began handing Dessalines the various articles of his clothing, which he assumed with a queer formality, as though he were being dressed by a valet. If he wanted medical help, he did not say so, and the doctor felt reluctant to approach him without invitation. Arnaud was on his hands and knees, vomiting in the bloody dirt. No one seemed to look at him, but Captain Maillart helped him up when he was finished.

The doctor thought then of the wounded mulatto officer—perhaps he could do something for him now—but the man had bled to death during the fight, or at any rate was now dead. The other prisoners stood looking dully at their boots. With his wounded arm, Dessalines made a short, chopping gesture in their direction.

"*Fé pyè yo sauté tè.*"

They began to move across the plain toward the camp, the hospital, leaving a squad behind with the prisoners. Presently there was another quick rattle of musketry, then the firing squad rejoined them at a brisk, energetic trot. Make their feet jump off the earth, Dessalines had said. It was certainly a vivid expression.

Red, the sun cracked against the horizon like the yolk of a spoiled egg. They were walking into the hot blaze of it. Now and then the doctor stumbled over something he did not especially want to identify. Riau's hand would come under his elbow to steady him. Already the smell of putrescence was general—decay ran so rapidly in this country. The first plump raindrop smashed into his face. Let it rain, he thought, let it all be washed away; he did not care if his pistols were wet nor even if he took fever.

The image of Choufleur's impaled, eviscerated body was ever present to his mind. Whether he opened or closed his eyes, he went on seeing it. There was nothing to do about it or to think about it. It was simply there, a part of himself, forever. A person must be composed of such moments—all he had seen, all he had known. Without knowing why he thought of Madame Fortier, wished that he could be in her presence and hear her voice. But for the moment he was alone, shoulder to shoulder with his speechless friends. They'd all seen such sights before, he thought, and doubtless they would go on seeing them.

Colonel Vincent, with the cheerful insouciance which caused so many of his acquaintances to love him, volunteered to go on a conciliatory mission to Rigaud. Toussaint concurred and the agent Roume wrote a safe-conduct for him. With this document as his only defense, Vincent debarked from a schooner off the south coast and rowed himself into the harbor at Les Cayes.

The safe-conduct did no more than inspire his immediate arrest. He was brought before Rigaud. When the colored general had grasped the essence of his message—that France continued to support Toussaint's authority over him, and that Toussaint's current order relieved him of his command—he produced a dagger from his clothes and made to stab Vincent on the spot.

Vincent, whose confidence in the safe-conduct had not been very great, had provided himself with another instrument: a letter from one of Rigaud's sons, who was being educated in France on a program similar to that of Toussaint's children. In this letter, the young Rigaud addressed Vincent as his "second father." When he had read this far, Rigaud reversed the dagger in his hand and offered the pommel to Vincent, crying, "Take my blood!—it belongs to you!" As Vincent declined the honor, Rigaud tried to stab himself. His subalterns disarmed him and hauled him away.

The Rigaudins were sick of war and knew they could not win it. Much of their property had been ruined by the general's scorched-earth tactic. When the content of Vincent's missives became known, Rigaud's last supporters fell away. The next time he rang the tocsin to summon his troops, next to no one responded to the alarm. Rigaud slipped out of Les Cayes by sea, meaning to make his way to France to plead his case. Shortly thereafter, Toussaint marched into Les Cayes without a battle and proclaimed a general amnesty for all the rebels who survived.

37

In dream he heard birdsong, and the purling of water; he was half asleep, half waking, turning on the bed. A harsh green voice spoke near his ear, *Ba'm manjé,* then after a moment, *M'ap prié pou'w.* The sound of the stream was a filament of dream that sought to draw him down again, but he shifted, opened his eyes with a start. For a moment he was unsure where he was. Paul stood at the end of the bed watching him soberly. The great green parrot, perched with its claws wrapped round the boy's forearm, gave him the air of some tiny antique falconer.

"*Ba'm manjé,*" the parrot repeated. Give me food.

The doctor shook his head and pushed himself up against the head-board, rubbing the point of his beard with his thumb. He spread his arms, and as Paul came forward into his embrace, the parrot flopped down onto the floor. Tocquet had acquired the bird from a trapper in the mountains, complete with clipped wings and a few Creole phrases, to amuse the children—though Elise affected to detest this pet. The doctor inhaled the warm scent that rose from his son's neck. Sophie hung in the doorway, dark curls flung across her face, putting her head into the room and then withdrawing it with a giggle. The doctor opened his right arm to invite her to him also, but she blushed and darted out into the hall. Paul followed. The parrot hopped across the board floor after the children.

Barefoot, his shirt hanging loose over his trousers, the doctor walked out onto the gallery with a yawn. Whatever he'd dreamed was lost to him now . . . Elise, already seated at the table, poured out a cup of coffee as he approached. A pack train of charcoal burners was just circling the pool toward the rear of the house, their ash-powdered donkeys bearing the fuel for the day. The doctor plucked a small *banane-figue* from the stalk in the center of the table and cut into the peel with his thumbnail.

Elise drew back slightly as the parrot lofted itself onto the table with a pump of its trimmed wings.

"Oh, the brute," she said, exasperated. Her face was full and flush, for she was three months pregnant. The parrot twisted its head to the side, riveting one eye on the banana stalk, which Elise pulled away. The children pressed against the table, giggling.

"*Ba'm manjé,*" the parrot said, and Paul extended a scrap of sweet cassava bread.

"Child, your fingers," Elise hissed at him. But the parrot accepted the bread quite decorously as Paul snatched back his hand. He and Sophie collapsed together, round-eyed.

"What was Xavier thinking?" Elise complained. "To introduce this creature to my house. Look. That beak is like a razor. And with a child to come."

"*M'ap prié pou'w,*" the parrot said, having finished the morsel of cassava. I will pray for you.

"After all, it is very devout," the doctor said, "especially for a parrot." He drained his cup and reached for the pot. "Most other parrots I have known have no such refinement—their conversation would be quite unsuitable for children."

"Oh," said Elise, withdrawing the banana stalk onto her lap as the parrot sidestepped toward it. "You may have the benefit of that thing's prayers all the way to Vallière. And leave it in the jungle if you like. Xavier," she said, for Tocquet was just then mounting the gallery steps. "Would you *kindly* get your harpy off the table?"

The parrot beat its wings again, and landed on the top of Tocquet's head. Grimacing, Tocquet disengaged its talons from his long hair, and shifted the bird down onto his shoulder, where it settled and began to preen.

Zabeth came out from the kitchen and set down a platter of fried eggs. Elise, with a resentful glare at the parrot, began to serve.

"Paul," she called. "Sophie, come—Paul, at least *you* must eat something before you go."

But the children had already run down the stairs and were splashing around the border of the pool.

"It is the excitement," the doctor said, wiping up egg yolk with a piece of cassava. "Of course, I'll carry something for him."

"You must," Elise said. She laid down her spoon, and straightened, poised. "Be careful—both of you."

"Of course, we take all precautions," the doctor said. "For the moment there seems to be nothing to fear."

A splintered sunbeam fell through the tossing fronds of coconut to warm them where they sat around the table. The doctor took more coffee, stirred in sugar. The trickle of water feeding the pool was the same sound he had been hearing through his dream. He yawned, abruptly covering his mouth. Tocquet served the parrot a bit of frizzled egg white from the tines of his fork. Elise glowered at him.

"*M'ap prié pou'w,*" the parrot said. The round eye glittered.

"As you know, my dear, and have often told me," Tocquet said, "I need all the prayers I can get."

"Oh, he is a little green-feathered Tartuffe, your parrot," Elise snapped, but she was smiling.

With a clink of harness, Bazau and Gros-jean led the doctor's mare and Tocquet's gelding into the yard below the pool. Paul and Sophie stopped their play and looked at the horses, suddenly solemn. Behind, a groom held Paul's donkey, which wore a small saddle of red Spanish leather which Tocquet had obtained during one of his obscure missions over the mountains.

The doctor excused himself and went into the house. He drew on his boots and, with a certain weariness, strapped on his pistols. Trailing the long gun, his saddlebags slung across his shoulder, he crossed the gallery and went down to his mare.

"Take these," Elise said, holding up the remaining bananas and a whole round of cassava. "For Paul."

The doctor climbed back to the porch rail to accept the food. The mare jibbed a little at the irregular shape of the banana stalk. The doctor put it into his saddlebag and stroked the mare's nose, murmuring. Tocquet broke from a long, slow hug with Elise, and trotted down the steps. With an unlit cheroot screwed into his mouth, he swung a leg over his horse. The parrot was still riding on his shoulder.

"Come, Paul," the doctor called. "We're going to say good-bye to your cousin."

Paul stopped his play and straightened, facing Sophie and touching her shoulder. He gave her two kisses, one on each cheek. They were still small enough that embarrassment did not prevent such demonstrations of affection. Paul marched to his donkey, brushing away the groom's attempt to help him up. With a firm grip on the mane, he mounted on his own, then leaned down to adjust the stirrups on the red saddle.

The doctor ran his finger under the girth that encircled his mare. She jibbed a little, again, as he got on. He stroked her withers absently. Sophie stood solemnly by the pool, a finger laid across her cheek, watching. Zabeth and Elise were at the top of the gallery steps, the black woman a bit more apparently pregnant than the white. Tocquet wheeled his horse in their direction. He touched his fingers to his hat brim, then, less obviously, to his lips.

They rode out, through the thickening coffee groves. Tocquet and Elise and the doctor had more or less abandoned sugarcane at Habitation Thibodet. In these times, when the armies ceaselessly requisitioned both men and nourishment, it was easier to turn a profit on the coffee. They'd put the low ground into yams and beans. Now, now that things were calmer, it might be possible to shift again to sugar.

A party of five, with Gros-jean and Bazau—they took no other escort, though the grown men were all armed. The doctor had been in the colony for eight years now, but this was the first time that no war was being waged anywhere within its boundaries, that he knew. Wherever they rode that day, it was warm and sunny and peaceful, with men and women working in the fields.

They had made a slightly late departure and, because of the boy, they did not press too hard, eager as the doctor was to reach their destination. In the afternoon they stopped at Marmelade. The doctor spent the evening exchanging botanical notes with l'Abbé Delahaye. He also learned that Moustique had been there not so long before, to return the stole and the silver chalice, and to claim Marie-Noelle and her child. Beyond these scraps of information, Delahaye had no remark to make on the subject of his rebel protégé.

At first light they saddled their horses and reloaded the short pack train; Tocquet had three donkeys, bearing coffee and some panniers of indigo he had scouted out somewhere, for trade across the Spanish border. They rode out through the morning mists and up into the mountains. Toward noon they were stopped on a high narrow trail by a patrol of Moyse's men, running out from Dondon. The officer, unknown to any of them, made a close inspection of Tocquet's goods, and asked him a number of narrow questions about where he was going with his wares and what he meant to do when he got there—they were not headed in the direction of a port.

Dismounted by the head of his mare, the doctor waited, irritated at the delay. He took off his straw hat and untied his sweat-drenched headcloth, then began to massage his peeling scalp with his fingers. One of the black soldiers looked at him closely, then went to whisper to his superior, who was interrogating Tocquet. The officer listened, then seemed to put a question; Tocquet nodded his assent.

"Ou mèt alé," the officer said. You may go on. He closed the packs which had been opened for inspection, and ordered his men to clear the trail.

They rode on. Tocquet was leading, the parrot rocking on his shoulder. Paul followed directly behind, then the doctor, finally Bazau and Gros-jean, flanking the pack animals. An hour later, when they stopped for water, the doctor asked Tocquet what he had said to the patrol.

"Nothing," Tocquet told him. "It was you. You are a person of influence—Toussaint's doctor. It may be that you are even a wizard of some kind. In any case you are not be impeded on your way."

Though he supposed he ought to have been pleased, the doctor had a rather uncomfortable feeling of exposure. He had come to prize the anonymity of his passages. Tocquet rinsed out his mouth and spat.

"Everything is very regulated nowadays," he said. He flipped his long hair back over his shoulder; the parrot squawked and shifted its claws. "I suppose that for a family man, and a man of property, it is a good thing."

They rode on. Tocquet would now meet both of those qualifications, the doctor reflected, though he did not seem to have been speaking of himself.

Toward evening they came into Dondon. There was an air of tension in the town, as if some action were in the offing, but no one interfered with them, and they found lodging for the night without difficulty. The doctor called upon Moyse at his headquarters, and put a question about the Fortiers.

"Caché," Moyse said briefly. Hidden.

"Oh?" said the doctor. "At their place near here, or at Vallière?"

"Pa konnen," Moyse said. He did not know, or would not say. His good eye was fixed firmly on the doctor's face; the loose lids wrinkled round the gray socket of the missing one. Moyse was not inclined to wear a patch.

"No one will harm them," Moyse finally said. "They are safe enough, wherever they are."

Accepting this statement, the doctor withdrew. He knew that the amnesty Toussaint had declared for the mulattoes was observed with less than perfect fidelity. In fact, there were rumors of massacres, though these were more likely to happen in the south, or along the coast. The Fortiers were remote from those troubles, and unlikely to be involved in conspiracy either. But to seek them out at their plantation near Dondon would amount to a day's delay. He would not make the detour, he concluded.

From Dondon to Vallière the road was more difficult (when it existed) and the route less evident. At one vexatious crossroads the four men argued over which way to go. The doctor, who was confident, persuaded the others; Tocquet assented with a shrug. Forty minutes later, when they emerged on the road he had predicted, Tocquet gave him a brief curious glance over his shoulder, but said nothing. The doctor was equally surprised at his own assurance. Formerly he might be lost for days at a stretch, whenever he rode out the gate of some plantation. Now it seemed that he had every peak and crevice, every crossroads firmly fastened in his memory.

Though the distance was negligible, the way was slow, and sometimes they had to stop and cut brush, or jack away fallen trees that blocked their passage. Today they kept going at the best pace they could manage, unwilling to spend the night in the jungle. Paul, who had soldiered on with great fortitude, finally grew too weary to keep riding. Bazau tied his donkey into the pack train, and the doctor took him aboard the mare. Paul collapsed against him, sleeping profoundly, his arms hanging slack and his loose mouth warm and damp against the doctor's shirt front. That afternoon there was no rain. At last they came riding up the rim of Trou Vilain under the light of a sickle moon.

Isabelle was all astir when she saw them come in, a whirlwind of hostess activity. She called the servants to bring more plates, stoke the kitchen fire again, wring the neck of another chicken. Paul had run to Nanon's skirts, before the doctor had a chance to greet her. He could not quite fix on his emotion. Instead of joy or relief, he felt an odd foreboding. Something was a little off-center—Isabelle too effervescent, Nanon too quietly reserved. No more than his fatigue, perhaps. Certainly his legs were watery beneath him, after that long day's ride. A chair was drawn up for him; there would be fruit, while they waited for chicken.

"Ehm," the doctor said awkwardly, glancing at Nanon's slim waist, still on his feet. "I believe . . . apparently . . . there has been an event."

"But of course," Isabelle cried cheerily. Was there something especially pointed in the look she gave Nanon? "Of course, you must see your children."

Lowering her head, Nanon turned from the table; she was not exactly beckoning, but the doctor followed. As they crossed the threshold, he took hold of her hand. Paul was nudging up behind them, alert now after his nap in the saddle, curious and eager. The doctor felt a flutter of nerves in his belly and throat. He'd noticed the plural, and thought now of a damaged twin, illness or some deformity. Nanon's hand was warm and firm in his own, and yet it expressed nothing. He stopped her for a moment.

"*Ma chère,* I was afraid for you," he said. "There was a story that reached Le Cap, of a woman in trouble with childbirth."

He thought he felt her weight shift toward him. But she reversed herself, with a slight pressure on his hand. "Come."

He followed her into the dark bedroom. She lit a candle, cupping the flame in her hand. She shushed Paul, who had surged up to the edge of the cradle. In the flickering light, the doctor saw two children curled together, sleeping. They looked healthy enough, though one would not have taken them for twins. The lighter boy had a curious pigmentation: a current of black pinpoints running over the milky skin of his face. The other, smaller one was almost altogether black.

"But they seem to be very well," the doctor said. Now he did feel the relief he wanted, though he was not sure why. He put his finger into the cradle and lightly touched the cheek of the bigger infant. The baby stirred, though without waking; the small hand came up automatically and closed around his finger.

"Do not wake them," Nanon murmured. "They will cry."

He turned to her, wondering. Her closed face. Again he felt himself on the brink of understanding, but it seemed better that he not cross over.

"Paul," he said gently, "go and get your supper."

When the boy had left, he disengaged his hand from the cradle and with the same finger lifted a heavy lock of hair from Nanon's face. There was an ache all through him—blend of a strange sadness with desire. She looked up at him. He cupped her ear.

"I wish to be married," he said.

Nanon turned, disengaging herself from his touch. Her face lowered like a flower wilting on the long stem of her neck.

"But what is it?" he said, confused, alarmed. Then he realized what she must be thinking: that he had found some eligible white woman and meant therefore to put her aside.

"No, no," he said. Both hands now on both her shoulders, to turn and bring her nearer to him. "I mean, to you."

*   *   *

He hung in darkness, over a torrent which roared in the sulfurous bowels of a cavern, twirling, left to a limit, then right to a limit, and very near to falling with each turn. He was hanging by just his left forefinger, and it was only the grip of the paler child, François, which kept him from pitching into the laval flow. Worst of all was his horrible, parching thirst. He had no strength to struggle, but somehow felt himself drawn upward. There was hope, then light. A gray light like the dawn. He saw the face of the black child, Gabriel, but larger, fixed like a stone idol. His own face was coming nearer to the parted lips of the child. At the moment of their kiss an immense flow of cool water poured from the infant's mouth into his own, quenching his thirst and refreshing him.

He woke like a shot, sweating and trembling, yet at the same time happy and assured. Nanon was twined completely around him, her body touching every surface of his own. This was sweet, but in reality he was quite desperately thirsty. Carefully he untangled himself, stroking her long back as she murmured in her sleep. He pulled on his breeches and groped toward the door. His blind hands found a water jug on a stand. He lifted it and drank deeply and wet his fingers to stroke them over his face and the few remaining sprigs of hair on his head. Through the crack in the door he could see a light on the gallery, and he slipped out of the room and went toward it.

Tocquet was sitting at the table, turning the pages of a heavy ledger in the light of a small oil lamp. The parrot perched on the top rail of his chair, both eyes closed and apparently sleeping.

"*Salut,*" Tocquet said as the doctor came up.

The doctor sat down across the table from him, without replying. The banana stalk from Thibodet was on the table, slightly blackened after three days in the saddlebag. After the exertions of the day and evening, the doctor was rather hungry. He peeled a banana and began to eat.

"This Fortier woman knows her business," Tocquet said, studying the close lines of script. "Someone has been making a good thing out of this place, and I do believe it must have been her. And her records are very meticulous. The plantings, the harvest, purchases and shipping. Every death and every birth—if it's only a cat, she has written it."

In the dark hills beyond the house, the *siffleur montagne* sang in a voice like water. The doctor inclined his head toward the sound.

"Of course, our lovely ladies of leisure have not been quite so exacting since. At least, not with the ledger."

"Isabelle is not to be discounted," the doctor observed.

"No," Tocquet said. "Nor yet Nanon." He turned back pages in the book. "But this is the hand of the other." He reversed the book, holding it open for the doctor's inspection. The words seemed to flutter in the wavering lamplight. The doctor leaned nearer, squinting.

To the quarteronée woman, Nanon, was born, 6 January 1800, a male child, quarteroné, to be called François.

"Well, then." The doctor sat back, noncommittal. Tocquet picked up a cheroot from the table and bent to light it from the flame of the lamp.

"You have the name of an eccentric fellow," he said, blowing smoke up toward the still fan blades overhead. "Yet he who takes you for a fool would be the greater fool himself."

"You flatter me," the doctor said.

"Do you flatter yourself? I know your dislike of the formula, but the union of a *quarteronée* with a *blanc* does not produce another *quarteroné*. Madame Fortier deduces a mixed-blood father. I am impressed with her perspicacity. Moreover, if two children had been born on this day, she would hardly have failed to make note of the second. As you are a master of medical science, it cannot have escaped you that those two children in there are not quite the same age, and that no kinship is apparent between them."

"Oh," said the doctor, tilting his head. The birdsong, which had stopped, now resumed again.

"I am satisfied that they are my children," he said.

"You are." Tocquet looked at him with a hint of a smile.

"You take what you're given," the doctor said. "As they are offered to me, I claim them."

Tocquet looked as if he would say something, but he did not. He got up and tipped ash from his cheroot over the gallery rail, then came and stood beside the doctor. Again he failed to find a word, but he was smiling openly now. He gave the doctor a couple of heavy pats on his bare shoulder, as one might reward a reliable horse or dog. Speechless still, he went into the house.

The parrot was still roosted on the chair rail, and part of a glass of rum remained on the table near Tocquet's place. The doctor reached for it and sipped. In the trees, the nightbird went on singing. The parrot stirred, ruffling the feathers of its neck. It turned its head to the right and the left, inspecting the doctor with one eye and then the other.

"*M'ap prié pou'w,*" the parrot said.

38

The war against the *gens de couleur* in the south was the bitterest, the angriest, that there had been since the first rising, but I, Riau, I did not own this anger. It was all around me, like the wind before the rain, but it did not blow inside of me. Other men were full of the spirit of rage. That same storm of anger took the colored men also, and threw them against our people like scraps of *bagasse* on the wind. There was such hate that men would throw down their guns and attack each other hand to hand. For that, some people called it the War of Knives, but as often men would throw the knives away too and fight with nails and teeth. That fight where Dessalines killed Choufleur was not the first of its kind, and not the last one either. But after Aquin no one wanted to listen to Rigaud any more, and the colored men could not call together enough men for a battle. We hunted them across the land like goats.

Sometimes, the war spirit came to Riau's head—Ogûn-Feraille, with his iron sword flashing points like shells exploding in the sky. It was that way at Grand Goâve, when Ogûn rode the body of Riau into the fighting, so that afterward I did not know what had passed, unless someone told me. That way also at the bridge of Miragoâne—without a spirit in the head a man could not go into that bloody water under the cannon, the slaughter was too frightening. But Riau was not many days in that battle before the doctor called me out to work in the hospital again, and Guiaou also.

After Aquin, after Rigaud ran away on his boat and Toussaint came to Les Cayes, the doctor left very quickly to go north, because he was hungry to find his woman again if he could. Toussaint went north again also, not long after, leaving Dessalines in command of the Grande Anse and all of the Southern Department. Since the army of the colored men was broken, no more of our men were being hurt, or very few. Those who were in the hospitals had either got better or died, so Riau and Guiaou were taken out of the hospital and sent back to the work of killing again.

There still was much killing to be done, and it was ugly work, and I, Riau, did not like it. Rigaud had kept his word in tearing up all the trees and poisoning all the streams everywhere on the Grande Anse where he retreated, and it was for us to paint that desert with another coat of blood of all the men he left behind when he sailed away, some said to France, until all the south was like the hell where Jesus sends the people who have made him angry. Dessalines ordered many men killed in the same way he had killed Choufleur, only without first breaking the neck. One must put the sword point into the *bounda* of the living man and drive the sword all the way up as far as it would go. Sometimes there would be hundreds killed that way in a single day, and sometimes it took them a long time to die, after the sword had been pulled out. There were no hospitals for them.

At other times boatloads of colored men were taken out on the ocean to be drowned. I liked this way even less than the other, because of the sharks, and the story Guiaou told of the Swiss and what became of them, all but him. The colored men went into the water with their throats cut sometimes, or with only light cuts about the arms and body, bleeding enough to bring the sharks. Sometimes Guiaou was on those boats himself, or not there really—Agwé would be riding in his head, because without his spirit he had great trouble crossing water. With the sunlight burning from the water, I saw how the curved *coutelas* rose and fell in Guiaou's hand, and I wondered, but Guiaou was only serving the colored men the way that they had served the Swiss. Afterward, we never spoke of it. It was a long time after before I would eat fish again, because I could not stop the thought of what the fish had been feeding on.

If a colored man stood firm and showed himself ready to fight to the death, sometimes Dessalines would not kill him. He found places for such people in the army, and they were well accepted there. But those who begged for mercy did not find it. Toussaint had published a promise of mercy from Les Cayes, but that promise was not very much respected. All during that time, Toussaint was somewhere else. When news came to him of the killings, he would throw up his hands and put on a face of misery and say, *I told him to trim the tree, not uproot it.* Often there were some whitemen watching when he said this, or one of the priests who were always near him in those days. Of course it was not possible that Toussaint did not know what Dessalines was doing. Still, it was Rigaud who had left all the trees in the south with their roots in the air, Rigaud who had sent his men to try to kill Toussaint so many times, when Toussaint was coming through the crossroads.

It was not possible, either, to leave the *gens de couleur* with men enough to make another army. Toussaint was thinking that if Rigaud had gone to France, maybe France would be persuaded to send out soldiers for Rigaud. I saw him thinking this, though he did not say it where I could hear, and I do not think he said it to anyone out loud. I saw myself that it was possible, and that we must do what we were doing in case it did happen. But I was glad when the order came from Toussaint to come away from that bloody place and bring my men back to Ennery.

At that time there were riding with me—Guiaou, Bouquart and Bienvenu. There were sixteen others too, under Captain Riau's order, but among those sixteen there were often changes, for sometimes some of them would be killed in a battle, or sent into someone else's command, or one of them might even run off to be a *marron* again, if there was still a place in the country where *marrons* could hide from Toussaint's army. Guiaou and Bouquart and Bienvenu were always there and none of them was ever badly hurt in the fighting. Also Quamba and Couachy, who were like brothers with Guiaou. Any one of these could lead the men, if Captain Riau was called to the hospital instead of to the battle. Bouquart especially led them well, because the other men admired his great strength and his fearlessness.

It did not take us very long to reach Ennery from the Grande Anse, because all of us had good horses now, taken from the colored men who had been killed. I looked for the doctor when I came to Thibodet, although I knew he would not be there, unless perhaps he had brought Nanon back from Vallière already, but there had not been time enough for that. Tocquet was gone from the plantation also, and they had taken the doctor's son Paul with them on this journey. So only the doctor's sister was there, with her child Sophie, but she received Riau into the house, as she would have any white officer. I saw that her spirit was very much changed since the time when she had driven Nanon away from Thibodet, and she seemed happier too, unless it was only the child in her belly that had softened her face.

Zabeth was carrying a new child too. This made Bouquart very proud, and he walked about picking his knees up high, like a warhorse on parade.

Captain Riau stayed in the *grand'case,* though for one night only. It seemed better to me, when the doctor's sister invited me. I did not want to refuse her offer, and also that way Guiaou could be the first to greet Merbillay and the children, which would please him. That night I dined with Elise on the gallery—no other guests had come but Riau. I did not know what I would say to her, without the doctor or any of the white officers there. But she spoke to me very naturally and asked questions in a way which made it easy for me to answer, with news of the south and other things she seemed to want to know about. Soon I was speaking as easily to her as to anyone, though I did not pretend to be making love to her when we talked, as Maillart or Vaublanc would sometimes do when they were there.

Afterward I lay in the room where the doctor slept when he was staying at Habitation Thibodet. The bed was fine, with a mattress made of feathers, which was too hot for the weather. We had been riding long that day, and in the evening I was drinking rum, but still my *ti bon ange* would not leave my body to go into the world of dreams. I lay thinking, I could not stop, I heard the house creak around its pegs, and outside the wind blowing through the long blades of the leaves. There was a crafty knocking at the back of the house, and I heard Zabeth giggling as she went out to be with Bouquart.

Riau must not think of Guiaou with Merbillay, he must divide himself from such a thought, and cover his mind with darkness, though the thought with its pictures would keep trying to push itself in, like a *djab,* a devil at the door. For Guiaou it must be the same, when he knew Riau was with Merbillay. Still it was better that neither of us had had to kill the other, the way Choufleur had finally had to die, even though the doctor would not kill him when he could have. Guiaou and Riau trusted each other, fighting in a battle or treating the sick. That was good. Also there were two men for the children instead of just one. It was only when we were at Thibodet at the same time that it was hard. Maybe that was only because it did not happen often that way, and that if we could build a *lakou* together to live there forever, it would go more easily, after a time.

In the morning when I woke, our children came running through the *grand'case* as if it were their own—Caco and Yoyo, because Marielle was too small for such games. Sophie had made a friend of Caco by way of Paul, and now that Paul was away she wanted these other friends to be with her still more. They ran screaming and laughing through the house, and afterward played by the pool where the doctor had set his floating flowers, while Riau took bread and coffee with Elise. It made me glad to see them, but I said to Elise that I would not return to the *grand'case* that night, because it was better that I sleep nearer to my men.

Who I slept with then was Merbillay, and the small one Marielle, and I did not think of anything but them. The next night I spent in the other *ajoupa*, where Bouquart and Bienvenu were staying, except that Bouquart had gone somewhere else with Zabeth. I played the *banza* there, and sang soft songs with Bienvenu, until it was time for sleeping. So it went for five or six days, a night in one place and a night in the other, and I saw Guiaou only by daylight. Then Toussaint called me to see him at that plantation he had bought for his family nearby, and he told me to ride with my men to Dondon.

All the way we rode, the country was quiet. Big gangs of people were working at every plantation which we passed. Toussaint had made new orders now. All the country was governed like the army. For those in the fields, the men of the hoe, it was now the same as for the men of the gun in the army. They must stay at their work, to which they were ordered, and if they ran away from the work they could be shot, like deserters from the army. Also the orders kept people from clearing new ground to make gardens for themselves and their families. Everyone was ordered to work cane or coffee, to make money to pay for the war. Except now there was not any war.

All the people looked peaceful, working this way. No whips snapped over them in the fields, and they had no other mistreatment. There was plenty of food for all, and no one was made to work at night, and the time of rest in the day's hot middle was respected everywhere. Still, the new orders seemed very tight to me. Sometimes we heard the people singing in the fields, and no one was whipping them to make them sing, but still there was the tightness in their voices.

Toussaint had made Dessalines captain-general to carry out those work orders in the south and in the west, along with all the other things Dessalines was doing there. In the north, he made Moyse the captain-general. I, Riau, did not know how Moyse would like the tightness of the orders. Toussaint had sent Riau to report to Moyse, but I felt that he wanted me to report to him about Moyse also, although he did not say so openly. But by the time we reached Dondon, a rising had already started.

This was a rising of all the field workers, and it poured down on to Le Cap like a wave, gathering more and more men as it passed over the plain, like the rising that had come against Hédouville. Moyse did not try to stop it. No, it was Moyse who had made it start. But I saw soon enough it was not a real *soulèvement*. There was much noise and waving of cane knives and torches, but no one was cut, and nothing was burned. It was my patrol, along with many others sent out by Moyse, that was charged to be certain there was no killing or burning and that the *blancs* at their plantations on the plain would not be harmed. They were not harmed, or their property either, but the *blancs* on the plain were very much frightened, and reminded that they were not master anymore.

Toussaint was master. It was his hand that moved Moyse in this affair. The rising was against the agent Roume, who had taken back the order he had once given which allowed Toussaint to take control of the Spanish side of the island. Moyse had stirred up all the field workers with the thought that the Spanish still held slaves, and that they were stealing people from our side, to make them slaves again across the border. That much was true, and I could join in that cry, but only with half my heart, because it was not a real *soulèvement*.

For Agent Roume, though, it was real enough. He was brought back to Dondon and shut up in a chicken house, until he gave the answer Toussaint wanted.

After it was over, there were big *bamboches* at Dondon and all over the plain. The people were happy, because they had a holiday from working in the fields, and they had shown their power, or believed that they had. There was rum and feasting, and cows and goats were killed for the *loa,* but I, Riau, did not go to the drums that night. I stayed with myself, thinking coldly. I did not know where Toussaint was, but I saw the idea in his mind—Moyse might make a false *soulèvement* into a real one. I saw that Toussaint expected me to warn him if that happened. But Moyse had done no more than what Toussaint had wanted him to do.

Soon after, we started across the Spanish mountains with a large part of the army, eight thousand men. Half went south under Paul Louverture, but I was with Moyse, striking north toward Santiago. We had all made our hearts tight and bloody for the idea of killing more whitemen who still held slaves. It was different than the war against the colored people. I felt so, and I could see that Moyse felt the same. We were all very much ready to fight, but in the end there was not much fighting. We met the Spaniards at the river called Guayabin, but the fight there did not last as much as half an hour before they ran away. There was one other fight, less than one hour, along that road, and then Santiago was surrendered to Moyse without any more fighting at all.

Moyse put the General Pageot in charge of the town, and we went on to join Paul Louverture at Santo Domingo City. Toussaint had crossed the border himself by then, and he was moving more men along the way his brother had opened. They had not much fighting to do on those roads either. It seemed there were not many people east of the mountains at all, neither whitemen nor their slaves. Nothing was there but cattle where we passed following Moyse, or horses and mules running half wild, and once in a long way a single herdsman's hut standing by a corral. In the towns there were more people, but they were not meaning to give any fight.

At Santo Domingo City, the Spanish General Don García made his surrender to Toussaint without any trouble. Anyway it had all been settled before by a peace paper between white people across the sea. So there was no reason for a battle. It must have been sweet for Toussaint to beat Don García so easily. All the time that Toussaint had been fighting for the Spanish, Don García had set Jean-François and Biassou above him. Now those two had disappeared, and Toussaint stood above the man who'd been their master, though it was in the name of France. Still, all of us who came with Moyse had seen Roume in that chicken house.

Toussaint ordered that there would be no vengeance taken on the Spanish people, the same as he had said about the mulattoes at Les Cayes. Here in Santo Domingo, the order was respected. I noticed this very much and I saw that Moyse had noticed it too.

It had been long, a very long time, since my spirit had mounted on my head. I had not gone to the drums after the false rising Moyse had begun to frighten Roume. There was no *bamboche* nor any drums after the Spanish gave up their country at Santo Domingo City. Toussaint would not allow it. It must be all quiet and strict discipline, as in the whitemen's army. All this time I had been alone with myself, Riau, thinking in ticks like that officer's watch which I kept always tightly wound in my pocket. This was loneliness. When I slept, I was wrapped in the dark, and no part of me traveled away into dream.

After the Spanish had surrendered, Toussaint told Moyse to divide his men in small patrols and send them around the northeast part to root out any Spanish soldiers who might not know of the surrender. I was to lead one such patrol myself, at the head of my twenty men.

This news lightened the weight I had been feeling on me for a long time then. The night before we set out on this errand, I dreamed. My *ti-bon-ange* was flying like a hawk among high mountains, with such swoops and sharp descents that my heart was many times swollen with fear. Those mountains were high and jagged and wrinkled like the mountains of Saint Domingue, but no trees were on their peaks, only mounds of snow and edges of ice. The sky was cold blue and there was no cloud, no sign of rain, and the cold was like the death when all the blood stops running in your body. In the life of my flesh I never had seen snow nor ice, though I had heard of these things from the whitemen. In my dream it struck me that the whitemen carried the seeds of this ice somewhere inside them, wherever else they went in the world, and the cold stabbed out through the blue of their eyes.

On the cold, cliff side was a sacrifice to Baron, bones hanging in chains against the stone. These were bones of a man, I saw, when my *ti-bon-ange* swooped near. Across a deep frozen gorge from the bones was a whiteman's fort built on a peak, with all the roofs and walls piled up with snow. The voice of Toussaint was in my ears, though Toussaint was nowhere to be seen. *Is it not to cut off a man's legs and command him to walk?* The voice was gentle and warm on the side of my head, but still it struck me through with fear. *Is it not to cut out a man's tongue and command him to speak?* The wings of my *ti-bon-ange* banked along the wall of the fort, and I saw within a small barred hole a figure of something I took to be an animal at first, but then it appeared to be a whitewoman, bony and shriveled, her hair in strings and her face all streaked with caca. She stared at the bones across the gorge, with eyes that had no understanding. Her eyes were more blunt and stupid than any animal eyes I knew.

Is it not to bury a man alive?

Toussaint's voice was still at my ear, so gentle it seemed I could not bear it. My dream sucked up into the cold sky, in a spiral like the flight of the *malfini,* until the world below was no more than a smudge.

When I woke, the watch had stopped, and I did not rewind it. My spirit was more clear than it had been for a long time, and it seemed to me that I knew the future. Or better, that there was no future, nor yet any past, but everything was already happening in the way that was to come. When I saluted Moyse at our parting, I saw his death and the part Riau must play in it. Moyse had been one-eyed for a long time now, and he was very near, that day, the place where he was bound to go. No power could change this for him, but on that morning even my sadness was as clear as glass. We rode up to the north, toward the coast and Puerto del Plata.

Old silver mines were in the mountains there, but these had long been abandoned. The mine holes were full of the bones of the Tainos whom the Spanish had made to work until they died. Farther on we met a squad of Spanish soldiers who stood ready to fight. They fired on us, but I, Riau, sat my horse unmoving, like Halaou with his bull's tail or his white cock in his arms, and the bullets bent their paths to go around me. The Spanish broke and ran away, pursued by their own fear. We did not trouble to chase them down and kill them.

On the third day we came to a small plantation in the hill where they were growing tobacco. There were slaves there still, with only a few white people over them. Just one family of *blancs* lived there, the father and two sons and the wife and *abuelita* both dressed in Spanish black. We let this head *blanc* know that France had taken his part of the island and so slavery was finished there now. The black people who were in our hearing did not seem very excited by this news, though they looked curiously at our horses and our weapons, and some of the young women gave us shy and secret smiles.

I thought maybe these people did not understand our language, so I told the head *blanc* he must repeat the words in Spanish. It seemed to me that he did so truly, though I did not have so very much Spanish in my head myself. Still there was no great movement among the black people when he spoke. I told the *blanc* we must bring the news to the others who were in the fields, and this we did. There were not so many slaves on this *habitation* anyway, something less than thirty men, sixty altogether with the women and the children.

At the drying shed we found the smuggler Tocquet, with Gros-jean and Bazau, and one of the white sons who was helping them to load their donkeys with leaf tobacco. Tocquet saluted me, with his cayman smile, and I took his hand. I was glad enough to see him, and especially Gros-jean and Bazau. As if they were *marrons* themselves, those three had never paid much attention to the border.

The head *blanc* spoke to the workers in Spanish with the words that I had given him to say. When he had finished, the slaves shrugged at each other and went to sit down on felled logs outside the shed. They smiled and muttered among themselves, but it did not appear that any great change had fallen upon them. They looked like they might go back to the same work once they had rested for a while.

Because I knew he understood Spanish better than I, I asked Bazau if the *blanc* had spoken truly. Bazau answered that he had.

Then I did not know what to think. I took off the tall hat I had got from the English hussar and rubbed the back of my head with my hand. The clarity of my dream was gone, for that moment. But there was another place which I heard of, not far off. Tocquet and his pack train started back to the west, but Riau and his patrol kept riding toward the north coast.

I thought, as we rode, that it was not all for nothing. At my left side was Bienvenu, whom I had set free from the headstall when he ran away from Habitation Arnaud before the rising. At my right side was Bouquart, whom I had freed from his *nabots*. And in the rear was always Guiaou, and it could be understood that Riau and Guiaou had each made the other more free than either one had been before.

At dusk we came to the last hills above a narrow plain which ran flat to the sea. This plain was a small, tight pocket with two mountain ranges between it and Fort Dauphin. I had heard that it was here, but never before seen it. We stopped, under cover of the trees. A ship was at anchor off the beach, and it seemed some sailors were camped on the shore. Nearer the mountains were clay houses, and the small green squares of rice fields, and the long, low shape of a barracoon. When the wind blew from the sea, we caught the sour smell of the people shut up there.

I kept my men well hidden under the trees, but later, long after darkness, when the fires in the camp had burned low, I slipped down with Bienvenu to look. About two dozen men were there, whitemen of the lowest type and a few blacks and mulattoes. The sailors in the beach camp made ten more. One could not tell how many were closed in that barracoon, and there were also some other slaves who were not shut up there, but were working in the rice. There was one small brass cannon covering the trail which led into the mountains to the west, and another one on the beach. The first cannon was watched by two men, but both were sleeping, and Bienvenu wanted to kill them then and there. This we could have easily done. I, Riau, had slipped into whitemen's camps by night, with Dessalines himself, and Moyse and some others, to do this work with knives. But tonight I did not want to do it. If the watch was changed before morning, the whole camp would take alarm.

We crossed a mud dike of the *rizières* to get back into the mountains. Those other slaves were standing on the dikes around us, unmoving, white-eyed, still as egrets standing in a swamp or horses sleeping on their feet in the field. They did not need to sleep like ordinary people, because they were already dead.

The hair was walking by itself on my neck and my arms when we passed among them, and this feeling in me reached out to greet the same feeling in Bienvenu. *Zombi.* It was true. Biassou had kept this place for a long time before he left the country, and it was said that Jean-

François also had used to sell slaves from the island, and still the same thing was always going on. Riau had heard of it for a long time, and knew more of it than he was willing to remember.

The sureness of my dream came back to me, but at the same time I needed to think and to plan as Toussaint would have done it. Four parties of five men each. Bienvenu would take his men to seize that cannon in the mountains and move it quickly to the cliffs above the sea. Bouquart and his men would break into the barracoon. Guiaou would lead a charge on horseback across the dike of the *rizières*. I, Riau, and my five men would handle the boats and the camp on the beach.

We moved an hour before full dawn, just as the light was turning blue. On the beach I waited for the shot that meant Bienvenu had got the cannon. It was easy enough to kill the *blancs* on the beach as they struggled up from their sleep, but the most important thing was to smash in the three longboats drawn up there and aim the cannon at the ship. I did not know how many men might be on that ship, or if there were more boats or cannon there.

The whitemen inshore had jumped up to meet Guiaou coming across the rice field and now they were being cut down by swords from horseback. The barracoons were open already, and the parties under Bouquart and Bienvenu had joined in this killing. The *zombis* were all still standing white-eyed and motionless in the *rizières*, except for two who walked stiffly toward the barracoons with buckets hanging from their arms, carrying grain and water. They did not seem to understand that the barracoons had been emptied out. There were no chains. The people had been coffled up with ropes and wooden yokes, so it was easy enough to cut them free.

Then the ship did fire a cannon, and we answered quickly from the beach, but our shot miscarried. Couachy, on the heights above, was the better gunner, and he managed to drop a ball from the cliffs onto the ship's deck. The ship's cannon fired another time, but without hitting anything that mattered. Then the ship loosed its moorings and sailed away without doing anything more.

It was over, except the *zombi*-master was hemmed up in a corner of the rice field, with the *zombis* gathered tightly around him. Guiaou's men were keeping well back, because they were all afraid of the *zombis*, and none more than Guaiou. The *zombi*-master was a blackman like us, and I knew him from the camps of Biassou, from long before I went to Bahoruco, though I did not care to remember his name. He was wearing a Spanish uniform still, with many ribbons and coins pinned over the front of it. I think he knew me also, for he seemed about to say my name, but I shot him twice, a pistol in each hand, and he fell over backward into the swamp.

Let the crabs take him. I loaded my pistols and put them in my belt. Now the *zombis* were all moving aimlessly around like ants do when one has kicked over the hill. Everything rushed up at me, swooping as in my dream, this *zombi* farm and the barracoon and the slave ship still waiting on the beach and the men in the tobacco who scarcely cared if they were free and Moyse's death bound soon to come and all the people across the border working quietly, tightly, under Toussaint's order. All this at once, and the same voice in my ear, but now the words were different.

What they did to us, we have learned to do to ourselves.

Where would it end? There could be no end. I saw this plainly at that moment, but I had always in my pocket the bag of salt I had gathered from the pans below Gonaives.

All my men were hanging back, afraid of the *zombis* still. The people freed from the barracoon were afraid of them too. I saw this had been the way of the *zombi*-master, using this fear to keep them down. All those people had been captured near the border, one at a time or in little groups, when they strayed too far from their villages, in the direction of the Rivière Massacre. They were mostly women, and children of all ages. Some of the older boys had taken up the guns of the dead whitemen.

It was true that the *zombis* looked frightening. There were thirteen of them, naked except for a cloth at the waist. They were starved to skin and bone and the cords that strung the bones together, and their eyes were more empty than the eyes of animals, like the eyes of that *blanche* I had seen in my dream.

I took some salt into my hand and went to the nearest *zombi*, holding him by his upper arm. He understood nothing, and I had to rub the grains against his mouth. But when he had once tasted it, a thread of life came into his eyes, and the stiffness began to leave his body, and he pushed at me for more. Then they were all pressing up around me, pushing, nuzzling, spilling the mound of yellow salt from my two cupped hands, their lips heavy and loose as the lips of horses.

All but one.

The people, my soldiers and those from the barracoon, were all looking upon Riau as if he were BonDyé himself. As they awoke, the *zombis* began to mingle with the people we had freed. They were given clothes from the dead men. It seemed that some of them were recognized from lives they'd lived before they were brought here to be among the dead. Some of the freed women from the barracoon had opened the supplies of the slave traders and were beginning to cook food. They had tapped a barrel of rum as well, so the mood was that of a *bamboche,* even though it was just barely morning. In the east, the sun had just pushed its edge above the sea.

I went to the last *zombi,* who had been, in his life, Chacha Godard. He moved away as I came near, moving a step for each step of mine, keeping our distance equal, as if an invisible stake was lashed between us. Perhaps it was so, for I had seen Chacha put into the ground, a corpse, and seen his body raised again, by Biassou, and made to move and to labor. I had wanted to see all those things at that time, but afterward there was nothing I could do to scrape the sight off my eyes.

Biassou had been gone for a long time now. He was supposed to have been killed in Florida. But still all this went on without him, and maybe it would take more than a handful of salt to undo it.

When Chacha struck the wall of the barracoon, he could not go backward anymore, and so I closed the distance. When I lifted my hand with the salt, his eyes rolled white, and his head whipped back and forth like the head of a panicked horse. He bit me when I forced the salt between his jaws, though not enough to break the skin. My hand jerked back, spilling salt upon the ground, but enough had passed his lips. His jaw worked and his body trembled. On the wet red of his lower lip, I saw the pieces of salt dissolving. Light came into his eyes then, and recognition, but no joy.

He turned from the wall, away from me, and began walking down toward the water. It was not the stiff *zombi* walk any longer. His hips and his shoulders swung with his step now, but still he walked very steadily, and his head and his eyes were fixed. Without breaking his pace, he passed the broken longboats on the shore and walked into the shallow surf, knee-deep, waist-deep, deeper. The sun was on the water, so bright one could hardly bear to look, and his head very black against it. A few people were quietly watching him, but many others were busy eating and drinking rum and so noticed nothing. Chacha kept walking into that bright mirror surface until the water sealed itself above his head.

At that moment a women on the beach was taken by Erzulie, and she began to sway and sing.

Tout kò-m se lò
Tout kò-m se lò
Tout kò-m se lò
Ezili sòti nan lamè-a
Tout kò-m se lò . . .

Erzulie of the Waters. People by the cookfire began to sway and clap their hands. They took up the singing too, though they had not seen what had begun it. They had not seen Chacha Godard go beneath the waters, but still they sang.

All my body is gold
All my body is gold
All my body is gold
Ezili comes out of the ocean
All my body is gold . . .

There was nothing to see in the ocean any longer, only the bright, tight surface of the water, like a sheet of hammered brass.

39

At a small mahogany secretary in his bedroom at the Governor's Residence in Le Cap, Toussaint sat writing, alone for once. He wrote in his own hand, for the matter was unsuitable for dictation. The high arched wooden doors had been opened onto the balcony by the servant who had brought in his coffee, so that daylight illuminated his hand and his page. It was early in the morning, still cool, and a small moist breeze moved through the garden.

"My dear sons, Placide and Isaac," he wrote, "I salute you from the country of your birth, your nation—" He stopped and blotted out the last phrase, "your nation," so heavily it was in no way legible. "May this letter find you healthy and industrious in the bosom of our great Republic, France."

He dipped his pen and lifted it from the well, tilting the nib for the excess to run off. Abstractedly he looked out over the balcony rail. In the sun-gilded garden, a servant was slowly sweeping up dried curls of leaves that had been blown down from the trees in the night.

"I wish always that both of you should make good use of the opportunity I must still deny myself, to live among the deepest roots of our fatherland, which is France." This statement was flawless, from the point of the view of the censors and spies who would certainly be reading it before (most likely) or after it reached the addressees.

"But duty, and the work I owe the nation, retain me here in Saint Domingue. I do not know what you have heard of our recent civil war. Nor is it right or necessary that you should know too much of *that,* although I hope and expect that you will profit from your schoolmasters' instruction in the art of war, that you will read and study Clausewitz and the other writers on this subject, and with your full attention."

The last quarter-inch of coffee in his cup had gone cold, but there was still a vestige of warmth in the cup on the tray. He poured and stirred in sugar, but forgot to taste the mixture, as the next phrase came to him. "Suffice it to say that the civil war which has just ended here, with victory to your old father's arms, has proved (if further proof were needed) that no conflict is more bitter than strife between brothers. As if the closer the kinship, the uglier and more ruinous the quarrel."

A wash of sadness spilled over him, unexpected. This was the very thought, if not the words, of Moyse. But that predicament, at the moment, did not bear thinking of. He must concentrate on another sadness—five years since he had seen his older boys. What did he know of them now? They wrote to him often enough, it was true. Their letters were correctly spelled, increasingly elegant in their penmanship and even in their style, and thoroughly unrevealing. The differences between the boys were flattened by this correspondence. Isaac, though the younger, was the bolder, more impetuous, braver (perhaps), certainly more foolhardy. *Tête bœuf,* Toussaint had called him formerly, bullhead, with a rap of his knuckles on the boy's hard skull, and not without a certain admiring recognition. Yet Placide, more hesitant, cautious, yielding in his manner, had also the greater capability, Toussaint believed. In Placide's instinct for self-effacement, he saw something of himself. Beneath those currents of elusiveness might be a tenacity greater than Isaac's. Or so it had seemed at the time of their departure. But what if the differences between the boys had really been rubbed away by their education? In the old days, before the Revolution in France, mulatto children sent for their education there had been neatly tapped into the mold of French chevaliers, until little remained of them but a set of borrowed morals and manners and assumptions which they did not realize would be useless, even harmful to them, when they returned to the colony . . . Lowering his pen to the paper, Toussaint glided into a Biblical homily, as smoothly as he might have done if the boys had actually been in his presence.

"I trust you remember the story of Jacob and Esau, which we read many times in our old cabin at Bréda when you were very small. How

Jacob through his deception stole the blessing and the birthright of his brother, disguising himself in the rough skin of a beast."

His thought wandered. Had Rigaud reached Paris, had he begun his intrigues there? On this subject, Toussaint's intelligencers had given no report.

"Be always honest, practice no deception, in your dealings with the world, but especially with one another. No matter what skin you are given to wear, be true to yourself, beneath it."

There. That was a nice piece of doubling. The censor could find nothing objectionable in this sermonette, but the message, the *pwen*, would fly past to reach, at least, Placide.

"I am pleased to tell you that peace and prosperity reign from one end of our colony to the other. Those disturbances you knew when you were small are at an end, once and for all. And how eagerly your mother and I look forward to your return!"

He stopped, bathed in a bitterness like gall. It was not so very long since he had actually tried to get the boys back. He had sent Huin, the French general whom he'd trusted with so many delicate negotiations, on a secret mission to spirit them out of their college and across the English Channel, where Maitland was waiting to receive them— under the protection of the entire British navy. Both boys, or at the least, Placide . . . but Huin had found no opportunity. Toussaint had felt himself suspected, if not detected outright in the scheme. And a failed attempt would have spoiled everything.

"But it is not for us to fix the day or the hour for that delightful event," he wrote doggedly. "Your parents must follow duty rather than desire, and you must complete your education thoroughly, for your country will have need of your most skillful services, when finally you do return.

"Your brother, Saint-Jean, is well and sends his greetings. Your mother sends her kisses, and I mine."

He signed, with the flourishing backward loop enclosing the customary three dots, lifted the sheet and flagged it in the air to dry the ink.

The anteroom to the private office in Government House had been furnished with a pair of tables so as to become, temporarily, a secretaries' suite. There the doctor, Riau, Pascal, and several other scribes labored over fair copies of the Constitution which Toussaint had recently engineered for Saint Domingue. Riau worked impassively, and the doctor envied his concentration—letter by letter, leaf by leaf. In such a task it was better *not* to see the forest for the trees. As for himself, if he winced at some especially terrifying clause, he was apt to drop a blot and spoil his page. Pascal, across the table, had gnawed his thumb to such a miserable state that the wound drew flies.

The door opened, and Toussaint walked in, alone, wearing his ordinary undecorated uniform, plumed bicorne in his hand, his head bound up in yellow madras. There was an excited burr of petitioners in the corridor (for the time being they were not admitted even to the anteroom), but Toussaint shut the door and cut it off. He circled the tables, looking over the shoulder of one scribe, then another, humming noncommittally. When he came to the doctor, he tapped him on the sleeve and beckoned. The doctor rose and followed him into the inner cabinet.

Toussaint produced a folded paper from inside his coat and held it out. "A fair copy only," he said, "there is no need to adjust the phrasing." His hand covered a rather ingenuine cough. "Of course you will make sure of the spelling."

"Of course."

The letter came unfolded as the doctor accepted into his hand, and he caught a glimpse of Toussaint's broken orthography, *sépa pou nou precisé lajour ni leure pou* . . . Fluent as Toussaint was in his language— he knew how to word the subtleties of his thought—his spelling was strictly phonetic; perhaps it had even worsened somewhat since his use of secretaries had increased. He wrote to his sons in his own hand, but always required a fair copy to be made—discreetly—lest his poor orthography embarrass him before the young collegians. The doctor was familiar with this work, and was rather flattered to be given it. He had mastered Toussaint's odd renderings to the point that he hardly ever needed to ask for a clarification of a word.

He sat down at the place Toussaint indicated—this task would not be performed in the anteroom—arranged a fresh sheet beside Toussaint's creased paper, and began the corrected copy. Toussaint pushed open the window behind his own desk. The cry of a crow came in with a wave of warm air, and the voices of carters encouraging one another beyond the wall.

The doctor wrote carefully. He was rather pleased to have been relieved of the Constitution for a time. The document had been approved by a committee of men whom all observers thought reduced to puppets. Its main thrust was to assign near-absolute powers to Toussaint Louverture, for the duration of his life, along with the right to appoint his successor. Who would perhaps be one of those sons to whom Toussaint had written today.

A tap on the door, and Riau presented himself, a sheaf of papers in his hand. He murmured that the Constitution was ready for the printer. The doctor felt himself begin to flinch, and he laid down his pen.

"Yes," said Toussaint. "Send it down."

Riau saluted and turned from the door, which Toussaint closed. The doctor, feeling that his tremor had passed, picked up the pen and went on writing. Before Toussaint could resume his seat, another tap came on the door. Pascal, announcing the arrival of Colonel Vincent.

"Yes," said Toussaint, in the same tone as before, as Pascal gnawed anxiously at the edge of his thumb's wound. "Let him come in."

Vincent closed the door behind him and turned to face the desk, shaking his head ruefully. "General," he began, "is there *any* way that I can dissuade you from this document you have prepared?"

"I think not," Toussaint told him. "For it is not my doing, but the work of the Assembly."

"The Assembly!" Vincent blurted out. "Raimond, Borgella—forgive me, General, I make no such accusation myself, but the men of the Assembly are *perceived* to be completely in your thrall, and that perception is likely to continue in France. Observe, this constitution gives you powers that a king might envy—might have envied even in the days before the Revolution. You have sole power to propose all laws, to conduct all enforcement, to bind and to loose—and this for the duration of your *life*? In effect, it is a declaration of independence."

"It is no such thing," Toussaint said quietly.

"How not?" said Vincent. "Sir, you assume to yourself every power of the state, save that to negotiate independently with foreign governments—which in truth you have done already, with England and the North American Republic—"

"Special laws." Toussaint raised his voice slightly, and moved to the edge of his seat. "The First Consul has himself declared the need for *special laws* to govern the colonies. The Assembly has drafted *special laws* to present for his approval. We are responding to the need he has . . . indicated."

Vincent took out a handkerchief and wiped his forehead. "If it is approval you sincerely seek," he said, "you would do better *not* to put this constitution into effect before approval has been obtained."

The doctor, though he could not quite render himself deaf, felt that he was approaching what he'd imagined Riau's state of mind to be: he looked no farther than the lines he must draw to make one letter, connect it to another letter to form a word. One word after another. In this way he was able to continue copying without a fault. When he had finished the copy, he would be able to leave the room, perhaps free to leave the building. Nanon and the children were waiting for him at the Cigny house.

Toussaint relaxed against the back of his chair, and set the tips of his long fingers together. "If the First Consul is uncertain of my Constitution," he said, "he will send out commissioners to negotiate with me."

"Say rather that he should send ambassadors," Vincent said. "As if to treat with a foreign power."

"Colonel Vincent," Toussaint said. "You of all people know how deep and abiding is my loyalty to France. I have fought and bled on many battlefields to conserve this colony for the French Republic. In taking command of the island's eastern part, I have more than doubled the territory belonging to France. I have restored peace, and a measure of prosperity—there will be more to follow. My Constitution is meant to do no more than to consolidate these gains—to France's benefit. All this you have seen with your own eyes."

Vincent opened his mouth, but no word emerged.

"Colonel, you know my heart, and my intention must be clear to you. I ask you to bring my Constitution before the First Consul and present it to him as I designed it—my ultimate service to the French Republic."

Vincent swallowed a mouthful of air, gasping like a fish hooked out of the water. "Of course," he said. "I shall do my best to satisfy your wish. But—"

"Excellent," said Toussaint, with his smile unconcealed for once. The teeth were uneven in his jaw. He disconnected his fingertips and spread his palms on the table. "With you as my emissary, I need fear no misunderstanding," he said. "Only, your departure may be slightly delayed, until the Constitution has come back from the printer."

"You have ordered it *printed*?" Vincent blanched. "General, to have it printed and promulgated before its approval—" With a sag of his shoulders, he cut himself off.

By dint of a massive effort of concentration, the doctor had completed his copy. He swiveled on his stool and presented it wordlessly to Toussaint, who spread it on the desk and signed it with his usual triple-dotted flourish. Folding the letter in three, Toussaint applied a wax seal and held it toward Vincent.

"I venture to add this private mission to your public one," he said. "A letter to my sons. And in this affair as in the other, I trust you absolutely."

Vincent clicked his heels and bowed. "I shall endeavor to be worthy of your trust."

With Moustique, Marie-Noelle, and Riau, the doctor walked into the Place Clugny. At first light the square was nearly empty, though a few of the market women had already begun to appear, beginning to furnish their stalls. One tall and stately woman with a basket of soursops balanced on her head, another leading a donkey with panniers of green oranges . . . Marie-Noelle's little son, called Jean-Baptiste, came trotting along behind the others. The dawn breeze coming from the sea ruffled the leaves of the *figuiers* planted round the edges of the square.

Moustique stopped, to the left of the central fountain, and handed Jean-Baptiste the gourd of water he had carried from the *hunfor.*

"Alé," he said.

The boy looked up at him, quizzical. He had a sweet, milk-chocolate colored face. His stomach protruded slightly under his shirt.

Moustique nodded. The boy moved in a leftward circle, pouring out the water till the gourd was empty and a damp ring in the dust had closed upon itself. He looked up, smiling, dangling the gourd.

"Poukisa n'ap fé konsa?" he said. Why do we do like this?

The doctor felt the quiet of attention of the market women who had continued to drift into the square while the child performed this small ceremony of remembrance. He did not look at them, but he felt their eyes.

"For the spirit of your grandfather," Moustique said. "He was killed here by the *blancs,* right on this spot."

"But my grandfather was a *blanc.*"

Moustique's face screwed up, then relaxed and cleared. "It is so," he said, going down on one knee beside the boy. "Still the other *blancs* killed him. He was a priest of God, an innocent man, and a martyr."

"The blood is of the martyrs," said Jean-Baptiste, in the recitative voice of catechism.

"It is so," said Moustique, "but water is greater. Greater than either blood or wine." He touched the child on his head, and stood up.

"Lamou pi fò pasé lahaine," Jean-Baptiste said.

"Yes," said Moustique, with some difficulty, as another contortion ran over his face. "Love is stronger than hate."

"Well," said the doctor, "he has learned a great deal since he came into your care." He glanced from Moustique to Marie-Noelle, who stood with her legs set slightly apart, rooted. A beautiful girl, with large clear eyes. She was pregnant again, and it became her.

The doctor lowered his eyes and looked at the ring of water sinking into the dust. Moustique had told him how such an offering of water might raise a spirit from its resting place. And at this moment he did feel the presence of the Père Bonne-chance, a sort of hum between the tendons at the back of his neck. A short, burly, balding man, with a smile that split his bullet head from one ear to the other. He had been a worldly man, excessively so for a priest (though the priests of Saint

Domingue were quite an irregular lot). If one judged by his death, which had been slow and gruesome, he had hardly lived up to his name for good luck, and yet in his worldliness he had done, in small, barely noticeable increments, considerable good. In his worldliness, he would certainly have appreciated the woman who had captured his son's fancy. *Lamou pi fò pasé lahaine,* indeed.

The moment had passed. Marie-Noelle twitched out a basket from behind her hip and ducked her head, with a smile. Taking Jean-Baptiste by the hand, she went off to do her marketing.

With Riau and Moustique, the doctor went out riding. The mission was to gather herbs, but they took a desultory way. For once there was no need for special caution—all was calm in all directions—and in any case both he and Riau carried their customary weapons, though they were not needed. Around noon, they swam in a spring-fed pool, and afterward ate the cold yams from their saddlebags with unusual relish.

Once they had eaten, Moustique seemed of a mind to turn back. But Riau lured them on ahead. *Pi devan,* he kept saying. A little farther . . . In fact there were attractions he seemed to have known in advance. Here a quantity of *herbe à crabe,* a specific against diarrhea, there a stand of *belle de nuit,* useful as a poultice to reduce the swelling of sprains. At last he brought them to a damp, shaded glen full of wild mushrooms enough to feed all the guests at the Cigny house and most of Moustique's *lakou.*

With their saddlebags bulging, they rode on, down the slopes of Morne Rouge, with the afternoon sunlight beginning to slant between the heavy, dark boles of the trees. Riau pulled his horse up before a great *mapou* tree, contemplated it for a long moment, then dismounted. From somewhere on his person he produced a whole egg, which he placed softly in a wooden bowl which lay before the mazy opening of the tree's branching roots. He walked on, leading his horse into the clearing.

It was an unremarkable spot, a wide space of packed earth, with a painted post driven in near the center. The doctor had learned enough of such matters to recognize a *hûnfor,* but that was not enough to explain the prickling he felt at the back of his neck—a stirring, collapsing sensation in the hollow just at the base of his skull. But it was Moustique, who also seemed somewhat out of equilibrium, who put the question.

"What is this place?"

"Bois Cayman," Riau said. He stood by his horse, with a casual air, not far from the *poteau mitan.* The doctor looked at the ground more closely. The dirt had been pounded smooth by many feet, but why did he feel this had happened quite recently? There were patches of sticky, cakey stain near the center post, some shards of broken clay vessels, and a scattering of black bristles.

"Bois Cayman," Moustique said in a shivering tone. "Why have we come here?"

Riau inclined his head, politely. "You brought me to see your son pour water," he said. "Sometimes, too, I serve in your mother's house on the hill, so in my turn I have brought you here, where Ogûn spoke through the mouth of Boukman, to inspire our first rising."

The tingling at the base of his head was a compound of fear and attraction—a mixture the doctor knew very well. He spoke without knowing he would do so. "Here is where the massacre of the white people was planned."

"No." Riau's voice was sharp enough to echo, but from what? There was no barrier anywhere to produce the ricochet.

"It is here that the spirits joined us to make one people," Riau said. "All we who are children of Guinée, and showed us how we must take our freedom."

The doctor stopped himself from replying. He saw that from Riau's point of view the slaying of a few hundred whites had been no more than a minor side-effect of the movement over the road toward liberty . . . as perhaps the destruction of thousands of Africans was only an unpleasant by-product of the manufacture of sugar. But that was another way of looking at it. His sense of disorientation increased.

"*Lamou pi fò pasé lahaine,*" Riau said, looking over his shoulder and all around. "There is a spirit who walks with you too." He was speaking directly to the doctor. "Balendjo, the traveler. Even now, he is near."

"But all this was long ago," the doctor said. "In ninety-one." His lips felt thick and awkward. He was speaking in spite of his sense that what Riau described was going on invisibly around him even now.

"They come here every year, I think," Moustique was saying. "August, at the middle of the month, so it has been, perhaps, six weeks?"

"No," said Riau, gathering in the space around him with an encirclement of both hands. His horse stirred its head at this movement, jingling the rings of the bit.

"It is now," Riau said. "Still, and always."

The doctor glanced at Moustique and saw that he was only feigning comprehension.

"Our dead do not leave us," Riau said. "They do not go away into the sky like spirits of dead *blancs.*"

At this Moustique nodded, for they both knew this litany.

"They are with us here, although invisible, *les Morts et les Mystères*," Riau said. He drew his sword and pierced the ground with its point. "They have their home beneath the surface of the earth—they are waiting beyond the gate, on the opposite side of the crossroads."

The doctor, who knew some portion of this reasoning from his conversations with Moustique, felt the small hairs rising on his forearms nonetheless. Moustique went on nodding rhythmically in the flow of Riau's words.

"At dawn or sunset, when the light makes the sea a mirror," Riau said, "then they are very near, *les Invisibles*, beneath the surface of the waters." He withdrew his sword from the ground and brushed the crust of dirt from its point. "When they come through the crossroads, then they move us," Riau said, looking very pointedly at the doctor. "That is how it is at Bois Cayman. And we must move as we are moved."

The doctor saw that Moustique had stopped nodding; the boy understood this last remark no better than he did himself. But Riau seemed satisfied, or finished, anyway. He turned, leading his horse after him out of the clearing. Under the trees again, he vaulted into the saddle, and took them on a spiraling route back home.

I, Riau, I did not know why I brought them to Bois Cayman at first, or even that I meant to do it. It was first one leaf, and then the other, the mushrooms, then we had arrived. Afterward I saw that I had wanted them to know, but especially the doctor, what was going to happen, what was happening already even then. I, Riau, had served at Bois Cayman once more this year, and with my spirit in my head. Six weeks before as Moustique had said, but that meant nothing. Time was nothing in that place. If Riau had brought his watch, it would have stopped ticking there, but I did not bring it. They did not understand what it all meant, but I was not sorry for bringing them there. I took them in and out again by such a twisted way that neither could have found the place again, alone.

At that time the division between Moyse and Toussaint was always growing greater. Moyse was made captain of the plantations in all the north, but he would not drive the men of the hoe to work as Dessalines did in the south and the west. Dessalines would drive, Dessalines would whip, Dessalines would kill any man who rebelled, and sometimes with torture equal to what the worst *blanc* could have dreamed. Dessalines had tasted it all in his own flesh, or much of it, and it seemed that he was willing to give it all back, and that he did not care in what direction he would give it. It began to be said that ten men who awaited an inspection from Dessalines could do the work of thirty under slavery.

Moyse looked at all this and said, *My old uncle can do what he wants, but I will not be the executioner of my people.*

By then, some people had begun to believe that Moyse really was Toussaint's nephew, because Toussaint was always so easy with him. Maybe Moyse believed it himself. But in truth, Toussaint was Moyse's *parrain* as he was mine, from our days at Bréda, and Toussaint had no blood tie with Moyse, any more than with Riau.

Moyse did not want to drive the men of the hoe to work, even on the lands which he now owned. He gave those lands to some whitemen to manage, and took a part of the money and did nothing more. Toussaint was very angry at this, and he let Moyse feel his anger. As captain of plantations in the north, Moyse ought to be managing his own land and making an example of how to squeeze more and more work from the men of the hoe, as Dessalines was doing in all the other parts of the country. Toussaint made his anger known, but Moyse was not in the humor to take that warning.

Moyse did not get much credit from the *blancs* for being captain-general of the north. He liked the *blancs* even less than they liked him, but still when he came to Le Cap he noticed how the *blancs* all preferred Christophe, who was commandant of the town at that time and had a more pleasant manner with white people. That was because Christophe had been a waiter in a *blanc* hotel, during slavery time, although I don't know how many white people understood this.

Moyse was not happy about Toussaint's Constitution. He heard what was in that paper from Riau, before it was printed and taken to France by Vincent, and after it was printed, the paper went on stinging him. This Constitution was a hard rule for the men of the hoe, because it bound them to stay working on the plantations for all of their lives under the hands of the army. The paper also said that Toussaint had power to bring more men into the country to work with the hoe, which meant that he would buy them as slaves. When they came here they must be made free, but it began to look like a strange kind of freedom.

From Toussaint's councils I knew that he did not really mean to put those new people into the fields. That part of the paper was meant to fool the *blancs* in France. What Toussaint planned was to bring in twenty thousand new men and put them into the army, to replace all the men who had been killed by the war in the south, because he was afraid a new army would come against us out of France, or maybe he already knew this was going to happen. Still, it meant that he would be paying to steal more people out of Guinée, as Riau and many others had been stolen.

Moyse was at Bois Cayman that year, and Joseph Flaville, and other officers of the army of the north, though not all of them. Toussaint did not know that they had gone there. Toussaint was not in the spirit of Bois Cayman anymore, or he did not seem to be.

I did not know what I would do when the thing began. At that time I had much freedom to move around the north with my horse soldiers. Even though Captain Riau was under command of higher officers, with the favor of Toussaint and the friendship of Moyse, I could often choose where I would be, sometimes at Ennery, or Dondon, or Le Cap.

Until the last day I thought that maybe I would take off my uniform coat and draw out my *coutelas* and begin killing whitemen again like before. Moyse expected this of Riau, and of Flaville also. That last day, I still did not know for certain, until we had passed Limbé, where Flaville commanded. There my heart turned cold and shrunken, and I knew my spirit was going to move me in another direction from Moyse.

We were going down to Ennery that day. But when we had come to Pilboreau, I took Guiaou away from the others, and told him he must ride without stopping to find Toussaint at Verrettes—he must not stop even for a moment at Ennery to see Merbillay and the children. Nothing was going to happen at Ennery, but he must tell Toussaint that the *ateliers* had risen and were killing whites all across the mountains from Limbé to Dondon, and all across the northern plain as well.

Guiaou looked at me without understanding. We had passed Limbé some hours before, and there was not any killing there. Guiaou had been at Bois Cayman that year himself, but since Agwé was riding his head the whole time, he did not remember anything afterward, himself, about what had happened or what it had meant.

"They are killing the *blancs*," I told him carefully. "But truly, it is a rising against Toussaint."

Guiaou's nose opened wider to breathe in my words.

"Go without stopping," I told him again. "Remember to tell him you come from me."

Guiaou nodded and turned his horse—I watched him canter down the slopes of Pilboreau. From Quamba I knew he had been afraid of horses when he first had joined Toussaint, but he was a good rider now, and his horse was strong. It would take death to stop him from reaching Verrettes. Toussaint had given him revenge for his scars and for the Swiss, and Guiaou was for Toussaint without any question.

With the rest of my men I rode east from Pilboreau to Marmelade. There was some confusion there, and when it ended, Bienvenu and

Bouquart and four of the men who were close to them had disappeared into the dust. They were *marrons* in their hearts, those two, and I thought they must have returned to Limbé. Though darkness had come, and the rain too, I took the other men on through the passes onto the plain again, until we came to Habitation Arnaud, because I knew the doctor was meaning to go there.

I found him already arrived, with Nanon and Captain Maillart and Isabelle Cigny. They were all making ready for bed, but I made them get up again, to return to Le Cap if they wanted to keep on living in their bodies. Moyse had come across the plain that same day toward Dondon, and everywhere he passed the *ateliers* would be rising, and Arnaud's people were going to rise too, whether or not he wanted to believe it.

At first only the doctor trusted what I told them—if he had not understood at Bois Cayman, he understood quickly now. He went outside at once and saddled his horse. Captain Maillart had been carrying on his love with the *blanche* Isabelle again, since she had come back from Vallière, and he did not want to go back to Le Cap so soon, where her husband was staying in her house, but with some talk I made him understand that it was necessary. With Arnaud, the trouble was that Flaville had protected him until now, but this time Flaville was very busy at Limbé, where three hundred *blancs* were killed that same night.

There was moon enough to see our road plainly. In time we began to see fires on the horizon, and after that there were not any more complaints. By morning we came through the lower gate into Le Cap. No one had attacked us. Twice there were bands who came near with knives and torches, but when they saw so many horse soldiers they went away again.

There was a rising in the town too, but Christophe took his men to put it down. I did nothing after those white people had been delivered, but took my men into the *casernes*. We had all been riding two days without a rest. When Christophe came in, he looked at me strangely, but he said nothing. Then there was nothing to do but wait. In another day, Bouquart and Bienvenu and the men who had gone off with them returned. I did not ask any questions of them, and they said nothing to me either.

If Moyse had had a little more time, even as much as one more day, he might have taken all the Cordon de l'Ouest from Limbé de Dondon and given Toussaint some real trouble. That chain of mountains had been the root of Toussaint's power from the beginning, and maybe Moyse thought the power would wither if the root were cut, or he might be able to take it for himself. But Dessalines, who was following Toussaint's order, brought his soldiers into Plaisance right away and broke the line. Wherever he went after that, Dessalines killed a great many of the men of the hoe who had rebelled, and Toussaint, who was coming up toward Le Cap from Gonaives, did the same thing.

When Toussaint came into the town, he ordered all the soldiers to parade on the Place d'Armes. I, Riau, stood at attention among my men, breathing as deeply as I could so that no part of my body would tremble. I had not seen Guiaou since I sent him to Verrettes, so I did not know what might be coming to me, but Toussaint was more terrible than I had ever seen him. People thought he was mounted by Baron de la Croix. He threw his plumed hat on the ground and tore the red cloth from his head and crushed it tightly in his fist, many times folded over.

"Here I stand," he screamed in a breaking voice. "The man that *Moyse* claimed would restore slavery. I stand before you—assassin of my brothers. Traitor to the French Republic. He who would make himself a king to rule a heap of corpses."

Toussaint was shaking from his heels to his shoulders as he paced the ranks of soldiers drawn up on the square. His mouth was bloody at the corners because his teeth had bitten into his cheeks. I thought he was coming straight for me.

"Step forward," Toussaint said, through gritted teeth.

But it was Bouquart who stepped out of the ranks from his place at my left side.

"Shoot yourself," Toussaint commanded.

Bouquart, standing very straight, picked up his pistol and blew his brains out through his ear. He fell down dead on the bloody stones. Toussaint walked on. Toussaint gave the same order many times. When it was enough for him, he ordered the ranks of soldiers to part. At one end of the square appeared three cannon. At the other came Joseph Flaville, bound among other prisoners Toussaint had taken on his way. All those cannon were loaded with grapeshot so that afterward no one could tell which scraps of meat and bone had belonged to one man or another.

In the echo of the shots I heard the high, shrill scream of a *blanche*. I turned to see Isabelle falling in a faint. The Captain Maillart caught her in his arms and carried her away. I did not know how she had managed to get herself there to see the killing, though I did know her reason. All the black people knew that she had borne a son of Flaville's at Vallière and afterward given it to Nanon, though none of the white people seemed to know it.

I was sorry that Bouquart was killed, and that Zabeth would have to find another father for the child they had made together. In the days that followed, I sometimes thought of Chacha Godard's head going down beneath the waters, and the same words in my mind—*what they did to us, we have learned to do to ourselves.* But I was not sorry that it had not been my time to go, that I could keep on breathing and living and sometimes kiss my children.

Moyse was not killed at once, even after so many others had died under Toussaint's rage. Toussaint met with him once in a friendly way, and pretended to believe that Moyse was not to blame for the rebellion. He even sent Moyse out with a party of soldiers to put down small risings that were still going on in corners of the plain and to the west of Le Cap. I thought then that Toussaint really did love Moyse, as much as his sons who had been taken away to France, and that he wanted Moyse to go off and hide in the mountains and save his life. But Moyse did not do this, either because he did not understand, or because he did not care anymore what happened to him. Instead he went to Port-de-Paix with his patrol, and there Maurepas arrested him and put him into the guardhouse.

There was a trial for Moyse at Le Cap, but all that time Moyse was kept in the fort at Port-de-Paix. Toussaint did not go to see him die, as he had watched Flaville and the others be blown to little rags of flesh, but he sent Riau in his place to watch it. I had no choice but to go. It was a lucky thing that Toussaint did not order me to be one of the firing squad.

When Moyse stood facing the guns in the Port-de-Paix fort, he called out in a loud, strong voice. Maurepas heard him, everyone did, but I thought his words were meant for Riau.

"Tell my old uncle," Moyse shouted. "Tell him my one eye has been looking into the other world for a long time. Tell him I see him walking there as well, among the shadows."

Then Moyse called on the men to shoot. *Feu! mes amis, feu!* he said. The muskets spoke together, and Moyse was silent.

I did not bring this message to Toussaint, and no one else did either. But it fell to Riau to tell Toussaint that Moyse was dead, which I had seen with both my eyes. When he heard this news, Toussaint put his face in his hands and wept without sound, and the water ran out from between his fingers. He had given the order himself, as I knew, but this time his grief was real.

40

The doctor threw the back of his hand half consciously toward the other side of his bed, and woke completely with a start of alarm when he found it cool and empty. Where was he? He sat up, bracing his back on the headboard, collecting himself one scrap at a time. The Cigny house, but he was still unused to the larger room he and Nanon now occupied on the second floor.

She was not there, but not lost either. Elise, who was also staying in the house at the moment, had insisted that he not see her all that day. This seemed a fond notion, given all the circumstances, but Nanon had accepted it with a secret smile, and if it pleased her the doctor had no reason to object. On the contrary, he was grateful for his sister's good will toward the enterprise, even if she had chosen to manage it with a very firm hand. In fact, all three women in the house had formed a temporary cabal, had shut themselves up in a room for the night and barred the door against the men.

He rubbed the fuzz on the back of his head, and shifted his bare feet to the floor. A warm band of sunshine came through a crack in the tall wooden doors to the balcony. He put on trousers and a loose shirt and went out to stand overlooking the street. Queer tremors of anticipation ran over him, though he laughed at this reaction. It was to be his wedding day.

The balcony doors of the next room were open wide, and the doctor put his head in cautiously to check the room before he entered. Paul and Paulette were sitting cross-legged on the bed nearest the window, telling each other a story in low whispers. On a smaller bed, wedged into the corner lest they should fall, François and Gabriel were sleeping. With a familiar twinge of slight anxiety the doctor tilted his head toward them to verify that they were breathing.

Gabriel was still somewhat the smaller, though he would not be so for long. Already he was heavier than François, as if a greater weight had been compressed into the smaller space of his compact, dark body. François was longer, leaner, and seemed in all ways more tentative, more fragile. Now Gabriel, snuffing, turned on his side and thrust a stubby black arm across the belly of his pale-skinned brother. François's mouth worked, as if at the breast. They stirred, nestled together, went on sleeping.

With a suppressed giggle, Paul and Paulette scurried out of the room, leaving the doctor alone with the smaller children. With a crafty hand, he enclosed one small rib cage, then the other, feeling the pump of respiration, the faint, steady beat of the heart. He had only to close his hand to extinguish the life. In his time he had seen infants this age or still younger impaled and hoisted upon spears. White, African, mulatto . . . it was the way in which one race announced its intention to wipe another wholly from the face of the earth.

The doctor raised his hands from the bed and looked at his tingling palms. The remembered horror did not frighten him today. It was part and parcel of the things he knew, a truth of the world he had come to live in. He was engaged to defend the lives of Gabriel and François and Paul with whatever power was in him. With that thought his hands grazed around his waist, but he had not yet put on his belt this morning, much less his pistols. He did not mean to bring his hand near any weapon, not today.

On the stairs he found himself thinking of a bit of prestidigitation Toussaint had recently adopted, since the latest rebellion and the executions of Flaville and Moyse. Toussaint before a throng of field hands or a division of the army, holding a glass container with a few grains of white rice sprinkled over unhulled brown, or a handful of white beans layered atop a quantity of dark-roast, unground coffee.

"Do you fear I am too close to the whites?" he was wont to ask. "Do you fear the whites will come to rule this country once again?"

It was, of course, a rhetorical question. A few brisk shakes of the jar, and the white grains disappeared entirely among the dark.

Downstairs, his way was blocked by Elise. Over her shoulder the doctor could see Paul and Paulette eating bananas, their eyes bright with amusement.

"What a creature," his sister chirped. "Do you mean to be underfoot all morning? Go out and find something to do with yourself."

"Let me take the boy, then," the doctor said mildly. He beckoned to Paul, and Elise removed her arm from the door frame to let the boy come through to him.

Together they walked down the slope toward the quay. On the waterfront, they turned in the direction of the Customs House. Profiting from the cool of the morning, the porters were busy in all directions. Some merchantmen of the North American Republic were taking on loads of coffee and raw sugar and molasses, while others disgorged barrels of flour, casks of wine or gunpowder, long, flat cases needing two men to carry, which the doctor knew contained new muskets. He called Paul nearer to him and took him by the hand. Whenever they came down to the port together, he was reminded of those weeks the boy had spent alone and abandoned in this area, surviving on the wits he could muster. Paul had never said much about it, though he had frequent nightmares in the first months following his recovery. Now he chafed at the restraint and soon broke free of the doctor's hand to scamper on ahead.

They passed the Customs House. Paul had stopped to gape at the cannon in the battery opposite the grove of trees which ornamented this area of the waterfront. The gunners smiled and saluted him. The doctor's son was well known to all of them. Paul came nearer, shyly at first, and was allowed to bestride a cannon and try the touch hole with his finger. The doctor took a seat beneath the trees. The sun, just fully risen in the east, struck metal reflections from the water. Against the dazzle he could make out sails coming in at the harbor mouth, and when he shaded his eyes, he could also see the smaller pilot boats bringing them in.

A porpoise broke the surface of the water, out ahead of the pilot boats. One rolling fin, then three, then five. One of them jumped clear of the water in a shower of shining droplets and fell back sideways with a tremendous splash. The doctor looked for Paul, to show him, but the boy had run farther along onto the parade ground between the Batterie Circulaire and the Arsenal.

The doctor leaned back beneath the trees, adjusting the brim of his straw hat against the glare. The increasing sun brought waves of warmth, and the breeze of the morning was dying. He felt calm, even drowsy, though at the same time he could still feel the wings of the butterflies stirring in his stomach. He turned his head idly in the direction of the town and saw a tall, erect figure approaching. As he watched, this form resolved itself into the person of Captain Maillart, wearing his best dress uniform complete with various decorations for valor he had lately been given, topped off with a dizzying orchid pinned to his lapel.

"Ah, you have absconded," he said, coming up to the doctor's bench, "but you won't evade capture. They'll have you penned up properly by the end of the day."

"I suppose you are right," said the doctor. "Let me say I am content to be made prisoner."

"Sooner you than me, my friend." The bench rails throbbed under the sudden shock of the captain's weight. "Well, *bon courage.*" Maillart produced his flask from an inner coat pocket. The doctor unscrewed the top and sipped and arched his eyebrows in surprise.

"That makes a change, does it not?" the captain said. "Corn whiskey, just in from Virginia."

The doctor sat back, withdrawing under his hat brim. The warmth of the whiskey spread in him. Despite the captain's teasing, he did not especially feel cornered. Though if he had not elected this marriage himself, he might have been brought to it by other means. During this oasis of peace, Toussaint had found time to turn his attention to the observance of proprieties (as his outward devotion turned ever more conservatively Catholic) and in consequence a great many men of whatever hue had found themselves contracting marriage with their long-term concubines, sometimes under a certain degree of duress. The doctor was content to have volunteered for his own mission before being conscripted—Toussaint had also appeared to be pleased. For once, he was in tune with the times.

They sat in a pattern of sunshine and shade. A flicker of warm breeze lifting the leaves around them suffused them with a citrus sent.

"Permit me to offer you a cigar."

Tocquet's voice. The doctor blinked his eyes open. Maillart had already accepted the proffer and was biting off the end of his cheroot with a great wrench of his slightly yellowed teeth.

"I did not expect to find you out and about so early," the doctor said.

In fact Tocquet had gone out the previous evening for a long night of gambling and who knew what else—seeing that the women of the Cigny house were disinclined to male society. He had invited the doctor, who had declined. Though he had stayed up late enough, comparing his botanical notes to a book on a similar theme he had recently acquired, Tocquet had not returned by the time he put out his candle.

"What is one to do?" Tocquet said. "The house is still untenable—the women." He snorted, cupping fire to Maillart's cigar and then to his own. "We shall all be relieved when you have settled your affair."

"Undoubtedly," the doctor said. "This once, as it is a special occasion, I accept your cigar."

Tocquet passed one to him and stooped down to light it. The doctor inhaled shallowly, and let out a rich plume of smoke, suppressing his impulse to cough. Tobacco was one vice he had never managed to acquire. The smoke rather dried his tongue. Maillart's flask went round again, and Tocquet kissed his fingers appreciatively at its savor, then turned to offer it to Riau, who had appeared, silently, imperceptibly, at his left hand. With a quick, bird-like toss of his head, Riau drank, and sat down, smiling, on the doctor's other side. Tocquet, who remained on his feet, leaned down to offer him a cigar and a light. Riau took it between his teeth and drew fire to the tip. He sat back, expansively fuming blue smoke. He too wore a dress uniform, with decorations derived from several services in addition to the French, and was crowned with the tall hussar's hat, which looked to have been given an extra-careful brushing for the occasion.

The doctor reclined against the bench rail, puffing his cigar infrequently, just enough to keep it alight. Captain Maillart began telling some story he had heard that morning from a seaman on his way across the docks. The doctor let his eyes sink, half attending. Paul, who had spotted Riau's tall hat, came running to his knee. Riau reached into his coat pocket and gave him something: a little pig fashioned from a piece of corncob, with sticks for legs and tail. Delighted, Paul ran with the toy back to the parade ground.

The voices of the children playing mingled with the shrieks of gulls. The doctor closed his eyes completely, pushed back his hat brim and let the red warmth play over his closed lids, listening to the drone of Maillart's voice and Tocquet's occasional remark. Between the cigar and the whiskey, he had become extremely thirsty.

Tocquet and Maillart broke off their talk. When the doctor opened his eyes, he saw that they were both watching Riau, who was balancing his way across the narrow aqueduct which fed the Fountain d'Estaing, placed in the harbor near the Batterie Circulaire to provision ships with fresh water. Riau stooped, into the glare that rebounded from the ocean's surface, and rose again and came toward them.

The others awaited him, with a certain solemnity. Riau reached them, holding a tortoise-shell dipper in both hands. With a barely perceptible flick of his fingernail, he spilled a few drops of water on the ground, then drank and offered it to the doctor, who gratefully tasted the cool, sweet water and passed the dipper on.

Slowly the conversation resumed; the flask made another circuit. The doctor's cigar was mostly consumed; he dropped it and ground out the spark with his boot heel. A moment later, Elise appeared, standing with her arms akimbo, under a parasol Zabeth held above the two of them.

"The pair of you," she said, meaning apparently the doctor and Tocquet. "What *are* you thinking—you are not dressed!"

The doctor looked down at his shabby trousers. *"Ma sœur,"* he said mildly, "it was you who expelled me from the house."

Unmoved by this reasoning, Elise stamped her foot and beckoned. Tocquet and the doctor followed her in the direction of the wardrobe.

At the makeshift altar in the white church on the hill, the doctor stood beside Tocquet, observing the benches with half his attention, wrinkling his nose at the scented water which Isabelle had dashed on his collar before he could prevent it—"It *may* cover the smell of drink," she'd said dulcetly as she made her retreat. Moustique held the Bible open in both his hands, discoursing on varieties of love: *eros, caritas, agape.* The doctor was struck by the evidence that he and Nanon had enough friends and wellwishers to fill a small hall. There was of course Maillart, with Vaublanc and the indestructible Major O'Farrel, also Riau with most of his cavalry troop. Toussaint was absent; he'd left the town on one of his lightning tours of inspection to some destination where he would be least expected, but Christophe was there, and Maurepas, who had come over from Port-de-Paix on a military errand. There were Elise and Arnaud and Claudette and Isabelle (though Monsieur Cigny was away, on his plantation at Haut de Trou), and there were Zabeth and Fontelle and her older daughters and Maman Maig' and a great many people from the *lakou* behind the church, whose names the doctor did not know.

A drum and a fiddle and a wooden flute took up a rickety version of a minuet, and to this music Paulette came down the aisle, walking slowly, with a shy pride, her hair pinned high on top of her head and her hand buried in an extravagant burst of orchids. Behind her stepped Nanon, her head veiled and demurely lowered. Save for the sinuous flow of her hips, she seemed completely disembodied by the wedding dress Elise had designed for her, its fabric rendered just slightly off-white by a brief drenching in weak tea, in token of the fact that Nanon's condition was other than perfectly virginal.

She reached his side. He could feel her warmth, and her scent was natural—again he regretted the splash of perfume. It all went very quickly: the vows, a bit of fumbling with the ring. Moustique raised a hand above them.

"Now we see through a glass darkly," he pronounced, "but then face to face; now I know in part, but then shall I know even as also I am known."

It was finished. At any rate, people were leaving the church. Tocquet had gone to join Elise, and the doctor and Nanon were bringing up the rear. Her hand on his elbow steadied him, for after all he was a little drunk. They emerged into the open air and paused on the first step below the doorsill, above the wedding guests, who had fanned out over the apron of ground before the church. There was Paul, observing Paulette in her transformation, with a certain covert admiration. Farther on, François rode Elise's hip, while Isabelle cradled Gabriel in her arms.

The breeze had freshened from the harbor, and the three crosses on the brow of the hill leaned into the wind. The doctor felt the hum in the hollow at the back of his neck, and with that the dead began to appear; intermingled with the living: nearest the crosses the Père Bonne-chance with his genial, slightly sheepish smile, and Moyse, the loose lid sagging over his missing eye, standing near Riau, and between Isabelle and Captain Maillart the figure of Joseph Flaville, and Choufleur was there too, looking more amiable than had been his custom, and the spirits of slaughtered children and those of the many men who had died under the doctor's hands when his skill was not sufficient to save them and those of other men he had killed with his weapons at moments of necessity or rage or fear. So many of them had been unwilling to share the world with one another—they had rather die—but after all, they had not left the world; they were still here, unseen among the living, the Invisible Ones, *les Morts et les Mystères*, and now, if for this moment only, they seemed disposed to harmony.

It occurred to Doctor Hébert that he had not yet kissed his bride. If not for her solid weight balancing his own and the warm touch of her hand in the crook of his elbow, he might have drifted away among the shades surrounding him. But he was happy now, and grateful, glad to be alive. He turned to her, and loosened the veil from the pins in her hair, and began to raise it from her face. As she lifted her face toward him, there was a sigh from their friends who were watching, and the wind caught the veil and tugged it free, light, airy, floating from the crown of the hill above the red roofs of the town.

Fort de Joux, France

September 1802

"You are unwell," Toussaint observed.

Caffarelli, who sat diagonally across the table from him, removed his handkerchief from his nostril to reply. Toussaint had placed himself with his back to the fire. Caffarelli was farther from the meager heat, nearer to that raw stone wall with its constant, dreary seepage.

"It is nothing," he said, honking slightly. "A cold."

"Take care lest it become more serious." Toussaint smiled. "You must take every care."

An unfolding movement of his hand seemed to indicate for Caffarelli's benefit all of the frosty, insalubrious conditions beyond the walls, surrounding the mountaintop and the Fort de Joux. To be patronized so, by the prisoner! It was outrageous. Caffarelli blew his nose, delicately, for his nostrils were chafed, and folded the handkerchief into his pocket.

"Oh," he said casually. "Once I have returned to the lowlands, I shall recover easily enough."

Toussaint said nothing.

"It is still warm there, below these heights," Caffarelli said. "You understand, it is only autumn, and a mild one too, once one has left these mountaintops." *As you can never hope to do,* he added with a silent smirk.

"Allow me to wish you a safe and pleasant journey," Toussaint said.

An unpleasant pressure spread beneath Caffarelli's cheekbones, behind his eyes and the bones of his forehead. He sniffed, swallowed the disagreeable slime.

"I shall not see you again, General," he said.

"No," Toussaint agreed. "I regret the loss of your company." He reached inside his coat and drew out two folded papers sealed with wax. "I ask you to deliver two letters for me," he said. "One to the First Consul. The other to my wife. If you would render me this small service . . ."

"Of course," said Caffarelli, in a milder tone than before. He glanced at the letters, then pocketed them. "I shall send you news of your family, as soon as I may. But even now I can assure you that they are treated with all consideration."

"Thank you," Toussaint said. "I will be glad of any news of them." He pressed the madras cloth to the side of his jaw.

"As we shall not meet again," Caffarelli repeated, "I wonder, General, that you do not take the opportunity to tell me something more substantial."

"But I have nothing more to tell," said Toussaint. "You have my memoir." He dipped his chin. "My letters."

"Yes, of course," Caffarelli said, and added in a flash of irritation, "for what little they may be worth."

But Toussaint only looked at him with his slightly rheumy brown eyes.

"Your secret pact with the English," Caffarelli said wearily.

"There is no such secret, as I have told you many times," Toussaint said. "You know all my dealings with the English, and they are clear as glass."

"Your treasure," Caffarelli said.

Toussaint blew out a fluttering, contemptuous breath, which made the flame of the candle waver.

"I have no wealth, in money," he said.

"But in your own memoir you record that at the outbreak of the revolt you possessed six hundred and forty-eight thousand francs."

"Sir, that was more than ten years ago, and surely you know the costs of war. That sum was all spent on the army, down to the very last sou."

"But what of the profits of your commerce since? Your exportations, the sugar and the coffee?"

"Commerce?" Toussaint's eyebrows lifted. "I was a planter, not a *commerçant.* What property I enjoy is not in money, but in land." He paused, considering. "In fact, I owe money which for the moment I am not able to pay. For purchase of those lands of which I have told you. For one plantation I still owe four hundred *portugaises,* and on another, seven hundred and fifty, I believe."

"And what of Habitation Sancey?" Caffarelli said quickly.

"Pardon?" said Toussaint. "What, indeed?"

"It was there that your chests of treasure were buried, is it not so?" Caffarelli lunged. "*Fifteen million francs,* General—and the Negroes who buried it were afterward shot."

Toussaint drew himself up. "I am long since exhausted with responding to that atrocious lie."

"Fifteen million francs, General," Caffarelli said again. "The sum which was voted by your central Assembly and paid into your treasury and of which no trace has been found since."

"You are bleeding," Toussaint informed him.

A tickle on his upper lip. Caffarelli tasted a thread of blood. He touched the area below his nose, and his finger came away stickily red. He smothered a curse as he reached for his handkerchief.

"The altitude," Toussaint said silkily. "And of course, your cold. But you will do better, as you say, when you have left the mountain."

Caffarelli, his whole face muffled in his handkerchief, made no reply.

"White people," Toussaint said, tilting an ear toward the grinding lock. "You *blancs* always believe that there is a gold mine hidden from you somewhere."

Outside, the castle bell began to toll. Under cover of the sound, Baille entered the cell, a long cloth bag slung over his shoulder, and relocked the door with his clattering key ring. He turned and faced the table and the fireplace. Caffarelli greeted him with a lift of his chin, swallowing blood as he did so.

"I have brought you fresh clothing," Baille told Toussaint, laying out garments on the table as he spoke. Civilian clothes, coarse woolens, brown trousers and a long, loose shirt such as a peasant would wear in his field.

"New orders have come, for your maintenance," Baille said. "If you please, put on this clothes at once, and I will take away the others. Also, I must take your watch."

Toussaint glanced up at him, then lowered his eyes to the rough clothing. "As you prefer," he said. He detached his watch chain from a buttonhole and laid the instrument on the table.

Baille cleared his throat. "I must also ask you for your razor," he said.

Toussaint was on his feet and trembling from head to heel. "Who is it who dares suspect I lack the courage to bear my misfortune? And even if I had no courage, I have a family, and my religion—which forbids me any attempt on my own life."

Baille's mouth came open and worked in a moist silence.

"Please leave me," Toussaint said. Baille obeyed.

Cautiously Caffarelli lowered his blood-stained handkerchief. If he kept his head tilted back, the bleeding did not resume, but he must strain his eyes against the lower rim of their sockets to see Toussaint, who had thrown his coat on the bed and was tearing off his linen. His upper body was taut and wiry, the black skin punctuated with a great many grayish white puckers and slashes.

"How many times have I been wounded in the service of my country?" Toussaint said. He touched his jaw. "A cannonball struck me full in my face, and yet it did not destroy me. The ball knocked out many of my teeth, and those that remain give me great pain to this day—although I have never complained of it before." He turned out his palm. "This hand was shattered in the siege of Saint Marc, but still it will draw a sword and fire a pistol."

Cafarelli stuttered without achieving a word. A gout of blood splashed out on his face; again he snatched up the handkerchief. Toussaint unbuttoned his trousers and let them fall. "Enough metal to fill a coffee cup was taken out just here, from my right hip," he said, "and still, several pieces remain in my flesh. That was when I was struck by *mitraille*—I did not leave the battle that day till I had won it." He flicked his finger here and there, from one scar to another on his torso and thighs. "From seventeen wounds in all (if I have not miscounted), my blood has flowed on the battlefield—and all of it spilled for France. You may so inform the First Consul."

Caffarelli found no answer. With a jerk, Toussaint pulled on the brown trousers Baille had provided. He shrugged into the shirt and sat down with a thump, leaning with his palms braced on the table top.

"Tell my jailer he may come for my possessions," Toussaint said. "One day there will be an accounting of all that has been taken from me, and of how my service has been repaid." He sat back, wrapping his arms around his chest. "You may go or remain—you are free to choose. Our conversation is at an end."

Caffarelli departed, though he had no heart to travel, that afternoon, even so far as Pontarlier. He stopped at the postal relay station at the mountain's foot. His nosebleed had dried and clotted unpleasantly, his head ached, he had a touch of ague, and he was unable to taste his food.

It was a cold, no more than a cold. In a matter of days he would regain full health and vigor, but for the moment he could not shake off the oppressive sense of his own mortality.

Of course he had taken the best private room the post hotel had to offer, which was not, however, so very fine or luxurious. Still there was a good fire in the grate, and the alpine chill of the Fort de Joux was already at a distance. By candle and the light of the fire, he struggled to finish his written report. His accounting to Napoleon would not be an agreeable one as, from almost any angle, it was a report of failure. The First Consul would not fail to recognize it as such. Caffarelli had come away without the information he'd been sent to obtain, and the Consul's sympathy for any failed effort, however strenuous, was notoriously low.

But after all, one must remember who was victorious and who defeated, who was master now, and who was in chains. Caffarelli dipped his pen for the final paragraph.

His prison is cold, sound, and very secure. He looked at the paper, and added, with next to no enjoyment of the irony: *He does not communicate with anyone.*

In the evening Toussaint's fever had returned, although he was not bothered by it. On the contrary, he had come almost to enjoy the sensation, as another man might enjoy the effects of wine or rum—pleasures which Toussaint had almost always denied himself. If this were weakness, it was weakness of the flesh. His body, faithful mount that it had been, had carried him a long way now, and he thought that it would not have to carry him much farther.

The fever repelled the cold of the damp cell. It was always succeeded by bouts of chills during which he must shudder and tremble, clutching the thin blanket to himself, while his loose teeth chattered painfully. The rattling of his teeth became the sound of the drums, and he heard the thin, high keening voice of a woman, calling upon Attibon Legba to open the road, to open the gate.

I am Toussaint of the Opening . . .

His arms spread expansively, in the form of the cross, and then regathered themselves around him. Now he was warm and still all over. The fire was still burning at his back (Baille, who grew more stingy by the hour, had complained again that he used too much wood) but the warmth came from within the molten core of fever. The damp wall opposite caught red glints of firelight, shimmered and ran before his eyes. Sometimes it seemed insubstantial as the laced roots of a *mapou* tree, or a curtain of vines or a hanging veil of water.

In the coziness of his fever, Toussaint chuckled at the thought of Caffarelli, his dumb persistence toward the buried gold he and his master imagined. He would have done better to look for buried iron. Toussaint had spent every coin he could scrape together packing the hills of Saint Domingue with iron—great caches of guns and the bullets to feed them. But as he had claimed to Caffarelli, there was no secret anymore. The weapons were all uncovered now; they were in active use.

The wall opened and the men began to emerge through the veil as from a cane field at the long day's end, pouring out in their hundreds, their thousands, through the corridors they had cut in the cane. Their skin was black and their chests and faces were marked with brands of ownership or punishment and also by the random slashes of the cane leaves. Some of them he knew by name and others were unknown to him except in the potency of their spirits, but to each alike he gave a musket, with the same words repeated, every time: *Take this, hold it, keep it always—This! This is your liberty.*

GLOSSARY

À LA CHINOISE: in the Chinese manner

ABOLITION DU FOUET: abolition of the use of whips on field slaves; a negotiating point before and during the rebellion

ABUELITA: grandmother

ACAJOU: mahogany

AFFRANCHI: a person of color whose freedom was officially recognized. Most *affranchis* were of mixed blood but some were full-blood Africans.

AGOUTI: groundhog-sized animal, edible

AJOUPA: a temporary hut made of sticks and leaves

ALLÉE: a lane or drive lined with trees

LES AMIS DES NOIRS: an abolitionist society in France, interested in improving the conditions and ultimately in liberating the slaves of the French colonies

ANCIEN RÉGIME: old order of pre-revolutionary France

ANBA DLO: beneath the waters—the Vodou afterworld

ARISTOCRATES DE LA PEAU: aristocrats of the skin. Many of Sonthonax's policies and proclamations were founded on the argument that white supremacy in Saint Domingue was analogous to the tyranny of the hereditary French nobility and must therefore be overthrown in its turn by revolution.

ARMOIRE: medicinal herb for fever

ASSON: a rattle made from a gourd, an instrument in Vodou ceremonies, and the *hûngan's* badge of authority

ATELIER: idiomatically used to mean work gangs or the whole body of slaves on a given plantation

AU GRAND SEIGNEUR: in a proprietary manner

BAGASSE: remnants of sugarcane whose juice has been extracted in the mill—a dry, fast-burning fuel

BAGUETTE: bread loaf

BAMBOCHE: celebratory dance party

BANZA: African instrument with strings stretched over a skinhead; forerunner of the banjo

BARON SAMEDI: Vodou deity closely associated with Ghede and the dead, sometimes considered an aspect of Ghede

BATON: stick, rod. A martial art called *l'art du baton,* combining elements of African stick-fighting with elements of European swordsmanship, persists in Haiti to this day.

BATTERIE: drum orchestra

BEAU-PÈRE: father-in-law

BÊTE DE CORNES: domestic animal with horns

BIENFAISANCE: philosophical proposition that all things work together for good

BITASYON: small settlement

BLANC: white man

BLANCHE: white woman

BOIS BANDER: tree whose bark was thought to be an aphrodisiac

BOIS CHANDEL: candle wood—a pitchy wood suitable for torches

BOKOR: Vodou magician of evil intent

BOSSALE: a newly imported slave, fresh off the boat, ignorant of the plantation ways and of the Creole dialect

BOUCANIERS: piratical drifters who settled Tortuga and parts of Haiti as Spanish rule there weakened. They derived their name from the word *boucan*—their manner of barbecuing hog meat.

BOUNDA: rectum

BOURG: town

BOURIK: donkey

BWA DLO: flowering aquatic plant

BWA FOUYÉ: dugout canoe

CACHOT: dungeon cell

CACIQUES: Amerindian chieftains of precolonial Haiti

CALENDA: a slave celebration distinguished by dancing. *Calendas* frequently had covert Vodou significance, but white masters who permitted them managed to regard them as secular.

CANAILLE: mob, rabble

CARMAGNOLES: derogatory expression of the English military for the French revolutionaries

CARRÉ: square, unit of measurement for cane fields and city blocks

CASERNES: barracks

CASQUES: feral dogs

CAY (CASE): rudimentary one-room house

LES CITOYENS DE QUATRE AVRIL: denoting persons of color awarded full political rights by the April Fourth decree, this phrase was either a legal formalism or a sneering euphemism, depending on the speaker

CLAIRIN: cane rum

COCOTTE: girlfriend, but one in a subordinate role

COLON: colonist

COMMANDEUR: overseer or work-gang leader on a plantation, usually himself a slave

COMMERÇANT: businessman

CONCITOYEN: fellow citizen

CONGÉ: time off work

CONGO: African tribal designation. Thought to adapt well to many functions of slavery and more common than others in Saint Domingue.

CORDON DE L'EST: eastern cordon, a fortified line in the mountains organized by whites to prevent the northern insurrection from breaking through to other departments of the colony.

CORDON DE L'OUEST: western cordon, as above

CORPS-CADAVRE: in Vodou, the physical body, the flesh

COUP POUDRÉ: a Vodou attack requiring a material drug, as opposed to the *coup à l'air*, which needs only spiritual force

COUTELAS: broad-bladed cane knife or machete

CREOLE: any person born in the colony whether white, black or colored, whether slave or free. A dialect combining a primarily French vocabulary with primarily African syntax is also called Creole; this patois was not only the means of communication between whites and blacks but was often the sole common language among Africans of different tribal origins. Creole is still spoken in Haiti today.

CRÊTE: ridge or peak

DAMBALLAH: Vodou deity associated with snakes, one of the great *loa*

DÉSHABILLÉ: a house dress, apt in colonial Saint Domingue to be very revealing. White Creole women were famous for their daring in this regard.

DEVOIR: duty, chore

DJAB: demon

DOKTÈ-FEY: leaf doctor, expert in herbal medicine

DOUCEMENT: colloquially, "take it easy"

DOUCEMENT ALLÉ LOIN: "The softest way goes furthest"; a famously favorite proverb of Toussaint Louverture

ÉMIGRÉ: emigrant. In the political context of the time, *émigré* labeled fugitives from the French Revolution, suspected of royalism and support of the *ancien régime* if they returned to French territory, and often subject to legal penalty. Most former slave and propertyholders who returned to Saint Domingue between 1794 and 1801 were considered to be *émigrés* in this sense of the word, though technically the term did not apply to all of them.

ENCEINTE: pregnant

ERZULIE: one of the great *loa,* a Vodou goddess roughly parallel to Aphrodite. As Erzulie-gé-Rouge she is maddened by suffering and grief.

ESPRIT: spirit; in Vodou it is, so to speak, fungible

FAIENCE: crockery

FAIT ACCOMPLI: done deal

FAROUCHE: wild, unconventional

FATRAS-BATON: thrashing stick. Toussaint bore this stable name in youth because of his skinniness.

FEMME DE CONFIANCE: a lady's quasi-professional female companion

FEMME DE COULEUR: woman of mixed blood

FILLE DE JOIE: prostitute

FLEUR DE LYS: stylistically rendered flower and a royalist emblem in France

FLIBUSTIER: pirate evolved from the wartime practice of privateering

GENS DE COULEUR: people of color, a reasonably polite designation for persons of mixed blood in Saint Domingue

GÉRANT: plantation manager or overseer

GHEDE: one of the great *loa,* the principal Vodou god of the underworld and of the dead

GILET: waistcoat

GIRAUMON: medicinal herb for cough

GOMBO: medicinal herb for cough

GOMMIER: gum tree

GOVI: clay vessels which may contain the spirits of the dead

GRAND BLANC: member of Saint Domingue's white landed gentry, who were owners of large plantations and large numbers of slaves. The *grand blancs* were politically conservative and apt to align with royalist counterrevolutionary movements.

GRAND BOIS: Vodou deity, aspect of Legba more closely associated with the world of the dead

GRAND'CASE: the "big house," residence of white owners or overseers on a plantation. These houses were often rather primitive despite the grandiose title.

GRAND CHEMIN: the big road or main road. In Vodou the term refers to the pathway opened between the human world and the world of the loa.

GRANN: old woman, grandmother

GRENOUILLE: frog

GRIFFE: term for a particular combination of African and European blood.

A *griffe* would result from the congress of a full-blood black with a *mulâtresse* or a *marabou*.

GRIFFONNE: female *griffe*

GRIOT: fried pork

GROS-BON-ANGE: literally, the "big good angel," an aspect of the Vodou soul. The *gros-bon-ange* is "the life force that all sentient beings share; it enters the individual at conception and functions only to keep the body alive. At clinical death, it returns immediately to God and becomes part of the great reservoir of energy that supports all life."[1]

GROSSESSE: pregnancy

GUÉRIT-TROP-VITE: medicinal herb used in plasters to speed healing of wounds

GUINÉE EN BAS DE L'EAU: "Africa beneath the waters," the Vodou afterlife

HABITANT: plantation owner

HABITATION: plantation

HERBE À CORNETTE: medicinal herb used in mixtures for coughing

HERBE À PIQUE: medicinal herb against fever

HOMME DE COULEUR: man of mixed blood; see *gens de couleur*

HOUNSI: Vodou acolytes

HÙNFOR: Vodou temple, often arranged in open air

HÙNGAN: Vodou priest

IBO: African tribal designation. Ibo slaves were thought to be especially prone to suicide, believing that through death they would return to Africa. Some masters discouraged this practice by lopping the ears and noses of slaves who had killed themselves, since presumably the suicides would not wish to be resurrected with these signs of dishonor.

INTENDANT: the highest civil authority in colonial Saint Domingue, as opposed to the Governor, who was the highest military authority. These conflicting and competing posts were deliberately arranged by the home government to make rebellion against the authority of the *metro pole* less likely.

ISLAND BELOW SEA: Vodou belief construes that the souls of the dead inhabit a world beneath the ocean which reflects the living world above. Passage through this realm is the slave's route of return to Africa.

JOURNAL: newspaper

KALFOU: crossroads

L'AFFAIRE GALBAUD: armed conflict which occurred at the northern port Le Cap, in 1794, between French royalists and republicans, as a result of which the royalist party, along with the remaining large property- and slave-owners, fled the colony

---

1. Wade Davis, *The Serpent and the Rainbow* (New York: Simon and Schuster, 1985), p. 181.

LAKOU: compound of dwellings of an extended family or inter-related families, often grouped around a central ceremonial area sacred to the ancestral spirits

LAMBI: conch shell, used as a horn among maroons and rebel slaves

LA-PLACE: Vodou celebrant with specific ritual functions second to that of the *hûngan*

LATANA: medicinal herb against colds

LEGBA: Vodou god of crossroads and of change, vaguely analogous to Hermes of the Greek pantheon. Because Legba controls the crossroads between the material and spiritual worlds, he must be invoked at the beginning of all ceremonies.

LES INVISIBLES: members of the world of the dead, roughly synonymous with *les Morts et les Mystères*.

LESPRI GINEN: spirit of Ginen

LIBERTÉ DE SAVANE: freedom, for a slave, to come and go at will within the borders of a plantation or some other defined area, sometimes the privilege of senior *commandeurs*

LOA: general term for a Vodou deity

LOI DE QUATRE AVRIL: Decree of April Fourth from the French National Assembly, granting full political rights to people of color in Saint Domingue

LOUP-GAROU: in Vodou, a sinister supernatural entity, something like a werewolf; a shape-changing, blood-sucking supernatural entity

MACANDAL: a charm, usually worn round the neck

MACOUTE: a straw sack used to carry food or goods

MAGOUYÉ: devious person, trickster, cheat

MAIN-D'ŒUVRE: work force

MAÏS MOULIN: cornmeal mush

MAIT' KALFOU: Vodou deity closely associated with Ghede and the dead, sometimes considered an aspect of Ghede

MAÎT'TÊTE: literally, "master of the head." The particular *loa* to whom the Vodou observer is devoted and by whom he is usually possessed (although the worshipper may sometimes be possessed by other gods as well).

MAL DE MÂCHOIRE: lockjaw

MAL DE SIAM: yellow fever

MALFINI: chicken hawk

MALNOMMÉE: medicinal herb used in tea against diarrhea

MAMBO: Vodou priestess

MAMÉLOUQUE: woman of mixed blood. The combination of *blanc* and *métive* produces a *mamélouque*.

MANCHINEEL: jungle tree with an extremely toxic sap

MANDINGUE: African tribe designation. Mandingue slaves had a reputation for cruelty and for a strong character difficult to subject to servitude.

MANICOU: Carribbean possum

MAPOU: sacred tree in Vodou, considered the habitation of Damballah

MARABOU: term for a particular combination of African and European blood. A *griffe* would result from the congress of a full-blood black with a *quarterronné*.

MARAIS: swamp

MARASSA: twins, often the sacred twin deities of Vodou

MARCHÉ DES NÈGRES: Negro market

MARÉCHAL DE CAMP: field marshal

MARÉCHAUSSÉE: paramilitary groups organized to recapture runaway slaves

MAROON: a runaway slave. There were numerous communities of maroons in the mountains of Saint Domingue, and in some cases they won battles with whites and negotiated treaties which recognized their freedom and their territory.

MARRONAGE: the state of being a maroon; maroon culture in general

MATANT: aunt

MAUVAIS SUJET: bad guy, criminal

MÉNAGÈRE: housekeeper

MITRAILLE: grapeshot

MONCHÈ: from the French "mon cher," literally "my dear," a casual form of address among friends

MONDONGUE: African tribal group, held in low esteem by slave masters. The Mondongues were known for their filed teeth and suspected of cannibalism.

MONPÈ: Father—the Creole address to a Catholic priest

MORNE: mountain

LES MORTS ET LES MYSTÈRES: the aggregate of dead souls in Vodou, running the spectrum from personal ancestors to the great *loa*

MOUCHWA TÊT: headscarf

MOULIN DE BÊTES: mill powered by animals, as opposed to a water mill

MULATTO: person of mixed European and African blood, whether slave or free. Tables existed to define sixty-four different possible admixtures, with a specific name and social standing assigned to each.

NABOT: weighted leg iron used to restrain a runaway slave

NÈG: black person (from the French *nègre*)

NÉGOCIANT: businessman or broker involved in the export of plantation goods to France

NÈGRE CHASSEUR: slave trained as a huntsman

NÉGRILLON: small black child (c.f. pickaninny).

NOBLESSE DE L'ÉPÉE: French aristocracy deriving its status from the feudal military system, as opposed to newer bureaucratic orders of rank

OGÛN: one of the great *loa,* the Haitian god of war. Ogûn-Feraille is his most aggressive aspect.

ORDONNATEUR: accountant

OUANGA: a charm, magical talisman

PAILLASSE: a sleeping pallet, straw mattress

PARIADE: the wholesale rape of slave women by sailors on slave ships. The *pariade* had something of the status of a ritual. Any pregnancies that resulted were assumed to increase the value of the slave women to their eventual purchasers.

PARRAIN: godfather. In slave communities, the *parrain* was responsible for teaching a newly imported slave the appropriate ways of the new situation.

PATOIS: dialect

PAVÉ: paving stone

PAYSANNE: peasant woman

PETIT BLANC: member of Saint Domingue's white artisan class, a group which lived mostly in the coastal cities, and which was not necessarily French in origin. The *petit blancs* sometimes owned small numbers of slaves but seldom owned land; most of them were aligned with French revolutionary politics.

PETIT MARRON: a runaway slave or maroon who intended to remain absent for only a short period—these escapees often returned to their owners of their own accord

LA PETITE VÉROLE: smallpox

PETRO: a particular set of Vodou rituals with some different deities—angry and more violent than *rada*

PIERRE TONNERRE: thunderstone. Believed by Vodouisants to be formed by lightning striking in the earth—in reality ancient Indian ax heads, pestles, and the like.

POMPONS BLANCS: Members of the royalist faction in post-1789 Saint Domingue; their name derives from the white cockade they wore to declare their political sentiments. The majority of *grand blancs* inclined in this direction.

POMPONS ROUGES: Members of the revolutionary faction in post-1789 Saint Domingue, so called for the red cockades they wore to identify themselves. Most of the colony's *petit blancs* inclined in this direction.

POSSÉDÉ: believer possessed by his god

POTEAU MITAN: central post in a Vodou *hûnfor,* the metaphysical route of passage for the entrance of the *loa* into the human world

PRÊTRE SAVANE: bush priest

PWA ROUJ: red beans

PWASÔ: fish

PWEN: a focal point of spiritual energy with the power to do magical work. A *pwen* may be an object or even a word or a phrase.

QUARTERRONÉ: a particular combination of African and European blood: the result, for instance, of combining a full-blood white with a *mamélouque*

QUARTIER GÉNÉRAL: headquarters

RADA: the more pacific rite of Vodou, as opposed to *petro*

RADA BATTERIE: ensemble of drums for Vodou ceremony

RAMIER: wood pigeon

RAQUETTE: mesquite-sized tree sprouting cactus-like paddles in place of leaves

RATOONS: second-growth cane from plants already cut

REDINGOTE: a fashionable frock coat

REQUIN: shark

RIZ AK PWA: rice and beans

RIZIÈ: rice paddy

SACATRA: a particular combination of African and European blood: the result, for instance, of combining a full-blood black with a *griffe* or *griffonne*

SALLE DE BAINS: washroom

SANG-MÊLÉ: a particular combination of African and European blood: the result, for instance, of combining a full-blood white with a *quarterroné*

SANS-CULOTTE: French revolutionary freedom fighter

SERVITEUR: Vodou observer, one who serves the *loa*

SI DYÉ VLÉ: If God so wills

SIFFLEUR MONTAGNE: literally mountain whistler, a night-singing bird

SONNETTE: medicinal herb

SOULÈVEMENT: popular uprising, rebellion

TABAC À JACQUOT: medicinal herb

TAFIA.   rum

TAMBOU: drum

THYM À MANGER: medicinal herb believed to cause miscarriage

TI-BON-ANGE: literally, the "little good angel," an aspect of the Vodou soul. "The *ti-bon-ange* is that part of the soul directly associated with the individual. . . . It is one's aura, and the source of all personality, character and willpower."[2]

TREMBLEMENT DE TERRE: earthquake

VÉVÉ: diagram symbolizing and invoking a particular *loa*

---

2. Davis, *The Serpent and the Rainbow*, p. 181.

VIVRES: life-stuff—roots and essential starchy foods

VODÛN: generic term for a god, also denotes the whole Haitian religion

YO DI: they say

ZAMAN: almond

Z'ÉTOILE: aspect of the Vodou soul. "The z'étoile is the one spiritual component that resides not in the body but in the sky. It is the individual's star of destiny, and is viewed as a calabash that carries one's hope and all the many ordered events for the next life of the soul."[3]

ZOMBI: either the soul (zombi astrale) or the body (zombi cadavre) of a dead person enslaved to a Vodou magician

ZORAY: ears

---

3. Davis, *The Serpent and Rainbow,* p. 181.

CHRONOLOGY OF HISTORICAL EVENTS

1789

JANUARY: In the political context of the unfolding French Revolution, *les gens de couleur*, the mulatto people of the colony, petition for full rights in Saint Domingue.

JULY 7: The French Assembly votes admission of six deputies from Saint Domingue. The colonial deputies begin to sense that it will no longer be possible to keep Saint Domingue out of the Revolution, as the conservatives had always designed.

JULY 14: Bastille Day. When news of the storming of the Bastille reaches Saint Domingue, conflict breaks out between the *petit blancs* (lower-class whites of colonial society) and the land- and slave-owning *grand blancs*. The former ally themselves with the Revolution, the latter with the French monarchy.

AUGUST 26: The Declaration of the Rights of Man causes utter panic among all colonists in France.

OCTOBER 5: The Paris mob brings King and Assembly to Paris from Versailles. The power of the radical minority becomes more apparent.

OCTOBER 14: A royal officer at Fort Dauphin in Saint Domingue reports unrest among the slaves in his district, who are responding to news of the Revolution leaking in. There follows an increase in nocturnal slave gatherings and in the activity of the slave-policing *maréchaussée*.

OCTOBER 22: Les Amis des Noirs (a group of French sympathizers with African slaves in the colonies) collaborate with the wealthy mulatto community of Paris, organized as the society of Colons Américains.

Mulattoes claim Rights of Man before the French Assembly. Abbé Grégoire and others support them. Deputies from French commercial towns trading with the colony oppose them.

DECEMBER 3: The French National Assembly rejects the demands of mulattoes presented on October 22.

1790

OCTOBER 28: The mulatto leader Ogé, who has reached Saint Domingue from Paris by way of England, aided by the British abolitionist society, raises a rebellion in the northern mountains near the border, with a force of three hundred men, assisted by another mulatto, Chavannes. Several days later an expedition from Le Cap defeats him, and he is taken prisoner along with other leaders inside Spanish territory. This rising is answered by parallel insurgencies in the west which are quickly put down. The ease of putting down the rebellion convinces the colonists that it is safe to pursue their internal dissensions. . . . Ogé and Chavannes are tortured to death in a public square at Le Cap.

1791

APRIL: News of Ogé's execution turns French national sentiments against the colonists. Ogé is made a hero in the theater, a martyr to liberty. Planters living in Paris are endangered, often attacked on the streets.

MAY 11: A passionate debate begins on the colonial question in the French Assembly.

MAY 15: The French Assembly grants full political rights to mulattoes born of free parents, in an amendment accepted as a compromise by the exhausted legislators.

MAY 16: Outraged over the May 15 decree, colonial deputies withdraw from the National Assembly.

JUNE 30: News of the May 15 decree reaches Le Cap. Although only four hundred mulattoes meet the description set forth in this legislation, the symbolism of the decree is inflammatory. Furthermore the documentation of the decree causes the colonists to fear that the mother country may not maintain slavery.

JULY 3: Blanchelande, governor of Saint Domingue. writes to warn the Minister of Marine that he has no power to enforce the May 15 decree. His letter tells of the presence of an English fleet and hints that factions of the colony may seek English intervention. The general colonial mood has swung completely toward secession at this point.

Throughout the north and the west, unrest among the slaves is observed. News of the French Revolution in some form or other is being circulated through the Vodou congregations. Small armed rebellions pop up in the west and are put down by the *maréchaussée.*

AUGUST 11:   A slave rising at Limbé is put down by the *maréchaussée.*

AUGUST 14:   A large meeting of slaves occurs at the Lenormand Plantaton at Morne Rouge on the edge of the Bois Cayman forest. A plan for a colony-wide insurrection is laid. The *hûngan* Boukman emerges as the major slave leader at this point. The meeting at Bois Cayman is a delegates convention attended by slaves from each plantation at Limbé, Port-Margot, Acul, Petite Anse, Limonade, Plaine du Nord, Quartier Morin, Morne Rouge and others. The presence of Toussaint Bréda is asserted by some accounts and denied by others.

In the following days, black prisoners taken after the Limbé uprising give news of the meeting at Bois Cayman, but will not reveal the name of any delegate even under torture.

AUGUST 22:   The great slave rising in the north begins, led by Boukman and Jeannot. Whites are killed with all sorts of rape and atrocity; the standard of an infant impaled on a bayonet is raised. The entire Plaine du Nord is set on fire. By the account of the Englishman Edwards, the ruins were still smoking by September 26. The mulattoes of the plain also rise, under the leadership of Candy.

There follows a war of extermination with unconscionable cruelties on both sides. Le Cap is covered with scaffolds on which captured blacks are tortured. There are many executions on the wheel. During the first two months of the revolt, two thousand whites are killed, one hundred eighty sugar plantations, and nine hundred smaller operations (coffee, indigo, cotton) are burnt, with twelve hundred families dispossessed. Ten thousand rebel slaves are supposed to have been killed.

During the initial six weeks of the slave revolt, Toussaint remains at Bréda, keeping order among the slaves there and showing no sign of any connection to the slave revolt.

In mid-August, news of the general rebellion in Saint Domingue reaches France. Atrocities against whites produce a backlash of sympathy for the colonial conservatives, and the colonial faction begins to lobby for the repeal of the May 15 decree.

SEPTEMBER 24:   The National Assembly in France reverses itself again and passes the Decree of September 24, which revokes mulatto rights and once again hands the question of the "status of persons" over to colonial assemblies. This decree is declared "an unalterable article of the French Constitution."

Late in the month, the Englishman Edwards arrives in Le Cap with emergency supplies from Jamaica, and is received as a savior with cries of *"Vivent les Anglais."* Edwards hears much of the colonists' hopes that England will take over the government of the colony.

OCTOBER: By this time, expeditions are beginning to set out from Le Cap against the blacks, but illness kills as many as the enemy, so the rebel slaves gain ground. The hill country is dotted with both white and black camps, surrounded by hanged men, or skulls on palings. The countryside is constantly under dispute, with the rebels increasingly in the ascendancy.

In France this month, radicals in the French Assembly suggest that the slave insurrection is a trick organized by *émigrés* to create a royalist haven in Saint Domingue. The arrival of refugees from Saint Domingue in France over the next few months does little to change this position.

NOVEMBER: Early in the month, news of the decree of September 24 (repealing mulatto rights) arrives in Saint Domingue, confirming the suspicions of the mulattoes.

Toussaint arranges the departure of the family of Bayon de Libertat from Bréda, then rides to join the rebels, at Biassou's camp on Grande Rivière. For the next few months he functions as the "general doctor" to the rebel slaves, carrying no other military rank, although he does organize special fortifications at Grand Boucan and La Tannerie. Jeannot, Jean-François and Biassou emerge as the principal leaders of the rebel slaves on the northern plain—all established in adjacent camps in the same area.

NOVEMBER 21: A massacre of mulattoes by *petit blancs* in Port-au-Prince begins over a referendum about the September 4 decree. Polling ends in a riot, followed by a battle. The mulatto troops are driven out, and part of the city is burned.

For the remainder of the fall, the mulattoes range around the western countryside, outdoing the slaves of the north in atrocity. They make white cockades from the ears of the slain, rip open pregnant women and force the husbands to eat the embryos, and throw infants to the hogs. In Port-au-Prince, the *petit blancs* are meanwhile conducting a version of the French Terror. The city remains under siege by the mulatto forces through December. As at Le Cap, the occupants answer the atrocities of the besiegers with their own, with the mob frequently breaking into the jails to murder mulatto prisoners.

In the south, a mulatto rising drives the whites into Les Cayes, but the whites of the Grande Anse are able to hold the peninsula, expel the mulattoes, arm their slaves and lead them against the mulattoes.

NOVEMBER 29: The first Civil Commission, consisting of Mirbeck, Roume, and Saint Léger, arrives at Le Cap to represent the French revolutionary government.

DECEMBER 10: Negotiations are opened with Jean-François and Biassou, principal slave leaders in the north, who write to the Commission a letter hoping for peace. The rebel leaders' proposal only asks liberty for themselves and a couple of hundred followers, in exchange for which they promise to return the other rebels to slavery.

DECEMBER 21: An interview between the commissioners and Jean-François takes place at Saint Michel Plantation, on the plain a short distance from Le Cap.

Toussaint appears as an adviser of Jean-François during these negotiations, and represents the black leaders in subsequent unsuccessful meetings at Le Cap, following the release of white prisoners. But although the commissioners are delighted with the peace proposition, the colonists want to hold out for total submission. Invoking the September 14 decree, the colonists undercut the authority of the Commission with the rebels and negotiations are broken off.

1792

MARCH 30: Mirbeck, despairing of the situation in Le Cap and fearing assassination, embarks for France, his fellow-commissioner Roume agreeing to follow three days later. But Roume gets news of a royalist counterrevolution brewing in Le Cap and decides to remain, hoping he can keep Blanchelande loyal to the Republic.

APRIL 4: In France occurs the signature of a new decree by the National Assembly which gives full rights of citizenship to mulattoes and free blacks, calls for new elections on that basis, and establishes a new three-man Commission to enforce the decree, with dictatorial powers and an army to back them.

APRIL 9: With the Department of the West reduced to anarchy again, Saint Léger escapes on a warship sailing to France.

MAY: War is declared between French and Spanish Saint Domingue.

MAY 11: News of the April 4 decree arrives in Saint Domingue. Given the nastiness of the race war and the atrocities committed against whites by mulatto leaders like Candy in the north and others in the south and west, this decree is considered an outrage by the whites. By this time, the whites (except on the Grande Anse) have all been crammed into the ports and have given up the interior of the country, for all practical purposes. The Colonial Assembly accepts the decree, having little choice for the moment, and no ability to resist the promised army. The mulattoes are delighted, and so is Roume.

AUGUST 10: Storming of the Tuileries by Jacobin-led mob, virtual deposition of the King, call for a Convention in France.

SEPTEMBER 18: Three new commissioners arrive at Le Cap to enforce the April 4 decree. Sonthonax, Polverel and Ailhaud are all Jacobins. Colonists immediately suspect a plan to emancipate the slaves (which may or may not have been a part of Sonthonax's original program). The commissioners are accompanied by two thousand troops of the line and four thousand National Guards, under the command of General Desparbés. But the commissioners distrust the general and get on poorly with him because of their tendency to trespass on his authority. Soon the commissioners deport Blanchelande to France.

OCTOBER: In the aftermath of a conflict between his troops and the *petit blanc* Jacobins of Le Cap, General Desparbés is deported by the commissioners to France as a prisoner, along with many other royalist officers. This event virtually destroys the northern royalist faction.

OCTOBER 24:   The Commission led by Sonthonax begins to fill official posts with mulattoes, now commonly called "citizens of April 4." By this tendency Sonthonax begins alienating the *petit blancs* Jacobins of Le Cap by creating a bureaucracy of mulattoes at their expense. In the end, Sonthonax closes the Jacobin club and deports its leaders.

The Regiment Le Cap's remaining officers refuse to accept the mulattoes Sonthonax has appointed to fill vacancies left by royalists who have either been arrested or had resigned.

DECEMBER: Young Colonel Etienne Laveaux mounts an attack on the rebel slaves at Grande Rivière. By this time, Toussaint has his own body of troops under his direct command, and has been using the skills of white prisoners and deserters to train them. He also has gathered some of the black officers who will be significant later in the slave revolution, including Dessalines, Moyse and Charles Belair.

Toussaint fights battles with Laveaux's forces at Morne Pélé and La Tannerie, covering the retreat of the larger black force under Biassou and Jean-François, then retreats into the Cibao Mountains himself.

DECEMBER 1:   Laveaux is sent to try to recall the disaffected Le Cap officers to the fold, but his efforts are ineffective.

DECEMBER 2:   The Regiment Le Cap, without cartridges, meets the new mulatto companies on parade in the Champ de Mars. Fighting breaks out between the two halves of the regiment and the white mob. The mulattoes leave the town and capture the fortifications at the entrance to the plain, and the threat of an assault from the black rebels forces the whites of the town to capitulate.

In the aftermath, Sonthonax deports the Regiment Le Cap en masse and rules the town with mulatto troops. He sets up a revolutionary tribunal and redoubles his deportations.

DECEMBER 8:   Sonthonax writes to the French Convention of the necessity of ameliorating the lot of the slaves in some way—as a logical consequence of the law of April 4.

1793

JANUARY 21: Louis XVI is executed in France.

FEBRUARY: France goes to war against England and Spain.

Toussaint, Biassou and Jean-François formally join the Spanish forces at Saint Raphael. At this point Toussaint has six hundred men under his own control and reports directly to the Spanish general. He embarks on an invasion of French territory.

MARCH 8: News of the King's execution reaches Le Cap.

MARCH 18: News of the war with England reaches Le Cap, further destabilizing the situation there.

APRIL: Blanchelande is executed in France by guillotine.

MAY: Early in the month, minor skirmishes begin along the Spanish border, as Toussaint, Jean-François and Biassou begin advancing into French territory.

MAY 7: Galbaud arrives at Le Cap as the new Governor-General, dispatched by the French National Convention, which sees that war with England and Spain endangers the colony and wants a strong military commander in place. Galbaud is supposed to obey the Commission in all political matters but to have absolute authority over the troops (the same instructions given Desparbès). Because Galbaud's wife is a Creole, and he owns property in Saint Domingue, many colonists hope for support from him.

MAY 29: Sonthonax and Polverel, after unsatisfactory correspondence with Galbaud, write to announce their return to Le Cap.

JUNE 10: The commissioners reach Le Cap with the remains of the mulatto army used in operations around Port-au-Prince. Sonthonax declares Galbaud's credentials invalid and puts him on shipboard for return to France. Sonthonax begins to pack the harbor for a massive deportation of political enemies. Conflicts develop between Sonthonax's mulatto troops and the white civilians and three thousand-odd sailors in Le Cap.

JUNE 20–22: The sailors, drafting Galbaud to lead them, organize for an assault on the town. Galbaud lands with two thousand sailors. The regular troops of the garrison go over to him immediately, but the National Guards and the mulatto troops fight for Sonthonax and the Commission. A general riot breaks out, with the *petit blancs* of the town fighting for Galbaud and the mulattoes and town blacks fighting for the Commission. By the end of the first night of fighting, the Galbaud faction has driven the commissioners to the fortified lines at the entrance to the plain. But during the night, Sonthonax deals with the rebels on the plain, led by the blacks Pierrot and Macaya, offering them liberty and pillage in exchange for their support. During the next day the rebels sack the town and drive Galbaud's forces back to the harbor forts by nightfall. The rebels burn the city. Galbaud empties the harbor and sails for Baltimore with ten thousand refugees in his fleet.

In aftermath of the burning of Le Cap, a great many French regular army officers desert to the Spanish. Toussaint recruits from these, and uses them as officers to train his bands.

AUGUST 29:   Sonthonax proclaims emancipation of all the slaves of the north.

This same day, Toussaint issues a proclamation of his own from Camp Turel, assuming for the first time the name Louverture.

SEPTEMBER 3:   Sonthonax writes to notify Polverel of his proclamation of emancipation. Polverel, though angry at this step having been taken without consultation among the commissioners, bows and makes similar proclamations in the south and west.

On the same day, the Confederation of the Grande Anse signs a treaty with the governor of Jamaica transferring allegiance to the British crown.

SEPTEMBER 19:   The British invasion begins with the landing of nine hundred soldiers at Jérémie. The surrounding area goes over to the British, but the eastern districts and Les Cayes are still held by mulatto General Rigaud for the French Republic.

SEPTEMBER 22:   Major O'Farrel, of the Irish Dillon regiment, turns over the fortress of Le Môle with a thousand men, including five hundred National Guards, to a single British ship. The peninsula goes over to the British as far as Port-au-Paix.

OCTOBER: A thousand more British soldiers land in the south, the mulattoes of the Artibonite revolt, and a new confederation of whites and mulattoes invites the English into the west. Similar events at Léogane mean that Polverel and Port-au-Prince are surrounded by the British invaders. From Le Cap, Sonthonax reacts by advising Polverel and Laveaux to burn the coast towns and retreat to the mountains, but they refuse.

OCTOBER 4:   Laveaux, walled up with a small garrison at Port-de-Paix, is being encroached upon by the Spanish from the east and the English from Le Môle, with his forces crippled by illness and fewer than seven hundred men fit for service. He writes to complain to Sonthonax of insubordination of the black troops.

Laveaux has left Le Cap under command of the mulatto Villatte, who established control of the town after the rebels of the plain had exhausted the plain and left it. Le Cap becomes the mulatto center of the north during the next several months.

DECEMBER: At the end of the month, Sonthonax joins Polverel at Port-au-Prince. Toussaint, fighting for the Spanish, occupies central Haiti after a series of victories.

1794

FEBRUARY 3: A delegation sent by Sonthonax, led by the black Bellay, is seated in the French Convention. Next day, the French Convention abolishes slavery, following an address from Bellay, in a vote without discussion.

FEBRUARY 9: Halaou, African-born leader of ten thousand maroons and newly freed slaves on the Cul-de-Sac plain, parleys with Sonthonax at Port-au-Prince.

MARCH: Halaou is assassinated by mulatto officers during a meeting with the mulatto General Beauvais. Leadership of Halaou's men is assumed by Dieudonné.

Intrigue by Biassou and Jean-François weakens Toussaint's credit with his Spanish superiors. Toussaint removes his wife and children from the Spanish to the French side of the island. Biassou lays an ambush for Toussaint en route to Camp Barade in the parish of Limbé. Toussaint escapes but his brother Jean-Pierre is killed.

MARCH 4: In France, Robespierre, chief of the French Terror, is arrested and subsequently executed.

APRIL: Toussaint, who now commands about four thousand troops, the best armed and disciplined black corps of the Spanish army, contacts Laveaux to open negotiations for changing sides.

MAY 6: Toussaint joins the French with his four thousand soldiers, first massacring the Spanish troops under his command. He conducts a lightning campaign through the mountains from Dondon to Gonaives, gaining control of the numerous posts he earlier established on behalf of the Spanish.

MAY 18: Toussaint writes to Laveaux, explaining the error of his alliance to the Spanish and announcing that he now controls Gonaives, Gros Morne, Ennery, Plaisance, Marmelade, Dondon, Acul and Limbé on behalf of the French Republic. The Cordon de l'Ouest, a military line exploiting the mountain range which divides the Northern and Western Departments of Saint Domingue, is under his command.

MAY 30: The British and their French colonial allies attack Port-au-Prince. A thousand whites under Baron de Montalembert come from the Grande Anse, twelve hundred confederates come from Léogane under Hanus de Jumécourt, and a fleet with fifteen hundred British troops attacks by sea. Commissioners Sonthonax and Polverel retreat to Rigaud's position in the south.

After their victory, the English ranks are decimated by an outbreak of yellow fever, which kills seven hundred men during the next two months and leaves many more incapacitated.

JUNE: An offensive led by British Major Brisbane fails to break Toussaint's Cordon de l'Ouest. Toussaint tries unsuccessfully to capture Brisbane through a ruse.

JUNE 9: Sonthonax and Polverel are served with a recall order from the French Convention; they sail to France to face charges derived from the many disasters which have taken place under their administration, including the sack and burning of Le Cap. Before his departure, Sonthonax gives his commissioner's medal to the maroon leader Dieudonné and invests Dieudonné with his commissioner's authority.

JULY 7: Jean-François, having lost various engagements with Toussaint's force on the eastern end of the Cordon de l'Ouest, falls back on Fort Dauphin, where he massacres a thousand recently returned French colonists, with the apparent collusion of the Spanish garrison.

SEPTEMBER 6: Toussaint's assault on the British at Saint Marc penetrates the town. He occupies Saint Marc for two days but is forced to retreat by a naval cannonade.

OCTOBER: Brisbane begins an offensive in the Artibonite Valley, disputing the natural boundary of the Artibonite River with Toussaint, supported by a Spanish offensive in the east. Toussaint uses guerrilla tactics against Brisbane, drives the Spanish auxiliaries from Saint Michel and Saint Raphael, and razes those two towns.

OCTOBER 5: Toussaint attacks Saint Marc again, capturing the outlying Fort Belair, and establishing a battery on Morne Diamant above the town. His fingers are crushed by a falling cannon. The British drive him from his new positions and he retreats to Gonaives.

NOVEMBER: Many of Toussaint's junior officers (including Moyse, Dessalines, Christophe, and Maurepas) are formally promoted by Laveaux. Laveaux tours the Cordon de l'Ouest and reports that fifteen thousand cultivators have returned to work in this region under Toussaint's control, and that many white colonists have returned to their properties in safety.

DECEMBER: Rigaud attacks the British at Port-au-Prince unsuccessfully, but succeeds in holding Léogane, the first important town to the south.

DECEMBER 27: Toussaint leads five columns to engage Spanish auxiliaries in the valley of Grande Rivière.

1795

JANUARY: Toussaint drives Brisbane from the town of Petite Rivière and leads a successful cavalry charge against British artillery at Grande

Saline. Mulatto officer Blanc Cassenave continues work on fortifications begun by the British at La Crête à Pierrot, a mountain above the town of Petite Rivière and the Artibonite River.

JANUARY 7:   Toussaint reports to Laveaux the success of his operations in the region of Grande Rivière. Most of the Spanish force has been expelled from this northern territory.

FEBRUARY 6:   Blanc Cassenave, arrested by Toussaint for a mutinous conspiracy with Le Cap commandant Villatte, dies in prison.

MARCH 2:   Brisbane dies of a throat wound he suffered during an ambush. Toussaint besieges Saint Marc once again.

MARCH 25:   Laveaux informs the French Convention that he has promoted Toussaint colonel and commander of the Cordon de l'Ouest.

JUNE: The Spanish try to purchase the loyalty of Toussaint's troops at Dondon. Jean-François writes a contemptuous rejection of Laveaux's attempt to convert him to Republican principles. Toussaint accuses Jean-François of slave trading.

Joseph Flaville, in a rebellion against Toussaint supposedly sponsored by Villatte, is defeated by Toussaint at Marmelade.

JULY 23:   The French Convention names Laveaux Governor-General. Toussaint, Villatte, Rigaud and Beauvais are promoted to the rank of brigadier general.

AUGUST 6:   Toussaint reports to Laveaux that he has gained control of the interior town of Mirebalais, and captured neighboring Las Cahobas from the Spanish.

AUGUST 22:   In France, the Constitution establishing the Directoire as national governing body specifies that the colonies are integral parts of the French Republic and to be governed by the same laws.

AUGUST 31:   Toussaint reports his defeat of a British assault on Mirebalais led by the white Creole Dessources.

SEPTEMBER 14:   Toussaint reports to Laveaux an alliance made with Mamzel, leader of the Docko maroons, a large band in the Mirebalais area.

Later this month, the British regain Mirebalais, defeating Toussaint's brother Paul Louverture, who was left in charge of the town.

OCTOBER 13:   News of the Treaty of Basel reaches Saint Domingue. By this treaty, Spain cedes its portion of the island to France, deferring transfer "until the Republic should be in a position to defend its new territory from attack." Jean-François retires to Spain. Most of his troops join Toussaint's army.

OCTOBER 25:   In France, after a lengthy trial, Sonthonax is formally cleared of all charges concerning his conduct in Saint Domingue.

1796

JANUARY: Having moved the seat of government from Port-de-Paix to Le Cap, Laveaux finds his relationship with Villatte deteriorating and begins to suspect the latter of plotting for independence. The mulattoes of the north are roused to further insubordination by the activities of Pinchinat, sent to Le Cap from the south by Rigaud.

FEBRUARY 12: Toussaint sends a delegation to Dieudonné with a letter meant to persuade him to join the French Republican forces. Dieudonné is overthrown by his subordinate Laplume, who turns him over to Rigaud as a prisoner. Laplume brings Dieudonné's men to join Toussaint.

MARCH 20: Villatte attempts a coup against Laveaux, who is imprisoned at Le Cap. Officers loyal to Toussaint engineer his release.

MARCH 27: Toussaint enters Le Cap with ten thousand men. Villatte and his remaining supporters flee the town.

MARCH 31: Laveaux, describing Toussaint as the "Black Spartacus" predicted by Raynal, installs him as Lieutenant-Governor of Saint Domingue. On the same day, Dieudonné dies a prisoner in Saint Louis du Sud, suffocated by a weight of chains.

MAY 11: Emissaries of the French Directoire arrive in Le Cap: the Third Commission, led by a politically rehabilitated Sonthonax and including the colored commissioner Raimond and whites Roume, Giraud and Leblanc. The new Commission brings thirty thousand muskets to arm the colonial troops, but only nine hundred European soldiers, under command of Generals Rochambeau and Desfourneaux.

MAY 19: The Third Commission proclaims that colonists absent from Saint Domingue and residing elsewhere than France itself are to be considered *émigrés* disloyal to the French Republic, their property subject to sequestration.

JUNE 30: Sonthonax proclaims it a crime to publicly state that the freedom of the blacks is not irrevocable or that one man can own another.

JULY 5: Toussaint's elder sons, Placide and Isaac Louverture, embark for France on the French warship *Wattigny.*

JULY 18: Unable for want of European troops to take possession of the Spanish part of the island, Rochambeau is stripped of his rank and deported to France.

AUGUST 17: Toussaint writes to Laveaux concerning his wish that the latter stand for election as a delegate to the French legislature, representing the colony.

AUGUST 27: Emissaries sent by Sonthonax to Rigaud and other mulatto leaders of the south create such ill will that a riot breaks out in Les Cayes, in which many whites are killed. Rigaud parades Sonthonax's proclamations through the streets of the town, tied to the tail of a donkey.

SEPTEMBER: Sonthonax and Laveaux are elected, among others, as representatives from Saint Domingue to the French legislature.

OCTOBER 6:   Members of the Third Commission write to the Directoire about their concern over the single-minded personal loyalty shown by the black troops toward particular leaders, especially Toussaint.

OCTOBER 14:   With further encouragement from Toussaint, Laveaux departs from Saint Domingue to assume his position in the French legislature.

1797

MARCH: In France, royalists, reactionaries, and proslavery colonists make significant gains in new elections.

APRIL: Toussaint successfully recaptures Mirebalais and the surrounding area and uses the region as the base of an offensive against the British in Port-au-Prince. British General Simcoe defends the coast town successfully and attacks Mirebalais in force. Toussaint burns Mirebalais and makes a rapid drive toward Saint Marc, forcing Simcoe to retreat to defend the latter town. This campaign is the last British challenge to Toussaint's control of the interior.

MAY 1:   Sonthonax arrests General Desfourneaux, leaving Toussaint as the highest-ranking officer in the colony.

MAY 8:   Sonthonax names Toussaint commander-in-chief of the French republican army in Saint Domingue.

MAY 20:   The newly elected French legislature convenes, with the proslavery colonial point of view energetically represented by Vaublanc.

AUGUST 20:   Toussaint writes to Sonthonax, urging him to assume his elected post in the French legislature.

AUGUST 23:   Sonthonax consents to depart, in his words "to avoid bloodshed."

SEPTEMBER 4:   In France, royalist and colonial elements are purged from the government; the Vaublanc faction loses its influence.

OCTOBER 21:   Toussaint informs the French Directoire that, after successful negotiation with Rigaud, the Southern Department has been reunited with the rest of the colony.

1798

MARCH 27:   General Hédouville arrives from France as agent of the French Directoire to Saint Domingue. His orders include the deportation of Rigaud. He lands in Spanish Santo Domingo, to confer with Roume, a survivor of the Third Commission stationed in the Spanish town.

APRIL 23:   British General Maitland begins to negotiate with Toussaint the terms for a British withdrawal.

MAY 2:   A treaty is signed by Toussaint and Maitland. British will evacuate Port au Prince and their other western posts, in return for which Toussaint promises amnesty to all their partisans, a condition which violates French laws against the *émigrés*.

MAY 8:   Hédouville arrives at Le Cap and summons both Toussaint and Rigaud to appear before him there.

MAY 15:   Following the British evacuation, Toussaint and his army make a triumphal entry into Port-au-Prince.

JUNE: Following his first encounter with Hédouville, Toussaint indignantly refuses to obey the order to arrest Rigaud.

JULY: During interviews with Toussaint and Rigaud at Le Cap, Hédouville seeks to weaken the power of both generals by turning them against each other.

JULY 24:   Hédouville proclaims that plantation workers must contract themselves for three-year periods, arousing suspicion that he plans to restore slavery.

AUGUST 31:   Toussaint signs a secret agreement with Maitland, stipulating among other points that the British navy will leave the ports of Saint Domingue open to commercial shipping of all nations.

OCTOBER 1:   Môle Saint Nicolas, the port of the northwest peninsula, is formally surrendered by Maitland to Toussaint. Following the transfer, Toussaint dismisses a number of his troops from the army and returns them to plantation work.

OCTOBER 16:   Instigated by Moyse and Toussaint, the plantation workers of the north rise against Hédouville's supposed intention to restore slavery.

OCTOBER 23:   Under pressure from the rising in the north, Hédouville departs from Saint Domingue, leaving final instructions which release Rigaud from Toussaint's authority. Commissioner Raimond, previously elected to the French legislature, accompanies Hédouville to France.

OCTOBER 31:   Toussaint invites Roume to return from Spanish Santo Domingo to assume the duties of French agent in the colony.

NOVEMBER 15:   Toussaint announces that plantation work will hence-forward be enforced by the military.

1799

FEBRUARY 4:   Roume brings Toussaint and Rigaud together at Port-au-Prince for a celebration of the abolition of slavery, hoping for a recon-ciliation between them. But Rigaud leaves the meeting in anger when asked to cede to Toussaint control of the posts he'd won from the Brit-ish in the Western Department (Grand et Petit Goâve, Léogane).

FEBRUARY 21:   In an address at the Port-au-Prince cathedral, Toussaint pro-tests the insubordination of Rigaud and warns the mulatto community against rebellion.

JUNE 15:   Rigaud makes public Hédouville's letter releasing him from obedi-ence to Toussaint.

JUNE 18:   Rigaud opens rebellion against Toussaint; his troops seize Petit and Grand Goâve, driving Laplume back from this area.

In the following days, the mulatto commanders at Léogane, Pétion and Boyer defect to Rigaud's party. Mulatto rebellions break out at Le Cap, Le Môle, and in the Artibonite. Toussaint rides rapidly from point to point to suppress them, placing Moyse and Dessalines in command at Léogane and Christophe in charge of Le Cap. At Pont d'Ester, mem-bers of his entourage are killed in a night ambush.

JULY 8:   Toussaint dispatches an army of forty-five thousand men to the south to combat Rigaud and his supporters.

JULY 25:   Toussaint breaks the siege of Port-de-Paix, where his officer Mau-repas was under attack from the Rigaudins.

AUGUST 4:   Fifty conspirators at Le Cap are executed after a failure to take over the town for the Rigaudins.

AUGUST 31:   In the midst of suppressing rebellion on the northwest peninsula, Toussaint narrowly escapes assassination near Jean Rabel. Returning in the direction of Port-au-Prince, he is ambushed, again unsuccessfully, at Sources Puantes.

SEPTEMBER 23:   Beauvais, mulatto commander of Jacmel, who had attempted to maintain neutrality in the Toussaint-Rigaud conflict, sails for Saint Thomas with his family.

NOVEMBER: Dessalines's offensive retakes Petit and Grand Goâve from Rigaud.

NOVEMBER 9:   In France, Napoleon Bonaparte assumes power as First Con-sul of the French Republic.

NOVEMBER 22:   Jacmel, key to the defense of the southern peninsula, is besieged by Toussaint's troops.

DECEMBER 13: In France, the new Constitution establishing the French Consulate states that the colonies will be governed by "special laws."

1800

JANUARY 18: Toussaint requests Roume's permission to occupy Spanish Santo Domingo according to the terms of the Treaty of Basel, citing the urgency of stopping the slave trade which continued to some extent on Spanish territory. Roume denies the request.

JANUARY 19: Pétion assumes command of Jacmel, entering the besieged town by stealth.

MARCH 1: Pétion evacuates the women of Jacmel.

MARCH 11: Pétion leads the survivors of the siege on a desperate sortie from Jacmel and manages to rejoin Rigaud with the shreds of his force, abandoning Jacmel to Toussaint. Rigaud retreats onto the Grand Anse, leaving scorched earth behind him.

APRIL 27: Under pressure from Toussaint, Roume signs an order to take possession of the Spanish side of the island.

MAY 22: Agé, a white general loyal to Toussaint, arrives in Santo Domingo with a symbolic force and is resisted by the population.

JUNE: A new group of emissaries from the French Consulate debarks in Spanish Santo Domingo, including General Michel, Raimond, and Colonel Vincent (the latter a white officer close to Toussaint). Their instructions are to keep the two halves of the island separate and to bring the black/mulatto war to a close—while at the same time conciliating Toussaint. Both Michel and Vincent are arrested briefly by Toussaint's troops, on their way into the French part of the island.

JUNE 16: Roume rescinds his order of April 27, 1800, in the face of Agé's failure.

JUNE 24: Colonel Vincent meets with Toussaint for the first time since his arrival, and informs him of the Consulate's intention to maintain him as General-in-Chief.

JULY 7: Rigaud is decisively defeated by Dessalines at Aquin—last of a series of lost battles.

AUGUST 1: Toussaint enters Les Cayes, Rigaud's hometown and the last center of mulatto resistance. Rigaud flees to France by way of Guadeloupe. Toussaint proclaims a general amnesty for the mulatto combatants. But Dessalines, left in charge of the south, conducts extremely severe reprisals.

OCTOBER 12: Toussaint proclaims forced labor on the plantations, to be enforced by two captain-generals: Dessalines in the south and west and Moyse in the north.

NOVEMBER 4: French Minister of Marine Forfait instructs Toussaint *not* to take possession of the Spanish portion of the island.

NOVEMBER 26: Roume, blamed by Toussaint for Agé's failed expedition to Santo Domingo, is arrested by Moyse and imprisoned at Dondon.

1801

JANUARY: Toussaint sends two columns into Spanish Santo Domingo, one from Ouanaminthe under command of Moyse and the other from Mirebalais under his own command.

JANUARY 28: Toussaint enters Santo Domingo City, accepts the Spanish capitulation from Don García, and proclaims the abolition of slavery.

FEBRUARY 4: Toussaint organizes an assembly to create a constitution for Saint Domingue.

JULY 3: Toussaint proclaims the new constitution, whose terms make him governor for life.

JULY 16: Toussaint dispatches a reluctant Vincent to present his constitution to Napoleon Bonaparte and the Consulate in France.

OCTOBER 1: The Peace of Amiens ends the war between England and France. Napoleon begins to prepare an expedition, led by his brother-in-law General Leclerc, to restore white power in Saint Domingue.

OCTOBER 16: An insurrection against Toussaint's forced labor policy begins on the northern plain and, in the coming weeks, is suppressed with extreme severity by Toussaint and Dessalines.

NOVEMBER 24: Moyse is executed at Port-de-Paix.

NOVEMBER 25: Toussaint proclaims a military dictatorship.

1802

FEBRUARY: Leclerc's invasion begins with a strength of approximately seventeen thousand troops. Toussaint, with approximately twenty thousand men under his command, orders the black generals to raze the coast towns and retreat into the interior, but because of either disloyalty or poor communications the order is not universally followed. Black General Christophe burns Le Cap to ashes for the second time in ten years, but the French occupy Port-au-Prince before Dessalines can destroy it.

In late February and March, the French forces pursuing Toussaint fight a number of drawn battles in the interior of the island, with heavy casualties on both sides.

APRIL 1: Leclerc writes to Napoleon that he has seven thousand active men and five thousand in hospital—meaning that another five thousand are dead. Leclerc also has seven thousand "colonial troops" of variable reliability, mulattoes but also a lot of black soldiery brought over by turncoat leaders.

APRIL 2:   Leclerc subdues the northern plain and enters Le Cap.

Early this month, the black General Christophe goes over to the French with twelve hundred troops, on a promise of retaining his rank in French service. But Toussaint still holds the northern mountains with four thousand regular troops and a great number of irregulars. Leclerc writes to the Minister of Marine that he needs twenty-five thousand European troops to secure the island—that is, reinforcements of fourteen thousand.

MAY 1:   Toussaint and Dessalines surrender on similar terms as Christophe. Leclerc's position is still too weak for him to obey Napoleon's order to deport the black leaders immediately. While Toussaint retires to Gonaives, with his two thousand life guards converting themselves to cultivators there, Dessalines remains on active duty. Leclerc frets that their submission may be feigned.

MAY: A severe yellow fever outbreak begins in Port-au-Prince and Le Cap in the middle of the month, causing many deaths among the French troops.

JUNE: By the first week of this month, Leclerc has lost three thousand men to fever. Both Le Cap and Port-au-Prince are plague zones, with corpses laid out in the barracks yards to be carried to lime pits outside the town.

JUNE 6:   Leclerc notifies Napoleon that he has ordered Toussaint's arrest. Lured away from Gonaives to a meeting with General Brunet, Toussaint is made prisoner.

JUNE 15:   Toussaint, with his family, is deported for France aboard the ship *Le Héros*.

JUNE 11:   Leclerc writes to the Minister of Marine that he suspects his army will die out from under him—citing his own illness (he had overcome a bout of malaria soon after his arrival), he asks for recall. This letter also contains the recommendation that Toussaint be imprisoned in the heart of inland France.

In the third week of June, Leclerc begins the tricky project of disarming the cultivators—under authority of the black generals who have submitted to him.

JUNE 22:   Toussaint writes a letter of protest to Napoleon from his ship, which is now docked in Brest.

JULY 6:   Leclerc writes to the Minister of Marine that he is losing one hundred sixty men per day. However, this same report states that he is effectively destroying the influence of the black generals.

News of the restoration of slavery in Guadeloupe arrives in Saint

Domingue in the last days of the month. The north rises instantly, the west shortly afterward, and black soldiers begin to desert their generals.

AUGUST 6:   Leclerc reports the continued prevalence of yellow fever, the failure to complete the disarmament, and the growth of rebellion. The major black generals have stayed in his camp, but the petty officers are deserting in droves and taking their troops with them.

AUGUST 24:   Toussaint is imprisoned at the Fort de Joux, in France near the Swiss border.

AUGUST 25:   Leclerc writes: "To have been rid of Toussaint is not enough; there are two thousand more leaders to get rid of as well."

AUGUST/SEPTEMBER: In his cell at Fort de Joux, Toussaint composes a report of his conduct during Leclerc's invasion, intended to justify himself to the First Consul, Bonaparte.

SEPTEMBER 13:   The expected abatement of the yellow fever at the approach of the autumnal equinox fails to occur. The reinforcements arriving die as fast as they are put into the country, and Leclerc has to deploy them as soon as they get off the boat. Leclerc asks for ten thousand men to be immediately sent. He is losing territory in the interior and his black generals are beginning to waver, though he still is confident of his ability to manipulate them.

As of this date, a total of twenty-eight thousand men have been sent from France, and Leclerc estimates that ten thousand five hundred are still alive, but only forty-five hundred are fit for duty. Five thousand sailors have also died, bringing the total loss to twenty-nine thousand.

SEPTEMBER 15:   General Caffarelli, agent of Napoleon Bonaparte, arrives at the Fort de Joux for the first of seven interrogations of Toussaint.

OCTOBER 7:   Leclerc: "We must destroy all the mountain Negroes, men and women, sparing only children under twelve years of age. We must destroy half the Negroes of the plains, and not allow in the colony a single man who has ever worn an epaulette. Without these measures the colony will never be at peace. . . ."

OCTOBER 10:   Mulatto General Clervaux revolts, with all his troops, upon the news of Napoleon's restoration of the mulatto discriminations of the *ancien régime*. Le Cap had been mostly garrisoned by mulattoes.

OCTOBER 13:   Christophe and the other black generals in the north join Clervaux's rebellion. On this news, Dessalines raises revolt in the west.

NOVEMBER 2:   Leclerc dies of yellow fever. Command is assumed by Rochambeau.

By the end of the month the fever finally begins to abate, and acclimated survivors, now immune, begin to return to service. In France, Napoleon has outfitted ten thousand reinforcements.

1803

MARCH: At the beginning of the month, Rochambeau has eleven thousand troops and only four thousand in hospital, indicating that the worst of the disease threat has passed. He is ready to conduct a war of extermination against the blacks, and brings man-eating dogs from Cuba to replace his lost soldiery. He makes slow headway against Dessalines in March and April, while Napoleon plans to send thirty thousand reinforcements in two installments in the coming year.

APRIL 7: Toussaint Louverture dies a prisoner in Fort de Joux.

MAY 12: New declaration of war between England and France.

JUNE: By month's end, Saint Domingue is completely blockaded by the English. With English aid, Dessalines smashes into the coast towns.

OCTOBER: Early in the month, Les Cayes falls to the blacks. At month's end, so does Port-au-Prince.

NOVEMBER 10: Rochambeau flees Le Cap and surrenders to the English fleet.

NOVEMBER 28: The French are forced to evacuate their last garrison at Le Môle. Dessalines promises protection to all whites who choose to remain, following Toussaint's earlier policy. During the first year of his rule he will continue encouraging white planters to return and manage their property, and many who trusted Toussaint will do so.

DECEMBER 31: Declaration of Haitian independence.

1804

OCTOBER: Dessalines, having overcome all rivals, crowns himself emperor. A term of his constitution defines all citizens of Haiti as *nèg* (blacks) and all noncitizens of Haiti as *blanc* (whites)—regardless of skin color in both cases.

1805

JANUARY: Dessalines begins the massacre of all the whites (according to the redefinition in the Constitution of 1804) remaining in Haiti.

ORIGINAL LETTERS AND DOCUMENTS

Quotations which appear italicized in the main text derive from the historical record, and are reproduced here in the original versions.

FROM CHAPTER 3, PP. 47–51:

Toussaint Louverture, général des Armées du Roy; à Monsieur Chanlatte jeune le scélérat, perfide et trompeur.

Quartier général ce 27 aoust 1793.

J'ai reçu vos trois lettres que vous m'avez écris par triplicat, *et qui me sont parvenus par trois de mes différents camps; et vous n'avez pas besoin de vous servir, de la voi de monsieur Vernet pour me fair parvenir vos letres, toutes celles qui me sont addressés directement oû non, me parvienne exactement.*

Je vous répondrai donc que je suis on ne peu des plus sensibles aux marques d'intérêt que vous prenez à ma personne. Je suis pénétré de votre humanité, vous m'en avez donnés des marques, par les cruautés que vous avez Commis par trois différentes fois envers mes gens en les martirisans de toutes manière. Mais je vous attend à la quatrième. Mes principes sont bien différents des vôtres, *et en mettant la main sur vôtre Conscience, vous saurez en faire la différence, et pour lors vous ne direz pas que vous êtes remply D'humanité; il n'est pas possible que vous Combattiez pour le droit de l'homme, après toutes les cruautés que vous Exercé journellement; non vous ne vous battez que pour vos interets, et satisfaire vôtre ambition; ainsy que vos traîtres projets Criminels, et je vous prie de croire que je n'ignore pas vos forfaits, et soyez persuadés que nous ne sommes pas si faibles de lumières pour nous laisser tromper comme vous voudriez nous le faire accroire, Nous savons bien qu'il n'y a plus de* Roy *puisque vous traitres républicains l'avez fait égorger sur un indigne échafaut; mais vous n'en etes pas encore où vous voulez, et qui vous a dit qu'au moment où je vous parle, il n'y en aye pas un autre? que vous êtes peu instruit pour un agent des commissaires. L'on voit bien que vos portes sont bien gardées, et que vous ne recevez pas souvent des nouvelles de France, vous en recevrez encore bien moins de la Nouvelle angleterre; je croirai bien que vous l'ignorez pas, mais étant trop lié avec les Commissaires d'interest, vous êtes trop politique pour travailler Contre, en divulgant la verité; faites vos Reflextions le tems n'est pas éloigné, où la Justice Divine va s'apèsantir sur les Criminels, et je désire sincerement pour l'interest que je prends à mes semblables, qu'ils puisse revenir de leurs erreurs.*

Quant aux Commissaires *ne m'en parlé pas, leurs stratagemes me sont connus et depuis leur arrivée dans la Colonie, nous avons suivis leurs démarches parjures, et ils ont développé leurs soi disant bonnes intentions; trop tard, setait dans le tems qu'ils nous fesait poursuivre et fesant endurer à ceux qu'ils atrapait des notres les plus grande cruautés, setait dans ce temps dis-je qu'il devait nous faire envisager ce qu'ils veulent nous faire croire aujourd huy pour nous tromper; et à ce sujet lorsque vous verrez les commissaires ils vous communiqueront certainement mes remarques à l'égard de leurs sage conduitte, en reponce, à un de leurs tentatives ordinaire auxquels je suis accoutumé ainsy que tous les État major et ma troupe.*

Je vous désire bien de la santé et vous engage pour un homme soi disant humain à ne pas gaspiller vôtre munition sur des malheureuses victimes de toutes Couleurs, comme vous faite tous les jours! C'est chez nous où Regne le *véritable droit de l'homme et de la justice! nous recevons tous le monde avec l'humanité, et fraternité, même nos plus Cruels ennemis, et leur pardonnons de bon coeur, et c'est avec la douceur que nous les fésons revenir de leurs erreurs.*

—Toussaint Louverture[1]

FROM CHAPTER 3, PP. 48–51:

Nous ne pouvons nous conformer à la volonté de la nation, vu que depuis que le monde règne nous n'avons exécuté que celle d'un roi. Nous avons perdu celui de la France, mais nous sommes chéris de celui d'Espagne qui nous 'témoigne des récompenses et ne cesse de nous sécourir; comme cela, nous ne pouvons reconnaître commissaire que lorsque vous aurez trôné un roi.[2]

---

1. Pierre Pluchon, *Toussaint Louverture* (Paris: Fayard, 1989), p. 94.
2. Pluchon, p. 93.

FROM CHAPTER 9, PP. 143–45:

Toussaint Louverture, général de l'armée de l'Ouest, à Etienne Laveaux, général par interim.

Le citoyen Chevalier, commandant de Terre-Neuve et Port à Piment m'a remis votre lettre en date de 5 le courant et pénétré de las plus vive reconnaissance, j'ai apprécie, comme je dois, toutes les vérités qu'elle renferme.

Il est vrai, général, que j'ai été induit en erreur par les ennemis de la République; mais quel homme peut se vanter d'éviter tous les pièges des méchants? A la vérité, j'ai tombé dans les filets, mais non point sans connaisance de cause. Vous devez bien vous rappelez qu'avant les désastres du Cap, et par les démarches que j'avais faites par devers vous, mon but ne tendait qu'a nous unir pour combattre les ennemis de la France et faire cesser une guerre intestine parmi les français de cette colonie. Malheureusement, et pour tous en général, les voies de réconciliation par moi proposées: la reconnaissance de la liberté des noirs et une amnistie plénière, furent rejetées. Mon coeur saigna et je répandis des larmes sur le sort infortuné de ma patrie, prévoyant les malheurs qui allaient s'ensuivre. Je ne m'étais pas trompé: la fatale expérience a prouvé la réalité de mes prédictions.

Sur ces entrefaites, les Espagnols m'offrirent leur protection, et pour tous ceux qui combattraient pour la cause des Roys, et ayant toujours combattu pour avoir cette même liberté, j'adhérai à leurs offres, me voyant abandonné des Français, mes frères. Mais une expérience un peu tardive m'a desillé les yeux sur ces perfides protecteurs et m'étant aperçu de leur superchérie scélérate, j'ai vu clairement que leurs vues tendait à nous faire entr'égorger pour diminuer notre nombre, et pour surcharger le restant de chaînes et les faire retomber à l'ancien esclavage. Non, jamais ils ne parviendront à leur but infâme! et nous nous vengerons à notre tour de ces êtres méprisables à tous les égards. Unissons-nous donc à jamais et, oubliant le passé, ne nous occupons désormais qu'à écraser nos ennemis et à nous venger particulièremet de nos perfides voisins.

Il est bien certain que le pavillon national flotte aux Gonaives ainsi que dans toute la dépendance, et que j'ai chassé les Espagnols et les émigrés de cette partie de Gonaives; mais j'ai le coeur navré de l'événement, qui a suivi sur sur quelque malheureux blancs qui ont été victimes dans cette affaire. Je ne suis pas comme bien d'autres que voient des scènes d'horreur avec sang-froid, j'ai toujours eu l'humanité pour partage et je gémis quand je ne peux pas empêcher le mal; il y a eu aussi quelques petit soulèvements parmi les ateliers mais j'ai mis de suite le bon ordre et tous travaillent comme ci-devant.

Gonaives, le Gros Morne, les cantons d'Ennery, Plaisance, Marmelade, Dondon, L'Acul et toute la dépendance avec le Limbé sont sous mes ordres, et je compte quatre mille hommes armés dans tous ces endroits, sans compter les citoyens de Gros Morne qui sont au nombre de six cents hommes. Quant aux munitions de guerre, j'en suis dépourvu entièrement, les ayant consommées dans les diverses attaques que j'ai faites contre l'ennemi; quand j'ai pris les Gonaives, j'ai seulement trouvé cent gargousses à canon dont je fais faire des cartouches à fusil pour attaquer le Pont de l'Esther ou sont campés le émigrés; je me propose de les attaquer au premier moment, c'est à dire quand le citoyen Blanc Cassenave se sera rendu avec son armée à l'habitation Marchand, au carrefour de la Petite-Rivière de l'Artibonite. . . .

Voilà, Général, la situation exact de tout; je vous prie de m'envoyer des munitions de guerre; vous jugerez par vous-même de la quantité qu'il me faudra dans la circonstance présente. . . .

Salut en patrie,
Toussaint-Louverture[3]

FROM CHAPTER 9, PP. 148–55:

Il est de mon devoir de rendre au gouvernement français un compte exact de ma conduite; je raconterai les faits avec toute la naïveté et la franchise d'un ancien militaire, en y ajoutant les réflexions qui se présenteront naturellement. Enfin je dirai la vérité, fut-elle contre moi-même.

La colonie de Saint-Domingue, dont j'étais commandant, jouissait de la plus grande tranquilité; la culture et le commerce y florissaient. Et tout cela, j'ose le dire, était mon ouvrage. . . .[4]

FROM CHAPTER 17, PP. 280–81:

Artibonite (6 février 1795) le 18 Pluviôse, l'an 3 de la République Française, une et indivisible.

Toussaint-Louverture, Commandant Général du Cordon de l'Ouest, à Étienne Laveaux, Gouverneur Général des îles françaises de l'Amérique sous le vent.

Citoyen Général,

Je réponds à votre lettre du 11 de ce mois. J'ai réçu les deux ordres que vous m'y annonciez, savoir le premier relatif aux commandants des paroisses dépendant de mon cordon, le second relatif aux commandants des autres paroisses.

---

3. Gerard M. Laurent, *Toussaint Louverture à Travers Sa Correspondance* (1953) p. 106.
4. Saint-Rémy, *Mémoires du Général Toussaint-Louverture, Écrits par Lui-Même, Pouvant Servir à l'Histoire de Sa Vie* (Paris: Libraire-éditeur, 1859), p. 29.

Cette mesure ne peut qu'être du plus grand avantage pour le succès des armes de la République. Je m'empresse de faire passer copie de celui qui concerne les commandants qui sont sous mes ordres et d'en ordonner la publication et l'affiche afin que personne n'en prétende cause d'ignorance.

Blanc Cassenave pendant sa detention a été atteint d'une colère bilieuse qui avait tout les apparences d'une rage effrénée; il es mort étouffé; requiescat in pace. Il est hors de ce monde; nous en devons à Dieu des actions de grâces. Cette mort de Blanc Cassenave a anéanti contre lui tout espèce de procédure, attendu que de son crime n'y a point de complice ni de participes. Vernet ne m'ayant pas encore fait passe le Procès-Verbal de sa mort, je lui écris de vous l'envoyer signé de l'officier qui le gardait et du médecin qui le voyait, et de m'envoyer copie de tout, pour que cela n'entraîne pas d'autre délai à cause de mon éloignement.

Je m'occupe de acquisition des mulets que vous m'aviez ordonnée pour Barthèlemy. . . .

Je vous embrasse de tout mon coeur, ainsi que le commandant de la Province, au souvenir duquel je vous prie de me rappeler.

                                                    Salut,
                                    Toussaint-Louverture[5]

FROM CHAPTER 17, PP. 282–83:

Au Fort Dauphin, le 20 novembre 1794.

Jean-François, général des troupes auxiliaires de Sa Majesté Catholique à Etienne Laveaux, Gouverneur-Général pour la République française, au Cap.

Votre lettre datée du 20 Brumaire de l'an 3 de la République me fait connaître les nobles sentiments avec lesquels vous l'avez dictée; elle commence avec le mépris que tous vous autres auraient toujours pour les gens de ma race. J'ay l'honneur d'être nommé général parmis mes amis et mes ennemis, titre glorieux que je me suis acquis par mes exploits, ma bonne conduite, ma probité et mon courage et vous me privez de cet honneur dans la première parole de votre lettre, en me nommant avec un air dédaigneux et méprisant Jean-François, comme vous pourriez faire dans ces temps malheureux où votre orgueil et votre cruauté nous confondaient avec les chevaux, les bêtes à cornes et les plus viles animaux, précisément dans une occasion où vous avez besoin de moi, et vous me proposé la perfidie la plus noire que vous cherchez à embellir avec des promesses séduisantes, menteuses et remplies d'artifices, et par lesquelles vous

_____

5. Laurent, p. 168.

faites connaître l'indigne idée que vous avez de mon caractère et mon procédé. Mon parti est pris, et je suis inébranlable une fois déterminé, je vivrai, je mourrai dans la belle cause que j'ai adoptée, et sans lâcher de faire l'apologie de Messieurs les Espagnols, je pourrai vous prouver que je n'ai que des louanges à faire d'eux les ayant toujours trouvés fidèles et religieux observateurs dans toutes leurs promesses.

Quoique je pourrai bien répondre à tous les chapitres de votre lettre, je les omets parce qu'ils sont presque tous détaillés dans un manifest que j'ai fait circuler à mes compatriotes dans lequel je leur fais connaître sans artifice, le sort que les attend, s'ils se laissent séduire par vos belles paroles . . . l'Egalité, la Liberté, &c &c &c . . . et seulement je croirai à celuy là jusqu'à ce que je vois que Monsieur Laveaux et d'autres messieurs français de sa qualité, accordent leur filles en mariage aux nègres. Alors je pourrai croire à l'égalité prétendue. Il ne me reste plus monsieur le général, que de vous demander la grâce de m'envoyer cette lettre de monsieur le Président que vous citez dans d'autres écrits que sont entre mes mains, dans laquelle il vous promet ma tête pour la rançon de tous les prisonniers espagnols, de vous prier de faire la guerre, en respectant les droits des gens et cette générosité observée anciennement par les noble guerriers français dont vous trouverez bien des exemples dans vos illustres ancêtres, et de vous instruire que jamais la trahison et la perfidie ne seraient le partage du général Jean-François.

Jean-François, Général de S.M.C.[6]

FROM CHAPTER 17, PP. 283–84:

Vous demandez si un républicain est libre? Il faut être esclave pour faire une pareille demande. Osez-vous bien, vous Jean-François, qui avez vendu à l'Espagnol vos frères, qui actuellement fouillent les mines de cette détestable nation, pour fournir à l'ostentation de son roi. . . .[7]

FROM P. 284:

Toussaint-Louverture à tous ses frères et soeurs actuellement aux Verrettes.

22 mars 1795

Frères et soeurs,

Le moment est arrivé où le voile épais qui obscursissait la lumière doit tomber. On ne doit plus oublier les décrets de la Convention nationale. Ses

---

6. Thomas Madiou, *Histoire D'Haïti* (Port-au-Prince: Editions Henri Deschamps, 1989), vol. I, p. 255.
7. Madiou, vol. I, p. 288.

principes, son amour pour la liberté sont invariables, et désormais il ne peut pas exister d'espoir de l'écroulement de cet édifice sacré. . . .

Art 6.—Le travail est nécessaire, c'est une vertu; c'est le bien général de l'Etat. Tout homme oisif et errant sera arrêté pour être puni par la loi. Mais le service aussi est conditionné et ce n'est que par une récompense, un salaire justement payé, qu'on peut l'encourager et le porter au suprême degré. . . .[8]

FROM CHAPTER 19, PP. 316–18:

Verrettes, le 23 pluviôse, l'an IV de la République française (12 février 1796)

Mon cher frère et ami,

Je vous envoie trois de mes officiers, pour vous porter un paquet que le général et gouverneur de Saint Domingue me charge de vous faire parvenir. Malgré que je n'ai pas le plaisir de vous connaître, je sais que, comme moi, vous portez les armes pour la défense de nos droits, pour la liberté générale; que nos amis les commissaires civils Polverel et Sonthonax avaient la plus grande confiance en vous, parce que vous étiez un vrai républicain. Aussi je ne puis croire aux bruits injurieux que l'on fait courir sur vous: que vous avez abandonné votre patrie, pour vous coaliser avec les Anglais, ennemis jurés de notre liberté et égalité.

Serait ce possible, mon cher ami, qu'au moment où la France triomphe de tous les royalistes et nous reconnaît pour ses enfants, par son décret bienfaisant du 9 thermidor, qu'elle nous accorde tous nos droits pour lesquels nous nous battons, que vous vous laisseriez tromper par nos anciens tyrans, qui ne se servent d'une partie de nos malheureux frères que pour charger les autres de chaînes? Les Espagnols, pendant un temps, m'avaient de même fasciné les yeux, mais je n'ai pas tardé à reconnaître leur scélératesse; je les ai abandonnés et les ai bien battus; j'ai retourné à ma patrie qui m'a reçu à bras ouverts et a bien voulu récompenser mes services. Je vous engage, mon cher frère, de suivre mon exemple. Si quelque raisons particulières, vous empêchaient d'avoir la confiance dans les généraux de brigade Rigaud et Beauvais, le gouverneur Laveaux, qui est notre bon père à tous, et en qui notre mère patrie a mis sa confiance, dois aussi mériter la vôtre. Je pense que vous ne me la refuserez pas aussi à moi, qui suis un noir comme vous, et qui vous assure que je ne désire autre chose dans le monde que de vous voir heureux, vous et tous nos frères. Pour moi, je crois que nous ne pouvons l'être qu'en servant la République

---

8. Victor Schoelcher, *Vie de Toussaint Louverture* (Paris: Karthala, 1982), p. 127.

française; c'est sous ses drapeaux que nous sommes vraiment libres et égaux. Je vois comme cela, mon cher ami, et je ne crois pas me tromper. S'il m'avait été possible de vous aller voir, j'aurais eu le plaisir de vous embrasser, et je me flatte que vous ne m'auriez pas refusé votre amitié. Vous pouvez vous en rapporter à ce que vous diront mes trois officiers; ce sera la vérité. Si, quand ils reviendront, vous voulez m'envoyer deux ou trois des vôtres, nous causerons ensemble, et je suis sûr que je leur donnerai de si bonnes raisons, qu'ils vous ouvriront les yeux. S'il est possible que les Anglais aient réussi à vous tromper, croyez-moi, mon cher frère, abandonnez-les, réunissez-vous aux bon républicains, et tous ensemble chassons ces royalistes de notre pays: ce sont des scélérats que veulent nous charger encore de ces fers honteux que nous avons eu tant de peine à briser. Malgré tout ce qu'on m'a dit de vous, je ne doute point que vous soyez un bon républicain: ainsi vous devez être uni avec les généraux Rigaud et Beauvais qui sont de bons républicains, puisque notre patrie les a récompensés de leurs services. Quand même vous avez quelques petites tracasseries ensemble, vous ne devez pas vous battre contre eux, parce que la République, qui est notre mère à tous, ne veut pas que nous nous battions contre nos frères. D'ailleurs, c'est toujours le pauvre peuple que en souffre le plus. Quand nous, chefs, nous avons des disputes entre nous, nous ne devons pas faire battre les soldats qui nous sont confiés les uns contre les autres, mais nous devons nous adresser à nos supérieurs qui sont faits pour nous rendre justice et pour nous mettre d'accord. Rappelez-vous, mon cher ami, que la République française est une et indivisible, que c'est ce qui fait sa force et qu'elle a vaincu tous ses ennemis. . . .

Croyez-moi, mon cher ami, oubliez toute animosité particulière; réconciliez vous avec nos frères Rigaud et Beauvais; ce sont de braves défenseurs de la liberté générale, qui aiment trop leur patrie pour ne pas désirer de tout leur coeur d'être vos amis, ainsi que tout le peuple que vous commandez.

Malgré que je n'ai pas l'avantage de connaître le commandant Pompée, je vous prie de lui présenter mes civilités.

Je vous embrasse et vous salue en la patrie, vous et tous nos bons frères.

Toussaint-Louverture[9]

FROM CHAPTER 19, PP. 338–39:

Paris, 22 fructidor an X (9 septembre 1802)

Vous voudrez bien vous rendre au château de Joux.

Vous y ferez une enquête pour savoir comment Dandigné et Suzannet se sont échappés. Vous verrez Toussaint, qui m'a fait écrire par le ministre de la

---

9. Schoelcher, p. 136.

Guerre qu'il avait des choses importantes à me communiquer. En causant avec lui, vous lui ferez connaître l'énormité du crime dont il s'est rendu coupable en portant les armes contre la République; que nous l'avions considéré comme rebelle dès l'instant qu'il avait publié sa constitution; que d'ailleurs le traité avec la régence de la Jamaïque et l'Angleterre nous avait été communiqué par la cour de Londres; vous tâcherez de recueillir tout ce qu'il pourra vous dire sur ces differents objets, ainsi que sur l'existence de ses trésors et les nouvelles politiques qu'il pourrait avoir à vous dire.

Vous ne manquerez pas de lui faire connaître que, désormais, lui ne peut rien espérer que par le mérite qu'il acquerrait en révélant au Gouvernement des chose importantes, et qu'il a intérêt à connaître.

Vous recommanderez qu'on ne se relâche en rien de la garde sévère qu'on doit faire pour empêcher qu'un homme comme lui se sauve.

Bonaparte[10]

FROM CHAPTER 19, PP. 341–42:

On m'a envoyé en France nu comme un ver; on a saisi mes propriétés et mes papiers; on a répandu les calomnies les plus atroces sur mon compte. N'est-ce pas couper les jambes à quelqu'un et lui ordonner à marcher? N'est-ce pas lui couper la langue et lui dire de parler? N'est-ce pas enterrer un homme tout vivant?[11]

FROM CHAPTER 24, PP. 408–9:

6 Messidor, an 4e

Par une de mes dernières lettres, cher général, je vous ai prévenu que vos enfans pourraient partir pour France sur le vaisseau de soixante-et-quatorze, le Watigny; comme nous devons le faire partir très prochainement, je vous prie de me les envoyer de suite; ils seront logés chez moi, j'aurai pour eux tous les soins de l'amitié jusqu'à leur départ. Vous pouvez compter sur toutes mes sollicitudes, sur celles du général Laveaux pour qu'en France on les elève de manière à répondre à vos vues. Soyez sûr que le ministre de la Marine, mon ami particulier, leur prodiguera tous les secours de la République. . . .

Sonthonax[12]

---

10. Colonel Alfred Nemours, *Histoire de la Captivité et de la Mort de Toussaint-Louverture* (Paris: Éditions Berger-Levrault, 1929), p. 73.

11. Saint-Rémy, p. 86.

12. Laurent, p.468.

FROM CHAPTER 24, P. 413:

Quartier Général des Cahos, le 30 *thermidor, l'an* 4 *de la République française, une et indivisible* (17 *avril* 1796)

Toussaint-Louverture, Général de Division et Commandant en Chef du Département de L'Ouest, à Etienne Laveaux, Général en Chef de Saint-Domingue.

Mon Général, Mon Père, Mon Bon Ami,

Comme je prévois avec chagrin qu'il vous arrivera dans ce malheureux pays, pour lequel et pour ceux qui l'habitent vous avez sacrifié votre vie, votre femme, vos enfants, des désagréments, et que je ne voudrais pas avoir la douleur d'en être spectateur, je désirais que vous fussiez nommé député pour que vous puissiez avoir la satisfaction de revoir votre patrie et être à l'abri des factions qui s'enfantent à Saint Domingue et je serai assuré et pour tous mes frères d'avoir pour la cause que nous combattons le plus zélé defenseur. Oui, général, mon père, mon bienfaiteur, la France possède bien des hommes mais quel est celui qui sera à jamais le vrai ami des noirs comme vous? Il n'y en aura jamais.

Le citoyen Lacroix est le porteur de ma lettre; c'est mon ami, c'est le vôtre, vous pouvez lui confier quelque chose de vos réflexions sur notre position actuelle; il vous dira tout ce que j'en pense, qu'il serait essentiel que nous nous voyions et que nous causions ensemble. Que des choses j'ai à vous dire! . . .

Je n'ai pas besoin par des expressions de vous témoigner l'amitié et la recon-naissance que je vous ai. Je vous suis assez connu.

Je vous embrasse mille fois et soyez assuré que si mon désir et mes souhaits sont accomplis, vous pourrez dire que vous aurez à St.-Domingue l'ami le plus sincère que jamais il y en ait eu.

Votre fils, votre fidèle ami,

Toussaint-Louverture[13]

---

13. Laurent, p. 424.

FROM CHAPTER 24, P. 415:

Aux citoyens de Saint-Louis-du-Nord

Liberté   Égalité

PROCLAMATION

Toussaint-Louverture, général de brigade et lieutenant au gouvernement de Saint-Domingue

J'apprends avec indignation, que des êtres pervers, désorganisateurs, perturbateurs du repos public, des ennemis de la liberté générale et de la sainte égalité, cherchent par des intrigues infâmes à faire perdre à mes frères de la commune de Saint-Louis-du-Nord le glorieux titre de citoyens français. Jusqu'à quand vous laisserez-vous conduire comme des aveugles par vos plus dangereux ennemis? O vous, Africains mes frères! vous qui m'avez coûté tant de fatiques, de travaux, de misères! Vous dont la liberté est scellée de la moitié de plus pur de votre sang. Jusqu'à quand aurai-je la douleur de voir mes enfants égarés fuir les conseils d'un père qui les idolâtre! . . .

Quel fruit espérez-vous retirer des désordres dans lesquels on cherche à vous entraîner? Vous avez la liberté, que pouvez vous prétendre de plus! Que dira le peuple français lorsqu'il apprendra qu'après le don qu'il vient de vous faire, vous avez porté l'ingratitude jusqu'à tremper vos mains dans le sang de ses enfants. . . .[14]

Ils osent, ces scélérats, vous débiter que la France veut vous rendre à l'esclavage! . . . comment pourriez-vous ajouter foi à des calomnies si atroces? Ignorez-vous ce que la France a sacrifié pour la liberté générale, pour les droits de l'homme, pour le bonheur, pour la félicité des hommes?

Faites bien attention, mes frères, qu'il y a plus de noirs dans la colonie qu'il n'y a d'hommes de couleur et d'hommes blancs ensemble, et que s'il y arrive quelques désordres, ce sera à nous, noirs, que la République s'en prendra, parce que nous sommes les plus forts et que c'est à nous à maintenir l'ordre et la tranquilité par le bon exemple.

---

14. Schoelcher, p. 175.

FROM CHAPTER 25, P. 428:

Toussaint-Louverture, Général en Chef de Saint-Domingue, à Etienne Laveaux, Représentant du peuple, Député de St.-Domingue au Corps Législatif.

Gonaives, le 4 prairial, an 5 de la République Française, une et indivisible (23 mai 1797)

Mon cher représentant,

Depuis votre départ et jusqu'à ce jour, je suis encore privé de la douce satis-faction de recevoir de vos chères nouvelles. Je vous ai écrit plusieurs fois et suis encore dans l'incertitude que mes lettres vous soient parvenues heureusement. Puisse celle-ci vous être remise aussi promptement que je le désire.

Pénétré de l'intérêt particulier que vous prenez à la colonie française, je vous dois compte de la position où se trouvent en ce moment les parties qui sont confiées à ma surveillance et à ma défense, et c'est avec la joie que m'in-spire mon attachement sincère et mon entier dévouement aux intérêts de la République, que je vous apprendrai l'heureuse réussite de mes dernières entre-prises sur les quartiers du Mirebalais, de la Montagne des Grands-Bois, de Las Cahobas, de Banica, Saint Jean et Niebel qui sont entièrement en notre possession en ce moment. Les anglais, nos ennemis, effrayés de la marche courageuse qu'ont dévelopée sur eux les braves défenseurs de la République en quittant ces points importants, n'ont pu s'échapper qu'avec une faîble partie de leur artillerie; l'autre est restée dans notre pouvoir. Resserrés dans de faîbles parties de la colonie, ils ne tarderont point à sentir leurs efforts impuissants et leur insuffisante opposition à la juste cause que défendent les républicains français. . . .

En vous réitérant parculièrement l'assurance de l'attachement que vous m'avez inspiré, je vous prie d'être l'organe de mes sentiments respectueux et de ceux de mon épouse, auprès de la votre et de votre chère famille, et croyez que les liens de notre amitié ne finiront qu'avec moi.

Salut et amitié
Toussaint-Louverture[15]

FROM CHAPTER 26, P. 451:

Toussaint-Louverture, général en chef de l'armée de Saint-Domingue, au citoyen Sonthonax, représentant du peuple et commissaire délégué aux îles Sous-le-Vent.

Quartier général du Cap français, le 3 fructidor, an V (20 août 1797)

---

15. Laurent, p. 430.

Citoyen Représentant,

Privés depuis longtemps de nouvelles du gouvernement, ce long silence affecte les vrais amis de la République. Les ennemis de l'ordre et de la liberté cherchent à profiter de l'ignorance où nous sommes pour faire circuler des nouvelles dont le but est de jeter le trouble dans la colonie.

Dans ces circonstances, il est nécessaire qu'un homme instruit des évènements et qui a été le témoin des changements qui ont produit sa restauration et sa tranquillité, veuille bien se rendre auprès du Directoire exécutif pour lui faire connaître la vérité.

Nommé député de la colonie au corps législatif, des circonstances impérieuses vous firent un devoir de rester quelque temps encore au milieu de nous; alors votre présence était nécessaire: des troubles nous avaient agités, il fallait les calmer.

Aujourd'hui que l'ordre, la paix, le zèle pour le rétablissement des cultures, nos succès sur nos ennemis extérieurs et leur impuissance vous permettent de vous rendre à vos fonctions, allez dire à la France ce que vous avez vu, les prodiges dont vous avez été témoin et soyez toujours le défenseur de la cause que nous avons embrassée, dont nous serons les éternels soldats.

Salut et respet.
(multiple signature)[16]

FROM CHAPTER 26, PP. 454-56:

5 *novembre* 1797

Toussaint-Louverture, général en chef de l'armée de Saint-Domingue, au Directoire exécutif de la République française

. . . Il tient à vous, citoyens directeurs, de détourner de dessus nos têtes, la tempête que les éternels ennemis de notre liberté préparent à l'ombre du silence. Il tient à vous d'éclairer la législature, il tient à vous d'empêcher les ennemis du système actuel de se répandre sur nos côtes malheureuses pour les souiller de nouveaux crimes. Ne permettez pas que nos frères, nos amis, soient sacrifiés à des hommes qui veulent régner sur des ruines del' espèce humaine. Mais vous, votre sagesse vous donnera les moyens d'éviter les pièges dangereux que vous tendent nos ennemis communs. Je vous envoie, avec cette lettre, une déclaration qui vous fera connaître l'unité qui existe entre les propriétaires de Saint-Domingue qui sont en France, ceux des Etats-Unis et ceux qui servent sous le drapeau anglais. Vous y verrez que leur souci de réussir les a conduits à s'envelopper du manteau de la liberté de manière à lui porter des coups d'autant

---

16. Schoelcher, p. 192.

plus mortels. Vous verrez qu'ils comptent fermement sur ma complaisance de me prêter à leurs vues perfides par la crainte pour mes enfants. Il n'est pas étonnant que ces hommes qui sacrifient leur pays à leurs intérêts soient incapables de concevoir combien un père mieux qu'eux peut supporter de sacrifices par amour de sa patrie, étant donné que je fonde sans hésiter le bonheur de mes enfants sur celui de ma patrie, qu'eux et eux seuls veulent détruire. Je n'hésiterai jamais entre la sécurité de Saint Domingue et mon bonheur personel, mais je n'ai rien à craindre. C'est à la sollicitude du gouvernement français que j'ai confié mes enfants. Je tremblerais d'horreur si je les envoyés comme otages entre les mains des colonialistes. Mais même si cela était, faites leur savoir qu'en les punissant de la fidélité de leur père, ils ne ferais qu'ajouter à leur barbarie, sans aucune espoir de me faire manquer jamais à mon devoir. . . .

Aveugles qu'ils sont! ils ne peuvent s'apercevoir combien cette conduite odieuse de leur part peut devenir le signal de nouveaux désastres et de malheurs irréparables et que, loin de leur faire regagner ce qu'à ses yeux la liberté de tous leur fait perdre, ils s'exposent à une ruine totale et la colonie à sa destruction inevitable. Pensent-ils que des hommes qui ont été à même de jouir des bienfaits de la liberté, regarderont calmement qu'on les leur ravisse? Ils ont supporté leurs chaînes tant qu'ils ne connaissent aucune condition de vie plus heureuse que celle de l'esclavage. Mais aujourd'hui qu'ils l'ont quittée, s'ils avaient un millier de vies, ils les sacrifieraient plutôt que d'être de nouveau soumis à l'esclavage. Mais non, la main qui a rompu nos chaînes ne nous asservira pas à nouveau. La France ne reniera ses principes. . . . Mais, si pour rétablir l'esclavage à Saint Domingue, on faisait cela, alors je vous déclare, ce serait tenter l'impossible; nous avons su affronter des dangers pour obtenir notre liberté, nous saurons affronter la mort pour la maintenir. *Voilà, citoyens directeurs, la morale de la population de Saint Domingue, voilà les principes qu'elle vous transport par mon intermédiaire. . . .*[17]

FROM CHAPTER 29, P. 490:

Un colon blanc qui possédait sa confiance voulut aussi se rétirer; il l'arrêta et luis dit: "Non, restez, vous n'êtes trop avec moi. Je pourrais bien le faire arrêté . . .; mais Dieu m'en garde . . . j'ai besoin de M. Rigaud . . . il est violent . . . il me convient pour faire la guerre . . . et cette guerre m'est necessaire. . . . La caste des mulâtres est supérieure à la mienne . . . si je lui enlevais M. Rigaud, elle trouverait peut-être un chef qui vaudrait mieux que lui. . . . je

---

17. Faine Scharon, *Toussaint Louverture et la Revolution de Saint-Domingue* (Port-au-Prince: Imprimerie de l'Etat, 1959), p. 102.

connais M. Rigaud . . . il abandonne son cheval quand il galope . . . mais il montre son bras quand il frappe . . . moi je galope aussi, mais je sais m'arrêter sur place; et quand je frappe, on me sent, mais on ne me voit pas. . . . M. Rigaud ne sait faire des insurrections que par du sang et des massacres . . . moi je sais aussi mettre le peuple en mouvement. Il gémit, M. Rigaud de voir en fureur le peuple qu'il excite . . . mais je ne souffre pas la fureur . . . quand je parais il faut que tout se tranquilise."[18]

FROM CHAPTER 30, P. 515:

"Quoi, n'ai-je pas donné ma parole au général anglais? Comment pouvez-vous supposer que je me couvrirais d'infâmie en la violant? La confiance qu'il a en ma bonne foi l'engage à se livrer à moi, et je serais déshonoré pour jamais, si je suivais vos conseils. Je suis tout dévoué à la cause de la République; mais je ne la servirai jamais au dépens de ma conscience et de mon honneur."[19]

FROM CHAPTER 31, P. 552:

Gens de couleur qui depuis le commencement de la révolution trahissez les noirs, que désirez-vous aujourd'hui? Personne ne l'ignore; vous voulez commander en maîtres dans la colonie; vous voulez l'extermination des blancs et l'asservissement des noirs! . . . Mais y réfléchissez-vous hommes pervers qui vous êtes à jamais déshonorés par l'embarquement et ensuite l'égorgement des troupes noires connues sous la dénomination des suisses. Avez-vous hésité à sacrifier à la haine des petits-blancs ces malheureux qui avaient versé leur sang pour votre cause? Pourquoi les avez-vous sacrifiés? Pourquoi le général Rigaud refuse-t-il à m'obéir? C'est parce que je suis noir; c'est parce qu'il m'a voué, à cause de mon couleur, une haine implacable. Pourquoi refuserait-t-il d'obéir à un général français comme lui, qui a contribué plus que n'importe qui à l'expulsion des Anglais? Hommes de couleur, par votre fol orgueil, par votre perfidie vous avez déjà perdu la part que vous possédiez dans l'exercice des pouvoirs politiques. Quant au général Rigaud, il est perdu; il est sous mes yeux au fond d'un abîme; rebelle et traître à la patrie, il sera dévoré par les troupes de la liberté. Mulâtres, je vois au fond de vos âmes; vous étiez prêts à vous soulever contre moi, mais bien que toutes les troupes aillent incessament quitter la partie de l'Ouest, j'y laisse mon oeil et mon bras: mon oeil pour vous surveiller, mon bras qui saura vous atteindre.[20]

---

18. Madiou, vol. I, p. 406.
19. Madiou, vol. I, p. 400.
20. Madiou, vol. I, p. 429.

FROM CHAPTER 33, P. 570:

à Christophe, commandant du Cap

Port Républicain, 29 Messidor an VII (15 juillet 1799)

La revolte du Môle, mon cher commandant, vient de s'opérer par les agents secrets du perfide Rigaud; ils ont des prosélytes partout, et partout ils opèrent le mal qu'il faut cependant arrêter dans sa source. Le Môle correspond directement avec le Fort-Liberté; il y sème la désunion, et j'ai la certitude que cette place devait aussi se soulever et arborer l'étendard de la révolte; au Cap même des agents y provoquent la rébellion; surveillez-les avec une rigueur étonnante; déployez le caractère dur que nécessitent les trames de ces scélérats; tous les hommes de couleur en général se sont donné la main pour culbuter St-Domingue, en les désunissant, et en armant les citoyens les uns contres les autres; ils servent la passion du rebelle Rigaud; ils ont juré de le servir et de l'élever le chef suprême sur des corps et des cendres; dans aucun cas ne molissez pas contre les hommes de couleur, et garantissez par une activité sans égal l'arrondissement que vous commandez, des horreurs qui menacent déjà quelques-uns.

L'arrondissement de l'Est doit faire encore l'objet de votre sollicitude dans des circonstances aussi critiques, vous savez combien sont remuants les habitants de cette partie de la colonie; faites former des camps qui fassent respecter cette place, et employez et faites même descendre des mornes les cultivateurs armés desquels vous croyez avoir besoin, pour également garantir cette place importante; les hommes de couleur y sont aussi dangereux que vindictifs; n'ayez aucun ménagement pour eux; faites arrêter et même punir de mort ceux qui seraient tentés d'opérer le moindre mouvement; Vallière doit être aussi l'objet de tous vos soins.

Je compte plus que jamais sur votre imperturbable sévérité; que rien n'échappe à votre vigilance.

Je vous desire une bonne santé.

Salut et amitié
Toussaint-Louverture[21]

FROM CHAPTER 36, PP. 619–21:

Les consuls de la République française aux citoyens de Saint-Domingue:

Paris, le 4 nivôse, l'an VIII de la République française, une et indivisible (25 decembre 1799)

---

21. Madiou, vol. I, p. 446.

Citoyens, une constitution qui n'a pu se soutenir contre des violations mul-
tipliées est remplacée par un nouveau pacte destiné à affermir la liberté.

L'art. 91 porte que les colonies françaises seront régies par des lois spéciales.

Cette disposition dérive de la nature des choses and de la différence des cli-
mats. La différence des habitudes, des moeurs, des intérêts; la diversité du sol,
des cultures, des productions, exige des modifications diverses.

Un des premiers actes de la nouvelle législature sera la redaction des lois
destinées à vous régir.

Loin qu'elles soient pour vous un sujet d'alarmes, vous y reconnaîtrez la
sagesse et la profondeur des vues qui animent les législateurs de la France.

Les consuls de la République, en vous annonçant le nouveau pacte social,
vous déclarent que les principes SACRÉS de la liberté et de l'égalité des noirs
N'ÉPROUVERONT JAMAIS parmis vous d'atteinte ni de modification.

S'il est dans la colonie des homme malintentionnés, s'il en est qui conser-
vent des relations avec les puissances ennemis, braves noirs souvenez-vous
que le peuple français seul reconnaît *votre liberté et l'égalité de vos droits.*

Signé, Le Premier Consul, BONAPARTE

Les mots suivants: «Braves noirs, souvenez-vous que le peuple français seul
reconnait votre liberté et l'égalité de vos droits» seront écrits en lettres d'or sur
tous les drapeaux des bataillons de la garde nationale de la colonie de Saint
Domingue.[22]

FROM CHAPTER 36, P. 679.

Rapport de Caffarelli au Premier Consul

Paris, le 2 vendémaire an XI (24 septembre 1802)

Mon Général,

Vous m'avez ordonné de me rendre auprès de Toussaint-Louverture pour
entendre les révélations qu'il avait annoncé vouloir faire au gouvernment,
savoir de lui quels traités il avait fait avec les agents de L'Angleterre, pénétrer
ses vues politiques et obtenir des renseignements sur ses trésors. Je me suis
attachés à remplir cette mission, *de manière à atteindre le but que vous désirez*
et si je n'y suis parvenu, c'est que cet homme profondément fourbe et dis-
simulé, maître de lui, fin et adroit, avait son thème préparé et n'a dit que ce
qu'il voulait bien dire.

Dès le premier jour il entama une conversation dans laquelle il me fit un

---

22. Schoelcher, p. 263.

narré fort long de ce qui était arrivé à Saint-Domingue. Cette conversation qui durait longtemps n'aboutait à rien, ne m'apprenait rien. Je le quittai, le prévenant que je reviendrais le lendemain pour savoir s'il n'avait rien de plus à m'apprendre. Je m'y rendais effectivement dans la matinée. Je le trouvai tremblant de froid et malade; il souffrait beaucoup et avait de la peine à parler. Je l'interrogeai de nouveau sur les révélations qu'il avait à faire, je le pressai de m'accorder un peu de confiance l'annonçant que je n'en abuserais pas. Il prit alors le mémoire ci-joint, il me pria de l'emporter et que j'y trouverais ce qu'il avait à me dire. . . .

. . . je l'ai vu montrer de l'élévation dans deux circonstances.

L'une, lorsqu'on lui apporta les habits et le linge qu'on avait fait faire pour lui.

La seconde, lorsqu'on lui redemanda son rasoir. Il dit que les hommes qui lui enlevaient cet instrument fussent bien petits puisqu'ils soupçonnent qu'il manquait du courage nécessaire pour supporter son malheur, qu'il avait une famille et que sa réligion, d'ailleurs, lui défendait d'attenter à lui-même. Il m'a paru, dans sa prison, patient, resigné, et attendant du Premier Consul, toute la justice qu'il croit mériter. . . .

. . . Les divers objets dont il est question dans ce rapport sont le résultat de sept entretiens, la plupart très longs dans lesquels les mêmes sujets ont été ramenés à plusieurs intervalles. Il a toujours répondu de la même manière et presque dans les mêmes termes.

Sa prison est froide, saine, et très sûre. Il ne communique avec personne.[23]

---

23. Nemours, p. 241.

CLASSIFICATION OF RACES IN COLONIAL SAINT DOMINGUE

From *Description Topographique, Physique, Civile, Polique et Historique de la Partie Française de l'Isle Saint Domingue* by Médéric-Louis-Élie Moreau de Saint Méry, 1797.

RÉSULTAT

De toutes les nuances, produites par les diverses combinaisons du mélange des Blancs avec les Nègres, et des Nègres avec les Caraïbes ou Sauvages ou Indiens Occidentaux, et avec les Indiens Orientaux.

I. *Combinaisons du Blanc.*

D'un Blanc et d'une Négresse, vient . . . . un Mulâtre.
D'un Blanc et d'une Mulâtresse. . . . . Quarteron.
D'un Blanc et d'une Quarteron . . . . Métis.
D'un Blanc et d'une Métive. . . . . Mamelouque.
D'un Blanc et d'une Mamelouque. . . . . Quarteronné.
D'un Blanc et d'une Quarteronnée . . . . Sang-mêlé.
D'un Blanc et d'une Sang-mêlée. . . . . Sang-mêlé, qui s'approche
continuellement du Blanc.
D'un Blanc et d'une Marabou . . . . Quarteron.
D'un Blanc et d'une Griffonne. . . . . Quarteron.
D'un Blanc et d'une Sacatra. . . . . Quarteron.

II. *Combinaisons du Nègre.*

D'un nègre et d'une Blanche, vient . . . . un Mulâtre.
D'un nègre et d'une Sang-mêlée . . . . Mulâtre.

D'un nègre et d'une Quarteronnée .... Mulâtre.
D'un nègre et d'une Mamelouque .... Mulâtre.
D'un nègre et d'une Métive .... Mulâtre.
D'un nègre et d'une Quarteronne .... Marabou.
D'un nègre et d'une Mulâtresse .... Griffe.
D'un nègre et d'une Marabou .... Griffe.
D'un nègre et d'une Griffonne .... Sacatra.
D'un nègre et d'une Sacatra .... Sacatra.

III. *Combinaisions du Mulâtre.*
D'un Mulâtre et d'une Blanche, vient .... un Quarteron.
D'un Mulâtre et d'une Sang-mêlé .... Quarteron.
D'un Mulâtre et d'une Quarteronnée .... Quarteron.
D'un Mulâtre et d'une Mamelouque .... Quarteron.
D'un Mulâtre et d'une Métive .... Quarteron.
D'un Mulâtre et d'une Quarteronne .... Quarteron.
D'un Mulâtre et d'une Marabou .... Mulâtre.
D'un Mulâtre et d'une Griffonne .... Marabou.
D'un Mulâtre et d'une Sacatra .... Marabou.
D'un Mulâtre et d'une Négresse .... Griffe.

IV. *Combinaisons du Quarteron.*
D'un Quarteron et d'une Blanche, vient .... un Métis.
D'un Quarteron et d'une Sang-mêlée .... Métis.
D'un Quarteron et d'une Quarteronnée .... Métis.
D'un Quarteron et d'une Mamelouque .... Métis.
D'un Quarteron et d'une Métive .... Métis.
D'un Quarteron et d'une Mulâtresse .... Quarteron.
D'un Quarteron et d'une Marabou .... Quarteron.
D'un Quarteron et d'une Griffonne .... Mulâtre.
D'un Quarteron et d'une Sacatra .... Mulâtre.
D'un Quarteron et d'une Négresse .... Marabou.

V. *Combinaisons du Métis.*
D'un Métis et d'une Blanche, vient .... un Mamelouc.
D'un Métis et d'une Sang-mêlée .... Mamelouc.
D'un Métis et d'une Quarteronnée .... Mamelouc.
D'un Métis et d'une Mamelouque .... Mamelouc.
D'un Métis et d'une Quarteronne .... Métis.
D'un Métis et d'une Mulâtresse .... Quarteron.
D'un Métis et d'une Marabou .... Quarteron.
D'un Métis et d'une Griffonne .... Quarteron.

D'un Métis et d'une Sacatra.............................Mulâtre.
D'un Métis et d'une Négresse ....Mulâtre.

VI. *Combinaisons du Mamelouc.*
D'un Mamelouc et d'une Blanche, vient ....un Quarteronné.
D'un Mamelouc et d'une Sang-mêlée ....Quarteronné.
D'un Mamelouc et d'une Quarteronnée ....Quarteronné.
D'un Mamelouc et d'une Métive......................un Mamelouc.
D'un Mamelouc et d'une Quarteronne.......................Métis.
D'un Mamelouc et d'une Mulâtresse ....Quarteron.
D'un Mamelouc et d'une Marabou, vient ....Quarteron.
D'un Mamelouc et d'une Griffonne.......................Quarteron.
D'un Mamelouc et d'une Sacatra ....Mulâtre.
D'un Mamelouc et d'une Négresse ....Mulâtre.

VII. *Combinaisons du Quarteronné.*
D'un Quarteronné et d'une Blanche, vient ....un Sang-mêlé.
D'un Quarteronné et d'une Sang-mêlé ....Sang-mêlé.
D'un Quarteronné et d'une Mamelouque ....Quarteronné.
D'un Quarteronné et d'une Métive......................Mamelouc.
D'un Quarteronné et d'une Quarteronne ....Métis.
D'un Quarteronné et d'une Mulâtresse....................Quarteron.
D'un Quarteronné et d'une Marabou ....Quarteron.
D'un Quarteronné et d'une Griffonne.....................Quarteron.
D'un Quarteronné et d'une Sacatra ....Quarteron.
D'un Quarteronné et d'une Négresse ....Mulâtre.

VIII. *Combinaisons du Sang-mêlé.*
D'un Sang-Mêlé et d'une Blanche, vient ....un Sang-mêlé.
D'un Sang-Mêlé et d'une Quarteronnée ....Sang-mêlé.
D'un Sang-Mêlé et d'une Mamelouque.................Quarteronné.
D'un Sang-Mêlé et d'une Métive ....Mamelouc.
D'un Sang-Mêlé et d'une Quarteronne.......................Métis.
D'un Sang-Mêlé et d'une Mulâtresse ....Quarteron.
D'un Sang-Mêlé et d'une Marabou ....Quarteron.
D'un Sang-Mêlé et d'une Griffonne ....Quarteron.
D'un Sang-Mêlé et d'une Sacatra........................Quarteron.
D'un Sang-Mêlé et d'une Négresse ....Mulâtre.

IX. *Combinaisons du Sacatra.*
D'un Sacatra et d'une Blanche, vient ....un Quarteron.
D'un Sacatra et d'une Sang-mêlée.......................Quarteron.

D'un Sacatra et d'une Quarteronnée . . . . Mulâtre.
D'un Sacatra et d'une Mamelouque . . . . Mulâtre.
D'un Sacatra et d'une Métive. . . . . Mulâtre.
D'un Sacatra et d'une Quarteronne . . . . Mulâtre.
D'un Sacatra et d'une Mulâtresse . . . . Marabou.
D'un Sacatra et d'une Marabou. . . . . Griffe.
D'un Sacatra et d'une Griffonne . . . . Griffe.
D'un Sacatra et d'une Négresse . . . . Sacatra.

X. *Combinaisons du Griffe.*
D'un Griffe et d'une Blanche, vient . . . . un Quarteron.
D'un Griffe et d'une Sang-mêlée . . . . Quarteron.
D'un Griffe et d'une Quarteronnée, vient . . . . Quarteron.
D'un Griffe et d'une Mamelouque. . . . . Quarteron.
D'un Griffe et d'une Métive . . . . Quarteron.
D'un Griffe et d'une Quarteronne . . . . Mulâtre.
D'un Griffe et d'une Mulâtresse . . . . Marabou.
D'un Griffe et d'une Marabou . . . . Marabou.
D'un Griffe et d'une Sacatra . . . . Griffe.
D'un Griffe et d'une Négresse. . . . . Sacatra.

XI. *Combinaisons du Marabou.*
D'un Marabou et d'une Blanche, vient. . . . . un Quarteron.
D'un Marabou et d'une Sang-mêlée . . . . Quarteron.
D'un Marabou et d'une Quarteronnée. . . . . Quarteron.
D'un Marabou et d'une Mamelouque . . . . Quarteron.
D'un Marabou et d'une Métive . . . . Quarteron.
D'un Marabou et d'une Quarteronne . . . . Quarteron.
D'un Marabou et d'une Mulâtresse. . . . . Mulâtre.
D'un Marabou et d'une Griffonne . . . . Marabou.
D'un Marabou et d'une Sacatra. . . . . Griffe.
D'un Marabou et d'une Négresse . . . . Griffe.

A NOTE ON CREOLE
ORTHOGRAPHY

Haitian Creole, which evolved from the contact of various African languages with French during the epoch of slavery on Hispaniola, is today, officially and in fact, the language of Haiti—a language which enjoys a vast reservoir of oral history and proverbs, and a rapidly growing written literature. In the latter half of the twentieth century, several systems for writing Creole were proposed and one of these has now been almost universally adopted.

In the colonial period, and for most of the nineteenth century, Haitian Creole had small status, and was considered to be a debased *patois* rather than a language in its own right; the official language of Haiti was French. The Creole of this period had no systematic orthography. To the extent that it was rendered in writing at all, it was written phonetically in a manner derived from French orthography.

Most of the Creole in this book is a similar phonetic rendering, which approximates the way Creole was recorded by travelers and historians during the period these events take place, from 1794 to 1803. In some cases Creole passages (e.g., Vodou songs) follow the more recent orthographies from the sources from which they are derived, but in general the orthography used in this book is not current.

PERMISSIONS ACKNOWLEDGMENTS

Portions of this novel have appeared, sometimes in a slightly different form, in *Granta, The Reading Room, The Idaho Review, Five Points, Virginia Quarterly Review, Agni, Gulf Coast, New England Review,* and the *Chattahoochee Review.*

Grateful acknowledgment is made to the following for permission to reprint previously published material: *Universal Music Publishing Group:* Excerpts from "Kalfou Danjere" words and music by Theodore Beaubrun, Jr., Daniel Beaubrun and Mimerose Beaubrun. Copyright © 1992 by Universal-Songs of PolyGram Int., Inc., a division of Universal Studios, Inc. (BMI). International copyright secured. All rights reserved. Reprinted by permission of Universal Music Publishing Group.

The lyrics on pages 185, 314, and 396 are reprinted from *Voodoo in Haiti* by Alfred Métraux, published by Schocken Books, a division of Random House, Inc., New York. The lyrics on pages 651–52 are reprinted from *Angels in the Mirror: Vodou Music of Haiti,* edited by Elizabeth McAlister, published by Ellipsis Arts. The other Vodou songs quoted in the text are amalgams, without a single source.

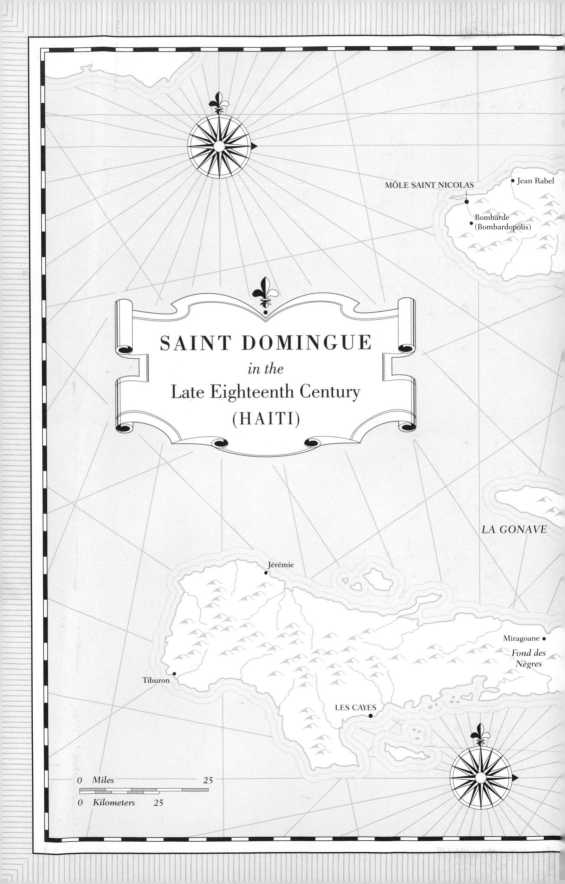

SAINT DOMINGUE

in the

Late Eighteenth Century

(HAITI)

MÔLE SAINT NICOLAS

Jean Rabel

Bombarde
(Bombardopolis)

LA GONAVE

Jérémie

Miragoane

Fond des
Nègres

Tiburon

LES CAYES

0   *Miles*   25

0   *Kilometers*   25